In memory of all my friends and family members who

have passed on. You were always there in support when

you were needed the most.

vi

Acknowledgement

Thank you to all my friends and family for all their
support.

CONTENTS

Preface

Growing up surrounded by the majestic Rocky Mountains, clear water, and beautiful blue skies, the title and idea for this book have always been in the forefront of my mind.

While this work is purely fiction, some readers might find some underlying truth in things and descriptions associated with this writing.

If you have ever been backpacking deep in the woods then you will understand how things can turn on you in a second or two.

The great outdoors is not for everyone. Please, if you're thinking about running off into the mountains and have no experience, take a course. Learn the basics, they could help you survive in an emergency situation. Above all, enjoy your surroundings and have fun. Remember what you carry in, you carry out. Leave nothing behind other than footprints. There is only so much wilderness left in our small world. Leave it as you found it so others may enjoy the pristine beauty that surrounds you.

I hope you enjoy *Grizzly*.

Chapter 1

The winter months in the town of Hillcrest were long and cold. Living close to the eastern edge of the Rocky Mountains, the community was subject to dull and chilly winter days. Snowfalls of a foot or more at one time were common. Twenty-year-old Brad had longed for the warmth of the spring air. He knew what that would eventually bring with it.

The beginning of March had not been much better. It had been cloudy most days followed by brief downpours of heavy rain later in the afternoons. The temperature had not been warmer than fifty-five degrees with very little direct sunlight; it always seemed to be overcast this time of the year. Brad knew that high in the mountains it would still be snowing. The spring runoff into the creeks and rivers were still at a minimum, and the snowpack was still above average.

Brad had been watching the height of the river water as it snaked through his hometown. The centre street bridge pilings were his guide. There was a gauge marked in feet and inches attached to one of the concrete pillars. The city had installed it ten years ago right after the big flood. It allowed the town to watch how fast the water was rising. They figured that if they kept an eye on things during runoff season, possibly an earlier warning could be issued to the local townsfolk. "A hundred-dollar fix for a bureaucratic screw-up," his father always said. Brad could hardly remember those events from the past. But he knew from his father, a local hunting and tour guide, it was a good way to tell you what was happening further up in the mountains. The higher the water got on the gauge and the rate it rose would indicate how long it was taking for the snowpack to melt in the mountains.

Brad was running late for his job at the local sawmill. He jumped in his truck and headed to work. He glanced at that marker about a mile from the mill site. As he floored the accelerator of his old Ford truck, the gauge read fifteen feet. The water was up a foot from Monday. "It's happening," he thought. The runoff from the rain was mixing with the now melting snow.

Brad pulled into the sawmill employee parking lot. He reported in, a smile on his face as he punched the time clock. Spring was just around the corner in the mountains and he could hardly wait. Brad walked into the mill's yard, wearing his work boots, hardhat gloves, safety vest, and tinted glasses. The small mill was running at full capacity. Brad looked skyward; the sun was poking through the clouds. A huge patch of blue sky directly to the west looked promising. Maybe he would stay dry on this shift. But then again, maybe not.

Chapter 2

Brad had been working at the sawmill since graduating from grade twelve. He was not sure what he wanted to do with his life. So, for the last two years he spent time working and sorting the fresh cut lumber into piles. His friend, Tommy, drove the forklift and, when a pile of lumber was complete, Tommy would use steel bands to bundle the boards. He would then hop onto the forklift and take the new bundles of lumber out into the yard.

Tommy and Brad had been friends since grade one. They were like brothers. Neither one had to say a word if the other detected a problem or a change in mood. A simple nod of the head was enough to say, "I understand." Throughout high school the two always enjoyed the outdoors. Camping, fishing, and hunting with Brad's father, both young men were well-versed on what the mountains could provide. On the other hand, they also knew how deadly things could be up there. The weather could change in an instant.

As part of the local search and rescue organization, both boys were involved in the search for a family three years prior—a family of four. A mother, father, and two girls had gone missing off the Rock Lake trail in July of that year. For two weeks, the Park Rangers, FBI, local law enforcement, and a team of volunteers scoured the trails and mountains leading to the four cabins at the north end of Rock Lake. Not a single sign of the family was ever found until the following year. The four bodies were eventually discovered wedged between a crack in the rockface of the Meadow Fork creek. Autopsies preformed showed all four had drowned. Brad and Tommy had discussed how stupid it was to hide in an area like that during a

storm. The raging water had rushed down the dry creek bed. The father's backpack got wedged between the rocks, trapping his wife and daughters aged twelve and fourteen. The water kept rising and they could not get out.

"What a horrible way to go," the boys had said, knowing that inexperience and the desperate attempt to get out of the rain had cost the family their lives.

"They were not the first," Brad's father had told them at the time. "They will not be the last. People go up there to take in the beauty of it all, and get away from city life, cell phones, and the stress of their jobs. They read a little on the internet and think they are expert mountaineers." Brad's father was always a proponent of people being certified before they were allowed a permit to camp in the national park. "These city folk just go to the local sporting goods store and have themselves outfitted with the cheapest gear they can afford. They think they know it all, then off they go, creating nothing but problems for themselves, the rangers, sheriffs, and the park's department."

Chapter 3

Ever since Brad could walk as a toddler, his father made sure he understood that potential danger could lie ahead no matter what he was doing. As Brad grew older, his father would take him into the mountains. During the two months of summer in his teens, while school was out, Brad would help act as an assistant guide. His father taught him how to hunt and fish—to live off the land—and build a shelter that could withstand some of the fiercest weather the mountains could throw at them. Brad felt at home in the mountains. He knew what he was doing and could survive anything. Tommy was almost as proficient, but always looked to Brad if things were getting sketchy. Tommy knew he could count on his friend if he needed him.

As their shift ended that day, the young men met in the lunch room for coffee. Brad was the first to sit down at the corner table, its surface was marred from years of use. There was also a rumour that old Pete, the owner of the sawmill was caught fucking his secretary on the very same table ten years ago. A smile came to Brad's face as he sat down. No one could prove it, but it was a hell of a story. All Brad knew was that Pete's wife, Anna, left him about ten years ago, so the timing fit with the rumours.

Tommy sat down with his buddy and added some sugar and cream to his cup of coffee. Brad watched as his friend stirred the mixture into the black liquid. He thought to himself, "Just more stuff to pack into the mountains. Maybe someday he will learn to drink it black like me."

"That was a good shift, buddy," Tommy said. "We managed to rack and stack twenty bundles today. That's a good shift in my books."

Both young men were still in their coveralls with hardhats on their heads. As they moved about, the sawdust that collected on their clothing dropped onto the floor and table. It was the way things were in the lunchroom. The sawdust would get cleaned up a couple of times a week but the men who worked at the mill did not care. At least they had jobs. The Vandenburg family had started the mill back in the late eighteen hundreds. They had employed as many of the local townsfolk as possible over the years. Even when the economy slowed down across the country, the Vandenburg family kept local people working. Old Pete Vandenburg had contacts overseas and always seemed to find a market for some of the specialty hardwoods that were harvested in the local area. The family was very well-respected in the community. When times were tough, the little sleepy town of Hillcrest seemed to chug along at its own speed.

"What do you think we should do on the May long weekend?" Tommy asked. "We both have three days off."

"Maybe we should round up the girls and head off into the hills," Brad said, "away from all the riffraff that will descend upon our little town in five weeks."

Chapter 4

Brad hated how crowded their town became on the weekends, especially the long weekends, but he knew deep down the people that showed up brought money with them and that was good for local businesses.

Brad had been dating Elizabeth for the last two years. Her father owned the hardware-sporting goods store in town. She had always worked in her father's store for as long as he could remember. During high school he never had the courage to ask her out. She was just one of those girls that always seemed to be too busy, or so he thought. Besides, he never liked the idea of being rejected, especially if Elizabeth said no. Then, back in April, almost two years ago, he decided to go shopping for a new hunting knife. Brad was smitten with the beautiful young woman behind the counter. He wanted something a little more manly than the knife his father had given him as a boy. He had carried that knife with him everywhere. However, Brad had outgrown it.

On his last trip to the mountains the previous fall, people had continuously bugged him about the picture of the forest ranger that was emblazoned on the handle. He swore to himself that he would never let them harass him again.

Elizabeth stood behind the counter in her father's store that day. She made direct eye contact with Brad when he walked in. Her father taught her how to greet customers. "Look 'em straight in the eyes," he would say. "You can tell if they are going to buy or steal from yah."

Brad noticed how beautiful she looked, her long-flowing auburn hair hanging below her shoulders.

"Can I help you?" she asked.

"I have not seen you since we graduated," Brad said. "You look fantastic."

"Thank you," Elizabeth said, her cheeks matching the auburn of her hair as they flushed from the compliment. "What have you been so busy with?"

"I have been so caught up at the mill," Brad replied. "And it just so happens that I am looking for a new hunting knife."

Elizabeth walked him over to the display case of knives they showed the general public. Nothing in the cabinet struck Brad's fancy.

"Do you have anything else?" he asked.

"Well," Elizabeth said, "we just had a new shipment of goods come in yesterday afternoon. I know dad had ordered the latest from Buck. Hang on and let me see if I can find the box in the warehouse."

Brad waited a few moments before Elizabeth returned with a carton about the size of a shoebox. Stamped on the outside of it was the world famous name Buck Knives. She cut the tape away from the top of the box and peered inside. There was a selection of smaller knives at the top of the box. She removed them. Then, he saw it—the Buck Huntsman. He had read about it in the latest edition of *Field & Stream*. It was the latest in Damascus blades offered by the world famous knifemaker. The blade was about ten inches long, the leather sheath was handstitched, and the handle was made out of solid walnut cut from the trees around Hillcrest. The brass rivets gleamed like gold against the dark handle. The pommel and guard were a perfect match.

"That's it," he said to Elizabeth. "That's the one I want. How much?"

She cut open the envelope taped to the box. It contained the invoice from the manufacturer. She knew her dad always put a markup on everything—forty

percent exactly. She moved to the calculator and ran a few numbers. "That will be four hundred and ninety-nine dollars," she said. "But because we know each other, I can give you fifteen percent off. How does four twenty-four sound, taxes included?"

Brad's bank account had taken a beating lately. The old Ford truck had needed an engine rebuild. He had just replaced the brakes, and now the four-wheel drive was acting up. "Can I give you two hundred dollars now?" he asked. "Can you put it on layaway for me? It's my birthday next week, and I get paid at the end of the month and can settle up then."

"Let me check with my dad," Elizabeth responded. Her dad was in the office upstairs. His office window overlooked the store. Brad saw the old man look out the window towards the counter, and then directly at Brad. Elizabeth returned. "My dad would be happy to accommodate your request."

Brad was elated. None of his friends would ever bother him again about the old knife. "I am thrilled!" he said. "The only thing that could be better than this is if you agreed to go to a movie with me on my birthday."

Elizabeth looked at Brad for a second, and then said, "Okay. What day is it?"

"The thirtieth. How about I pick you up at seven o'clock in the evening here in front of the store? Besides, the thirtieth is also payday and I'll be able to give you the rest of the money for my new knife."

They shook hands and Brad noticed Elizabeth's hand was soft but she still had a good grip. "Must be from working in the store all these years," he thought. He found himself thinking about her more and more as the days passed.

The following week, he stopped at the store with an inexpensive bouquet of flowers. He left them with

Elizabeth's mother, Joan. Elizabeth was busy with another customer that day and Brad had to get to work.

"That nice young man was here and left these for you," Joan said to Elizabeth after the latter was finished with the customer.

Elizabeth opened the card attached to the flowers. It read, "Can't wait until the thirtieth and thank you for being so kind. – Brad."

The morning of the thirtieth started like every other day. Brad got up, showered, and went to the kitchen to have breakfast before heading out for his shift at the mill.

On the table was a gift from his father plus a card attached to the top. Brad opened the card. It read, "When your mother was still alive she said that she wanted you to have this on your twenty-first birthday. I have been keeping it safe and sound for you until this day. You make me very proud. Happy birthday, son! Love, Dad."

Brad tore open the wrapping paper and opened the box. Inside, he found his grandfather's .45 calibre M1911 semiautomatic that he carried with him during World War II. It was now Brad's. He removed it from the box and placed it in his right hand. "Grandpa," he said aloud, looking at the ceiling, "someday I will make you proud. I hope you're looking after mom."

Chapter 5

Brad took the gun back to his room and tucked it between his mattress and box spring. He had thirty minutes to make it to the mill. Earlier that morning, Tommy had called and asked if Brad wanted to go to the local pub to celebrate his birthday after they finished their shift.

"Sorry, buddy," Brad replied. "I have a date tonight."

Brad's shift ended at 6:00pm. He had an hour to get home and change, shower, wash the sawdust off, dress, and pick Elizabeth up by seven. He also had to stop at the bank and deposit his check. With no time to waste, he floored the old truck as he left the mill's parking lot, dust kicked up behind the wheels. A smile crept to his face. In an hour, he would be in the company of Elizabeth. He could hardly wait.

Brad got to the store at exactly 6:59pm. He pulled up right in front. There was no sign of Elizabeth. He stepped out of his truck and went inside the store. And there she was, removing her purse from behind the counter.

"Hello!" Brad said, trying his best to hide his enthusiasm. "You look fantastic."

Joan was standing at the far end of the store. "You kids have fun tonight," she said. "Oh, and happy birthday, Brad. I sure enjoyed my flowers last week."

Brad's heart sunk. Those flowers were for his date. He was so excited and overwhelmed that he forgot all about his new knife.

"Let's go," Elizabeth said. "Mom is just bugging you. My flowers were beautiful, thank you."

Brad and Elizabeth left the store. Being the perfect gentleman that he was, Brad opened the

passenger door to his truck and helped Elizabeth inside. His four-wheel drive was extremely high off the ground. The lift kit had added another eight inches to its height. Brad quickly made his way to the driver's side. He got in and looked over.

"How does Dusty's sound for dinner before we go to that movie? The movie starts at nine so that gives us two hours."

"That sounds great," Elizabeth said.

Dusty's was the local BBQ restaurant. They had mean burgers and awesome ribs and steak. The two young adults arrived five minutes later. Brad parked just a few stalls away from the front door. He got out, walked around, and opened Elizabeth's door. She slid down off the seat and dropped to the ground, stumbling and falling into Brad's arms. He caught her, allowing her to catch her balance. She stood up, straightened out her blouse, then kissed Brad on the cheek.

"Thanks," she said softly. "Your truck is pretty big."

They went into the restaurant, finding a table in the back. It was Brad's birthday and he wanted to make sure that Elizabeth felt as special as he did. The waitress came over with two glasses of water and a couple of menus. Brad knew what he wanted from the time he walked in. Elizabeth took her time. When she had decided what she wanted she placed the menu on the corner of the table.

The waitress returned and said, "What can I get you kids?"

"I'll have your chef's salad with grilled chicken," Elizabeth said.

Brad ordered the twenty-ounce T-bone steak, medium rare, with baked potatoes and the works. After all, he did not get a chance to have lunch today; they were

far too busy at the mill. He and Tommy had racked and stacked twenty-five piles of lumber—a new record.

"How about a glass of wine or beer?" Brad asked Elizabeth.

"Sure," she replied. "I'll have a glass of Chardonnay with my salad."

"Nothing for me, thank you," Brad said. "I'll stick with the water. I'm driving this gorgeous lady around tonight." His father had taught him well. They sat for an hour and a half chatting about high school and what their plans were for the future. They both enjoyed their meals. Brad glanced up at the clock on the wall. "My God," he exclaimed, "where has the time gone? If we are going to make the movie we better get going or we are going to end up in the front row." Friday nights were always busy, especially when a new movie came to town.

They arrived at the theatre just in time to get their tickets and find two seats at the back of the room. The theatre was small with maybe two hundred seats in total. What more could you expect for a community of only five thousand people? The only saving grace was that after two weeks a new movie would come to town. There was a constant turnover of new flicks.

Brad looked around after they had taken their seats. There, in the middle of the theatre, were two empty seats. Walking up the aisle were Tommy and Donna.

"Hey buddy," Tommy said, waving at Brad. "Happy birthday!"

"Elizabeth, how are you?" Donna said, coming all the way up to the backrow. "How are your mom and dad?" Donna and Elizabeth had been friends all through high school. The girls engaged in idle chitchat for a minute or two. Donna bent over and kissed Brad on the cheek. "Happy birthday!" she said. She returned to her

seat beside Tommy just as the lights went out and the curtains opened.

The movie was a new war flick: guy goes to war, guy gets wounded, girl works in hospital, guy falls in love, guy gets killed in the end, woman gets left alone standing on a beach looking endlessly out into the ocean. Brad looked down and found Elizabeth's hand in his. He did not remember her putting her hand in his, or was it the other way around? It did not matter to him. She was holding his hand and it felt great. The movie ended and, as always, there was popcorn and empty containers scattered all over the floor. Brad and Elizabeth found their way out the front door where Tommy and Donna were waiting.

"Come on, buddy, let's go for a quick ice cream with the girls," Tommy said. "I know you won't go for a drink, especially if you're driving Elizabeth around. Her father would kill you."

"Her father?" Brad thought to himself. "What about my father?" That's how Brad's mom had died. A drunk driver hit her car when Brad was only eight years old. Brad looked at Elizabeth. "Would you like to go with these two for an ice cream?"

"Sure," Elizabeth said.

It was now 10:50pm. They had ten minutes to make it to the ice cream parlour before it closed. The four arrived just as the the exterior sign was being turned off. Old George Williams had owned the joint for forty years. The kids rushed in. All four ordered medium sundaes each with their own unique topping.

"Let me get this," Tommy said to his buddy. "It's your birthday." Tommy paid for the four of them.

They went outside to sit at one of the many picnic tables that adorned the parking lot. The four young adults sat down. Tommy reached into his pocket and pulled out two candles, one in the shape of a two and the other a

16

number one. Tommy stuck the candles into Brad's sundae and lit both.

"What are you doing with candles in your pocket, you goofball?" Brad asked.

The girls had talked last week and Elizabeth had mentioned to Donna that she and Brad were going to the movie. The meeting at the theatre had been set up by the girls. Brad smiled at his buddy and Tommy nodded his head. There were no other words needed. The three of them sung happy birthday to Brad as he blew out both candles. The four young adults sat for another hour, talking and finishing their treats. It was after midnight when Brad finally pulled up to Elizabeth's house.

"I had a wonderful time tonight," Elizabeth said.

"So did I," Brad said. "It was amazing. I cannot believe you girls and how fast the time went."

Elizabeth slid across the seat closer to Brad. "I really enjoyed myself," she said again.

He looked deep into her eyes. He felt the same and wanted to show her how much. He leaned in and kissed her lightly at first. She responded and kissed him back. This time it was far more passionate. Their tongues met for the first time and Brad felt a stirring in his pants. The porch light flickered on and off a few times and there stood Elizabeth's father in the open door.

"I should go," she said.

"I understand," Brad said.

He got out of his truck and walked to her door, opening it then helping her out. He walked with her to the front door of the family home where her father stood.

"Home safe and sound, Mr Eaton," Brad said.

Elizabeth turned and said, "Good night."

Brad wanted to kiss her again, but did not dare push the envelope with her father standing right there.

"Good night," Brad said.

17

He walked back to his truck. He heard the front door close behind him. The porch light had been turned off. He opened his driver's door, then slid behind the wheel. Brad looked down at his seat, and there laid out was a beautifully wrapped gift with a card attached. "Damn," he thought to himself, "she must have been hiding this in her purse all night." Brad opened the card Elizabeth had written: "Happy Birthday to a wonderful guy. I hope you enjoy your gift." Brad carefully opened the paper that contained a plain cardboard box. He removed the box from the paper, then tugged at the tape that kept it sealed. The flaps broke open, he peered inside... the box contained his new hunting knife and his original two-hundred-dollar deposit. Brad was in love, and it was not with the knife. He was officially twenty-one years old; it had been one hell of a day.

Chapter 6

Donna and Tommy had been a couple all through high school. Donna had caught Tommy's attention one day when the fire alarm rang. Everyone in the school was evacuated to the field behind the school while the officials figured out what was going on. It turned out that Mr. McLean's Science class was experimenting with a new shipment of Bunsen burners. The oil used in manufacturing them had not been cleaned off before being shipped to Hillcrest High School. When all the burners were lit simultaneously, the oil burning off the twenty or so Bunsen burners triggered the school's smoke detectors and fire suppression system in the classroom. The students from that class came running outside, soaking wet. Donna was among them. Tommy noticed that she was cold and shaking, and he walked over to her, offering his sweatshirt to keep her warm. From that point on, they became inseparable.

Donna came from a family of misfits. Her brother was in prison for stealing cars. Her mother was a drug addict and was frequently in the hospital for various reasons. Tommy always believed it was a way for her to obtain more prescription pills. If she got caught high somewhere, she had an easy excuse. Her father worked as a used car salesman at Hillcrest Motors, the same place where Brad had bought his truck. Her father had several affairs over the years, and her mother seemed not to care, as long as money continued flowing into the household, enabling her drug habits. Donna's younger brother Billy was a good kid. There were ten years between Matt, the brother in jail, and Billy. Donna, the middle child, was seven years younger than Matt. She never really had anyone to watch over her. The day

Tommy offered her his sweatshirt, she felt like someone actually cared about her.

Tommy and Donna spent hours talking about their upbringings, and as soon as she graduated, Donna found a job at the local library as an assistant. While it did not pay much, it was enough that she could afford her own little apartment and put food on the table. Tommy was always good to her. He sprung for the new furniture. After all, he was spending a lot of time there, and if he was going to spend the night, he wanted a nice television to watch. So long as his Donna was safe. She had confided in him to such an extent that one evening she told Tommy about an evening her older brother Matt had come into her room.

The house was dark, her mother was high, Billy, her younger brother, was asleep in his room. Her father, she assumed, was out with one of his flings because she had not heard him come in. Matt came into her room, she said, and laid down beside her on the bed. She was still half-asleep when she realized that his hand was on her breast. He had his cock in his other hand and was masturbating. He removed his hand from her breast and reached between her legs. She screamed, jumped out of bed, and grabbed the baseball bat that she used for the girls' softball league. Matt had rolled onto his side on her bed and she struck him across his back with all her might. The bat hit with a heavy thud and she heard her brother gasping for air. She had broken a couple of his ribs and one punctured his lung.

Donna took her brother to the hospital that night. The emergency room staff operated, removing his rib from the lung. They sewed him back together and reinflated the lung. The hospital staff then called in the cops. The emergency room doctors believed Donna's father had laid a beating on Matt. When he came to he told everyone he had been walking along the top of their

fence to get at the crab apples and slipped. His father was not responsible. Matt never approched his sister in that way ever again.

When Tommy heard the story from Donna he vowed to her that if he ever met Matt in the future, Matt would never forget him. That was a promise Tommy would live to keep. He and Brad had gone over Donna's story many times. It always ended the same way.

"If I do something stupid, buddy, make sure you look after Donna for me," Tommy said.

Brad promised he would. He knew what it was like to carry hate for someone. They were brothers, even if the blood was not the same.

On Friday nights, Tommy would show up at exactly 6:15pm, bearing groceries for the week. He brought plenty of greens and fruits for Donna, as well as meat and potatoes for himself. Donna would prepare a meal for Tommy every Friday night. Together, they would tidy up the dishes after dinner, and by 8:00pm, they would find themselves in the new king-size bed that Tommy had bought.

Tommy would always say to Brad, "You know the story of the librarian? Well, it's all true."

The reality was that Donna was the hottest and only girl Tommy had ever been with. She had gone out and gotten herself a couple of tattoos and some body piercings. The tattoos were a heart with the date of the event at the school, and both of their initials. The other was a pair of wings just above her butt crack. Tommys favorite, though, were the rings in her nipples and the barbell in her belly button. She kept things spicy for the two of them and Tommy loved it. When she got dressed in the morning to go to work, no one but Tommy knew what was under her clothing. She was the perfect librarian. She would come home, let her hair down and

Tommy knew what was in store for him. No wonder he hardly went home.

Chapter 7

"So how about it?" Tommy said. "What do you think about the long weekend in May?"

"Sorry," Brad said. "I was drifting. I am in. Let me check with Elizabeth. I think the four of us could have a blast. Have you spoken to Donna?"

"I'm sure it'll be okay," Tommy said. "She's in for anything I do and vice versa."

"Okay, we have five weeks to plan this. Let's see if we can get an extra day off and get out of here before it gets too crowded and maybe make it four days. Wonder if old Pete will give us the extra day off."

Both young men left their requests in the office dropbox before going home that day. When they showed up for their shifts the following day, inside each of their lockers was an envelope. The envelopes contained written approvals and a crisp one-hundred-dollar bill for each of them plus a handwritten note: "Thanks for hitting twenty-five lifts the other day. Enjoy your days off! Signed, Pete."

"Wow an extra day off and a bonus of one hundred bucks!" Tommy exclaimed. "How much better could that be?"

The boys chatted as they dressed in their coveralls; the girls were in. Both had no issues getting the extra day off. It was going to be a fantastic time—four days off in the mountains with his buddy and the girls. "Can't get any better than that," Brad thought to himself.

Chapter 8

The following five weeks were uneventful. The boys worked their tails off at the mill, while the girls were busy at their respective jobs. Tommy received a message from Donna during their shift on Wednesday two days before they were to leave. Donna was upset. Her Aunt Mary had dropped off her cousins, Mark and Marcy, with Donna's mother. Mary and her new boyfriend were headed for Vegas for the long weekend and there were no kids allowed on this weekend of adult debauchery. Mary had not given her sister any notice. They just showed up on the family's front doorstep. Joann, Donna's mother, answered the door. She was high as a kite. The new oxy she had just taken half an hour ago was kicking in.

"What are you doing here?" Joann asked.

"Trevor and I are heading to Vegas for the weekend," Mary said. "It's a spur-of-the-moment thing, and we can't take Mark and Marcy with us. You know what Vegas is like. Besides, you owe me. Remember who stayed and looked after your kids when you were in the hospital?"

Joann had been hospitalized eight years ago because of a drug overdose. Donna's father, Clifford, could not handle the three children on his own, so he had called Mary and asked for her help with the children while Joann dried out. Mary was only too eager to assist at the time. Her own marriage was falling apart. Tony, her husband, was an aloholic, and she told him if things did not change she would be filing for a divorce.

Mary had arrived the same day that Clifford had called. She had arrived from Hillsboro that evening around 6pm. She immediately set to work making dinner for the children, but there was hardly anything in the

fridge. She found a jar of spaghetti sauce in the pantry and some noodles. "That would have to do until Cliff gets here from the hospital," she thought to herself.

The kids were all sitting watching television when their father got home from Hillcrest Memorial Hospital. The facility had twenty emergency beds and a small operating room. The newest wing, on the second floor, housed old folks with dementia. The first floor was reserved for recovering patients. There were two surgeons in town and that was more than enough for Hillcrest's population of five thousand.

Clifford had arrived home around 9:30pm that night. "Hello, Mary," he had said. "Thank you for coming. It's been a hell of a day. Kids, it's time for bed."

After the usual "Dad, I don't want to," they were all finally behind closed doors. It was 9:45pm. The two adults sat at the kitchen table.

"How is my sister," Mary asked.

"You know the situation," Clifford said. "Nothing has changed. Joann keeps getting these prescription drugs, and this time she took way too much. They want to put her into a rehab program and she is refusing to go. Says nothing is wrong with her. I'm fed up with all the bullshit. It's been going on for too many years."

Mary got up and walked over to Clifford. She stood behind him, put her hands on his back, and massaged his neck and shoulders. After a moment, Clifford stood up, turned towards Mary, and drew her close. He embraced her and kissed the top of her head. "Thank you," he said.

She looked up at him and he looked for a second or two deeply into her eyes. He recognized the chemistry that was occuring. After all, Joann had not been romantic in years. He had to get it from elsewhere. He bent down and kissed his sister-in-law. She responded and engaged

25

in one of the deepest kisses she had ever encountered. Tony was only interested in his next drink. Here was her brother-in-law paying attention to her.

She got down on her knees, unzipped Clifford's trousers, and reached in for his manhood. Clifford was not saying a word. His head was tilted back and he was just letting Mary go about her business. She placed his semi-hard cock in her mouth and started to suck on the head. It was getting harder and she was not even working at it. She swirled the tip of her tongue around his shaft. Clifford was hard as a rock. She stood up, unfastened her jeans, and bent over the kitchen table. Clifford placed the tip of his cock at her entrance and in one slow, continuous thrust was deep inside his sister-in-law's hot and wet mound. He thrusted hard, grabbing her hips. She pushed back against him. Mary looked over her shoulder. "I'm going to cum," she said. That was enough for Clifford. He gave her one last thrust and deposited his hot load deep inside Mary.

Hearing a noise behind them they both turned their heads. There stood twelve-year-old Donna. "Dad, I don't feel good," she said.

Still coupled and deep inside Mary, Clifford shouted, "Go to your bed! I'll come check on you shortly."

Donna returned to her bedroom, and waited for her father to come and check on her. She waited an hour for her father to come and see how she was doing. He never showed. She was so tired, eventually Donna fell asleep even with her stomach cramps and aching back.

Later that night, she awoke to hear moaning coming from her parents' bedroom. She eventually fell asleep again only to awake in the morning, pull back her covers and find blood between her legs and on her bedsheets. Donna screamed at the top of her lungs. Her aunt Mary came running into her room.

"Oh, honey," she said. "It's okay! You're a young woman now. Let's get you into the shower and I will explain what is happening to your body."

Donna sat with her aunt at the kitchen table. Her Aunt Mary was sitting in Joann's housecoat. She explained how ladies got their periods about every twenty-one days or so. It was normal and part of being a woman. Joann had only mentioned to Donna once what eventually would happen when they were shopping for her first training bra. It was never brought up again.

Clifford had left early that Friday morning. He had two deliveries at the car lot and needed to be there.

"Here, honey," Mary said to Donna, reaching into her purse. "Take this pad and put it in your underwear. It will catch what is flowing for the time being, and we will go to the drugstore later."

Her aunt stayed for another two weeks with Donna's family. The moaning would continue to come from her parents' bedroom. Joann eventually dried out and was sent home with the promise she would go for counselling. As the years went by Donna came to realize what she had seen that night in the kitchen. She never spoke of it to her father, but she knew someday she would confront them both. She was just waiting for the right time.

Mary dropped off her two children.

"You have to help me, Donna, this weekend," Joann said to Donna over the phone. "I just can't handle it. Your aunt just dropped off Mark and Marcy and I can't look after these kids alone. I need you, please."

When Donna finally got a hold of Tommy, she said, "I can't go this weekend. My Aunt Mary just left her two kids with mom, and she is having a fit. Mom needs me to stay in town and help look after Mark and Marcy."

Tommy thought for a second. "Sweety," he said. "Don't worry about a thing. Let's take them with us this weekend. It will take the stress off your mother, and maybe they will learn something."

"Tommy, I love you," Donna exclaimed. "I can't wait till Friday!"

Chapter 9

Donna went to her parents' home right after her shift at the library that day. Mark and Marcy were sitting and watching TV.

"Hello you two," Donna said. "Where's mom?"

Marcy spoke and said, "In the bedroom."

Donna made her way down the hallway and noticed the bedroom door was closed. She opened the door and found her mother passed out on the bed. An open bottle of pills sat on the nightstand beside her head. She shook her mother. "Mom? Mom, wake up! It's Donna."

Eventually, Joann started to come around. "What do you want?" her mother said. "I was sleeping."

"Mom, you asked for my help with Mark and Marcy."

"What are you talking about? They are with your aunt in Hillsboro."

"No, mom, they are in the livingroom. You asked me to help you look after them this weekend."

"I did not," she exclaimed. "They are not here."

"Okay," Donna said. "Go back to sleep. I'm sorry I woke you up."

Donna looked back at her mother and swore she would never be like her. She closed the bedroom door and walked to the kitchen. Donna found a pen and piece of paper. "Mom, dad," she wrote. "I have Mark and Marcy with me. Tommy and I are going to the mountains this weekend. See you Monday night." She signed the note, "Love, Donna."

The kids were engrossed in some kind of horror movie. Donna walked into the living room and turned off the television. "Who is up for an adventure this weekend?" she asked.

"We are, we are!" they exclaimed.

"Fantastic!" Donna said. "Let's grab a few things from the garage."

The three of them went outside to the detached garage and found two sleeping bags and the old tent Donna and her brothers played in when they were younger.

"There," she said. "We have a roof over your heads and a nice warm spot for you to curl up in."

Donna loaded a few more things into the trunk of her car. Mark and Marcy jumped into the backseat, did up their seatbelts, and they headed for Donna's apartment. Donna made the kids dinner that night. Tommy had been over and dropped off a few extra grocieries. Donna rolled the two sleeping bags out on the floor of her small livingroom. This is where the kids would sleep tonight. Tommy would be there at 6:00am, Friday morning. They needed to be ready to go when he arrived.

"Hey you two," she said. "Tommy will be here in the morning real early. It's bedtime now."

It was only nine o'clock but they finally agreed to bed down. Donna made her way to the bathroom and finally had a chance to get out of her work clothes. She closed the bathroom door and started the shower. She climbed in and drew the shower curtain behind her. She washed her hair, letting the soapy water run across her breasts. She made sure that the day's grime was gone. Too bad Tommy was not in the shower with her. She was horny. Donna took the shower wand off the wall and set it to massage. She let the water work its magic on her clitoris. She got out of the tub, wrapped a towel around her long, blonde hair, then finished drying off. She made her way to her bedroom.

"Goodnight," she said to the kids. There was no response. They were already fast asleep.

Donna laid her head on her pillow. It had been a long day. Six in the morning came fast. Donna woke to Tommy kissing her cheek. He had let himself in with his key and had tiptoed around the sleeping kids and found Donna sound asleep behind her closed bedroom door.

"Morning, sweety," he said. "Did you miss me last night?"

"Of course I did," Donna said. "Why don't you crawl in under the covers with me and I'll show you how much?"

Tommy laughed. "There will be plenty of time for that later," he said. "We have to meet Brad and Elizabeth by 6:30. They're going to be waiting for us in the parking lot of Elli's Diner." The plan was to have a quick bite to eat and then hit the road. "I'll go wake up the kids," Tommy said. "You get ready, honey."

Tommy went out to the living room and woke Mark and Marcy. "Uncle Tommy, you're here!"

Tommy had known the children from the time he and Donna had started dating. "Come on, you two. We have to get ready. Your uncle Brad and Elizabeth are waiting for us."

Tommy rolled up the sleeping bags and gathered the things that Donna had put in the trunk of her car. He loaded everything into the back of his Jeep Cherokee. Thursday evening he had run around and picked up extra food and supplies for the four of them. He knew what they would require for the three full days in the mountains. No one was going hungry under Tommy's watch. He went back up to the apartment. It was six twenty-five. Donna was dressed and her backpack was loaded. The kids had a duffle bag that contained their clothes that Mary had packed for the weekend at Joann and Clifford's.

"Lets go," Donna said.

They locked the apartment door as they left. Tommy heard the deadbolt engage. All four piled into Tommy's jeep with the remainder of what they were taking. By the time they got to Elli's Diner it was six thirty-five.

Chapter 10

Tommy pulled into Elli's a little too fast. He hit the brakes and came to a skidding stop beside his buddy's truck. The dust was thick as he got out and stepped over to Brad's truck. "Howdy partner," he said to Brad. "Sorry we're a little late. The kids were still sound asleep when I got to Donna's. Morning, Elizabeth! You look stunning today." They all laughed.

"Come on, let's get a bite to eat," Brad said. "Elli has the grill all fired up."

The three of them walked over to Tommy's jeep. The kids and Donna had gotten out. Donna gave Elizabeth a big hug and told her she was amazing. Brad had explained to Elizabeth what had happend when Mary dropped off the kids to Donna's mother's house. Tommy and he had discussed the situation as soon as Tommy hung up the phone and calmed Donna down. Brad gave Mark and Marcy a rub on the head. "How are you two doing?" he said.

"We're good," Marcy replied.

"Mom and her new boyfriend, Trevor, are in Vegas and we're not allowed go," Mark exclaimed.

"How awesome is that?" Brad stated. "Now you get to go camping with us."

The six of them marched into Elli's Diner and sat at a table large enough for eight. Brad, Tommy, Elizabeth, and Donna were dressed in their hiking gear. Brad's new knife hung from his belt. Elli came over to the table. "It looks like you kids are headed off to the mountains," she said.

"Yeah," Tommy said. "We're headed for the hills but thought we'd stop for some good home cooking before we get out of dodge."

Elli laughed. "What will you all have?" she said.

Mark and Marcy ordered pancakes. Tommy, Brad, Elizabeth, and Donna all ordered the breakfast special—Elli's world famous omelete that came with your choice of toast and hashbrowns. The girls both ordered wholegrain while Tommy and Brad ordered brown bread. Tommy also asked for a plate of sausages as a side. Fifteen minutes later their meals were out in front of them. Tommy reached for the sausages and placed a couple on both Mark and Marcy's plates. "You two need more than pancakes," he said.

The kids poured strawberry syrup all over everything—it was their favorite. They all ate until everything was gone. Tommy and Brad were discussing where they would go once in the park. With Mark and Marcy along plans had to be modified so the children could keep up. The trail had to be easy. The girls chatted about their time at work that week and how great it was to get Friday off on top of Monday.

"Wow! Four days of R-and-R," Donna said with a big smile. "I need it."

There were two sausages left on the plate when everyone was done. "Here," Tommy said to Mark. "You're a growing boy. Let's wrap these in a few napkins and you put them in your pocket for later. You might need them on our hike."

Mark readily agreed and took the sausages from Tommy and put them into the front pocket of his jacket. He zipped up the pocket and said, "I'm not going to starve." Tommy and Brad split the bill fifty-fifty. Brad did not mind helping his friend pay to keep he and Donna happy. Brad knew everything and it was only twenty bucks. Old Pete had given him a hundred cash. The kids left Elli five dollars on the table and they were gone.

Chapter 11

The drive from Elli's Diner to the park gates was exactly one hour if you could maintain sixty-five miles an hour. The twinned highway leading to the park connected to Hillcrest Boulevard, the main street that ran through town. As they got to the west end of town to connect to the highway Brad glanced at the railroad bridge piling. The gauge read twelve feet. If the gauge ever read zero the water would flow over the bridge and Hillcrest would be underwater again. The water was up three feet from five weeks ago. "That's a good sign," Brad thought to himself. Things were warming up in the mountains. The runoff had started in earnest. After all it was the long weekend of May.

Brad and Tommy floored their vehicles as they made their way towards the ramp connecting to the highway. The sky was bright blue and there was no rain in the forecast. The boys drove beside each other on and off making faces at one another. Mark and Marcy got in on the action, however Elizabeth and Donna thought it somewhat childish so they refrained from their men's antics.

As they got closer to the park, the hills and area surrounding Hillcrest changed from rolling topography to huge mountains thrust up from the earth's crust during the creation of the world.

"What a beautiful sight," Elizabeth said. "I can never get enough of seeing this."

The boys pulled up to the park gates. Each had a search-and-rescue sticker mounted to their windshields. The ranger manning the gate waived them both through. There was no charge to enter the park if you were on the search-and-rescue team.

"Just another half hour," Tommy said to the kids and Donna. "We will be at the parking lot and then our real adventure begins."

The kids let out a woop and said, "Fantastic!"

"I have to pee," Mark said.

"Can you hold it?" Tommy asked.

"Okay," was the comeback from Mark. "But I don't want to pee my pants."

Tommy passed Brad on the way to the Rock Lake parking lot. He arrived about five minutes ahead of Brad and Elizabeth and pulled up to one of the park restrooms. "There you go little buddy," he said to Mark. "Go pee while we go and park the jeep."

A few minutes later, Brad and Elizabeth pulled in beside Tommy and Donna. Brad got out and spoke to Tommy at the rear of his truck. "What's the hurry?" Brad asked.

"Oh, Mark had to pee and I did not want to stop on the side of the highway," Tommy answered. "Now the girls are in there too."

Brad laughed. He opened the tailgate of his truck and pulled back the tarp that covered his and Elizabeth's backpacks. Both were neatly packed with everything they would need for the weekend including an extra day's supply of freeze-dried stroganoff. His father always said, "Plan for the worst just in case." To have a little extra food, especially the dehydrated kind, never hurt. Tommy was busy trying to organize the stuff that Donna had brought for Mark and Marcy. He tied a rope around the small tent and one sleeping bag for Mark to carry. Marcy would carry the duffle bag of clothes and her sleeping bag the same way. Tommy fashioned the ropes in such a way that the children could carry everything on their backs. The ropes would slide over their shoulders just like a regular backpack. Tommy

looked over at Brad and noticed he was putting something into the top pocket of his well-used pack.

"Is that what I think it is?" Tommy said.

"Yup," Brad said. "I brought grandpa's .45 cal with me. I really want to try it out. Since it is illegal to have a firearm in the national park you did not see anything, right buddy?"

"I get it," Tommy said.

The children and Donna returned from the washroom. Mark spoke up right away and said, "It stinks in there."

"What do you expect for an outhouse?" Tommy said. "Running water and heat? You're in the mountains now. Just wait, it is only going to get better." He turned and winked at Brad. Brad laughed. Mark and Marcy had never really been camping deep in the mountians. Since their mother divorced Tony, Trevor had taken the family to one of those drive-in family vacation spots once where they slept in a tent surrounded by other families doing the same thing for a week. They had flush toilets and showers just a few hundred feet away from their site. The beach was close by and Trevor said they were camping. That was the extent of Mark and Marcy's camping and that was two years ago. Mark was only ten at the time and his sister was eight.

"Come here, little man," Tommy said, placing the ropes around Mark's shoulders. "You get to carry the tent and your sleeping bag. This load is a little heavier than your sister's. Come on, Marcy, your turn." He placed the load he had fastened together over her shoulders and onto her back. "Oh," he said. "Just a minute. I have something else to add." He fastened a bear bell to each of their bundles. The bell hung just below their sleeping bags, fastened with a plastic quick tie. The kids walked around for a few moments going *jingle jingle.*

"I sound like Santa," Marcy said.

"Perfect," Tommy thought. "She does not have a clue what it's really for."

Mark spoke up and said, "How come we have these?"

"It's so I can find you in the dark," Tommy said.

Brad looked at Tommy and said nothing. Both knew why everyone carried bear bells.

Brad, Tommy, and Elizabeth's packs not only contained all the food, clothing, and gear they would need for the next three nights, but they also carried bear spray, whistles, and each had a hunting knife. Elizabeth carried Brad's old forest ranger knife. And Tommy had one of those survival knives. You could screw off the top, which was a compass, and inside the handle was a sawblade, matches, fishing line, and a few hooks. Donna's pack contained her clothes, sleeping bag, and a can of hairspray.

Brad noticed his father's passenger van off in the corner of the parking lot. He had arrived earlier that day with four couples that had hired him to take them to Angel Glacier for the weekend. Brad walked over to the van and placed a note under the windshield wiper blade. It read, "We have headed up to Rock Lake for the weekend. See you Monday night sometime. Love, Brad." He walked back over to Tommy and said, "You guys all ready to go?"

"You bet," Tommy said.

They headed towards the trailhead marked *Rock Lake*. The arrow pointing the direction said ten miles. With Marcy and Mark in tow, Brad knew that a casual three-and-half-hour hike for him and Tommy would turn into a six-hour marathon. "What the heck," he thought to himself. "It's 10:00am, and we will be there at the latest by 4:00pm." The six of them headed up the trail and all you heard was *jingle jingle jingle*.

Chapter 12

Tommy's father, Chris, had been a helicopter pilot during the war in Iraq. He never spoke much to Tommy of his three tours over there, but the Air Force had trained him to fly Apache gunships.

That worked in his favour when he returned from his time overseas. The park's service needed a pilot to fly the brand new Bell 505 they had just acquired. Chris (gunner) fit the bill perfectly. He knew how to take orders and, man, could he fly a chopper. He would get the job as chief pilot for the forest service if he passed the checkout ride on the new 505.

During his test flight with the new 505, there had been a bank robbery in Hillsboro. While going through the certification process, and in the air with the factory instructor from Texas, gunner heard radio chatter about the robbery. He looked over at the instructor. "I cannot let this go," said Chris. The next moment they were off and over Hillsboro in a matter of minutes. Gunner took the new bird to an elevation of seven thousand feet. He radioed to the Hillsboro dispatch that he was in the area and asked for a description of the suspect vehicle. Dispatch had come back and said that they would soon have their own bird in the air and did not require civilian or ranger intervention. They thanked Chris for his concern, though. Chris looked around and noticed a black Corvette heading northbound on route 55. The Corvette had to be traveling at 100mph or more. The driver in control was erratic and passed every car he came up on. Gunner and the instructor watched as the 'vette, ran a family in a Dodge Caravan off the road. The Corvette just mannaged to get by a logging truck it was passing. If the father of the three children in the van had

not hit the ditch, there would have been a head on collision.

"That has to be the idiot they're looking for, no question about it," Gunner said aloud. "Hang on! We're going in."

"No, you can't do this," the instructor said. "Don't do it, gunner, or you'll fail your checkout ride and certification."

Gunner ignored what he heard through the headset. As the chopper decended from seven thousand feet, gunner radioed into Hillsboro Dispatch once again. "Ma,am," he said. "I have a fix on a black Corvette headed northbound on highway 55, approximately forty miles from Hillsboro. This guy is going to kill someone. He just ran a family off the road in a blue Dodge Caravan. Please send help."

"Roger!" came the reply.

Approximately forty miles north of Hillsboro was the dispatcher's message.

"Roger," came gunner's reply.

The Corvette was going faster now. It was actually pulling away from the helicopter. "This guy thinks he is going to outrun me?" Gunner thought to himself. "I'll get him on Canyon Meadow Curve." The car had to follow the road, gunner did not. He pointed the chopper west and was over Canyon Curve as the Corvette came around the bend. Gunner radioed into dispatch. At Canyon Meadow Curve, dispatch had sent their four patrol cars to gunner's first location. The chopper and Corvette were ten miles further down the highway. Dispatch radioed their patrol cars to head towards Canyon Curve. State police and the FBI were on their way. An ambulance had been dispatched to check on the family in the Caravan.

Gunner looked over at the flight instructor. He was as white as a sheet and hanging onto the grabrails

41

located over the door. "You're going to kill us!" he yelled.

"Here we go!" gunner replied.

He dropped the chopper horizontally across the highway. The new bird, the instructor, and gunner were in direct path of the oncoming Corvette.

Johnny Robbins, a career criminal and a two-time loser, wasn't about to return to prison. It was a do-or-die situation for him. He floored the Corvette—130, 140, 150, 160 MPH—the speedometer read as the distance closed between the Bell 505 and the Corvette. Gunner could now see the face of the driver behind the wheel. "This guy is not taking me seriously," he thought. The instructor was undoing his seatbelt, preparing to exit the running chopper. "Hold on," Gunner said. The instructor froze. Gunner applied full power just as the Corvette was mere feet away from the new bird. Johnny Robbins had his middle finger in the air. Gunner could see his eyes through the windshield now. "He's mad, crazier than a bedbug in Iraq," he thought.

The Corvette passed inches below the skids of the brand new chopper. The downwash from the rotor blades had kicked up a ton of dust and turbulence. As the Corvette passed below the chopper's skids, it lost all traction. The air in the front of the car wasn't stable enough to keep the downforce running smoothly over the clean lines of the stolen car. Johnny's middle finger soon came down out of the air as he placed both hands on the wheel. He did his best to maintain control, but as the Corvette's wheels left the ground, there was no going back. The Corvette sailed off the corner of Canyon Meadows curve at a speed of approximately 130 mph. It rolled several times as Gunner and the instructor watched from their vantage point a couple of hundred feet in the air. It was one hell of a wreck. "At least no one else is going to get hurt," Gunner said aloud.

The instructor looked at Gunner and said, "Just wait until I'm done with you. You'll never fly again."

Gunner set the new bird down on the highway. Traffic was now stopped in all directions. He shut down the engine and waited for the authorities to arrive. Five minutes later, state police, Hillsboro P.D, and the Hillsboro news van were on the scene. The instructor was on his cellphone to Texas. The check for the new bird hadn't even been processed yet. Someone was in a heap of trouble, and the situation was about to escalate. Police and emergency rescue teams made their way to the shattered Corvette. Inside the totaled car was Johnny Robbins, wearing blue coveralls, a bag of cash, and a loaded 9mm. "We have a pulse," said one of the EMTs. The factory-designed roll cage had done its job. There was nothing left of the car, but the passenger compartment had stayed somewhat intact. Using the jaws of life, they cut Johnny Robbins from the mangled metal and fiberglass that surrounded him.

The news crew descended on Gunner as the cops tried to gather statements. "Tell us in your words what happened," Christie Mathews from WWHB News asked as she reported live. Gunner relayed his story, and just as he was about to finish, he explained that if it weren't for the new Bell 505, being as nimble and light as it was, the outcome might have been different.

"She's one hell of a bird," he concluded his conversation with the reporter. Chris gave a thumbs up, his other hand on the windshield of the 505.

The FBI had finally arrived at the scene and took Gunner and the instructor to their car for statements. Christie rushed over to the ambulance attendants. They had Johnny Robbins on the stretcher, and he was conscious. "Did you rob the bank?" Christie asked.

Johnny responded, "I am going to kill the motherfucker that was flying that helicopter," as he

pointed. "I did nothing, I am innocent. I was out for a nice drive, and this stupid fucking idiot landed in front of me on the highway. I am innocent," he screamed.

The news report went viral within an hour, and every single wire in the country carried the headline: "HERO PILOT Saves the Day." By the time Gunner and the instructor flew the 505 back to the Ranger station, the instructor's cell phone was ringing constantly. It was Texas. The story had become national news, and pictures of the hero pilot, his hand on the windshield of the new Bell 505, were everywhere.

"I understand completely," the instructor said as he ended his call with Texas. Walking over to Chris, he extended his hand. "Congratulations," he said to Gunner. "You check out and pass with flying colors. Let's just keep what I said earlier to ourselves." The instructor signed off on the checkout ride for Chris, presenting him with his certification in front of Superintendent Gerard and the rest of the staff inside the ranger station.

Gunner was hired and had been flying the new 505 weekly for the forest service since that day. He was a proud man, but he never showed his feelings to anyone or spoke about what he felt. He simply did what was right and did it well.

Johnny Robbins went to trial, was found guilty, and was sentenced to life in prison. "Three strikes and you're out," the judge said in delivering the verdict.

Bell sent Gunner a check for $50,000 and a release agreement. Chris was featured on the front page of the new brochure for the 505, his hand firmly on the windshield. The caption below the picture read, "She's one hell of a bird." Orders were pouring in, with every agency in the country wanting a new 505.

Chapter 13

Johnny Robbins had been in prison for the last five years since the "incident" as he called it.

He swore he was innocent and claimed to have only borrowed the car from his long-time friend, Jackson Hall. Robbins even testified in his own defense at the trial of the century in Hillsboro. The news media had tried and convicted Johnny long before he got to the courtroom, but he was determined to put up a fight. Robbins had a list of prior convictions dating back to when he was 12 years old, including setting the Hillsboro fire department's garbage cans alight.

Johnny had been one of those kids who had been in and out of the system his entire life. He had even faced a murder trial when he was twenty years old, but the prosecution couldn't make their case stick. He had served time for burglary and had a stint for grand theft. It was during this time that he met Jackson Hall. Hall was serving a ten-year sentence for corporate embezzlement.

The towns of Crestview, Hillsboro, and Hillcrest formed a triangle in the state where they were born. Johnny was the notorious figure in Hillsboro, and Jackson had a similar reputation in Crestview, though he was a decade older than Johnny. Their paths crossed while serving time in prison, where they formed a bond and looked out for each other. Both men completed their sentences without parole, having learned how to navigate the system. Jackson was released three months ahead of Johnny, and they maintained a connection through a secret code they had developed, ensuring secure communication.

A few months after Johnny's release, he received a call from Jackson. "Hey man, it's Jackson," the voice said. "How you doing?"

Johnny hesitated for a moment and then replied, "You got something to say to me, brother?"

Jackson's response was, "The fucking garbage stinks when it's on fire." It was the code, a memory etched in Johnny's mind. Jackson proposed a meeting on the following Tuesday, right in front of 451 Front Street in Hillsboro. "How about two o'clock?" he asked.

"Works for me," Johnny confirmed.

"Don't be late," warned Jackson. "We'll lose the job. You'll need a pair of blue coveralls. You can order them from Amazon for twenty bucks. Here's the stock number." Johnny jotted down the details, counting down the days until the appointed Tuesday arrived.

Standing at the Front Street address in Hillsboro, Johnny wore his blue coveralls and checked his watch. It was exactly 2 pm, and the anticipation was palpable.

A black new Corvette pulled up in front of 451 Front Street, and Jackson Hall stepped out, wearing a pair of blue coveralls and driving gloves. "How you doing, man?" greeted Jackson. The two men embraced and shook hands, the contrast of Jackson's driving gloves against Johnny's white hands standing out. "Hey, man," said Jackson, "I'm having a little trouble with the old lady, and I need some time to cool her down, you know what I mean?" He pointed to apartment 301. "Here's a hundred bucks. Why don't you take my new wheels and go for a spin? Come back in two hours, and we'll talk about that job."

"You're kidding," exclaimed Johnny, "that's your Corvette."

"Yup," confirmed Jackson, "all mine. I told you the job is going to pay well, real well. If you haven't noticed, I've been doing great since I got out. See you in two hours," he added. "Wait, here's the security fob you need to start the car," Jackson said, handing it to Johnny. Attached to the fob was a red disk with the number 22. Johnny got into the new car, pushed the start button, and sped off. "Back in two hours!" he yelled over the roar of the engine as he disappeared down the street.

Johnny drove around for a few minutes, passing by the Hillsboro Savings and Credit Union. In front of the bank, several local police cars were parked, and a crowd of people stood around. As he drove by, people pointed at the Corvette, clearly noticing the striking vehicle.

The police swiftly got into their cars, activating their lights and sirens, and initiated a pursuit. Meanwhile, blocks away, Jackson Hall had changed out of his blue coveralls and driving gloves. He reached the end of the block where he had previously stashed a duffle bag containing $150,000 in cash along with a black ski mask, all of which he had hidden in a mailbox. Jackson hastily stuffed his rolled-up coveralls, gloves, and ski mask into the duffle bag and then boarded bus number 99, which was headed to the airport. "Not bad for a day's work," he thought as he settled in.

Johnny drove as fast as the Corvette could go, the vehicle's engine running hot. He felt betrayed by his former prison buddy, suspecting that he was being set up. Determined to evade the pursuing police, he aimed for the open highway. He took Route 55, knowing it would lead him out of town, and he planned to abandon the car after managing to outpace the pursuing officers. The anger and frustration burned within him. He considered Jackson dead if their paths crossed again.

After the crash, the police managed to recover a 9mm handgun and a bag of money from the robbery. However, upon counting the cash, they discovered only $100,000. The situation was growing more complex and dangerous by the minute.

The count came up short by one hundred and fifty thousand dollars. The bank reported a loss of two hundred and fifty thousand dollars that day and received an insurance payout for the difference. They would have to wait until the trial was over as the $100,000 was held in evidence and could not be released.

Jackson Hall had orchestrated a setup against his friend and was now as free as a bird. Johnny Robbins tried to plead his case, explaining how Hall had framed him. He maintained his innocence, insisting he was set up. The police conducted a brief investigation into his claims. However, it was confirmed that on that day, Hall was in California on the beach with his business partner, Maria Hernandez. They co-managed a local surf shop together. Jackson was nowhere near Hillsboro when the robbery occurred, and multiple witnesses, including Maria Hernandez, could vouch for his absence. Furthermore, they visited apartment 301, which had been vacant and under renovation for the past three months. This lead turned out to be a dead end.

In addition to the witness statements, there was bank surveillance footage showing a masked Johnny wearing blue coveralls during the bank robbery. These were the same coveralls he was wearing when he was pulled from the wrecked Corvette. The authorities had amassed sufficient evidence, and Johnny's protests were futile. He was innocent, yet no one would believe him.

There was speculation that the missing one hundred and fifty thousand dollars was hidden

somewhere between the bank and the crash site. Some locals even attempted to locate it, but the money remained undiscovered. Johnny refused to divulge its location, though he claimed he had no idea where it was. He was trapped in a hopeless situation.

Five years passed since the incident. On May 15th, Johnny walked into the prison library. There, he spotted an old copy of Pilot Magazine on the table. The front cover featured a photograph of a hero pilot with his hand against the windshield of a new Bell 505. "Read the story inside," read the caption. Johnny read the article and then tore out a page containing the pilot's picture. He folded it and discreetly placed it between the cheeks of his ass. Johnny had a plan.

Chapter 14

The last five years for Gunner had been mostly routine, except for the divorce from Tommy's mother. She had started an affair with an asshole while Chris was serving his country overseas. When Chris returned, he noticed that she wasn't as receptive to his advances as she once was. They spent hours talking, and she always claimed everything was fine. One day, Gunner left the house early, telling her about the job interviews he had lined up and how he would be home by five that night. However, his last interview called and canceled, changing his plans.

Chris got back home at 3:00 pm. There was an appliance repair van parked in front of the house. The van had a sign on its side that read, "Your fridge don't work? Call Dirk." Chris entered the house through the side door. Everything was quiet, and the fridge was in its usual spot in the kitchen. A tool belt lay on the kitchen table. It all seemed strange. Gunner walked down the hall and opened the bedroom door, where he found his wife, Bonnie, sleeping against Dirk's chest.

In a fit of anger, Chris chased Dirk out of the bedroom, and the man ran out into the street completely naked, leaving behind a chaotic scene.

The ruckus had brought the attention of some of the neighbours. Chris stopped following the prick that had fucked his wife. He returned to his home, grabbed the dick's clothes and toolbelt, and threw them on the front lawn. Dirk stood behind his van as he slipped into his pants. He got in his service vehicle and drove away. How was he going to explain this one to his father who was about to retire? It was a family business and Dirk

was going to take it over.

Two months later, Bonnie initiated divorce proceedings. She received half of Gunner's military pension and the fifty grand that Bell had sent Chris for the photo. On a positive note, Chris retained ownership of the house, along with its mortgage, and he also got custody of their 15-year-old son, Tommy. Tommy would live with his father full-time, as Bonnie was granted supervised visits twice a month due to being declared an unfit mother after her nervous breakdown.

Fast forward five years, and it was now Friday at 10:00 am as Gunner approached the Bell 505 helicopter. He was already two hours into his shift. The chopper was beginning to show signs of its age. The bright red and blue paint scheme, which the park's department had adorned it with, was starting to display wear and tear.

Despite her age, the helicopter had accumulated several thousand hours of flight time. It had undergone a couple of rebuilds, received a new windshield, and had been equipped with new rotor blades. There was also an incident where a goose collided with the passenger side front windshield. Chris had spotted the bird coming towards him and banked hard to avoid it. Unfortunately, the goose followed the same direction he did, resulting in a gruesome scene. Blood and feathers swirled around the cockpit, and the bird's body ended up on the front passenger seat. On the bright side, it made for a good meal the next day.

Placing his hand on the door handle of the Bell 505, Chris addressed the helicopter, "What do you say, girl? Are you ready to start your day?" With that, he hopped into the pilot's seat and began going through his checklist. He flipped a few switches, and the glass displays in the cockpit flickered to life. A few more

switches, and the jet engine emitted its characteristic whine as it roared to life. Overhead, the main rotor began to spin faster and faster, causing the 505 to vibrate. Chris meticulously checked all his gauges: oil temperature was perfect, pressure was perfect, and the fuel tank was full. The mechanics always made sure she was topped up.

On the centre screen of the 505, a computer overlay displayed the route he was about to fly, providing Chris with the necessary guidance for his upcoming journey.

The computer program was so advanced that it allowed him to fly even in complete fog without clear visibility through his windshield. The computer's capabilities extended to determining his precise location and projecting his flight path over a 3D map of the terrain. It was an extraordinary piece of technology, one that the Air Force had been utilizing for a quarter of a century. He pondered about the other novel advancements that had been developed in the meantime. He speculated that eventually, some of these innovations would filter down to civilian use, much like fax machines that were initially invented between 1843 and 1846. Historically, the military always received technology ahead of the general public.

Speaking aloud, Gunner addressed the helicopter, "Come on, girl, let's start our day." He pressed the red button on the cyclic control and spoke clearly into the microphone attached to his helmet. "This is Charlie Gulf Romeo Romeo, requesting a vector from RS 1 to Crystal Springs National Park." His words were transmitted through the communication system, initiating his flight plan for the day.

His radio sprung to life, and he heard the voice of Air Traffic Control at Hillsboro Municipal. "Roger,

Charlie Gulf Romeo Romeo," they communicated, "you are cleared for a heading of 330 at an elevation of 3000 feet. Watch for traffic to your right, a 172, at 3500 feet. Enjoy your flight, sir."

"Roger," Gunner replied, "have a great day." He pulled back on the collective control, increasing the altitude of the helicopter. Utilizing the rudder pedals under his feet, he smoothly turned the helicopter's nose to the 330-degree heading. Adjusting the cyclic control forward, he directed the helicopter over the tree line adjacent to the Ranger Station.

While the Bell 505 was capable of reaching a maximum altitude of 22,500 feet, the tallest mountains within his jurisdiction reached only 17,300 feet. The helicopter handled these altitudes with ease, not even breaking a sweat. Gunner reminisced about the time he had to rescue two climbers from the top of Mount Eisenhower four years earlier. It was a testament to the capabilities of his reliable aircraft.

Today's mission involved a routine patrol aimed at spotting wildlife and identifying any potential issues that the public might encounter over the long weekend. Gunner's role was to identify problems, radio the information to the ground teams in their four-wheel-drive vehicles, and coordinate solutions. As he approached the park boundary, he glanced at his watch—it was now 10:45 am.

Flying over the Rock Lake parking lot, his eyes caught sight of several cars. Among them were his son's vehicle and his friend Brad's. Both cars had "S and R" painted on their roofs, making them easily distinguishable. Gunner chuckled to himself, thinking, "At least search and rescue is here before we even need them." It was a recurring scenario; every year, there

would be one or two couples who managed to get lost during the first extended weekend of summer. This time, he hoped it wouldn't be the case.

With a gentle pull on the collective lever using his left hand, Gunner increased the engine power. The Bell 505 started climbing and reached an altitude of 4500 feet. He began his patrol along the outer boundaries of the park, a task that would take around an hour to complete. The park spanned 2500 square miles, with some areas remaining untouched by human presence.

As he changed his flight path, Gunner found himself flying over Angel Glacier. He spotted a group on the trail leading towards its face—Brad's father, Kevin, along with his companions. They all wore backpacks and winter jackets, standing out against the landscape.

Angel Glacier rested at an elevation of 8,700 feet, nestled within a sheltered valley between two mountain ranges. The glacier's main expanse lay between these rising mountain ranges, with two smaller glaciers branching from the main body—one to the east and another to the west. From Gunner's perspective, the glacier resembled an angel with outstretched wings. Above the Bell 505, a towering 9,000 feet of mountains were adorned with a blanket of spring snow. It was a breathtaking sight, one that Gunner couldn't help but marvel at. "Beautiful," he thought, "nothing like this in the desert."

As he flew over the group below, his radio crackled to life. Kevin's voice came through, "How's she look?" he inquired.

Gunner replied, "Better than last year. Lots of spring snow still around. It looks like you might run into several other hikers." The camaraderie between Kevin and Chris had grown strong since their sons became

friends.

"Roger," Kevin acknowledged. "We'll be here for a few hours and then head down to Glacier Creek Campground. It's a bit chilly up here," Kevin said.

Gunner responded, "Roger. Enjoy your weekend." The connection faded as the radio returned to static, leaving Gunner to continue his patrol and enjoy the magnificent sights spread out beneath him.

Brad's father had booked and registered their tour with the park's branch months in advance, adhering to all the proper protocols. Therefore, they were precisely where they were meant to be. Following a path that traced Angel Creek, Gunner guided the helicopter over the campground area. He circled the site twice, quickly observing that the firewood bins were devoid of supplies.

"Charlie Gulf Romeo Romeo to ground support, do you read?" Gunner transmitted through his radio, awaiting a response. After a brief moment, the radio crackled to life.

"Go ahead," came the reply.

Gunner reported, "I noticed the bins are not stocked at GCCG. We have a group up at Angel Glacier, and they are going to get mighty chilly tonight without your help."

"We're aware of the situation," came the response. "We encountered an issue with Toby's quad this morning, but we're on our way."

Gunner acknowledged, "Roger, thanks, boys." Toby and Brent had relatively straightforward responsibilities. Both had been employed by the park's branch for the past three years. Their task involved loading custom-designed trailers with firewood in the

parking lot, ensuring the campers had sufficient supplies for their stay, and then connecting the loaded trailers to their quads and transporting the firewood to the designated campgrounds within the park boundaries. This method efficiently prevented the destruction of forests by weekend campers wielding axes. The park's branch had introduced substantial fines for anyone caught cutting down trees, rendering such practices unnecessary. The firewood was already provided, waiting for campers upon their arrival.

The firewood supplied by the park came from dead trees and those affected by disease, which had succumbed to the natural cycle of life. This approach allowed the park to clean up after nature had taken its course. Moreover, this method served to mitigate the risk of wildfires in the area, contributing to a self-sustaining program. With ample deadfall each year and a steady stream of campers paying for camping spots and wood, the arrangement was mutually beneficial. This approach ensured that the forest could continue to provide for generations to come—an arrangement that was beneficial to everyone involved and a wise decision overall.

During his flight, Gunner spotted several bighorn sheep dotting the landscape. In the meadows, elk could be seen grazing. He observed deer sipping from the edges of abundant water sources. Occasionally, he caught glimpses of mountain lions, though there were no wolves in sight that day. Wolves had been reintroduced to the park two decades ago, but they proved to be more elusive than the mountain lions.

Yet, Gunner's favorites among the wildlife were the bears. The park hosted a small population of black bears and around twenty grizzlies. Over the years, the black bears had grown accustomed to the presence of

humans passing through their territories. They could usually be discouraged with the noise of banging pots or the blare of an air horn. Grizzlies, on the other hand, feared little except each other. In the rare instances when Gunner had flown over a grizzly, the bears would hold their ground. Casting a glance upwards, they would continue their activities at their own pace. The noise from the helicopter was treated as an annoyance, barely affecting them. Grizzlies exhibited a profound indifference to whoever or whatever crossed their path. They stood atop the food chain, and this reality was evident in their demeanor. Evolution had ensured their dominance.

Chapter 15

Jingle, jingle, jingle was the sound that resonated from Brad, Elizabeth, Tommy, and Donna. Marcy and Mark contributed to the chorus, accompanied by a hint of weariness expressed through a whining tone, "I'm tired, how much further do we have to go?" As they ventured an hour into their hike towards Rock Lake, the children's persistent jingling began to test Brad's patience.

Sensing the group's fatigue, Tommy suggested they pause a few hundred feet ahead at Trappers Gulch. It was an ideal spot to step off the trail, catch their breath, and relish the surrounding scenery. As the six hikers ascended further along the trail, moving away from the parking lot, they encountered patches of snow nestled deep within the forest. Sizeable remnants still covered the forest floor in shaded areas. Brad recognized that these areas typically took longer to thaw. The trees would retain the snow on their branches throughout the winter, accumulating until it became too heavy for them to bear. At that point, the snow would tumble from the top of the tree, creating a buildup at its base. This accumulation would create a well-like depression with icy walls, making it virtually impossible to escape without a rope and a helping hand.

The configuration of each tree's accumulation varied based on the size of its branches. Despite the winter conditions, solitary hikers would traverse these trails.

Over the years, some hikers had become disoriented in these conditions. Springtime had witnessed the discovery of bodies at the base of sizable

spruce trees. These unfortunate individuals had slid into the depressions formed by the snow accumulation at the trees' bases and found themselves trapped. The predicament was dire—cold, hungry, and with no means of escape. In Brad's relatively short lifetime, three bodies had been discovered this way. It was a chilling way to meet one's end—stranded, unnoticed, until it was too late. Ultimately, these individuals succumbed to hypothermia as they drifted into a final, fatal slumber.

Moving off the path, the group of four adults and two children ventured about fifty feet before settling down, overlooking Trappers Gulch. Tommy expressed his awe, "How beautiful is that?" he remarked to Marcy and Mark.

"Look over there. Do you know why they call it Trappers Gulch?" Mark inquired.

Brad answered, "Well, back in the olden days, fur traders passed through this area. This is where they would hunt for foxes, mink, and any other fur-bearing creatures."

Marcy questioned further, "Did they kill them or just shave off their hair?"

Donna explained, "No, honey, they had to kill them. That's why today we have fake fur. The trappers harvested a significant number of animals during those times. If it wasn't for the park, these animals wouldn't be alive today to have new babies."

"I hate trappers," Marcy exclaimed.

Amidst the conversation, Mark interjected, "I'm hungry." Responding to Mark, Tommy, Brad, and Elizabeth retrieved some trail mix from their pouches and generously shared with Donna and the two children. Despite the snacks, Mark's hunger persisted, and he

voiced, "I'm still hungry."

Tommy had a suggestion, "Why don't you eat the sausages in your pocket?" Mark realized he had forgotten about them and unzipped his pocket to uncover the napkin-wrapped sausages.

With a plan in mind, he contemplated, "I'll eat one now, and I'll save the other for later."

As they prepared to depart, the sound of the approaching 505 became audible in the distance, steadily growing louder. Excitement ensued as Tommy urged, "Come on, you guys. Maybe if we hurry, you can wave to Grandpa Chris." Rejoining the trail, they made their way forward, though their efforts fell just short. By the time they returned, Gunner had already flown over his own son, girlfriend, their friends, and the two children.

Gunner hadn't activated the 505's FLIR infrared system; there was no need for it on this particular flight since no one was lost. "Sorry, kids. Maybe we'll see Grandpa next time," Tommy consoled.

Meanwhile, Chris continued flying directly toward Rock Lake. As he approached, a movement caught his eye in the meadow beside the old trapper's cabin—it was a sow grizzly and her two cubs. An exclamation of excitement escaped Gunner, "Fantastic!" he declared aloud. This sighting marked the twenty-second grizzly he had encountered. The population of these majestic creatures was evidently thriving within the park, a testament to the success of the conservation efforts. With a quick press of the black record button on the dash, the 505's cameras captured a series of images that would later be downloaded and reviewed. Observing the mother and her cubs retreating into the forest about a mile away from the Trapper's Cabin, Chris couldn't help but praise, "Great. She and her offspring are headed

away from the possibility of human contact this weekend. Good girl," he affirmed aloud.

Gunner initiated a bank with the 505, aligning its nose towards Hillsboro. With the fuel running low, he soared over the parking lot once more, witnessing its transformation into a bustling hub of activity. The area was now teeming with people, SUVs equipped with barbecues, and a scattering of lawn chairs. It resembled a parade day scene in a Walmart parking lot.

Gunner contacted Hillsboro Municipal Airport through the radio, "Charlie Gulf Romeo Romeo requesting a vector to Shell for refuelling," he announced.

A swift response followed, "Roger." Further instructions were provided, "Charlie Gulf Romeo Romeo, heading 140 degrees. Please contact ground control 10 miles out."

Acknowledging the instructions, Gunner replied, "Roger Romeo Romeo out."

As he approached the airport, Gunner reached out to ground control as instructed. They guided him over the eastern region of the airport's outer boundaries, a route that he wasn't fond of due to its proximity to the landfill serving the three communities. The stark contrast from the breathtaking scenery he had just experienced was disheartening.

"Charlie Gulf Romeo Romeo, turn right heading 240, and we will have someone meet you at the pump. No traffic in the area," the instructions came through. Following their directions, Gunner adjusted his course accordingly.

Approaching the designated landing area in front of the gas pumps, Gunner deftly hovered the 505 for a

few moments before gently touching down. He reviewed his gauges to ensure everything was in order and subsequently powered down the helicopter. Attendants emerged from the building situated behind the gas pump, and with a smile, Gunner stepped out of the 505. Its main rotor, which had been spinning, had now come to a stop.

Greeting the attendants, Gunner instructed, "Fill her up and check the tires, will you, boys?" They shared a chuckle at his request. As they set about their tasks, Chris entered the building. He needed a restroom break and had a couple of phone calls to make. The time was swiftly approaching 2:30 PM.

Roughly thirty minutes later, the attendants had successfully refueled the 505. They also took care to wash the windshield and eliminate any lingering moisture with their squeegees. Gunner expressed his gratitude, "Thanks, boys. Send the bill to the park's branch, as always." Chris then embarked on a brief walk around the 505, inspecting it thoroughly for any discrepancies that might have arisen during his morning flight.

Chris opened the door, climbed into the cockpit, and spoke aloud, "Let's go home, girl." Air traffic control granted him clearance to ascend to 6,000 feet, directing him on a heading of 140 degrees. This trajectory would lead him directly over Hillcrest and guide him to the ranger station's helipad.

From his vantage point at 6,000 feet, Chris enjoyed a sweeping view of the three adjacent communities: Hillsboro, Hillcrest, and Crestview. They formed a symmetrical triangle, all conveniently located within an hour's drive of each other. Nestled in the center of this geographical triangle was the aging Benchmark mine, a once-productive site now characterized by decay

and neglect. The mine's tailings covered its grounds, while settling ponds had transformed into havens for bullrushes and local ducks. Benchmark mine had yielded millions of dollars' worth of gold, silver, and copper over its active years, and the surrounding communities had emerged as a result of its existence.

The mine sat just a half-hour's drive from either community, yet each town was separated by an hour's travel from the other. The forefathers seemed to have employed a clever strategy in their planning. Although the mine employed around 40% of the workforce in each town, every community had its distinct characteristics.

The mine owners played a significant role in shaping the infrastructure and major recreational facilities of each town. This investment proved lucrative, especially during events like high school football matches between Hillsboro and Hillcrest or their ice hockey games. The mine profited from the need for food and drinks during these gatherings. The three towns engaged in spirited competition, fostering a rivalry that the Benchmark mine capitalized on.

As the mine's resources dwindled, the communities were compelled to diversify their economies. Hillcrest, for instance, transformed into a thriving tourist destination just before the entrance to the National Park. The local Rotary Club even organized tours of the old mine site. For twenty dollars, participants could experience a ride on the historic donkey train, venturing a few hundred feet underground. During the stop, a guide would provide a historical overview of mining practices from the past.

The mine's transformation into a popular tourist attraction turned it into a bustling spot throughout the summer. Hillsboro, with its local airport and major

banks, played a pivotal role in the region's economy. Crestview, on the other hand, had evolved into the primary hub for the area. Serving as the central distribution point, they received and distributed various goods to the surrounding regions. From food and clothing to hard goods and even the railroad, everything passed through Crestview. Surprisingly, these changes had led to even more employment opportunities than during the mine's heyday. Despite the mine's closure forty years prior, the three communities not only endured but thrived. Life in the region was good.

As the clock struck 4:00pm, Gunner gently landed the 505 on the helipad outside the Forest Service's main office. He retrieved the SDS memory card from the main computer, then shut down the helicopter. His day wasn't over; there was still paperwork to be done.

Chapter 16

The kids trudged on with their hike towards Rock Lake, taking breaks approximately every hour. Mark and Marcy, however, continued their complaints, expressing how cold they were. Clouds began to gather over Prospectors Pass, their fluffy white forms raising no immediate concern. Rain wasn't likely, at least.

Their journey had lasted for three and a half hours so far, not accounting for their breaks. The trail led them around a corner, guiding them downhill into the valley where Rock Lake nestled. The valley sprawled out before them, its grass turning a vibrant shade of green. A gentle ripple shimmered across the lake's surface. Rising from the lake's centre stood a towering cluster of rocks, reaching heights of about a hundred feet. The view from this vantage point was breathtaking.

Tommy eagerly pointed out, "Look, kids, we're almost there!" Donna chimed in, noting her sore feet. Brad and Elizabeth exchanged glances; they were only 25 minutes away from setting up camp. Nature's beauty surrounded them, and it was time to savor the experience. At last, they reached the lake's shoreline.

The group of four young adults and two children made their way to the designated camping area designated by the National Park Service. They chose a spot with a picnic table and a flat area for their tents. Their backpacks were laid on the table, while Tommy helped Mark and Marcy remove their rope harnesses and set their gear with the others. Brad and Elizabeth proceeded to set up their tent for the next three nights.

Brad retrieved the flexible fiberglass poles from

their bag. These poles were designed with a high-tension rubber bungee cord running through the center, allowing them to be easily connected. After connecting the two-foot poles to create two ten-foot lengths, Brad inserted them through the ridge cap that formed an X at the top of the nylon tent. He gently bent each pole down, securing them into the four pockets on the base of the tent.

"Looks perfect," he remarked to Elizabeth. They agreed on the tent's placement and Brad asked for his axe. With the axe in hand, he drove six fourteen-inch metal rods through the eyelets stitched into the tent's floor fabric. He pulled the fabric tight, securing it in place. "There you go, Elizabeth—your home away from home," Brad announced as he finished the setup.

Brad turned his attention to helping Tommy and Donna set up their tent. Then they moved on to setting up the kids' tent. After everything was set up, the three tents formed a semicircle around a fire pit, with a picnic table placed nearby.

"Doesn't get much better than this," Tommy commented.

Brad and Tommy decided not to use the tent flies since there was no rain in the forecast. They saved the extra tarps for other purposes. Mark suddenly exclaimed that he needed to use the bathroom. "I have to poop," he said. Tommy handed him a plastic bag from his backpack and instructed him on what to do.

"Come on, it's this way," Tommy said, leading Mark away from the campsite towards some fallen trees behind the huckleberry bushes.

"What, where's the toilet?" Mark asked incredulously.

"Right here," Tommy replied. He explained that

Mark should find a sturdy log to support his weight and secure a plastic bag to one side using push pins. "Now we need to find a stick in the shape of a Y..."

"Here's one," Mark said.

Perfect. Now, place the Y-shaped stick on the other side of the plastic bag just like this. Make sure the bottom of the Y keeps the mouth of the bag open," Tommy explained. "You hang your bum over the edge of the log and you poop in the bag." Mark followed the instructions and positioned himself over the bag, using the stick contraption.

"Here's the roll of toilet paper. Don't use too much, it's all we have," Tommy warned.

"Ugh, gross," Mark muttered, though he had no other choice. He completed his task and returned to Tommy on the other side of the bushes.

"Are you all done?" Tommy asked.

"Yup, that was pretty gross," Mark replied.

"Where's the bag and toilet paper?" Tommy asked.

"Huh?" Mark was puzzled.

"Go get the bag and your poop. Don't forget the push pins and toilet paper. Bring everything here," Tommy instructed.

Mark retrieved the bag, pins, and toilet paper. Tommy then showed him how to tie a knot in the top of the bag, securing its contents. Tommy jokingly declared Mark an official mountain man.

Returning to the campsite, Mark proudly held up the bag, announcing, "My poop!" Marcy, curious, asked about it, and Mark teasingly waved the bag at her. Marcy

screamed and called her brother a pig.

Amused by her reaction, Mark playfully chased Marcy around the campsite with the bag in his hand. The fun continued until Mark slipped, and the bag accidentally broke open.

Mark's playful antics took a rather unpleasant turn when the bag broke and there was feces on his hand. "Get another bag," Tommy instructed, clearly less amused now. Tommy guided Mark through transferring everything to a new bag and cleaning up the mess. "Once you're done, go wash your hands down by the water," Tommy said, his tone more serious. The incident put an end to Mark's earlier teasing of his sister.

Within the camping area, the park had buried a 45-gallon drum with a screw-on lid. This drum served as a waste disposal system for campers. Visitors were required to use it for waste and garbage while they were at the site, and they had to carry out all waste with them when they left. Tommy opened the drum, kicked the bag inside, and securely screwed the lid back on. Brad and Tommy shared a hearty laugh, knowing that they had a similar experience a decade ago when Brad's father, Kevin, had brought them to the same spot. It seemed that both generations of boys had their initiation into wilderness living right there. Brad and Tommy had their first shit in the woods almost in the same location. They, too, were mountain men.

Mark, having returned from washing his hands, joined Brad for a fishing expedition. "Did you see any fish?" Brad asked.

"Fish? I didn't see any fish," Mark said. "Where are they?"

"Come on, little man," Brad said. "We need to

catch some dinner or we're going to starve tonight." Brad explained the strategy to Mark, emphasizing that they were aiming to catch dinner for everyone at the campsite. Leaving the others at the campsite, Brad and Mark made their way to the edge of the clear lake, ready to try their luck.

Brad engaged Mark's observational skills, asking him what he saw in the water. "What do you see, little man?" he asked Mark.

As Mark looked more closely, he noticed movement in the water, prompting him to wonder aloud about what he had seen. "What was that? Something just went by. I saw something in the water."

Brad pointed out a small creek flowing into the lake and explained that this was where the fish gathered. "Do you see this little creek that flows into the lake? That is where all the fish hang out. The creek brings dead bugs and stuff from the forest and the fish wait right out there for their dinner. But tonight, they're going to be our dinner instead."

Brad rolled an old log over, and on the bottom side, there were about ten grubs that had been busy breaking down the soft wood. Brad opened the small tin box he had brought down to the water. "Here, take this old pill bottle and put those white wiggly things in the container," he instructed Mark.

"Cool," said Mark, and soon he had them all rounded up and in the bottle. Brad had assembled his rod and placed a hook on the end of the fishing line, tying it just like his dad had shown him years ago.

"Now," he said, "we need a little piece of wood that will act as a bobber." He took his new buck knife from its sheath and cut two notches into a small piece of

wood. "There," he said, "see how that looks?" Mark was paying close attention.

"Now we're going to place that piece about five feet from the hook. See," Brad said to Mark, "now give me one of those grubs you have in the container." Mark handed one to Brad; it started to wiggle, and Mark dropped it—the thing disappeared among the rocks they were standing on. "Grab another one," said Brad. This time Mark hung on a little tighter.

"Here, Uncle Brad," he said.

"Now watch," said Brad. "You take the grub and you push the hook in here, and it comes out here, but not very much. The fish are smart, and if they think something is not right, they won't bite. See how the hook is hard to see? That's what we want—to trick the fish. We're after cutthroat trout; they're smart, but we are smarter." Brad placed the bait on top of the piece of wood and placed the whole setup into the creek. "Now, Mark," Brad said, "if we have done this right, we are going to have fresh fish for dinner." Brad let out the seven-pound test line as the piece of wood was carried by the creek out onto the lake. He and Mark watched as the small piece of wood was carried about thirty feet offshore. "Now, this is the trick," he said to Mark.

Brad gave the rod a quick, light flick, and the hook with bait rolled off the piece of wood into the water five feet below the surface. "Now we... boom, fish on!" said Brad. His light rod bounced, its tip fluttering back and forth. He set the hook and slowly turned the handle on the reel while keeping tension on the line. "Do you see him?" said Brad as the line moved back and forth in the water.

"There it is!" exclaimed Mark. "I see it."

Brad continued to keep the tension on the line until the fish was near the shore. In one quick motion, he lifted the rod high into the air, and the fish came flying out of the water onto the rocks at their feet. "Quick, grab a hold of him," said Brad to Mark. The fish was flopping all over the place. Mark got a hold of the cutthroat and held it up. The fish wiggled about, but there was no way Mark was going to let it go.

Brad laid his rod down and took the fish from Mark's hands. Brad showed Mark how to remove the hook from the edge of the cutthroat's jaw. "You stick your finger in here," said Brad. "This is the gill slit. See, when your finger is in here, he can't get away." Mark paid close attention; his hands were covered in slime, and his uncle was handling the fish with one finger and a thumb. "Now," said Brad, "you never let anything you are going to eat suffer." He laid the trout out on a rock. Brad picked up a fist-sized stone.

He hit the first catch of the afternoon in the head. The trout stopped moving. It was a perfect two-pounder. "Now, little man, do you think you can catch one on your own?" Brad asked Mark.

Mark said, "I want to try. I think I can do it." Brad handed Mark his rod and reel. He watched as the boy placed a grub on the hook just as Brad had shown him. "Do I put it in the creek like this?" The hook fell off the wooden float Brad had made.

"Try again," said Brad. "Push the button on the reel so the line goes out... There you go, see... keep letting out the line. That's it, very good, keep letting it out." The piece of wood drifted out thirty feet. Mark turned the handle on the reel, and the line went tight. "Now just give it a little jerk." The hook and grub dropped into the lake below the homemade float. "Now

we wait," said Brad.

Five minutes later, Mark had hooked his first fish. He fought it like a pro. As he got it closer to the shore, the line went slack. He turned the handle on the reel and brought the line to the surface. The fish was gone. "Try again," said Uncle Brad. Mark went through the same routine. He lost two that day, but he and Brad were going back to the campsite with three two-pounders. There was going to be a feast tonight. Mark was learning fast.

Mark carried those fish into camp on a stick Brad had found lying on the ground.

The stick was passed through each gill slit and out through the mouth. "Look, look what we caught!" Mark was as proud as a peacock.

Donna said, "Those look wonderful! Hold on, I want to get a picture of the fisherman and his catch." She pulled out her cell phone and snapped a few shots. Soon, they were all posing for pictures with Mark.

Brad noticed that the picnic table had been set for dinner. Donna and Elizabeth had taken the sleeping bags off the backpacks and laid them out in their respective tents. They organized the canned food for the evening's dinner, counting on Brad to bring back some fish. Tommy was gathering firewood from the stocked area that the park's service filled every two days. He had a good stack already split and ready to go for the evening. He was just returning with another armful that he needed to split.

Brad looked around; everything looked in order around the camp. "Come on, little buddy," said Brad. "I am going to show you how to clean these fish."

Marcy asked, "Can I come?"

"Sure, let's go down to the lake and get these babies ready for the frying pan." Brad took a plastic bag from his pack.

Marcy and Mark led the way to the water's edge. Brad kneeled down next to some large rocks. "Hand me those fish," he said to Mark. Brad reached for his new knife, unsnapped the sheath, and held the knife firmly in his left hand. "Remember how I showed you how to hold the fish?" he said to Mark. "Put your thumb in the gill slit, just like this. Now we rinse off the dirt." He moved the trout back and forth through the water. "Now we are going to gut this sucker and clean out the inside."

Mark watched intently as Brad ran the blade of the knife up the belly of the trout, cutting about a half inch into its body cavity. He opened the sides of the fish, exposing its internal organs. Marcy screamed and ran back to the campsite. Brad reached in and pulled out everything he could see. He tossed the guts into the lake. "See this black line that runs up his spine?" said Brad. "You run your thumb along that and clean it all out." He rinsed the fish in the lake. "See how nice and clean it is inside?" Mark looked. "Let's remove the head too. Your Auntie Donna does not like them looking at her when she cooks."

He took the Buck Huntsman and, in one quick stroke, the head fell to the water's edge. Brad grabbed it and tossed it ten feet off shore. "There," he said, "the whitefish will clean that up. Let me do another one, and you can try the final one," he said to Mark. Brad cleaned a second fish, removed its head, and spent another twenty minutes helping Mark clean his first fish. When all three were cleaned to Brad's liking, they put the fish into the plastic bag and returned to the campsite.

Marcy was complaining and saying she did not

want fish because they were gross. Tommy had lit the fire in the provided pit. It was the top of a 45-gallon barrel, about 12 inches deep. Several holes were cut into its sides to provide a fresh supply of air to the fire as it burned inside. "How many matches?" asked Brad.

"One," was Tommy's reply. It was always a competition to see if the fires they made were done right from the start or took more effort and more matches.

"Way to go," said Brad. He took two cans of beans from his pack and made two holes in the tops of each can. He dropped the half grill that was attached to the fire ring across the flames. Instantly, he had a surface he could cook on. "Let's wait a bit for the fire to die down, and we'll have some nice coals to cook on," he suggested.

"Perfect," said Tommy.

"I'm hungry," said Marcy.

Elizabeth took a couple of hotdogs from their package and wiggled them in front of Marcy. "How about these?" she said.

"Yes, hot dogs are my favorite. I want some too," said Mark. Elizabeth put four hotdogs down on a plate. She took small squeeze bottles of ketchup, mustard, and relish from her pack, along with a semi-frozen ball of dough. She worked the dough into a roll about a foot long and cut it up into 12 equal pieces. Placing the cut dough on a plate, she covered her work with a plastic bag.

Donna searched through Tommy's pack and found a package of pre-made salad. Tommy took a collapsible water jug from his pack and asked Marcy to go fill it up at the creek. "Take this cup, use the water from the creek, and then fill up the jug," he instructed. Tommy took the cap off and placed it in her pocket.

Mark and Marcy went to the creek together and started filling the jug.

Chapter 17

The four young adults sat at the picnic table, observing Mark and Marcy as they filled the jug with cup after cup of fresh water. "That will keep them busy for half an hour," Tommy said, and they all shared a laugh. Suddenly, there was movement at the top of the trailhead that led to the meadow where the kids were camping. Brad took out his binoculars and looked closely. He spotted six older adults, burdened with large backpacks. It took the three couples at least half an hour to reach the campsite that the kids had established.

"Howdy, I am Seamus O'Riley," said the man at the front of the group with a thick Irish accent. "We're from Ireland and have c'mere ta enjoy this beautiful country. Can you tell us how to get to RL01 and RL02?"

"Well," Tommy replied, "you're on the right path. You have about a mile to go. You'll find those two rental cabins at the north end of Rock Lake. This is the south end. Just keep going down this path," Tommy pointed. "It will take you along the lake and eventually to the cabins. They're pretty small," he added. "How long are you folks staying?"

Seamus responded, "We'll be there for a couple o' days, then we'll head to California. You kids look like you know what you're doing. Thanks for the information." With that, the group of six continued on their way.

Mark and Marcy returned with the water jug half full, their shoes soaked. "What happened to the rest of the water?" Tommy asked.

"The jug was too heavy," Mark explained. "We

had to let some out."

Tommy took the lid from Marcy's pocket, screwed it back onto the jug, and placed it on the picnic table. "Time to start preparing dinner," Brad said. He and Tommy got up and moved towards the fire pit.

"Did you notice anything about that group?" Tommy asked.

"Yeah," Brad replied, "obviously newbies. All their gear was brand new, even their boots. Did you notice they didn't have any bells on their packs? I didn't even see a bottle of bear spray."

"Well, hopefully whoever outfitted them sold them a bottle and it's in one of their packs. God knows they were weighed down, they had a lot of stuff."

Meanwhile, the group of six tourists continued down the path that Tommy had pointed out. They followed the trail across the creek, past the old Trapper's cabin that had stood there for over a century. Its roof had long since collapsed, and the walls were sloping inwards, while the door frame was askew. They continued for another half mile until they eventually reached RL01, one of the rental cabins.

In the 1970s, the park's service had constructed four cabins at the north end of Rock Lake. These cabins were fairly well-built for their time and were situated on concrete blocks. To bring in the materials necessary for each cabin's construction, the old Sikorsky H-34 helicopter owned by the park's department was utilized. This helicopter, although fuel-hungry and challenging to pilot, was a formidable workhorse capable of carrying substantial loads.

The materials for each cabin were carefully secured in netting beneath the Sikorsky helicopter. Items

ranging from windows, 2x4s, plywood, shingles, woodstoves, and bunks were airlifted to each of the four designated locations. The distance between each cabin was approximately one hundred feet. Cabin one was positioned on the east shore of Rock Lake, while cabins two and three were located on the lake's northern end. Cabin four was situated on the west shore, directly across from cabin one. These four cabins became the prized assets of the park's branch, commanding a rental price of five hundred dollars per night during high season and two hundred dollars per night during the off-season and winter months.

Seamus and his party of five had paid a total of two thousand dollars, plus tax, for a two-night stay in their chosen wilderness retreats. The park's brochure showcased a photograph from the mid-70s, depicting families sitting on lawn chairs, reveling in the serene scenery during their vacations. Seamus, residing in Ireland, had easily booked his accommodations online the moment he saw those compelling images. Upon confirming his credit card payment, he swiftly received a confirmation along with a unique combination code. This code would grant him access to the key box for each of the cabins he had reserved: RL Cabin One's code was 2428, and RL Cabin Two's code was 2429.

As the group stood gazing at RL01, they noted its dimensions of 16 feet by 20 feet. The cabin's original cedar shake roof had long been replaced with a modern green tin roof. The once-present curtains in the windows had been substituted with sturdy plywood shutters, which were hinged on the exterior of the cabins. When opened, these shutters were propped up by chains suspended from the roof trusses.

Seamus took out his phone and dialed the combination on the lock box, securely fastened to the

railing of cabin one. He entered the digits 2428 and deftly manipulated the lever. The lock box sprang open, revealing an aged key affixed to a National Parks key chain.

Seamus unburdened himself from his backpack and ascended the cabin's stairs. He slotted the key into the lock, giving it a subtle jiggle until the mechanism yielded and the door creaked open. Within, the interior hosted a pair of plywood bunk beds as well as a solitary wood stove. This stove had been carefully situated in a corner, surrounded by old tin flashing that extended from floor to ceiling. These protective measures were implemented to ensure that the occupants of the cabin wouldn't inadvertently spark any disastrous fires. Placed in the center of the room was a well-worn picnic table.

All four cabins mirrored this layout, maintaining identical arrangements with one exception. Seamus's attention was drawn to the picnic table's surface, where numerous people over time had carved their initials into the wood. Stepping back outside, he enthusiastically declared, "It's perfect!" He then assisted his wife, Aileen, in removing her backpack.

Meanwhile, Shawn, Briana, Caitlin, and Caitlin's girlfriend, Cathleen, were assigned to stay in Cabin RL02. The quartet made their way to the front of Cabin Two. Shawn deftly entered the combination code 2429 into the lock box, retrieved the key, and unlocked the door. The group entered the cabin, backpacks still strapped to their shoulders. For the next two nights, this cozy abode would serve as their home, immersing them in an authentic experience reminiscent of the American pioneers.

Chapter 18

Chris entered the ranger station with the SD card tucked into his pocket, a clipboard in hand, and a photocopied map of the park. Using a red felt pen, he had carefully traced the flight route he had taken earlier that day on the map. He submitted the marked map and proceeded to fill out his daily report, detailing the day's events and observations.

Reaching into his shirt pocket, he retrieved the SD card and handed it over to Betty, the computer expert stationed at the office. Betty promptly stamped the card with the date and time of its submission before placing it on the corner of her desk. In exchange, she handed Chris another blank SD card, all set for his use the next morning. "Pretty routine day," Chris remarked to Betty, "Everything's in my report."

Betty acknowledged his words and added the card to her collection. Her task for the following morning would involve typing up Chris's report, ensuring that the flight's details were accurately documented for the official records of the park's service. With such documentation, future generations would be able to read about Gunner's day and get a glimpse of what the park looked like during this period in history. Chris's efforts were contributing to the preservation of history, allowing future readers to appreciate his insights and experiences.

As the clock struck 5:00 pm, Chris prepared to head home. Betty, on the other hand, remained immersed in her tasks, working diligently to catch up on the extra workload that had accumulated due to the extended weekend.

Due to the demands of the weekend, everyone was on call and had to work both Saturday and Sunday, including the office staff. Betty found herself occupied with cataloging the day's permits, a task that took longer than anticipated. By the time she completed the task, it was already 6:20 pm, well past her scheduled shift end at 5:30 pm. She diligently logged her hours on the time sheet situated at the front desk, ensuring her work was properly documented.

Turning off the lights in the office and securing the main door, Betty made her way down the stairs to the parking lot. Walking around two hundred feet, she arrived at the Superintendent's residential quarters and entered the premises. In the kitchen, her partner and Superintendent, Bob Gerard, greeted her.

"Honey, I've made dinner. How was your day?" he inquired, looking up from his task.

Chapter 19

The Cessna 172 that passed by Gunner earlier in the day was carrying two passengers and the pilot. The passengers, Johnny Robbins and Matt Jones, the latter of whom happened to be Donna's brother, who had been sent upstate for grand theft. Robbins had concocted a plan after reading about the heroic pilot, and now that plan was coming together. He had lost another five years of his life, and it was time for payback. Matt had crossed paths with Robbins and Jackson Hall in Big Sky State Prison. It was Matt's first extended federal sentence, while it was Hall's second and Robbins' third. Following the infamous incident and the subsequent "Trial of the Century," Johnny found himself back at Big Sky with a life sentence. Matt, on the other hand, had managed to navigate his way through prison life reasonably well. Despite a few attempts on his life in the prison yard, he decided he'd had enough. Manuel Hernandez, the leader of the Hispanic gang known as the Blades, was someone you definitely didn't want to antagonize. They had earned their name, the Blades, for a very good reason. When Hall and Robbins completed their second terms, there was a noticeable void left behind. Matt's back was no longer covered. While Matt did associate himself with the White Brothers and they respected the unspoken code, he was ultimately just a hillbilly from the golden triangle—expendable in their eyes.

There had been two attempts on Matt's life. On both occasions, the assailants were Hispanic. Each time, Matt managed to fend off his attackers, though he inevitably found himself in the infirmary afterward, where they patched up his wounds. Matt had a connection to Jackson Hall, who was involved with

Hernandez's sister, Maria. Hernandez had gone to great lengths to threaten Hall, even attempting to eliminate him personally. However, the guards intervened before any fatal harm could come to Hall, and he was released from prison before Hernandez could see his plan through. Left with limited options, Hernandez aimed to send a message by targeting Matt. He believed that by doing so, he would finally capture Hall's attention. Matt's name was on the hit list, and any Blade member who had the opportunity was instructed to act. But within the unwritten code of prison life, particularly within the federal system, a stark principle held true: if someone attempted to take you out, retaliation was fair game, and no one would intervene should you seek retribution. Matt patiently bided his time, waiting for the opportune moment. Eventually, Manuel Hernandez made a critical error—he positioned himself with his back exposed in the open commissary. Engaged in conversation with his two lieutenants, Hernandez discussed their plans to shake down individuals in the prison yard later that afternoon.

Among the newly arrived prisoners, a fresh batch had quickly understood that relinquishing their lunches, cigarettes, and any illicit items they had managed to smuggle inside was a small price to pay for their continued survival. Balancing his food tray, Matt navigated his way toward the table where Hernandez was seated. Timing his move perfectly, he discreetly retrieved the makeshift knife he had ingeniously crafted using an old toothbrush and a razor blade. The blade had been heated and fused into the toothbrush handle, forming a deadly weapon.

With a swift and calculated motion, Matt drew the blade from his shirt sleeve, its fine edge finding its mark against Manuel Hernandez's neck. The two

lieutenants accompanying Hernandez reacted, but their response was too slow. In rapid succession, Matt slashed the razor's edge across Hernandez's neck, severing the vital vein not just once, but twice. In a flurry of chaos, Matt dropped the makeshift weapon as blood spilled from the gaping wound, saturating Hernandez's fingers and spilling out of his neck. Hernandez's head collided with his serving tray, his final moments accompanied by guttural gurgles. With a final, surreal display, his gravy-covered head jerked, his eyes rolling back, and then his life was extinguished.

The immediate aftermath was pandemonium, as the guards leaped into action. The dining area was promptly locked down, the eruption of violence triggering an urgent response. Amidst the frenzy, Matt's actions were captured on the facility's security cameras, solidifying the shocking event in recorded history.

For an entire week, the two lieutenants engaged in heated debates, vying for supremacy and control over the Blades' operations. The power vacuum left by Hernandez's demise had to be filled, and tensions escalated as each contender sought to solidify their position. The uncertainty hung thick in the air, casting a palpable sense of danger over the prison yard.

Ultimately, the matter was brutally settled on the unforgiving grounds of the yard. In a macabre turn of events, Diego Martinez emerged victorious by strangling the life out of Lucas Garcia. The very barbell that Garcia had been using for his workout became the instrument of his death, wielded by Martinez's hands. The cold-blooded act solidified Martinez's dominance and signaled his ascent to the throne of the Blades.

Meanwhile, Matt found himself facing the consequences of his own actions. The fallout from

Hernandez's assassination resulted in an additional fifteen-year sentence being tacked onto his prison term. Through the efforts of his public defender, his charge was negotiated down to manslaughter, a lesser offense that carried a somewhat lighter weight of guilt.

The subsequent trial of Diego Martinez, however, proved to be a different spectacle altogether. Martinez took to the stand, weaving a tale that aimed to present the incident as an unfortunate accident. According to his account, the barbell had slipped from his grasp while he attempted to intervene and save his friend. Tragically, the barbell had descended, its weight inadvertently crushing Lucas Garcia's throat, and Martinez professed to feel deep remorse over his friend's untimely demise.

Curiously, during the trial, a significant piece of evidence was conspicuously absent. The state's prosecution, curiously, had no footage to present—a video that could have potentially corroborated or contradicted Martinez's version of events. It was revealed that the camera responsible for capturing the weightlifting area had malfunctioned on the very day of the incident. The timing of the malfunction seemed to border on the uncanny, raising questions about the veracity of Martinez's narrative.

Diego approached Matt a few days after his trial. They were standing in the shower, both their bodies wet and covered in prison tattoos. Diego's new lieutenants blocked the doorway. At first Matt thought that he would be fighting for his life, or at the very least protecting his asshole. Diego walked towards Matt, his hands open and to his sides. He extended his right arm and grasped Matt's hand in a firm gang-like shake. He drew him close and whispered in his ear, "Manuel was a fucking prick and I now got what I want. If you ever need anything you

let me know."

Word got out that Matt was untouchable. He had developed quite a reputation. Over the last five years, Johnny Robbins had befriended Matt to a point that the rest of the prisoners also stayed away from him. Johnny went to Matt's cell and showed him the picture he had torn from the Pilot Magazine. "This is the guy," he said to Matt. "It looks like he is from the Golden Triangle. That's the son of a bitch that put me in here for life. You get me out of here and there is fifty grand in it for you."

"Are you serious?" Matt said. "Fifty grand cash?"

"Cash," said Robbins.

It was Thursday morning and in another few hours they would be out in the yard. The staff in the prison would be running on holiday hours with fewer guards, maintenance staff, and only one person in the infirmary. Matt knew this was the only opportunity he and Robbins would have. Matt approched Diego in the commissary and extended his hand. Diego extended his and Matt slipped a small handwritten note into Diego's fingers. Nothing was said. Diego and his lieutenants left the table and found a quiet area out of the view of the CCTV cameras. The note read, "Robbins and me… Needs to look bad. Infirmary today." Diego put the note in his mouth, took a drink of water, chewed for a couple of seconds, and swallowed the evidence. The plan was in motion.

The prisoners were escorted to the exercise yard at 2:00pm that afternoon. Johnny and Matt were walking across the yard to get to the bleachers. Their plan was to pretend to sit and discuss how they were going to escape. They made it to the centre of the yard and were swarmed by a group of fifteen Blade members. Diego's first

lieutenant pulled a thin plastic shank from his belt line. Matt and Johnny saw what was coming. They both pulled their shirts to the side while grabbing the skin below. They stretched the skin as far as they could. The homemade blade pierced Matt's shirt twice as it entered his side. Johnny was next—he was hit three times. The men let out groans as they released their clothing and skin. Both fell to the ground. The blades had collected blood from each of their members that morning after Matt's note had been read. They stored it in a plastic bag. Diego removed the bag from under his shirt and poured its contents over the two victims. The gang members turned and walked away. The plastic bag and homemade shank were buried under the leg of the weight lifting bench.

In all it took no longer than thirty-five seconds to get the job done. In the middle of the yard lay Johnny and Matt, writhing in pain and covered with blood. The prison siren sounded. The prisoners were ordered to stand along the fence line of the yard. The guards pointed their M16s at the prisoners. The guards that were trained in first aid geared up in their riot gear. They carried two stretchers out into the yard. Matt and Johnny lay there in two bloody heaps. Both pretended they could hardly breathe. They were loaded onto the stretchers and carried from the yard to the jeers of the rest of the inmates. Both men were rushed to the infirmary. There was blood everywhere.

Jane Kennedy, the only nurse left on duty for the afternoon took one look at the wounds and blood. She immediately called for an ambulance from the Metro General Hospital. She applied direct pressure to both of their wounds with the help of one of the guards. Both prisoners had laboured breathing and the extent of what she was looking at was way beyond her training.

"Their lungs have collapsed!" she said. She gave both men 10 cc of morphine.

It took the EMTs seven minutes to arrive at the prison, another five minutes to clear security, and two more to make it to the infirmary. Both EMTs pushed wheeled stretchers through the doorway of the infirmary. Matt and Johnny were loaded onto their respective gurneys. The EMTs started IVs using Ringer's lactate. Both men were loaded into the waiting ambulance. The lights and sirens were switched on as the ambulance left the prison gates. It took six and one half minutes to arrive at the emergency department of Metro General. The EMTs had radioed ahead and the emergency room doctors, nurses, and staff were ready when Johnny and Matt were wheeled into the operating room.

Both men were doing their best to pretend to be out cold from the shock and the injection of morphine they had been given. The nurses cut open their respective prison-issued shirts, then started to clean the wounds. Both men acted like they were having difficulty breathing and the doctors ordered chest x-rays. In both cases, x-rays showed the prisoners had gotten lucky and the knife had missed their left lungs.

Matt received twenty stitches, Johnny twenty-five. The men were given another shot of morphine each. Both men fell asleep after the second shot of the drug. They were sent to recovery, handcuffed, to their hospital beds with a guard posted outside their room.

Matt awoke at 5:00pm, Johnny at 5:30. Matt looked over at Johnny and winked. "How you doing?" he said.

"Perfect," Johnny replied, "other than this pain in my side." Both laughed. By pulling at their skin and stretching it as far as they could, the blade Diego had

used went right past their ribs. When the skin was released it looked like the wounds were right through the rib cage and into their lungs. Diego had done a good job and with Matt and Johnny doing their part the flesh wounds they received in the yard looked fatal. The plan was working. Johnny removed the IV from his arm. He reshaped the needle and used it to release the cuff that bound his wrist to the bedrail. He was free.

"I'm going with you," Matt said.

"No," Johnny said, "this is somthing I need to do on my own. I don't need deadweight."

"I want my fucking money," Matt said. "I don't go with you, and there won't be a place you can hide where I won't find you."

Johnny reluctantly agreed. "We need to get rid of the guard." Johnny placed two pillows under the sheets of his bed and adjusted them so they looked like the profile of someone sleeping on their side. He then stood behind the door to the room. Johnny nodded his head and Matt knocked the pee bottle off the table beside his bed. It hit the floor with a thud and then bounced a couple of times. The guard outside the room, who had been sitting with his chair leaned back against the wall, heard the commotion coming from inside. He bounced out of his chair, undid the snap on his holster for the 9mm he carried, and burst into the room. Robbins hit the guard across the head with the shelf he had taken out of the closet in the room. The guard crumpled to the floor and was out cold.

Robbins got out of his hospital gown, removed the guard's uniform, and dragged the guard into Johnny's bed. He laid the guard on his side facing away from the door and cuffed both his hands to the bedrail.

"Hurry up," said Matt. "We don't have much time."

Johnny dressed in the guard's uniform. He checked the gun belt and found the 9mm intact, its clip contained ten rounds. There was a taser in a holster on the other side. In the back of the belt were handcuffs and a flashlight. He put the guard's boots on; they were two sizes too big. He tossed Matt the keys for the cuffs.

"There you go, kid. I am out of here."

"Not so fast!" Matt said, as he tore his IV line from his arm. "There are car keys on this ring." He continued and unlocked his handcuffs. "You want to get out of here then the deal stands. You're taking me with you. Go find me some clothes."

Robbins left the room and made his way down the hall. He found a door marked employees only. He opened it and found a room with lockers and a small dining table. He rummaged through a few lockers, eventually finding a pair of pants, a shirt, and shoes he thought would fit Matt. He stuffed everything into an empty garbage bag and returned to the recovery room. He opened the door to find Matt standing over the guard. He had hit him again with the IV pole that had held his lifesaving Ringer's lactate.

"He was coming around," said Matt. "What a joke. They thought we were going to die." Both men laughed.

"Come on," said Robbins. "I saw a stairwell."

Johnny opened the recovery room door. Once again looked down the hall, it was clear the nurses were still at their station. The men made their way into the stairwell and down to the ground floor. Matt was now in the lead as they ran into the parking lot. There in the

authorized parking zone sat a State penitentiary cruiser. The prisoners walked to the car. Matt tried the keys in the driver's door and it opened.

"You better drive," he said. "It would not look good if the guard was on the passenger side of the vehicle."

Matt climbed into the backseat, and Johnny Robbins got behind the wheel. In fifteen minutes they had overpowered the guard and were driving out of the parking lot. Both men had split some of their stitches open and blood oozed into the cotton bandages covering the sides of their chests. It was 8:30pm and the streets were dark. As they headed out of town they passed a 24/7 drugstore. Its sign flashed open and Robbins pulled upfront.

"Be right back," he said.

Johnny walked into the store and found bandages, cleaning alcohol, Tylenol, and two cans of coke. He made his way towards the cash register. Johnny looked around, and in the store's parabolic mirror, he saw the pharmacist busy counting out a prescription. He whispered something to the young female cashier. She said, "Excuse me?" He whispered again, and the girl leaned over her counter so she could hear him better.

Robbins removed the taser from his belt and pressed it against the girl's neck; then he pulled the trigger. She dropped like a sack of potatoes and lay quivering behind the counter. He punched a few keys on the till, and its cash drawer opened. He emptied the cash drawer, then stuffed the money into his front pocket. He made his way back to the car as casual as could be. "We are out of here."

By 9:00 pm, the hospital was swarming with state

police, FBI, local law enforcement, and the prison warden. They were looking for a three-time loser and a murderer. They would leave no stone unturned.

Johnny continued to drive west, Matt was busy in the back seat rebandaging his wounds.

"There," said Johnny, pointing towards a farmhouse visible from the highway, illuminated by two yard lights - one shining over the farmyard and the other lighting up the front of a massive Quonset. To the right of the building, a windsock hung limp on a thirty-foot pole. "There must be a plane," he thought to himself.

Johnny pulled up in front of the house and turned on the car's overhead flashing red and blue lights. Inside the house, Eric Taylor and his wife, Cathy, were enjoying the latest episode of Wheel of Fortune. Suddenly, their living room was lit up like the Fourth of July.

"What the hell?" exclaimed Eric, grabbing his loaded Remington 12-gauge. He opened the front door.

Johnny Robbins stood beside the penitentiary cruiser and screamed at the top of his lungs, "I need help quickly, my partner was attacked."

Eric, now focused on the uniform and the car with state markings, set his shotgun beside the front door and ran to assist the two men. Johnny opened the back door, and both men lifted Matt's arms over their shoulders, helping him to the front door, his legs dragging behind him.

"Quick, Cathy, call 911, these boys need help," Eric shouted.

Cathy reached for the phone, but as she did, Johnny Robbins struck 65-year-old Eric across the back of the head with the butt of the 9mm he carried. Eric

staggered but didn't go down. He managed to make it to the living room couch and sat down.

"Drop the phone," said Robbins.

Cathy wasted no time in putting the phone back on its cradle and ran to her husband's aid. Johnny turned towards the open front door, the shotgun neatly placed beside the entrance.

"Get out there and turn those damn lights off," he said to Matt. "Put that car in the barn. We don't want anyone to see it."

Matt turned the car's overhead lights off, then opened the barn doors. He pulled the car inside and noticed a workbench to the side of the old tractor, with parts scattered everywhere. Matt grabbed a hammer, some pliers, and a roll of grey duct tape from the pegboard above the workbench.

By the time he returned to the house and closed the front door, Johnny Robbins had the shotgun in Eric's mouth.

"Where's the plane? Where's the fucking plane?" Robbins shouted.

Finally, Cathy spoke up. "Our son is the pilot, and he won't be home until the morning. There's a dirt landing strip behind the Quonset. He lands there," Cathy said. "Leave my husband alone."

Matt threw Johnny the roll of duct tape.

"Get in those chairs," Robbins ordered as the couple moved into the two rocking chairs on either side of the couch. He bound their hands and feet with the duct tape and placed a strip across Eric's mouth. Cathy he left alone.

"I am going to take a shower," he said to Matt.

"You keep an eye on these two. Maybe make us something to eat."

Johnny walked down the hallway, found the bathroom, and turned on the light. On the wall across from the doorway, he noticed a picture frame with a series of medals fastened to a black felt background. He closed the door, removed the service belt, and let the uniform drop to the floor. Then, he climbed into the shower and let the water run over his body, then his head. Robbins removed the bandages covering his wounds, washing the fresh blood from his side. Eventually, he rinsed himself off and stepped out of the shower.

"That feels better," he said aloud. He searched the bathroom and found some gauze and bandages. He covered his wounds again, wrapped himself in a towel, placed the service belt over his still wet shoulder, and made his way back to the living room.

"Your turn," he said to Matt. "Go get cleaned up. We want to be presentable for these kind folks."

Matt went down the hall and closed the bathroom door.

Robbins noticed a fresh sandwich on the kitchen counter. He went over and ate the whole thing in a matter of two minutes. Then, he opened the fridge and took a container of milk from the top shelf. Unscrewing the cap, he drank directly from the jug. He heard the shower start and knew he would be alone with his captives.

Cathy Taylor was at least ten years younger than her husband. She had managed to maintain her figure and scored a seven out of ten in the looks department. Robbins walked into the living room with a large carving knife he found in a kitchen drawer. He stood in front of Cathy, the holster still around his shoulder, and knife in

his hand.

He looked over at Eric. "You some kind of war hero?" he asked. Eric was thinking clearly now. He mumbled under the duct tape fixed to his mouth.

"Leave him alone!" Cathy shouted. "Have you not done enough?"

"Oh," said Johnny. "We are just getting started. I will let you know when I have had enough."

Robbins ran the tip of the knife across Cathy's cheek. It left a nice red line as he pressed it firmly and down her face.

"No!" she cried.

Eric was jumping in his chair and trying to yell under the tape on his mouth. Johnny ran the blade under the button holes on Cathy's blouse. With a little pressure each button fell to the floor.

"No!" she exclaimed. "No! Not in front of my husband!"

Robbins opened her blouse. Cathy was wearing a white lacy bra, her breasts moved with each heavy breath she took. Johnny placed the blade under the front of the bra between her breasts and slowly drew the knife towards him. The material strained against the blade until finally the blade broke through the material. Cathy's breasts hung free, her nipples grew hard in the cool air. Johnny's hard-on was noticeable under the towel still around his waist. Eric continued to struggle against his restraints. Johnny slapped Cathy as hard as he could.

"Do I have your attention?" he said. "You're going to suck my cock and I'm going to cum in your mouth. You fucking bitch. Do you understand?"

95

"You whore!" he said. He slapped her again. This time the blow knocked her out. Cathy sat motionless, bound in her chair, cum and vomit dripping from her chin. "See, that wasn't so bad," he said as he looked over at Eric.

Under the duct tape, Eric was yelling, "You're dead! You're fucking dead if I ever get my hands on you!"

Johnny wrapped the towel back around his waste and placed the 9mm back into the holster. He placed the belt around his shoulder then sat down on a kitchen chair. Matt had been in the bathroom for about twenty minutes. When he reappeared, he was wearing Eric's bathrobe. Cathy's head was moving in circles as she was coming around. The television screen flashed with the words "alert." Matt grabbed the remote control and turned up the volume.

"We interrupt this program for this emergency broadcast!" The reporter came on and announced that two prisoners had escaped from Metro General Hospital. There were mugshots of both Matt and Johnny in the top-righthand corner of the screen. "Be on the look out," the reporter said. "It is believed the fugitives could be driving a stolen county prison car, licence plate number CP 2061. Both men are believed to be armed and dangerous. Do not approach! If you spot them call your local authorities immediately."

Eric threw his head back. The bastards were standing right in his living room and there was not a thing he could do about it.

97

Chapter 20

The fire had died down, leaving behind a nice base of coals that provided a constant source of heat. "Let's get that dinner cooking," Brad said to everyone. "Is anybody hungry?"

Mark and Marcy were the first to pipe up. "We are starving."

Elizabeth brought over the pan that contained the dozen dough pieces she had made. Carefully, she took the dough from the pan and placed it on the plastic bag, which was now resting on the seat of the picnic table. She then put the pan on the grill directly over the fire and added half a cup of oil. When the oil was hot enough, she added the dough pieces back into the pan. She covered the entire setup with a multipurpose lid that came with the well-used cooking kit Brad had packed. The kit contained a large pot, frying pan, and a smaller pot that all nested together into a neat stackable assortment of everything you could ever need when deep in the woods.

Donna had washed and wrapped some potatoes in tin foil, and Tommy had packed them away deep in one of his backpack pockets. She eventually found them and laid them out for Brad to cook when he was ready.

She also had a bag of salad, and she set out to wash it down by the creek. Tommy, Marcy, and Matt had returned from the edge of the huckleberry bushes, where they had managed to find a few long sticks they could use to cook the hotdogs.

Fifteen minutes after covering the dough, Elizabeth removed the lid to reveal twelve beautifully cooked sweet and soft dinner buns. "Perfect," she

exclaimed.

"They smell fantastic," said Brad.

She removed the pan from the grill and scooped the buns out onto a paper plate. "Here you go," she said to Brad. "It's your turn."

Brad tossed the potatoes on top of the coals. He placed the frying pan back on the grill and added a little oil and two tablespoons of butter from a Tupperware container the girls had set out on the table. He placed the two cans of beans directly on the grill, one on either side of the frying pan. When the oil was hot, he added the three trout. They sizzled as they hit the oil.

"Look, little buddy," Brad said to Mark. "We are going to have a feast tonight, and it's all because of you."

Mark stuck out his chest. "Yup," he said. "I am the best fisherman in the forest."

Marcy had run down to the creek to see what Donna was doing. Tommy sat on the corner of the picnic table as he sharpened the sticks with his hunting knife. "There," he said. "Ready for hotdogs."

Donna and Marcy returned from the creek, the salad freshly washed in ice-cold water. The water that ran in the creek this time of the year came directly from the snowpack higher in the mountains. It was pure and was the life source of Rock Lake.

"Oh my, look at those buns," Donna said to Elizabeth. "Good job."

"Thanks," came Elizabeth's reply.

Brad turned the fish using a fork from the table. "Now," he said, "my secret herbs and spices." He took a package from the pocket of his pack and dusted the trout, dropping the spices using his fingers and thumb. He

sprinkled the concoction over the cooking fish. Tommy could never figure out what the secret spices were. From the time they were kids, Brad's father had sworn him to secrecy. He was never to reveal what it took to take trout from just fish to this incredible fish. He laughed to himself, "Dad's secret of using lemon pepper shake and bake would never leave his lips. Okay, Marcy and Mark, time for you two to cook your hotdogs."

Tommy placed the dogs so the sharpened point of the sticks ran the whole length of the tube steaks. "Here you go," he said, "now go over by the fire, and Uncle Brad will show you where to hold them over the coals."

The beans were starting to bubble through the slits Brad had made in the tops of the cans. He removed the Buck Huntsman from its sheath and quickly used its point to turn the potatoes sitting in the coals. "Here," said Brad to the children. "Hold your hotdogs over here. Keep turning them, that's it, you don't want them to burn."

Five minutes went by, and Mark and Marcy had blistered their hotdogs to a point where they were starting to split open.

"Okay," said Brad, "everything is ready. You kids take your food up to the table."

Mark and Marcy walked up to the table, their hotdogs moving back and forth on the end of the three-foot sticks. "You two sit here," said Donna.

"Everyone have a seat," said Brad. "I will be right there."

Brad took his knife and speared the first potato. It pierced the tinfoil with ease and through into the heart of the spud. "They are done, perfect," he said to himself. He walked to the table with the tinfoil-covered potato on

the end of his knife and placed it on Elizabeth's plate. He did that three more times until all the adults had a hot baked potato sitting in front of them.

Brad returned to the fire, using a pair of socks as oven mitts, carrying the baked beans to the table. One more trip to the fire, and he returned with the frying pan of freshly cooked trout. He removed the lid, and the aroma of the cooked fish filled the air. The flesh was falling off the bones just the way it should be. This was the first meal of the season outdoors, and it had to be perfect.

"Dig in," he said, "before it starts to get cold." He took his knife and worked the blade under the lid and around the rim of the cans of beans. He scooped some out onto Mark and Marcy's plates. Elizabeth handed Donna the buns; she took two and broke them open. She slid a hot dog neatly onto each bun directly from the sticks Tommy had made. "There you go," she said. "The ketchup and stuff are right here."

The hotdogs stuck out from the ends of the dinner buns about an inch on either side. The kids bit the ends off and ate them without any condiments. Now they looked like mini dogs similar to those slider burgers you could get in the city. The four adults helped themselves to what lay before them. Donna placed some salad on the children's plates and sprinkled a nice raspberry vinaigrette on the greens. The feast was on.

Halfway through their dinner, coming down the path, they heard *jingle, jingle, jingle*.

A young couple came around the corner and waved. "We have been smelling your cooking for the last half an hour. Who's the chef?" Everyone pointed at Brad.

"Hang on," said Brad. "We have far too much for all of us. We are just about finished here." He wrapped the third trout into some tinfoil and walked over to the couple. "I am Brad," he said as he extended his hand.

David Smith extended his hand to meet Brad's. "This is my fiancée, Tammy," he said.

"Pleased to meet you," she said.

"Where are you headed?" Brad asked.

"RL04 is our destination for the weekend," said David.

"Here, take this lake trout. It's fresh, just a couple of hours ago," said Brad, "one of my specialties. You two better get a move on; we only have about an hour and a half before dusk."

Brad returned to his friends, and David and Tammy were gone from sight in minutes.

"Come on, little buddy, you have to try some of this leftover fish you caught," Brad said. "Marcy, please try just a bite for your Uncle Brad."

Both kids put a piece of fish into their mouths. It was amazing, and Marcy had forgotten about what she had seen when they were being cleaned. "More, please," said Mark.

Tommy scraped everything he could from the pan onto Mark's plate. "Me too," said Marcy.

Tommy divided what he had dished out equally between the two children. They devoured the last of the evening's meal. "I don't like hotdogs," said Marcy.

The adults laughed. Brad had done a good job, and there was not a single bun left. Elizabeth was proud of herself. Brad and Tommy rubbed their bellies, and

Mark jumped in and started rubbing his as well.

"What's for dessert?" said Mark. They all laughed again; the kid had a hollow leg. Donna got up and reached into Tommy's pack. She pulled out a box of Hostess Ding Dongs. "There," she said, "fresh, made by Uncle Tommy."

Elizabeth and Donna refrained from dessert; everyone else dug in. Mark ate two.

Chapter 21

Betty sat down at the kitchen table with her lover, Superintendent Bob Gerard. He had prepared a nice meatloaf and was just taking it out of the oven.

"My day was okay," she said. "It was so busy. I did not have time to get everything done. We issued so many permits today. Three out of the four cabins at Rock Lake were booked. The last couple that came in to get their paperwork for RL04 did not show up until 2:00pm. I hope they get to the cabin before the sun goes down. They were a nice young couple," she exclaimed.

"Plenty of time," said Bob. "If they are that young, they are probably running all the way up there. How big a piece of meatloaf would you like?"

"Normal," said Betty.

Bob put a small piece on her plate and scooped some mashed potatoes beside the meat. "Gravy, honey?"

"Sure, I love your gravy," she said with a wink. He laughed.

"Here is a nice piece of corn on the cob, fresh from California this week," he said. "It's peaches and cream, your favorite."

Bob dished up a plate for himself and sat at the head of the table. "How was your day?" she asked.

"I was out with the rest of the wardens. The ten of us made our rounds, checking to make sure everyone was in compliance. You know, the usual stuff. Park passes, fire permits, camping permits, fishing licenses... We had our hands full. You should have seen Emerald Lake," he said.

Emerald Lake was about five hundred feet from the main parking lot. "It looked like Walmart. The city folks would arrive for the day and carry their crap down to the water's edge and set up shop. They were stacked on top of each other. It's not like the good old days," he said. Twenty years ago, you could pull in with your family, grab your picnic basket and BBQ, and head down to the water. You might see ten other families. Today, with the way the population had grown in the area and the government's policy on immigration, there was a mix of every type of family you could think of. Some would set up inexpensive tents for the day. Others played loud music and danced to the cheers of their friends. It was not Bob's cup of tea, but so long as they all followed the rules, the parks department could not limit who came and went.

Bob had worked for the department for almost forty years, Betty thirty-five as the office administrator. Bob had lost his wife to cancer ten years ago. Betty's husband was housed in the new wing at the Hillcrest Hospital. He had been in the dementia ward since it had opened. Betty had managed to get him a bed there. It made it much easier for her to see him. When he was housed at Metro General, she could only get by twice a month. Now she paid weekly visits. The poor man did not know who she was anymore, but it did not matter to Betty. They had had a good life together when they were younger and had raised two children.

She was okay with her decision to start an affair with Bob. The reality was Betty's husband would never come back from his constant fog. Bob was available since his wife had passed away. They both had worked together for the last thirty-five years and knew each other well as friends. Betty had struggled with the decision to move her husband back to Hillcrest. It was Bob who had

convinced her it would be a good idea. They had talked at great lengths about their respective spouses until one day they both recognized the sparks that were being generated between them. "Life goes on even in your early sixties," Bob would say. "Those feelings you have when you're a teenager never go away when you're in the company of the right person."

Bob poured both of them a glass of red wine, and they continued talking about their future together. They had managed to keep the affair fairly confidential. At least none of the staff ever talked about Betty coming out of the superintendent's quarters at seven thirty in the morning to start her workday. The general consensus of the staff was that they were old enough to know what they were getting themselves into. Bob and Betty never showed any affection toward each other in public or at work. That was their policy. After all, Betty had two grown children and her reputation to protect.

After they had finished dinner and the dishes, Betty went to the washroom and ran the tub. She filled it with bubbles and slid beneath the surface, letting the events of the day drift from her mind. Bob came in an hour later and stepped into the separate shower stall. He rinsed the day's grime off his sixty-three-year-old body. By the time he had finished and dried off, Betty was waiting for him in the master bedroom. Bob walked in, dropped the towel from his waist, and climbed under the sheets. They made love for the next hour, "not bad for two old folks," he thought to himself.

When he and Betty were both satisfied, Bob rolled over and turned off the light. It had been a long day. "I love you," he said as they both drifted off. It had been a long day.

Chapter 22

Brad's father, Kevin, had successfully guided his four couples to Glacier Creek Campground by 5:00pm. The group was exhausted from their day's tour, which had commenced in the parking lot at 6:00am. They had hiked to the head of the Glacier and down to the campground, completing the journey in less than 12 hours. "Not too bad for a group of office employees," Kevin commented aloud. "You folks did great today."

"Thanks," they replied.

Glacier Creek Campground catered to those who appreciated nature but still desired some comforts of home. The parks department maintained washroom facilities on-site, complete with running water, showers, and actual flushing toilets. Power was supplied by solar panels on the roof, and water was pumped and heated through a series of tubes, stored in insulated tanks during the day. This system, though expensive when installed, had paid for itself many times over. The permits issued to each couple cost one hundred dollars per day, more than enough to cover the costs of general cleaning, supplying toilet paper, and annual maintenance.

Toby and Brent had ensured the firewood bins were full, and the washrooms had been cleaned and disinfected, proving to be a godsend for the group as each member eventually found their way to use the facilities. "We better get those tents up," said Kevin. "This area is reserved for us." The group wasted no time getting organized. Kevin pushed two picnic tables together and hung a big blue tarp over both, stretching it tight and tying it to four spruce trees at each corner. Having brought hundreds of groups here over the years,

Kevin knew the place like the back of his hand.

Twenty years ago, there was only a single outhouse that sat over an open pit. Things had changed dramatically over the years of his guiding, some for the better and some for the worse. The three couples set up their shelters for the evening, and food had been laid out on the picnic tables. Kevin had gathered wood and built a large fire in the provided pit. He also set up his tent, laid out his foam pad and sleeping bag, and then it was time to prepare dinner.

Each couple had brought some nice strip loin steaks, and there was even an extra one for Kevin. The men stood around the fire, waiting for it to die down so they could use the coals to cook on. The ladies had set up their own single-burner propane stoves, and each woman whipped up something unique to go with the steaks their men were cooking.

Within a half an hour, all nine adults were sitting at the table. Kevin marveled at a perfectly cooked strip loin, covered in sautéed mushrooms. There was wild rice, corn on the cob, and someone even grilled some garlic bread. Two bottles of red wine graced the table, and plastic glasses were passed around. As they were filled, one of the husbands raised his glass and said, "Here's to Kevin, one hell of a guide."

Kevin raised his glass and replied, "Here's to you folks and to nature."

They all looked around, surrounded by the snow-capped mountains. Glacier Creek flowed in the distance, its gentle murmur adding to the tranquil ambiance. Squirrels chattered in the background, and the meadow surrounding them was transitioning to a vibrant green. This was life, exactly as it was meant to be.

Kevin raised the wine glass to his lips but didn't take a drink. He hadn't touched a drop since that fateful night when Emily's life was tragically taken by the drunken son of a bitch. He missed sharing the wonders of the world with her dearly. There remained a hollow spot in his heart reserved just for her.

His private life was not a matter of concern for this group or any others. He smiled, a quiver in his lip. "She's beautiful," he said softly.

Chapter 23

Prison Warden Martin Perkins had interviewed his guard in the presence of the FBI after surgeons had put twenty stitches in his head. They took cranial X-rays and fortunately found there were no fractures. He was suffering from a concussion and was still groggy when Perkins started asking questions.

"What the hell happened, David? You're one of my best guards," Perkins inquired.

"I don't know, sir," was his reply. "I remember hearing a noise from inside the room. It sounded like a thud, no, it was more like someone had jumped down from a six-foot ladder," he said. "I heard the commotion, stood up from my chair, undid the snap on my holster, and walked into the room. Both men were still handcuffed and in their beds, sir. Then everything went black. I woke up cuffed in the first bed. My clothes were gone. Where's my holster, sir? My gun, the taser? My extra rounds? My keys were in my pants."

"It's okay, son," said Perkins reassuringly. "We will find them."

The FBI had set up a perimeter around Metro General, extending for 50 miles. There was no way these convicts were going to get away. A call came into the FBI from Metro PD; they had been dispatched to Adams Pharmacy. There had been a robbery, and the FBI might be interested in speaking to the witness they were questioning. The Feds dispatched two cars with four of their best local agents.

They arrived at the drugstore to find EMTs and local cops swarming the joint. Sitting in a chair beside

her cash register was Debbie Williams. The pharmacist stood holding her left hand. Debbie was crying and shaking hysterically.

"Can you tell us what happened?" Agent Miller asked.

"I already told those guys standing at the door," she said, pointing with her index finger as her hand shook.

The agents noticed two distinct burn marks on the side of her neck. Agent Miller took the lead. "You three, look around, see what you can find. You guys at the door, do not let anyone in here. This place is a crime scene."

"Please, Debbie," he was looking at her name tag, "can you tell me what happened?"

"One of you guys came in here," she said. "He bought some bandages, cleaning alcohol, and coke. He whispered at me, I could not hear him. He leaned across the counter, I leaned in so I could hear him, and the next thing I knew, I was laying on the floor. It felt like I was going to die," she said, rubbing her neck.

"Did you see anything?" Miller asked the pharmacist.

"No, I was out back filling prescriptions," he replied.

Agent Anderson came back to the front of the store. He had been in the office used to count the daily receipts and place the stock orders. Inside the room was a closed-circuit camera setup. The entire store was monitored, and the television screen was split into six segments. Miller could clearly see the pharmacist holding Debbie's hand as the numbers ticked by, recording the time.

"Get that guy in here," said Miller, pointing to the pharmacist on the screen.

Agent Anderson complied and returned with Henry Tomas in his white coat, the company logo emblazoned on the outer pocket.

"Can you play this back for me?" said Miller.

"Sure," said the pharmacist. "We had the system installed last year on the suggestion of our underwriter. Damn insurance is getting expensive. We are saving a thousand dollars a year by having our security system."

He hit rewind on the machine, and the images on the screen started moving backward. The time on the screen showed 8:35pm. A minute later, a man wearing a state pen guard's uniform walked through the front door. Everyone stood in the small room, watching the video.

The guard walked around, gathered a few things, and walked up to the till. As he leaned across the counter, he placed his hand flat against the smooth surface. The video clearly showed the taser being pulled from the guard's holster and pressed against Debbie's neck. The guard then ransacked the cash register, gathered his things, and left the building.

"Call the identification team," Agent Miller ordered. "I want the counter and that till dusted for prints, and I want it done now."

"Can I take this?" he said, pointing to the memory card on the side of the machine.

"Sure," said the pharmacist. "Anything to help."

As the four agents left the pharmacy, they looked back. "Send her home," said Miller, pointing to Debbie. "We have what we need."

The agents returned to their office downtown.

Metro PD had the entire mall locked down when the Identification department of the FBI showed up. The IDENT boys entered the drugstore and went to work in the areas of interest. They pulled a nice set of prints from the counter and prints from the till. They took a large piece of adhesive tape and placed it across the counter directly over the dusted prints. Slowly, the agent removed the tape as not to smudge the work he had just done. He held the tape up to the light, smiled, and said, "Gotcha." He placed the tape back onto the white backing paper he had removed it from. The print stood out like an old black and white photograph. The agent opened his case and scanned the sheet. He pressed send, and the scanned image was sent to the agents back at the downtown office.

"Run this now," said Miller. In a matter of minutes, they had a match. An image came up on their computer screen. It was Johnny Robbins.

The IDENT boys called a few minutes later. "Did you see the camera outside the liquor store?"

"No," said Miller.

"Well, it is pointing straight into the parking lot. Might be worth having a look at it."

The Identification team moved down to the liquor store. Garmech Bawa sat behind the counter, an old television sitting above the bright turban he wore on his head.

"Can we look at your tape?" the agents said, flashing their ID.

"Sure, sure," said Bawa, not wanting to cause any issues with the authorities. The agents rewound the old VHS recorder to 8:30 and watched.

A car left the parking lot at 8:32, and another

pulled in at 8:34. The car said "STATE PENITENTIARY" on the side. A prison guard got out of the driver's side and entered the drugstore. There was someone in the backseat, but the image was blurred.

"We need to take this," said the agents. "It's evidence."

"Sure, sure," said Bawa. "No problem."

The IDENT team returned to their office and used some of the new video-enhancing equipment they had received last month. The pixels from the grainy image came together on their computer screen. They visually compared it to the image of Donna's brother, Matt, and then ran both through the computer. A series of X's appeared on the screen over each image. The computer flashed "Match." The IDENT boys called Agent Miller upstairs. "We can place Matt Jones in the car. He was definitely with Robbins at the time of the heist."

"Thanks, boys," said Miller. "Nice work."

The roadblocks and perimeter that had been set up around Metro General had turned up nothing. The Feds could now place both convicts at the drugstore.

"Run the perimeter in a hundred-mile circle from the Pharmacy, not the Hospital. They can't be that far," said Miller. "I want these bastards."

It was 11:00pm.

Chapter 24

Matt stood wearing Eric's bathrobe in front of the television. He and Johnny watched the emergency broadcast of their daring escape from Metro General. They were number one on the FBI's Most Wanted list. There was a dragnet out and the Feds were going to get their men. That was a promise Agent Miller made to the TV news crew as they left the pharmacy.

"We will see about that," said Johnny Robbins.

Matt looked over at the senior Robbins for some sort of solace. "What do you think?"

Robbins responded, "They don't have a chance in hell."

Matt turned and looked over at Cathy. Her breasts were visible and only slighty covered with her blouse. Her head was still moving in a slow circle as she mumbled. "My turn," said Matt. Eric started to move violently against his restraints. The rocking chair was bouncing on the floor. He took the butcher knife Robbins had used to free Cathy's buttons from the kitchen table. He cut through the duct tape on Cathy's wrists and ankles. Red welts had formed on her face, and the vomit was drying on her chin and pants.

"Come on. "We are going to get you cleaned up and make you presentable." Matt picked up Cathy under the arms and in one quick move turned and placed her left arm over his shoulder. He slid his other arm under her legs and carried her down the hallway. Eric was going crazy. He continued to bounce up and down in the chair and was yelling under the duct tape covering his mouth. Robbins had enough of the noise. He had stuff to

think about. He walked over to Eric with the guard's service belt over his shoulder. He removed the taser from the holster and pressed it against Eric's chest directly over his heart. Robbins pulled the trigger. The taser made a snapping sound and Eric shook in the chair, straining against his restraints before he passed out.

Matt propped up Cathy on the counter in the bathroom. He ran the bathtub and checked to make sure the water was not too hot. Matt removed Cathy's blouse and broken bra. He leaned her against the mirror and removed her slacks and panties, placing the butcher knife on the top of the toilet. He noticed that Cathy's pubic area was completely bald. "Oh sweetheart," he said. "I love what I see." He picked her up and placed her in the warm water. Cathy started to slide under the water. Matt straightened her up and started to wash her face with the cloth he had used earlier. Cathy started to come around as the water ran down her face. She sat upright in the tub and looked over at Matt. Her left eye was swelling shut from one of the blows Robbins had delivered. "I am sorry," he said. "I am not like Johnny." He wet her hair using a glass he found beside the sink. He then shampooed her hair into a nice lather. Then, using the glass, he poured water over her head, rinsing the shampoo into the bath water. "There," he said. "Doesn't that feel better?" Cathy was shaking. She did not know what to expect.

Matt reached down between her legs, the soapy water hiding where his fingers were exploring. "No," she said.

"Sweetheart," said Matt, "you know I am not like Johnny. I would never hurt you. Come on, let's get you out of this water." Matt pulled the plug and Cathy stood up. He took a fresh towel from off the shelf over the toilet. He dried Cathy and wrapped her in the towel. He

116

took another and massaged her hair, wrapping the towel around her head. "There," he said, "don't you feel better?" Cathy nodded her head slightly. Matt opened the bathroom door and took the knife from the top of the toilet. He stepped into the hallway and took Cathy's hand and escorted her to the master bedroom.

"No, no!" she said to Matt.

He pushed her onto the bed and closed the bedroom door. Matt removed the belt from the bathrobe. She noticed all of his prison tattoos as the robe fell open. Matt took the belt and bound Cathy's hands over her head. He then fastened the ends of the belt to the brass headboard. Matt tore the towel away from Cathy's body. Her breasts moved as she breathed. "You're so beautiful," Matt said. He looked through the closet in Cathy and Eric's room. Cathy was moving and kicking at Matt. He found two leather belts that he used to fasten her legs to the footboard.

"No, you bastard!" she said. "You dirty rotten bastard!"

Matt did not want to hear it. He took the towel and stuffed it deep into her mouth. He let Eric's bathrobe fall to the floor. Cathy stared at him, tears flowing down her cheeks. "I know you have missed me," he said to Cathy. Matt placed his head between her legs. "Oh, look at that. You really have missed me." He used his tongue on Cathy's vagina and sucked on her clitoris for a few minutes. He stuck two fingers inside her then played with her ass. He removed the towel from her hair. Her wet locks fell onto the pillow. "Oh, honey, I have missed you," he said. Matt was as hard as a rock. He removed the towel from Cathy's mouth; it was getting in his way.

She screamed, "No, you fucking bastard!"

Robbins turned up the television in the living room so he did not have to listen to Matt's sexual exploits. Matt took the knife and placed it to Cathy's throat. He kissed her and Cathy did not move. Matt proceeded to rape Cathy not once, but twice, in the matter of an hour. The tears poured down her face. She was in shock, her face was swollen. Her vagina was bleeding from Matt's forceful thrusts. She did not want him to penetrate her. Her body was beaten and bruised, but she was still alive. "See?" said Matt. "I am nothing like Johnny." He fell asleep beside his bound captive. Cathy eventually gave into the pain and the overwhelming exhaustion and closed her eyes before drifting off.

Chapter 25

Brad removed the cooking grill from the firepit and added more logs. He and Tommy walked the 300 feet to the firewood bin the park's department kept full. The young men gathered the driest wood they could find and both carried an armful back to camp. Donna and Elizabeth had carried the cooking pots, pans, and eating utensils down to the creek so they could be washed. Marcy and Mark sat on the picnic table bench, poking their hotdog sticks in the fire. Sparks would jump into the air as they poked about. When the tips of the sticks caught fire, they would wave them in the air and make circles until the flames went out and smoke poured from their tips.

"Look," said Marcy, "I can write my name in the air."

Mark was not to be undone, "Me too."

Brad and Tommy dropped the fresh wood they had just returned with then set about making sure the tents were ready for the evening. Brad unzipped the door to his tent and peered inside. Elizabeth had set out their foam pads and laid their sleeping bags out beside each other. Brad looked and said to himself, "Well, that's a good start." He went into the tent, unzipped both sleeping bags, and then zipped both together, making one large bag both he and Elizabeth could fit into. "There, that's better," he said aloud. "If she gets cold tonight, I can share my body heat with her." He tossed the tent fly towards the head of the sleeping bag, then placed his flashlight under the corner of the foam padding. He went back outside, zipped the front door of his tent closed, and then sat with Marcy and Mark, watching the fire.

Tommy checked the kids' tent, and all was laid out for them. He quickly peered into his and Donna's tent; there was nothing for Tommy to do—she always set it up perfectly. There was even a plastic rose laid out on their sleeping bag. She always brought it with her when they camped in the forest. "Perfect," Tommy said aloud as he did the zipper back up on their tent.

Donna and Elizabeth returned from the creek. The evening's cooking utensils were spotless and ready for the morning meal. Donna put everything on the top of the picnic table. They gathered the paper plates, plus the remainder of the fish carcasses, and threw them into the now raging fire. It only took a few minutes. The evidence of what they had eaten that evening was gone.

Brad kissed Elizabeth and said, "Honey, thank you for all your help today. Dinner was perfect." Brad opened his backpack and found the one-hundred-foot climbing rope he always had with him. "Come on, buddy, I will need your help," he said to Tommy. They walked to the edge of the large spruce trees, thirty feet or so from the edge of their campsite.

"There, this one will do," said Brad. Tommy handed his friend a rock that weighed about a pound. Brad tied it to the end of the rope. He uncoiled a length and then started to windmill the rock around in a circle.

He looked up at a large branch about twenty feet in the air and released the rope. The rock sailed into the air over the branch and carried the rope back down to the ground. "That will work," said Tommy. Tommy went back to the campsite and gathered his tent fly. He returned, and the young men set about attaching the fly to the rope. They gathered all the backpacks and set them into the fly, then hoisted everything to the bottom of the branch. Tommy tied the rope around the base of the tree

as Brad held the rope steady. "That will do it," Tommy said. All their food, clothing, and whatever else they brought with them now swung twenty feet in the air. No bear is ever going to get at that. Brad's father had taught the boys well.

Brad and Tommy returned to the fire and sat beside their girls. It was dusk, and soon the stars would be shining overhead. It was starting to get cool. Tommy threw more wood on the fire; sparks jumped into the air. Mark and Marcy giggled with excitement. "Just like the Fourth of July," said Mark as he poked his stick back into the fire. They all sat around chatting and singing as dusk descended upon them.

"Look up there," said Brad to the kids. "Do you see the big pot in the sky?"

"Where, where?" the kids said.

"Follow my finger," said Uncle Brad as he pointed to the heavens. "You can see a big pot with a handle attached to it. Look hard."

All the adults gazed up at the night sky as well. Donna said, "I can see it."

"Where?" said Marcy.

"There," said Mark. "I see it too."

"Now," said Brad, "that pot is called the Big Dipper. If you follow the handle to its tip, you can see a real bright star at the end."

"Oh yes," the children said.

"That's the North Star," said Uncle Brad. "If you can see that, you will always be able to find your way home. The sailors used it to find their way across the ocean."

"Wow," said Mark. "That's cool. How come they did not use GPS?" he said.

"Because it had not been invented," said Tommy. "Everything was done with a sextant, a piece of paper, and a pen made out of a feather."

The children laughed. "You said sex," Marcy giggled.

"Oh, never mind," said Tommy. He was talking way above their pay grades. Someday they would learn this stuff in school, he hoped.

"Time for bed, you two," said Donna, looking at Marcy and Mark.

"Do we have to?"

It's time for bed and we have a big day ahead of us tomorrow."

The children made their way to the kids' tent. Donna was right behind them. She unzipped the door, and the kids crawled inside. "Take your shoes off right here at the door," she said. "You do not want to be tracking dirt inside. Leave your socks on so your feet don't get cold." The duffle bag containing their clothing was inside by the doorway. "Make sure you put clean socks on in the morning."

"Okay," said the kids. They climbed into their respective sleeping bags without undressing.

They pulled the top of their bags over their heads. "It's cold," said Marcy.

"You will warm up soon," said Donna. "Your sleeping bags are good to twenty-below, just give them a few minutes to warm up. Good night. I love you," she said, then zipped up the doorway. She returned to the fire and sat beside Tommy, holding his hand. "Thank you,"

she said, and leaned in to kiss him.

Tommy held her close and said, "You're welcome."

The four adults sat outside, poking at the fire and talking about their lives. By the time the fire died down, it was 11:30. "I don't know about you, Brad," Elizabeth said, "but I am exhausted and ready to hit the hay."

"Us too," said Tommy. The two guys stirred the coals from the fire as they poured water over the red hot coals. The steam rolled into the air. "That ought to do it."

The girls had already made their way into their respective tents. By the time Tommy and Brad joined their girlfriends they were inside their sleeping bags warming things up for their men. Brad undressed down to his underwear and crawled into the sleeping bag with Elizabeth. "I hope you do not mind," he said. "I figured if the bags were zipped together and you got cold I could keep you warm."

"No," she said. "I am going to keep you warm." Elizabeth rolled over into Brad's arms. She was naked. "I love you," she said as she worked her way on top of him. She moved seductively over Brad's body. She bent her head down towards his and kissed him long and deep. Her long hair she ran back and forth across his chest. She pulled his member from his underwear. Brad was hard as a rock. His full eight inches never ceased to surprise Elizabeth. "You're so big," she said, as she slowly sat on top of Brad's throbbing penis. Brad grabbed her hips and guided her down ever so gently so as to not hurt her. In just a few strokes, nature had provided all the moisture Elizabeth needed to accommodate Brad's extra large manhood. Brad held her hips firmly. He thrust into her as deeply as he could. She moaned, "I am going to cum."

"Me too," he said. In one final thrust he felt the warmth of his load deposit deeply into Elizabeth. He continued to twitch as she orgasmed on his penis. "That was amazing," he said as he drew Elizabeth close and kissed her deeply.

"You always make me feel so good," said Elizabeth. She rolled off Brad's body and lay on her side. Brad laid on his side and spooned his woman. He held her close and then put his nose in her hair. It smelled like a combination of her strawberry hair conditioner and smoke from the fire.

From Tommy and Donna's tent they heard, "You are such a stud, Tommy! Do it, do it… Oh! I love it!" said Donna. Elizabeth giggled. Brad had to bite down on his tongue to keep from laughing out loud. He and Elizabeth drifted off. The day's events had caught up to them both and they needed some sleep.

Chapter 26

David and Tammy continued down the path that followed the contours of Rock Lake as they made their way towards RL04. David carried the lake trout in his right hand. Moisture had run out of the tinfoil and was dripping everywhere.

"Do you want any of this?" David asked Tammy. "I am getting covered in slime."

"No way," she said. "You know I do not like fish. Who knows what they did to it before giving it to you? I know you were being nice taking it from that guy, but do you think it's smart to eat it?" she said.

David thought for a moment and tossed the whole works into the brush beside the pathway.

"There," he said. "The crows will clean that up in the morning."

He removed his backpack and stepped to the shore of Rock Lake. He washed both of his hands in the ice-cold water. He stood up, and Tammy helped him with his backpack. They walked another six hundred feet down the trail towards the Rock Lake Cabins. They rounded the last corner and could hear music, and there was a slight smell of smoke. There sat Seamus O'Reilly and his entourage trying to get a fire going.

David and Tammy stopped for a moment and introduced themselves.

"It looks like you're having a little trouble with your fire," David said.

"Oh, negh," said Seamus, "all be good."

"Have a good night," said David and Tammy. "We will be over at RL04 on the other side of the lake."

They continued down the trail until the path opened into a small clearing. RL04 lay directly in front of them. David stood at the lockbox and dialed in the combination. The box opened, and David retrieved the key.

"Come on, honey, let's see where we will be spending the next three nights."

Seamus took one look at the fire he was trying to start. The kindling he was using was the size of his arm. He eventually took all the wood out of the firepit and split it down using the new hatchet he bought a few days ago. He had everyone round up some small dry twigs from under the trees and bring them over to him. He went inside the cabin and retrieved the brochures he had taken from the ranger station after speaking with Betty. He crumpled them up into balls and stuck them into the middle of the fire pit. He placed the dry twigs and smaller kindling on top of the crumpled park brochures. He struck a match and lit the final brochure. The pamphlet started to burn, and he stuck the whole thing on top of the crumpled balls of paper. As it burned, he noticed the writing on its cover: "You are in Grizzly Country."

Seamus smiled; there had not been a grizzly in Ireland for over twelve thousand years. The balls of paper burst into flames and ignited the twigs. The kindling started to burn. No one was going to question his fire-starting abilities.

"It's time to eat," he said to his group. "Let's do some cooking." The eight adults huddled around the fire.

The steaks were brought out and cooked two at a time in a frying pan over the open fire. Seamus's wife,

Aileen, brought out two loaves of French bread and a jar of bramble jelly they had brought from the old country. Shawn and his wife, Briana, had made a batch of boxty. It was the poor man's bread of the old days, made with mashed potatoes, flour, baking soda, milk, and eggs. The boxty was cooked in half an inch of oil and looked like biscuits when they were done. They were a perfect complement to the jar of bramble jelly. Caitlin and Cathleen took on the job of cutting up raw vegetables - carrots and celery. They made up a nice vegetable dip.

When the steaks were all cooked, the eight adults sat at the picnic table outside RL01. Their plates overflowed with the evening's dinner. Seamus quickly ran inside and brought out six plastic cups and a bottle of single malt Irish whiskey. He poured two good shots into each glass and passed them around.

"Cheers," he said aloud. "Here's to us being pioneers in this great land."

They all raised their glasses and threw back the alcohol.

"That is good," said Shawn. "Let's dig in."

David and Tammy entered RL04 and removed their packs. It was dark and difficult to see inside the cabin. David took a lighter from his shirt pocket and used it to see into his backpack. He removed his propane lamp and bottle. He turned the valve on the side of the lamp, then held the lighter to the hole below its mantle. The lamp flickered and came to life. He adjusted the valve, and a warm glow enveloped the cabin. David and Tammy set about organizing themselves. It was time to have a quick bite to eat before going to bed.

Chapter 27

Gunner made it home around 7:00pm. He had a couple of stops to make and had picked up a few groceries. He walked into his home and into the kitchen. There on the table was a note from Tommy: "Gone to Rock Lake with Brad and the girls, home Monday evening sometime. Love, Tommy."

Chris had not expected to see his son. Donna had garnered most of Tommy's attention over the last couple of years. There were many times over the last two years that Chris had peered into Tommy's room late at night to find that his son had not come home. "Well, at least I know where he is, and he has settled into some sort of responsibility."

Tommy had taken the divorce hard. He loved his mother. When Gunner was away overseas, Christine had been both a mother and a father to Tommy. Christine had allowed Brad's father to pick him up on weekends. Tommy would go with Brad and Kevin on weekend camping adventures. The boys were extremely close all through school, and while Gunner was away, Kevin took on the role of a surrogate father. Chris was away serving his country, and the least Brad's father could do was help Tommy learn to be a man.

When Tommy was away from the house on weekends, Dirk would come over and visit Christine. Dirk and Christine had big plans. Dirk's old man was retiring from the appliance repair business he had started thirty years earlier, and Dirk was taking over the family business; a very successful business. The old man's business serviced Hillcrest Hillsboro and Crestview. He had grown it into a five-hundred-thousand-dollar-a-year

venture that returned one hundred percent on fixed costs. Dirk was set for life. He and Christine had talked about buying a new home and making a life together. They continued their affair until that fateful day Chris had come home from being interviewed to find the dick and his wife in bed with each other. The entire town had talked about gunner chasing Dirk from the matrimonial home. Someone had even snapped a couple of pictures as the asshole was putting his pants on behind the company van. The pictures ended up plastered all over social media. Dirk was the talk of town. Well, actually three towns. More women came out of the woodwork. It seems that Dirk had been fucking as many of the company's customers as he could. One woman even claimed that Dirk fathered her daughter and filed a lawsuit for support plus childcare. Dirk's father cut him out of the will and was forced to fire his own son to save his business. Sales plummeted to less than half before the scandal. Dirk's father was eventually forced to sell the entire business to his competitor for twenty cents on the dollar. Dirk declared bankruptcy, trying to avoid paying child support. It had made it back to Gunner that the dick was living out of his van somewhere in California. When Christine found out she was not the only one, she had a nervous breakdown. The money Gunner had made from the helicopter photograph went to pay for her lawyer and a shrink.

Christine now lived in Crestview, an hour away from Hillcrest, and her son Tommy. As Tommy had grown older, he came to understand how his father felt about things and what was right and wrong, especially when it came to relationships. He would never do that to Donna; he saw the destruction an affair could cause. Tommy was a one-woman man, and Donna was the benefactor of his devotion. Gunner could not knock his son for not coming home. Tommy learned how to be

loyal from Chris. He was proud of his son but did miss his company when he was not around.

Gunner took a Hungry Man dinner out of the freezer and tossed it in the microwave on high for 12 minutes, then sat down to eat. He needed to find another woman he could share his life with, but who could he ever trust? Chris had remained single since the divorce and concentrated on his new career as the chief pilot for the Ranger Service. He sat and watched television for a couple of hours and then hit the sheets. He had an early start in the morning and wanted to be fresh and alert for the daily events.

Chapter 28

Johnny Robbins was fast asleep on the couch in Eric and Cathy's living room when the sheriff's car started down the driveway to the farmhouse. The young deputy had been instructed to check all the farmyards within his quadrant of the search area.

Robbins heard the noise of the car traveling across the gravel driveway and jumped to attention. He went over to Eric and shook him. Eric started to come around.

"Come on, old man, I need your help," Robbins said. He pulled the 9mm from its holster and used the scissors that sat on the coffee table to cut the restraints from Eric's wrists and ankles, then tore the duct tape from his mouth.

"The cops are here," said Johnny. "Get rid of them."

Eric stood up groggy and went to the front door of his house. He turned on the porch light then opened the front door. Robbins stood on the other side of the wall, pointing the 9mm at Eric's back.

"Say the wrong thing, and I put one in your spine," said Johnny. "The second one will be in your wife."

Sheriff Lucas Clark radioed in his location before stepping out of his cruiser.

"Good evening, Eric," he said as he approached the front steps of the farmhouse.

"Evening, Lucas," said Eric. "It sounds like you boys have your hands full tonight."

"You heard?" said Lucas.

"Yup, I saw the news before I fell asleep on the couch. You having any luck finding those cons?"

"Not yet," said Lucas. "You see any strange activity tonight?"

"Not a thing," said Eric. "All has been quiet around here except for the coyotes yipping in the fields."

"Yeah," said Lucas. "Everyone has said that."

Lucas and Eric's son, James, had gone to junior high together. Lucas followed the law enforcement path, while James followed the academic road that would lead to becoming a medical doctor.

"How's Cathy?" said Lucas.

"Good," said Eric. "She is sound asleep."

Eric grabbed his nose with his thumb and fingers. He blew some snot from his left nostril and wiped his nose with his sleeve.

"Well, you know what to do if you see anything strange," said Lucas.

"Sure do," was Eric's reply. "Good luck in finding those prisoners."

Lucas turned and went back to his cruiser. Eric entered the house, locked the door, and turned off the porch light. He watched as Lucas turned his car around and headed back towards the highway.

Lucas radioed into headquarters, "Taylor farm, all clear."

"Roger," came the reply.

The radio operator looked at the county map, she circled the Taylor farm and put an X through the circle.

The sheriff's department was striking out.

"I gotta use the can," said Eric.

"Piss in the kitchen sink," said Robbins. Eric went to the sink, undid his fly, and urinated in the sink. "Back in the chair, old man," said Johnny. Eric shuffled towards the rocker. As he turned to sit in the chair, he took a swing at Johnny Robbins. Johnny dodged the fist that was coming his way and pulled the trigger of the 9mm. The bullet hit Eric in the chest, and he collapsed in a heap on the floor. Blood poured from the fresh wound. "You idiot," said Johnny. "I did not want to shoot you."

Eric rolled onto his back and looked Robbins in the eyes. Eric's breathing was labored.

Matt had heard the gunshot and sprung up from the bed, waking Cathy in the process. Matt ran down the hallway naked. He and Johnny stood over Eric as the old man took his last breath.

"Stupid son of a bitch," said Johnny. "He wanted to be a hero. Now we got a mess to clean up."

Matt removed Eric's wallet from the rear pocket of his jeans. "Guess you won't be needing this anymore," he said. It was five AM on Friday morning. The convicts had things to do.

Chapter 29

Brad awoke around 2:00am and thought he heard a noise outside the tent. He listened intently and did not make a sound. He heard heavy breathing and then the footsteps of something moving several feet away. He reached for his Buck Huntsman, unsnapped the clip that held it in the sheath, then removed the blade. He was ready. The noise disappeared into the evening. Brad lay awake as adrenaline coursed through his system. He was prepared to fight anything or anyone to the death to protect Elizabeth. Eventually, he dozed off again. His girl still cuddled up to him, completely oblivious to the noise he had heard earlier.

Tommy woke to hear screaming from the children's tent next door. He bolted out of the sleeping bag in his underwear. By the time he unzipped the front of his tent, Brad was standing in front of the children's tent with his Buck Huntsman in his hand. Marcy was still screaming as the boys pulled back the open doorway to the children's tent. Tommy turned on his flashlight and used it to illuminate the inside of the tent. Marcy was sitting upright, tears rolling down her cheeks. "Where's Mark?" Tommy asked.

"I don't know," she said. "I woke up, and he was gone. The door was open."

Tommy yelled, "Mark! Mark!" There was no answer. Brad looked at his watch. It was 3:30am. Both young men stood wearing nothing but underwear.

"Where the hell would he have gone?" said Brad. They both ran to the opposite ends of the campsite, peering into the forest. "Mark! Mark! Where are you?"

By this time, Donna and Elizabeth were standing outside, wrapped in their jackets, their legs bare to the cool night air.

"Mark!" the girls screamed at the top of their lungs. Tommy and Brad kept shouting. Tommy shouted at the women to be quiet.

Brad said, "Over here."

Brad made his way to Tommy's side. Tommy was moving the beam of the flashlight back and forth across the line of trees in front of them. *Jingle, jingle,* they heard, then "I am here." Tommy and Brad made their way to the tree line, and Mark started walking toward them, *jingle, jingle,* as he walked.

"What are you doing in the forest this time of night?" asked Brad.

"I had to pee," was Mark's reply.

Tommy was furious and said, "Mark, I told you if you had to go to the bathroom, you go behind the huckleberry bushes."

Mark said, "I did not have to poop, just pee."

"What are you doing carrying the bells?" said Brad.

"You told me that if I had the bells, I would not get lost. It's really dark, and I could not see very well when I opened the door," he said.

Tommy and Brad both looked at each other, standing there in their undergarments. "Come on, little buddy," said Brad. "You get back to bed." The two young men stood relieving themselves, a steady stream of warm fluid flowing from their members. Brad looked over and said to Tommy, "At least he is listening. He took the bells with him, thinking if he got lost, we would

find him. Don't be too hard on him."

"Yeah, I guess," said Tommy.

By the time the young men had finished pissing on the grass, the girls had gone back to bed. Tommy peered into the kids' tent and said, "If you have to go, make sure you stay close, okay?"

Mark and Marcy both said, "Okay." Tommy did the zipper back up and made his way back to the tent he shared with Donna. He brushed his feet off and then did the zipper up on the doorway. He crawled in with his girl.

"Damn, it is chilly out there," he said.

"Come here," was Donna's reply. "I will warm you up."

Brad and Elizabeth drifted off, listening to Donna call out Tommy's name over and over again. Elizabeth spooned Brad. Life was good, and everyone was safe.

Chapter 30

Matt and Johnny spent the next half hour rolling Eric's body up in a sheet of plastic and cleaning the blood off the floor in the living room. His body was carried down into the cellar and hid behind some old boxes. The blood they soaked up with dish towels they found under the sink. A little warm water with some bleach and the place looked like new. Matt looked at Johnny and said, "I am going to get some more rest."

"No way," said Robbins. "It is my turn. You take the couch."

Matt hesitated but then agreed. Robbins made his way to the master bedroom. Cathy was stretched out on the bed, tied to all four corners, tears flowing down her face, a sock stuffed back in her mouth. Johnny removed the sock. Cathy coughed and looked at Johnny. "Where's my husband? I want to see my husband," she said.

Johnny took the sock and placed it back in her mouth. "There is plenty of time to see your husband later," he said. Johnny played with Cathy's breasts. He removed the taser from its holster and ran it across her nipples. Cathy shook her head from side to side. "What's wrong?" he said. "I heard you like it rough." He moved the stun gun down between her legs and noticed some dried blood. "Well, this just will not do," he said. He got up and Cathy noticed his cock was hard and moved from side to side as he walked. Johnny unfastened both of the belts holding her legs to the footboard. He bent her legs back so her ankles were up by Cathy's ears. He refastened the belts to either side of the headboard. Cathy was now bent as far back as she could go. Her hands were purple from being tied earlier by Matt. Johnny looked at

137

the shape of her ass as he climbed back onto the bed. "You are so nice and firm," he said. He started playing with her asshole. It was tight and he wanted a piece of that. "Just a minute," he said and bounced off the mattress and opened the bedroom door.

He made his way to the bathroom, his hard-on pointing the way. He scanned the shelves and found some clothespins and a jar of KY jelly. He returned to the bedroom then closed the door. Looking at Cathy, he said, "You're going to like this." Her breathing was laboured, being twisted into the position Johnny had left her in. Robbins took two clothespins and fastened them to her nipples. He removed the lid from the jar of KY and put a big dollop on the end of his index finger. He held it up for Cathy to see. She shook her head from side to side, the end of the sock moved like a trunk on an elephant. He placed his finger around the tip of her ass, then massaged the jelly into position before shoving his finger inside her. "There," he said, "that is much better." He stuck another finger in her ass until eventually he had three inside her. He moved them back and forth and when he was ready, he mounted Cathy.

He plunged his cock deep inside her ass. He thrust as hard as he could, the clothespins on her nipples moved back and forth as he gave her everything he had. Her head moved side to side, tears flowed again from her eyes. The pain was incredible as Robbins raped her. He looked down and removed the sock from her mouth. He bent forward to kiss her, his cock deep inside her ass. "Are you ready?" he said, thrusting as though Cathy was enjoying her situation. He placed his lips on hers and started to cum. Cathy bit down as hard as she could through Johnny's lower lip. He screamed in pain as he deposited his load deep in Cathy's ass. He punched Cathy on the side of her head, breaking her eardrum. She

released her grip on Johnny's lip and spat blood into his face.

"Come on, you motherfucker," she said. "Try it again." She looked like a rabid dog. She had reached the point that nothing could be worse than what she had endured at the hands of both men. Death was going to be a welcome relief to the horror she had endured at the hands of the criminals in her house. Robbins pulled out of her ass. He wiped the blood from his lip as it started to swell. He grabbed the taser and placed it against Cathy's vagina and pulled the trigger. Fifty thousand volts shot through her body.

Johnny screamed, "You fucking bitch! I am going to kill you!" Cathy's body jerked from the electricity that coursed through her body. Her eyes rolled in her head as she passed out.

Chapter 31

James, the son of Cathy and Eric, had been at a medical convention in Las Vegas. He was interning at Metro General as a trauma surgeon, and Vegas was the hub for five days of cutting-edge technology he wanted to be on the forefront of. Metro General had invested a lot in their local prodigy. It had been twenty years since the local area had produced someone with James' intellect, dexterity, and talent. He was one of those kids who excelled no matter what he set his mind to. In school, he was in the ninety-seventh percentile category. There was actually a time he was isolated in a room with two instructors watching him take his SATs; they believed he was cheating. He aced them and won a scholarship to Metro University, which shared its campus with the hospital.

James had never been interested in the farm life his mother and stepfather had laid out before him. Instead, he went the academic route. His mother encouraged him every step of the way. Eric had hoped his stepson would take over the family farm someday. After all, they had done very well over the years and had a few million socked away for retirement.

James received his private pilot's license on his sixteenth birthday. On his 25th birthday, the day he graduated from med school, Eric handed his stepson the keys to a brand new Cessna 172. Eric was proud of his stepson, and it didn't matter if James would run the farm or not. He was making something of himself, and the plane would help free up more time.

It was 7:00am on a Friday morning when the farm came into view. The GPS system had taken James

on a direct route from Vegas to the family farm. James had to be back at Metro General Saturday morning, and he wanted most of Friday to catch up on some sleep.

Eric had made a 1500-foot gravel landing strip behind the big Quonset. The strip ran east to west and had been hardpacked using the farm tractor and roller. Eric kept aviation fuel on hand so that James could top up when he needed to. The rules for a private landing strip were far more lax than the federally or municipally approved airports. James could land, top up with fuel, roll the Cessna into the Quonset, and be sitting at the dinner table with Cathy and Eric in 30 minutes.

James flew over the family farm and rocked his wings. He noted the direction of the windsock, then banked the 172 for the final leg of his approach. He was landing with the rising sun directly to his back. "What a beautiful morning," he thought as the extra-large tires made contact with the gravel runway. Dust kicked up behind his plane as he turned around and headed back towards the Quonset. He radioed Hillsboro Municipal Airport and closed his flight plan. He locked the brakes, flipped a few switches, and shut the engine down in the 172. It had been an uneventful flight.

He left Vegas at 5:00am on an instrument flight plan, then switched to a visual flight plan after the sun came up. He clambered out of the cockpit and grabbed his duffle bag, which contained five days of dirty laundry. He would top up later that day. He was tired and needed to rest. He made his way to the front of the house and opened the front door. Cathy sat at the kitchen table in her housecoat with a big floppy hat on her head. James ambled inside, "Hello, Mom," he said as he dropped his bag in the front entrance. Cathy's hands moved across the top of the table, and she raised her head.

James saw his mother's face. It was bruised, her eye swollen shut. "Oh my God," he said to his mother, "what happened?" Then everything went black.

James awoke, his hands bound behind his back, duct tape over his mouth. He was bound to a kitchen chair and was looking directly at his mother. It took a moment for him to focus. The back of his head throbbed from the impact caused by the butt of the 9mm Robbins used to knock James to the ground. His eyes focused on his mother.

The barrel of his father's shotgun was now stuck in his mother's mouth. Duct tape was wrapped around her head, holding the barrel in place. The gun was held in place on the table with several layers of the gray tape. A string ran from the trigger of the shotgun to the kitchen sink. The string was tight and looped through a handle on an upper kitchen cabinet door. It was finally fastened to the handle of the red bucket his mother used for cleaning. The sprayer faucet had been pulled out to its maximum length. It rested on the edge of the bucket, held in place by a piece of duct tape. The bucket sat perched over the edge of the counter.

James blinked and stared at his mom, tears rolling down her eyes. He struggled against the bindings that held him in place to the chair. He mumbled through the tape on his mouth.

Johnny Robbins and Matt Jones sat in the other two kitchen chairs, wearing Eric's clothing. Both men looked at Cathy. Her floppy hat now lay on the kitchen floor. Both winked at her. They then focused their attention on James.

"You're going to fly us to Hillsboro," said Robbins. James shook his head from side to side, indicating no.

Johnny stood up and removed the stun gun from a wall plug just above the kitchen counter. It was once again fully charged, its green light indicating it was ready for use. Johnny walked towards Cathy and held the stun gun close to her face and pulled the trigger. It snapped and crackled as it came to life. He looked over at James. He was not moving his head this time.

Johnny said, "You see that bucket over there? The tap is set to drip a couple of times a minute. The way I figure, it will take about four hours for the bucket to fill up and fall off the counter. When it does and the bucket falls to the floor, pulling the string... Boom!" He yelled at the top of his lungs. Robbins then smiled. "There goes your mother's head. Are you going to fly us to Hillsboro?"

James nodded his head up and down, confirming he would indeed fly the two convicts anywhere they wanted.

Cathy, her eye now swollen shut, looked at her son, the barrel of the gun deep in her mouth. She was exhausted, and her son was doing everything to save her.

Johnny stood and fastened the service belt containing the 9mm, extra rounds, and the holster for the taser around his waist. He took the stun gun and put it into place on his hip. "Now," he said, "you have four hours to get us there and get back here to save your mother. Don't be a hero, or I will put a bullet in your head."

James nodded his head up and down. Robbins removed the duct tape from James's mouth. "Where's my father?" he asked.

"Your father is busy right now; we sent him to Hillsboro to meet us. You can fly him back when you get

us there."

Matt used a kitchen knife to cut through the tape on James's feet and hands. The three men got up and walked outside to the plane. "I need to add fuel," said James. "With the three of us and the return trip, I am going to need every drop."

"You have 10 minutes," said Johnny. "Remember, the longer you take, the less time your mother has."

James worked as fast as he could, topping up the two tanks in the wings of the 172 as quickly as possible. "I have to file a flight plan," he said to Robbins. Matt and Johnny looked confused.

"No flight plan," said Matt, "we don't want anyone knowing where we are going."

Johnny went to the barn and returned with a gas can, a package of matches, plus a couple of Colt cigars Eric kept on his workbench. "Better top up this gas can," he said to James. "We might need it."

The three men clambered into the cockpit of the 172. Johnny sat in the backseat, the gas can behind James. Matt sat in the front passenger seat. They closed the doors, and James yelled, "Clear!" The engine came to life. The three men slipped the plane's headsets over their ears, then adjusted the microphones so they were in front of their mouths. James applied power and turned the 172 toward the homemade runway. "We are going to need the whole length," he said into the microphone. Johnny reached over, tapped him on the shoulder, and said, "Go ahead."

They taxied to the end of the field, and James turned the 172 toward the west, adjusted the flaps, and applied full power. The 172 rolled down the gravel strip

until it reached rotation speed. James pulled back on the yoke, and the plane lifted into the air.

"We will follow the highway," said James. "If I keep her under 500 feet, we should be clear of radar. As we get closer to Hillsboro, the mountains around us for sure will keep us hidden."

It was around 10:30 as Hillsboro came into view on the horizon. James's radio crackled to life. "Unidentified aircraft, this is Hillsboro Municipal Airport. Identify yourself?"

"What was that?" said Matt.

"They have seen us," James said. "Their radar must have picked us up. I have to respond or the next thing you know, we will have F16s chasing us. They don't like unidentified planes in the air since 9/11; they will shoot us down."

Johnny pulled the gun from its holster on his hip and held it to James's head. James pushed the talk button on his yoke. "This is Charlie Romeo Bravo Echo Delta. We are a chartered 172 taking real estate photographs."

"Climb immediately to 3500 feet," came the reply, "and squawk your ident code."

James pulled back on the yoke. The 172's nose lifted, and he climbed until the altimeter read 3,500 feet. He was approximately 1,500 feet above the ground. The town of Hillsboro sat at an elevation of 2,100 feet.

It was 10:40am when James noticed the Ranger station's chopper fly below him, approximately 500 feet lower and a half-mile away. "Lucky bastard," he thought to himself.

"There, over there," Matt pointed. "Fly that way."

James pointed the nose of the 172 in the direction his passenger was pointing. "There is the old mine," said Matt. "I told you we would find it," he said to Robbins. "You see that road down there that runs right to the mine? It's nice and straight. Set it down there."

James looked. "The trees were pretty close to the road," he said.

"Set it down there."

James flew over the road and concluded that he could make a safe landing as long as there were no crosswinds. He dropped down, lowered his flaps, and set the Cessna down on the gravel road leading to the Benchmark Mine. He brought the plane to a stop. Johnny Robbins lit up a cigar and offered the other one to Matt. The two men took deep drags and exhaled the smoke into the cockpit's cabin.

Johnny Robbins unscrewed the cap on the gas can that sat behind James's seat. He shook the jug until some gas spilled out on the 172's floor. "Let's go," Robbins said to Matt.

Matt opened the plane's door. Johnny took his cigar and tucked it into the cover of the matchbook he had used to light up. He placed the matchbook and lit cigar into the storage pouch on the back of James's seat. "Thanks for the lift," said Robbins as he closed the door of the plane.

James was finally on his own. He looked at his watch. He had approximately one and a half hours to make it back to the farm to save his mother. He hit the throttle on the 172, and it roared down the gravel road, dust filling the air. Johnny and Matt covered their faces with their shirts. The 172 jumped into the air. James had performed a perfect short-field takeoff.

As soon as he was above the trees, James got onto his radio. "Mayday, mayday, mayday," he called out into his microphone. "This is Charlie Romeo Bravo Echo Delta, mayday." James needed to tell the authorities that he had been kidnapped, and his mother's life was in danger.

The cigar that was tucked into the matchbook had burned down to a point where the red-hot tip reached the head of the matches. The matchbook went up instantly and burned through the plastic on the back of James's seat. Burning debris dropped onto the gasoline-covered floor, and it ignited in a giant fireball. The plastic gas can melted and poured its contents out onto the floor.

"Mayday, mayday, mayday," James said, his priority now on the flames and smoke filling the cabin. The heat was getting intense.

Hillsboro Municipal responded, "Echo Delta, mayday, go ahead."

He kept his finger on the transmit switch for his radio. He couldn't see out of the plane's window as the flames grew so intense that he could feel his clothing starting to burn. "Mayday, my mother, my mother!" he screamed as the plane's nose lowered towards an open field twenty miles from the Benchmark mine.

"Echo Delta, go ahead... Echo Delta, are you there?" There was no reply.

Calls started to come into the tower. Some people had seen a small plane on fire, and it had crashed. Hillsboro Tower called the fire department, explaining that they had reports of a small plane going down. Calls came into 911 from the general public that a small plane had crashed in a field. The department responded with two tankers and a crew of eight, including Captain

Anderson.

It took the firetrucks thirty minutes to arrive on the scene. There, in the field, was the crumpled mass of the 172. The pilot's charred body lay behind the flight controls. "Poor bastard," said Anderson aloud. "Let's get some water on this and put her out." Anderson got on the radio to his dispatch office. "You better get a hold of the FAA and the NTSB; we have a crash. The pilot is dead, and we do not see any other bodies or passengers. Tail markings CRBED."

"Roger," came the response from dispatch. "Remain on scene; we will advise."

Robbins and Jones walked the two miles to the Benchmark Mine. It would open for tours by noon. They had an hour or so to come up with a new plan. So far, they were batting a thousand.

Chapter 32

Saturday morning arrived swiftly. The squirrels began chattering just as the sun started to rise. Brad rolled over in his sleeping bag, inadvertently exposing Elizabeth to the cool morning air.

"No," she protested, "it's too early." She hastily tugged the edge of the bag back over herself. Brad couldn't help but smile as he climbed out of his sleeping bag. He got dressed and, when ready, quietly unzipped the tent's door flap and slipped outside.

He found Tommy tending to the coals in the firepit. "Good morning, buddy," Tommy greeted him. Both young men were early risers. "How did you sleep last night?"

They both chuckled. Speaking in hushed voices so as not to disturb the kids and their girlfriends, Brad replied, "Well, it was great until I heard Marcy screaming her head off. I thought someone had died."

"Me too," agreed Tommy. "It's the first time the children have been this far into the woods. I'll talk to her later. We can't have her doing that for the next two nights."

"No kidding," Brad agreed. "What do you say we get this fire going again?"

Tommy took out his pocket knife and picked up a piece of wood from the ground. He skillfully shaved slivers of wood off the piece he held in his hand. Once he had a small handful ready, he turned his attention back to the firepit. He poked around until he found a few embers still glowing from the night before.

"There," he said to Brad. Tommy bent down and gently blew on the section of wood that was barely warm. As he did, smoke appeared, and eventually, the wood started to glow a brighter red. When he felt it was ready, he placed it back into the firepit, adding his bundle of wood shavings on top of the glowing embers. Taking a deep breath, he blew a steady stream of air across his handiwork. The embers glowed beneath the pile of shavings, and in seconds, it ignited his little bundle of fire starter. Brad handed him some small pieces of wood, which Tommy placed over the now burning shavings, and before long, the fire crackled back to life.

"We could survive anything," Tommy said to Brad. They walked over to the pile of wood the park department had supplied and gathered up an armful each. They repeated this a couple of times until they felt they had enough wood at their campsite for the day. Brad took the water jug from the table, and both young men walked down to the creek, taking their time filling the jug to the brim.

"What do you say we build a raft today?" Tommy suggested. "Maybe we can float over to the island and take in the view from there."

"Sure, I'm up for anything," Brad replied. "That will also keep the kids busy." They returned to the campsite, ready for a new day of adventure.

Tommy placed the water jug back on the picnic table. "There we are, all set. How about some coffee?" he asked.

"My thoughts exactly," said Brad. Both men walked over to the tree where their backpacks were tied and suspended twenty feet in the air. Tommy pulled on the rope, creating enough slack for Brad to undo the end wrapped around the tree. They slowly released the rope

through their hands until the backpacks were lying on the ground. They removed them from the tent fly.

The young men carried the packs back to the picnic table. Brad opened the nesting cooking set he had left out on the table. He took the largest pot out of the set and filled it with water. He placed the grill back down over the freshly lit fire.

Tommy rooted around in his pack and found the package of coffee he brought. He took two handfuls of coffee grounds and dumped them into the open pot of water. Brad placed the lid on the pot, and the young men sat and stared at the fire.

Within 10 minutes, the water had started to boil, and the aroma of fresh coffee filled the air. Brad found the two socks he had used the night before as oven mitts. He took the pot of boiling coffee off the grill and placed it on the bench of the picnic table.

They dug into their packs and found their respective coffee mugs. Brad and Tommy had been using them since they were boys, and Brads' father took them out on their first camping trip. Back in the day, they only held hot chocolate. The mugs were as old as their experiences in the woods.

Brad removed the lid from the pot and peered inside to make sure the coffee grounds had settled to the bottom. He dipped his mug into the steaming black liquid, and with a quick flip of his wrist, it was filled. Tommy handed Brad his mug, and with the same motion, he filled his friend's cup.

"Here you go, buddy," Tommy said. Brad took the mug and placed it on the table. He opened a pocket on his pack, finding his sugar and dry creamer. Tommy stirred the works into the hot liquid with his pocket knife.

He sipped from the edge of the rim. "That's perfect," he exclaimed. Brad smiled, flashing back to the Staff Lunchroom. "Someday Tommy might drink his coffee black, but for now, he's happy, and that's what matters."

Brad added more water into the pot and placed it on the edge of the grill next to the fire. It would stay nice and hot until the girls got out of bed. Brad started to recall the events of last night. "You know," he said, "I think I heard something last night."

"What, when?" said Tommy.

"Maybe around two. Yah, I think it was two."

The noise was coming from behind Brad's tent. The boys walked behind Brad's tent and stared at the ground. There, in the soft dirt, was one of the largest grizzly tracks they had ever seen. There was only one print visible.

The rest of the ground was hard enough that you could only see where the claws from each foot had disturbed some of the gravel.

"I knew I heard something," Brad said, "Looks like a big sucker." He laid his hand across the print in the dirt. It was two and a half times the size of his spread hand. "Let's just keep this to ourselves," he whispered to Tommy. He stood and rubbed his boot across the pawprint.

"Don't want to worry the girls or the kids over nothing," said Tommy. "Looks like it was sniffing around and moved down the path. He's long gone by now."

Chapter 33

By the time Johnny and Matt had walked the two miles to the Benchmark Mine, it was 11:30am on Friday morning. A few cars had passed them on the gravel road, but no one stopped to ask if they needed a ride. The men choked down the dust as they made their way to the small parking lot that was being used for tourists. Four signs in front of the ticket office, snack shack, and souvenir store were marked "staff parking," and each stall was full. Behind the building, there was a donkey engine and two open passenger cars. A wooden platform allowed ticket holders to board the open railroad crew cars easily, making it convenient for passengers during loading and unloading. At least those who paid for the one-hour tour of the inner workings of the old mine.

Robbins took the lid off a garbage can situated at the foot of the ticket office stairs. He removed the green plastic garbage bag and placed the service holster containing the 9mm, stun gun, flashlight, and two extra clips into the bag. Johnny and Matt then tried the front door, and to their surprise, it was unlocked.

"Sorry, we're not open until noon," yelled Bert, the volunteer who ran the engine. Three other employees emerged from the kitchen area, holding steaming cups of coffee.

"Sorry about that," Matt apologized. "I guess we're a little early. We're here for the tour."

There were too many employees around for the convicts to stage a surprise or potentially steal a car. Matt and Johnny had to play it cool. Johnny spoke up, "Our car broke down a couple of miles from here, and we

walked two miles hoping someone might be able to let us use a phone."

"Sure," said Bert. "Come on in." Johnny made his way to the phone on the counter and placed a call that lasted about two minutes.

"You boys look a little thirsty," said Bert. "How about a coffee?"

"That would be great."

"Have a seat at the table over there, and I'll have one of the girls bring out a couple of cups. We're expecting a big crowd today, and everyone is a little busy getting ready for our noon tour."

Bert headed back into the kitchen and asked Lisa to bring out two cups of coffee for the gentlemen seated in the small dining area. It was 11:40, and Bert needed to do his safety walk, service the electric engine, oil the bearings, and check the lighting, all before the crowds arrived. "See you gentlemen later," he said as he exited through the back door, dressed in blue coveralls and an old engineer's cap. Lisa arrived at the table with two piping hot cups of coffee.

"The sugar and cream are in those containers," she informed them. "I'm just taking a fresh batch of cinnamon buns out of the oven. They're quite popular. Would you two like a couple with some fresh butter?"

Matt, reaching for Eric's wallet he had been carrying, asked, "How much are they?"

"They are five dollars each, but well worth it," she said. Matt opened Eric's wallet and removed a twenty-dollar bill.

"Will this cover the buns and coffee?" he asked.

"More than enough," said Lisa. "I will be back

with your fresh buns." She turned and started walking away.

Matt said, "I would not mind those fresh buns."

Robbins laughed. "Me too," he said. "What do you figure, thirty, thirty-five?"

"Nah, she's too confident," he said. "Got some experience. Probably forty."

The remainder of the staff scurried around, preparing for the crowds. The parking lot was filling up, with around twenty cars outside now and people starting to mill around. A few stood in front of the ticket window. Lisa returned with two beautiful cinnamon buns, steam still rising from them. "Enjoy, gentlemen," she said. "I put a dollop of butter on each. If that's not enough, just yell at Tammy. She looks after this area during the day. I have to get back to work."

The convicts dug into their fresh buns, and within minutes, both had finished eating. "That was really good," Robbins said as he belched. "We better grab us a couple of tickets for that train." They finished their coffees with a couple of large gulps. Johnny grabbed the green garbage bag, and they exited the building.

The prisoners stood in line with several other couples and families in front of the ticket office. The office window opened exactly at noon. The sign on the wall displayed the prices: Adults twenty dollars, Children ten dollars, Seniors ten dollars. Sweaters or jackets were recommended.

When it was Matt and Johnny's turn, Matt requested two tickets. The woman behind the window said, "That will be forty dollars." Matt checked his wallet and found only thirty dollars in cash. He removed Eric's Visa card and handed it to the clerk. She pushed the card

into the reader and then handed the machine back to Matt. "Just enter your pin number," she said.

"Damn it," Matt said out loud. "I just got that card, and I left the number back in my car."

"Then just tap it," she suggested. Matt was puzzled. The clerk took the card from the machine, tapped the computer chip over the screen, and the ticket dispenser spit out two adult vouchers for the 12:30 boarding of the Benchmark Express. "Here you go," said the agent. "Two tickets and your credit card. Enjoy your tour. Next."

Matt and Johnny took their time scanning the crowd that was forming on the platform. They moved behind an older couple, husband and wife, who looked like they had been married for fifty years. The woman, short in stature, carried a large leather purse over her shoulder, with the zipper open. Johnny, standing behind her, could see its contents.

It was now 12:25. The PA system crackled to life. "Ladies and gentlemen, boys and girls, welcome to the Benchmark Mine. Your roundtrip tour will take approximately one hour, and it gets a little cool the deeper we go inside, so if you think you need to put your jackets on, do it now. There are no washrooms, so if you have to go, please use the facilities inside. We will be leaving in five minutes. All aboard!" came the call at 12:30. The people standing on the platform boarded the open cars, making their way to respective bench seats. The wooden seats were similar to church pews, worn and showing their age. After all, this was the same equipment that took the miners underground when Benchmark was fully operational.

The elderly couple took the second-to-last bench, and Johnny and Matt sat behind them in the last seat of

the final car. The woman placed her purse between the outer wall of the rail car and her hip after taking it from her shoulder. She cuddled close to her husband, and he placed his arm around her shoulder while adjusting the collar of her jacket. "There you go, honey," he said. "Don't want you getting a chill."

She rested her head on his arm. "Thank you, you're always looking out for me."

Johnny reached from the back seat in between the wall of the car and the seatback. He slowly and cautiously placed his hand into the open purse. The engineer started ringing the bell on the train. Clang, clang, clang. Johnny's hand found its mark in the old woman's purse.

The loudspeakers mounted in the back of the engine came to life. "Good afternoon, ladies and gentlemen. I am your tour guide, Lisa. You are about to experience what it was like for the men who worked in the Benchmark Mine so many years ago. Please stay in your seats and keep your arms and legs inside the cars at all times."

The train started to move with a loud shudder and bang as the slack was taken up in the couplers holding the cars together. Robbins removed his hand from the purse and elbowed Matt in the ribs. The men jumped from their seats as the train reached the end of the platform.

In his left hand, Johnny held the green garbage bag, and in his right hand, he held a fistful of tissues. He turned his right hand over and opened his fingers, revealing a set of car keys in the middle of the tissues. "Let's get the hell out of here," Robbins said. "We have an hour before that old lady knows it was us."

The convicts made their way to the parking lot, where now there were thirty cars in front of them. Johnny pushed the lock button on the key fob. In the distance, they heard a car horn and saw headlights flash. They reached a white Chrysler 200, and Johnny pushed the unlock button. The door locks released, and the men climbed into the car. Johnny tossed the green plastic bag into the back seat and pushed the button on the dash to start the engine. He put his foot on the brake pedal and shifted the car into drive. They had less than an hour to make it to Hillsboro and ditch the car. Their latest plan was working.

Chapter 34

Jackson Hall hung up the phone. "I have to go," he said to Maria Hernandez. "Can you and the staff handle the shop?"

"Where are you going?" she asked.

"It's unfinished business," he replied. "I have no choice."

Maria knew well enough not to ask any questions when Jackson's voice changed like that. She hated these unexpected business trips. Her brother, a long-time gang member of the Blades, had been killed in prison. She had pulled herself out of the gang life and become a respectable citizen, running an incredible surf shop on the coast of California. At least that's what she portrayed. She caught a glimpse of Jackson when she was up at the prison visiting her brother, Manuel.

She was talking to her brother when Jackson came into the visitors' area of the Big Sky prison. Jackson sat down. He was chatting with a blonde woman, but he kept looking past his visitor and glancing in Maria's direction. She caught him looking at her. Every time she looked back in his direction, he was looking her way.

Maria was a stunning woman with long black hair. She stood about five-foot-two and was built like a centerfold model. Maria was struck by Jackson's rugged looks and blonde hair. It was love at first sight. Maria stood and said goodbye to her brother after her half-hour visit was up. Prison rules forbid any contact; she couldn't even shake his cuffed hands. "It was good to see you," she said, then glanced in Jackson's direction. She

memorized the prison number on the front of his shirt.

Maria was good with numbers; that's what she did for her brother. She managed the money for the Blades on the outside. She always had a head for numbers, and she was going to use her gift this time for her benefit.

When she returned home, she sat down and wrote a long letter.

"Dear P 204376, I noticed you were looking in my direction when I was visiting my brother on the weekend. My name is Maria; I am single and live in California. Tell me about yourself. Here is a picture of me just in case you forget who you were looking at."

The letter ended with a lipstick-stained set of red lip prints, a quick spray of perfume, and her signature. Maria addressed the envelope to the Big Sky prison, attention Prisoner 204376. She put her return address on the envelope and then mailed her letter.

Three days later, Jackson Hall was sitting reading a book when the mail cart pushed by old Jasper stopped in front of his cell. "Gots a letter for a Jackson Hall, smells real purdy," he said. Jasper handed the letter through the bars to Hall's waiting hand. The letter had been opened by the prison screening department. Everything that came and went from the prison went through the department. They constantly watched for contraband and also screened letters about past crimes and ones that were being planned. The cons knew this, and so did the folks on the outside. Each individual inside had developed their own code when speaking to someone in the real world.

The screening department had their hands full deciphering what was actually being said. They were

responsible for helping to solve 286 unsolved crimes, plus they had thwarted 479 future crimes of prisoners who had been released. In the department's office, on the same floor as the prison wardens, there was a banner stapled to the wall that read, "NOTHING IS WHAT IT SEEMS."

Jackson opened the letter; the prison had done a perfect job in using a razor blade to cut through the top of the envelope. There was no need to tear it open; all he had to do was reach inside. The smell of perfume permeated the air. He unfolded the letter, and Maria's picture dropped onto his lap. He read the letter, smiled, and opened the shoebox that sat on the shelf above his toilet. He added the letter to the fifty or so other letters he had received from other women interested in the famous Jackson Hall.

Jackson had been featured on the front page of Forbes Magazine. The caption read, "Corporate embezzlement hurts everyone." The feature article spoke about how big corporations were stealing from the little man on the street. The CEOs then stole from the companies they owned or managed. Jackson was a force in bringing down several key players in the corporate fraud business. He assisted the FBI in helping track funds and money transfers from large organizations. Jackson was not a popular individual in the world of big business.

His own companies moved millions of dollars a month through banks, businesses, and stocks and bonds. Jackson Hall was the star of how to do it when he was assisting the FBI. That came to an end very quickly when the feds started to investigate him for embezzling just over one hundred million through his own corporations. The government caught on very quickly. Forensic audits of the last ten years revealed his companies shorted the IRS twenty million in tax revenue.

Hall's companies would put money into stocks and short what they reported in capital gains. The difference would be diverted to offshore accounts in the Bahamas. It was a perfect plan. Take a little here, take a little there. The biggest money-maker for Jackson Hall's companies was in private loans to developers. They charged twice the interest rate of the chartered banks. Who knew what the actual cost of building a new office tower or local mall was? No one. It was easy to bury money in these projects and pad the bills if you knew the right people. Everyone got a cut.

If the developer fell short on their loan payments twice in a row, Hall's companies would foreclose. They would resell the partially finished projects to another developer. That would double their initial investment without lifting a finger. There was so much paperwork involved; no one would ever know how it was done. That was until the Feds hired someone smarter than Jackson Hall and paid them a bonus for every crook they took down.

Hall received ten years for embezzlement. His companies were forced into bankruptcy and were sold off to his competitors.

They loved the fact that the fair-haired golden boy who had turned in so many in the financial world was just as dirty as those he finked on. Jackson had learned a lot from his father, who was a bank manager in Crestview. Being street-smart and a troublemaker as a teen in town boded well for his adult career. His arrest records were expunged when he turned eighteen and sealed. His father shipped him off to Harvard Business School. It was like adding an extra layer of thick icing to the best chocolate cake in the world. Jackson Hall emerged from Harvard a proper gentleman dressed in pinstripe suits. There was nothing stopping him.

Jackson picked up a pen and a sheet of paper. "Dear Maria," he wrote, "how could I ever forget those beautiful eyes and long black hair. My name is Jackson Hall. Thank you for your lovely letter; the perfume is driving me crazy. When I close my eyes, I can see you; now I can smell you. I have six months left on my sentence, and then I am as free as a bird. Please write back. Love, Jackson."

Over the next six months, their love letters got more frequent and far more intimate. Maria was in love with a man she glimpsed only once. Manuel Hernandez had found out about the letters through Jasper, the mail delivery guy. Jasper just happened to mention one day that Jackson was getting a lot of letters from Maria Hernandez. Manuel had paid Jackson a visit with a couple of his lieutenants. They turned up several letters and a couple of nude pictures of Maria. They beat the hell out of Jackson that day and left him lying in a pile on his cell floor. No one was going to fuck with and distract the woman who managed the Blades' finances.

Two weeks later, Maria was standing at the entrance to the prison as Jackson Hall walked out into the sunlight. He still had a black eye from the beating he took from Maria's brother, but he was now a free man. He did all his time and was not required to report to a parole officer. "Let's get the hell out of here, sweetheart."

They climbed into Maria's new Dodge Challenger and made their way to the closest hotel. They spent two days making love and ordering room service. Life could not be any better. Five years later, he received the call he had been waiting for. "Maria, I have to go. I love you; I should be back in less than a week."

Maria walked Jackson out to his new Mercedes-

163

Benz convertible and kissed her lover goodbye. "Hurry home," she said. "I will be waiting for you."

Chapter 35

Matt and Johnny reached the city limits of Hillsboro in forty-five minutes. They took their time, trying not to draw attention to themselves as they drove through town.

"When do I get my fifty grand?" Matt asked. "I got plans."

"Soon," Johnny replied. "We're almost there."

They continued through town and finally arrived at 451 Front Street.

"I'm going to park around the block," Johnny said. "We can walk back to the apartment building."

They left the car keys on the dashboard in plain view and wiped down the areas of the car they might have touched with their shirts. Johnny grabbed the green bag from the back seat. They walked away from the car and crossed the street to the local 7-11.

"Go inside and purchase a roll of duct tape and maybe some of those nylon quick ties if they have any," Johnny instructed Matt.

Matt went inside, grabbed two large Slurpees, two hotdogs, a roll of tape, and a bag of large nylon ties. He placed everything on the counter, and the clerk rang it all through, saying, "That will be seventeen ninety-five."

Matt pulled out Eric's credit card and tapped it against the machine. "Keep the receipt," he told the clerk as he returned outside. Johnny was waiting at the corner of the building.

"The cops just drove by," Johnny said. "We've got to keep a low profile. They'll be looking for us hot and heavy."

The two men made their way back to 451 Front Street. This was the apartment building where Johnny had met his friend Jackson Hall on the day of the incident.

"This is where it all started," Johnny said to Matt. "I hate that fucking prick Hall. He framed me, and someday he's going to pay."

They entered the lobby of the building. To the right of the entrance was an intercom system with the apartment numbers and names of the tenants. Johnny found apartment 301 on the board, listed under Hernandez.

Johnny pushed the intercom button. "Yes," came the reply, sounding like a very old man.

"Papa John's pizza. We have a delivery," Johnny said.

"I did not order any pizza," the old man replied.

Johnny lied, "The delivery was ordered by someone named Maria."

The buzzer sounded, and both men entered the building. They made their way to the third floor and found apartment 301. Johnny told Matt to stand back in case someone looked through the peephole and got suspicious.

Johnny reached inside the green garbage bag and withdrew the stun gun from its holster, hiding it behind his back. He nodded toward Matt and knocked on the door.

"Pizza delivery," he said.

The door opened wide, and there stood sixty-year-old Jesus Hernandez, Maria's father, his arms and neck covered in tattoos, his white muscle shirt stained with morning coffee that had dribbed from his chin.

"Where's the pizza?" Jesus managed to say just as Johnny removed his hand from behind his back and placed the stun gun against the old man's chest. Johnny pulled the trigger, and the old man hit the ground, flopping about like a chicken missing its head. Johnny and Matt dragged Jesus out of the doorway and into the apartment. They closed the door behind them, locked it using the deadbolt and chain, then placed the old man in a kitchen chair.

The two men bound Jesus's feet to the legs of the chair and pulled his arms behind him, fastening them together with the nylon ties. They then secured his arms with tape to the back of the chair. Johnny took the roll of tape and wound it around the older Hernandez's mouth. He also placed a strip around his eyes.

"There," he said. "When the old man wakes up, he won't know what hit him."

"What about my money?" Matt asked.

"I told you soon, did I not?" Johnny replied.

"Yeah," said Matt.

"Just chill. I have to make a call."

Johnny picked up the phone and dialed a number from his memory. Jackson Hall answered. "The fucking garbage stinks when it's burning." Hall laughed. "I'll be there Saturday night. I'm driving straight through."

Johnny hung up the phone. "Now we wait," he said to Matt. "Let's just relax. All is coming together just as I thought it would. I'm going to take a shower and see

if I can change these bandages on my side. I recommend you do the same when I'm done. Keep an eye on the old man."

Johnny found the bathroom. It was a mess and not anywhere near as nice as Cathy's and Eric's farmhouse, but it would do. After all, the convicts were in a bit of a tight spot. He showered and found some clean bandages on a shelf in the hallway. He left them out on the bathroom counter for Matt.

"I'm done," said Johnny as he walked into the living room wearing a towel. "Your turn. I left some bandages out for you on the counter."

The old man's head was still bent forward; he was still out cold. Matt made his way to the bathroom. He, too, cleaned up, replaced his bandages, and returned to the living room. The two men raided the fridge and ate what they could. Matt cooked up some bacon and eggs and made a fresh pot of coffee. Johnny made himself a sandwich.

The two men sat in the living room watching the Friday afternoon game. It was now 3:00pm. Both men soon dozed off as the events of the last day and a half had finally caught up with them.

At 7:00pm, they awoke to thumping coming from the kitchen. It was Jesus bouncing up and down in the chair he was tied to. Johnny walked over to the taser that was plugged into the wall above the kitchen counter. He removed the gun from the wall socket and then walked over to the old man.

He placed the probes of the gun over Hernandez's heart and then pulled the trigger. Johnny held it for ten full seconds against his victim's chest. The old man was thrown backward by his own violent

movements, and Johnny had to catch the back of his chair before he fell to the floor. When Johnny straightened out the old man, smoke was coming from the two burn holes in his white muscle shirt. Matt watched the events unfold from ten feet away, still wearing their bath towels. Matt walked over and asked, "Who is this guy? He's got more tats than I do."

Johnny threw a cup of water against the old man's face and shirt, and Jesus started to come around. Johnny zapped him again, and the old man's head slumped forward. Through the wet material, Matt could see the outline of a large chest tattoo. Matt pulled the wet shirt away and looked. The tattoo read "BFE," and under the letters, it said "President."

"Holy fuck, do you know who this is?" said Matt. The BFE meant Blades Forever. President meant that before the two convicts sat Jesus Hernandez, the father of the most notorious gang ever to hit the streets. "Fuck me," said Matt. "This fucking guy is connected. I killed his son in prison."

"I know," said Johnny. "Jesus, meet Matt. Matt, meet Jesus." Johnny laughed. "Don't worry, kid. He hasn't seen your face. I got you covered."

"Where's my goddamn money? I got to get out of here," said Matt.

"You will have your money in the morning. What do you say we order a pizza?" The old man's wallet sat out on the counter, and there was five hundred dollars in it. "Let's order from Chester's. They make the best pizza and wings in town," Johnny suggested. Johnny picked up the phone and ordered two medium pizzas with the works and two dozen hot chicken wings. "Can you also have your driver pick up a six-pack of Coors?"

"We'll ask the driver," came the reply. "Your total is forty-two dollars."

"Tell your driver there's a forty-dollar tip if he brings the beer," Johnny said before hanging up the phone. Within minutes, the streets below were alive with cop cars, lights flashing. There had to be five cars that went by the apartment.

"We're dead," said Matt. The men turned off the lights and television and sat quietly in the living room. Off in the distance, they could hear the muffled sounds of a bullhorn and then some gunshots.

The buzzer rang on the intercom inside the apartment, and Matt was going out of his mind. Johnny answered. "Can I help you?"

"Chester's pizza delivery," came the response. Johnny buzzed the driver in. He stood in the open doorway, the lights still out in the apartment. The driver, not much older than 21, arrived at the door in two minutes.

"Sorry it took so long," said the young man. "There are cops everywhere."

"What's going on?" asked Johnny.

"The cops just shot up a white Chrysler with two black dudes in it. Things are quite a mess around the corner," the delivery boy replied.

"Thanks, kid," said Johnny. "The girlfriend and I are starving. You know how it is." Johnny winked.

"Here's your beer, wings, and pizza." Johnny handed the driver a one-hundred-dollar bill from Jesus' wallet.

"Does that cover everything?"

"Yes, sir, more than enough. Have a good evening." The driver left, and Johnny closed the door. He locked the deadbolt and refastened the chain.

Johnny looked over in Matt's direction as he turned on the light. "Guess we won't be going anywhere for a while. May as well enjoy another game. Turn on the tube," said Johnny.

The cons sat and ate everything they had ordered. When the half dozen beers were finished, Johnny walked down the hall to the bedroom and made his way onto the bed. Matt curled up on the couch with a blanket he found in the hall closet. It was 2:30 in the morning, and it was time to get some more shut-eye.

Chapter 36

Saturday morning came early. Gunner was up, showered, and dressed in his Park's uniform before the birds started to chirp outside his windows. He adjusted the shoulder flashes on his shirt. The four gold bars on each shoulder were the only thing that set his uniform apart from the Rangers and staff on the ground. He grabbed his jacket off the back of the kitchen chair, turned, and exited his house, locking the door as he left. He enjoyed the drive to work. The town of Hillcrest was still asleep at this time of day.

He pulled into the local doughnut shop's drive-thru. He ordered a large coffee with two cream and two sugars. "You better give me one of those long johns as well," he said to the girl in the window.

"That will be three seventy-five," she said.

"Here's five; keep the change."

Chris was feeling good. He had an excellent sleep Friday night. The nightmares were few and far between now. He never spoke to anyone about them. When he got back from his second tour, Gunner would wake up in a cold sweat. He had visions of going down in his chopper. He had been shot at, missiles had been launched at his Apache, his main rotor had even started to come apart once, but he always made it home. This dream was different. He was out of control, and there was nothing he could do about it. Over the years, he had managed to put it out of his mind for the most part.

He pulled up to the Ranger Station Headquarters at 6:00am. The lights were all on inside. He got out of his truck and looked over to the helipad. He walked past

172

Betty's car and then placed his hand on its hood. The steel was cool, and the car had not moved from its position on Friday. The 505 had been washed and shined up by the part-time ground crew. It was ready for the day's events.

He walked into the office, and there sat Betty at her desk. "Good morning, Chris," she said with a big smile.

"You're in bright and early," came Gunner's reply with a wink. Betty knew that Gunner was aware of the affair she was carrying on with Superintendent Robert Gerard. The two never spoke of it, but both knew the other was aware.

Chris went about checking the daily forecast. He filed his flight plans with Hillsboro. By 7:30am, he had reviewed most of the reports that had come in Friday afternoon. Betty turned and said to Chris, "Did you see this yesterday?" She was pointing to her computer screen.

"What?" said Chris. "What are you looking at?" Betty enlarged the image, and Chris came over to see what she had been looking at.

"There," she said. "See?" The 505's camera had picked up an image Gunner had not seen with his own eyes. It was only two frames of the entire video. Chris stared at the image. Peering from behind the old abandoned trapper's shack on the Rock Lake trail was the head of the largest grizzly he had ever seen.

"Shit," he said. "That is one big fellow."

"That's the largest one I have seen," said Betty. "If you compare the scale to the logs, he has to be a seven-footer, maybe more. That might explain why Momma Bear and her cubs took off yesterday. I thought

173

it was the chopper that scared them off, but if that guy is hanging around, then she ran because of him."

"How many folks do we have up at the Cabins this weekend?" asked Chris.

"There is a half dozen in RL01 and RL02, they are from Ireland. A nice young couple in RL04. No one in RL03," replied Betty. "Not until tonight."

"I will make a couple of extra passes through there today," Chris said.

"Good idea. We want to make sure we have a neutral area," added Betty.

"Affirmative," said Chris. "I will let you know if anything pops up. I will fire up the infrared just to be on the safe side. If he's still around, my girl will pick him up."

The door opened, and in walked Superintendent Robert Gerard. "Good morning, you two. How are things looking for the day?"

Gunner piped up, "Betty was just showing me a couple of shots from the video yesterday. Looks like we had some bear activity up at Rock Lake."

"Show me the pictures," he said to Betty. The two of them scanned the computer screen.

"Wow, that's a big one," said Bob. "Gunner, I am going to go up with you. I want to have a look for myself. I am going to act as your spotter today."

"Sure," said Chris. "Give me a bit; I have to recalculate the weight and balance. It's going to cut down on my flight time, but I am looking forward to having you along."

Chapter 37

The fire trucks had finished extinguishing the several fires that had ignited around the Cessna 172. The fuel tanks in the wings had ruptured when the plane hit the ground, and fire had burned not just the plane but also the surrounding ground. Anything that could burn was incinerated.

"Good job, boys," said Captain Anderson. "Looks like we have everything under control. Let's secure the area." They drove wooden stakes into the ground at the perimeter of the burn marks and ran yellow tape around each stake until the entire area was surrounded. The tape read, "Fire Investigation - Do Not Cross."

"The boys from the NTSB should be here within the hour," said Anderson. "Truck #2, return to the station. Truck #1 and I will stay here until they arrive. We have enough police presence, and the coroner is on his way."

Anderson communicated with his crew through the radio in his half-ton truck. "Roger," came the reply from Engine #2, "we are returning to the station."

Captain Anderson was just finishing his paperwork when the NTSB investigators arrived on the scene. The rest of the fire crew were standing and talking to the police, pointing and speculating on what had actually happened. There were a few cars that had stopped, and some of the general public were there. The crowd was getting a little bigger. These kinds of things did not happen around Hillcrest, so people were on their phones, chattering away to friends.

The news crew from Hillsboro had also arrived on the scene. Christie Jones ran her fingers through her hair, shook her head, and then held her microphone close to her mouth. The camera operator counted down: 3, 2, 1, "You're on."

"This is Christie Jones, live on the scene. There has been a small plane crash 20 miles outside of town. Authorities are trying to determine what has happened," reported Christie. "Just a minute," she said, "I see Captain Anderson. Captain, can you tell us what happened? Do you know who or how many people were on board?"

Anderson turned and addressed the reporter. "All I can tell you at this time is we have a burned plane on the ground. There is only one deceased individual in the remains of the plane. We do not know any more than that at this time."

"This is Christie Jones reporting live from the crash site," she concluded. The camera panned to the plane and focused on the charred numbers on the tail.

The two investigators made their way under the tape and walked towards the burned-out wreck. The smell of aviation fuel and burned grass filled the air. Agents Williams and McFadden put rubber gloves on their hands and moved about the mangled pieces of metal. Agent McFadden took a series of pictures.

"You can see where it clipped the tops of the trees before it hit the ground," said McFadden. "At least we don't have to climb through the bush on this one."

"You remember..." started Williams.

"Yeah, yeah," said McFadden. The two men made their way to the charred cockpit. The windows had been melted by the fire.

"Poor bastard. He's still hanging on to the wheel. What's left of it," said McFadden. They put on surgical masks and then pried the pilot's door open. James's body was burned beyond all recognition.

McFadden took his camera and shot another twenty or so pictures. "You ready?" said Williams.

"I guess," said McFadden. Agent Williams reached inside and did his best to remove James's hands from the controls. The burned flesh fell to the floor as Williams continued. He managed to release the pilot's death grip. James's arms stayed outstretched, burned into position by the raging fire that had consumed the interior of the cabin.

"It got awfully bloody hot in here," said Williams. He moved James's body, and the charred skin on his stomach burst open. His intestines tumbled out into the hands of Agent Williams. "I was afraid of that," he said. McFadden took more photographs.

They laid a sheet of plastic out on the ground beside the plane. Both men took hold of James's legs and upper body. They carried his body to the plastic sheet and laid him on his side. The back of his shirt and seat of his pants were still somewhat intact. Agent McFadden reached into the right back pocket and retrieved a wallet. He opened the wallet and found a pilot's license. "James Taylor, M.D. Well, we know who he is. Better get the sheriff's office to notify the next of kin. We don't want them hearing about it on the five o'clock news."

McFadden walked to the two sheriff's deputies and read the name and address to the officers. He then returned to the scene so he and Williams could continue their investigation. The coroner was asked to come and assist with the body. The three men placed James's charred remains into a black plastic body bag. They had

to fold his arms so the body bag could be zipped shut. It was not a pretty sight. The coroner and his assistant carried James's body to their waiting car.

"Something is just not sitting right with me," said Williams. "It is just too hot. You see how the aluminum has melted in the back seat? It has burned through the floor. There had to be an accelerant in the cabin. Something is fishy," he said, moving the pilot's seat forward as best he could. "Look," he said to McFadden, "you see that? Grab your camera."

There was a small piece of burned red plastic that had melted and attached itself to the melted aluminum. "That's a gas can," said Williams, "or what's left of it. This guy committed suicide. He wanted this to look like an accident. Bloody doctors, they are always overstressed. Probably a big insurance payout somewhere."

Agent McFadden got on the phone and contacted Hillsboro Control Tower. "We have an ID," said Miller. "Did you guys play back air traffic control's tapes?"

"Affirmative," was the reply. "We are downloading to you now."

Miller's phone beeped. "Got it," he said. "The pilot's name was James Taylor, M.D."

There was dead silence at the other end. Then a voice spoke. "I knew that kid. He was a rising star. He was so bright, had the world by the tail. Worked at Metro General Hospital. His folks have a farm. He often flew in and out of there."

"Interesting," said McFadden. He walked over to Williams and pressed play on his smartphone. The two men listened to the recording twice. "My mother... My mother... save..." and the recording ended.

Anderson got on the phone and called the FBI. "You guys might be interested in this one." The Sheriff's office had been contacted by the deputies at the crash site. "We have an ID on the pilot they reported."

"Roger. We will dispatch a car."

Lucas Clark was still on duty. He had pulled an all-nighter and was looking at a full double shift. "Car 2433, what's your twenty?" Clark responded.

"We have some bad news," said the operator. "There has been an accident. James Taylor's plane has gone down. There were no survivors. Can you go by the Taylor farm and deliver the news to his parents?"

"10-4," said Clark. His childhood friend was gone. It was now up to him to tell Jame's mother and father. Lucas turned his cruiser around and headed for the Taylor farm. He pulled up to the front door of the farmhouse. He radioed dispatch that he had arrived. He got out and noticed that it was quieter than normal. "Hello? Hello?" Lucas shouted. There was no reply. He walked up to the front door and knocked on the glass window. There was no answer. Lucas looked around, his gut told him something was not right. He tried the door handle. It was not locked. The door opened. "Hello?" Lucas said as he walked inside. He looked to his right. There, at the kitchen table, sat Cathy Taylor, a shotgun taped into her mouth. He studied the situation. He followed the string from the trigger to the red bucket that sat on the edge of the counter. Water was dripping out over the rim and onto the floor. He realized that if the bucket fell the string would be drawn tight, pulling the trigger of the gun. He moved cautiously into the kitchen. Cathy looked at him, her one eye swollen shut. She mumbled. "Do not move," said Lucas. He made his way to the bucket. The faucet head was hooked just barely to

the rim of the bucket. It had prevented it from falling to the floor. He held the bucket in his hands and reached for the knife he carried on his service belt. He shouted, "You're going to be okay, Mrs Taylor." He cut the string from the handle of the bucket. It fell, hitting the floor with a thud. Cathy jumped as water poured everywhere. "It's going to be okay. Do not move." Lucas turned his attention to Cathy. "Don't move you poor woman. Hang on! I am here." He worked his knife around the duct tape. He was finally able to remove Cathy's mouth from the barrel of the shotgun. She moaned and took a deep breath. Lucas moved the gun to the side and, as he did, the tape holding the stock to the table tore. Lucas stumbled. The shotgun went off. The blast went past Cathy's left shoulder. The bird shot blew a hole into the wall behind her. She lost control of her bowels and messed herself. "Oh my God," said Lucas. "You're going to be okay. I have you." Lucas used the microphone attached to his shoulder. "Dispatch Car 2433, 10-53! I repeat, 10-53! I need an ambulance now! Do you read? I need an ambulance now!" He cut the tape from Cathy's wrists. She moved her arms from behind her to Lucas's hand.

"Help me," she said, her throat dry. "Help me, please. Where is Eric?" she managed to say.

"I don't know," said Lucas. "But we will find him." In the distance, Lucas could here the sound of sirens. The cavalry was on its way.

Chapter 38

Tommy and Brad sat at the picnic table speaking softly. They did not want to wake anyone up before they were ready to get up. "Let's stoke that fire," Brad said. "I am getting a little hungry." Tommy threw a couple of split logs on the fire. Sparks jumped into the air.

"So what do you think about that print?" Brad held his index finger against his lips. He shook his head. "Obviously the grizzly had moved on. Nothing here for it," said Tommy. "It must have been pissed off when it could not reach our backpacks."

Brad laughed. "Right."

How many times over the years had the boys heard stories of stupid hikers that would leave their packs in their tents or on top of picnic tables? Tents would get ransacked, packs would get shredded, people injured. Their supplies would get destroyed and it was always the bear's fault. There had been several cases where the park's department had to relocate problem bears. Once they started coming into campsites and found a food source they became habituated. Parks had to trap the bears, tranquilize them, and fly them into remote locations so they would not return and become a nuisance. Each bear would be tagged with an embedded computer chip in the right rear flank. Any bear trapped was scanned for the chip. If a bear was caught and already had been chipped, they were flown further up into the mountains. If there was a third time, the bears had to be destroyed. It pissed Brad off that people were so stupid. Tommy's father had relocated many bears over the years. Parks used a cargo net slung under the 505. It was a labour-intensive exercise, not to mention

the closures of affected areas while the park was trying to capture the respective culprits.

"Dad taught us well," said Brad. "Nothing to eat, so the bears just move on. Just like they should."

"I am going to start the bacon," said Tommy. He reached into his pack and pulled out two packages of semi-frozen bacon. The frozen cold pack had done a respectable job in keeping the meat he and Donna brought from spoiling. He zipped up the foil-lined cooler pack. "Now," he said, "my turn to do the cooking." He took the frying pan from Brad's nested cooking set and sat it on the grill over the fire. He opened the packages with his knife and dumped the contents into the pan. The bacon sizzled immediately. He broke the bacon apart with his knife. "You okay with pancakes this morning my brother from another mother?" he said.

Brad smiled. "Whatever you're cooking is fine by me." Donna and Elizabeth were starting to stir in their respective tents. The smell of cooking bacon permeated the air. Donna emerged first from her slumber.

"Good morning, sweetie," said Tommy. Her hair was in a bit of a disarray. Her sweater hung crooked off one shoulder.

"Morning," she said. "I need coffee." Tommy took his mug and dumped out the last mouthful that he had not finished. He lifted the lid of the pot and dipped his mug into the black liquid.

"Your wish is my command," he said.

"You are amazing," she said.

"It was a joint effort this morning," said Tommy.

"You are amazing too, Bradly," said Donna.

The zipper on Brad and Elizabeth's tent opened.

Elizabeth emerged into the sunlight, squinting and rubbing her eyes. "Good morning," she said.

"You look amazing," said Brad.

She had brushed her hair before getting out of the sleeping bag. Even deep in the forest she wanted to be presentable for her man.

"Is that coffee?"

"You ready for a cup?" Brad asked.

"I have to pee first," she said. "Donna?"

The two girls made their way behind the huckleberry bushes. They dropped their jeans, squatted, and relieved themselves. Donna had a tissue in her pocket. She tore it in half. "Here you go," she said to her friend. The girls wiped themselves, stood up, pulled their jeans up, and kicked some dirt over the used tissues. "That feels better," said Donna.

They made their way back to the picnic table. Brad handed his girl a steaming cup of coffee. Elizabeth added some powdered cream and two lumps of sugar. Brad took the buck huntsman from its sheath and then stirred the contents for his girl. "There you go, beautiful. Breakfast will be ready soon."

"What are you two making?" asked Elizabeth.

"Bacon, pancakes, and scrambled eggs," said Tommy.

Donna dug threw Tommy's pack. She found the instant pancake mix and bag of powered eggs. "Would you like me to mix up the batter for the hot cakes?" she asked Tommy.

"Sure," came Tommy's reply. "I am going to be done cooking the bacon soon." Tommy poured the extra

grease from the cooking bacon into a tin can he had saved from the trash barrel. "Good thing we had those beans last night." The grease sizzled and popped as he poured it into the can he had rinsed out. Donna whipped up the pancake batter in one of the pots. Elizabeth took the package of powered eggs and added enough water to turn them into something that could be cooked and scrambled.

"That's sure a lot of bacon," Donna stated.

Tommy smiled, "Sure is." Tommy finished the bacon and then loaded it all onto a plate sitting on the table. He added a little grease from the can into the frying pan. He poured some batter into it. When the surface of the hotcakes were full of bubbles, Tommy flipped them over. "Perfect," he said aloud. He repeated the procedure another four times until he had a stack of piping hot pancakes hidden under a piece of tinfoil. He took the last of the grease from the can and lined the frying pan. He dumped the egg mixture into the pan, then stirred the contents with a fork.

"Smells pretty good for powered eggs," said Brad. The girls had dug into Tommy's pack. They brought out maple syrup and butter. Brad reached into his pack and pulled a special bottle. He handed it to Elizabeth. "I brought this for you." She looked at it. Brad had remembered that strawberry syrup was her favorite.

"Oh, Brad, you are just the best!"

Tommy finished his cooking. He placed the pan with scrambled eggs in the middle of the picnic table. "I think we are ready. There is just one thing missing." He took the last empty pot and walked over to the kids' tent. He unzipped the doorway, stuck the pot inside, and banged it at least ten times with his knife. He yelled, "Come and get it."

Mark and Marcy said, "No, it's too early!"

Tommy banged the pot again. It was 9:10am, Saturday morning. "Time to get up!"

Chapter 39

Lucas held Cathy's head. "You poor woman," he said, as he stroked her hair. He bent down and used his knife to cut the duct tape from her ankles. The smell of excrement filled his nostrils. The sirens were growing louder. "What happened?" he asked in the gentlest voice he could muster.

"Two men," she whispered. Cathy burst into tears. Her ear was ringing from the shotgun blast. "They raped me! Oh, my God, they raped me!"

Lucas took the blanket from the couch and draped it around Cathy's shoulders. The EMTs were the first to arrive, pulling up right to the front door and entering the house promptly.

"Ma'am, are you all right?" EMT Adams inquired. Cathy shook her head from side to side.

"We are going to need oxygen and the stretcher," EMT Adams informed his partner. The younger man went back to the waiting ambulance, opened the back doors, and retrieved the gurney himself. By the time he had found the oxygen bottle, three additional sheriff's deputies arrived on the scene.

"I could use a hand, gentlemen," the young EMT said. Two of the deputies assisted in carrying the gurney and oxygen bottle into the house. The third deputy, Sergeant Baker, made his way into the home just before the rest of his men.

"What do we have, Lucas?" he asked.

"Cathy, this is my Sergeant. He needs to ask you some questions before we can take you to the hospital."

186

Baker took a seat in one of the kitchen chairs, opened his notebook, and began his inquiries. Meanwhile, EMT Adams placed the oxygen mask over Cathy's nose and mouth, reassuring her that it would make her feel better.

"How many were there?" Baker inquired.

Cathy held up two fingers. Baker shouted at his three deputies, instructing them to secure the place. The men pulled out their guns and methodically went room by room, searching the farmhouse.

Lucas descended into the basement to conduct his own search.

"Did they touch you?" Baker asked Cathy. She nodded in affirmation, her swollen eye and tears revealing the ordeal she had been through.

"Where is your husband?" Baker questioned.

Cathy shook her head, signaling she didn't know. She removed the oxygen mask and whispered, "They took my son, forced him to fly them somewhere."

"When was that?" Baker pressed.

"This morning, early. I'm not sure what time," Cathy replied, tears streaming down her face.

"All clear," came the response from the two deputies on the main level. Lucas returned from the basement, handed Baker a note, and said, "Search all the buildings."

"Do you know where your husband is?" Baker inquired again.

Cathy shook her head. Baker looked at her sympathetically, saying, "I am sorry, so very sorry." Cathy went into hysterics, and the EMTs administered a

shot of Droperidol to calm her down. They lifted her onto the ambulance stretcher.

The EMTs hit their lights and sirens and headed for Metro General Hospital. The sheriff's deputies were instructed to search all the buildings on the property, and Baker made a call to dispatch.

This was not a call that would go out over the radio; the news hounds and public had too many police scanners. The phone rang in the sheriff's office.

"This is Baker; I need to speak to Chief Parker," Baker said.

The call was immediately transferred to the Chief's office. The phone rang once, and then the Chief answered.

"Chief Parker."

"Sir, we have a situation here at the Taylor Residence. It does not look good. We have a body in the basement, and I believe I know where the convicts were last night."

"I will contact the Feds and state police," said Parker. "Secure the scene and do not let anyone touch anything."

The two deputies returned from the Quonset.

"There is a State pen guard's car in the building over there," one of the deputies reported.

"Fuck me," said Baker. "It was them. How the hell did we miss them?"

"Lucas, you were here last night," Baker continued. "You went to all the farms in this area."

"I spoke to Eric myself," Lucas said. "It's in my report. It was all quiet. He stood right there and talked to

188

me. He grabbed his nose and shot snot all over the place."

"He grabbed his nose? Show me how he grabbed his nose!" Baker demanded.

Lucas took his thumb and placed it on one nostril and his index finger on the bridge of his nose.

"Christ almighty," Baker exclaimed. "They were here. They were in the house when you came to check."

"That's not possible," Lucas argued.

"I am telling you, they were already here." Sergeant Baker, a veteran of the Gulf War, recognized Lucas's gesture. "That is the sign we used for when something stinks! Eric was hoping you would pick up on it."

"I did not know," Lucas admitted, shaking his head in disbelief. "I thought he might have had a cold. I am so sorry." He lowered his head in disbelief.

Baker made his way into the basement. Behind some old boxes, he found Eric's body.

"I am sorry, brother, that we missed your signal," Baker said softly. "I promise you we will do everything in our power to catch these motherfuckers. Your wife is in good hands now."

Chapter 40

Mark and Marcy made their way to the picnic table. "I have to pee," said Marcy.

"Me too," said Mark.

"Come on, you two, I will take you," Donna offered. She handed a tissue to Marcy. They headed towards the huckleberry bushes. Marcy went around the back, and Mark relieved himself just before the edge of the bushes. He rushed back to the picnic table. There was no way he'd let his sister eat all his breakfast.

"Uncle Tommy, can I have mine now? I am hungry," Mark requested.

"Sure, little man. Did you sleep well last night? You put a pretty good scare into all of us. Tonight, you won't be drinking a lot before bed," Tommy advised.

"I am sorry," Mark said. "I really had to go."

Marcy and Donna returned, and Marcy joined her brother in gobbling down pancakes, bacon, and eggs. Elizabeth had mixed up a batch of Tang orange crystals in the last pot. She took two red plastic cups from her backpack and filled them halfway. "Here you kids go," she said. "Make sure you wash out your cups when you're done. We don't have too many, and you need to use them for the rest of the day."

The sun was just starting to rise over the eastern edge of Prospector Pass. "It's going to be a beautiful day. Look at that sky," Brad remarked. "We might get up to 65 or 70 degrees today."

Tommy stoked the fire. "Honey, are you done with your coffee?" he asked Donna. She took her last

gulp and handed the old mug to Tommy. "I think I'll have another," he said. "Buddy, how about you?" Tommy asked Brad.

"Sure, when Elizabeth is done, I'll have another with you."

Elizabeth handed Brad his mug. "I'm finished too."

Tommy and Brad refilled their mugs. "I'm going to walk down to the water," Brad said.

"I'll go with you," Tommy replied. The two young men made their way to the edge of Rock Lake. The trail leading to the north end of the lake was to their right.

"Look there," said Brad. "You see that?"

The two men walked over. In the middle of the trail was a pile of bear scat. They had a quick look, noticing squirrel fur, shoots of grass, and things they didn't recognize within the pile of bear dung. "Looks like it has not been eating well," said Brad as he kicked the pile into the shrubs. "We don't need the kids seeing that."

The young men stood on the edge of the lake, sipping their coffee. "Might be a good day to build a raft and take everyone over to the island for the day," Tommy suggested.

"I was thinking the same thing," Brad replied. They turned to head back to the campsite and noticed the girls and kids walking towards them, each carrying something that needed to be washed. "We will do the dishes," Donna offered, since the boys had done all the cooking that morning.

The young ladies and kids made their way to the creek.

They washed everything in the ice-cold water. Mark and Marcy stood on the edge of the lake, watching as bits of pancake and egg floated out into the water. It didn't take long until Mark said, "Look at all the fish." The lake's surface rippled as the trout fought for the scraps floating on or near the water's surface.

"Cool," said Marcy. "There are so many."

"You kids take these things back to Uncle Tommy," said Donna. Mark and Marcy headed back to the campsite with all the clean dishes. Donna looked at Elizabeth and said, "I don't know about you, but I need to get cleaned up." The girls made their way to the edge of the trees, where the creek flowed out from deep in the forest. It was a perfect spot with the creek shallow as it rippled over the rocks. Some fallen trees nearby provided places to hang their clothes.

The girls stripped down and waded into ankle-deep water. Donna was the first to squat and splash water onto her private parts. "My God, it's so cold," she said. Elizabeth soon followed suit. They each found a suitable rock to sit on and washed their bodies as best they could, but the cold water made their nipples hard. Donna's piercings glistened in the sunlight.

"I wish I could wash my hair," Elizabeth said.

Donna came over to her friend. "Tip your head back," she said. Elizabeth complied. Donna bent down and scooped up water in her cupped hands, repeating the process several times until her friend's hair was thoroughly soaked.

"Can you do mine?" Donna asked. Elizabeth exchanged places with her friend. When both were satisfied with their washing, they sat on the rocks, letting the cool mountain air dry their bodies. They dressed and

returned to the campsite.

Brad commented, "Where did you two go, the spa?" Both girls grabbed their brushes and combed each other's hair.

"Tommy, can you put some more wood on the fire?" said Donna. "That water gave me a chill." Tommy stoked the fire by adding more wood. The heat radiating from the burning logs soon warmed the girls.

Off in the distance, they heard a jingle. Two women in their mid-thirties came around the corner, loaded down with large backpacks. Each had walking poles in their hands, and they both wore those silly white canvas hats. "Hello," they said as they were walking by. They paused for a moment.

"How long have you all been here?" asked the taller of the two.

"Just since yesterday," said Elizabeth. "We're up for the weekend. Where are you two headed?"

"Oh, we're staying at RL03 until tomorrow morning."

"Well, have fun," they all waved to each other, and the two ladies continued down the trail.

Rachel and Susan had been friends for about a year, having met in a divorce support group. This was going to be the spiritual outing they needed to put their lives back on track. Both were fed up with men and relationships and needed a break from their lives. Rock Lake was the perfect spot to get away from the crap they had endured.

Chapter 41

Matt woke up around 7:30 on Saturday morning. His neck was sore from sleeping on the couch. He looked over into the kitchen at Jesus Hernandez. His head was moving back and forth. He had pissed in his sweat pants and his breathing seemed to be laboured.

Matt walked down the hall to the bedroom. He put his foot on the edge of the bed and pushed it a couple of times. "Wake up!" he said to Johnny Robbins who rolled over.

"What time is it?"

"7:35, Saturday morning."

"You see any cops outside?" Robbins asked.

"No. I stayed away from the window. You go have a look if you're that interested."

"How's the old man doing? Did he give you any grief last night?"

"He has pissed all over himself. He sounds funny when he is breathing."

Johnny got up from the bed and the two men made their way to the kitchen. Robbins took a look at Jesus then removed the duct tape from his mouth. Hernandez took a deep breath. Johnny filled a glass with water then put it to Jesus's mouth. The older Hernandez gulped down the cool liquid, some of it running from either side of his mouth and down onto his stained white muscle shirt. When the water was gone, Johnny returned the glass to the counter.

Jesus cleared his throat. "You're fucking dead!"

he said with his thick Hispanic accent. "I know who you are! I'm going to kill you! I'm going to kill your family! You're dead, do you hear me?! Fucking dead!"

Johnny took the stun gun from the outlet on the wall, its green light indicated that it was ready for use. He put it against Jesus's neck and pulled the trigger. The older Hernandez shook violently before passing out.

"Not today, old man," said Johnny. He grabbed the roll of duct tape and wrapped it around Jesus's head.

Matt looked at Robbins. "When do I get my money? It's time for us to go our separate ways."

"You can have your money after I have a shower," said Robbins. "Turn on the TV and see if you can get the news." Robbins made his way to the bathroom. He sat on the toilet and relieved himself. Those spicy chicken wings the night before had given him an upset stomach. He showered and found some clean clothes in Jesus's closet. The smaller Hernandez made it difficult to find something that fit. Johnny returned to the kitchen. Matt was glued to the television in the living room. "What does the news say?"

"They have the whole area surrounded," said Matt. "News says the cops killed two guys in a stolen car that fit our description. The dudes went down in a hail of bullets last night. Oh, there was a reporter standing outside that farmhouse. That chick made it. They took her to Metro General."

"No way," said Robbins. "That fucking bucket should have dropped! I cannot believe she made it. Can't win 'em all, I guess. Give me a hand here."

The two men pulled the fridge from between the cabinets and the wall. They moved it to the centre of the kitchen floor. Johnny reached behind and unplugged it

from the wall.

"Find me a sharp knife," he said to Matt.

Searching through the drawers, Matt found a utility knife, one of those with a retractable razor blade. "What about this?" he asked Robbins.

"Perfect, give it to me," Johnny said as he got down on his hands and knees. Robbins cut into the linoleum on the floor and peeled it back. "Give me a butter knife," he said.

Matt handed him a butter knife. Johnny wedged it between the cracks in the plywood flooring and pried the wood until an area about the size of a folded newspaper started to come loose. He worked his fingers under the lip of the plywood and pulled. The wood came loose, and Robbins tossed it aside. Matt looked on with enthusiasm.

"What is that?" he asked.

Johnny put his arm into the hole and reached in as far as he could. He looked back at Matt and smiled. He withdrew his arm, holding a dusty old black duffle bag. Johnny stood up and carried the bag to the kitchen table. Matt's eyes were wide open as Robbins opened the zipper and the flap on the bag to reveal a large pile of cash.

"Would you like twenties or hundreds?" said Johnny to Matt.

Matt stared in disbelief. The money he had been promised was right there in front of him. Johnny took five bundles of one hundred dollar bills from the bag and placed them on the table. Each bundle had a band around the bills that read ten thousand dollars.

"Do you want to count it?" asked Johnny.

"No," said Matt. "How much is in that bag?" he asked.

"That is irrelevant," said Robbins, "but I will tell you that my father always said to save half for a rainy day. A deal is a deal," he said to Matt. "I am paid up in full. You're on your own from here on in, kid."

Matt grabbed a paper bag from under the kitchen sink and placed his money inside it. Matt took the bag into the living room, dressed in Eric's clothing, and made his way to the front door.

"Good luck," he said to Johnny.

"You too, kid," said Robbins.

Matt unhooked the chain on the door and unfastened the deadbolt. He peered into the hallway, making sure the coast was clear. In a minute, he was down the stairs and outside in the fresh air, the top of the paper bag rolled up in his right hand. He walked down the sidewalk, the sunlight warming his face. It felt good to be free. He walked down the block and across the street to the 7-11. He poured himself a cup of coffee and grabbed a breakfast sandwich from the display case. He made his way to the till and pulled out Eric's credit card.

The cashier rang in the total. "That will be four twenty-five," said the clerk.

Matt tapped the card against the machine, and the unit flashed "declined."

"Try again," said the clerk.

Matt tapped the card again, and the machine again read "declined."

"Oh, here," he said, handing the clerk a five-dollar bill from Eric's wallet.

Matt walked through the store's doors to the outside world.

The brown paper bag under his arm, coffee in one hand, Eric's wallet, and his breakfast sandwich in the other, he stopped in front of the garbage can. Then he dropped Eric's wallet into the slot in front of the bin. He made his way down the street, eating his sandwich and sipping on his coffee. He sat on the bus bench, waiting for the next scheduled stop. In the distance, he heard sirens. He stood up and noticed a cab coming down the road. He waved it down and climbed into the backseat.

"I will give you one hundred bucks if you take me to 24 Mountain View Road in Hillcrest," Matt said to the driver.

"Sure thing," was the driver's reply.

As they left the bus stop, Matt looked down the road through the back window. He watched as three sheriff's cars pulled into the 7-11. "Damn," Matt said out loud. "There are cops everywhere."

The cab driver nodded his head. "There were two convicts that escaped from the hospital a couple of days ago. They say they shot them last night in a stolen car."

Johnny counted out his money. There was just over half a million dollars sitting on the kitchen table. Jesus Hernandez started to stir again. Robbins placed the stun gun over the heart of his captive's chest once again. He pulled the trigger and held it until the gun no longer made a sound. The elder Hernandez and former president of the Blades was gone. Johnny plugged the stun gun back into the wall socket. He turned his attention to the body of Jesus.

"Do not ever fucking threaten me, you fucking motherfucker," he kicked the side of the chair, and it

tipped over. With a thud, Jesus's head hit the floor. Johnny made himself a couple of boiled eggs, toast, and coffee. He then sat watching the latest news. When he had finished, he looked out the window of the apartment and smiled. His plan was working, and working well.

Chapter 42

Kevin woke up at 5:45am. As Brad's father, he was always up before everyone else. Since his wife had been taken by a drunk driver, Kevin had to play the role of both parents. He always made sure breakfast was ready for his only son, and he was never late for school. When he was away on hunting trips or acting as a tour guide, Jasmine acted as a live-in nanny. She filled the role as a parent in Kevin's absence. She was wonderful to Brad. She had come over from the Philippines. Kevin had gotten lucky when he spotted an ad in the local paper advertising a nanny for hire. She was in her mid-thirties when she first started working for Kevin. The insurance check he received for his wife's death amounted to two million dollars, less the thirty percent the lawyers took to settle the case. So the thousand dollars a month Jasmine wanted to live in and help care for Brad was nothing. She had her own separate bedroom in the house. She worked for Kevin until Brad had turned sixteen. She helped nurture Brad when a mother's love was needed.

Kevin never told his son about the amount of money he received for his mother's death. He wanted his son to grow up with morals, values, and a purpose, not a silver spoon in his mouth.

Kevin dressed in his tent then unfastened the zipper on the door. He peered outside; it was dark and quiet. He crawled out of his tent into the crisp morning air. He looked to the east and could see the outline of the Princeton Mountain Range. It was going to be a beautiful day.

Kevin walked over to the firepit. He stirred the coals with a large stick someone had left lying around.

When he found some embers, he placed small pieces of kindling over them and took a deep breath. He blew a stream of air across the embers until they glowed red-hot. The kindling caught fire, and flames once again illuminated the inside of the firepit. He gathered more wood and stoked the fire until the wood started to snap and pop.

Kevin made his way to the restrooms. He went inside, used the toilet, then had a quick shower. All the backpacks were lined up against the south wall just like he had instructed. He put his pack on the counter. Kevin removed his towel and shaving kit. He dried himself off, shaved, and redressed using a clean shirt. He heard the click of the solenoid as fresh water was pumped into the hot water tank. The solar panels on the roof were doing their jobs and keeping the batteries topped up. "All the comforts of home in the middle of nowhere," he said aloud. He had to wipe the mirror twice with his towel. The steam kept fogging it up. "There," he said, "nice and presentable for the paying masses." He took his backpack from the counter and walked outside to the fire. Everyone was still asleep.

He took his old pot from the backpack and filled it with water plus a handful of coffee grounds. He placed it next to the fire. In ten minutes, the water was boiling. He removed the lid from the pot and watched the grounds settle to the bottom.

Kevin reached into the side pocket of his pack and then removed his dented old mug. It was identical to the one he gave Brad years ago, except Kevin's was about twenty years older and had a few more miles on it. He dipped his mug into the black liquid. Steam filled the air, and the aroma of fresh coffee filled his nostrils.

"Here's to you, son," he said.

Kevin watched as the sun climbed further into the sky. Daybreak was an amazing sight. It was too bad he had no one to share it with.

Chapter 43

The cab pulled up to 24 Mountain View Road. Matt reached into the brown paper bag and removed a one hundred dollar bill from one of the bundles. He handed it to the driver.

"Thanks for the lift," Matt said.

The driver accepted the cash. "Anytime, buddy. Have a good day."

Matt exited the cab and made his way down the block. He turned right at the end of the street, then walked a couple of doors down until he was standing in front of his old family home. Matt was not stupid enough to give the cab driver the actual address of where he wanted to go. He had learned that the first time he had been caught.

Matt walked up the sidewalk to the front door. He peered inside. All was very quiet. There was no car in the driveway. His father must be at the car lot; Saturdays were some of his busiest days. Matt made his way to the side entrance. The plaster fisherman still stood guard to the right of the doorway. He tilted it to the side and reached under its base. Matt removed the key from the hidden slot his father had carved there years before.

"Nice to see some things never change," he said out loud. He unlocked the door and went inside. The house was quiet. He made his way down the hall and peered into Donna's room. It now looked like a home office. He walked to Billy's room and quietly opened the door. The bed was unmade, and Billy was nowhere to be seen. Matt's room, across the hall, was still as tidy as the last day he had been sent to the state pen. He made his

She kissed him back, her tongue deep in his mouth. Matt rolled off Joann. He rested on his father's side of the bed. Joann put her head on her son's shoulder. She ran her finger across Matt's chest. "So, my beautiful boy, what do you have for mommy today?"

Matt knew that was the signal she used for "I want to get high".

"I have something real special for you, mom." He got up and opened the brown paper bag. He took five one-hundred dollar bills and rolled them up into a neat little bundle in the shape of a cigarette. "Here," he said to Joann, as he slipped her three oxy. She gulped them down with a little water from the half-empty glass on the night stand. Matt waited for ten minutes. His mother's eyes were closed. She was breathing deep. Matt took the rolled hundreds and spread his mother's legs once again. He placed the rolled bills into her vagina. He knew his father would never look there. Matt placed the covers back over his mother.

She extended her arm. "Matt, I love you," she managed to mumble as the oxy was kicking in. Matt picked up Eric's clothing. He grabbed the paper bag and exited the master bedroom, closing the door behind him. He showered, shaved, and found some of his favourite clothing just where he had left everything.

He took an old baseball cap off the back of the shelf placed it on his head then exited the family home. He put the key back under the fisherman after locking the door. He made his way down the street with the brown paper bag in his hand. The kids at school never understood Matt when he said he loved his mother. From the time he was fourteen he had made sure Joann got everything she needed. Clifford, Matt's father, had neglected Joann for years. As Matt had come of age and

206

was getting into trouble, he found a way to keep his mother happy and himself satisfied. All he had to do was keep her supplied with something that would make her high and keep her hooked. It was perfect.

Matt walked down the street with a bit of a skip in his step. He wondered how many other boys loved their mothers like he did. He never did figure out why his sister did not love him too. He shrugged his shoulders and smiled. "What an awesome day it was turning out to be."

Chapter 44

Chris had figured out the new weight and balance for the 505. He and Superintendent Robert Gerard made their way out to the chopper. Gunner did his walk around to make sure everything was in order. He climbed into the left front seat, Bob took the right. Chris looked over his shoulder to make sure his emergency kit was still in place, buckled into the backseat. It was a medium-sized bright red duffle bag that contained emergency supplies: bandages, a flare gun, a flashlight, a small hatchet, emergency blankets, matches, a few chocolate bars, and some dried soup mix that made up most of the kit. The military had made sure their pilots were always prepared. That stuck with Chris even in civilian life.

The two men put on their headsets, then locked the 505's doors. Chris flipped a couple of switches. The dash lit up, and the radio crackled. The lights flashed under the belly of the chopper. Chris hit the start button. He watched the electronic gauges start to move as the engine came to life. The familiar whine of the turbine was like music in his ears. The main rotor started to turn. The tail rotor spun at almost three times the speed of the big blades overhead. They needed to, so they could keep up with the torque produced by the large main blades.

Superintendent Gerard knew enough not to say anything while the pilot in command went through his checklist. Gunner put his clipboard down between his seat, then flicked the radio button.

"This is Charlie Gulf Romeo Romeo requesting a vector to Rock Lake."

"Roger," came the reply with instructions on

altitude and direction. "No traffic in the area. Have a good day, sir."

"Roger! Charlie Gulf Romeo Romeo out."

Gunner pulled back on the controls, applied some pressure to the left rudder pedal on the floor, then pointed the nose of the 505 in the direction they wanted to go. As they approached Hillsboro, Bob looked out the window and to the right.

"You see that down there?" he said to Gunner. "Some poor bastard put his plane into the field down there. It looks like they are still cleaning up the mess."

Chris thought for a moment. "I wonder what happened," he said into the microphone. "I passed a 172 yesterday. Could not be the same plane though because I saw three folks in the cabin."

"Realtors out taking pictures. That's what they told Control in Hillsboro. Obviously not the same plane," said Gerard. "The crashed plane had only one soul on board."

They continued towards the park boundary. Once they hit the park airspace, Gunner was free to fly in whatever direction they wanted to go. It was restricted airspace.

"Head over to Crystal Lake," said Gerard. "I want to see if we have a full house or not."

Gunner adjusted the course to intercept the edge of the lake. Two thousand feet below them, the parking lot was full. People were out setting up day-use tents and their BBQs.

"Look at that," said Gerard. "It's a full house and not even 10.00 am."

"A busy weekend for sure," said Chris as he

pointed the nose of the chopper to the staging area and parking lot for Rock Lake and the Glacier Creek campground. It too was full. People would hike in for a couple of miles, sit, then take in the views. Few ever hiked the distance to Rock Lake for the day and back. It was just too far. Glacier Creek Campground was even further. City folks just never ventured that far unless they were spending a few days in the woods.

Bob checked his clipboard. All four cabins were rented at Rock Lake for the rest of the weekend. There was a group of six booked into Glacier Creek for two more nights. If he saw more people than what Betty said there should be in the areas, he would send some of the Rangers to check for park passes. No passes meant five hundred dollar fines for each and every person in the area who were not supposed to be there. It was the superintendent's way of making budget without saying he needed to collect fines to protect the environment.

They flew over the southern end of Rock Lake. Both men noticed three tents. A fire was burning, and people were milling about. The chopper was about 2500 feet above the campers when they all started to wave.

"Those folks are not registered," said Gerard.

Chris smiled. "I think I know who they are," he said. He descended until he was five hundred feet above the lake, the nose of the chopper pointing at the tents. Droplets of water moved out and away from the downforce of the rotor blades. The group of six were waving. One young man stood saluting the 505 with his right hand.

"That's my kid," said Gunner. "He is with search and rescue."

"Got it," said Gerard, "not making any money off

of them." Chris rocked the 505 back and forth, in essence waving back to the group on the shoreline. He applied power then climbed back over the island in the middle of the lake. They made their way to the cabins on the north shore, and there were some folks milling about. "Nothing out of the ordinary here," said Gerard. "Not even a duck."

Gunner turned the 505 to head up to the Angel Creek Glacier. He flew through the narrow valley and climbed to 6500 feet. There, at the base of the glacier, were about twenty people. They were posing for pictures, and tents were set up along the edge of the tree line. Four big fires were burning, but there was no one standing around them.

Superintendent Gerard got on the radio. "Gerard to Rangers 2, 6, and 8, do you copy?"

"Loud and clear," came the reply from all three men.

"We have unregistered traffic at the foot of Angel Glacier."

"Roger," came the reply, "we will head up in the ATVs and find out what is going on."

"Roger that," said Gerard. "We are heading to Glacier Creek Campground. Let me know what happens."

"Roger."

Bob looked over at Chris. "Set us down in the campground. The guys might need some backup later."

Chris nodded his head.

It took twenty minutes to fly the distance to the Glacier Creek Campground from the face of Angel Glacier. Chris set the 505 down on the other side of the

camp washrooms. There was a small helipad there they often used for simulated rescues and actual events. He let the turbine cool down for a few moments before shutting the engine down.

From around the corner of the building came a man clean-shaven and wearing a fresh plaid shirt. Kevin stood with a cup of coffee in his hand. Gunner and Gerard unlocked the 505's doors then climbed out. The two men walked towards Kevin. Chris extended his right hand. The handshake was firm and friendly.

"Superintendent Gerard, this is a good friend of mine, Kevin," Chris said. "He guides here in the park."

"Please call me Bob," Gerard said to Kevin as he shook his hand.

"You gentlemen up for a cup of coffee?" asked Kevin.

The men started walking towards the eight registered adults. "Kevin is the father of my son's best friend, the one I told you about," Chris said.

"For God's sake, it's a small world, isn't it?" said Gerard. "We just saw the kids about an hour ago over at Rock Lake. Looked like they were enjoying themselves."

Gerard made his way into the washroom and used the facilities. Kevin and Chris stood around the fire. Kevin introduced his pilot friend to his entourage. Gerard made his way to the campsite after finishing his business.

"Hello," he said to the eight adults. "I am Superintendent Gerard with the Parks Service. Sorry for dropping in on you like this."

"We were just about to have brunch," said one of

the ladies. "We have plenty. Coffee and a cinnamon bun, gentlemen?" she asked.

Chris looked at Bob; he nodded his head slightly. "Sure," said Gerard. "We have a while to wait until the rest of my guys get here."

The eleven adults sat around the fire for an hour or so. They chatted about how beautiful the park was and how much they appreciated what Bob did to preserve the wilderness. There was no mention at all of Chris and him buzzing around the park in his helicopter.

In the distance, they could hear the quads coming up the trail. It was Toby and Brent with more loads of wood, plus cleaning supplies in their trailers. The two young men pulled in front of the washrooms. They got out their mops and buckets.

Gerard approached the two young men, and the three of them chatted for a minute. Toby and Brent drove the quads and trailers over to the wood storage area then unhooked the trailers. They took a gas can off Brent's trailer and topped off the ATVs. Gerard got on his portable radio and contacted Rangers 2, 6, and 8; they were still twenty minutes away from Glacier Creek Campground.

"Roger," said Gerard. "We will meet you at the base of Angel Glacier. Come on," he said to Chris. "We have work to do." Chris and Bob jumped onto the two quads, leaving Toby and Brent behind to finish cleaning the washrooms and unloading the trailers of firewood. The two quads disappeared up the trail and out of sight within minutes.

The young men went about cleaning the washrooms. Forty minutes later, three Park quads came into view. The rangers riding them were equipped with

nine-millimeter handguns. Shotguns were housed in plastic scabbards bolted to the fenders of the machines, and they wore the types of helmets you might see on a motorcycle cop in Los Angeles. Each machine was stenciled with the name "warden" on each side. The three wardens did not stop. They drove through the campground and disappeared out of sight.

Superintendent Gerard and Gunner were the first on the scene. As they pulled around the corner and into the middle of the twenty or so young adults, an older-style helicopter lifted off. It looked similar to the ones you see on the television show M*A*S*H, except on its skids instead of injured soldiers, there were three Styrofoam containers on each side. Each had been sealed with grey duct tape and was fastened down with ratchet straps. The chopper flew directly over Gunner and Gerard. There were no tail numbers on the bird.

Superintendent Gerard and Chris got off their respective ATVs. "What is going on here?" yelled Gerard. The two men soon found themselves surrounded by twenty-two young Asian men. They were dressed in puffy down jackets, gloves, and ski pants. Each wore heavy winter boots. There was a stack of about fifty Styrofoam coolers at the face of the glacier. Each measured two feet by four feet. Raging fires burned off in the distance in front of a half dozen cheap tents. The Asians had dug out an area with some axes and shovels in the face of the Glacier.

There, before Gerard and Gunner, was all the evidence they needed. One of the coolers was full of ice the Asians had chipped from Angel Glacier. "Ice poachers," Gerard said to Chris. "Did you get a tail number?"

"There were no markings," said Chris. "He's a

rogue."

Black market glacier ice was the latest thing. A cooler of ice that was thousands of years old and pure would fetch one thousand dollars in California. By the time the ice made it to Hong Kong, it was worth five thousand dollars a cooler. Nightclubs could not get enough of it. Beverages glowed blue that contained glacier ice under fluorescent lighting. It was shipped in refrigerated planes, the same kind that flew sides of beef overseas.

"You are all under arrest," said Gerard.

The Asians looked at each other somewhat confused. One man stepped forward and spoke perfect English. "You and what army are going to arrest us?" he said, translating so the others understood. They all smiled, and the circle tightened around Chris and Bob. The two wardens stood with their backs to each other, having no weapons with them.

One of the other men got into Gerard's face. "We mine ice. You no stop."

Gerard replied, "No, you are under arrest for destroying National Park property."

The man who spoke perfect English translated again.

"You stupid man," said the second Asian, as he spit in Superintendent Gerard's face. "We mine. You no stop."

Gerard replied again, "I said, you are all under arrest!"

The man who spoke perfect English laughed. Then, suddenly, they all heard the three other quads approaching. The three rangers drove up and quickly

assessed the situation.

They removed their shotguns from the plastic scabbards, cocked their guns, and walked into the middle of the group. "We've got a problem, boss," said Dan Thompson, Ranger number Two. The crowd of men had stepped back.

"Put your cuffs on that one right there," said Gerard, pointing to the second Asian that had spit in his face. "He's under arrest for assaulting a federal conservation officer," he added as he wiped spittle from his face. Thompson turned the smart ass around and placed his hands behind his back, ensuring the cuffs were extra tight.

As he turned him back around to face Gerard, he said, "You are under arrest, as I said, you little fuck." Gerard moved his head forward quickly, his forehead striking the Asian across the bridge of his nose. Blood gushed from the Asian's nose and ran down his puffy down jacket. "You understand now?" the Superintendent asked. The Asian man nodded his head as he held his bleeding nose. Gerard bent down and grabbed a handful of snow to wash his face. Chris looked at his boss but didn't say a word.

Gerard ordered his men to take the rest of the Asians and dismantle their camp, gathering their belongings. It was a slow process, but eventually, everything was packed up and put into a big pile in the middle of what was once their camp. Gerard looked at his watch; it was 12:30 Saturday afternoon. It would take his men seven hours to march their prisoners down to the staging area.

"Chris, you take this guy," said Gerard. "I want the translator with me. Gentlemen, you march these guys down to the staging area; I will meet you with a bus and

the state police in seven hours."

They placed handcuffs on the translator and sat him on Gerard's machine. The smart ass was placed on the back of the ATV Chris was driving. Chris took the lead down the pathway towards Glacier Creek Campground, rounding a corner and ducking as the ATV bounced out of control, slightly off the pathway. A large branch caught his passenger, and the smart ass rolled off the back of the machine.

Chris stopped, walked back to the Asian that had spit in his boss's face, and Gerard pulled up right behind the chaos.

"You okay?" he yelled to Gunner.

Chris looked up and winked, replying, "Yes, sir, I am, but this guy got hit by that branch." He grabbed the Asian by the arm and wiped a couple of leaves from his hair, turning the smart ass toward Gerard. The Asian's face was all cut up from the branch, and his eye was starting to swell.

"Be careful," said Gerard as he winked back, following the unwritten code shared between enforcement officers.

Gunner and Gerard made it back to the Glacier Creek Campground in record time. Bob got on his radio and spoke to Betty, requesting her to send two sheriff's cars to the staging area. "In five hours, send a bus up there; we will have another twenty prisoners that need to be processed. It's going to be a long day," he told her.

"Roger," said Betty. "I will stand by the radio."

Chris and Bob turned the quads over to Toby and Brent. "We are taking these guys down with us in the bird," said Chris. They then asked Brent to take Chris's emergency kit with him in one of the trailers since there

wouldn't be enough room for the duffle bag with four men in the helicopter.

The prisoners were loaded into the 505. The eight adults and Kevin stood and watched as Gunner started the shiny bird. When the whine of the turbine was just right, Chris lifted off. He raised the chopper one thousand feet above the treetops and then headed down the mountain. They arrived over the staging area forty-five minutes later. Two sheriff's cars were in the staging area parking lot.

Chris hovered the 505 a couple of hundred feet over the road leading into the parking area. When he was comfortable that all was clear, he set the 505 down on the only piece of pavement in the whole area. The pavement had been placed there years before as another emergency landing area, strictly for search and rescue operations. The two sheriffs approached from the sides of the 505. They opened the rear doors and unfastened the seatbelts the Asians were wearing. Gerard reached around and handed a piece of paper to one of the sheriffs. The deputy raised his thumb in the air. The rear doors were closed, Chris applied power, and lifted off. He pointed the 505 in the direction of the Hillsboro airport and radioed for a vector to the fuel station at the airport.

"Roger," he said. He looked over at Bob, who was rubbing the bump on his forehead. "I hate this route. Nothing but garbage down below." The two men laughed. There was a lot of garbage down below, and they had just been instrumental in cleaning up a big pile of it. Bob tapped Chris on the shoulder, and nothing more was said.

Chapter 45

Cathy woke up on a Saturday morning in the intensive care unit at Metro General Hospital. Her right eye was swollen shut, with the surrounding skin and eyelid displaying a dark purple hue. Her ear ached, and she noticed the IV line taped to the side of her wrist. Her body felt sore, especially her private parts. She tried to sit up but quickly fell back onto her pillow. Her throat was parched, and she desperately needed a glass of water.

Through the window, she could see the nurses' station. There were two nurses visible. The senior nurse noticed Cathy's movements and rushed into her room. She held Cathy's hand gently and asked if she wanted to sit up. Cathy managed to whisper a yes. The nurse used the remote control to elevate the head of Cathy's bed by about a foot. Cathy nodded, indicating that it was comfortable. She then requested some water.

The nurse handed her a cup with a bent plastic straw. Cathy held the cup with both hands, feeling the coolness of the plastic against her skin. She took a sip through the straw, and the ice-cold water soothed her dry throat. It was the best-tasting water she had ever had.

A younger nurse entered the room with Dr. Hansen. Cathy recognized him from the graduation parties she had attended with James and Eric. Dr. Hansen was about twenty years older than her son and specialized in trauma and emergency procedures. James had done his practicum in the hospital's ER under Dr. Hansen's guidance.

Dr. Hansen held Cathy's hand and expressed

sympathy for what she had been through. He mentioned that they had conducted a thorough examination when she was brought in and had sent samples to the lab and the FBI for DNA analysis. Cathy whispered her understanding. Then, she asked about Eric.

Dr. Hansen gently broke the news that there was nothing they could do for Eric, and he hadn't survived. Cathy had a vague memory of hearing something like this before but thought it was a dream. Her mind raced, memories of the past few days flooding back. She remembered a gunshot in her house, but the timeline was a blur. She asked about the date, trying to piece together the timeline of events.

"It's Saturday," Dr. Hansen replied.

Cathy requested to see James, thinking he should be back to work today. Dr. Hansen's grip on her hand tightened as he delivered the devastating news. James had been in an accident, a crash, and he hadn't survived.

Overwhelmed, she started to sob and shake. Dr. Hansen instructed the nurses to get her an extra blanket, and they gently covered her, trying to provide comfort in the face of such devastating news.

"The FBI wants to talk to you," said Hansen. "Do you feel up to it?" Cathy nodded her head in the affirmative. "Okay, I will call them and let them know you're awake. It's going to take time, Cathy. I have you on some antibiotics and some saline to rehydrate you. You should start to feel a little better soon. I would also like you to speak to Dr. Lewis. She is a psychiatrist. She was a friend of James. Is that okay?" Cathy nodded her head again. "I'll see you later this afternoon. If you need anything, have these ladies call me."

"Thank you," Cathy whispered.

The nurses brought Cathy a tray with the morning breakfast and placed it on the table beside her bed. They adjusted it so the tray was across Cathy's lap but not touching her body.

"Eat what you can, Mrs. Taylor," said the older of the nurses. "The FBI should be here soon. You want to build your strength back up."

"Okay," was Cathy's reply.

The Feds arrived about an hour later dressed in black suits and dark blue ties. They knocked on Cathy's hospital room door before entering.

"Mrs. Taylor, I am Agent Miller. This is Agent Williams. We are the lead investigators on your case." They flashed their identifications. "Do you mind if we ask you a few questions?"

Cathy nodded her head. Tears started to flow down her cheeks once again.

"The doctor told me you are aware that your son and husband are no longer with us."

Cathy yelled. "What are you talking about?" She wiped the tears from her face.

"Can you tell us what happened?" Miller pulled out his notepad and a ballpoint pen.

"Two men showed up. We were watching Wheel of Fortune. I'm sorry, I don't remember the day."

"Could it have been Thursday night?" asked Miller.

"That's right," said Cathy. "Wheel of Fortune is on Thursdays. Eric noticed flashing lights in the yard. He got up and came in with two men. One was a sheriff, I think."

"What did his uniform look like?"

"It was brown. No, I think it was blue. I'm not sure, but one was in a uniform. He had a holster with a gun and flashlight. He also had one of those taser things."

"Good, Cathy," said Miller. "Do you mind if I call you Cathy?" She nodded. "What else do you remember?"

"It was awful. They were bastards! Eric tried to help and they hurt him!" Her mind flashed back to the events of Thursday night. She was shaking. "They made me do things. Oh, Eric! He watched! Oh, my God, no! One of them took me to the bathroom and gave me a bath."

"Did you go willingly?" asked Willams.

"What do you mean?" she asked.

"Did you fight with them when he took you into the bathroom?"

"I don't think so," she said. "I do not remember. I woke up a few times and I was tied up in my own bed."

"Do you remember anything else, Cathy? It's really important."

She thought and said, "Yes. One of them tried to kiss me. I bit the motherfucker." Her fear was now turning to anger.

"Where did you bite him?" asked Miller.

"On the lip. I wouldn't let go. Then everything went black."

"Can you tell us anything else?"

"James," she said. "They made James fly them somewhere."

"Did James volunteer to fly them?" Miller asked.

"Volunteer?" Cathy said. "I had a shotgun in my mouth! Yes, he volunteered! He was trying to get them away from me!"

"I see," said Miller. "It sounds to me like James did not have much of a choice."

"That's exactly what I'm saying!" said Cathy. "He volunteered to save my life!"

"Cathy, just one last question. I have a book with me with some pictures in it. Could you have a quick look and see if any of them look familiar to you?" Miller handed Cathy a book that contained thirty mugshots of local criminals. She looked through each page carefully and examined the photos. She pulled two pictures from the pages and handed them to Miller. Johnny Robbins and Matt Jones had been identified by their victim. "Thank you, Mrs. Taylor. You have done well. Do you know where Eric keeps his wallet?"

"He always had it in his back pocket," she said. "He never went anywhere without it."

"Thank you," said Miller. "We have put a trace on his credit cards. We could not find it when we searched your house. Is there anything else?"

Cathy looked over at the younger of the two agents. "They took everything from me that meant anything! Please kill the bastards! Kill them for Eric and James!"

Chapter 46

Rachel and Susan continued down the path that ran along Rock Lake. They crossed the creek and were soon out of sight. Brad looked at Tommy. "Notice anything about those two?" he said.

"Yah," said Tommy, "they are man haters, couldn't look at you or me."

"Bet they are divorcees," said Brad.

"Or maybe they are batting for the same team," said Tommy. The boys laughed. Donna and Elizabeth just shook their heads.

Mark spoke up and said, "Do they play baseball?"

Susan rounded the bend first, and they were just about at the old Trapper's cabin. She looked back at Rachel. "Another half mile and we will be at RL03," she said. She turned back towards the path then noticed something shiny lying in the middle of the trail. She stopped. Rachel walked up beside her. "What's that?" Susan said. "Let me check; you stay here."

Rachel watched intently as Susan moved towards the item in the middle of the trail. It was covered with dirt and had some bright, shiny silver spots visible. It was the size of a small French loaf of bread. She moved it with her foot, and it rolled over, fluid running out over her boot. "What is it?" Rachel asked.

Susan bent down and picked up a stick about two feet long. She poked the package until it split open, revealing its contents. "It's a damn fish," she said as she turned to address her friend. "Do not move," Susan said.

She held her hand up to her friend. "For God's sake, do not move, Rachel." Rachel knew instantly something was wrong. She turned back to face down the trail. A large male Grizzly was moving quickly in their direction. "Get your bear spray ready, your bear spray, get it ready."

Rachel was frozen, not moving. Susan was reaching for her spray as the huge boar passed her friend, knocking her and her backpack to the ground. The Grizzly was snapping its jaws as it lunged at Susan and took her to the ground. She screamed as the bear dug its claws into her stomach. Its six-inch claws tore through Susan's jacket and shirt, going deep into her body. She did her best to roll over and tried using her backpack for protection.

The bear paused for a moment as Susan lay silent. The bear put both of its front legs on her backpack then jumped up and down. The large male weighed around 700 lbs. It was the dominant male in this area, and nothing was getting in his way of a meal.

As the bear jumped up and down, Susan felt her ribs break under the strain. The packages of food she had in the backpack broke open, and their contents spilled into the interior of the nylon shell. The bear paused again, its large snout sniffing the now-wet nylon. The bear started to drool, saliva dripping from its mouth. Rachel had managed to get to her knees in time to see the Grizzly sniff the backs of Susan's legs. The Grizzly got to her foot, which was covered with fluid from the package of fish. It opened its jaws and then bit down hard.

The bear shook its head. Susan and the backpack became airborne. The Grizz shook her like a ragdoll and bit through her jeans and into the back of her right calf

tearing her pants and muscle undearneath. Susan screamed. She could not take it! The bear dropped her leg and moved to her head. Susan placed her hands over her neck as the bear put her entire head in its mouth. Its breath smelled rotten.

She froze as the Grizzly bit down. She felt its teeth scraping across her skull. One lower canine tooth entered Susan's right eye socket. The bear shook Susan by the head until she laid motionless. The attack took three minutes but it felt like hours. It looked up. Rachel was on her feet and running in the opposite direction. Her can of bear spray lay beside the trail. The Grizzly was on her in a couple of seconds. She was knocked to the ground again. Rachel laid on the dirt as the bear bit into the back of her neck. It shook her like Susan until her neck snapped. She lay motionless on the edge of the pathway. The bear turned then and made its way back to Susan. It grabbed her by the shoulder and dragged her to the side of the old Trapper's cabin and proceeded to sniff at the backpack. Blood pouring from Susan's leg, the bear scratched at the dirt. It covered Susan with leaves, sticks, and mud it could throw up with its front feet. He would come back later for a feast when his fresh kill was a little more tender. The bear returned to the package on the trail. It used its front claws to open the foil to get at the fish inside. The Grizzly laid down on the pathway, its mouth foaming. He flicked his tongue into the foil and the lake trout Brad had prepared the evening before spilled out. The bear ate every scrap and licked the foil clean. It lay there for a minute before getting up and lapping up some water in a puddle beside the pathway. It looked back at Rachel and then ambled off into the bush.

He would be back.

Chapter 47

Chris dropped the 505 in front of the fuel pumps at the Hillsboro Airport. He needed to top up before he and Superintendent Gerard could head back to the staging area in the park. They still had a few hours before the rest of the rangers would walk the bad guys out of the woods to the waiting bus.

Bob went into the filling station office. He made a couple of phone calls. Gunner engaged in idle conversation as the two attendants went about their business servicing the 505.

"Better top her right up," Gunner said. "We still have a long day ahead of us."

Chris asked the two young men if they had ever seen an old 47 in or around the airport.

"What's a 47?" they asked.

"You know, one of those old egg beaters. It looks like the helicopters on the old TV show M*A*S*H."

"That old thing," both young men nodded their heads. "Yup... see that building across the field, the pale blue one with the old folding door?"

Chris looked over the rims of his sunglasses.

"Norman Fisher owns one like that. He has been working on it for two years. He just got it certified a month ago. Did most of the work himself. You know he is a certified aviation mechanic."

"I don't know him," said Chris. "Where does he work?"

"He works for Blue Sky Air, over in their shop."

227

"Thanks," said Chris. "I am looking for an old chopper, something I can play with in my downtime. Maybe I will look him up sometime."

Chris went into the office; Bob was just finishing his last call.

"I have a lead on that rogue chopper," said Chris.

"I just gave a report to the Sheriff's office," said Gerard. "What's up?"

"Just a hunch, but we need to follow up on it." He looked at the cashier. "Do you folks happen to have a courtesy car we could borrow for about a half an hour?"

"Where are you headed?" she asked.

"Just thought we would go over to the main terminal. Maybe grab a nice lunch."

"Take the golf cart. Here's the key," she said. "If you're not going off the airport property, you're welcome to use it. Just take it easy; the guys have taken the governor off the engine, so it's pretty fast."

"Great," Chris replied. "We should not be any longer than a half an hour."

The golf cart was equipped with a radio, which would allow them to communicate with the control tower and ground control. Bob and Chris made their way to the golf cart.

Chris radioed the tower and explained that they needed to cross the runway.

"Who is this?" asked ground control.

"We are Charlie Gulf Romeo Romeo," said Chris, "except we are in your golf cart. We have some business we need to conduct."

"Roger," came the reply. "There is no traffic currently in the area. Use caution and proceed."

Chris turned the key. The flashing strobe light mounted on the six-foot pole above their heads lit up. It blinked every second and could be seen for two miles, day or night.

The two men made their way across the tarmac, then made a beeline for the pale blue building. They pulled up to the front of the large folding doors. Chris got off the cart and walked to the side of the building, Bob right behind him. They peered through an old broken window. There, inside, was a Bell 47, the same kind of helicopter they had seen only a few hours earlier.

"That looks like it could be our rogue," said Chris. The two men tried the side door, and it opened. They walked in.

"Hello?" said Chris. "Hello." There was no reply. The men walked around the old Bell 47.

"It can't be the same one," said Gerard. "This one has numbers on it."

Chris looked closely. The one he had seen had no numbers. Something did not add up. What were the odds of two old 47s being in the same vicinity at the same time?

"Look at this," Chris said as he turned the flashlight for his cellphone on. "Looky here." He had his hand on a homemade lever in the cockpit. He moved it back and forth. Someone designed black shields that slid back and forth over the registration numbers on the sides of the 47.

"Look at the way the springs work," said Chris. "You can't even see them. This is our rogue," he said to Bob. "I wonder who owns it."

229

"I think I know." The two men looked around a little more. In the backroom, they found six empty Styrofoam containers, a bed, a small kitchen, and a washroom in the corner.

"This has to be our guy," said Bob. "The guys at the filling station said his name is Norman Fisher; he works for Blue Sky Aviation. This is just getting way too easy. You made my day."

The two men made their way back over to the service station on the other side of the airport. Chris returned the key to the cashier.

"I think we'll just order a couple of burgers here," he said as they walked back to the cafeteria. The two men ordered bacon cheeseburgers, fries, and two large cokes with extra ice. Bob made one more call and came back to the table. He looked at Chris.

"Sheriff says they should be here in an hour. They need the judge to issue a search warrant; it's Saturday, and he is out fishing."

"Naturally," said Chris. The two men waited 15 minutes for their burgers. By the time the food arrived, Chris was getting lightheaded. He had put on a lot of miles, and the day was not over yet.

Chris and Bob sat, enjoying their meals and sipping on their cokes. It had been forty-five minutes since Gerard had called the sheriff's office. He looked at his watch.

"Maybe another fifteen minutes, half an hour. That's cutting it close to get back and meet the bus and my men."

Two men walked into the cafeteria, sporting pilot shirts and black slacks. One of the men had four gold bars on his shoulder flashes; the other had three.

230

"Pilot and copilot," Gunner said to himself.

The two men sat down on the other side of the room. Gunner heard one of them say, "Oh, we do not fly out until Sunday. Hotel six, that is the closest?" He thanked the waitress. Two deputies walked in twenty minutes later and stood in the doorway. Gunner and Bob stood up.

"I got this," said Bob as he left a twenty on the table. The four men walked outside. An old restored McDonnell Douglas DC-3 sat two hundred yards away from the 505. Bob and Chris filled out statements, then signed them.

"We will leave the rest up to you and your office," said Gerard. "We will check back in with you later." The superintendent and his chief pilot climbed back into the 505. They were off to the staging area; they had tickets to write.

Chapter 48

Johnny picked up the phone and called his friend, Jackson Hall.

"The garbage stinks when it's burning," Johnny remarked.

Hall laughed. "How's the drive going?" he asked.

"I am about two hours out," said Jackson.

"Where do you want to meet?"

"Pick me up in front of the apartment building."

"Sounds good," replied Hall. "See you in about two hours. Did you make all the arrangements?"

"Done," was Johnny's brief reply. He hung up the phone.

He went back into Jesus' bedroom and went through his closet. He found a suit, a nice black shirt, socks, and underwear, laying everything out on the bed. Johnny stood in the shower for a half hour, peeling the bandages from the wound on his side, letting them drop into the tub. The hot water ran over the stitches, doing a good job of removing some of the dried blood. He exited the shower, wiped the mirror with a towel, and turned sideways to examine his wounds. The doctors had done a good job stitching him up. He found some Polysporin in the bathroom drawer and applied a liberal amount to his side. The stitches glistened when coated with the ointment. He took the last of the bandages and applied them over his wound. Johnny shaved, then used some aftershave from a bottle on the counter.

"Cheap shit," he said out loud, "but better than

232

nothing." He dressed in Jesus' clothes, which were a little tight but would have to do for now. Johnny found some black leather shoes that were real snug. He ran some hot water in the kitchen sink, then soaked them for five minutes. When the leather was more pliable, he placed the shoes back on his feet. He walked around the apartment, leaving a trail of water with each step. In a few moments, he felt the leather starting to stretch and conform to his own feet.

Jesus' body lay on the kitchen floor. Johnny found a bottle of bleach under the kitchen sink. He wiped down the counters, poured some in the bathtub, and sprinkled a little on the bed. He returned to the kitchen and then dumped the rest on Jesus' body.

"There, that ought to do it," he muttered.

He turned his attention to the black duffle bag. Johnny took the taser from the wall and placed it back into the holster. He checked the 9mm and extra clips. When he was satisfied, he placed the utility belt on top of all the cash and closed the zipper on the bag. Johnny stood looking out the window until he saw the Mercedes convertible containing Jackson Hall pull up in front of the building. Johnny opened the apartment door, then peered both ways in the hallway. The coast was clear. He exited the door, then used the keys Jesus had left in a bowl on the counter. He locked the deadbolt, placed the shoulder strap of the duffle bag around his neck, and slid Jesus' sunglasses over his ears and onto his nose. Johnny made his way down the stairs to the waiting convertible. Jackson Hall popped the trunk for his friend. Johnny placed the black duffle bag inside, closing the lid.

Johnny opened the passenger door and slid onto the tan leather seat. He looked over at Hall and raised his left fist. Hall raised his right fist, and they bumped them

together.

"Good to see you," said Hall. "How is Hernandez?"

Johnny shook his head side to side. "What about Maria?" he asked.

"She does not have a clue," said Hall. "Told her I would not be back for a few days."

"Okay," was Johnny's reply.

The two men drove from in front of the apartment building and around the corner. Traffic had been slowed as a street sweeper was going about its business cleaning up blood and broken glass from the police shooting the night before.

Jackson handed Johnny a wallet. It contained cash, credit cards, his new PIN number, and a California driver's license. The picture was Johnny's but had been altered; it showed him with blonde hair and a mustache. The ID read Justin Wayne.

"I look like a surfer," Johnny said as he placed the wallet in the breast pocket of his jacket. "That's the best picture you could come up with?"

Jackson laughed, "You did not give me much time. Those clothes look like shit."

"Best I could do under the circumstances," was Johnny's reply. "Head to Hillcrest; I have some unfinished business there."

Jackson made his way out onto the highway and headed to the town of Hillcrest.

"Pull in there," said Johnny, as he pointed to the Hillcrest Mall. "One-stop shopping, pick me up in two hours."

Johnny walked into the mall and made his way to Audrey's hair salon. He walked in and sat down. There was only one other person in the place. Audrey was almost finished styling her client's hair.

"Be right with you," she said as she sprayed some styling stuff in the woman's hair. The lady looked at Johnny. She smiled, then paid for her cut and left the salon.

"What can I do for you?" said Audrey.

"Can you dye my hair and make it blonder?" asked Johnny. "Trim it up; I need to be presentable for my business meeting on Monday."

"Sure," said Audrey. "Have a seat." She cut Johnny's hair, then bleached it to lighten it up. "I am going to do your eyebrows as well," she said. "If you're going to go that light on top, you cannot have dark eyebrows."

"Whatever works," said Johnny. It took Audrey an hour to finish up, but by the time she was done, Johnny looked like a new man. There were three new clients waiting their turn. Johnny wanted to use his new credit card. The total was eighty-nine dollars. "Please add a twenty-dollar tip." Audrey turned the machine towards Johnny then asked him to enter his pin number. Johnny entered the four digits he had memorized an hour earlier. The transaction went through.

He walked out of the salon and into Ken's Menswear. He found two new suits, size 42 regular, that fit perfectly. Two new shirts, black and dark blue, a nice western belt, and a new pair of black cowboy boots.

"How much is that hat?" he asked the clerk.

"Two hundred dollars," he replied.

"What's the total so far?"

The clerk ran everything up. "Nine hundred and thirty-five dollars," he said.

Johnny asked, "If I pay you an extra hundred bucks, can you hem the pants and steam the shirts while I wait? I have a big date tonight."

"Yes, sir," said the clerk.

Johnny sat in the changeroom, waiting for the first suit to be finished. The clerk came in and handed him a shirt, then his first new suit. Johnny dressed. He ran the belt through the loops in the pants, slid his feet into the new cowboy boots, and pulled on the suit jacket. Johnny then put the new cowboy hat on his head and tilted it forward. He walked out of the changeroom, leaving Jesus' old clothes on the floor.

Johnny waited at the till for the clerk. In ten minutes, the other suit and shirt were ready, placed in a cheap garment bag. The clerk met Johnny at the till, hanging the new clothes on a chrome hook over the counter.

"You forgot your old clothes," he said.

"No, that's okay," said Johnny. "Please donate them; I will not be needing them anymore."

"Sure," said the clerk as he rang in the total. "That will be one thousand and thirty-five dollars." Johnny handed him his credit card. The clerk handed him the machine, and Johnny entered his pin number. The sale went through. The clerk handed Johnny his credit card.

"Thank you, Mr. Wayne," the clerk said. "Hey, are you any relation to...?" Johnny held his finger to his lips.

"He was my father."

"I thought I could see some similarities," said the clerk. Johnny laughed as he reached into the wallet Jackson had given him. He handed the clerk a crisp one hundred dollar bill.

"That's for looking after me and keeping this to ourselves."

"Yes, sir, Mr. Wayne, I understand completely. If you need anything else, come back."

Johnny grabbed the rim of the new cowboy hat and said, "Thanks, partner," as he took the garment bag. He put it over his right shoulder and exited the mall. He found Jackson parked fifty feet from the main entrance.

"It's four o'clock," said Jackson. "The bank closes at five."

"I know," said Johnny.

Jackson Hall drove up to the Hillcrest Savings and Loan Branch, one of the banks that his father managed years before. He pulled into the third stall from the front door. Johnny got out of the Mercedes, and Jackson handed Johnny a key. Johnny asked Jackson to open the trunk.

Johnny entered the bank wearing his new suit, with the duffle bag over his shoulder. He made his way to the customer service desk.

"Howdy," he said. "I would like to access my safety deposit box." The female clerk asked him for his ID, and he pulled out his California driver's license.

"Welcome to the branch, Mr. Wayne. I see it's been five years since you've been in."

"Yes, ma'am," said Johnny. "California has been

keeping me busy." He signed the access card as she turned it around for him. Johnny signed the card "Justin Wayne," and the signatures matched perfectly. Johnny was escorted to the safety deposit room, where he placed the duffle bag in the middle of the table.

Johnny opened the zipper and worked at the lining on the inside of the bag. He found the key he had placed there five years earlier. He looked around until he saw box number 888, specially designed by Jackson's father for business partners. Each would have their own keys, and one without the other could not access the box. It rented for a thousand dollars a year. All the special boxes in the respective banks made a profit of close to a million a year. Johnny placed both keys in the colored slots; his was blue, Jackson's yellow. He turned both keys at the same time and heard the lock click. He pulled on the keys, opening the door about the size of a shoebox. Johnny reached inside and pulled out the metal strongbox, placing it beside the duffle bag. He opened the lid on the box and looked inside. Johnny reached in and pulled out a single key, about three inches long, with several shallow holes drilled into both of its sides. There was a computer chip forged into the wide end of the key. Johnny placed the large key in his pocket, then loaded three hundred and fifty thousand into the strongbox, keeping one hundred thousand in cash. He placed the strongbox back into the safe, closing the door and turning the keys. He looked into the duffle bag; it was much lighter now. Closing the zipper, he exited the safety deposit box room.

The clerk walked him to the front of the bank. "Is there anything else I can do for you, Mr. Wayne?" she asked.

"Do you have a knife?" asked Johnny.

"I have a letter opener at my desk," she said.

"That will work," said Johnny. They made their way to her desk.

"Can I get you a coffee, Mr. Wayne?"

"Sure, two cream and two sugars, please." She left Johnny for three minutes with the letter opener in his hand. He reached into his pocket and pulled out the large key. He pried the computer chip from its flattened end and loosened the heel of his boot just enough to slip the chip into its hollow center. He placed the key back in his pocket.

The clerk returned with his coffee. "Thank you," said Johnny. "You have been awesome."

"Anything I can do or the bank can do, let me know."

"I think that is all for today, little lady, unless you want to give me your phone number."

"Oh, Mr. Wayne," she said. "Sure." She handed him a business card that read "Vicky Andrews, Customer Service Specialist." It had her work number and cell phone number.

"Why, thank you, Ms. Vicky," said Johnny, and he tipped his hat. "I should be ambling along."

"Well, you have a good night," she replied.

Johnny winked. "I am planning on it. Good day to you, miss." Johnny exited the bank and climbed back into the Mercedes. He tossed the bag into the backseat.

"You got it?" asked Jackson.

Johnny reached into his pocket and pulled out the large key, laughing. Jackson couldn't go with Johnny into the branch; someone could have recognized him.

Johnny knew Jackson was at his mercy, so he made sure his thumb stayed over the area where the chip had been.

"Got it," Johnny said as he tucked it back into his pocket. "Come on," he said, "I am starving. Let me buy you dinner. I know a great little place."

The two men pulled into Elli's Diner exactly at 5:00pm. "Pop the trunk," Johnny said, "I want to put the bag in there." The two men walked in and sat down at a booth. Elli, the owner, walked over and asked if they would like dinner or lunch menus.

"Dinner, ma'am," said Johnny as he tipped his hat. Elli returned with two dinner menus and glasses of water.

"You gents want anything stronger than water?" she asked.

Jackson piped up and said, "How about a couple of beers?"

"Tap is okay, or would you prefer bottles? I serve Miller."

"Tap is fine," the men responded. Elli came back a few minutes later and took their orders. BBQ ribs and smoked chicken were the daily specials.

"You got a full rack, a giant thigh, mashed or baked potato, and salad for $19.95," Elli explained.

"Two specials," said Johnny. Twenty minutes later, Elli came out with both their meals and placed them in front of the men. Johnny asked, "Do you own this place? I notice your name tag says Elli."

"Sure do," she said. "I've been serving customers around here for thirty-five years."

"Well," said Johnny, "then you are the one I need to speak to." He reached into his pocket and pulled out a crumpled piece of colored paper he had been carrying with him since leaving the hospital. He unfolded the paper to reveal the magazine article of the hero pilot, with a picture of Gunner standing beside the new 505. "Do you happen to know this man?" Johnny asked.

"I sure do," said Elli. "Why?"

"I am a producer from Hollywood," he said.

"Sure you are," came Elli's reply.

Johnny pulled out his wallet and handed her his driver's license. She looked at it and said, "Your last name is Wayne?"

"Yes," said Johnny. Jackson was biting his tongue to keep from laughing.

"Is... was your father..." Elli began, but Johnny held his finger to his lips.

He looked around and said, "Please," he said. She handed back his license.

"His name is Chris, but he goes by Gunner. He works for the forestry department, flying their helicopter. His son and girlfriend were in here yesterday. They were headed up to Rock Lake in the National Park. The warden's office is just south of town, about twenty miles from here."

"Thank you," said Johnny. "You have been very helpful." Elli went back into the kitchen.

"Do you know who that is out there?" Elli asked Enrique, her cook and friend of thirty-plus years.

"Who?" asked Enrique.

"That's the kid of that famous actor that made

241

westerns," said Elli.

"Sure it is," said Enrique.

"Well, he showed me his ID," said Elli.

"Right," said Enrique. "Your order is up." Elli grabbed the plate of chicken fingers and fries and took it to table six.

Chapter 49

The sun was warm and glistened off Rock Lake. The water was almost perfectly calm. Brad, Tommy, Elizabeth, and Donna walked down to the edge of the water, with Mark and Marcy only a few paces behind.

"If we can find a half dozen or so logs, we can lash them together and float over to the island," Tommy said, carrying his axe.

The four adults pushed, pulled, and dragged six large pieces of deadfall to the edge of the water. Each log was approximately eight inches in diameter and maybe seven or eight feet long.

"They're not perfect, but they'll do the job," Brad said. Tommy returned to the campsite, and the climbing rope he brought was still attached to the lower portion of his pack. He undid the straps that held it in place and returned to the water's edge.

"Do you think this will be enough?" he asked Brad.

"More than enough, buddy," Brad replied. He had trimmed the dead branches off the logs, and the children had stacked them into a nice little pile.

The six pieces were laid side by side, with the first three feet of each log resting in the water.

"Now we need four smaller ones to go across here and here," Brad pointed to both ends of the raft. Donna and Elizabeth went back into the trees and dragged out four dead trees, each about three inches in diameter. Tommy quickly trimmed off the dead branches and handed the pieces to his buddy.

Brad laid one across the width of the logs, marked it with his Buck Huntsman, and handed it back to Tommy. With two blows, Tommy cut the end off the first branch-sized log. He had three more to go. When they were all the same length, Brad removed his boots, then his socks, and rolled up his jeans. He waded into the ice-cold water.

"Man, you women are brave," he said. "It's cold."

The girls laughed. "Get your hair wet," said Elizabeth.

"No thanks, not right now," Brad replied.

Brad slid the small log under the front of his raft. He placed another on top directly over the bottom log. He used a portion of Tommy's climbing rope to lash the front of the raft together. He pulled, and Tommy pushed until the back end of the raft was just hanging onto the shore. Brad slid the next small log under the back end of the raft, and Tommy placed the other small log directly over the back one. They fastened everything together like Brad had done at the front.

"Perfect," said Brad as he jumped up and down on the floating end. "Stable as any boat I've ever been in."

Rock Lake had a maximum depth of forty feet, and the water was so clear you could see right to the bottom. The young men fashioned two paddles from the leftover small logs, forming the paddle blades using wood they split from a chunk of firewood. All were lashed together using a couple of large nylon ties.

"Look at that," said Tommy, holding up his paddle. "Almost as good as going to the outfitter store."

"Almost," said Brad as he held up his.

It had taken them two hours to put the raft together. Mark and Marcy had been running back and forth to the tents, going at least a dozen times. Donna spoke up first.

"Tommy, I don't think it's a good idea to put the kids on the raft. What if they fall in?" she said.

"I agree," said Elizabeth. "Probably not a good idea. Why don't you and Brad go? Donna and I will head back to the fire and make some lunch for Mark and Marcy. Are you two hungry?" she asked the children.

"Starving!" exclaimed Mark.

"Okay, ladies, you win. Tommy and I will check out the island alone. Come on, buddy, let's see if this thing floats." The two men now had no boots or socks on. They knew if they fell in, their boots would fill with water and take them to the bottom. Brad stood on the front of the raft, and his weight made it easier for Tommy to wiggle the back of the raft off the shore. As the raft started to float, Tommy jumped on. It wasn't as stable as they had originally hoped, but they caught their balance. Tommy paddled from the right side, and Brad from the left. Soon, they were headed for the island.

No one had ever gone to the island before. Really, the only time you could get to it was in the middle of winter. The shoreline surrounding the island was identical to the rest of the lake, except that the ground thrust up almost immediately. The rocks rose a couple of hundred feet above their heads. They guided the raft to a suitable area where it could be beached.

The young men put their boots back on and spent the next twenty minutes clambering to the top of the island. They looked back towards their campsite, where the children sat at the table eating Kraft Dinner and

hotdogs. Donna was on the shoreline, waving and taking pictures with her cellphone. The young men waved back.

"Cool, you can see everything from here," Tommy said.

They looked down over the western edge of the rocks, and both noticed something unusual at the same time.

"What is that?" Brad asked.

"Not sure," replied Tommy, "but let's go have a look."

The men climbed down to the entrance of a den. The opening was about four feet high and three feet wide. They peered inside and saw sticks, twigs, grass, and a few bones lying about. The cracks in the rocks were full of dark brown fur, and scat covered the floor. The smell coming from within was overpowering.

"Grizzly den," said Brad, examining the fur. "The bear is a smart one."

"It must have the whole area to itself," Tommy remarked. "I think it dens up here just after the lake freezes over. I don't believe it would be swimming over here on a regular basis, not this time of the year."

"Strange," Brad added. "There's no food for it here, so you must be right. It dens up after the lake freezes over, then comes out of hibernation when it's warming up but the lake is still frozen over, allowing it to get to the surrounding land. Smart. Very smart."

The two young men made their way back to the raft and paddled back to the eastern edge of the lake. "Do you think that bear made the track around your tent, Brad?" Tommy asked.

"I would bet on it," replied Brad. "This is its

territory, no doubt about it."

The friends beached the raft and then returned to the campsite. The children had finished eating, and Donna and Elizabeth sat at the table playing cards. "How was your adventure, Huck Finn?" Donna asked.

"Uneventful, but it sure is a beautiful view from up there," Tommy replied. The young men roasted a few hot dogs and ate them directly off the sticks Tommy had carved the night before. The sun was moving deep into the western sky.

"I can't wait for dinner," Tommy said. "I picked up some really good-looking T-bone steaks. They're all thawed and ready for the grill."

"We brought some steak as well," Brad said. "Looks like another feast tonight."

"What time is it?" Donna asked.

"Only four thirty," Tommy replied.

The young adults sat playing cards while Mark and Marcy had gone into their tent for a nap. It was quiet, and Donna spoke up.

"It's so beautiful here; I love it."

"Me too," said Elizabeth as she drew a card from the deck. "Gin," she declared.

Chapter 50

The bus was already at the staging area when the 505 returned and set down on the emergency landing pad. Chris and Bob waited for the main rotor blade to stop turning before exiting the helicopter. The parking area was only one-third full now. The two sheriff's deputies had returned. Superintendent Gerard was back on his turf now. The airport was out of his jurisdiction, so he had to rely on the deputies to serve the warrant and arrest the perpetrators. Here in the park, the charges that would be laid fell on his shoulders. Gerard would issue the summons, and the bus would haul the perps into Crestview where they would have to post bond before being released. This late on a Saturday afternoon, Bob knew the thieves would end up being the guests of the State until Monday. He smiled, at least he would have a little satisfaction knowing they would not be back that weekend.

The first quad appeared in the staging area. The ranger drove over to Chris and Bob.

"They are about a half mile behind me," he said.

The bus was ready, with lights on in the interior. Twenty-five minutes later, the entourage marched out of the woods and into the parking lot. The twenty individuals were loaded onto the bus. They were dirty, tired, and cold. The rangers went through the group, gathering IDs, and they sat writing tickets. Each one amounted to twelve thousand dollars: five hundred dollars for camping without a permit, five hundred dollars for having a fire in an unauthorized area, five hundred dollars for cutting down trees for firewood, five hundred dollars for littering in the National Park. The

best was saved for last: destroying a National Heritage site, ten thousand dollars. Twelve thousand dollars multiplied by the twenty individuals added up to $240,000. Not bad for a day's work, and Gerard had not finished with the two main characters.

The majority of the young men were Asian students from overseas, attending school in California. They were privileged kids from another part of the world. They were all handed their individual summons and IDs back. Gerard stood outside the bus at the foot of its steps.

The doors closed, one of the sheriff's cars took the lead, and the second followed the bus out of the staging area. Superintendent Gerard turned to his men.

"Gentlemen, I am proud of you all. We had a good day. I will get the boys to go up there tomorrow and clean up the rest of the mess. Someone's got to get that shit out of there. Once again, it's up to our office. Thank you for your dedicated service. Come on, Chris, I am almost ready to call it a day."

Bob and Chris returned to the 505. In minutes, they were airborne and headed back to the Ranger Station. By the time they landed, it was 7:00pm. The two men walked into the station, and Betty sat at her desk. The Sheriff's office in Crestview called; they needed to speak to Bob about those first two guys. Bob called into the office and faxed them a list of all the charges, including assaulting a federal conservation officer. The Sheriff's office had been holding the two men pending further investigation. Time was limited before the two men had to be released.

"How did it go with the warrant at the airport?" Bob chirped into the phone. Robert nodded his head. "I understand," then he hung up. Gerard turned to Chris and

shook his hand.

"Thank you," he said. Chris asked about the airport and if they caught the guy.

"Not yet," said Gerard, "but they are watching the hangar."

"Damn," said Chris, "it would have been nice to wrap this whole thing up in a neat little package today. I will have my report to you in the morning. You and Betty have a good evening."

"We will," said Bob. Chris left the station, then jumped into his truck. Betty looked at Bob, the strain of the day was all over his face. She walked up to him then brushed his hair from his forehead.

"Oh, honey, you have a big red bump on your head. What happened?"

"Nothing, dear, just a little rough air. Come on, let me make you dinner," said Betty. They exited the Ranger Station, locking the front door behind them. The 505 sat off in the distance, its main rotor blades moved ever-so slightly in the evening air. It was time to relax and put their feet up.

Chapter 51

Susan woke up just as the sun was starting to set. The back of her leg was causing excruciating pain. She reached down, then stopped. Something was wrong. She thought for a moment and it suddenly hit her. She had been attacked by a Grizzly!

"Oh, my God," she said to herself. Susan collected her thoughts. She could only see out of her left eye. Still wearing her backpack, she started to move and realized she was covered in sticks, leaves, and mud. She moved until her head poked out from under the debris. She had a splitting headache. She tried to get up but the pain in her stomach forced her to lay back down. She reached down past her chest. Susan felt warm blood soaking through her jacket and shirt. She touched something soft and not familiar.

Susan moved back and forth until she had freed her shoulders from the straps holding her pack in place. She tried to stand up and fell back to the ground. She looked at her right leg. The calf muscle was torn free. It was hanging by a few strips of skin. Blood started to flow again from the open wound. It had stopped and coagulated when she had been buried under the debris. Susan had not been moving for many hours. She had no idea how long she had been unconscious. Removing her belt and looping it around her thigh, she pulled with all her might to try and stop the blood flow. She just did not have the strength, though. Picking up one of the sticks that covered her, she used it to twist the belt around itself. She felt it tighten around her flesh. The blood slowed to just a few drips, and she tried standing again.

Susan collapsed halfway onto the trail that led to

the Rock Lake cabins. She could not walk no matter how hard she tried. She could see Rachel laying on the pathway, blood had pooled all around her. The can of bear spray lay twenty feet ahead of her. She crawled on hands and knees until she held it in her hand.

"Rachel?" she whispered. "Rachel, can you hear me?" There was no reply. Susan's reality was setting in. She was in shock but her primal instincts were kicking in. Survival was her number one priority. She needed water. She had lost a lot of blood. Her thirst was her body's way of trying to replenish some of its fluids.

Susan turned and crawled back up the pathway. She scooped water into her mouth from the same puddle the bear had drank from. Suddenly, something bumped her right cheek. She reached up with her right hand. Her eye dangled from its socket by its optic nerve. She wept as she ran her hand over that side of her head. Her scalp had been torn away from her skull. It flapped over her ear. She pushed it back into place. Her brown hair was matted with dried blood. She scooped more water into her mouth. She looked forward. She only had a half mile to go to the four cabins; she could make it. There had to be people there. Susan got on her hands and knees. She inched forward one foot at a time.

"I can do it," she said out loud. She clutched the can of bear spray in her left hand as she headed towards the north end of Rock Lake. "I have to make it," she said to herself. "Someone has to save Rachel."

Chapter 52

Twenty-seven-year-old Matt continued down the street with the brown paper bag tucked under his arm. It was now midafternoon. The clothing he wore fit like a glove. He had not put on any weight while he was in prison and had managed to keep himself in pretty good shape while in the joint. He worked out every day and had watched the amount of carbohydrates he consumed. The only thing he had gained was more prison tattoos plus a dislike for authority.

From the first time he had been busted Matt continued down the wrong path. He had made a bunch of appearances in front of judges that had given him chances to straighten out his life. Nothing seemed to work. Matt started dealing drugs to the kids in school when he hit thirteen. It started innocently enough, a couple of joints here and there. He would buy them for five dollars each and sell them for ten bucks, doubling his money. He learned that if he bought his own rolling papers he could break up the joints. He would add some stolen oregano from the grocery store then turn two joints into four. The stupid kids in school did not know any better. It provided Matt with quick money and it was easy.

The first time he had been caught the principle had called Joann. When she arrived at the school the police were already there. Matt's mother walked into the principal's office. Matt's locker had been searched. Laying on the principal's desk were ten nicely rolled marijuana cigarettes. Joann went crazy in front of the police and the head of the school.

"When your father finds out what you have been

doing you will not make it to your next birthday!" Joann yelled. She apologized to the principal, and looked at the cops and shook her head. "I am sorry," she said to the officers. "This is just awful."

The principal and two deputies stepped out into the hallway. Within minutes they had come back into the office. The principal looked at Matt. "Young man, you are suspended for one week." The cops took the ten joints, saying they would hold them for evidence. If Matt ever caused another problem they would show the judge what they had. It was agreed that Joann and Clifford would handle things at home. No charges were being laid.

Joann grabbed Matt by the scruff of the neck and hauled him outside to her car. "Where did you get that stuff?" she asked Matt.

"I have a friend that sells it to me."

"Can you get more?" she asked her thirteen-year-old son.

"Yes," he said. "Anytime I want."

Joann handed her son twenty dollars then dropped him off on the next corner. "I will see you at home," she said.

Matt went to his source. He bought four new joints. He returned home and handed them to his mother.

"Your father does not need to know what happened," she said. "We will keep this to ourselves." She retreated to her bedroom alone and lit the first joint her son had supplied her. Matt never said a word to his father and whenever his mother handed him money he would return home with more pot.

Over the next year Matt expanded his little

enterprise. He only sold to four kids in the school he could trust. They sold to everyone else. The less exposure Matt had the less chance he had of getting caught. His supplier eventually had Matt selling ecstasy, coke, and assorted types of pills.

On Matt's fourteenth birthday he had skipped class and gone home early. Joann was making him a homemade cake when he entered the house. "You're home early," she said.

"The teacher was sick and they did not have time to find a substitute." Matt took two pills out of his pocket.

"What are those?" Joann asked.

Matt looked at his mother. "Something new," he said. "They are better than the joints. These are for you mom for everything you do for me." Matt needed to see how they affected someone. After all, if you're going to supply shit you better know what you are selling. His mother took the two pills then walked over to the kitchen sink. She swallowed them with a mouthful of cool water.

Matt's cake sat on the counter half-finished, the icing drooping from the sides. Joann sat down at the kitchen table. She started to feel a warmth building up inside her. She was getting lightheaded. The pills were kicking in. She looked at Matt.

"Your father has been cheating on me," she said. "I know he has. I can smell the whores on him when he comes home. He never touches me anymore. What is wrong with my tits?" she asked as she unbuttoned her blouse. Matt sat looking at his mother's bare chest. Joann tilted her head back and laughed. "Maybe you're more of a man than your father," she said.

She stood up, her breasts exposed and her nipples

hard. She took Matt by the hand and led him into his bedroom. That was the first time Matt was abused sexually by his mother. He enjoyed it. If his father was not going to keep his mother happy, he would. All he had to do was keep her supplied with pills and he would get what he wanted in return. Years of mental and sexual abuse had added up in Matt's psyche. He was unaware of it.

Matt turned right at the end of the block and walked another mile until he arrived at the Burger Baron drive-in. He walked up to the window. "I will have a double cheese with extra bacon, loaded. One order of onion rings and a chocolate shake." He reached into his pocket and pulled out a one-hundred dollar bill. He handed it through the window.

The young girl said, "I do not have that kind of change, sir. I will have to get my manager."

The manager came to the window and looked at Matt. He went to the cash drawer. He removed eighty-five dollars. The manager handed the money to his cashier and she gave it to Matt. His order was placed on a red plastic tray. Matt turned and made his way to a picnic table. He placed the brown paper bag from under his arm beside the food tray and sat down.

Matt dug in and took his first bite of the burger. It was just like he had remembered. The onion rings were hot. He closed his eyes and reminisced about the old days when he would hang out here and sell a few joints. As Matt took his second bite of the hamburger four deputy sheriffs' cars pulled into the lot. One drove up on the grass twenty feet from the table Matt was sitting at. The manager was on the phone in his office.

"Yes," he said. "They are here now. No, I will not hang up." He had recognized Matt from his picture

on TV. The deputies stood behind their drivers' doors, their guns drawn and pointing directly at Matt. The two families sitting at the other picnic tables scooped up their children and disappeared. Matt was alone staring down three 9mm berettas and a Remington 12-guage.

"Matt Jones, you are under arrest! This is the Hillcrest sheriff's department. Do not move."

Matt looked up from under the brim of his old ball cap. He reached for the milkshake and sucked hard on the straw. The coolness of the icecream felt good in his dry throat.

"Do not move!" He was ordered again. "We will shoot!"

Matt put both his hands flat on the table. He tilted his head in the direction of the cop with the shotgun. Matt moved his hand in the direction of the brown paper bag. He slowly put his hand inside.

"Don't do it! Do not do it!" said one of the deputies.

Matt pulled his hand quickly from the bag. He held two bundles of one-hundred-dollar bills. The four deputies opened fire, striking Matt eight times. Matt's body was thrown off the seat onto the ground. Blood pooled around his body and soaked the asphalt around him. His eyes stared blankly towards the sky. The one-hundred-dollar bills had been blown out of his hand by a single shotgun blast. They blew around in the light breeze, drifting across the parking lot.

Matt was never going back to prison. Just like he promised.

Chapter 53

Kevin and his group had watched the Rangers march the group of young men down the trail and out of view. He was asked if he knew what had happened. Kevin could only speculate. "I am guessing they were camping without permits. The warden's department does not take kindly to that."

The group of nine had planned on hiking up to Big Horn hot springs. However, the day's events had put a damper on them getting away on time. By the time the Rangers, Quads, and violators had marched by, it was 2:30. Gunner and the superintendent had taken off earlier with two other men in handcuffs. Kevin knew things must have been pretty serious but could not let on to his campers.

"Is there anyone that would still like to go to the hot springs?" Kevin asked. "If we travel light, we can be there in two hours. That would give us an hour to splash around then make it back here as the sun starts to set." Four of the eight still wanted to go. "Ok," said Kevin, "then grab your day packs and bathing suits. Gale and Jerry, are you okay looking after things around here while we are gone?"

"No problem," Jerry said, "we have everything under control." Gale had developed some pretty good blisters the day before. She had not said anything about them.

"Great, then we will leave everything in your hands. See you around 7-7:30," said Kevin.

The group of five made their way past the washrooms and landing pad. Kevin took the lead as they

made their way up the narrow pathway. A small sign posted at the trailhead read 'Hot Springs Five miles.'

The hike into Big Horn Hot Springs was uneventful. The four adults were in pretty good shape for city folk. They had no problem in keeping up with Kevin even when the trail became a little steeper. As they descended from Razorback Ridge down into a large ravine, the smell of sulfur started to fill the air. "It smells like rotten eggs," Kevin said. "The Indigenous folks say it's got great healing power."

They arrived at the edge of the main pool. Water flowed from a small creek one hundred yards uphill from between cracks in the rocks. Kevin paused then looked at his group. "Hundreds of years ago, the natives would come here," he said. "You see how all these rocks have been placed in a circle like this? Those people knew what they were doing," he said.

The depth of the pool in the middle was no more than four feet. Rocks lined the outer edge. Bigger rocks had been placed along the edge that ranged from being underwater by a foot to maybe two feet. "See how they placed those rocks there so you can sit on them," Kevin said. The group was fascinated by what they were seeing.

Kevin pointed to a wooden blind the park's service had made from fallen trees. It was in the shape of a V and stood eight feet high. "There is the change room," Kevin pointed. The ladies went first, leaving their packs by the edge of the pool.

They returned from behind the blind wearing bikinis and stepped gently across the rocks before making their way into the hot water. "It's perfect!" they exclaimed. The two men quickly changed and joined their spouses in the 105-degree water.

As Kevin sauntered off, he looked back and said, "You guys enjoy yourselves; I will be back in half an hour."

Kevin made his way to his usual vantage spot where he could keep an eye on the pool but be inconspicuous. Over the years, he had witnessed many things but never said anything. This was couples' time. He had a job to do, and that was to look after those who hired him. He scanned the area looking for wildlife with his old binoculars. "Nothing today," he said to himself.

Thirty-five minutes later, he returned to the pool's edge. "We should probably be thinking about heading out," he said. The ladies stepped out of the water first, their bodies pink from the hot water. When they had changed, the men had their turn. It was 5:35 by the time everyone was ready to go.

"I feel so weak," said Lisa.

"That hot water will do it to you every time," said Kevin. The five adults made their way back toward the Glacier Creek Campground. The four city folks moved slower now, and Kevin followed up from the rear. He smiled to himself, knowing their legs and feet felt like they weighed twice as much. It always happened to him when he stayed in the hot springs for an extended length of time.

They were at mile marker two when Garth, Lisa's husband, stopped in the middle of the trail and raised his finger to his lips. A sow Black Bear and two cubs were wandering up the pathway directly at them. Kevin quickly saw what Garth had been looking at and made his way in front of him. Kevin removed his daypack from his shoulders and reached inside. He pulled out a clear plastic bag containing several orange cartridges and a small blue handle with a trigger. Kevin removed the blue

handle and one orange cartridge, screwing them together as he yelled at the Black Bear and her cubs.

Waving his hands in the air and making himself as big as possible, Kevin shouted at the Sow, while the four adults cowered behind him. The Black Bear continued in their direction, sniffing the air. "Hey! Hey!" Kevin shouted as he moved toward the Sow, knowing that she would do whatever was necessary to protect her offspring.

The bear stood on its hind legs, trying to see what was making all the noise. Kevin was aware that Black Bears had poor vision, and from his years of experience in the bush, he knew they couldn't see well up to about forty yards ahead. In this case, the bear and her cubs were around fifty yards away, and Kevin didn't want them getting any closer to his hikers.

He pulled the trigger on the blue handle, and there was a puff of smoke as something shot out of the orange end, sailing over the Sow's head as it stood on its hind legs. It exploded with a loud bang about ten feet from the bear. The Black Bear dropped to all fours, turned, and ran up the hill, with her cubs right behind her. Kevin looked at the others and smiled. "Works every time," he said.

"What is that?" asked Garth.

"It's called a bear banger. I've been carrying them for years."

"Why do all the sporting goods stores push bear spray?" asked Lisa.

"That's a good question," Kevin replied. "The best I can figure is that there's more money in it for them. By the time the bear is close enough for your bear spray to be effective, it's going to be within 10-15 feet. Kind

of silly, if you ask me."

The five adults walked the last two miles back to their campsite, where Gale and Jerry had laid out the table for dinner. The fire and coals were ready for cooking. "How were the hot springs?" asked Gale.

"Amazing," said Lisa. "And you should have seen the bear and cubs."

"Really?" asked Gale. Lisa pulled out her cellphone and played the video she had recorded of the encounter. The Sow was standing on its hind legs as Kevin fired the explosive over its head.

"Look at that," said Gale. "They ran like scared rabbits. Those poor fluff balls."

Kevin smiled and then said, "They always do. Better them than us."

Chapter 54

Joann woke up around 5:30. The three oxy her son Matt had given her had now worn off. The events of the early afternoon were a blur. She was confused. Matt could not have been there. "He is in prison," she reasoned with herself. She pulled back the blankets on the bed then made her way to the washroom. Joann sat on the toilet and relieved herself. She had a chill and decided the best thing to do was run the tub. A soak would do her some good, especially before she tackled what was left of the day.

The water was nice and warm. Joann added her favourite scented bubble bath to the running water. She slid into the tub, the water still running from the faucet. The bubbles were thick and covered her breasts. When she was satisfied with the depth of the water, she manoeuvred her right foot to work the handles on the taps. She closed the leavers and let the warm water sooth her aching body. Joann layed back as far as she could, her head now just poking over the top of the bubbles. She closed her eyes and thought about nothing. The bubbles eventually started to dissipate. Joann relaxed even more. She let her head slide under the water. She laid beneath the surface. The warm water enveloped her. For a split second she thought, "It would be so easy just to stay here."

She sat up and took a deep breath. She reached for her shampoo bottle then washed her hair. She slid back down and rinsed the lather from her hair. She was feeling more human. The chill had disappeared as she reached for her loofa and soaped it up. She washed under her arms at first, then reached down to her private area.

She felt something.

"Strange," she thought, as the loofa drifted on the surface. Joann reached between her legs and with her finger explored what it was she felt. She pulled at it thinking it might have been a tampon. She was confused, as she removed the item from her vagina. She looked in disbelief at what looked like a coloured cigarette. Joann brought the item closer to her eyes. She then recognized what she held in her hand. Joann unfurled five single, one-hundred-dollar bills. She laid them on the side of the tub, all lined up in a neat row. Matt had been there. She remembered small bits and pieces. Her son left her the money in the only place Clifford would never find it.

Joann closed her eyes again then tried to remember the events of the afternoon. It was no use. Her mind was almost void of anything that occured. She heard Clifford and Billy come in through the side enterance of the house. Someone slammed the door.

"Matt, is that you?" she yelled. "Matt?"

"Joann, it's me and Billy," Clifford shouted through the closed bathroom door. "We are home from the car show."

Billy and his father had enjoyed a wonderful father-and-son day wandering through the weekend show. The antique cars were something Billy and his father shared a passion about. Billy was not going to go down the same path as his older son, not if Clifford could help it.

"I will be out in a minute," Joann yelled back, as she pulled the plug, allowing the water to drain. She stepped out of the bath and towelled herself off. She scooped up the five one-hundred-dollar bills. She opened the bathroom vanity doors. Joann folded the money so it

would fit inside the bottom of her Q-tip box. She moved the ear swabs around until the money could not be seen. She placed the box back under the sink way in the back corner and covered it with some facecloths.

Joann wrapped herself in the biggest towel that was laying out. She ran the blow dryer, brushing her hair until she was happy with the results. She opened the door and walked back into the master bedroom. She slipped into her tracksuit. Joann walked into the kitchen where Billy and Clifford sat.

"How was your day?" she said, looking at Billy.

"We saw some real neat cars," he said to his mother.

"Good for you, Billy. I am happy you enjoyed your day." Joann looked at Clifford. She snarled, "Too bad you could not take the same interest in your older son when he was that age."

Clifford hung his head. He had not been home more than a half an hour and his wife was already berating him. "Things were different then," he said, trying to defend himself.

Joann walked away and sat down in the living room. She grabbed the remote control and turned on the six o'clock news. There was a red banner that flashed across the bottom of the screen. "Breaking news," it said. The reporter came on live from in front of the Burger Baron.

"This is Christie Mathews reporting live from in front of the Burger Baron drive-in. Authorities have just shot and killed escaped convict, twenty-seven-year-old Matt Jones. Again, authorities have shot and killed escaped criminal, Matt Jones." The camera panned to a stretcher being loaded into the back of an ambulance.

The sheet covering the body was soaked in blood.

Joann turned up the volume. Tears were running down her cheeks. Clifford stood at the end of the couch watching the report. Christie Mathews interviewed two men live that said exactly the same thing. "This dude was just sitting there eating his hamburger. The cops pulled up and shot him. There were bullets flying everywhere."

"This is Christie Mathews reporting live from the Burger Baron in Hillcrest. Now back to our regular program."

The next report was about the influx of visitors to the community over the long weekend, as well as the car show. Joann wiped the tears from her eyes. She looked at Clifford and said, "You killed our son! It's your fault! You were not the father he needed!" She got up from the couch and made her way back into the master bedroom. Joann turned then locked the bedroom door. "You bastard!" she screamed through the closed door.

Clifford closed his eyes, opened them, and walked over to Billy. "I did the best I could," he said to his youngest son.

"I know, dad," said Billy.

Clifford had tears in his eyes. He held his youngest son's head in his hands. "Look at me," he said to Billy. "I love you and do not ever forget that."

"I won't," said Billy. "What are we going to have for dinner?" Clifford's youngest son was completely detached from the reality of the moment. Billy had become quite self-sufficient in his young age. He could not count on his mother for anything. Matt had been in prison on-and-off for most of Billy's life. His father was never home and Donna only came by when her mother called.

"How about pizza?" said Clifford.

"Can we get wings too?" asked Billy.

Joann took her tracksuit off and lay naked on her bed. She closed her eyes for a moment and then opened them. She sat up and took the bottle of oxy that was sitting on the nightstand. She placed it to her mouth and let the remaining fifteen pills slide onto her tongue. She choked as she took two gulps of water from the glass her son Matt had touched last.

She laid there naked as the oxy started to kick in. She felt the warmth starting to envelop her body once again. This time it was different, it was faster. Her body started to convulse. She grabbed at the sheets and closed her eyes. She started to drift off deeper than she had ever gone. This trip was going to be her last.

Chapter 55

Susan crawled in the darkness, the moon providing just enough light for her to make out the trail. Her jeans were worn through at the knees, exposing her skin. Every movement caused excruciating pain. Her calf muscle dangled, flopping back and forth as she struggled forward. Susan's hands were covered in blood and dirt, and her eye hung from its socket, now swollen shut. Her hair was matted in a clump on top of her head, but she was still alive.

As she crawled around the last corner to the cabins on Rock Lake, she could hear people talking, and the smell of something cooking filled her nostrils. She paused for a moment, then yelled, "Help me!" Her throat was dry, and it came out more like a whisper. She tried again, "Help me! I've been attacked by a Grizzly!" There was no response. She could see people standing around a large fire. Susan took a rock and started to tap the side of the bear spray, making a loud clicking sound. She tapped it repeatedly, yelling, "Help me! Help me!" as loud as she could.

The crowd around the fire fell silent, and suddenly, a white beam of light illuminated the pathway in front of her. Soon, the light reflected off Susan's face, and the voices grew louder. The first person to reach Susan was Seamus. "My God, Lassi," he said as he knelt down beside her. Shawn and Briana quickly joined him.

Briana's light was directly on Susan's face when she rolled over to her side. Her head hit the ground, causing the torn skin on her scalp to flop down past her ear, and her eyeball rocked back and forth. "Help me," Susan muttered. "My friend and I were attacked by a

bear."

Briana turned and vomited her dinner. "Don't worry, Lassi, I've got you," Seamus said as he placed his arms underneath her and picked her up. "Quickly, tell Aileen to open the door and clear off the table." Shawn carried the can of bear spray, and Briana ran back to RL01. Seamus did all he could to comfort Susan during the seventy-yard journey back to his cabin.

By the time they arrived, Caitlin and Cathleen were at the foot of the stairs. Aileen and Briana were in the entranceway. "Oh my, oh my," said Aileen. Seamus carried Susan up the stairs into the cabin and laid her down on the table inside.

Caitlin and Cathleen, trained nurses from Ireland, quickly took over. "Elevate her legs," they instructed Shawn. "That's it. Just about a foot."

"Help me," Susan muttered.

"We have you," said Seamus, "you are safe." Susan mentioned her friend, and they exchanged worried glances.

Susan's scalp wound was open to the bone and bleeding profusely. Caitlin grabbed the flap of skin and hair, adjusting it to cover the exposed bone on Susan's skull. "Get me one of your T-shirts," she yelled to Seamus.

Seamus rummaged through his backpack and found a clean shirt he had been saving for the hike out. "Here," he said, handing it over.

"Cut it into strips. You have to help me and Cathleen."

Aileen held Susan's hand while Shawn stood nearby, watching the nurses go to work.

"Now, hand me one of those," Caitlin said, pointing to the strips of cloth Seamus had torn from his shirt. "There, put it under her chin. Now tie it around the top of her head. That's right, just like that. Now another one." As Caitlin adjusted the loose eye, she looked down at Cathleen, who had assessed the torn calf muscle and was now lifting Susan's shirt. Her stomach was exposed, with her bowels protruding from an eight-inch gash torn into her gut by a claw. Cathleen shook her head, and Caitlin took another strip of cloth, placing it over the loose eye and around the back of Susan's head.

"Water... can I have some water...?" asked Susan, who was losing consciousness.

Cathleen did her best to tuck the exposed bowel back into the opening and instructed, "Get me some plastic wrap, Shawn." He returned with a roll they had bought for leftovers and pulled out about two feet, following Cathleen's instructions. "That's it. Put it down over my hands," she said. "Now, I'm going to remove my hands, and you put pressure right over the top. Got it?" Shawn held the plastic wrap in place as Cathleen carefully removed her hands.

"Seamus, we need to roll her on her side," Cathleen said. She pulled more plastic wrap from the roll and continued, "Now, around her back and back over. Let's do that a few more times." Shawn moved his hands as the wrap wound around Susan four times. Cathleen was satisfied that it would hold the wound somewhat closed.

"There," she said. "I think that will do for now." Susan had passed out as the nurses continued to work. "I need water! This leg muscle is full of dirt and stones. Briana, we need water. Get us some water!"

Briana got two bottles of fresh water and placed

them on the table. She could not look. "Here," she said.

Cathleen did her best to wash the muscle clean, and she placed it back in position on Susan's leg. Cathleen noticed the skin tissue had changed color and was dying. "She is going to lose this," she muttered to Caitlin. "We can only do what we can," she said. Cathleen wrapped more plastic wrap around Susan's leg. The wrap was holding, at least for now. "Give me a couple of those strips," she said to Seamus. She wrapped them around Susan's leg, just in case she started to move about when she woke up.

"I am going to loosen this belt," said Caitlin. "Maybe if we can get a little blood down there, it might save some of the muscle." She loosened the belt by backing off the branch that had been tightened hours earlier by Susan herself. Blood seeped out under the plastic wrap and onto the table. "Tighten it back up! That's arterial blood, look at the color."

"I see it," said Cathleen. The nurses looked up at everyone. It had taken twenty minutes to assess and cover Susan's wounds.

"We have to get some water into her. She has lost a lot of blood. Shawn, lift her head," Caitlin instructed. She put one of the water bottles to Susan's lips. The cool water hit her mouth, and Susan started to choke. "That's it," said Caitlin. "Wake up, my dear. You need to drink some water." They tried again and again, and Susan managed to swallow a couple of tablespoons' worth in her unconscious state. A little was better than nothing.

"We need to get her to a hospital, or she will die," said Cathleen.

"How are we going to do that?" said Seamus. "There ain't no phones. They nay work up here!"

"You have to do something. She is dying!" shouted Cathleen.

Chapter 56

Brad, Tommy, Elizabeth, Donna, and the children sat around the fire after enjoying a hearty dinner of steak with pork and beans. Donna had whipped up a batch of biscuits. The icepacks that had been keeping things cold had now thawed out and were not much use after two days. The weather had been warm. Brad looked up at the sky.

"It's going to be a cool night," he said to everyone.

Mark was curious, "How do you know that?"

Brad pointed to the sky, "You see how there are no clouds? If there were clouds in the sky, they would act like a blanket and keep the warm air closer to the ground. But because there are no clouds tonight, the warm air is going to rise and draw the cool air in from the mountain tops."

Tommy added more wood to the fire. "You kids might want to leave your jackets on tonight when you are sleeping. They will keep you nice and warm."

Brad and Tommy took the backpacks and set them into the tent fly. Before starting to pull on the rope, Brad reached into the side pocket of his pack and removed his Grandfather's M1911. He tucked it into the back of his belt, pulling his jacket down to conceal it. He exchanged a nod with Tommy, and nothing more was said between them. The day's events had given them enough reason to be cautious, especially after finding a Grizzly bear footprint outside one of their tents and discovering the bear's den on the nearby island half a mile away.

The boys hoisted the backpacks aloft into the tree and tied the rope off as they had done the night before. By then, darkness had settled in.

It was dark when they returned to the girls. The pots, pans, and utensils had all been washed and neatly stacked on the edge of the table. Donna asked, "Who wants some roasted marshmallows?" as she opened a fresh bag.

Mark and Marcy were the first to eagerly volunteer, grabbing the sticks that had been used to cook the hotdogs. Donna placed two marshmallows on each stick and instructed them, "Be careful they do not catch on fire. You want to keep turning them until they turn nice and brown."

The kids followed her instructions, although Mark lost focus, holding his stick into the air until the two white orbs burst into flames, consumed by the fire as they dripped onto the ground. Donna took the stick away from Mark, cleaned it in the fire, and put two fresh marshmallows on it before handing it back to him, cautioning, "Be more careful this time."

Marcy proudly waved her browned marshmallows under Donna's nose. "How are those?" she asked.

"Perfect," came Donna's reply.

Elizabeth reached into her left pocket and pulled out a bag of Graham Wafers. From her right pocket, she retrieved a bag containing three Jersey milk chocolate bars.

Elizabeth took a wafer and broke it in half. She placed a piece of chocolate across it, saying to Marcy, "Bring your treats over here." Marcy walked over, and Elizabeth slid the first marshmallow off the stick on top

of the waiting chocolate.

"Now," she said to Marcy, "just give it twenty seconds and watch. See how the chocolate is melting. Now it's ready. You can have the first one." Marcy devoured the concoction. She made another and handed it to Brad.

"Honey, you are such a good cook," he exclaimed.

Elizabeth said, "Oh, Brad."

He replied, "Not you, Marcy." He winked at Elizabeth, and Marcy giggled.

Mark had managed to ignite several more marshmallows that evening. He discovered that he could move about with them burning, and it looked like he was carrying an old-fashioned torch. Everyone eventually had their fill of the special treats.

It was 10:30 when Donna looked at her watch. "It is way past your bedtimes," she said to the children.

"Ahhh, do we have to?" It sounded like they had been rehearsing their mutual reply for years.

"Now," said Donna, "we do not want any sleepy heads in the morning."

The children ambled towards their tent. "Remember to leave your jackets on. It's going to get chilly tonight. I will check on you in ten minutes."

Brad and Tommy stacked the last of the split wood onto the fire. Sparks and embers jumped into the air as the new wood started to burn. Donna got up to check on the children. She removed her phone from her pocket, turning on the flashlight. She walked to the children's tent and peered inside. They were already asleep. Donna did the zipper up to the tent and returned

to the picnic table, joining her friends and lover.

"Thank you," she said to everyone. "Thank you for making today something special for those two." Tommy put his arm around Donna and kissed her on the cheek. She turned her head so his next kiss could be on her lips.

"No need to say thank you," said Elizabeth. "Friends look after friends and family."

"You know I did not have much family time," said Donna, "this is just nice. It feels right."

"You're welcome," said Brad. The young adults sat around and chatted about the days in high school, including the day that the Bunsen burners had set the school on fire.

Tommy smiled and said to Donna, "I remember that day so well. Your t-shirt was so wet... your nipples... oh, never mind." He caught himself.

The fire had died down and the girls had gone into their respective tents. Brad and Tommy agreed to let the fire burn itself down tonight. The smoke should keep anything that is roaming away. The young men clambered into their tents. The ladies were waiting for their men.

Brad removed his jacket and placed it at the foot of the bed. He removed the M1911 from his belt behind his back and tucked it under the edge of his side of the sleeping bag. He removed his shirt and pants, climbing in with Elizabeth. She lay there naked, waiting for him. They made love.

"It's warm in here," Brad whispered.

"No," said Elizabeth. "It is hot in here." They both laughed as they lay beside each other, catching their

276

breaths, the events of the day filling their heads.

From the tent next door came the words, "Oh, Tommy, that's it! Right there!" Elizabeth started to giggle and Brad was smiling as they both drifted off.

Brad awoke at 4:00 am, again hearing noise coming from outside. He reached under the corner of his sleeping bag and removed the M1911. He flipped the safety lever off with his thumb. Kevin, Brad's father, had shown him how to use his grandfather's old army pistol when Brad was sixteen. He hadn't forgotten what his dad had taught him.

Brad could hear lapping noises, sounding like a dog drinking water from a bowl. "Damn, that bear is back and licking up the stupid burnt marshmallow," Brad thought. Slowly, he started to move the zipper on the tent door. He peered into the darkness; the fire was out, and moonlight cast shadows. He could hear light grunting sounds, but something didn't feel right.

Turning his attention toward Mark and Marcy's tent, he saw it suddenly collapse, and could hear the nylon being shredded accompanied by the kids' screams. From Tommy's tent, Brad heard the words, "What the fuck?"

Brad unfastened the zipper all the way and jumped outside in his stocking feet. He was just in time to see a grizzly bear carrying off one of the sleeping bags from the children's tent. Brad fired his gun into the air, and the grizzly turned, with the bag in its mouth. An arm was visible hanging from the top of the bag. Brad fired the gun again, and the bear dropped the bag with its contents, then ran toward the pathway leading to the north end of Rock Lake.

Tommy, now standing in his underwear, was

shouting as he ran to the children's tent. He pulled back the torn nylon to reveal Marcy, wide-eyed and shaking hysterically, tears rolling down her cheeks. "Where's Mark, Tommy?" Marcy asked.

Tommy looked back at Brad, panic in his eyes. "Where's Mark?" Tommy asked again. Brad pointed his gun in the direction of the sleeping bag laying on the ground. Donna and Elizabeth, now outside with their jackets wrapped around them, joined the scene.

"I need a flashlight," Tommy beckoned. Donna reached for her cellphone and handed it to Brad, who walked over to join Tommy at the shredded tent. Tommy picked up Marcy, along with her sleeping bag, and carried her back to Donna.

Returning to Brad, Tommy asked, "Are you ready?"

Brad replied, "Ready."

The two young men walked toward the heap of torn material that had once been a sleeping bag. An arm hung motionless above the material. As they got closer, the cellphone's flashlight illuminated what they had seen from the edge of the campsite.

"Fuck me," said Tommy. "No." Tommy bent down as Brad scanned the trail to make sure the grizzly wasn't coming back. "Mark? Mark, are you okay?" Tommy called out.

There was no reply.

"Mark!" Tommy said as he pulled apart the torn bag. "Mark, it's Uncle Tommy. Mark!" The arm moved. "Mark, are you okay?"

Mark worked himself free from the shredded material. The boy stood up, half of his jacket torn. "What

happened?" he asked.

Brad and Tommy looked at each other in disbelief. "Are you okay, little buddy?" asked Brad as Tommy turned Mark to inspect him for wounds. There wasn't a scratch on the kid.

"Look at my jacket," said Mark. "Mom is going to kill me. Now what am I going to do for breakfast?"

"Breakfast?" said Tommy, surprised. "You're worried about breakfast?"

"I had my last sausage in my pocket. I was going to have it for breakfast."

Tommy and Brad exchanged glances.

The Grizzly had smelled a source of food emanating from the kids' tent. Tommy had forgotten all about the sausages he handed to Mark at Elli's Diner. The bear had smelled the greasy napkins that contained the last bit of food from two days prior.

Tommy held Mark in his arms as Brad scoured the trees and the pathway. The three of them walked back towards the campsite. The cold night air was taking hold as their adrenaline subsided. The girls were yelling, "Is Mark okay?" The young men started to shake.

"I have to get dressed," said Brad.

"Me too," said Tommy as he handed Donna her cellphone.

"Where are my runners?" asked Mark.

"Just sit here and be quiet for a minute," Brad said. He walked over to Elizabeth. He placed his grandfather's gun in her hand. "I need to get dressed," he said. "If you see anything, just point and pull the trigger."

The two young men wasted no time putting on

their clothes and boots. When they were back outside, Brad took the M1911 from Elizabeth's hand. The girls went into their tents and changed. Marcy followed Donna inside and crawled into bed. She was still shaking from the near-tragedy that had just occurred.

Tommy and Brad gathered more wood from the pile that Toby and Brent had delivered to the site two days earlier. They took small pieces and placed them on the dying fire. Tommy knelt down and blew until he found some embers. He placed small bits of wood on top of the glowing embers and blew. The wood burst into flames. The two friends piled fresh wood onto the fire and watched it start to burn.

Brad looked to the east. The outline of the mountains was now visible. "It will be light in an hour or so," he said to Tommy.

Mark spoke up, "I need my shoes. My feet are cold."

Tommy walked to the shredded tent and rummaged through the torn nylon. "I found them," he said as he walked back to the picnic table. "Here, put this around your shoulders." He placed Marcy's sleeping bag around Mark. Tommy held Mark's runners open as he slipped his feet into them. "How's that?" asked Tommy.

"Better," came Mark's reply. The two young men sat on either side of Mark. Brad had the M1911 tucked into the back of his belt. Brad looked across the top of Mark's head at Tommy. Tommy looked into Brad's eyes. The young men had screwed up, and they knew it. It almost cost Mark his life. Nothing more was said. The bear was only doing what bears do. It was foraging for food, and Mark smelled good enough to eat.

Chapter 57

Johnny Robbins and Jackson Hall settled their bill for dinner with a crisp one hundred dollar bill. Johnny tipped his hat in Elli's direction as the two men made their way past the crowded front entrance. They got into Jackson's convertible. Their next stop was the Big Crow Indian Reserve, where the Natives had built a beautiful casino six years ago. Jackson Hall and one of his shell companies had provided the funding for the construction because there wasn't a regular financial institution willing to take on the risk of the thirty-million-dollar project. Jackson had needed a front to help with some of the extra cash he had to launder.

Jackson had made an agreement with the Band Council, stating that his architect would be involved in the design of the casino and hotel. It would incorporate many historical features with significance to the indigenous people of the area. The facility would also contain several new security features, including state-of-the-art safes in hotel rooms for high rollers, a cash room with topnotch security, and high-tech security cameras placed throughout the property.

One unique feature was the special room designed beneath the indoor swimming pool. It had solid concrete walls that were four feet thick and was twenty feet by twenty feet in size. The room was secured with an electromagnetic lock that could only be opened using a specialized chipped computer key and security code. It was a state-of-the-art technology feature at the time of the casino and hotel's construction. The council had been told that the room would contain computer equipment to track the casino's daily income. Jackson's company

would have access to the daily receipts, with Hall's company charging only five percent interest on the loan instead of the usual ten percent. They would submit an annual bill until the complete thirty million had been repaid with interest. Jackson's company would also take twenty percent of the daily profits, and in the event the project failed, the Natives would transfer complete control to Hall's company, which would lease the land back to Jackson for a dollar a year for one hundred years.

The council voted eight to three in favor of the proposal, and the project was expected to employ hundreds of band members, making Jackson Hall a hero in their time of need. The arrangement included a private suite for Mr. Hall's exclusive use anytime he wanted. Jackson Hall would be a silent partner in the venture with access to everything to ensure his company was not being cheated.

Jackson and Johnny drove to Hillsboro and then west on Highway 22. The Big Crow Casino and Hotel was located thirty miles from Hillsboro, right in the middle of nowhere. The casino was a quarter mile off the highway, and its strobe and searchlights lit up the night sky. A giant metal teepee sat on the corner where you turned off public land and entered the Reservation. The hotel and casino featured beautiful green-tinted glass windows, reminding everyone of the native grasses in the area.

A huge waterfall sat forty yards from the front entrance, and a manmade creek flowed from the pooled water at the base of the falls, leading towards the parking lot before disappearing underground. Several footbridges spanned the creek, connecting the parking lot to the main entrance. Atop the waterfall was a statue of a giant golden eagle clutching a lake trout in its talons. Jackson pulled the Mercedes up to the front doors, and

the canopy overhead was adorned with blue LED lights, creating the illusion of a midafternoon summer sky. The revolving front doors of the casino were outlined in gold leaf.

Two valets, dressed in tuxedos, approached the convertible and opened both doors of the vehicle at the exact same time. As Johnny stepped out, adjusting his cowboy hat, Jackson popped the trunk and handed the valet his Mercedes fob. In return, the valet handed him a tag, and Jackson retrieved his suitcase from the trunk. Johnny slung his duffle bag over his shoulder. The valet on the passenger side signaled, and two young men in blue coveralls and black gloves appeared—one pushing a luggage cart and the other driving Jackson's car over to the VIP parking lot. Jackson and Johnny were escorted into the lobby and then to the front desk.

Jackson looked at the clerk's name tag and removed a black card with gold writing on it from his wallet. He presented it to the beautiful front desk clerk, Judith Manymoons. She recognized the card as something incredibly special, as only one had ever been issued by the casino. She knew that the man holding it was to be treated with the utmost respect and could have anything he desired. When she applied for the job she had gone through the rigorous training program all employees underwent, knowing that there was one special guest who was to be treated equally as the Chief. The man who held that card was responsible for bringing prosperity to the Nation. Johnny stood by Jackson's side as Judith processed their check-in.

"Mr. Hall," she said, "your suite is 1026, and it's ready for you and your guest. Here is your access card. Max will escort you to your room." She summoned the room valet, and Max led the way with the luggage cart to the bank of elevators in the main lobby. Max swiped

a card, and the elevator took them up to the tenth-floor penthouse suites.

When the elevator doors opened, they stepped out onto a grand balcony. From there, Johnny had a breathtaking view of the casino floor, bustling with people ten stories below. "Right this way, gentlemen," Max said, guiding them to the end of the hallway and opening the door to their suite. As the lights came on, it revealed a lavish two-bedroom penthouse suite with a stunning view of the mountains in the distance.

Jackson removed two one hundred dollar bills from his wallet and handed them both to the room valet. "That's for both of you," he said. The valet expressed his gratitude, and their bags had been placed on the king-size beds in their respective bedrooms. After the employees left and closed the door, Max, the room valet, handed a twenty-dollar bill to the young bag valet in the blue coveralls as a tip.

In the bedroom that held his duffle bag, Johnny retrieved the taser from its holster and placed it in his jacket pocket. Jackson, on the other hand, left his bag untouched. He had something important to share with Johnny.

"I have something to show you," Jackson said to Johnny. "I have everything arranged for tomorrow at 3:00 PM. The guys will be waiting for us at Hillsboro Municipal Airport in an old DC-3. Where's the key?" Jackson asked.

Johnny tapped his pocket and replied, "Right here."

"Come with me." The two men left the suite and made their way back to the elevator. Jackson swiped his black card and selected the basement floor. "I know the

last five years have been shit."

"You have no idea. Agreement or no agreement, I lost five years of my life. I assume this is where the Corvette came from that day?"

Jackson smiled and admitted, "Well, I didn't get it from a dealership." He had worn a set of blue coveralls on that fateful day and simply drove away with a new car that should have been in the VIP parking lot. "This is going to make it all worth your while. I told you when we opened the account with the safety deposit box that someday I would make it up to you. You protected my ass in the joint and when we were growing up."

Johnny said nothing. He remained reserved, knowing that Jackson had set him up that day to obtain a second key for the safety deposit box. Jackson had needed that key to access the hidden money stashed away, and Johnny had no idea about the full extent of the plan. The two criminals had used the safety deposit box to conceal the proceeds Jackson was skimming from his company. Johnny's share was a twenty percent cut for his silence, but the money kept piling up. The casino was the perfect cover. It was not federal land Jackson fronted its construction. The FBI investigation against Jackson and his companies led to Jackson's downfall and imprisonment. Money was missing but no one knew where it was other than Jackson Hall.

The elevator doors opened and the two men exited into the basement corridor. "This way," said Jackson. He had devised a plan where he would give Johnny the computerized key. Johnny had no idea what it was for; he just had instructions to put it in the safety deposit box.

Johnny knew it was important to Jackson so hiding his key in the original safety deposit box made

sense. If Hall needed the computerized key back he needed Johnny to go with him. Johnny was then assured of his cut. They walked to the end of the corridor arriving to a set of doors that were chained and locked.

"Service entrance," said Jackson. "It goes up a flight of stairs to the outside of the building. This way." They walked twenty feet down a dimly lit hallway. There was a card reader mounted on the wall, its light glowing red. Jackson took his black card and ran it through the machine. The single steel door unlocked. He held it open. "After you." Johnny entered the room. Jackson reached over and turned on a light switch. In front of the two men was a large safe door. It had a digital keypad with a key slot beside it. Jackson stood in front of the keypad. "I need the key." Johnny reached into his pocket and handed the key to Jackson Hall. Johnny stood behind Hall as he entered the numbers 64729. Jackson placed the key in the lock and turned it.The keypad flashed red and then the word "Error" flashed on its screen. "What the hell?" Hall turned to face Johnny as the stun gun found its mark. Jackson Hall hit the ground as Johnny zapped him one more time. Jackson blacked out.

Johnny removed the key from the door. He used the key to pry the rubber loose from the heel of his boot. The small computer chip fell onto the floor. Johnny picked it up, placing it into the slot of the key he had pried it from. As his father had taught him, "Trust no one." Johnny stood in front of the door. He entered 64729 in the keypad and inserted the key into the slot, turning it.

The light on the pad turned green and the door started to open automatically. Johnny had to drag Jackson Hall out of the way as the door opened completely on its own. The fluorescent lights overhead flickered while Johnny stood looking at fifty cardboard

boxes all neatly stacked together. Each box weighed approximately fourty pounds and measured two feet by two feet.

Johnny tore open the closest box and peered inside. Neatly wrapped in bundles of ten thousand dollars were piles of one hundred dollar bills. There was two million in cash in each box. Johnny removed his belt from his pants, placing it around Jackson Hall's neck. He twisted it until his friend turned blue and stopped breathing.

"Twenty percent just won't cut it this time."

Johnny dragged Jackson's body into the room with the money. He took Jackson's wallet, his black card, the valet tag, plus his cellphone. Placing two bundles of hundreds into his breast pockets, Johnny realized he was going to need a truck, a really big truck. He also needed a new plan.

Chapter 58

Clifford answered the front door. It was the pizza delivery guy.

"Here's your pizza and wings," the driver said, handing the food over to Clifford. "That's twenty-five bucks."

Clifford handed the driver thirty dollars and said, "Billy, go get your mother and tell her dinner is ready."

Clifford made his way to the kitchen table, placing the pizza and wings in the middle. He searched for three clean plates. Joann had not done any of the dishes from last night or the morning. He shook his head as he laid out the mismatched china. Clifford had worked hard at the dealership to keep a roof over their heads no matter how poorly he had been mistreated.

Billy returned to the kitchen table and said, "Mom's door's locked."

"Did she answer you?"

"No, I don't think so."

Clifford got up and went to the bedroom door and knocked. "Joann? I ordered dinner. You have to eat. I know it's not a good time, but you have to keep your strength up. Joann? Answer me." The silence from the bedroom was deafening. Clifford knocked harder on the door. "Joann? Answer me." Still nothing. Clifford went and found his house keys. The lock on the bedroom door had been keyed when Matt was a boy after Clifford had caught him stealing twenty dollars from his sock drawer. Clifford fiddled with the key in the lock and opened the bedroom door.

Joann lay on the bed completely naked, the empty bottle of oxy lay in her open left hand. White foam dribbled from her open mouth. Clifford shook his wife. "Joann? Wake up! Wake up!" There was no response. He lifted her eyelids. Her eyes had rolled back. All he could see was white. "You have done it this time, you really have." He picked up the phone beside the bed and dialed 911.

The operator answered, "State your emergency." Clifford explained what had happened. "An ambulance is on its way, sir. Do not hang up." Clifford stayed on the phone.

"Billy, go to the front door," Clifford shouted from the bedroom. "I've called an ambulance for your mom."

Billy put down his chicken wing, sauce dripping down his chin, and went to open the door. He stood there with the door open. This was not the first time he had to let the EMTs into the house.

The ambulance arrived five minutes later. The two attendants ran into the house with their emergency boxes. Billy led them to his parents' bedroom and pointed towards his mother, but did not go into the room. The two EMTs quickly assessed the situation.

"Do you know how much she took?" one of them asked.

"No," Clifford said. "I don't. The prescription had been filled on Monday."

The second EMT was on his radio to the hospital. They were ordered to inject Joann with naloxone.

"Hand me the Narcan," said Tim, the senior of the two attendants while holding a stethoscope to Joann's naked chest. "I hardly have a pulse."

Evan handed his training officer the hypodermic needle containing a premeasured amount of lifesaving drug. Tim opened an alcohol swab with his gloved hands and carefully cleaned a large vein on Joann's arm. He removed the plastic cover from the needle as Clifford suddenly blurted out, "Our son was killed today. She took the news pretty hard."

"I am sorry," Evan offered his condolences.

Tim inserted the needle deep into Joann's vein and administered the antidote. "Now we wait," he said to the worried husband. He instructed Evan to prepare the stretcher for Joann's transport.

Tim then placed the end of his stethoscope on Joann's chest, listening intently. He looked up at Clifford and nodded. "Her heartbeat is stronger. The antidote is working." He quickly radioed the hospital with Joann's vitals.

Evan returned with the stretcher, and the two EMTs carefully lifted Joann onto it. They covered her with a white sheet and then a wool blanket. Clifford handed Evan Joann's tracksuit. "Here, you better take these as well," he said. "I will meet you guys at the hospital."

"We are going to Hillcrest Memorial first to stabilize her, and then to Metro General."

"I need to find someone to look after Billy."

The EMTs wheeled Joann down the hall, out the front door, and into the waiting ambulance. The wheels of the gurney locked securely into position on the floor of the vehicle. Tim continued to monitor Joann's condition in the back of the ambulance as Evan drove, sirens blaring and lights flashing, on their way to provide her with the urgent medical care she needed. In a swift

six-minute journey, they arrived at the newly expanded Hillcrest Hospital. Joann was promptly wheeled into the emergency room, where medical staff were ready to take action. Knowing the urgency of the situation, they immediately administered another injection of Narcan through Joann's IV.

The emergency room doctor recognized the severity of Joann's condition and decided to call for Life Flight, the hospital's helicopter service, to transfer her to Metro General. Hillcrest Memorial Hospital, being in a rural area, lacked both the specialized equipment and the expertise required to manage an overdose of this nature and potential complications.

An hour later, the Life Flight helicopter touched down on the helipad at Metro General Hospital. Joann was quickly wheeled into the bustling emergency room, where Dr. Hasen, his gloved hands raised, was standing by, ready to provide immediate care. The helicopter crew promptly relayed Joann's current vital signs to the medical team, ensuring they had all the information they needed to begin their efforts to save her.

"Tube her," said Hansen. "I want everything out of her stomach."

The two nurses swiftly and skillfully worked to insert a tube down Joann's throat and into her stomach. With precision, they flushed warm fluid down the tube for fifteen seconds and then activated the vacuum. As the vacuum operated, a mixture of the fluid and the remnants of the oxy Joann had consumed began to travel up the clear plastic tubing, effectively removing it from her system.

"Good work, girls," said Hansen. "Her breathing is really shallow. I want to intubate her when we get her cleaned out. This girl's going to make it." he said.

The nurses removed the suction tube and replaced it with an intubation tube, connecting Joann to a respirator. With the assistance of the respirator, her breathing became more controlled, and her color gradually returned to her face. The medical team continued to monitor her closely, ensuring that she was stable and receiving the necessary care.

"Let's move her to recovery," Dr. Hansen said.

Joann was wheeled into the same room as Cathy Taylor. Cathy was sound asleep as the nurses wheeled Joann into the recovery room. The sound of the ventilator eventually woke Cathy. She looked over at her new roommate. She was having difficulty remembering her conversation with the FBI agents. She was also having trouble with what she believed was her period. She needed to use the washroom.

Cathy tried getting out of bed on her own. It was no use; she needed help. She pushed the call button on the side of her bed. The nurses looked up from their station through the large glass window. Two came to Cathy's aid, assisting her to the bathroom. She sat on the toilet and defecated. When she urinated, it hurt. She stood up with the assistance of one of the nurses. Blood filled the toilet.

Cathy was escorted back to her bed. Dr. Hansen was informed of what the nurse had seen. One half-hour later, Cathy was under sedation back in the operating room. Dr. Hansen had run an endoscope into her rectum.

"There's the problem," he said. "The bowel wall has a small tear in it. I'm going to try and cauterize it." He worked diligently with his equipment. "There, it looks like we've got it. Increase her antibiotics to three times a day. I don't want to see an abdominal infection."

The operation took about forty-five minutes. Dr. Hansen removed his gloves and gown. He shook his head and said, "Poor woman."

Cathy was wheeled back into the recovery room. Her bed was five feet from Joann Jones. There was no curtain separating the two beds. The nurses had to have full view of both their patients through the large glass window from the station. Dr. Hansen retired to the hospital cafetiera for dinner. He was proud of the work he had done.

Chapter 59

The DC-3 pilots finished their coffee and burgers in the tiny cafeteria at the Hillsboro Municipal Airport. "Cab is here," shouted the waitress. The pilots left thirty dollars on the table. They got into the cab and asked if there were any better hotels in the area. The cab driver suggested the Big Crow Casino. "You can get anything you want there. I can have you there in an hour." The two pilots readily agreed; they had time on their hands. Jackson Hall had not booked them until 3:00 pm Sunday morning. They did not have to be back at Hillsboro Municipal until 2:00 tomorrow.

Their company, Calmer Air, was a small charter service based out of Modesto, California. The charter service had been in business for twenty-seven years, running several different types of aircraft. They had developed a reputation for not asking questions about destinations or whom they carried, so long as the premium payments were made for their services. Their pilots were instructed not to ask anything that might incriminate the company. "Load and Go" was the company motto.

The first plane Calmer Air had purchased twenty-seven years prior was a twin-engine Cessna. Arthur Anderson, the CEO, had big aspirations back in the day. When the banks would not fund his new company, he turned to a few people he knew, which eventually led him to Jesus Hernandez. Hernandez needed a way to get some of his shipments from Mexico back up to the States. The fledgling company was an opportunity, and both men saw the potential. Jesus came up with two hundred thousand dollars. It was a lot of money back

then, and Arthur was in business. The used twin-engine Cessna 425 was purchased for $180,000 at a government auction, and the extra twenty grand Arthur used as seed money.

Officially, Calmer Air was a charter service; unofficially, the business flew drugs into California. Calmer Air expanded over the years, hiring pilots that needed hours and knew how to keep their mouths shut on those special bonus runs. The pilots Jackson had hired were getting a one million dollar bonus for their flight on Sunday, all in cash. Sixty percent went to the pilot, forty percent to the co-pilot.

The taxi pulled up to the Big Crow Casino. "Here's two hundred," said the pilot. "Pick us up tomorrow right here at 1.00 pm."

"Yes, sir," the cabbie responded. "See you Sunday." The two men got out, each carrying wide leather briefcases. They were escorted to the front desk.

"Can I help you gentlemen?" asked the front desk clerk, Judith Manymoons.

"Sorry, we do not have any reservations," the pilot responded.

"Hmm," said Judith, "we are pretty booked with it being the long weekend. How long are you planning on staying?"

"Just one night," the two men replied.

"I can get you into a suite on the 10th floor. That is all I have. It's $2500.00 for the night."

The two pilots looked at each other. The co-pilot reached into his leather case, removing his wallet. He handed Judith the Calmer Air's corporate credit card. "Are you on business?" asked Judith.

The pilot responded, "Yes, we are. We turn around tomorrow afternoon."

"Well," said Judith, "I can give you the corporate rate of $2000.00."

The pilot asked her if she could charge the card $2500.00 and give them $500.00 in cash. "We would like to try out your casino. Just make sure the invoice reads $2500.00 for our accountants," he explained.

"Sure, no problem," Judith said. "I understand." The two men each received a plastic swipe card. The pilot took five hundred in cash, placing it in his front pocket. "The elevators are to your right. Have a good evening and good luck," said Judith.

The two men made their way to the elevators. The doors opened, and there stood Johnny Robbins dressed in his new outfit, his cowboy hat adjusted so you could not see his eyes. The two pilots got into the elevator with Johnny and pushed the button for the tenth floor. Nothing happened. Johnny swiped Jackson's card then pushed the button for the tenth floor. "Thank you," uttered the pilot.

"It's a secure floor," said Johnny.

"This is our first time here," said the pilot extending his hand. "I am Carl, this is Randy."

"Justin Wayne," Johnny said extending his hand. "Pleasure to meet you. You here for very long?"

"No," said Carl. "We fly out tomorrow at 3:00 pm." The elevator doors opened on the tenth floor. The men parted in opposite directions.

Johnny entered the suite he and Jackson Hall were to be sharing. "Fuck," he said aloud. Those two are the pilots Hall had booked to fly them out of Hillsboro

Sunday afternoon. He sat at the table for several moments, his head in his hands. Johnny looked around; he had to devise a plan to get rid of Hall's body. He needed to get the cash from the vault to a truck then onto the plane. The pilots now knew him as Justin Wayne. Johnny had fucked up; he needed to think this one through. There was one hundred million at stake.

Chapter 60

Cathy woke up in her bed in the emergency department, unable to recall falling asleep. The nurse monitoring her came in. "You did well," she said. "You came through with flying colors."

Cathy looked confused. "Dr. Hansen had to perform a small operation. You had a couple of ruptured blood vessels in your rectum. He cauterized them, and you are going to be just fine," said the nurse.

Cathy's memories of the events leading up to her being in the emergency department came flooding back. Tears formed in her eyes. "Thank you," Cathy mumbled.

Dr. Lewis, the hospital psychiatrist, walked into the room. The nurse pulled the curtain between Cathy's bed and the unconscious Joann. "I am Dr. Lewis," she said as she held Cathy's hand. "Dr. Hansen asked me to come and see you. It sounds like you had a bit of a setback a few hours ago."

Cathy nodded her head. "How are you feeling now?" asked Lewis.

Cathy looked at her through her one good eye. Her ear still throbbed from the events before. Cathy swallowed hard. "How do you think I am feeling? I have lost my husband and my son. I was raped by two criminals; they stuck a shotgun in my mouth. How the hell do you think I feel?" Cathy pushed Dr. Lewis's hand away.

"Would you like to talk about it?" Lewis asked.

"No," said Cathy. "Leave me alone."

"I will come back another time," said Dr. Lewis.

"Don't bother," said Cathy.

Dr. Lewis left the room, then went to the nurses' station. She filled out her report and added it to Cathy's chart. It read in part: severe emotional trauma, a possible threat to herself or others. Should be monitored closely for any rapid decline in cognizant function. Dr. Lewis signed, dated, and timed her report. She had seen several cases like this in her career. The victims never did recover fully. The trauma was just too great to whitewash the events her patients had endured.

The nurse walked back into the room. She opened the curtain so Cathy could be seen through the observation window. Cathy looked over at the woman in the bed next to her. Her wrists were in restraints. "What happened to her?" Cathy asked the nurse.

The nurse walked back to Cathy's bedside. "I am not supposed to say anything, but she tried to kill herself."

"Thank you," said Cathy.

An hour later, the food service cart was wheeled into the hallway outside Cathy and Joann's room. The attendant walked in with a tray. The food was covered in round sanitized white plastic covers. "Here you go," said the male food server. "Dr. Hansen took the liberty of ordering this especially for you." He placed the tray on Cathy's bedside stand. He adjusted it so the table was directly across Cathy's waist. "Try and eat," he said, "it will make you stronger. I will be back later to see how you did."

"Thank you," Cathy replied.

The attendant left another tray beside Joann's bed before he left the room. The smell of the food filled Cathy's nostrils. She fumbled for the button to raise

herself up. Her left arm was still hooked up to an IV line.

She grasped the remote and held it up to her good eye, pressing the button to elevate her torso. She looked down at the covers on the tray. The thought of food was making her sick; however, she knew she needed to get something into her stomach. She removed the covers: mashed sweet potatoes, gravy, pureed turkey, pureed cauliflower with cheese sauce. There was chocolate pudding with a container of skim milk for dessert. Dr. Hansen wanted to ensure nothing rough was coming down Cathy's pipes, destroying his work. The nurses watched through the window as Cathy worked at feeding herself. The smell of the food permeated the air in the room. It triggered something in Joann's brain. She started to stir. Her eyes opened. Joann stared blankly at the ceiling. Her mouth was dry, her throat was sore. Joann reached to touch her lips. Her hand, restrained and tied to the bed, rattled as she moved it. She tried the other hand. It too was tied to the bed. Joann looked side to side. She was in the hospital. Her thoughts turned to the news she had seen on her living room television; she started to sob. Cathy saw that her roommate was awake. She pushed the call button for the nurses. Soon, two nurses were attending to Joann. They elevated her torso so she was sitting upright. Joann asked for some water. The nurse put a straw to Joann's mouth. She drew the water in. It was cool and soothed her throat as she swallowed. "Thank you," Joann said.

The nurses left the room. Dr. Hansen was paged to the emergency department recovery area. His attempted suicide patient was awake. Hansen found his way back to Emergency. He reviewed the two charts for Joann and Cathy before entering the room. Dr. Hansen stood beside Joann's bed, introducing himself. "You gave us a bit of a scare," he said. Joann smiled. Hansen

said, "If it was not for the helicopter crew, things might have been different."

"Are these necessary?" Joann shook her restrained arms.

"Just for now," said Hansen. "I would like you to talk to our hospital psychiatrist, Dr. Lewis, before I order the restraints removed. Please understand where I am coming from. We pumped enough Oxy out of your stomach to kill a horse." Joann laughed. Dr. Hansen let Joann know her husband was on his way from Hillcrest.

"I do not want to see that bastard," she said. "He killed our son."

Dr. Hansen was taken aback by Joann's comment. "You take it easy," he said, "we will talk soon." Hansen made his way over to Cathy's bed. "It looks like someone has her appetite back."

Cathy looked at Hansen. "I would love some coffee," she said.

"I think I can arrange that," was Hansen's reply. "You did good," he said of the operation. "We stopped all the bleeding. We just have to watch what you eat for the next few days."

"I understand," said Cathy. "Thank you. How do you turn on that TV?" she asked.

Dr. Hansen left the room. Shortly thereafter, a nurse walked in with a remote control. "Here you go," she said to Cathy, handing her the remote.

Cathy looked over at Joann. "Do you mind if I turn on the television?"

Joann looked over. "No, go ahead," she said. "By the way, I am Joann."

301

"I am Cathy Taylor." The ladies sat upright, watching the Saturday night movie.

"We interrupt this program for breaking news." A large red banner flashed across the bottom of the screen. "The Sheriff's department, in cooperation with the FBI, has issued an alert for this man, escaped convict Johnny Robbins. It is believed Robbins is in the vicinity of Hillcrest, possibly Hillsboro." Cathy watched intently without saying anything. That was one of the bastards that had hurt her and Eric, she thought to herself.

"Sheriff's deputies killed his accomplice late this afternoon," said the reporter. A picture of Matt Jones flashed on the screen with the words 'shot dead.'

Joann screamed, "That's my son! My poor boy, my boy! He would never, ever do anything! They are liars!"

Cathy looked over at Joann. "Your son was shot and killed by the sheriffs today?"

"Yes, yes!" said Joann. "It was my husband's fault!" It was all perfectly clear to Cathy now. She now knew who her roommate was. Joann screamed again, "My boy, I love my boy! He would never do anything to hurt anyone!"

Cathy turned off the television. The nurses had paged Dr. Hansen that Joann was hysterical. He ordered the nurses to give her 3 mg of diazepam. The head nurse walked in, giving Joann the pill the doctor ordered with a mouth full of water. The nurse lowered the head of her bed so Joann now laid flat, her hands still bound to the bed rails. Cathy watched the whole drama unfold right beside her. She said nothing. The nurse left the room as Joann sobbed. Soon the warmth of the pill filled her body as she fell into a deep sleep. All was calm.

Cathy looked over, moving her tray as she climbed out of bed. She looked out at the nurses' station. One nurse sat monitoring a computer screen, maybe she was filling out a report; it did not matter. The others could be in another room. It was no concern to Cathy as she walked over to Joann's bedside, pulling her IV pole with her. Cathy removed Joann's pillow out from under her head. She placed the pillow over Joann's face and pressed it down over her nose and mouth using both of her hands. She whispered, "You gave birth to that motherfucker. You won't be giving birth to any more now, will you, you fucking bitch?" Cathy held the pillow and her hands in place until Joann stopped breathing. Cathy looked up; the nurse was still staring at the computer. She removed the pillow and placed it back under Joann's head. Cathy made her way back to her bed. She pulled the covers over herself, adjusting her IV line. She smiled as she started to drift off. Revenge felt sweet.

Chapter 61

Seamus and Shawn gathered a few things: a flashlight, two bottles of water, and a fully charged cellphone. "We will do our best as soon as we get a signal. Hopefully, we'll get through to someone. We will turn around and come back," Seamus said. He kissed his wife, Aileen. "Do your best," he said to Caitlin and Cathleen as they tended to Susan.

Her bleeding had now slowed; the girls had done a good job with what little they had. Susan still lay unconscious on the table inside RL01. "We will do everything we can for her. Hurry; she needs to get to a hospital."

Seamus and Shawn left the security and pandemonium behind them as they made their way down the trail running along the edge of Rock Lake. From time to time, the flashlight would shine on blood pools in the middle of the trail. "That poor girl," Shawn said. "She lost a lot of blood. It must have been a horrible thing for her to endure. It's up to us; we need to find a signal."

The two men continued down the path. The moonlight cast shadows in front of them. "What's that?" exclaimed Seamus as he pointed the beam from the flashlight toward an object. They were very close to the old Trapper's cabin. "It's just the old cabin," Seamus said as he continued with his friend. The beam of light caught something lying directly in the middle of the pathway. Seamus focused the beam of light; his eyes took a moment to adjust, Shawn stood beside him. The two men were looking at a backpack lying on its side. Rachel's head was visible, her legs jutted below the pack. The two men watched as Rachel's legs moved.

"Hello? Hello, Missy? Are you okay?" Seamus said in his thick Irish accent. The two men took a couple more steps towards Rachel. "Missy? Missy, are you okay?" Rachel's legs moved again. "She's alive!" Seamus said as he kept the light on the backpack. The men started to run towards Rachel, then stopped dead in their tracks. The light from the flashlight caught something on the other side of the backpack.

"What the hell," said Shawn.

The two men watched as the dominant male Grizzly's eyes reflected the light coming from the flashlight. It raised its head, its muzzle covered in blood. It had been laying behind the pack, feasting on Rachel's tender internal organs. The Grizzly stood up; something was hanging from its mouth. Rachel's legs moved again. As the bear was feasting and pulling on her internal organs, it moved Rachel's body. It had fooled Seamus and Shawn into thinking she was alive. The Grizzly was snapping its jaws. The two men started to take a few steps backward when they heard a noise behind them. Seamus quickly turned the light down the path from the direction they had just come.

There was a huge Grizzly walking in their direction. Seamus pointed the light back at Rachel's body. The other Grizzly was now standing over Rachel as it urinated on her corpse. The Grizzly the men first encountered was the one that had dragged Mark from the children's tent. It had eaten the sausage it tore from Mark's jacket and had been scared off by the two shots fired from Brad's M1911. It had ambled up the path and found a ready supply of food just laying there.

The large Grizzly behind Seamus and Shawn was the bruin that actually had attacked Susan and Rachel earlier in the evening. The two Grizzlies had fought

before over territory. The younger one behind the two men now walked with a limp from the last run-in he had with the older male. Both had scars from the fights they had in the fall over the Sow that had wandered through. The elder Grizzly had chased off the younger one, getting the hard-won right to pass on his bloodline. Now the older Grizzly was back, eating the meal the younger one was headed for.

Standing on the path, Seamus and Shawn were trapped; they had no place to run. The two men scrambled off the path into Rock Lake. Seamus dropped the flashlight as the men dove for cover in the freezing forty-degree water. The two Grizzlies charged at each other. The fight lasted for five minutes or less. The younger of the two males won this round. The elder male limped into the woods, still hungry; he did not have the strength to take on his rival this time. The territory now belonged to the younger male bear.

The two men did all they could to keep their heads above the water. Seamus was the first to start coughing as he sucked water into his lungs. He reached for Shawn, trying to keep himself afloat. The ice-cold water was sapping the strength of both men. Shawn desperately tried to break the grip Seamus had on him as he was forced underwater. The new hiking boots both men wore, plus their fleece clothing, weighed them down. They settled ten feet below the surface, their boots on the rocks. Seamus could see the moon through the clear water as he looked up, knowing he could not make it to the surface. Shawn was motionless. Seamus watched as the air from his lungs, lit by the moon, bubbled to the lake's surface. He tried to inhale. Water flooded his lungs. His body twitched once. The surface of Rock Lake became still.

The younger Grizzly went back to Rachel; he was

hungry. The moon shined brightly overhead. The boar had won the right to be the dominant male this time. He was going to get his fill.

Chapter 62

Johnny knew he had screwed up. It was imperative that he come up with some sort of plan. There was one hundred million waiting to be carried out of the hotel basement. He had until Sunday afternoon to get rid of Jackson Hall's body and get his money to the airport.

Johnny called down to the front desk. "Can I help you, Mr. Hall?" was the answer at the other end of the phone.

"This is Justin Wayne, Mr. Hall's friend. I was wondering if it would be possible to arrange an in-room massage."

"One moment, sir, I will put you through to the Spa." Johnny heard the phone click.

"Hotel Spa, Francis speaking, may I help you?"

"Francis, this is Justin Wayne. I'm calling from upstairs; the front desk put me through to you. I'm in room 1026. I was wondering..." Johnny paused.

Francis interrupted, "The front desk mentioned you would like someone to come up for an in-room massage. Is that correct?"

"Yes," said Johnny, "is that possible?"

"One moment, sir." The line went quiet. A few minutes passed, then Francis came back on the line. "Mr. Wayne, one of my girls was just finishing her shift, but she has agreed to stay. Her name is Barbara. She is very good and has been with us for five years. Would you like me to send her up?"

"That would be great," Robbins replied, "just

charge it to my room, please."

"Absolutely," said Francis, "is there anything else?"

"No," said Johnny, "thank you."

Johnny hid Jackson Hall's suitcase in the closet. He undressed, wrapping a towel around his waist, leaving his cowboy hat on his head. Shortly, a knock came to the suite's door. Johnny opened the door with a big smile on his face. There stood Barbara; she was maybe thirty years old. The uniform buttons on her white blouse were unfastened, so her cleavage was showing. Her auburn hair was long and pulled back in a ponytail. She carried a black duffle bag over her right shoulder.

"Howdy, little lady, I'm Justin Wayne," Johnny said. "What's your name?"

"I'm Barbara, may I come in?" She made her way past Johnny; it had been a long time since she had made a room call. They never went well. The guests always wanted more than just a regular massage. "Francis tells me you're looking for a full massage, is that correct?"

"Well, ma'am, it's been a long day. I need to relax."

"Tell me about it," Barbara said. "I was just getting off my shift..." She stopped herself.

"I understand," said Johnny. "Your line of work must be exhausting."

"It can be," Barbara said.

"I'll tell you what," said Johnny, using his best western drawl. "Since you're off your shift and decided to come and look after me, how about I make it worth your while?" Barbara looked at Johnny; she knew what was coming. "If you give me the best massage I've ever

had, I'll pay you $10,000 in cash. How does that sound?" Barbara had been propositioned before. It was always one hundred dollars. Once she was offered five hundred. No one ever offered her ten thousand. The subject of sex had not been mentioned. "How about it? The best massage I've ever had for ten thousand?"

Barbara looked at Johnny. "No sex, right, Mr. Wayne? If I got caught I'd lose my job, not to mention my self-respect."

"Sex?" said Johnny. "Who said anything about sex?"

Johnny took Barbara by the hand and escorted her to his bedroom. They stood on opposite sides of the king-size bed. Johnny started to fold down the sheets on his side. Barbara did the same on hers. Barbara opened her black bag, removing a large freshly pressed sheet. She laid it across the bed. "The hotel hates it if my lotions stain the regular sheets. I hope you do not mind?"

Johnny said, "You are the expert."

"Why don't you take your hat off and lay down in the middle of the bed?" Barbara suggested. Johnny removed his hat. He went one step further and let the towel from his waist drop to the floor. He stood in front of Barbara naked for a few seconds, just long enough for her to get a good look at his package. The bandages on Johnny's side were starting to come loose. Johnny climbed onto the bed; he laid across the clean sheet on his stomach. "Mr. Wayne," she said, "I am going to apply some oil to your body. You will feel it start to get warm as I start to work my magic."

"Please be careful of my side," said Johnny.

Barbara removed her runners, then straddled herself across Johnny's legs. She settled just below his

buttocks before she rested her weight down on him. Johnny felt the oil being drizzled onto his skin. Barbara let the bottle drop beside Johnny. She worked his neck muscles first, then his shoulders. The oil was warming; Barbara's touch was soothing. "How does that feel, Mr. Wayne?"

Johnny groaned as Barbara kneaded her fingers into his back. "Wonderful," said Johnny. "The lady downstairs said you knew what you were doing."

Barbara turned around so now she was looking at Johnny's legs. She applied more oil, working it deep into his muscles. She finished the backs of his legs and asked him to roll over. Barbara reached into her duffle bag, removing a large towel. She placed it across Johnny's waist, trying to be as professional as possible all the while trying to hide her excitement of making ten thousand dollars. Not to mention the fact Johnny was one of the most well-hung men she had ever seen.

Barbara climbed on top of Johnny. She lifted Johnny's head, placing a pillow under his neck. "What happened here?" she asked, pointing to the bandage on Johnny's side.

"Just had my appendix taken out a few days ago," he said.

"There," she said, "now just relax." Johnny closed his eyes. Barbara placed more oil on his chest and went to work with her magic fingers. Johnny could feel her nails from time to time as she pressed harder, working the oil deeper into his tissues. Johnny opened his eyes. He placed his hands on Barbara's hips. He looked at her; she stopped.

"I do not think it's very fair that I am the only one naked in the room," Johnny said. Barbara looked down

at Johnny, "besides, I know you have had a long day, I would like to return the favor. Maybe you will let me give you a massage?"

"Mr. Wayne, that is a very unusual request." However, she did not want to upset her client. She needed the money.

"Please," said Johnny.

"You cannot tell anyone," Barbara said.

"Who am I going to tell? Why would I ruin a good thing?"

"Do you have the money here?"

Johnny asked her to hand him is suit jacket. Barbara got off the bed, removing the jacket from the back of the chair. She handed it to Johnny. He reached into the left breast pocket, removing a bundle of one hundred dollar bills he had taken from the box in the basement. There was a bank band wrapped around them stamped $10,000 dollars. He reached into the right pocket, pulling out another bundle.

"That's twenty grand," he said. "It's for you if you let me give you a massage."

Barbara smiled. She reached for the elastic, holding her hair back, then removed it. She shook her head. Her hair flowed down past her shoulders. She removed her company blouse and black slacks. Barbara wore a white lace bra and an ultra small thong for underwear. Johnny noticed a small wet spot in the front of her underwear. Barbara climbed back onto the bed. Johnny rolled onto his side.

"Lay here," he instructed. "On your front."

Barbara complied. Johnny reached for the bottle of oil. He ran some onto her shoulders and neck, moving

Barbara's hair out of the way. He placed his hands on her neck, working his hands around until he found her Adam's apple. Johnny worked his fingers, pressing firmly. Barbara did not complain. Johnny unfastened her bra with one hand while working the oil into Barbara's skin.

"How does that feel?" Johnny asked.

"You have amazing hands, Mr. Wayne," she said. Johnny worked more oil into her back. Barbara moaned. "You have no idea how good this makes me feel." Johnny pulled her thong down, sliding it off her feet. He took the bottle of oil and applied a liberal amount to Barbara's ass. Johnny worked the oil into her cheeks and crack until he found what he was looking for. "Oh, Mr. Wayne, I am not that type of girl. I can't. My husband, what would he say?"

Johnny leaned forward. "I will not tell him if you don't," he whispered in her ear.

Barbara moaned. "I just don't know if..."

Johnny pulled Barbara up by her hips. She was on her knees, her head down in the pillow. Johnny spread her legs apart. He was hard. Barbara was not fighting to get away. Johnny slid his cock into her wet mound in one smooth stroke. Barbara gasped as she took Johnny's extra large manhood. He thrust deeply into her womanhood; Barbara pushed back. It was not enough for him. He took the bottle of oil, shoving the tip into Barbara's ass. She moaned. Johnny took two fingers, sliding them into her tiny hole. He could feel his cock moving deep inside her.

"Oh, Mr. Wayne, you are so big," she said.

Johnny removed his manhood from Barbara's quivering pussy and placed the tip of his cock on her ass.

313

Barbara reached back, spreading her cheeks so Johnny could have complete access. He slowly entered her ass. Barbara lifted her head from the pillow. Johnny reached for her hair, wrapping it around his hand. He pulled back so Barbara's neck was streached to its limit. Johnny thrust hard, pulling on her hair. Barbara pushed back, rocking her hips.

"You feel so good! Pull my hair harder, Mr. Wayne!" Johnny complied. He used both hands in her hair now as he pulled her head back. "I'm going cum!" Barbara said. "Give it to me harder!" Johnny thrust with everything he had. He exploded deep in Barbara's ass. "Oh, I can feel that," she exclaimed. "You are so hot." Johnny withdrew, rolling onto his side. Barbara lay on her side, looking into Johnny's eyes. "That was amazing," she said. "You give one hell of a massage," exclaimed Barbara.

"From now on you call me Justin," he said. He laid on his back. Barbara laid on hers, resting her head on Johnny's shoulder.

"I do not ever do this kind of thing," Barbara said. "I am not that kind of girl."

Johnny kissed her cheek. "It's okay," he said. "Your secret is safe with me."

Barbara laid beside Johnny. She opened up about her past, her job, and her family. Her husband was not working and had been laid off. He had not touched her in months. Her brother lived in their back bedroom. Between the two of them they barely had enough money to pay the rent and put food in the fridge.

"What does your brother do?" Johnny asked.

"He drives a delivery truck. He works for Crestview Foods. Sometimes I see him for lunch when

he delivers to the casino."

"How big is his truck?" Johnny asked.

"I don't know," Barbara said. "I have only seen it a couple of times. It has one of those roll-up doors on the back. Kinda like a truck you would rent for moving except it is refrigerated."

"He must work hard."

"Hardest working man I know," Barbara said with a laugh. "Tell me a little about yourself. Where did you get these tattoos, Justin?"

Johnny told her he was an investor. He and his business partner had come to move some files from the casino. However, his partner had been called away this evening on some urgent business. He left for New York on the 7:00pm connecter out of Hillsboro.

"That's too bad," Barbara said. "Do you have a lot of files to move?"

"There's just fifty boxes, about two feet by two feet in the basement of the casino. My company has to review the receipts to make sure we are being paid back what the Natives borrowed to build this place."

"Where do you have to take the boxes?" asked Barbara.

"Just to the airport. Then we will fly them to California. Our accountants go through everything and we bring them back putting them into storage."

Why don't the accountants just come here?"

"It could take months. To take them away from their families that long would not be fair."

"I understand. Family is important. I bet my brother, David, could help you."

315

"I'm leaving tomorrow. Maybe some other time." Johnny waited a moment, hoping he had done his job well enough that Barbara would take the bait.

"Let me call him," she said, jumping up from the bed. She left the bedroom. Johnny could hear some muffled conversation from the other room. Barbara came back into the bedroom with a smile on her face. "He has to pick the truck up in Hillcrest in the morning. But you have to pay for the gas. He said he will be here by 10:00am. Is that okay?"

Johnny smiled. "That is fantastic. I'll look after him."

"Now where were we? If you think that you're getting out of here without fucking me again tonight you have another thing coming, cowboy."

Johnny laughed. "Anything you want, little lady." He had a new plan and it was working.

Chapter 63

Kevin and his group sat around the campfire after enjoying their evening meals. It had been an interesting day. The park's service had landed their helicopter next to where they were camping. The Glacier Creek Campground had been a hive of activity today. Everyone speculated on what had been going on at the Angel Glacier site. Questions were being thrown in Kevin's direction. He did his best to deflect and speculate. After all, he was not there. He did not see what was taking place. All he knew was that whatever was taking place warranted intervention from the park's service. They would not have sent more wardens up to the Glacier and march everyone down past the campground if trouble had not been brewing. The conversation soon turned to the hotsprings and the black bears they spotted on the way back to the campground. "How old do you think they were?" asked Lisa.

"The mom had to be five, maybe six years old, the cubs maybe two weeks out of the den. Definitely a mature female, but she looked thin to me," Kevin said. Lisa played her video again on the screen of her phone. The exploding bear banger could be heard by all who could not see the image on her phone.

"Have you had to scare many bears away in the past?" asked Gale.

"Not really," explained Kevin. "Generally, a little shouting and making some noise will send them in the opposite direction. It's the bigger bears, the grizzlies, you have to be really cautious of. They are the kings of this jungle. You do not want to piss off one of those critters, and do not ever get between a mother grizzly and

her cubs. For that matter, any sow and her cubs. Out here, they will do whatever is necessary to protect their young. I have seen females fight larger male bears that have come too close to the babies. They do not give up, even when the odds are stacked against them in winning a fight."

"How long have you been coming up here?" asked Jerry.

Kevin responded, "Forty-plus years now. My father would bring us up here when we were young. His father, my grandfather, would bring him up here when he was a boy. My grandfather trapped in these woods before it became a national park."

"Your grandfather was a trapper?" asked Jerry.

"He was," said Kevin. "He and his friend, Joseph Manyguns, worked two lines in this area for years. They were pretty tough dudes being up here in the middle of winter." Kevin pointed to the washrooms. "They would laugh at the creature comforts the park's department has installed for the general public today."

Lisa piped up, "Do you think the park's department should not have put washrooms in for us to use?"

Kevin looked at her; he knew he'd said too much. "Not at all, times change," he said. The group sat around watching the flames burn down. Backpacks were rounded up and stored in the restrooms. It was midnight when Kevin finally crawled into his sleeping bag. It had been a long and busy day. He closed his eyes, drifting off into another world where he didn't have to worry about anything or anyone.

Chapter 64

"Holy shit, that was close," Tommy said, looking over at Brad. The girls were in their tents changing. Marcy was buried in Tommy and Donna's sleeping bag.

Brad nodded his head. He put his hand on top of Mark's head and rubbed his hair. "What did you think of that, little buddy?"

Mark looked over at Brad. "That bear had real bad breath. It woke me up, but I was okay. It was a little bumpy when he dragged me in the sleeping bag. I'm sorry, Uncle Tommy."

"What do you mean?" Tommy asked.

"I should have eaten all my sausages, but I saved that one."

Tommy looked at Mark and his torn jacket. "Do not worry. When we get back to town, Uncle Tommy is going to buy you a brand new jacket."

"Cool," said Mark.

Donna and Elizabeth soon joined their men and Mark around the fire. "What are we going to do?" asked Donna.

Tommy and Brad looked at each other. "When the sun comes up, you and Elizabeth are going to take the kids back to the staging area," said Brad. "When you get there, your cellphones should be in range so you can get a signal. You will need to get a hold of the park's department. Tommy's dad needs to get up here with the helicopter. We have to track that bear and make sure it has left the area. Tommy and I will head up to the cabins at the end of the lake to warn the folks up there. The bear

is probably long gone, but we have to be sure."

Elizabeth spoke up. "You want us to go alone back to the staging area?"

Brad looked Elizabeth in the eyes. He put his hand behind his back. "Here," he said, "you take Grandpa's gun with you. Just do not tell anyone you have it. It's illegal to carry it in the park."

Elizabeth took the M1911 from Brad's hand. "I will put it inside my pack."

"Just take one pack, leave everything here," said Tommy. "Travel light. Brad and I will figure a way of getting everything out of here. The sun will be up in two hours. Let's put some water on, make some coffee, and maybe some breakfast."

Brad and Tommy went and lowered the backpacks from the sling in the tree. The boys brought them over to the picnic table. By the time they got back to the fire, the pot of water was starting to boil. Brad took the bag of coffee from his pack then scooped a few handfuls of grounds into the boiling water. "This batch is going to be strong," he said. "We all need to be alert."

Donna and Elizabeth had talked while their men retrieved the packs. Elizabeth would take the lead, Donna the rear. Mark and Marcy in between them. If they came across any bears, Donna would take the gun out of the pack and hand it to Elizabeth; she would do the shooting. Her father had taken her to the gun club several times, teaching her how to use a 9mm, just like the one they kept under the cash register in the store. Tommy removed a can of bacon from his pack. He opened the lid and then placed the contents in a frying pan beside the boiling coffee. The young men scrambled up some powdered eggs. The girls toasted some bread on

the marshmallow sticks. Breakfast was ready in thirty minutes.

Tommy went to his tent to wake Marcy up. He opened the flap and peered in. Marcy was curled up in a ball crying. Tommy went inside and held her hand. "You are going to be okay," he said.

Marcy looked up at Tommy. "Did you see that bear?" she asked. "It could have eaten me. It almost ate Mark."

"I did see the bear," replied Tommy. "Uncle Brad saw the bear too. Let me explain what happened, honey. During the winter time, bears go to sleep in their dens for a long time. When they wake up, it's spring, and they are very hungry. That bear could smell the sausage your brother left in his pocket."

"He left a sausage in his pocket?" she asked.

"Yup, one from Friday morning when we stopped for breakfast. Remember he put two in his pocket?"

"I remember," said Marcy.

"Well, the silly bear could smell that sausage. He did not want to eat you or your brother. He just wanted that sausage he could smell." Marcy stopped crying. Tommy looked her in the eyes. "That bear had a pretty good sniffer. He took the sausage right out of Mark's pocket. The bear was only hungry, sweetheart. You would be too if you slept that long. Guess what?" exclaimed Tommy. "We made breakfast for all of us."

"Really?" she asked.

"You bet," said Tommy. "And when you're finished, then you girls and Mark are going to go to the Jeep so Auntie Donna can make a phone call. You will

be able to sleep in her apartment tonight. Maybe even have a nice hot bath with bubbles. What do you think of that?"

"I am hungry," said Marcy.

"Well then, little missy, let's eat. We have lots of things to do today."

Marcy and Tommy appeared from the tent. Everyone sat down at the picnic table. The air was cool, and the sun was rising in the east. The stars grew faint. Mark's torn jacket was the talk of breakfast. "Uncle Tommy is going to buy me a new jacket," he said.

"You bet I am, little buddy," was Tommy's reply. "Finish up your breakfast because you have some walking to do."

The four young adults and two children finished eating. "Do not worry about dishes," said Brad. "Tommy and I will look after everything." Brad pulled Elizabeth aside. "When you get in range with the cellphone, make sure you call the Ranger Station right away. We need Tommy's father up here with the helicopter. If that bear tore down one tent, it will do it again looking for more food. Tommy and I will track it the best we can. Tell the Ranger Station we went to the north end of the lake to warn the rest of the folks in the cabins." Brad kissed Elizabeth deeply. "Keep Grandpa's gun close, honey. I love you."

Donna and Elizabeth gathered the children. They hit the trail lightly and quickly.

Brad and Tommy sat at the picnic table, watching their loved ones head up the trail back to the staging area and Tommy's Jeep. "Holy fuck, buddy, that was a close call," said Tommy.

"I could hear the damn thing outside our tents,"

was Brad's reply, "it could have happened to any one of us. Thank God that sausage was in Mark's pocket, at least it focused on that long enough so you could get a couple of shots off. It could have been a lot worse. We need to warn everyone up at the cabins. Let's get these dishes out of the way and get everything back into the sling. We need to head out right away."

The boys packed everything back into the sling and hoisted it up into the tree. Tommy and Brad each found long two-inch round dead trees. They took them back to the campsite, trimming the branches off of each with Tommy's axe. Tommy cut his tree down to six feet; Brad's was maybe a foot longer. The boys pointed just one end with a few light chops with the axe. They both now could carry their homemade spears as they walked towards the cabins. Nothing would get closer than six feet. Brad checked to ensure his Buck Huntsman was tight in its sheath. He looked at Tommy.

"You ready?" he asked.

"Let's do this," Tommy said.

The two young men started up the trail leading towards the Rock Lake cabins. Brad looked at his watch; it was 6:10am. The boys stopped at the creek, filling their water bottles. They continued along the trail until the old trapper's cabin was in sight.

"What the hell is that?" asked Tommy, pointing.

There was a bundle of tinfoil in front of them. Brad knelt down; he picked it up and held it to his nose. "Fish," he said to Tommy. "I think this is what I gave that couple last night. Look here, do you see the blood? They must have tossed the foil away after eating the fish, but where are the bones?"

He and Tommy walked further up the path, and

they stood side by side as they came across Rachel's body. "Oh my God," said Tommy, "look at her." They were about twenty yards away. It took a second or two for everything to register.

"That looks like one of the girls from last night," Brad said. "The ones that did not want to talk to you or me. I recognize the pack." Blood covered the trail. Rachel's clothing and belongings were scattered everywhere. The young men walked slowly towards the body. Brad used the end of his spear to move a piece of torn clothing away from Rachel's stomach. Her body cavity was empty. "She has been partially eaten." Tommy vomited next to his friend. There was a blood trail leading up the path.

"I wonder where her friend is," said Tommy, wiping the corner of his mouth. Brad pointed with his spear. His father had taught him well in the art of reading signs.

"Up the path that way," said Brad, "it looks like she was being dragged. See here," he pointed to the marks leading away from Rachel's body.

"What do we do?" said Tommy. "We can't just leave her here."

"We have to," said Brad, "there is a maneater on the loose. I sure wish I still had my gun," said Brad.

"That would have made me feel a little better about things," said Tommy.

They continued up the trail towards the cabins. Brad noticed two sets of boot prints heading south.

Look here," he said, "someone was here last night." Tommy looked at the heavy prints in the middle of the drag marks left by Susan. The two young men continued down the pathway to RL01. They came out

into the small clearing. It was very quiet; no one was up yet. There was a blood trail leading to the stairs of the first cabin.

Tommy knocked on the door. "Hello? Hello?" he said. "Is there anyone there?"

The door flew open. It was Seamus's wife, Aileen. "Are you the doctors?" she asked.

"Doctors?" asked Brad. "No, we are not doctors. We just came to warn you folks about a bear."

Caitlin and Cathleen now stood with Aileen. "We have a girl in here. She was attacked. We sent our husbands, Seamus and Shawn, to get help. Where are they? Did they send you?"

"No," said Brad. "One of our tents was destroyed this morning. We chased off a very large grizzly. It ran up the pathway towards the cabins. We came here to warn you. We came across her friend," said Brad.

"How is she?" asked Caitlin. Tommy shook his head side to side. Brad had made his way up the steps. The young men could see Susan lying on top of the table inside the cabin.

"We are nurses," said Cathleen with her Irish accent. "We have done everything we can for her. If she does not get to a hospital soon, it will be too late."

"Did you see my husband?" Aileen asked again.

Briana was shaking standing by Susan. "My husband too, did you see him?"

"No, I am sorry," said Brad, "there was no one else on the trail." Tommy looked at Brad; neither one of them mentioned the boot prints they had seen. "We sent our girlfriends back to the trailhead. They are going to call the Ranger Station," explained Brad. "My friend's

father here flies the park helicopter." Brad looked at his watch; it was almost 8:00 am. He knew Donna and Elizabeth had at least another two hours before they made it to the Jeep and phone service.

"Have you seen any bears around here?" asked Tommy.

"No, nothing," the ladies said.

Susan started to moan; she was coming around. The voices had roused her from her unconscious state. She started to choke. Caitlin rushed to the table. She held Susan's head upright. "Do not move," she said. "You have been in an accident."

Cathleen held a cup of water to Susan's lips. "Drink," she said, "you need to get some fluids back into you." Susan started to drink the water, then gulped it down. She started choking again. "Just a little at a time. There you go, that's the way," said Cathleen.

"What happened?" asked Susan. Brad and Tommy watched from the doorway.

"You had an accident," said Aileen.

"No," said Susan, "there was a bear. A big damn bear. Where is Rachel?" Both boys were shaking their heads side to side.

"Seamus and Shawn have gone to look for her," Briana said, reaching for Susan's hand.

"Where am I?" asked Susan.

"In the cabin at Rock Lake. We are going to get you to a hospital."

"I am so cold," said Susan.

Donna kept checking her cellphone as Elizabeth and the children followed her. Its battery was getting

low. They were still an hour away from the Jeep when she held the phone over her head. One bar appeared on the screen. She dialed the number for the ranger station. There was a pause, and the line went dead. "Try again," said Elizabeth. Donna pressed redial.

It was 8:30 am on Sunday morning. Betty was tired but diligently back in the office early. She had let Bob sleep in, as he had a pretty full day on Saturday with the ice poachers. "Glacier Creek Ranger Station, Betty speaking," she said, answering the phone. The static was bad on the line.

"Betty, this is Donna Jones. I am Tommy's girlfriend." The static got worse. "There has been a grizzly bear situation." The line went dead. Donna tried calling again; her phone said no signal.

Betty wrote down what she had heard. She got on the phone calling Gunner.

"Chris speaking," he said, answering his cell. Betty explained the call. "I am about fifteen minutes away," said Gunner. "I know the kids were up at Rock Lake yesterday. Bob and I saw them. How did she sound?"

"The line was real bad," said Betty, "it was hard to understand her."

"10-4," said Gunner, "I will be at the office soon." Chris floored the accelerator pedal on his truck. He arrived at the Ranger station in ten minutes. He hit the brakes, then slid on the gravel into his parking stall. A small cloud of dust enveloped the surrounding area as he came to a stop. Chris ran into the office. "Betty!" he shouted, "have you heard any more?"

"Nothing," she said, "the phone has been quiet since I got the original call."

"Okay," said Gunner, "I am going to make a pass over there first thing just in case. I am sure everything is all right. I know my boy can look after himself and those with him." Chris grabbed his paperwork. He signed in, then reviewed the weather forecast quickly. He made his way out to the 505. Chris felt a sense of urgency but was not rushed. His military training had taught him to keep a calm head while under stress. Chris was not one to get flustered easily. He opened the door to the 505 and looked in the rear seat. Toby had put the emergency kit back where it belonged. Gunner nodded his head. He slid into the pilot's seat. "Good morning, girl," he said aloud. "Looks like we are going to have a busy Sunday."

Chapter 65

Johnny Robbins and Barbara made love two more times after she had called her brother. She left Johnny's suite at midnight. "I have to get home, Justin," she said to Johnny as she ran her fingers across the bandage on his side. "I had a wonderful time."

"So did I," said Johnny. "Can I call you sometime?"

Barbara gave Johnny her cellphone number. "Please," she said, "text me only. My husband likes to listen in on my phone calls."

Johnny added Barbara's number to Jackson Hall's list of contacts in his cell phone. "Thank you," he said. "I will give you a call when I meet with your brother, David."

Johnny placed his cowboy hat on his head then wrapped himself in a towel. He escorted Barbara to the door of the suite. She kissed him on the cheek. "Thank you, Justin. I am glad you were happy with your massage."

Johnny closed the door behind her; he had work to do. He quickly changed into his western clothing, gathered up what he needed - his duffle bag with the cash, gun, and taser - then made his way to the elevator. He swiped the black card then pushed the button to the basement of the hotel. Johnny was now alone. There were no security cameras in the basement. There was no need for them. Laundry, pool service, a maintenance room, and receiving of supplies were the only things that took place in the basement. The only security camera Johnny had to worry about was in the elevator.

Johnny made his way to the vault door. He entered the code 64729 then placed the large key into the slot, turning it slowly. The electronic lock hummed as the bolts in the door slid out of position. The door swung open. Johnny stood looking at an empty room. Jackson Hall's body was not there. The fifty boxes and all that cash were gone. Taped to the back wall was an envelope. A giant smiley face drawn in ink looked back at Johnny. Robbins removed the envelope from the wall. He opened it. Inside it read, "Dear Asshole. I have waited a long time to get to my money. The next time you try to kill someone, you're going to want to make sure they are dead. I faked it, I held my breath, you fucking prick. If you look above the door, there is a panic button. So if I ever got trapped inside my vault I could simply press it from within and the door would open. One of my own designs. Do you think I am stupid?" Jackson wrote. "By now the cops should be on to you. I look forward to reading about your state execution." Jackson Hall had signed the letter with the initials JH.

"Fuck, fuck!" said Johnny out loud; the sound of his own voice echoed off the bare walls in the vault. He turned, looking above the doorway, and a small button was just visible and bright red in color. He had been outplayed by his partner, his ex-partner. Johnny left the vault. He locked the door behind him. Johnny made his way back into the hallway. The chain and lock that had been around the handles on the doors leading to the outside stairway were now missing. Jackson Hall had gotten away with one hundred million in cash. If Johnny had been smarter, he would have at least gotten his cut of twenty percent. He had nothing, only the cash in his bag. The twenty grand he had taken from the vault he spent on Barbara. Johnny was pissed, his mind was racing. He adjusted his hat, pulling the brim down so his eyes could not be seen. He stopped in the hotel laundry

room, grabbing a fresh pair of blue coveralls. He rolled them up and placed them in a plastic hotel laundry bag. Johnny rode the elevator to the main floor. The doors opened. There were several state police and sheriff's deputies standing in the lobby, along with four FBI agents at the front desk. Johnny's first reaction was to run, but he played it calm. Johnny walked towards the casino entrance and scanned the room, locating the two pilots he had met earlier in the evening. He walked towards them. The men had just lost five hundred dollars at the blackjack tables. Johnny walked right up to them.

"How's it going tonight?" he asked.

"Not worth a damn," came the reply.

"Gentlemen, I believe this might be our lucky night," Johnny said to the two pilots. "My name is Justin Wayne, and I believe my partner, Jackson Hall, is the one that booked a flight with you tomorrow at 3:00pm." The two pilots looked at each other and did not say anything. Johnny looked them both over. "I have a proposal for you," he said. "Whatever your bonus is, I will double it." The two pilots looked at each other. The three men went to a quiet corner of the casino floor.

"Who the hell are you?" asked Carl, the captain.

"I told you I am Jackson Hall's business partner. Jackson had to leave early, some type of family emergency back in California. So, if you fellows trust me, I will double your bonus." Johnny tried to remain calm as he scanned the casino floor. The state police were walking into the gaming area. He had to convince the pilots to work with him; time was running out. "Gentlemen," Johnny said, "how about three million for 3:00pm? Does that work?"

Carl looked at Randy. The two pilots extended

their hands. "Three million at 3:00pm, Hillsboro Airport, sounds good to us." Johnny shook their hands and then exited through an emergency exit outside into the parking lot. Johnny made his way to the valet stand. He handed the attendant the tag for Jackson's convertible. Johnny watched as the attendant opened the metal door behind him.

"I am sorry, sir, we are a little short-staffed tonight. I will personally get your car for you." The attendant left his station. Johnny reached into the cabinet as soon as the valet's back was turned, taking the first electronic fob he got his hands on. Johnny slipped behind the waterfall with the Giant Eagle on top of it. He quickly removed his suit and then slipped into the blue coveralls he had carried from the basement.

Johnny placed his clothes and hat into the used laundry bag. He headed towards the parking lot, where he watched as the valet started the Mercedes. The convertible was quickly surrounded by FBI agents with guns drawn, screaming at the driver to put his hands out the window. Johnny pressed the stolen fob until he heard the familiar chirp of an alarm and saw the headlights flash. Johnny had stolen the keys for a grey BMW. He got in the car, started the engine, put it into drive, and headed towards the exit.

At the exit, there was one sheriff's car with a deputy standing outside, checking people as they drove out. Johnny pulled up to the sheriff, saying, "What a crazy night. Did you see that?" He pointed back to the big takedown happening in the parking lot.

The deputy nodded and asked, "Where are you going?"

"Car wash," was Johnny's reply. "Part of the service around here." The deputy waved Johnny through.

Johnny adjusted the rearview mirror as he headed towards the highway. He smiled and said to himself, "Stupid cops." He had a whole new plan, and it was working.

Chapter 66

Clifford, Donna's father, arrived at Metro General Hospital later in the evening. He had tried to find someone to look after Billy; however, everyone he knew seemed to be out of town for the long weekend. Billy had fallen asleep in the backseat as his father did his best to get to the hospital as quickly as possible. Clifford lowered the driver's side window about an inch so his son would have some fresh evening air. He locked the car and then made his way into the Emergency Department.

Clifford approached the front desk, where there were a half-dozen patients waiting to see doctors. One gentleman had his arm in a sling, and his hand was bandaged with rags soaked in blood. The receptionist asked, "Can I help you?"

"I am Clifford Jones, and I believe you have my wife here, Joann Jones. She would have been brought in by helicopter, an overdose," he said.

"Oh yes, Mr. Jones, please have a seat, and I will try to find the doctor for you," replied the receptionist. Clifford took a seat, one chair away from the guy with the bleeding hand.

Over the PA system came the page: "Doctor Hansen to ICU one, STAT." There was a flurry of activity down the hall, almost out of sight from where Clifford sat. The page went out again: "Dr. Hansen, ICU one, STAT. Code blue."

Clifford noticed several people running back and forth. Someone yelled, "We need a crash cart." Dr. Hansen ran to Joann's bedside and checked for a pulse.

There was none.

He opened her hospital gown, and with urgency, he yelled to the nurses, "Charge the paddles!" He placed the paddles on Joann's chest. "Clear!" he shouted. The nurses who had been forcing air into Joann's lungs stood back. Dr. Hansen shocked Joann. Her body jumped off the bed, but there was no response. Again, Hansen shouted, "Clear!" Joann's body jumped again. Nothing happened. "Give me the epinephrine," Dr. Hansen commanded. He removed the plastic cover from the needle and injected the lifesaving fluid directly into Joann's heart. He threw the empty needle to the floor, then grabbed the paddles. "Clear!" he shouted again, hitting Joann with the maximum amount of voltage the machine could put out. Her body arched, shook, and then lay limp. Joann's lips had turned blue. Hansen wiped his forehead, looked at the clock on the wall, and said, "Time of death, 11:56pm." He pulled the sheet over Joann's face and shook his head. "I just don't understand. She was doing so well," he muttered, while the nurses nodded in agreement.

Someone from the nurses' station came into the room and informed Dr. Hansen, "Dr. Hansen, there is a Mr. Jones here to see you. He is asking about his wife."

Dr. Hansen looked up and said, "Thank you." He made his way out of the ICU room, down the hall, and into the lobby. "Mr. Jones?" he inquired aloud.

Clifford stood up and extended his hand to meet the doctor's.

Dr. Hansen, speaking to Clifford in the hospital lobby, explained the unfortunate news: "I am Dr. Hansen. I was your wife's attending doctor. I am sorry. We did everything we could for her. She passed away about 10 minutes ago."

Clifford looked stunned. He hadn't expected to hear such news. Joann had been in and out of emergency departments before. "What happened?" he asked.

"I do not know," said Dr. Hansen. "She just stopped breathing."

"Can I see her?" Clifford pleaded.

"Follow me," said Hansen. The two men walked into the ICU, and Dr. Hansen pulled back the sheet so Clifford could see his wife.

Clifford kissed her on the forehead and whispered, "Oh, Joann, you finally did it this time." Tears filled his eyes. Despite the difficulties they had faced in their marriage, he still loved her in his own way.

"I am sorry for your loss," Dr. Hansen said. "Do you have any children?"

"Yes, we have... had three. One was killed yesterday. I think that's what pushed her over the edge," Clifford explained.

"My God," said Hansen. "That is terrible."

"Yeah," said Clifford. "Killed by the cops. He was a misunderstood kid."

Cathy, lying in the bed on the other side of the room, could no longer contain herself. She started to laugh. "I am glad they are both dead," she blurted out. "I am glad she is dead. The bitch got what she deserved."

"What do you mean?" said Hansen.

Clifford yelled at Cathy, "What are you saying!?" he shouted.

Cathy wanted to make sure both men knew she was responsible for Joann's death. "I held a pillow over the bitch's head. She can't have any more kids now, can

she?" She burst into laughter.

Clifford sat in the chair beside Joann's bed, his head resting in his hands. He looked up at Dr. Hansen and asked, "What the hell happened here!? Was no one watching over my poor wife!?"

Cathy continued her outburst, shouting, "Your poor wife? You motherfucker, you helped spawn the devil himself! An eye for an eye! I am God's willing servant!"

Dr. Hansen, alarmed by Cathy's confession, escorted Clifford to the nurses' station. "We obviously have a problem here," he said. "I need to call the authorities. I think we have a crime scene here."

"My God," said Clifford. "My wife was murdered in your care. I am going to sue this whole fucking place!"

Dr. Hansen had the head nurse call the FBI and the local Sheriff's office, requesting their presence at the hospital. He retrieved Joann's chart, changing the cause of death from "unknown" to "possible homicide," checking the box for an autopsy request. Dr. Hansen then made his way back to the lobby. Clifford was on the phone. Hansen stood back, allowing Clifford Jones some privacy while he spoke to the other party. After hanging up, Clifford approached Dr. Hansen.

"The FBI and Sherriff's department will be here soon," Hansen said. "They will want to question the two of us plus the woman in the bed next to your wife."

"I have to check on my son," said Clifford. "He is in the car sleeping."

"I understand. Do what you need to do. But the police will need statements."

337

Clifford left the lobby, making his way across the parking lot towards his car. He jumped in the air, clicking his heels together, a rare expression of relief amid the chaos.

He had just gotten off the phone with the life insurance company he had been making payments to for the last three years. Clifford had insured Joann's life a full thirty-six months earlier for two hundred and fifty thousand dollars. He had just been informed that murder was considered accidental death. Pending the insurance company's investigation, the policy contained a clause that paid double in the case of an accident. Clifford Jones had just fallen into a pile of cash. The agent said, "Someone will be in touch on Monday so they can complete the paperwork."

Clifford opened the driver's door of his car. He reached over and then shook Billy awake. His son stirred. "What? Are we here?" asked Billy.

Clifford looked at his son and smiled. "Your mother is dead, Billy. She passed away about half an hour ago."

"Oh, okay," said Billy. "Can I go back to sleep now?"

"Sure," said Clifford. "I have to go talk to the police." Billy did not comprehend what his father had just told him. The only thing that mattered was getting back to the dream he was having.

Clifford made his way back to the hospital lobby. He sat waiting for the authorities. Dr. Hansen had been busy with Cathy and the nurses. Cathy now lay in her bed, her arms restrained to the bed rails. She was shouting at Dr. Hansen, "Do you want to fuck me too!? Come on, you bastard, you want to fuck me!" Cathy's

338

mind had snapped. Two nurses had to hold Cathy's arm still as Dr. Hansen injected Cathy with midazolam. She instantly relaxed and then fell asleep.

Hansen looked at the two nurses. "Is there a full moon tonight?" he asked.

"As a matter of fact, there is," came the reply.

"Good," said Hansen. "I thought it was just me thinking this was a crazy night." Hansen took Cathy's chart. He signed paperwork to transfer her to the psychiatric ward, under the care of Dr. Lewis. The authorities could deal with her there. "Do not move the body," he said to the nurses. "The FBI will want to investigate this situation further."

Chapter 67

Brad and Tommy watched as Susan swallowed more water. "We are going to go to the other cabins to inform the rest of the people about the situation," Brad said.

"There are only two more people over on the other side of the lake, at the last cabin. A husband and wife," said Aileen. "If you see our husbands, let them know we are concerned and they should get back here right away."

"We will do that," said Tommy as the two young men made their way out of the entrance of RL01. "We will be back," they shouted.

Brad and Tommy made their way down the clearing past RL03. It was eerily quiet as they approached the last cabin on the west side of the lake. Brad walked up the stairs to RL04 and knocked on the door. David Smyth opened the door, rubbing his eyes. "Can I help you guys?" asked David. "Hey, you're the dudes from the other end of the lake."

"What's up?" Brad looked at David. "How was the fish?" he asked.

David paused for a moment. "You came all the way over here this early in the morning, woke me and Tammy to ask me about your stupid fish? We did not have any," he said in a stern voice. "The package you gave me was leaking all over the place, so I tossed it away."

"Where did you throw it?" asked Brad. "It's really important."

"Why?" asked David. "Did you lose something?"

"No," said Brad. "Where did you throw the package?"

"That old trapper's cabin or whatever it is, the one that is all falling apart," said David. "Somewhere around there."

Brad looked back at Tommy from the top of the stairs. Tommy spoke first. "There has been a bear attack," he said.

"What do you mean?" asked David.

Brad spoke next. "Someone is dead because of your actions," he said to David. "Her body is lying on the trail. Her friend was also attacked and could die. She is in Cabin number one."

Tammy now stood beside David in the doorway. "We had no idea," she said. "It was your fish. You should have eaten it or thrown it back into the lake. It's not our fault someone got hurt. We did not want your stupid fish in the first place."

Brad could see that he was going to get nowhere with Tammy. He walked down the stairs, standing beside Tommy he looked back. "You better hope the girl in cabin one does not die."

Brad got the information he had come for. The pieces of the puzzle had come together. David and Tammy threw the fish away. The bear found it. The two women came across the bear and fish. The bear protected its food source. It was that simple, well almost. Brad and Tommy started walking back to RL01, spears at the ready. "Can you believe what that bitch said?" Brad looked at his friend.

"No, I cannot. People need to be accountable for

their actions. She is in denial. They are the ones that just threw it into the woods. What the hell did they expect to happen? This whole thing is just one big clusterfuck right from the beginning. Maybe I should not have offered them our leftovers," Brad stated.

"It's not your fault," came Tommy's reply. "They are adults. They could have said no. Once they accepted your offer, they were responsible for what they took. It should have ended up in the garbage bin outside their cabin, not beside the trail."

The boys made it to RL01. In the distance, they could hear the sound of the 505's rotor blades cutting through the still mountain air. Gunner was fast approaching the campsite he had seen his son at the day before. He lowered the nose of the 505 then dropped down over the south end of Rock Lake. He spun the helicopter around so he was facing the campsite. The chopper hovered over the lake. The downdraft from the rotor blades kicked up water from the surface. The windshield was covered with water droplets, so Gunner had no choice but to turn on the wiper blades to clear his view. He held the 505 at 60 feet. He moved the bird from left to right, trying to get a better line of sight.

The campsite that had been bustling with activity and his son the day before was quiet. Nothing... there was no movement. One tent had collapsed, the other two moved from the wash of air coming from the 505. "Something is not right," Chris thought to himself. He turned the 505 so it pointed north. He added power then climbed over the mountain of rocks in the middle of the lake. He headed to the North end and the four cabins.

Standing on the shoreline were two men waving their arms; both carried what looked like large sticks, one had a t-shirt attached to its end. The t-shirt was waving

back and forth in a frantic fashion. As Gunner got closer, he could see that it was his son Tommy and his friend Brad. Tommy stood bare-chested, indicating that his father should find a place to land. Gunner knew that was impossible in this location. There was not enough room to set the skids down in the clearing in front of the cabins without the rotor blade hitting the buildings. He hovered at an altitude of 100 feet, looking directly at his son just 75 feet from the shore. The women from RL01 came running outside. Chris had a bad feeling as he watched the women waving frantically for him to land.

Tommy removed his boots and pants. Gunner watched as his son dove into the ice-cold water of Rock Lake. The cold water took Tommy's breath away as he surfaced. Tommy swam as quickly as he could; he made it 50 feet from shore before his arms started to get heavy. Gunner dropped the 505 just above his son, so the right skid was touching the surface of the water. Tommy used all his strength to climb onto the skid as his father held the 505 steady. Tommy held on with everything he had as his father turned the 505 towards the rocks in the middle of the lake. Gunner lowered the 505 over the rock island in the middle of the lake. Tommy climbed off the skid, he crouched as his dad set the 505 down on two flat rocks.

The helicopter was balanced precariously. His father backed off on the power as Tommy opened the 505's passenger door and climbed in. Tommy closed the door as his father applied power. Tommy grabbed the passenger headset and placed it around his ears. He adjusted the microphone as he looked over at his father. Tommy was shaking from the cold.

"What the hell is going on?" Chris asked his son as he turned the 505 back towards the north end of the lake.

"There has been a Grizzly attack," said Tommy. "There is a dead girl on the path. One girl is chewed up pretty bad. She is in the first cabin. She needs to get to a hospital bad."

"Are you and Brad okay? Where is everyone else?"

"We sent the girls and kids down to the staging area so they could make cellphone contact."

Chris nodded his head. "Donna got through to the station, but the call was bad." Tommy nodded his head. "How are we going to get her out of there?" Chris asked his son. "Can she walk?"

"No, Dad, she is in a real bad state, lost a lot of blood. The ladies there are nurses. I think they are from Ireland. They have looked after her all night. Their husbands went to get help."

"Roger that," said Chris. Gunner radioed into the office. He explained to Betty what had occurred, "Send the medics and ambulance to the staging area for Rock Lake," he stated. "I will not have enough fuel to make it to the hospital by the time we complete the rescue."

"10-4," was Betty's reply. "They are on their way."

Tommy was still shaking. The cold water had taken a lot out of him. Sitting in wet underwear did not help much either. "You're quite a sight, my boy," said Chris. "I am proud of you."

Tommy nodded his head. "Thanks, Dad."

"What is that over there?" Chris pointed to the raft the boys had made to get to the island.

"We put that together yesterday to get over to the island."

Chris nodded. "I have an idea," he said. "Reach behind you, in the emergency bag. How much rope is there?"

Tommy pulled out a coiled length of climbers' rope. "One hundred feet," said Tommy as he held it in his hand.

Gunner looked over at his son. "We are going to use your raft as a sling. I am going to set you down on the raft. You tie the rope to both ends, then attach it to the hook under the helicopter, the one we use to drop the bears. Stay on the raft. I will take you back to the cabins. You and Brad get the girl onto the raft. I will fly her to the staging area. Sound like a plan?"

Tommy nodded his head; his adrenaline had kicked in. Gunner hovered the 505 over the wooden raft. His son opened the door as it vibrated on its hinges from the main rotor's downdraft. Tommy climbed out with the rope. His father moved the helicopter away as his son fastened both ends of the rope to the raft.

When he had finished, Tommy stood with a loop of rope in his hands. If everything worked according to plan, the raft would hang about 20 feet below the 505. Tommy stood with the loop in his hand as Gunner lowered the helicopter just above his son. Tommy reached up, clipping the loop of rope into the hook in the belly of the helicopter. Gunner applied power, and Tommy laid flat on the logs as the 505 lifted the raft and Tommy from the surface of the lake. The raft started to turn under the helicopter, but it was staying in one piece. Brad and Tommy had done a good job lashing it together.

Chris took it easy as he made his way back to the cabins. He flew at a height of one hundred feet, just in case the whole works fell apart and his son ended up back

in the water. The 505 arrived in front of RL01, the raft twirling in the wind. Tommy looked over the edge, Brad was looking up. Chris lowered the 505 so his son could step off into waist-deep water. Tommy made his way to shore as his father hovered the 505 in position. Tommy looked at Brad. "We have to get her onto the raft. Dad will take it from there."

The four women, Brad, and Tommy rolled the now unconscious Susan into a sleeping bag. They zipped it up. Tommy removed two shoulder straps from one of the backpacks in the cabin. He held them firmly in his mouth. "On the count of three," said Brad. "We all lift at the same time." The six of them had no issue lifting the 130lb Susan from the table and out the cabin door. They carried her to the water's edge. Brad removed his clothing. The boys stood looking at each other for a second. Tommy looked out at his father. Water was being sprayed everywhere from the downdraft, the raft turned on the rope like a spinning ride at the fairgrounds. Tommy raised his thumb in the air. Brad took one end of the sleeping bag, Tommy the other, as they carried Susan into waist-deep water. They approached the raft. Tommy used his body to stop it from spinning. It almost knocked him over when it made contact with his side. Gunner lowered the raft to the surface of the water. The two young men slid Susan onto the raft. Tommy used both shoulder harnesses to tie Susan down to the logs. That way, she would not slip off the makeshift gurney during the flight down to the staging area. The boys stood back so Gunner could see them. Tommy and Brad raised their thumbs into the air. Chris applied power to the 505's engine, then climbed away from the cabins. David and Tammy had watched the whole event unfold from the front step of cabin four. They never lifted a finger to lend a hand. The 505 moved slowly south, the raft moving in circles. Eventually, the helicopter was out of sight.

The two young men stood waist-deep in the freezing water, wearing only their briefs. The four women from Ireland stood on the shore, watching Tommy and Brad high-five each other. They were numb, cold, and exhausted, but both had smiles on their faces. The boys made their way out of the water. The ladies invited them into the cabin so they could dry off and warm up beside the woodstove. As they gathered their clothing and boots, Brad looked over at RL04; the door was now closed, and David and Tammy were nowhere to be seen.

Gunner had no choice but to take his time. The raft spun under the 505 and also moved like a pendulum. He could not take any more risk than he already had. The fuel monitor on the glass display in front of him showed 1/3 full. He still had 15 minutes ahead of him to make it to the Staging area. "It's going to be close," he said to himself.

By the time the 505 had made it to the emergency helipad at the Rock Lake staging area, emergency services had arrived. The two attendants had cleared an area in the parking lot close to their ambulance. Chris lowered the makeshift gurney containing Susan right in the middle of the parking lot. He pressed the switch that worked the hook release, dropping the rope into the EMTs' hands. He swung the 505 around and set it gently down on the emergency helipad. He looked at the fuel gauge; it read less than 1/4. Before shutting down, he radioed headquarters. "I am going to need a fuel truck up here," he explained to Betty. "I just do not have enough to make it back to Hillsboro." Betty confirmed that she would send someone out.

Four wardens had been dispatched to Rock Lake to close off the area. They needed Gunner back in the air if they were going to track down the Grizzly. "Roger

that," said Chris. "I am not going anywhere for a while." He shut down the 505. Chris stepped out of the helicopter, making his way to the parking lot.

Donna, Elizabeth, Mark, and Marcy met him by the raft. Donna gave Chris a great big hug. "Boy, do we have a story to tell you," she said.

"It sounds like it," said Gunner. "I am glad you are all safe and sound." The ambulance pulled out of the parking area, siren and lights flashing. "Tell me what happened."

Chapter 68

Johnny Robbins was furious. He had made a mistake, perhaps his belt wasn't tight enough when he strangled Jackson Hall. He replayed the entire scenario in his mind as he sped away in the grey BMW. "Fuck me," he muttered to himself, "a hundred million dollars on the line, and what if that son of a bitch doesn't show up at the airport?" How would he pay the pilots? It didn't matter now; he was determined to find Hall and get his money. He still had a hundred grand in cash left in his duffle bag. There was also the money in the safety deposit box reserved for a rainy day. He should have been a millionaire many times over by now.

Johnny had let his dick overrule his better judgment. He should have followed his father's advice: never trust anyone. How could he have been so foolish? Johnny slammed his fist against the steering wheel in frustration. He reached into his pocket and pulled out Jackson Hall's cellphone, scrolling through the contacts until he found Barbara's number. He sent her a text message: "Had a wonderful time, but sorry, I have to cancel on your brother. Something has come up. Please apologize for me. Thanks, Justin."

A few minutes later, he received a response. "Are you okay? Can I help?" Barbara asked.

"Not okay," Johnny replied. "Meet me at Elli's Diner at 8:00am. I'll explain everything in the morning."

Johnny found a secluded spot by the side of the road and parked the stolen BMW under the branches of a large ponderosa pine tree. He reclined the driver's seat as far as it would go, turned off the ignition, and laid his

349

head back on the seat. He needed some sleep and a new plan.

Chapter 69

Jackson Hall's neck was sore, and his eyes were bloodshot when he woke up on the floor of his vault. It was pitch black, and he couldn't see a thing. His phone and wallet were gone. Jackson fumbled around in the darkness until he found his lighter. With a flick of the igniter, the room came to life with a faint orange glow. He could see the fifty boxes containing his one hundred million dollars right in front of him. Reaching over the doorframe, he found the panic button he had installed when the saferoom was built and pressed the red button. The door locks released, and the door swung open on its own. Fluorescent lights flicked on, illuminating the room.

Jackson closed the lid on his lighter and placed it back in his pocket. All the boxes were intact, except one. Two bundles of hundreds were missing from the neatly packed bills. Jackson knew he had to act quickly. He didn't know how long it would take for Robbins to reappear, but he presumed that Johnny would be in the casino, spending Jackson's hard-earned cash.

Jackson Hall stepped out of the saferoom and placed a chair in front of the door so it wouldn't close. He made his way to the maintenance room and picked up the receiver of the black phone hanging on the wall. Jackson pressed 0, and a voice from the front desk answered.

"May I speak to Judith, please?" Jackson asked, his voice somewhat hoarse.

"One moment," came the reply. The line went silent for a few moments, and then Jackson heard a click.

"Judith speaking."

"Judith, this is Jackson Hall. I checked in a while ago. I need a favor. There are some boxes in the basement I need to move. Do you know anyone with a truck?" Jackson inquired urgently.

There was a pause. "You're in the basement, Mr. Hall?"

"Yes," replied Jackson.

"I will check with the valet service..."

"No," said Jackson. "This has to stay between you and me. I will make it worth your while."

"How many boxes do you have?"

"Fifty."

Judith thought for a moment. The small rental car company that maintained a desk in the hotel lobby always kept a small one-ton moving truck in the back corner of the hotel's lot along with their regular rentals. The truck was popular with the folks on the reservation.

"When do you want to move the boxes?" she asked.

"Right away," said Jackson. "It's very important."

"Okay," said Judith. "The small rental car company in our lobby has a small moving truck with a roll-up door. They keep it here, but they are closed right now. I will call you right back. I have an idea."

Judith promptly called the manager of the budget franchise.

"Hello?" responded Casandra, the manager of the franchise.

"Casandra, this is Judith Manymoons. I am sorry to wake you, but we have a bit of an emergency. We have a client that needs the moving truck right away. Is there any way?"

"You woke me up because someone needs a moving truck at this time of night?"

"He says he will make it worth your while. He's a bigtime player and developer."

Casandra thought for a moment, clearing the cobwebs from her mind. "The contracts are in my top drawer. Make sure you photocopy the guy's license and credit card. The keys for the van are hanging behind my desk in the locked cabinet. The extra cabinet key is taped under the right top drawer. You let this guy know that the rate is double the usual $19.95 an hour."

"No problem," said Judith. "I will make sure when he returns, the tank is full again. I am sorry I woke you up. Goodnight."

Judith called the extension Jackson had used to contact her. The phone rang once.

"Hello," said Jackson.

"Mr. Hall, this is Judith. I managed to get through to the manager of the rental car company. She said you can use their small moving truck, but it will be double the rate. It works out to $39.90 an hour. Is that okay?"

Jackson laughed. "That is just fine. Can you bring the truck around to the basement's exterior entrance? Someone is going to have to unlock the chain on the doors. Oh, and Judith, can you ask a couple of your coworkers you trust to come downstairs? I will need a hand putting the boxes on the truck. There is a hundred dollars each for the guys who want to help. I don't think it will take any longer than twenty minutes with the four

of us."

Judith did not want to disappoint the most valuable client the casino had. "I am just going for my break," she said. Judith promised she would bring the truck around to the basement entrance herself.

"I will have a couple of my friends come down and help you, Mr. Hall." Judith clocked out for her break. She went to the rental car booth then retrieved a contract and keys for the moving van. Judith went outside to the valet stand where she waited for two of her closest friends, Hank and Irvin. The two young men came from around the edge of the waterfall wearing their blue coveralls, smelling of marijuana.

"Do you guys want to make an extra hundred bucks?" asked Judith.

"Sure," said Hank. Irvin nodded his head.

Judith handed Hank the key for the locked doors in the basement. "Mr. Hall will meet you by the doors. You make sure you treat him with respect. Open the doors up and wait for me," she instructed the two young men.

Jackson Hall made his way back to the chained doors. He quickly grabbed a bundle of hundreds from the open box Johnny Robbins had so kindly pried open. Jackson placed $10,000 in cash in the breast pocket of his suit. He waited in the basement corridor by the chained doorway. Ten minutes seemed like two hours for Jackson Hall. Finally, he heard voices and saw two men approaching in his direction.

"Mr. Hall?" asked Hank.

"You found me, gentlemen," said Jackson. "Judith said she would send two of her best guys."

Jackson could hear the truck pulling up to the entrance outside. Hank put the key Judith gave him into the lock that held the chain in place around the door handles. He quickly removed the lock and then the chain from the doorway. Irvin pushed the large panic bar down, opening the first exterior door. The fresh cool evening air rushed inside. Hank opened the second door and used his foot to kick down the door stopper so it would not close. The three men looked up a flight of eight concrete stairs. Judith stood at the top.

The truck was right where it should be, with the rear roll-up door within easy reach. Judith made her way down the concrete stairs. "Good to see you again, Mr. Hall."

"Good to see you too, Judith. Thank you so much for your assistance this evening. Let me show you what I need to move." Jackson walked ahead of his three assistants. He entered the vault first. Jackson grabbed the open box, holding it close to his chest, as he placed his chin on top of the flaps so no one could see inside.

Judith spoke, "I did not know this room was here."

"These are my old company files," Jackson exclaimed, his chin moving across the top of the box as he spoke. "They are very confidential. Let's get them loaded up." Hank reached for the box Jackson was holding. "That's okay, son," said Jackson. "I have got this one." The two young men each took a box and carried them up the stairs to the back of the waiting van. Jackson carried the open box up the stairs to the front of the cab. He opened the door and placed his box on the driver's seat.

He turned and found Judith right behind him. "The manager asked me to get a copy of your credit card

and driver's license."

"No problem," said Jackson, reaching for his wallet. "Oh damn," he said, "I must have left my wallet in the room. I will meet you back at the front desk, Judith."

"Sounds good, Mr. Hall. My break is almost over, and I do have to get back to work."

"See you in a bit," said Jackson. "Oh, Judith, this is for you." Jackson handed Judith ten one-hundred-dollar bills. "Your customer service has been exceptional this evening."

"Thank you, Mr. Hall," Judith said.

She made her way back down the basement stairs and shouted out to Hank and Irvin as she headed to the elevator. "Don't forget to chain and lock the door when you're done! Bring me the key!"

"Yes," said Hank.

The young men had the 49 boxes out of the basement and onto the back of the truck in twenty-three minutes flat. It was just enough time for Jackson to write his note to Johnny Robbins, leaving it in the vault for him to find. Jackson smiled as he closed the vault door. He shook the hands of the two young men who had just assisted him. He handed each a one-hundred-dollar bill and then gave them both two hundred more as a bonus. "Gentlemen," said Jackson, "thank you for your help. My accountants will be happy."

Jackson made his way up the concrete stairs. The doors closed behind him, and he heard the chain being wrapped through the handles. The evening air felt good in Jackson's lungs as he moved the open box onto the passenger seat. Jackson jumped behind the wheel of the running truck. He placed the shift lever into the drive

position and then pressed down on the accelerator pedal. Jackson smiled, "Fuck you all," he said aloud as he drove out of the casino parking lot and into the night air.

Jackson made his way to the nearest truck stop, where he made a twenty-second anonymous call from a payphone to the FBI. "Johnny Robbins was seen at the Big Crow Casino," he said before hanging up. Jackson then bought himself a cup of coffee, plus a burger and fries to go. "Do you folks sell those disposable cellphones?" he asked the clerk.

"We do, sir, but I only have this one left. It is pretty expensive. But look, it has a camera."

"How much?" asked Jackson.

"It is four hundred dollars," said the clerk, "with two hundred anytime minutes."

"I will take it," said Hall. Jackson left the counter area with his purchases. He walked back across the parking lot and jumped back into the moving truck. Jackson sat eating his burger while sipping on his coffee. He noticed four black sedans speeding down the highway towards the casino, followed by four local sheriff's cars with their red and blue overhead lights flashing. Jackson started the moving truck and then drove out onto the highway. "Fuck you all," he said aloud one more time. He was sitting on one hundred million in cash. It was time to implement his ultimate plan.

Chapter 70

Brad and Tommy were feeling pretty good about themselves. They had hopefully helped save Susan's life. Now, at the very least, she had a fighting chance after the Grizzly had mauled her. The two young men stood shaking on the shore of Rock Lake. Aileen, the wife of Seamus, invited Brad and Tommy back into Cabin One, where they could warm up by the woodstove.

"Come in," she said, "dry off and get dressed. You boys deserve a nice warm breakfast. How does scrambled eggs, pancakes, and sausage sound?" she asked.

"Awesome," said Tommy, "I am starving."

Brad and Tommy stood by the woodstove inside Cabin One. Aileen and the other ladies were rounding up the ingredients for breakfast. Briana wondered aloud about the whereabouts of Seamus and her husband, Shawn.

"We will have a look for them on our way back to our campsite," said Brad. "It's strange that we did not see any signs of them. Mind you, we were a little preoccupied with the events that were unfolding."

"You don't think..." Briana began.

Brad interrupted Briana, "No, don't worry, they will be fine. I bet they are at our campsite looking for us."

"Well, please, when you see them, please tell them to come back."

"They would have seen the helicopter and heard it," said Tommy. "Hard to miss that."

The men dressed as soon as they had dried off. Caitlin had poured each a cup of coffee. It was strong and had been on the stove all night. Aileen put her frying pan on the stove and browned up some sausages, all the while talking about the events of the evening. The table in the cabin was still covered in Susan's blood.

"She is one tough lady. What she and her friend went through, I do not think I could have survived that," said Aileen. "You boys are heroes."

"No," said Brad, "we just did what was necessary to get her on the helicopter. You ladies looked after her and dressed her wounds long before we got here. You're the heroes."

"Well, let's just hope she will make it." Aileen removed the sausages from the frying pan. Brad and Tommy sat on the front steps of RL01. They sipped their coffee while the ladies prepared the rest of the breakfast. When the pancakes and eggs were done, Briana carried out two paper plates, each containing two sausages, a pancake, and scrambled eggs. Everything had a nice coating of Canadian Maple syrup drizzled evenly across its surface.

A plastic fork was tucked neatly under the edge of the pancake on each plate; the handles hung in the air, waiting for someone to engage them.

"Here you go," Briana said.

"Thank you," came Tommy and Brad's replies.

The four ladies came outside with their plates in hand. Aileen spoke first. "What is the next step?" She looked at Brad. "Is that helicopter coming back?"

Brad looked at Tommy. Tommy said, "That pilot is my father. By now, he has gotten that lady to an ambulance or hospital. They will be sending some park

359

rangers this way to escort you all back out to the staging area. Unfortunately, as you know, we have no phone service here or radios. All I can tell you is that would be normal protocol in a case like this. The trail to Rock Lake will be closed. They will hunt the Grizzly responsible for the attack and dispatch it. They will autopsy its carcass. You ladies will have to stay here until help arrives." Tommy looked at his watch. "I expect that help will arrive by 3:00pm this afternoon, no later than that."

"We have to walk out of here?" asked Briana. The ladies all looked at each other. "What if the bear comes back?"

"Don't worry," said Brad, "the wardens know what they are doing. You will get home safely. Just do not leave this area until help arrives."

"We will stay put," said Aileen. "You can count on that."

"Brad and I will head back to the south end of the lake. We have to pack up our stuff. We will join you and the rangers on the hike out later today." Brad nodded his head. The young men finished their coffee.

"Thank you so much for breakfast," said Tommy. "I did not realize how hungry I was."

"Me either," came Brad's reply.

"Well, we should be heading out. There is a lot to do before help arrives. We will see you later." Brad and Tommy stood up from their positions on the steps of Cabin One. They shook the hands of the ladies then said their goodbyes. The two young men made their way back down the same trail that brought them to the cabins. It would take them south, back through the area where the attack had occurred, and to their campsite. They carried their sharpened poles; each felt nervous, but neither said

360

a word. After all, they were part of the search and rescue team, and they knew what they were doing.

Chapter 71

Susan woke up in the back of the ambulance. The IV fluids the EMTs had started in her left arm were working. "Where am I?" she asked the attendant sitting beside her. "I cannot see out of my eye." She reached for the bandages the nurses in the cabin had wrapped around her head.

The EMT touched her on the shoulder. "Just leave that in place for now," said the EMT. "We are going to get you to Hillsboro General. You are in an ambulance. There was a bear."

Susan nodded her head. "I remember," she said. "It hurts so much." Susan started to shake. Her body was in shock. The EMT radioed into Hillsboro General with Susan's vitals.

The EMT was instructed to inject three cc's of morphine into the IV line. "This will make you feel better." Susan watched as the EMT injected the IV line. She felt warmth in her arm, and soon it spread throughout her body.

She closed her eye as a tear ran down her cheek. "Thank you," she mumbled.

The ambulance made it in record time to the emergency department at Hillsboro General. Dr. Steven Hobbs was on duty. The staff waited for the EMTs to wheel Susan into the Emergency Department. Dr. Hobbs stood with his gloved hands in the air as Susan was brought in on the ambulance stretcher.

"Get her on the table now!" Hobbs shouted as the EMTs moved her from their gurney. He took one look at her and knew instantly that the injuries she had sustained

were well beyond his capabilities. "Call for Life Flight!" he instructed. "This girl is going to need reconstructive surgery. We need to get her to Metro General. Get me a blood type STAT!" he yelled.

Dr. Hobbs looked at the plastic wrap surrounding Susan's midsection. The anesthesiologist arrived as Hobbs triaged his patient. "She has had 3ccs of morphine," Hobbs said.

"Okay," said the anesthesiologist. "Let's keep her in a champagne state. We do not want her too far under." He placed a mask over Susan's face.

Dr. Hobbs cut away the plastic wrap from Susan's stomach. The gash opened, exposing her intestines. "Flush this," he instructed the nurse standing beside him. The nurse used saline and a red rubber squeeze bulb to follow the doctor's instructions. "I don't know who looked after this girl initially, but they saved her life." Hobbs called for the surgical stapler. He put two clamps on either side of the wound. "Pull these together," he instructed the nurse. Hobbs used his fingers to push Susan's internal organs back into position as he ran staples up the shredded skin.

A nurse came back into the operating room. "We have type O," said the nurse.

"How many units do we have?" shouted Hobbs.

"Three," came the reply.

"Start a unit now!" Hobbs instructed. "I want a line of antibiotics as well. Find another vein." The operating room was a flurry of activity. "Let's look at that leg," said Hobbs.

He cut away the bloodied field dressings. The flesh from Susan's calf muscle hung by a tendon. There was no skin left around the open wound. "Moisten some

pads," he instructed. "Wrap this back up." He cauterized a couple of bleeding vessels. "She needs a substantial graft. This is not looking good."

Hobbs then turned his attention to the plastic wrap and towel on Susan's head. He cut away the plastic wrap. The towel and blood had dried to Susan's hair and skin. "Saline!" he shouted. "Come on, we do not have all day!"

Administration came on the PA system. "Life Flight just called in. They will be here in ten minutes."

Hobbs removed the now blooded wet towel from around Susan's head. Her scalp peeled back as some of her hair remained stuck to the cotton fabric of Seamus's shirt.

"Scissors!" Hobbs shouted, holding the towel in his hands. "Cut the hair!" he instructed the nurse. "That's it, perfect." He threw the towel to the floor. Susan's eye hung from her socket. "Flush the orbit," he said. White pus oozed from the opening. "Flush the skull." The nurse saturated the open wound on Susan's head. "Look at that," said Hobbs. "You can see the scrape marks from the teeth across the top of her skull." Hobbs pulled the scalp back into position. "Stapler," he said, placing a small plastic cup over Susan's protruding eye. "Let's wrap her up," Hobbs said.

The PA system crackled again. "Life Flight is two minutes out." The anesthesiologist looked at Hobbs.

"Discontinue the General," said Hobbs. Dr. Hobbs stood back, folded his arms across his chest, looking directly at Susan. "Good job, everyone. We have done what we can for her here. Where are those other two units of whole blood? I want them going with her." The sound of the Life Flight helicopter could be heard

inside the hospital. "Let's get her to the helipad."

The EMTs from Life Flight stood outside the operating room beside their specially designed gurney. One of the nurses pressed a red button on the wall, opening the doors to the operating room. Susan was gently transferred to the helicopter's gurney. Dr. Hobbs signed off on her release and included the chart for what he had done. The two bags of whole blood were placed in a cooler and handed to one of the EMTs as Susan was wheeled out of the surgical suite and then into the waiting chopper. Susan's stay at Hillsboro General lasted a total of forty-seven minutes.

Hobbs stood, looking at the mess in the surgical suite. The PA system crackled. "Dr. Hobbs to emergency room two." Hobbs had barely enough time to remove his bloodied gown and gloves before he was summoned again. Hobbs walked into Emergency room Two. There sat Tamika Mills. Her finger was wrapped in Kleenex.

"How can I help you?" asked Dr. Hobbs.

"I cut my finger with a kitchen knife," she said.

"Let's have a look," said Hobbs as he unwrapped the Kleenex. "It looks like you're going to need a couple of stitches."

"It hurts so much," said Tamika. "Will it leave a scar? I think I am going to pass out."

Dr. Hobbs took a hypodermic needle with some local anesthetic and injected it around the cut on Tamika's finger. He smiled and could hardly contain himself as he placed two stitches across the tiny cut. "There, there," he said. "It's all better now."

Tamika looked down at her finger. Dr. Hobbs wrapped the finger in a quick layer of gauze. "Do you think I need a sling?" asked Tamika.

Hobbs looked at her and replied, "No."

"What kind of emergency room doctor are you?" shouted Tamika. "My finger feels like it's going to fall off."

Hobbs wrote her a prescription for Tylenol-3 and left instructions to soak the wound in hydrogen peroxide starting the next day. "Good luck," said Hobbs. "Your regular doctor can remove the stitches in 14 days." Hobbs made his way to the supply room. He entered, then closed the door behind him. He placed his hands on the closed door and laughed. If only his last patient could have seen Susan. He laughed until he had tears running down his cheeks. Life had a way of keeping him balanced.

Chapter 72

Johnny Robbins arrived at Elli's Diner. Several cars were already in the parking lot. He removed his duffle bag from the car and found a table for two in the back of the restaurant. Two young ladies were running around the dining room, doing their best to keep up with the demands of the patrons. Johnny ordered a cup of coffee while he waited for Barbara. He looked at his watch; it was 8:10, and she was late. Johnny was getting nervous. He had changed back into his western duds as soon as he woke up in the stolen BMW. He sat with his hat low on his forehead.

At twenty after eight, Barbara parked her red Mustang convertible and walked into Elli's Diner. She scanned the crowd of people until she saw the man in the cowboy hat sitting in the back. Barbara made her way over to Johnny's table.

"I am so sorry I am so late. My husband was questioning me this morning, and I had a tough time getting away. How are you, Mr. Wayne?" she asked.

Johnny looked up. Barbara was wearing a light summer dress, and the top three buttons were not fastened. Her cleavage was in full view for Johnny to see. She had a light perfume on that smelled something like roses. Johnny stood. "Please have a seat," he said as he walked around the table. He pulled Barbara's chair away from the table so she could sit down.

Barbara spoke up, "Are you always such a gentleman?"

Johnny laughed as he sat back down. "Only when a lady is present." The two engaged in idle chat about

their evening's activities. The waitress came over, took their orders, and poured Barbara a cup of coffee.

When the coast was clear, Barbara asked, "What is wrong? Can I help you with something?"

Johnny spoke up. "You know last night when I told you I had to get that paperwork to my accountants?"

"Yes," said Barbara.

"Well, that was not completely the truth. It is paperwork, but not the kind you were thinking. I know you have figured out who I am," said Johnny. "I know you know who my Dad was."

"Yes," said Barbara. "I believe he was that famous actor."

"That's right," said Johnny. "Since he passed away, I have managed his estate for my stepmother. I invested in that casino out there. Fifty million dollars. It was all cash. The natives could not get a loan, so the deal was I would lend them the 50 million, and they would pay back 100 million in three years. All in cash. I was here to collect. There was a room downstairs in the basement. Every month, the management would deposit 2.7 million into a vault downstairs."

"All in cash?" asked Barbara.

"Yes," said Johnny. "My business partner is trying to screw me. After you left, I went to check on the funds. Everything was gone. The entire vault was cleaned out."

"Oh, Mr. Wayne," said Barbara, "that is awful."

Johnny said, "Call me Justin, I think we are close enough," he laughed.

"Justin, what can I do?" asked Barbara.

"Well," said Johnny, "I believe that my money is going to end up at the airport today around 2:30 or 3 o'clock. It was going to be loaded onto a plane and then flown to California. There it was to be loaded onto a truck and taken to my bank. I have people all lined up for Monday morning. Things are just a huge mess right now."

"Why would your business partner try and screw you?" asked Barbara.

"None of it is his money. It's my money. Dad had earned it from his movies. All that interest. Folks will do anything to take advantage of a situation. One hundred million is a lot of dough. I guess I should not trust anyone." Johnny hung his head low.

Barbara reached across the table. She held Johnny's hand. "Justin, you can trust me. I swear, I will do anything that you ask of me. It is not fair that someone is trying to take advantage of you and your father's money like that."

"Thank you," said Johnny.

The waitress brought over their respective breakfasts. She placed each meal down in front of them. "I am famished," said Barbara. "You made me work up an appetite."

Johnny laughed. "I am rather hungry myself." The two of them enjoyed their meals. Johnny was taking his last sip of coffee when the sheriff's deputy walked into Elli's Diner. Johnny noticed the deputy speaking to Elli herself. Elli shook her head from side to side.

"Time for us to go," said Johnny, as he pulled his hat further down on his forehead. Barbara and Johnny left the table, leaving twenty-five dollars behind to cover the bill. Johnny glanced out the windows, his duffle bag

over his right shoulder. Two other deputies were inspecting the grey BMW in the parking lot. Johnny pulled on Barbara's arm. "I am just going to use the washroom before we leave." He entered the men's room, making his way into a stall.

Johnny removed the blue coveralls from his duffle bag. He wrapped the taser and 9mm in the coveralls then pushed the whole works out the small open bathroom window. Johnny removed his western blazer, rolled it up, and placed it inside the duffle bag. The keys for the BMW he removed from the front pocket of his pants. Johnny casually walked out of the washroom. Barbara and three other people were standing at the cash register. The ladies had been asked by the lone sheriff inside the restaurant to open their purses. The men were told to empty their pockets onto the counter. Johnny realized the cops were looking for something specific. "The keys," he thought to himself. Johnny removed twenty dollars from his wallet. He wrapped the keys for the stolen BMW into the bill as he approached the group of people being searched as they were leaving the restaurant. The lady in front of Johnny started complaining that the cops had no right to search anyone. They needed a warrant. The deputy was engaged in conversation with the woman as Johnny took the opportunity to drop the folded twenty with the keys into the pickle jar on the counter marked TIPS.

Barbara stood in the doorway of Elli's, watching Johnny in line. Johnny tipped his hat at Elli standing behind the counter. "Thank you, ma'am," said Johnny. "Our breakfast was fantastic." The sheriff finished with the folks in front of Johnny, and it was now his turn. "Howdy," he said to the cop.

The sheriff looked at Johnny. "Do you mind if I look in your bag?"

"Not at all," said Johnny. "What's going on?"

The sheriff responded, "We are looking for an escaped con."

"Oh," said Johnny, "I sure hope you catch him."

"Sir, could you please empty your pockets? Do you have any ID?" the cop asked.

"Sure," said Johnny.

The cop said, "You look familiar."

Johnny presented his California driver's license that Jackson Hall had given him the day before. "Here you go," said Johnny.

The sheriff looked at the license. "Are you related to that actor?"

"Sure am," said Johnny.

"Here you go, Mr. Wayne. No wonder you look familiar. I am sorry to delay you."

"I understand," said Johnny.

The sheriff asked if Johnny would sign his notebook. "The guys in the department won't believe that I met the son of the Duke."

"Sure," said Johnny. "Who do I make it out to?"

"Andrew," said the sheriff. Johnny took the pen and notepad from the cop. "To my friend Andrew," he wrote. "All the Best, Justin Wayne." Johnny handed the sheriff his pad and pen back. There were now more people standing behind Johnny. "Have a great day," said the sheriff, not searching Johnny's bag. "Thank you for your understanding." Johnny nodded his head and tipped his hat. "Oh," said the cop. "Do you mind removing your hat for a second?" Johnny complied. The cop smiled and

waved to the door. Barbara held Johnny's hand as they left the building.

"Get your car and meet me around the side," said Johnny.

"Sure," said Barbara. They kissed in the middle of the parking lot for the entire world to see. Johnny walked around the back of the building. He picked up his coveralls and placed them into his duffle bag just as Barbara drove the Mustang around the corner of the building. Johnny opened the passenger door. He threw the duffle bag into the back seat and got into Barbara's car. Johnny closed the door and then kissed her on the cheek. "How about we go somewhere private, little lady?" he said.

"I know just the place," said Barbara, as they drove out of Elli's back parking lot.

Chapter 73

Tommy and Brad had been on the trail heading back to their campsite at the South end of Rock Lake for approximately 10 minutes.

"What are we going to do with the body of that girl?" asked Tommy. "We can't just leave her there."

"No, we cannot," said Brad, waving his pointed stick in the direction of the pathway. The young men took their time, watching for movement in the trees along the trail. They rounded the bend and came across scattered belongings that had been tossed aside like discarded garbage. Rachel's body was gone. There was a new blood trail leading from the path up the slight incline to the trees behind the old trapper's shack.

Brad crouched down, looking at the undergrowth leading from the trail. Blood was splattered on several leaves. "There," he pointed. "It looks like the Grizzly dragged her up that way."

"Well, that will give the rangers a place to start when they get here," said Tommy.

Brad and Tommy stacked several rocks on the side of the pathway. They topped the small pile of rocks with a stick and broke the end so it hung down. Brad pointed the broken end towards the blood trail, then placed a large flat rock on top of the stick so it would not move. "There," said Brad. "That will make it easier for them to track the bear."

"Perfect," said Tommy. He gathered some of the bloodied clothes, tins of food, and an old pair of sneakers. Tommy placed the belongings beside the pile of rocks they had made. "Looks like we have done what

we can, buddy. Let's get back to our site and wait for the Rangers to arrive. I am sure they are going to have a few questions for us."

The young men continued towards their campsite. They arrived at the creek that crossed the path, flowing into Rock Lake when they noticed in the distance that their tents were not standing. "It looks like we have had some company," Tommy said. "Shit, you would think with firing the gun, the damn Grizz would have been running for the hills."

"I agree," said Brad. "Something is not right. The bear dragged off that girl into the bush and then came back to our site. No, it just does not feel right." Both boys knew that a Grizzly would defend its kill. They were never far away from their meal source. Brad's father had taught them that when they were just boys. If they ever came across a dead deer, they were to look for bear signs and then stay clear of the kill site.

The boys walked up to their campsite. They placed their sharpened sticks on the picnic table, then took in the damage. Both remaining tents had been knocked to the ground. Tommy's had been shredded, and Brad's tent was in a little better condition, with a single tear along the back wall. The backpacks still hung in the tree, suspended like piñatas.

"Well, at least we have our packs and food. Let's get a fire going and put some coffee on," said Brad.

The friends chopped up some kindling, lit the fire, and stacked several pieces of wood until smoke filled the air. Tommy and Brad then started to gather the scattered remnants of their shattered campsite. Tommy found the coffee pot; it now had a small dent in its side. "I will go and get some water," he said.

"Cool," was Brad's reply. "I will get the packs down from the tree."

Tommy picked up his sharpened stick and made his way to the water's edge. He removed the lid of the coffee pot and rinsed it in the cold, clear water of Rock Lake. Tommy pressed the lid of the coffee pot into place, then picked up his stick and turned to head back to the fire. Tommy looked up to see Brad standing next to the tree that held the backpacks aloft. He was not moving. Tommy noticed about ten yards from his friend some movement at the edge of the trees.

Tommy's instinct kicked in. Brad watched as the old Grizzly stood on its hind legs, snapping its jaws and smelling the air. It had fresh wounds under its neck, with hair torn away and coagulated blood in its fur. The Grizzly was the biggest he had ever seen. The bear dropped to all fours and began approaching Brad.

Tommy ran as fast as he could, shouting. He dropped the coffee pot and waved the sharpened stick he carried. Brad had a second to decide what he was going to do. He grabbed the rope holding the backpacks aloft. Brad jumped up, holding onto the rope, his boots scrambling against the bark of the spruce tree. His weight pulled the backpacks higher into the tree. He scrambled hand over hand, his boots scraping the bark of the tree as the Grizzly drew closer. Brad wrapped his legs around the tree, hoping to gain more traction as the bear lunged towards the base of the large spruce.

The bear stood on its hind legs, swiping at Brad with its right front paw, its jaws snapping as its head moved from side to side. The backpacks were now drawn tight against the branch 15 feet above Brad's head. He managed to scramble just high enough that he was out of reach of the big bruin.

Tommy stood twenty feet away, shouting and waving his pointed stick above his head. The Grizzly turned and dropped to all fours. It now stood stomping its front paws into the ground, with saliva dripping from its mouth. Tommy shouted at the top of his lungs, "Get out of here! Get!"

The Grizzly stood its ground. It stood up on its hind legs for a second time, with its back turned to Brad, who was hanging from the rope in the tree. Tommy was close enough that the Grizzly could be on him in a matter of seconds. The big bruin dropped to all fours, swiping at the air with its left paw. Brad struggled to hang from the rope, his legs wrapped around the tree. Tommy took one more step towards the bear, spear ready in his hands. The bear lunged at Tommy.

In one motion, Tommy plunged the spear into the Grizzly's neck. His spear broke as the bear knocked Tommy to the ground, with a portion of the broken spear visible, sticking out of its brown fur. Blood was dripping off the broken end of the homemade lance. The Grizzly let out a howl as it stood over Tommy.

"Don't move!" Brad yelled to his friend. "He is right on top of you."

Tommy had rolled onto his chest, his fingers interlaced with his hands, protecting the back of his neck. Brad was yelling from his position, hanging from the rope. The Grizzly was focused on Tommy. Brad let go of the rope, dropping to the ground. He reached for his Buck Huntsman, pulling the blade from its sheath as the Grizzly placed both of its front paws on Tommy's back. Its claws tore through Tommy's shirt. Tommy felt his skin start to tear, but he did not move. There was no way Brad was going to let his friend get killed right before his eyes, not without him trying his best to prevent it.

Brad took two steps. As he did, he raised the Buck Huntsman above his shoulders. With both hands on the handle of his knife, he plunged the blade deep into the neck of the Grizzly. Brad withdrew the blade and struck the bear a second time. He felt the blade hit the bones in the bear's spinal cord. The Grizzly turned its head, blood pouring from its nose. The bruin collapsed on top of Tommy. It took two more breaths as blood poured from the wounds both young men had inflicted.

Brad removed the blade, holding it in his right hand. Blood ran down the blade onto the handle, coating Brad's hand as he knelt beside his friend's head.

"Are you okay, Tommy? Tommy, are you okay?"

Tommy moved slightly. "Brad," he whispered. "Is that you?"

"It's okay, buddy. We did it. The Grizz is dead." Brad placed the Buck Huntsman back into its sheath. "Hang on, buddy," he said to Tommy. Brad stood up and placed both hands into the bloodied fur of the largest bear he had ever seen. He pulled with all his might as the bear rolled onto its side and off of Tommy's back. Blood soaked Tommy's torn shirt.

"Can you move?" asked Brad as he knelt beside his friend a second time. Tommy removed his hands from the back of his neck and then rolled away from the body of the bear. Tommy knelt on his hands and knees, looking up at Brad.

"What the hell happened?" asked Tommy.

"The Grizzly was on you," said Brad. "I jumped down and used my knife on him."

Tommy looked at his friend, tears welling up in his eyes. "You saved my life. You fricking well saved

my life with a knife."

"Well," said Brad, "you were trying to save mine with a pointy stick. Thought I would return the favor."

The events of the moment had just started to set in, and the young men began to shake.

"Let me have a look at your back," said Brad. He took his knife from the sheath, running it through Tommy's shirt until it hung from his sides. Six distinct lines ran down Tommy's back; the skin was torn, but the wounds were only a quarter inch deep. "Stay here," said Brad, "I am going to get the first aid kit." Brad stepped over to the tree, unfastening the rope he had just been hanging from, letting the backpacks drop to the ground. He searched through his pack until he found the small first aid kit his father had given him - a just-in-case gift for Christmas one year. Brad opened the kit for the first time, running back over to Tommy. "Let's see what we can do with this." Brad took a small spray can from the kit, marked antiseptic, and sprayed Tommy's back. The wounds foamed, then bubbled, turning white briefly under the heavy coating of spray he applied. "It doesn't look too bad," said Brad, "he just scratched you. But you are going to have a few scars that you can tell our grandkids about." The boys laughed. Brad found some gauze and tape in the kit, placing the bright white pads over his friend's wounds and taping them in place. "How's that feel?" Brad asked.

Tommy looked up from his position. "Better, pal," he said. Brad extended his right hand to Tommy. They locked hands as Brad pulled his friend to his feet. The two young men now stood over the carcass of the biggest Grizzly they had ever come across.

"Son of a bitch," said Tommy, "we did it. We got the mankiller." The young men examined the bear.

"Look at its sides," said Tommy. "Look at the wounds, did you...?

"No," said Brad, "those are not from me. It looks like it was in a fight with another Grizz. You don't think?" The boys stood there pondering the situation.

"Do you think there might be another?" asked Tommy.

"Shit," said Brad, "look at the size of this thing. What would have been stupid enough to take this guy on?" Brad walked his friend back over to the picnic table. "Stay here, buddy, I will go gather the packs. We need to find you a clean shirt." Brad spent the next ten minutes gathering the packs and carrying them back to the picnic table.

"Here," he said to Tommy, "put on my sweatshirt. It will keep you warm. How about I fix us some coffee, and we wait until the cavalry arrives?"

Tommy looked back at Brad. He said, "Sounds like a good plan to me."

Chapter 74

Chris, Donna, Elizabeth, and the children walked towards the 505. It would take a fuel truck at least an hour to arrive. Chris thought to himself, "The rest of the wardens should be here soon."

Mark spoke up and said he saw a bear. "It had real bad breath," he said to Gunner, "and look, it tore my jacket."

"I bet it did," Chris replied as he rubbed the top of Mark's head. Donna had pretty much filled Chris in at that point. He was shocked to hear the Grizzly had pulled Mark from the tent. Chris looked at Donna and Elizabeth. "When the rest of the Rangers arrive, they will not have any problems tracking it down."

"Do you think they will shoot it?" asked Elizabeth.

"The bear attacked a girl on the trail," said Chris, "the Rangers will know what to do when they see it."

Chris stepped into the cockpit of the 505 and radioed Betty to see how things were going. He had a nagging urge to get back into the air so he could check on his son. Betty said that the fuel truck was about 10 minutes away. The rest of the Rangers had loaded up and left Emerald Lake. They should be arriving soon. The Rangers had to load the ATVs back onto the trailers, gather weapons, and then make their way to the staging area of Rock Lake.

It was not long after Chris got off the radio with Betty that the sound of a large truck could be heard in the distance. A cloud of dust could be seen behind the trees as the noise of the vehicle grew nearer.

"Well girls, it looks like I have to get back to work. That is my fuel truck." Donna and Elizabeth gathered Mark and Marcy, who were fighting with two sticks as though they were swords. "Are you girls going to head back to town?" asked Gunner.

Donna spoke first, "I want to stay until Tommy and Brad get here to the parking lot. They should be packing up our stuff by now. So it will only be a couple of hours."

Elizabeth agreed, "We will keep the kids occupied until then."

The fuel truck pulled up into the parking lot just below the Bell 505. The driver got out then waved to Gunner.

"Well girls, I will see you at the end of the day."

The driver from the fuel truck unrolled 100 feet of hose from the rack on the back of the truck then made his way to the helicopter.

"Heard you were looking for a little fuel," said the driver.

"It's been a crazy morning," said Chris, "thanks for coming as quickly as you did."

"No problem," said the driver, "anything for the department."

The fuel hose was connected to the 505, and the driver returned to his truck, set the gauge to zero, and flipped the switch for the electric fuel pump. The hose moved slightly as fuel started to flow up to the waiting fuel tank of the helicopter. As the chopper was being refueled, Chris watched as five Rangers began arriving in the parking lot.

They began unloading their gear along with the

services' four ATVs. Someone was going to be riding double today. Chris headed down to meet his fellow Rangers. They all gathered around the last trailer containing the ATV marked "supervisor." The guys all shook hands.

"We are back again," said Dan Thompson. "This is a busy place. Frickin' long weekends. I heard you have had an exciting morning so far. Betty has filled us in."

"It's been interesting," said Chris.

"How's the girl?"

"Don't know," said Gunner. "The attendants were working on her as they pulled out of the parking lot. All I can tell you is she was still alive when they left."

"Well done," said Dan. "Bob has given us instructions to wait for him. He wants to do a briefing then get the ball rolling. He is about 15 minutes behind us."

The Rangers went about setting up barricades at the entrance to the Rock Lake pathway system. The signs they posted said, "Closed, do not enter, Bear in area." By the time the ATVs were unloaded, the men were ready to go, and Bob Gerard pulled into the staging area with his overhead lights flashing red and blue on top of the F150 he drove. Gerard pulled alongside his group of men, getting out of the Park's service truck marked "supervisor."

"Morning, gentlemen," he said as he looked at his watch. It was 11:10am, Sunday morning. Bob shook Gunner's hand. "Good job," he said. "She has made it to Metro General. Betty just called me on my cell as I was arriving."

"That's great news," came Chris's reply. "She has a good chance then."

Bob then addressed his five men. "This morning we were informed that there had been an attack up at Rock Lake. Sounds like we have a Grizzly that has turned." The men understood what that meant. The bear had gone from its natural instincts. To finding food from humans, or humans being the food.

"We need to get this one, and it needs to be done by the end of the day," said Gerard. "It won't be long until the press catches wind of this. By then, I want it wrapped up. My orders are to shoot to kill. We will autopsy it after it is brought down. Gunner, you take the lead in the air. Scout out the area, then direct the crew where needed."

"Roger," came his reply.

"Is the chopper fueled?" asked Gerard.

"Just finishing. We will be ready to go in a few minutes," said Chris.

"Good. I will act as your spotter," said Bob.

As the meeting was wrapping up, a bright red Mustang pulled into the parking lot. Its top was down. Music from the radio was loud, catching the attention of the group of Rangers. Barbara drove her car to the corner of the parking lot, pulling in beside the washrooms. Johnny spoke up, saying, "It sure is not very quiet here, honey."

"I am sorry," said Barbara, "I like to come here because it normally is very quiet. Let's go somewhere else."

"Hang on, little lady," said Johnny. "I want to see what is going on."

He placed his hand on hers as she was about to restart the car. Johnny scanned the area and noticed the

505 on the emergency pad and the fuel truck below it. They looked at the group of Rangers huddled together. Then it hit him like a ton of bricks.

Johnny pulled his duffle bag from the backseat. He removed a crumpled piece of paper, unfolding it. He stared at the picture of Chris standing beside the new 505. The caption read "hero pilot." He glanced up then looked at the picture again. He knew then and there that the man standing 100 feet away was the pilot responsible for sending him to the pen. Johnny had vowed revenge. After all, he had done nothing wrong that day.

"This is a perfect spot," Johnny said to Barbara. He watched as the Rangers broke up and went about getting things finished before they headed up Rock Lake Trail.

Chris walked over to the fuel truck driver. "How much did she take?" Chris asked.

"Seventy-eight gallons," he said.

"Shit," said Chris, "that was close..." the 505 only held eighty-five gallons, give or take a few ounces. "She was pretty dry," said the driver.

Chris said, "Do you have plans over the next few hours? I am thinking we might need to do this again. Looks like we are going to be busy." The fuel truck driver responded by saying it was Sunday and his schedule was clear. So long as the Department paid his invoice, all was good. Gunner responded, "I will let the office know you are going to hang around in case I need you again."

Bob Gerard had just finished up with the rest of the Crew. The Rangers started up the four ATVs, one pulling a narrow utility trailer used to carry all their excess gear. Bob Gerard turned to his men, waving them

up the trail. The Rangers engaged the ATVs, creating a cloud of dust that drifted towards the Mustang.

Bob Gerard turned towards Gunner and the 505. He raised his right arm, moving it in a circle. Gunner knew that was his signal to fire up the bird.

Gerard walked across the parking lot in front of the Mustang, making his way to the outhouse beside Johnny and Barbara. Johnny looked over at Barbara and said, "I am sorry, honey. I am going to help these guys. It's my duty. Meet me at the airport at 2:30. Do not be late. I promise I will make it up to you."

"How will you get back?" Barbara asked.

"These guys will give me a ride, do not worry. I know what I am doing." Johnny stepped out of the car, placing the strap of the duffle bag over his shoulder. "See you at 2:30," he said as Barbara started the car, its music blasting into the air. She waved over her shoulder as Johnny made his way into the outdoor biffy.

Johnny opened the bag, placing his hand inside. Bob Gerard stood with his zipper down, relieving himself in the only urinal. Johnny stood behind him and slightly to the side.

"Looks like you boys have something big on the go this morning," said Johnny as he approached.

"We have had an incident with a bear," replied Robert without turning around, focused on the task at hand. Johnny heard the stream of urine hitting the porcelain. It was now or never. Johnny swiftly placed the stun gun on the Ranger's neck and pulled the trigger. Bob crumpled to the ground, his penis still hanging out of his pants and dribbling piss all over the old concrete floor. Johnny quickly removed his own shirt and then Robert's. He took Robert's supervisor utility belt and

fastened it around his waist. The final pieces of attire were Robert's supervisor ball cap and sunglasses. Johnny turned to look in the stainless steel mirror.

"This is going to have to do," Johnny said aloud. He placed the 9mm from his bag, tucking it into the belt behind his back. Robert's utility belt also contained a 9mm Glock, which was standard issue for the department. Johnny placed his clothing into the duffle bag. He then took the stun gun off the counter and placed it over Robert's heart, pulling the trigger a second time. Robert's body convulsed, then lay completely still.

"Have a nice day," Johnny said as he exited the outhouse, carrying the duffle bag in one hand as he made his way towards the running Helicopter. Johnny walked past Donna, Elizabeth, and the kids, tipping his hat.

"Good morning, ladies," Johnny said. "Don't worry about a thing."

The girls waved back, saying, "Good morning." Johnny walked up the slight incline and around to the passenger side of the 505. He pulled on the door latch as Gunner concentrated on his gauges. Johnny tossed his black duffle bag into the backseat, then climbed onboard. Johnny looked to his right as he fastened the doorlatch. Gunner continued to go through his preflight. Johnny reached up and took the headset off the hook above the door, placing it on his head. He adjusted its microphone.

Gunner looked over at his passenger for the first time. Something was not quite right. Johnny Robbins turned towards Chris and pulled Robert's sunglasses from his eyes. Robbins shouted into the microphone, "Do you remember me, you fucking cocksucker?" Fate had brought the two men together again. Robert Gerard's 9mm was now pointed directly at Gunner's midsection. "I told you I would get you someday. Now you are going

to pay," Johnny threatened.

Chris looked at the passenger, and then it came to him. This was the individual who had stolen the Corvette years ago.

"Sorry," said Chris, "who are you?"

Chapter 75

Jackson Hall awoke seven hours later, the remnants of the meal he had bought at the truck stop scattered all over the floor of the moving truck. Jackson's neck was stiff, and he could hardly turn his head. He adjusted the mirror on the windshield, noticing that his eyes were bloodshot, with some vessels having burst when Robbins had his belt around Hall's neck.

"Damn," Jackson said out loud, "I'm lucky to be here." The moving truck was now surrounded by big rigs, and their trailers provided the perfect cover. It would be difficult for anyone to see where he was parked unless they slowly drove through the parking lot. Jackson felt comfortable enough to get out of the truck and head in for a bite of breakfast. How could he go wrong if all these truckers were eating there? The food must be good. The burger he had last night was okay.

Jackson walked into the restaurant, making his way to a table. The place was buzzing with activity. Men and women sat discussing their loads and destinations. The pay was shit. Jackson sat, just listening. The waitress came over with a menu, carrying a pot of coffee in her hand.

"We have ham and cheese omelets on special this morning for $10.95, and that includes your coffee with a choice of toast," she offered. Jackson did not take the menu from her hand.

"That sounds perfect," he said, "sign me up."

The waitress looked at Jackson. "Looks like someone had a rough night."

"Yeah," said Hall, "spent too much time at the

Casino."

The girl nodded. "I understand. I think their drinks are stronger than normal."

"That might explain my headache," said Hall with a smile. The girl turned and walked behind the counter. She placed a slip of paper containing Jackson's order on one of those revolving circle things. The short-order cooks just spun the holder, removed the slip, and then laid out the meal, tagging the slip back onto the plate. It only took five minutes, and the client was eating.

"Order up!" came a shout from the back. The waitress took Jackson's meal over to his table.

"That was fast," he said.

"We know how busy you guys are. Fast home-cooked meals so you can get back on the road," she said.

"No, no," said Jackson. He stopped himself. "You're right." He looked up through his bloodshot eyes. "Nothing better than home cooking." The waitress topped up Jackson's coffee, making her way to other tables and topping up everyone's coffee until her pot was empty.

Jackson enjoyed his breakfast. He sat, listening to the conversations. There was a young guy, maybe in his mid-thirties, two booths away. Each of the booths had a phone hanging from the wall above the condiment containers. The phones were set up so the drivers could swipe their credit cards to make long-distance calls to their dispatch office.

He watched the young man talking on the phone; his voice grew louder. "You can't expect me to keep running backhauls empty." He slammed the phone back onto the receiver. Jackson walked over to the young man's booth.

"I couldn't help overhearing your conversation," said Hall.

"I am sorry," said the young man. "I have a six-month-old kid at home. They keep running me empty on backhauls, so I don't make as much. It pisses me off. Do you know how expensive diapers are these days?"

"No, sorry, I do not," said Jackson. "But this might be your lucky day. Mind if I sit down?"

The young truck driver nodded his head. Jackson sat and took a sip of his coffee before he spoke.

"I rented a moving truck yesterday. Been having nothing but trouble with it." Jackson knew the authorities would be looking for it since he never went back to sign the paperwork with Judith. "I'm stuck in the parking lot here, waiting for them to send out a mechanic, or someone with another truck. There is nothing I would like better than to tell them to shove that moving truck up their asses."

"What have you got?" the driver asked.

"Just some small boxes that have my company files. There are fifty of them, about this size," Jackson moved his hands to show the size. "I need to get them to the Hillsboro airport. My pilot heads out at three today."

The young driver looked up, "Your pilot?" he asked.

"Yes," said Jackson. "I will pay you two thousand dollars cash to get my stuff there."

"How about four thousand?" said the truck driver.

"Three," said Jackson.

"Thirty-five hundred," said the driver, "and you

help me load it onto my truck."

"Deal," said Hall. Jackson picked up the tab for the driver's breakfast.

"I will meet you out in the parking lot," said the driver. Jackson paid both bills and then made his way out into the parking lot where the driver stood. "That's my rig over there," the driver pointed to a new tractor with a beat-up trailer attached to the back. "I bought it brand new, and the payments are killing me."

"There is my rental truck over there," said Hall.

"I will back the semi to your tailgate," said the driver. "We can just transfer the boxes from one truck to the other in a few minutes."

The semi driver opened the swinging doors to his trailer before starting the tractor. Jackson had made his way to the rental truck, rolled open the backdoor, and then stood inside, waiting for the truck driver to back his trailer against Jackson's bumper. Jackson watched from his viewpoint in the back of the moving van. The semi driver backed his 45-foot trailer into position with the precision of a surgeon. The driver stopped within two feet of Jackson's bumper. There was just enough room for a man to slip between the two vehicles. Jackson heard the air brakes lock on the trailer. The driver appeared and then climbed into the empty 45-foot trailer.

Jackson handed each box to the driver until all 49 were loaded onto the semi. "I thought you said you had 50 boxes," said the driver.

"The other is in the cab," said Jackson.

"Do I get a discount if we only load 49 into the trailer?"

"Nice try," said the truck driver.

The truck driver jumped down out of the trailer, and Jackson followed. Sweat was forming on Jackson's brow. He wiped the droplets of moisture away with the back of his sleeve. "Guess I am getting old," Jackson said to the driver.

"Grab your stuff," said the driver. "I will meet you in the cab of my truck after I get these doors locked."

The driver pulled the rig ahead so he could close and then lock the doors of the trailer. Jackson Hall gathered his things from the cab of the truck, plus the remaining open box. It had been laying out of sight on the floor, passenger side. Hall made his way to the cab of the semi, opening the passenger door. Jackson slid the box onto the floor, ensuring his jacket lay on top of the unsealed box. He climbed aboard, closing the door behind him.

The driver pulled out his briefcase from behind Jackson's seat. The sleeper behind the seats was large and looked more like a motorhome's interior. The driver opened the case, removing a booklet of invoices. He wrote out "Moving boxes. Total three thousand five hundred dollars." He tore the receipt from the booklet, leaving a carbon copy for himself, and handed the receipt to Jackson.

Jackson read it and said, "Perfect," looking at the driver.

The driver smiled and said, "We do not move until I get paid."

"Oh," said Jackson.

"I've been burned too many times," said the driver. "I have your load on my truck, so if you do not want to pay me, that's no problem."

"No, no," said Jackson. He reached for his jacket

and removed a bundle of 100-dollar bills. He counted off thirty-five, handing them to the driver. Jackson then counted out ten more, placing them on the dashboard in front of his seat. "There is an extra grand for your efforts," he said as he placed the rest of the bills into his pocket. "You get that so long as I am at the airport no later than 2:30."

The driver smiled, tucked his 35 one hundred dollar bills into his shirt pocket, looked at his watch, nodded his head, found first gear, and let out the clutch. They were off in a cloud of dust. The driver looked over at Jackson and said, "I like your style."

They pulled out onto the highway. The dust followed behind the trailer for about fifty feet, trapped in the vacuum of air created by the trailer. Jackson looked into the side mirror of the semi, and two sheriff's cars were just pulling into the truck stop. Jackson smiled and said to the driver, "I like your style too."

Chapter 76

Kevin's crew was having a lazy Sunday morning. The group had watched the Rangers march a group of individuals past their encampment the afternoon before. The park's helicopter had been there on Saturday. So Sunday was looking pretty tame by comparison. The plan today was to break camp around 9:00am. The group, led by Kevin, would make their way through Twin Valley Gorge, making their way to the valley that contained Rock Lake. Kevin had figured that the way this group was moving, it would take them approximately six hours to make the hike. RL03 had been reserved for Kevin's group and their final evening. The view down the lake from that stop in front of RL03 was the best the entire group of cabins had to offer. Eight bunks awaited the entourage inside the rustic cabin. Kevin would pitch his tent alongside the cabin, as he had done many times before for the evening.

Kevin sipped on a hot cup of coffee as his group started to stir. He had once again started a fire as he waited for everyone to join him to start their day. It was not long until the smell of bacon and sausages filled the air. Blueberry pancakes were the breakfast of choice on this beautiful Sunday. Jerry whipped up the batter, Gale did the cooking. Two pancakes per person with a nice shot of maple syrup. Kevin looked at his watch; it was 8:00am. He knew there was no way they would be ready to go by 9:00. By the time everyone had eaten, taken their showers, and done their morning due diligence, it was 10:30. The tents were packed away, sleeping bags rolled up, backpacks were loaded. The campsite was left spotless as the group marched toward the path leading to Twin Valley Gorge.

Kevin stopped as he got to the head of the trail that would lead his group through the rugged terrain. "Who wants to take the lead?" he asked. The group discussed things for a moment or two. It was decided that Kevin would stay in the lead, since a bear had been spotted on the other trail yesterday. Kevin led the way up the winding pathway until finally they reached the gorge.

Millions of years of erosion had formed a forty-foot-wide gap hundreds of feet high. The site was stunning. Kevin turned to his group. "The natives found and used this pass to make their way between the two valleys," he said. "If you look closely, there are paintings on the walls further ahead." Cameras were quickly made ready as the group proceeded through the gorge. A small amount of water flowed through the rocks in the middle of the pass. "She is pretty tame right now," said Kevin, pointing to the water. "I have seen it when the water is four feet high and flowing so fast that it's not possible to walk through here."

"When does the runoff start?" asked one of the tourists.

"Soon," said Kevin. "Things are a little late this year with the winter we had. All it will take is a good rainfall to hit that snowpack up there, and the torrent will start to flow. Park's always keeping an eye on things so people do not get stuck up here. We are over 8,000 feet above sea level right now."

The group stopped for pictures, taking in all the native paintings Kevin pointed out. Deer, elk, fish, and bears adorned the walls in red ochre paint. There were handprints scattered throughout the walls. Kevin led his group to a large white rock in the middle of the gorge. He took off his backpack, opened it, and removed a clear plastic bag with charcoal he had taken from the firepit.

"Time for a break," he said. "Is anyone curious about how they got all those handprints everywhere?"

The group stood around as Kevin took a lump of charcoal and placed it in his mouth. He started to chew, then took a swig of water from his bottle, swished the mixture in his mouth, and placed his hand on the white rock. Kevin blew the mixture from his mouth across his hand. When he removed his hand, the outline left behind was a perfect match to his fingers and palm.

"Who is next?" Kevin asked, smiling. His teeth and mouth were black with charcoal.

Chapter 77

Susan started to come around as the Life Flight helicopter approached the Metro General Helipad. IV lines hung from poles attached to the stretcher. She reached for the bandage covering her head, but one of the Life Flight EMTs held her hand back.

"We are almost there," the female EMT said, but the noise of the rotor and engine made it too loud for Susan to hear what was being said. The EMT rested her hand on Susan's shoulder, and Susan lay motionless. A sudden calm came over her. The Life Flight chopper landed on the pad at exactly 12:10, and hospital staff stood behind the glass doors waiting for the engine to shut down before approaching.

By the time the main rotor had stopped turning, the Life Flight crew had Susan unloaded and were waiting to transfer her to the hospital gurney. Time was of the essence, and the chopper crew had been trained on how to maneuver around the flying ambulance while it was running. The hospital staff had limits and rules they needed to follow.

Susan was transferred to the hospital gurney, with a chart containing all her vitals recorded on the flight. The chart also contained information sent from Hillsboro General. The cooler with two units of blood was given to a hospital attendant. The female EMT rested her hand on Susan's shoulder again, saying, "Good luck. You are in good hands."

Dr. Hansen stood in the emergency operating room with his gloved hands in the air. A team of nurses, an optical surgeon, and an anesthesiologist also stood at

the ready. Susan was wheeled into the surgical suite at 12:17, and Dr. Hansen quickly reviewed the charts.

"Let's get her under," Hansen said to the anesthesiologist. Dr. Baily, the ophthalmologist surgeon, stood on the right side of the bed, Hansen on the left. Dr. Baily called for scissors, and Dr. Hansen continued his assessment. He cut away the gauze on Susan's calf. Her leg was swollen, and fluid oozed from the temporary staples. Her leg was red, and when Hansen squeezed the calf, the staples ruptured, and a yellowish pus burst out onto the table. Hansen shook his head. Susan was going to lose her leg. Infection had spread, and the muscle was dying.

Hansen took a surgical marker and drew a line around Susan's leg just below the knee. Dr. Baily had removed the bandages from Susan's head, and her eye hung from the optic nerve.

Dr. Baily shook his head as he examined Susan's eye. The nerve was damaged beyond repair, and there was no way to save her eye. He couldn't help but express sympathy, saying, "This poor gal. It's amazing she survived the attack."

Dr. Hansen ordered the nurses to shave Susan's head so he could better assess her scalp wound. Her hair was matted with blood and dirt. Dr. Baily clamped the optic nerve, and with a simple snip of his surgical scissors, the eyeball dropped into his gloved left hand. He then placed it in a blue dish, which he handed to one of the nurses. Hansen began the amputation of Susan's leg with a surgical saw. He carefully cauterized the vessels and folded a flap of skin over the open wound, leaving her with a stump that would provide a good attachment area for a prosthetic leg. After performing ninety-eight stitches, Susan's stump was closed.

Dr. Baily stayed in the operating room to assist with the head wound. He removed the surgical staples that Hillsboro had hastily used to close the scalp. Baily pulled back the scalp to reveal teeth marks across Susan's skull. They flushed the wound, ensuring that the scalp was properly repositioned. Baily inserted a sterile eye prosthetic into the eye socket and placed two small sutures in Susan's eyelids to keep them closed temporarily. When Susan was well enough, these stitches could be removed, allowing for a proper glass eye to be used in her socket. Hansen examined Susan's stomach wound, and while it was not aesthetically pleasing, the staples used by Hillsboro had securely closed the wound. The surrounding tissue appeared pink, indicating that it was healing well. Any scar tissue could be addressed by a plastic surgeon at a later date.

"Let's clean her up and get her into recovery," Hansen announced. He, Dr. Baily, and the anesthesiologist walked into the scrub room together.

"Good job, gentlemen. Thank you for your assistance," Hansen said. "With a good round of antibiotics, I think she has a good chance."

The three doctors discarded their disposable scrubs, and Hansen suggested, "Come on, gentlemen, I'm buying coffee."

Chapter 78

Chris looked over at Johnny Robbins. Robbins screamed into the microphone attached to the headset as he waved Robert's 9mm at Gunner's chest.

"Let's go! Get this thing off the ground. Take me to Hillsboro now," said Johnny.

Gunner remained calm. He pulled back on the collective as the 505 lifted into the air. Johnny ordered Chris to fly his scheduled route out of the park. Everything had happened so quickly that he was not sure how his plan was going to unfold.

Gunner pointed the 505 in the direction of Rock Lake. He nosed the helicopter forward. The 505 gained speed as it climbed, maneuvering through the mountains. They passed the ground crew within the first 5 minutes of lifting off.

"Where the hell are you going?" asked Johnny.

"I have to report in," said Chris. "They are expecting me to give them reports of the trail. There was a bear attack, they are hunting it. I am supposed to be the eyes in the sky."

"Damn it," said Johnny. He thought for a moment. "Go ahead," said Robbins. "No funny stuff."

Gunner radioed into base. Betty was quick to reply, "Go ahead." Chris reported he was in the air, fully fueled, and he had just passed the ground crew.

"We are code 99," said Gunner.

There was a brief delay in the reply from Betty. The radio then crackled, "Roger, code 99, all is clear."

"Roger," said Chris. "Will advise as I move further up the mountain towards Rock Lake."

"10-4," came Betty's reply.

Johnny was agitated. "What's a code 99?" he demanded.

"Code 99 means all is clear and things are good. Don't worry, pal, you're the one holding the gun. I ain't that stupid," said Chris. "If I do not report in, then the office is going to think something is wrong."

Soon the radio crackled again. "Base to command one. Base to command one." There was no reply. "Base to command two."

"Go ahead," came the reply from the ground crew. Johnny listened intently.

"Base to command two, switch to channel 5."

"Roger," came the reply.

Betty waited a few seconds as she adjusted her radio to Channel 5. "Command two, how do you receive?"

"Loud and clear."

"Command two, air one reports code 99, all is clear. Will advise as they progress to Rock Lake."

"Roger, Base, code 99, all is clear. Air one will report as they progress."

The radio in the 505 automatically switched between the frequencies used by the park's service. It was quite a piece of equipment. It constantly scanned the channels parks used, locking in as required. It allowed the pilot to keep his hands on the controls but still communicate throughout the range of channels the ground crews had to switch to manually.

Johnny felt a little more relaxed as he heard the Rangers communicate back to their base station. Johnny spoke into the microphone, "Okay, okay," he said, "I believe you."

Command two was Dan Thompson, second-in-command to Robert Gerard. Thompson raised his left hand into the air, the quads following slowed and came to a stop behind him. Thompson got off his ATV, then walked over to the other men. Thompson drew a line across his neck with his hand. The other rangers shut down their quads. Thompson stood in front of the group of men.

"Air one just reported a code 99," he said.

"Code 99? What is that?" asked one of the junior rangers as he reached for the code book in his breast pocket.

Thompson spoke again. "Base has confirmed that the Code 99 had been issued by Air one."

Having Thompson switch to Channel 5, this was not a drill. Air one was in trouble; something was going on, and Gunner could not report the situation. Code 99 had never been used since the park service had received their first chopper. This was no mistake; something was amiss. Thompson ordered one of his men to turn around and head back to the staging area. There was to be no chatter on the radio. Communication was to happen using code only until advised otherwise. Thompson needed to figure out what was going on, then report back to base.

Thompson mounted his ATV, waved his left hand in the air, motioning forward. The four remaining Rangers continued up the trail as Scott McLean, the most junior of the Rangers, turned his quad around and headed

back to the staging area.

Scott arrived twenty minutes later. The parking lot was quiet. He was to stay put and watch for suspicious activity. Donna, Elizabeth, Mark, and Marcy were sitting in the back of Tommy's jeep, the open hatch just above their heads. Scott pulled his quad in beside the washroom. The two cups of coffee he had on the way up to the staging area were working their magic. He had to relieve himself. Scott shut down the quad. He dismounted and then walked into the restroom. There, lying on the floor, was his Superintendent, Robert Gerard. His shirt, hat, utility belt with his gun, and radio were missing. Robert's breathing was shallow. There were burn marks on his neck and chest from where Robbins had discharged the stun gun against Gerard's skin. Scott knelt beside Bob, his hand on the superintendent's back. He shook Robert.

"Boss, boss, are you alright?" Robert moaned but did not move. Scott got on his radio. "Ground 5 to base," he said.

Betty responded right away. "Base, go ahead."

"Command one is down, we need an ambulance to Rock Lake staging area."

Betty composed herself. "Roger," she said. "Command one is down."

"10-4," came Scott's reply. Scott rushed out of the washroom, shouting to the girls on the far side of the parking lot. "Help, I need help!" he yelled. Donna and Elizabeth came running. The three of them entered the washroom. Donna assessed the situation.

"There is a blanket in the jeep and some water. I will go and get it," she said, then ran as quickly as she could. She told Mark and Marcy to stay put and not to

403

leave the jeep. She had to help a man in trouble. The children promised they would not go anywhere.

Donna returned to find Elizabeth cradling Robert's head. She had moved him onto his side. Robert had a large lump on his forehead from hitting the ground. His eyes were closed tightly. Elizabeth stroked his hair.

"You're going to be all right," she whispered. Scott helped Donna with the blanket as they covered Robert.

"Thank you, girls," Scott said. "There should be an ambulance here soon."

Scott's radio crackled. It was Betty.

"Ground 5, what is the status of Command one?" she asked. Her love for Robert overruled the guidelines set out for emergency procedures. Scott replied that Command one was alive and unconscious. "Roger," replied Betty.

In the 505, the radio had picked up the communications. Johnny listened intently. Robbins shouted into the microphone, "Turn this thing around. Who the fuck is Command one?" he shouted. "Head to Hillsboro airport," he demanded.

Gunner looked over at Robbins. "Not until I know my son is alright. He is at Rock Lake. It is a twenty-minute ride." Robbins pulled the trigger on the 9mm. The bullet ripped through the door beside Gunner. Chris looked over at Robbins. "You're going to have to kill me," he said. "Unless you can fly this thing, I would suggest you think twice." Gunner was calm and cool in his wording.

Johnny lowered the gun to his lap. "Fuck, fuck, fuck," he said into the mic. Chris was in control, and there was nothing Johnny could do about it. His plan was

falling apart. The 505 made its way up to Rock Lake. Chris had the bird running at full power. He maneuvered the 505 swiftly through the narrow valley. The 505 rocked from side to side as they moved left and right. Rock Lake was coming into view. Chris dropped the nose of the 505, backed off the power, and reduced altitude. The 505 flew directly over Brad and Tommy's Campsite. Chris turned the 505 to face what was left of the tents. The 505 hovered one hundred feet above the water. Tommy was laying on his stomach on the picnic table. Brad was waving to Gunner. Johnny now held the gun in the air, pointed directly at Chris. "Is that your kid?" asked Robbins.

"My son is the one on the picnic table. The one with the blood on his back."

"You have seen him," said Robbins. "Now head for the airport."

Brad could see the passenger waving a gun at Chris. There was a flash from the muzzle. Gunner removed his hands and feet from the controls as he fought with Robbins. The gun discharged again. Two bullets hit Gunner's chest. The 505 spun out of control. It tilted to the right then slammed into Rock Lake. Johnny Robbins was knocked unconscious on impact.

The cabin of the 505 was filling with water quickly. Brad ran to the edge of the lake. Steam and smoke rose from the engine as the cold water came in contact with the hot manifolds. Gunner was in trouble, and Robbins was below him as the 505 continued to fill with water. Robbins was starting to move. Brad swam the 20 yards to the downed chopper. He pulled hard on the door next to Gunner. It was jammed. Chris watched as Brad tried to open the door. Robbins was moving, and the 9mm was laying next to his leg. Chris grabbed the

weapon and fired at the door lock of the 505. Brad opened the cockpit door. He watched as Gunner tried releasing his seatbelt, but the weight of his body would not allow the mechanism to let go. Gunner was trapped.

Brad reached for his Buck Huntsman. He pulled the knife from its sheath and quickly cut through the nylon webbing of Gunner's seatbelt. The 505 was almost completely submerged as Chris slid out the door. Brad noticed holes in Gunner's shirt. The two men stood on the 505's skid as it went under the water. Gunner looked back through the open door. He could see Robbins was still strapped in his seat. Robbins's eyes were open, seemingly looking into nothing. Fuel started to make its way to the surface of the lake.

Brad and Gunner moved off the skid and slowly made their way to shore. Brad reached around as his feet hit the bottom. He placed Gunner's arm over his shoulder, walking Chris the rest of the way to shore. Chris stood on the shoreline, two holes in his shirt, the material darkened with gunpowder residue and bright red blood. Chris groaned as he unfastened the buttons on his shirt. He pulled at the material, exposing his light bulletproof vest. The two rounds Robbins had fired at Gunner pointblank were stuck in the material three inches apart. Gunner removed his vest. Two large red circles had formed around his ribs. His skin had split open from the impact of the bullets. He was having trouble breathing. Brad looked in disbelief. The rounds had not penetrated his skin.

"That's going to leave a mark," Chris said. Brad shook his head. The vest was not standard issue for the department. Gunner had bought it with his own money. He only wore it when things were out of the norm. This morning had been one of those instances where he listened to his intuition.

"My son, how is my son?" asked Chris as he tried to catch his breath.

Brad shook his head. "The bear got him pretty good. His back is torn up." Chris and Brad made their way to the picnic table. Tommy was awake; the noise of the crash had kept him alert. Gunner clasped his son's hand.

"Dad, are you okay?" asked Tommy.

"I will be fine, son, just a little trouble breathing, maybe a couple of broken ribs. How are you feeling?"

"Sore, Dad, that Grizz was on me pretty good. Brad took it down with his knife."

Chris turned to Brad. "Is that true?" he asked.

Brad nodded his head. "I got lucky," he said. "Think I severed its spine. It dropped like a ton of bricks."

"Hang in there, Tommy," said Gunner. "Help is on the way. We will have you out of here in no time." Gunner looked back toward the lake. Oil and fuel floated on the surface of the water. Chris was happy to be alive. "Thank you, Brad. I do not think I would have gotten out of there without you."

"Who was that guy with the gun?" asked Brad.

Gunner replied, "The asshole I helped bust years ago. I am still trying to piece it all together. When he got into the bird, I thought it was Superintendent Gerard. The whole thing does not make sense. The guy should have been in jail."

In the distance, on the other side of the creek, a wet man in a partial ranger uniform crouched behind some shrubs, watching the three men by the picnic table. Johnny Robbins needed a new plan.

Chapter 79

Bob Gerard was being made as comfortable as possible when the ambulance pulled into the staging area for Rock Lake. Donna stood outside the washroom, waving to the driver. The EMTs pulled up to the washroom, then rushed out of the ambulance.

"In here," exclaimed Donna, "he's in here." The two men walked into the washroom, one carrying a black plastic box with a red cross painted on the lid. Elizabeth and the young warden stood aside as the EMTs assessed Bob. There was some blood running from his right ear. There was a huge lump on his forehead. Four burn marks were visible from where Robbins had used the taser. Gerard's pupils were fixed and dilated.

"What is going on around here?" asked one of the attendants. "This is the second call we have had in six hours. Does anyone know what happened to him?"

"No," said the young warden Scott, "I found him like that. He is my Superintendent."

"We need to get him to the Hospital," said the most senior of the attendants. "He has a bleed on the brain. We need Life Flight. He won't make it by road."

The youngest EMT radioed into dispatch, explaining they had a critical patient. Life Flight would be there in twenty-five minutes. It would take another hour to get Gerard to Metro General. It was his best chance for survival. The pressure had to be removed from his brain before everything shut down.

The EMTs broke open chemical cold compresses. They squeezed the three packages then shook them before placing them around Bob's head,

taping all into position. The whole works then were wrapped in gauze. The idea was that the cold would help shrink the blood vessels in Bob's head and slow down any bleeding.

By the time the EMTs had loaded Gerard onto a spine board and stretcher, the sound of the Life Flight helicopter could be heard in the distance. The EMTs rolled Bob across the parking lot just below the emergency helipad Gunner had used earlier in the morning. The Life Flight crew maneuvered directly overhead, then gently set down on the emergency pad. Two attendants exited the helicopter while the pilot stayed at the controls. The attendants met the Ambulance EMTs and were given Bob's last vitals. The four attendants then carried Bob Gerard to the waiting helicopter on the spine board. The sliding door on the Life Flight chopper was closed. The two ambulance attendants crouched 100 feet away as it lifted off. The noise of the rotor blade was deafening. The chopper was soon out of sight.

Elizabeth, Donna, and now the children stood in the parking lot. The EMTs soon joined them. "We did everything we could for him. Let's hope for the best." The moment was a somber one. The warden Scott stepped away from the group. He radioed into Betty, informing her of the events that were unfolding.

Betty confirmed receiving the message. She folded her arms across the top of her desk, laid her head across her arms, and then began to sob. Betty composed herself after a few moments. She needed to be professional. She radioed Air One. There was no response. "Air One, come in please," she said into the microphone. The channel used specifically for the 505 was dead.

410

Betty switched to the ground channel. "Base to Command Two," she said.

A few seconds went by, then Command Two replied. "Read you loud and clear, go ahead."

"Command One is down. I have not heard from Air One," Betty replied.

"Command Two to Base, I saw Command One get into Air One. What do you mean Command One is down?"

"Command One found in the washroom in the staging area of Rock Lake. Command One is now on the way to Metro General. Life Flight is involved."

"10-4," said Command Two.

Dan Thompson raised his left arm from the handlebars of the ATV he was driving. The other three Rangers following closely behind slowed then came to a stop behind Thompson's ATV. Thompson removed his helmet; the radio receiver hung from his ear. He dismounted, walked behind the quad, and then reported to the other Rangers what Betty had told him. The men were stunned. They were all sure Command One had gotten on Air One. They watched him get onboard. Now Air One had not been heard from. There was no contact whatsoever.

"Keep your eyes peeled," said Thompson. "There is more going on here than just a bear attack."

Thompson got back on his ATV. He adjusted the earpiece for his radio, then ensured the microphone was still in place on the side of his neck. He raised his left hand, pointing up the trail to Rock Lake. The three Rangers and Thompson ambled up the mountain on their quads. One hour later, they were descending down the mountain. Rock Lake was clearly visible in the distance.

Two tents were collapsed at the south end of the lake, a small children's tent was torn. The quads made their way into the camping area of Brad and Tommy. Gunner sat on the picnic table, holding his son's hand as the Rangers came running over. Chris had his shirt and vest off; two distinct bruises had formed on his ribcage. Blood oozed from the center of each. His breathing was shallow but controlled. The men glanced at Tommy's back.

"What the hell happened?" asked Thompson.

Brad spoke first. "Tommy was attacked by the biggest grizzly I have ever seen. It has to be the one that attacked those women. Gunner flew in here this morning. There was someone in the chopper with him. Chris was shot. The helicopter went down over there in the water," Brad pointed to the lake. "The guy is still in there."

Thompson shook his head. "Is that true?" he asked Gunner.

Chris nodded his head. Chris then quietly whispered, "Get my son out of here. He needs medical attention."

"So do you, my friend," said Thompson. "What direction did the bear go?" Thompson asked, looking at Brad.

"It's laying over there behind the bushes. I put my knife in its neck." Thompson looked in disbelief. He waved to the other Rangers to go and check. They returned in minutes. The grizzly was dead, all right. A pool of blood had formed around the front of the carcass. Thompson got on his radio. They needed more help.

"Command Two to Base," he said. "Command Two to Base." There was no reply. The valley was blocking the radio signals from getting through. Thompson put his hand on Tommy's shoulder. "Hang in

there, kid," he said. "We are going to get you out of here."

Chapter 80

Susan awoke in the recovery room of Metro General. Her eye was bandaged, and her leg tingled. The recovery room nurse noticed she was moving. She walked over to Susan's bedside.

"You are in the recovery room at Metro General," said the nurse.

Susan looked over at her. "How did I get here?" she asked.

"The Life Flight helicopter brought you in. There was a bear..." the nurse stopped.

Susan nodded. "I remember," she said. The events of the last two days were a blur. Some were clear, others not so much.

"Are you in any pain?" asked the nurse, as she looked at the IV hanging and dripping into Susan's arm.

"My leg feels funny," she said.

"I am sorry," said the nurse.

"Sorry for what?" asked Susan.

"For what has happened to you," came the nurse's reply. The nurse put her hand on Susan's shoulder. "The doctor had to remove your leg," she said. "The tissue was infected and dying."

"What are you talking about?" Susan panicked, throwing back her bedsheet. Her leg was gone; in its place was a stump wrapped in white gauze, stained with dry blood.

"My God, what have you done to me!?" she

yelled. Susan pulled the bandage from her eye. She felt for something, anything where her eye should be. The eyelids had been stitched together. Susan panicked. She screamed, then started thrashing about in her bed.

The nurse called Dr. Hansen. Hansen arrived in the recovery room five minutes later. He administered a shot of diazepam directly into the IV line. "There," he said. "That will make you feel a little better."

Susan felt the rush of the injection. "You butchered me," she mumbled as she started to doze off. Hansen wrote an order to transfer Susan up to the psychiatric ward. His job was done. This patient would need more than his skills could provide.

Dr. Lewis received the transfer request signing off on moving Susan. It had been a busy weekend for the young Dr. Lewis. She had received a trauma patient the day before named Cathy. That patient was now the center of a murder investigation. The FBI wanted to interview Cathy, but Dr. Lewis had made sure that did not happen until she could be confident Cathy understood what was happening.

The orderly wheeled Susan into the psychiatric ward at exactly 2:30pm on Sunday afternoon. Susan was out cold; the injection Dr. Hansen had given her had not worn off. The orderly stopped at the nurses' station, handing Susan's transfer orders to the Nurse in Charge.

"Oh yes," said the nurse. "We have a bed for her in a semi-private room. Yes, here it is, Room 626, bed B."

The orderly rolled Susan into Room 626. He leveled the gurney to the exact height of the bed Susan was to be transferred to. Two nurses came into the room; between the three of them, they slid Susan over to her

new bed and then raised the rails on either side so she would not roll out onto the floor. The nurses left the room as the orderly adjusted the gurney to take back to the emergency room. He was as quiet as he could be so as not to disturb the patient on the other side of the room.

As he pushed the gurney through the doorway, he heard, "I am God's servant!" and the rattle of restraints.

"So am I," said the orderly. "Have a wonderful day."

Chapter 81

Kevin and his group enjoyed the uneventful hike through Twin Valley Gorge. Everyone had participated in leaving some kind of impression on the rock, spitting charcoal over their hands, and then signing the dates. The charcoal markings would soon be a fleeting memory when the next storm blew through the area, bringing with it rain. The creek bed would flood, washing away any trace that humans had been there.

It was around 3:30 on Sunday afternoon when Rock Lake came into view. The surface of the water shimmered in the afternoon sun. The four cabins could clearly be seen at the north end of the lake. The island in the middle looked isolated and serene. Kevin noticed the south end was busy with activity. He pulled out his binoculars, stopped, and concentrated on what he was seeing. There were three quads and what appeared to be rangers. Some other folks were milling around. From the vantage point Kevin and his group had, the 505 could be seen under the crystal-clear water.

The group was quiet as Kevin removed his two-way radio from his pack, then turned it on. He switched to the frequency that the parks department used. He held the walkie-talkie up, then pressed the button on the side of the unit, speaking clearly.

"This is Guide 101 to Parks on the south end of Rock Lake, how do you read?"

The radio crackled to life. "This is Command Two, go ahead."

"Dan, is that you at the end of Rock Lake?" asked Kevin.

"Roger," said Dan Thompson. "We have a situation here. Can you relay a message to Base for us? Before the mountains block your signal."

"10-4," came Kevin's reply. Dan Thompson explained to Kevin what had happened. They needed a helicopter to take Tommy and Gunner to Metro General. There was a recovery that needed to be done. Kevin knew that meant someone had died in the crash.

"Roger," came Kevin's reply. "Guide 101 to Park Base, Guide 101 to Park Base, how do you read?"

"Park Base, go ahead," said Betty.

Kevin relayed the information Dan Thompson had given him. "Roger," said Betty. "Two patients require Life Flight, Rock Lake."

Kevin's group stood watching in awe as he took charge, relaying message after message. A second Life Flight helicopter had been dispatched. The GPS coordinates had been relayed to Kevin by Dan Thompson. The Life Flight crew, while experienced in rescue missions, were not that versed in mountain flying. This mission would press the pilot and copilot to their limits. The turbulent winds, updrafts, and narrow valleys made for difficult flying.

The Life Flight crew consisted of four people: the pilot, copilot, and two EMTs. On the flight out to the park boundaries, the copilot had calculated that with the current weight, the addition of two extra patients, and altitude, the chopper would be at its maximum operating capacity, even with the expended fuel. The pilot made the call to set down in the staging area for Rock Lake. He set down on the same pad Gunner had used earlier in the day. The two EMTs disembarked from the Life Flight helicopter. They knelt on the ground as soon as they

exited, heads down, as the pilot added power, lifting off in a matter of seconds.

Dan Thompson, his crew, and Brad had taken down the three tents. They carefully moved Tommy and Gunner to the edge of the clearing, allowing room for the chopper to set down now that the tents were gone. It would be tight, but if the chopper came in with its tail facing towards the north end of the lake, then they could make a safe landing.

It had taken approximately one hour for the bright red Life Flight helicopter to arrive at the coordinates that had been relayed by Kevin to the park office and Betty. The rangers on the ground heard the helicopter off in the distance. Dan shouted to everyone to get ready. Brad stood on the edge of the campsite. The rangers stayed with Tommy and Gunner.

The red chopper came into view, turned over the island, and flew slowly towards Brad. Brad raised his arms in the air as he backed himself towards the firepit they had used to cook everyone's meals the evening before. The pilot watched as Brad moved his arms back and forth as the chopper got closer and closer to the ground. Water and now dirt filled the air due to the downdraft from the large rotor blades. The pilot turned on the wiper blades as he focused his attention on Brad's movements.

Brad stood directly in front of the helicopter, his arms cocked at the elbows, moving them back and forth. When the bird was over solid ground and Brad had assessed there would be enough room for them to load Chris and Tommy, he crossed his arms in front of his chest. The pilot reduced power, setting the bright red bird down exactly where Brad had instructed him to. The air wash from the rotor blades was strong; small bits of grass

419

and dirt blew into the air as the pilot let the chopper reduce speed to idle.

The copilot opened his door then exited the bright red machine. He then slid open the side door, removing a portable stretcher. Brad met the copilot and directed him to the rangers. Together, they all helped load Tommy and carried him back to the waiting helicopter. Gunner managed to walk under his own power to the side door as he watched his son being strapped down to the floor.

"Sir," said the copilot to Gunner, "I would like you to take the front seat. Do not touch anything. I need to start some IVs and get some vitals for the hospital." Gunner got into the front passenger seat. Dan Thompson closed the door, then gave a thumbs up to Chris. The sliding door was closed.

Brad made his way to the front of the chopper, standing about 50 feet from the revolving blades. Brad crouched, raising his right arm, moving it in a circle. The pilot applied power as the rangers crouched off to the side. The Life Flight chopper lifted off then backed slowly over Rock Lake. The pilot added more power and was soon high enough to turn. He headed towards the island, adding more power and altitude as he banked the red machine to the left, turning once again towards the rangers and Brad.

The chopper was now 500 feet above the lake as it flew directly over the Rangers. The wind from the downdraft moved the trees, and the sound was intense as the bird went out of sight.

"Well done, gentlemen," said Dan Thompson. He looked at his watch; it was 3:55 on Sunday afternoon. They had done everything they could for Chris and his son. It was time to focus on the recovery of the body in

the downed 505.

The rangers mounted their quads, taking them down to the edge of the lake. Brad watched as the youngest of the wardens removed a wetsuit, mask, snorkel, and fins from the small trailer behind his quad. Soon, the young ranger was dressed in the wetsuit. He waded into the freezing water, taking the mask and snorkel, placing them on his head. He moved backward slowly into the water, with fins attached to his feet.

He then removed his mask and spat in it, using his fingers to swirl the saliva around on the glass. He then rinsed the mask in the lake and sealed it to his face as he placed his lips around the mouthpiece of the snorkel. The young warden gave a thumbs up to Dan Thompson. He rolled onto his stomach and then moved towards the downed 505.

When the young warden had made it over the chopper, which was 10 feet below the surface, he took a deep breath, arched his body, and descended. His head pointed directly at the 505, with his legs now above his head as he kicked the fins. He was soon by the open door of the downed bird. The water was crystal clear, and there was no mistaking what he was looking at. The cabin of the 505 was completely empty. There was no body buckled into the passenger seat, as Brad had told them. The young ranger spotted a 9mm lying on the floor. He picked it up and then headed to the surface.

The young ranger removed the snorkel from his mouth. "I have a gun," he said, "but there is no body."

Brad yelled, "He can't be far. The water is calm." Dan Thompson raised his hand in the air, moving his palm in a circle. This indicated to the diver that he was to do a search around the 505. Holding the 9mm in his hand, he swam in ever-increasing circles around the

421

downed 505. On his second pass, he spotted a black duffle bag laying at the bottom.

The young ranger again headed directly towards it. He picked up the bag, and it was quite heavy, making it difficult to make it back to the surface. Struggling, the ranger rolled onto his stomach, holding the bag and gun in one hand. He placed the snorkel in his mouth and then began swimming back to shore.

"He has something," Thompson yelled to Brad and the other Ranger. The diver made his way to the shore, where he could stand. The diver stopped and stood facing his party on the shoreline. He held the gun in his left hand. He tried lifting the duffle bag, and it was full of water. The young ranger removed his fins and then walked out of Rock Lake with everything he had found.

He handed the gun to Dan Thompson. His fins he dropped on the rocky shore. The bag he dragged out of the water, laying it beside his fins. Water ran out of ventilation holes in the side of the bag.

"What have we got here?" said Thompson. Dan crouched beside the bag as the members and Brad gathered around. Thompson unfastened the zipper, then pulled back the flap on the top of the duffle bag. There were waterlogged twenties and hundreds floating in what was left of the draining water. Thompson moved his hand about then pulled out a waterlogged stun gun, a 9mm, and a pair of blue coveralls.

"There has got to be a hundred grand in here," said Thompson. "What do you make of this?" he said aloud. Thompson turned to Brad. "Are you sure that you saw a body in the passenger seat? Maybe it was just this bag."

Brad thought for a moment. "I saw someone," he

said to the Rangers. "I thought he was gone. His eyes were as big as saucers. I know I did. He shot Gunner. My priority was Chris, and when I got him out, I did not look back. I had to get him to shore. The water was so cold it was sapping my strength."

Thompson looked at his men. "Gentlemen, we need to assume that whoever shot our pilot is out there somewhere. He can't go far. We need to get some eyes in the sky. Damn," said Thompson as he looked at his watch. It was now 6:30. He said, "Looks like I am not going to get that prime rib tonight." The sun was now behind the west mountains, and it would be dark in a few hours. "Gentlemen, looks like we will be spending the night. Let's get set up so we can discuss our options for the morning. This guy is not going anywhere."

Johnny Robbins had watched for several hours as the diver entered the water. He had removed his wet clothing, laying everything out where no one could see him. Johnny watched as the Rangers set up camp. Robbins looked at his watch; it was now 6:10pm. He had missed his appointment with Barbara, all because he needed to fulfill his need for revenge.

Johnny needed a plan. He peered through the bushes as Dan Thompson stood on the shoreline, binoculars pressed to his eyes. Thompson held a walkie-talkie close to his mouth. Johnny could not hear what was being said, but he assumed it was about him. Thompson scanned the shores of Rock Lake and then the mountains surrounding the area.

"10-4," said Kevin as he and his group had now finished setting up in RL03. The Irish ladies from RL02 and RL01 had come over, introducing themselves. Aileen had asked if they had seen their husbands.

Kevin had responded with a "No, but we'll

definitely keep an eye out for them." Dan Thompson had been talking to Kevin about the current situation and bear attacks. Thompson had alerted Kevin to the fact that a suspect in the shooting of his friend Chris could be in the area. Kevin was to be on high alert for bears, even though the suspected bruin was dead. Kevin and Dan agreed to check in every four hours.

Kevin's group had been worried about what they had seen. They set up in the cabin as planned. This was going to be their last night together. Kevin pitched his tent beside the cabin as he had done on many other guiding trips. The fire was lit, and it was time for dinner. Kevin stood on the shoreline looking out south across Rock Lake. He scanned the shore from his vantage point.

"Nothing," he said to himself.

"What do you see?" asked Jerry.

"Just a beautiful bunch of mountains," said Kevin. "Here, have a look for yourself." Kevin handed Jerry the binoculars.

Jerry scanned the lake. "Gorgeous," he exclaimed. "I hope everyone is okay at the other end."

"All is good," said Kevin. "The Rangers are spending the night at the other end. Everything is just fine. They are waiting for the sky crane helicopter to arrive in the morning. Someone has to get that wrecked helicopter out of the lake. The boys will have to work the slings to help out."

The smell of bacon soon filled the air. The ladies were preparing a creamy bacon pasta with garlic bread, wine, and coleslaw. Kevin went to his pack. He removed a freeze-dried pouch of chili.

"What is that?" asked Gale.

"Chili," said Kevin.

"Do not be silly," said Gale. "We have a ton of food here, go put that away."

"Yes ma'am," came Kevin's reply. He walked back to his tent, placing the chili into his backpack. He smiled to himself. This was one of the best groups he had out in years. He had not cooked for himself the whole trip.

Johnny Robbins dressed in his damp clothing. He watched as the Rangers prepared meals for themselves. From time to time, the smells would drift towards him. He suddenly realized that he had not eaten since Barbara and he met at Elli's Diner. The air was getting cool. Johnny watched as the Rangers sat around a large fire. He could hear the mumble of their voices. Johnny glared, and then it hit him. He had a plan, and it was a damn good one. He looked at his watch; it was 7:15pm on Sunday.

Chapter 82

Barbara had followed Justin's instructions to the letter. She was at the airport, waiting for Justin Wayne to show up as he had promised. She sat in her car as a large semi-trailer emblazoned with the DOT logo pulled into the taxiway beside the big silver DC-3. Two men in uniforms met the individuals who climbed down from the cab of the truck. Jackson Hall shook both of the uniformed men's hands, and then the two men disappeared into the plane. Shortly after, the rear door of the plane opened.

The pilots stood inside the fuselage as Jackson Hall was handed box after box from the back of the semi-trailer. The truck driver would drop a box into Jackson's waiting arms, and he stacked them on the ground. Barbara counted the boxes, and as they were unloaded, there were 49 in total. When everything was unloaded from the back of the trailer, she observed the man who had been catching the boxes go into the cab of the semi. He returned with another box identical to the rest.

The driver of the semi closed the rear doors of the trailer, and he stood beside the man who had caught all the boxes. The semi driver held out his hand, and Barbara watched the older gentleman count out some money. He counted out even more money, folded the bills, and placed them into the front pocket of his pants. He shook Jackson Hall's hand and then returned to the cab. The roar of the diesel engine could be heard easily as black smoke was pumped into the air from its twin exhaust stacks. Minutes later, the semi had pulled off the tarmac, driven through the open gate, and was soon out of sight.

The man on the tarmac removed his jacket and

picked up a box, carrying it to the open door of the DC-3. Barbara watched as he did that 49 times. The pilot and copilot took turns at the open door, and it took about an hour for everything to be loaded onto the DC-3. The man on the tarmac moved slower and slower as he moved the boxes.

"This must be the money that Justin told me about," she said to herself. "One hundred million." She looked at her watch. Her lover was late. The final box was handed to the co-pilot. Jackson picked up his jacket from the tarmac and wiped his brow with it. He stuck his head into the open door of the DC-3. Within minutes, the three men headed into the little café beside the tarmac. Barbara heard Jackson Hall say he would buy everyone a burger before they left.

Barbara sat looking at the big plane. She had to do something. After all, her lover and new friend had counted on her. He had shared privileged information, and she could not let him down. Barbara looked around and noticed the golf cart by the entrance to the café. She had been on a couple of golf tournaments with the casino. Once every six months, the casino would hold an employee appreciation day on the golf course that the natives owned. Half the staff would go one time, and the other half the next. It was a great morale booster.

It didn't matter if you could swing a club; it was just a fun time. She had learned how to drive a cart the first time out. Barbara exited her car, then opened the trunk, removing her umbrella. She walked up the sidewalk towards the café entrance, glancing towards the golf cart as she got closer. Barbara noticed the key tag dangling in the ignition switch. She had a fleeting thought.

She went inside the café and ordered a coke to

go. "Please fill the glass with ice," she asked the waitress. Barbara looked around; the three men were sitting in the back, talking and laughing. Barbara paid for her soft drink and then exited the café. When she was sure no one was looking, she jumped onto the golf cart. She turned the ignition to the on position, jammed her umbrella against the accelerator pedal, and then wedged it against the seat. She aimed the steering wheel at the DC-3, then jumped off the cart as it started to move.

Barbara ran towards her car. The golf cart bounced as it headed towards the DC-3, gaining speed. Every time it would change direction just a little more. Barbara looked back over her shoulder. The golf cart was no longer pointed towards the middle of the plane. "Damn," she thought, "is it going to miss it altogether?" She stopped, then watched as the electric cart plowed into the tail of the DC-3; it hit with a loud bang. The cart flipped onto its side. The DC-3 shuddered slightly as parts of its elevator and tailwheel broke free.

Barbara hurried into her car, and she drove to the other side of the parking lot where there were other cars. She could hide amongst them, and hopefully, no one would see her. Barbara waited, and all was quiet. No one came out of the café. She sat in her car for an hour until finally, the three men emerged from the café, laughing. The older man who had removed his jacket had his hands on the shoulders of the pilot and copilot as they walked down the sidewalk towards the DC-3. It took only seconds until she saw all of them running towards the plane.

The wounded DC-3 sat there, the golf cart wedged sideways partway under its belly. The man with the jacket was running around, waving his fists in the air. The pilot and copilot were assessing the damage. The pilot was soon holding his phone to his ear. The copilot

picked up Barbara's umbrella, holding it in front of him so the man with the jacket could see it. She could not understand what was being said but knew that the situation was becoming chaotic. She looked at her watch; it was 4:10pm, and there was still no sign of Justin.

Barbara was scared; she didn't want to get caught. However, she did want a piece of the $100 million that Justin Wayne had told her about. Barbara tried the number Justin had called her from, but no one picked up, and it went to voicemail. The message was not from someone she knew, and she didn't recognize the voice. Barbara listened to the prerecorded message.

She decided it was best not to say anything and hung up. What had she gotten herself into? Thoughts flooded her mind. It didn't matter anymore. She wanted out of her marriage, and Justin Wayne was her ticket to freedom. After all, they had spent a wonderful evening together. How could he not want to carry on with what they had started?

Barbara watched as the Airport Maintenance crew and security from the main terminal showed up to inspect the damaged DC-3. A large forklift was soon on the scene. It lifted the tail of the DC-3 just high enough so the golf cart could be dragged out from under the fuselage. A crowd had formed on the tarmac, with someone taking pictures.

Barbara drove out of the parking lot. She knew the old plane was not going anywhere for a while. There was a motel just down the road that would be a good place to sit and wait for Justin to call her. She pulled into the parking lot of the Wheel Inn Motel and made her way to the office.

"Do you have a room for the night?" she asked the clerk.

"Sure do," came the reply. "That will be $49.95 for the room, and we will need to put a security deposit on your card of $500. Are you paying with Visa or Mastercard?"

"I would like to pay with cash," Barbara said.

"We need your credit card for our own security and any possible damage," exclaimed Steven Butler, the co-owner of the Wheel Inn Motel.

"I am separated from my husband," said Barbara. "If I use my card, he could find out where I am. He is mean and abusive, and I cannot risk that. I guess I will have to go somewhere else." She turned to leave.

"Just a minute," said Steven. "I think we can make an exception in this case." His business was slow since the natives had opened their casino. He was not going to let an opportunity walk back out the door. Besides, she was good looking. Thoughts ran through Steven's head. "I will take $300 cash," said Steven. "When you check out in the morning, I will give you the $250 back if everything is okay with your room." Barbara reached into her purse, pulling out three one hundred dollar bills Justin had given her the evening before. "That will be room ten," said Steven, handing Barbara the key. "Would you mind signing our guest book?" Steven turned the ledger towards Barbara. She signed the book as Barbara Wayne. "Thank you, Mrs. Wayne." Steven turned the ledger around towards himself. "Enjoy your stay."

Barbara opened the door to Room 10; it was showing its age. The carpet was worn, the furniture was dated, but at least it was clean. Barbara placed her purse on the nightstand, then laid on the bed. In minutes, her eyes closed as she drifted off. The stress of the afternoon had gotten the best of her, and she needed a break.

Chapter 83

Susan woke up in the psychiatric ward of Metro General. She looked around with her one good eye. Across the room was a lady who was strapped down to her bed. Her arms and feet were bound in leather restraints. Cathy noticed Susan's movements, and Susan started to cry.

"What's wrong?" asked Cathy.

"Look at me," said Susan. "They butchered me. I can't believe they did this to me. I am going to sue someone."

"I feel the same way," said Cathy. "There is nothing wrong with me, and they have me tied down to this bed."

"Why are you here?" asked Susan.

Cathy replied that she came in with some cramps and a little bleeding. The next thing she knew, she was on this ward tied down to her bed. "I need to get out of here," said Cathy. "My husband and son are going to wonder where the heck I am."

"They don't know you are here?" said Susan.

"No, I came to the emergency on my own. My husband was busy on the farm. My son is a pilot and will be home soon. I am making chicken for dinner."

Susan spoke up. "They cannot keep you here against your will. How do you feel now?" she asked.

"I am fine," said Cathy. "None of this makes any sense to me. Can you help me?" asked Cathy.

"What do you mean?" said Susan.

"I need to get out of here."

"Look at me," said Susan. "I only have one leg. How could I help you? I don't want to live anymore."

"Oh honey," said Cathy, "everything will be all right."

One of the duty nurses entered the room. "I see you're awake," she said to Susan. "Can I get you anything?"

"I am really thirsty," said Susan.

"That is natural," said the nurse. "You have been through a lot. Would you like ice in your water?"

"Yes," said Susan. The nurse left the room then returned with a cup of water and a package of cookies. The nurse lowered the side rail of Susan's bed then moved the portable table over the bed and Susan's stomach.

"There you go, dear," she said, as she adjusted the height of Susan's head. "How does that feel?"

"Better," said Susan as she reached for the water. Susan's depth perception was off, and she knocked over the glass of water. The water ran all over the table then onto her sheets. Her bed was soaked. The nurse pressed the call button over Susan's bed.

"Orderly to unit 626," she said. "I am sorry," said the nurse. "I should have told you to be careful. It's my fault. Your perception is off. That is going to take some getting used to."

Susan was crying. "Why me?" she said. "Why is all this happening to me?"

The orderly showed up a few minutes later. The nurse was standing by Susan's bed. "Let's get her into

this wheelchair. I will go get the clean sheets. If you want to strip the bed and clean up the water," said the nurse. Susan sat in the wheelchair as the nurse left the room. The orderly stripped her bed, placing the wet sheets in a plastic bag. The orderly wiped up the water on the floor, mattress, and little table then left the room.

Cathy watched from her bed as Susan sat with her head down, her hospital gown damp with water. Cathy said, "Let's get out of here."

"Where am I going to go?" asked Susan.

"I will take you with me," said Cathy. "You do not want them touching you again, do you? Can you come over here and unfasten these things on my arms?"

Susan used her good leg and arms to maneuver her way to the side of Cathy's bed. Susan reached up from her wheelchair then unfastened the restraint on Cathy's right wrist. Cathy quickly unfastened the restraint on her left wrist then went to work on the restraints on her ankles. Cathy jumped out of her bed. Her hospital gown open in the back.

"Come on, sweetheart," she said to Susan. "Let's get you out of here."

Cathy poked her head into the hallway. When the coast was clear, she pushed Susan in front of her. The two women were quite a sight. Cathy's backside was clearly visible. Susan sat in the chair at the mercy of Cathy's pushing. The bloody bandages on her stump stood out against the light blue of her gown.

Cathy found the stairwell. She opened the door then backed onto the landing. The door closed behind them. Susan spoke. "Now what?"

Cathy turned the wheelchair towards the stairs. "It will be all right, dear." Cathy raised the front wheels

off the ground and tilted the wheelchair back. With a thump, the back wheels landed on the first step heading down. Susan winced in pain.

Cathy bent forward then whispered into Susan's ear, "I am God's servant." Cathy released her grip on the handles of the wheelchair. Susan and the wheelchair tumbled to the next landing. Susan was thrown from the chair, and her neck hit the wall, severing her spinal cord. Susan's body lay motionless. Cathy walked by her, making her way to the basement. She mumbled as she passed Susan's body. "I told you I would get you out of here. Now you do not have to worry anymore. God told me what to do."

Cathy opened the door to the basement, and she could smell the hospital laundry. The air was warm and damp, and the scent of bleach reminded her of Sundays when she did laundry at home. She looked down the hallway, and two people in purple uniforms went through a doorway.

Cathy made her way into a large room where the hospital washing machines and dryers were all running. On the tables were folded sheets, blankets, towels, and facecloths. She spotted a rack with some clean hospital uniforms. All had been neatly pressed. The names of the owners were written on the tags which hung from the top buttonhole of each garment.

Cathy took a dark green outfit that looked like it would fit her. She slipped into the pants, tied up the string that held them in place, and then placed the smock over her now naked torso. There were several pairs of street shoes located by the laundry room entrance. She found a pair that would fit. She could hear voices coming down the hallway.

Cathy exited through a doorway that said

"service entrance." She found herself standing outside on a concrete ramp. The service entrance was used for receiving supplies that the hospital laundry required. The fresh air felt good in Cathy's lungs. She slipped the shoes onto her feet and then walked the length of the ramp, making her way into the hospital parking lot. The hospital was now on full alert. Susan's body had been found in the stairwell. Cathy was nowhere to be found. Security had implemented a search for Cathy. They were looking for a blonde woman wearing a hospital patient gown with her eye swollen shut. They were to approach her with caution. After all, she had escaped from the psychiatric ward.

Cathy watched as a city bus pulled into the parking lot. She made her way to the bus stop. The bus stopped, and the doors opened. Cathy climbed aboard as several people exited through the back door. She stood in front of the bus driver.

"Damn," she said, "I forgot my purse."

The driver looked up. "No problem," he said. "It looks like you've had a long day," he added, pointing to his own eye.

"I bet that hurts."

"Catch me tomorrow, are you new?" he asked.

Cathy responded, "No, I just transferred here. It's been a long day."

"Ah," said the driver, "that's why I didn't recognize you. Where are you headed?"

"Home," responded Cathy as she sat down. The doors closed on the bus, the air brakes released, and they were off. The roar of the diesel engine filled the passenger compartment. Cathy could hear the shifting of the gears as the bus gained speed. She looked back

towards the hospital. Then she shouted aloud towards the driver, "I am God's servant!"

The driver looked in his rearview mirror. "You all are in my book," he said to Cathy as they headed down the road. "Without you folks, I would have lost my Marian. God bless you all."

The bus made its way towards downtown Metro. Cathy looked out the window until she recognized the area. She and Eric had bought a townhouse here. It was a place that her son James could use while he was doing his internship at Metro General. The townhouse had two bedrooms and a front drive garage.

It had been a perfect second home for the family. Cathy and Eric would often use the second bedroom on weekends when they came to the big city to go shopping. Cathy thanked the bus driver as she disembarked, promising to pay him tomorrow after her shift. She walked a short distance from the bus stop until she stood in front of the townhouse.

Cathy made her way up the sidewalk, then climbed the two stairs to the front porch. There was a two-person swing that Eric had installed a week or so after they bought the place. Its wooden framework was painted bright white. Cathy had purchased matching cushions that rested in place on the swing. It was perfect. Eric and she spent many nights waiting for James to come home and tell them how his day had gone. Cathy sat down.

She fumbled under the right armrest until she found what she was looking for. Cathy slid the secret compartment door open. It swung towards her leg. Inside the hollowed-out portion on the hidden compartment door was the key to the front door of the townhouse. "Eric was so smart," she thought to herself. Cathy

removed the key from its hiding place, stood up, and opened the front door.

The air inside smelled a little stale. James had been away at a conference. Cathy and Eric had not been to town for two weeks. Cathy turned on the interior lights. She made her way into the kitchen. She ran the water for a few moments, grabbed the glass sitting beside the sink, and proceeded to drink two full glasses of water. She filled the glass a third time, then left the kitchen.

Cathy made her way to the master bedroom. She placed the glass of water on the nightstand, laid down on the bed, closed her eyes, and was soon drifting off into a world that held no bias.

Chapter 84

Jackson Hall was furious. The DC-3 was grounded, loaded with his precious cargo, and he needed to get it out of there fast. The two pilots had been on their cellphones with the corporate head office, and the security guards were investigating the incident with the runaway golf cart. The bottom line was that the DC-3 sat wounded on the tarmac and was going nowhere fast. It could take days to get the parts they needed to get the plane up and flying again, and that didn't include the inspection by a certified aeronautical engineer, which could take another week to find someone qualified on DC-3s. Frustrated, Jackson made his way back into the small café and asked to use the phone.

Jackson dialed the number for the surf shop in California. "Catch-a-Wave, Maria speaking," was the answer he heard.

"Hello, honey," said Jackson. "Sorry I haven't called. I lost my cell phone. The plane I was supposed to be on has mechanical trouble. It looks like I'm going to be delayed."

"Where are you?" Maria asked.

"Hillsboro Airport," came Jackson's reply. "I just needed to hear your voice."

"Can I do anything for you, sweetheart?" asked Maria.

"It's okay, honey," said Jackson. "I'll figure something out. How are things at the surf shop?"

"We are so busy," said Maria. "The breakers are rolling in today. I'm waiting for my second shipment of

439

wax. We can't keep it on the shelves."

"That's good, honey. I'll let you know when I'm out of here. Love you."

"I love you too. I have to go, sweetie. There are two customers standing in front of me." The phone line went dead.

Jackson smiled, then hung up the receiver. He turned to walk out the door, and then it hit him. He thought for a moment, "What was the logo on the side of that truck?"

Jackson picked up the receiver and dialed 0. "Operator, may I help you?"

"I am looking for a number for a trucking company," Jackson said. "I believe it is DOT Trucking."

There was a pause. "I only have Delivery-on-Time Trucking listed," said the operator. "Would you like that number?"

"Yes," said Jackson. "That is most likely it." The operator gave Jackson the number, and he wrote it down on the back of a napkin. Jackson wasted no time calling the number.

"Delivery-on-Time Trucking, Stacy speaking. May I help you?"

"Yes," said Jackson, "I was wondering if you might have a truck that could come out to the airport. I have a bunch of boxes that I need to ship to California."

"What size are the boxes?" asked Stacy.

"Approximately two feet by two feet," Jackson replied.

"How many do you have?" she asked.

"Forty-nine," said Jackson.

"Are the contents hazardous?"

Jackson laughed. "No, they are files for my company," he said. "I just need them picked up and sent to an address in California."

"We can do that for you, sir," said Stacy. "When would you like them picked up?"

"Can you get your driver here by 5:00pm?" Jackson asked.

"Yes," Stacy replied. Jackson looked at his watch; it was 3:00pm on Sunday. The truck would arrive in less than two hours.

Jackson had little time to implement his next step. He made his way out to the plane and spoke to both pilots. The cargo needed to be unloaded so repairs could be carried out. A certified mechanic was on his way to supervise the repairs, and a large forklift had just arrived. It maneuvered to lift the tail of the DC-3 off the ground, and it would then drive backward to the closest hangar where the cargo could be unloaded, and the plane repaired. Jackson and the pilots followed in a security car sent to escort the forklift along the taxiway.

Inside the damaged plane, Jackson and the pilots watched as the forklift operator fastened large straps around the damaged tail and the forks of his machine. Slowly, he backed away from the spot where the DC-3 had been parked. The DC-3 was hauled to the open hangar, her tail backed into the large open hangar door. Repairs could be carried out here, even if the weather turned nasty. Jackson and the pilots stood by in a security car as the forklift operator drove to the side door of the wounded plane. The boxes of files were unloaded onto pallets and shrink-wrapped tightly around the stacked

boxes. After securing everything, the forklift operator placed the loaded pallets in the middle of the hangar floor. Jackson looked at his watch; it was now 4:20pm. The DC-3 would be ready for the maintenance crew when they arrived.

Jackson walked over to the pilots and handed each of them a fresh $100 bill. "It's been a rough afternoon, gentlemen. Why don't you go get yourselves a drink? I have a few calls to make, and then I will join you."

The pilots took the cash, waved, and said, "See you in a while." Jackson was left alone in the hangar with the forklift operator, who sat at the only desk in the northwest corner of the building. The forklift operator sat in the worn-out office chair with his feet up on the desk.

"I need your help," said Jackson.

"What can I do for you?" asked the operator as he sat up behind the desk.

"Do you know anyone that has a plane around here that can handle my boxes?"

"No, sir. All I do is drive the forklift. I don't like to spend much time getting to know folks. It can get you into trouble. I just do my job and go home."

"Where do you live?" asked Jackson.

"Did you see that old motorhome on the side of the building? That's my pad," said the operator. "She runs like a Swiss watch. Picked her up for three grand. The airport lets me park here and tie into the power, water, and sewer lines. I get that for free, so long as I keep my cell phone on 24/7 for emergencies, just like yours."

"Not a bad gig," said Jackson.

"Sorry I could not help you," said the operator.

"That's okay," said Jackson. "You have been a bigger help than you know. Would you be interested in selling your motorhome?"

"No," said the young man. "Where would I sleep tonight?"

"You said you paid three grand for it, right?" Jackson inquired.

"Yes," said the forklift driver.

"How about I give you ten thousand for it, but you have to help me load my boxes inside it?"

"No way," said the kid, "that's my house."

"How about twenty thousand cash?" said Jackson. "You can stay in a hotel for a night or two until you find new digs. I saw a hotel down the road, I think it was called the Wheel Inn. Didn't look too expensive."

"Yeah, I know the place," said the kid.

"$20,000 cash," Jackson repeated himself.

"Cash?" asked the kid with a blank look on his face.

"Yes," said Hall, "all cash, but you have to help me load the boxes."

"Sold," said the forklift operator. "I have to get my stuff out of there before I give you the keys."

"Don't have time," said Jackson. "What's in there?"

"My clothes and a little food in the fridge," came the reply.

"Tell you what," said Jackson, "let's make it $25,000, and you leave everything there. You look my

443

size," he added, laughing.

The kid looked at Jackson. "You got a deal, mister. I don't know why you're in such a hurry, but I don't care. We have a deal," said the operator. "Where's my money?" he asked Jackson.

"You bring the motorhome around to the door, and by the time you do that, I'll have your money on the desk for you," Jackson assured him.

The kid stood up, shook Jackson's hand, and said he would be a couple of minutes unhooking the utilities for the motorhome before he could pull around. "No problem," said Hall. The kid left the hangar.

Jackson fumbled with the shrink wrap surrounding his precious boxes containing his hard-earned cash. He reached inside the box he had taken money from before, pulling out three bundles of one hundred dollar bills, each with a band that said $10,000. He placed the money in his jacket pocket just as the kid pulled around with his motorhome.

"There she is," said the kid. "Isn't she a beauty?"

Jackson looked at the old Class C motorhome and smiled. Her paint was blistered, but she had character. "She is beautiful," said Hall.

The kid jumped on the forklift and started it up. He picked up the first pallet of Jackson's files and maneuvered the loaded forklift over to the open side door of the motorhome. The two men loaded all 49 boxes into every corner of the old motorhome until there was no room to move. Jackson took the 50th box and placed it on the passenger seat. He turned to find the operator standing behind him.

Jackson reached inside his jacket pocket and removed the three bundles of cash. "Kid, I want to thank

444

you for all your help. I don't even know your name," said Hall.

The kid's eyes were as big as saucers. "Andrew Jackson," he said.

Hall started to laugh. "Your parents named you after a President?"

"Yeah, I get that all the time."

"Well, Mr. President," said Hall, "here is thirty grand, but you can't tell anyone about our deal."

The kid looked at the three bundles of one hundred dollar bills. "Not one word," said Andrew. "Here are your keys. Do you want me to show you how everything works?"

"No," said Jackson Hall. "I have a deadline. I have to get to California with these files, or my accountant will have my head."

"Drive safely," said the kid. Jackson waved out the window as he turned around and headed through the open maintenance gate. Jackson pressed the accelerator pedal, and the old motorhome picked up speed as he hit the highway. A cloud of blue smoke followed behind him.

Andrew Jackson walked back to his desk in the corner of the hangar. He looked at the damaged tail of the DC-3 from his desk and placed the three bundles of one hundred dollar bills on the desk in front of him. He smiled and laughed, then picked up the phone and dialed a number he had known for twenty years.

"Hello," came the answer.

"Norman, it's Andrew. You're not going to believe the kind of day I'm having."

Chapter 85

Johnny Robbins, also known as Justin Wayne, waited until all was quiet, and everyone was asleep in the Rangers' Camp. He slowly walked down the path toward their tents. The quads were laid out, making it easy for him to steal one. That's all he needed to make a quick escape. By the light of the moon, Johnny made his way to the Rangers' ATVs. The ignition switches of each machine sat between the gauges on the handlebars. Johnny went to each one. There were no keys.

"Fuck," he said to himself. "I can't walk out of here. Not now, and they are going to be looking for me in the morning." Johnny was beside himself. Barbara was going to be waiting for him, or would she? Johnny was way overdue. He made his way back to his hiding spot. The plan he had formulated had fallen apart. Johnny laid down in the grass, then dozed off. He was exhausted.

Monday morning came early. Johnny was awoken by the noise coming from the Rangers' Camp. He could smell the fire and bacon cooking. The Rangers were standing around drinking coffee. Brad was mixed up in their conversation about when the sky crane would arrive. It was a big chopper with twin blades in the front and back, with a crew of three. It was always brought in by the department when heavy equipment needed to be lifted for the park. The last time was when they brought in the materials for the Glacier Park campground washrooms. One flight, one load. It was an awesome machine.

The Rangers were on the ready for the sky crane. The number one priority was to get the 505 out of Rock

Lake before her fuel purged from the tanks into the pristine waters of the lake. The parks department did not need an environmental disaster on their hands on top of everything else.

The young Ranger who had made the dive on the 505 the day before was again suited up. He was on the ready for the sky crane to show. Time was money, and the department's budget was going to take a hit on this call. He knew it and was looking for a promotion. He did not need to be told to get ready.

Johnny watched as the men ate. "Something was going on," he said to himself. One of the Rangers went around to each of the quads. He started each of them, one by one. The headlights from each machine glowed in the morning light until the Ranger went around and turned each machine off. They were warmed up and ready for action if the Rangers needed them in a hurry.

The young ranger, dressed in his wetsuit, excused himself from the rest of the men. Nature was calling, and he needed to take a dump. He was looking for a place to go. Johnny watched as the young park's official made his way towards Johnny's hiding spot. Johnny watched as the young man made his way towards a log laying about 5 feet from Johnny. The ranger stripped off his wetsuit, lowering it to his ankles. He then sat down with his ass hanging over the edge of the log.

The Ranger carried a plastic bag in his right hand. He sat with his back facing Johnny. This was going to be Johnny's one and only chance. Robbins reached for a large rock that was laying on the ground. Johnny crouched then moved slowly, not making a sound. When he was within reach, he smashed the heavy rock across the back of the ranger's head. The ranger grunted as Johnny hit him a second time. The ranger fell off the log

head first into the bushes in front of his makeshift outhouse. Johnny hit him a third time for good measure, blood covered the ground. Johnny could see the white bone of the ranger's skull. Robbins stayed low as he stripped off the ranger's wetsuit. He grabbed the light utility belt that held his waterproof radio, mask, and flashlight. Johnny stripped off his own clothes, then quickly dressed in the ranger's gear. Johnny's timing was almost spot on. He heard the roar of the helicopter in the distance. Johnny stood from his hiding spot. The Rangers in the camp spotted Robbins when he stood up. Johnny waved. From the distance, he looked just like the young ranger. The radio on Johnny's hip sprung to life. "This is Sky crane one, we are two minutes out. Is your diver ready?"

Johnny pushed the button on the walkie-talkie. "Roger," he replied.

There was another message that came through. "You got this one kid. Just hook up the line to the rotor shaft, and we can get out of here."

"Roger," came Johnny's reply. Within minutes, the sound of sky crane's huge rotors could be heard slicing through the air in the distance. Johnny walked into Rock Lake, placing the diving mask over his eyes and nose. He again waived to the other rangers on the shore. The sky crane was soon overhead. The downwash from the swirling blades was incredible. The huge helicopter maneuvered overhead. The wreck of the 505 could be seen clearly from their position one hundred feet above. The winch line was lowered from the belly of the twin-blade behemoth. Johnny watched as the cable was lowered with expert precision in front of him. Johnny waived his hand with his thumb pointing down. The winch operator knew more line was required. When the cable laid across the top of the 505, Johnny dove

down the 10 feet then secured the hook to the main rotor shaft. Johnny surfaced then raised his thumb in the air. The sound of the sky crane's engines got louder as the big bird took on the weight of the 505. The pilot raised the 505 just high enough above the surface of Rock Lake that the water poured from her open doors. The mangled rotor of the 505 hung like dead branches from a tree. Johnny maneuvered himself over to the 505, then climbed onto the roof. He clung to the shaft of the downed bird's rotor. He moved his hand in a circle. The sky crane applied more power until the 505 and Johnny hovered over the surface of Rock Lake.

The pilot radioed to the winch operator. "Are we clear?" The response was negative. "The diver is on the downed bird." Johnny kept moving his hand in a circular direction. His thumb pointing towards the sky.

"He wants us to go up," said the operator.

"What?" said the pilot? "That is against everything in the book."

"He is insisting," said the winch operator.

"Turn on the cameras," said the pilot. "If this guy falls off and gets hurt, we are not taking the blame."

"Roger," said the operator. Johnny kept moving his hand and thumb. The sky crane rose into the air with the 505 and Johnny suspended below its belly. The pilot maneuvered the large bird through the pass and back to the staging area for Rock Lake. The 505 slowly spun while attached to the cable, Johnny clinging on for his life. The pilot placed the downed 505 right in the middle of the parking lot. Johnny signaled for the sky crane to come down more so the cable became slack. Johnny released the hook from the rotor of the 505 then waived off the sky crane.

Johnny's radio crackled. It was the pilot. "Never seen anything like that. You have got one hell of a set of balls." Johnny climbed down from the 505, stood, and saluted the men in the sky crane. The winch operator retrieved the cable and soon the big bird was out of sight. Donna, Elizabeth, and the kids watched the whole event unfold in front of their eyes.

Johnny walked over towards Donna in his wetsuit. The kids and Elizabeth had begun walking towards the wrecked 505. "Did you guys like the show?" asked Johnny as he rubbed Mark's head.

Marcy and Mark both said "cool" at the same time.

"Well, thank you, little lady," Johnny said to Marcy. He continued walking towards Donna. The next thing Donna knew, Johnny's fist had come down across her jaw. Donna lay in a heap beside Tommy's jeep. Johnny's hands made their way through her pockets until he found what he was looking for. He took her car keys and cell phone. Mark and Marcy were screaming and crying. Elizabeth was running towards her friend laying on the ground. Johnny opened the door of the Jeep, placed the keys in the ignition, then drove away in a pile of dust. By the time Ranger Scott had reacted and run over to Donna, the jeep was out of sight.

Johnny looked at the clock on the dashboard; it read 10:00am. "Fuck," he said out loud as he hit the steering wheel. He picked up Donna's cell phone. Johnny called Barbara's number he had memorized. "Where was she, did she go home to her husband?" The phone rang three times.

"Hello?" said Barbara.

"Honey, it is me... Johnny."

"What happened to you?" she asked. "I waited for you at the airport just like you asked."

"Where are you now?" asked Johnny.

"I am at the Wheel Inn. I hit a big plane with a golf cart. They had loaded it with all your boxes. It's not going anywhere."

"Good girl," said Johnny. "I will be there in a couple of hours. Can you find me some pants, shoes, and a shirt? I will explain everything when I see you."

"Okay," said Barbara, then the line went dead.

Chapter 86

Kevin awoke to the sound of the sky crane off in the distance. He moved slowly in his sleeping bag, taking in his surroundings. Some small droplets of water had formed on the walls of his small tent from his breathing overnight. He hadn't heard any movement from the cabins. Kevin unzipped the tent door and stepped out into the bright sunlight, just in time to see the sky crane heading over the trees with the 505 hanging below. He grabbed his binoculars, steadied himself, and watched as the giant bird disappeared into the distance.

Kevin walked toward the only outhouse that served the cabins, situated behind RL02. He was still shaking off the evening's sleep. He liked to call it morning brain fog. Looking down at his feet, he noticed a large footprint in the dirt, clearly belonging to a massive Grizzly. He put his hand down in the print to make a comparison. The print was at least two and a half times the size of Kevin's hand. He looked around and saw more tracks, all around the back of the cabins.

"What the hell," he thought to himself as he heard movement coming from inside RL03. Kevin made his way into the outhouse to relieve himself. When he stepped back into the fresh air, Gale was waiting.

"Good morning," said Kevin. "Did you have a good sleep?"

"Yes," replied Gale, holding half a roll of toilet paper.

"Is your husband up?"

"Yes," she said, "he's on the front step." Kevin made his way around to the front of the cabin.

"Good morning," said Jerry.

"Morning," replied Kevin. "Looks like a big bear has been around here over the last 7 hours or so. I noticed some big tracks out back."

"Do you think it might still be around here?" asked Jerry.

"I doubt it," said Kevin. "With all of us around here, it should be long gone. Just keep your eyes peeled and let the rest know if you see anything. I'm going to get on the radio and speak to the guys at the end of the lake."

"Okay," said Jerry.

Kevin walked back to his tent, retrieved his radio from his pack, and turned it on. He pressed the button on the side of the walkie-talkie.

"This is Guide 101 to Parks at the end of Rock Lake, how do you read?" he inquired.

"Loud and clear," came Dan's reply.

"I see you managed to get the service chopper out of the water this morning."

"Yeah," said Dan, "all is good. We were a little concerned about a fuel spill, but all went well. How are things with your party?"

"We are just getting going here," said Kevin. "We will be having breakfast then heading your way."

"Roger," said Dan, "we have some more clean-up to do, then load the carcass of the Grizzly the boys put down. We need to get it into town and do the forensics. I am sure that the lady who was attacked with her friend would like to know the outcome. We will be heading down the path to pick up her girlfriend's remains before

anything. We don't want your party walking through there until we have taken our photos and gathered her remains."

"10-4," came Kevin's reply. Dan Thompson and the other Ranger mounted their quads. Brad rode the quad that the young Ranger who did the diving had been using. Brad took the lead as he knew where the attack had taken place, plus the location of Susan's friend's remains. The men crossed the small creek where the girls had bathed themselves the day before. Water splashed onto Brad's face as the front wheels hit the moving water. Brad turned his head to the left to keep his vision clear. There in the bushes beside the lake lay the body of Ranger Gary Smith. The young Ranger and diver for the parks department lay in a bloody heap, naked, the back of his head beaten to a pulp. Brad stopped, and the rest of the Rangers behind him followed suit.

Dan Thompson was right on Brad's ass, shouting, "Why are you stopping?" Brad stepped off the quad and pointed behind the bushes. Thompson dismounted and walked over to Brad, expecting to see Susan's friend.

Thompson looked, then really focused, and yelled into the air, "No!" as he ran to the body of Smith. Thompson fell to his knees beside the young man he had been mentoring for the last three years. Tears welled up in Dan's eyes as he looked towards the sky. "Why! Why!?" he said out loud. "He was a good kid!" Thompson gathered his thoughts, then stood to his feet. The other Ranger now stood beside Brad, looking at the body of his fallen comrade. Dan Thompson needed to get a message to Betty. The imposter who rode out on the fallen 505, hanging below the Sky Crane, needed to pay. Dan Thompson was going to make sure the bastard was not going to get away with killing a member of his

department. Dan pointed to Ranger Erickson.

"Ted, I need you to get up to Lookout Pass. The radio will work there. Get a message out to the office and Betty. We have a murderer on our hands. Tell them to send the state police. We will secure the area. We need to catch this bastard."

"Roger that," said Ted.

"Get back here as soon as you can," said Thompson. Ted mounted his quad and turned it around. He headed back through the campsite and up the trail to Lookout Pass. Dan Thompson walked over to the quad with the trailer and opened the plastic container on the front of the trailer hitch. He removed a blue plastic tarp.

The men and Brad covered Gary Smith's body. Thompson looked at Brad and the remainder of his men. "That will have to do until help arrives. Brad, can you please show us where the body of that lady is?"

Brad nodded his head. The sky was bright blue, the sun growing stronger as it rose from the east. "It is going to be one hell of a day," Brad said to himself as he worked the throttle of the ATV. The old trapper's cabin was only 10 minutes away, depending on the condition of the trail and how fast he could travel. The soft rubber tires threw dirt up as they traveled north. Branches from the shrubs and trees brushed against Brad's arms as the trail grew narrower. He was not looking forward to the grim reality of what lay ahead.

Kevin soon heard movement coming from RL01. The ladies from Ireland had opened the front door. The fresh mountain air rushed in. Aileen stood in the doorway. Kevin turned from looking down the lake. "Good morning," he said.

"Good morning," said Aileen. "Have you seen

456

our husbands?"

"No," said Kevin.

"They did not return last night," said Aileen. "We are so worried. It's been two nights. I am afraid they got lost, or something worse has happened to them."

Kevin turned his radio back on and pressed the button on the side of his walkie-talkie. "Guide 101 to Parks. Guide 101 to Parks."

Dan Thompson stopped his quad for a moment as Brad continued up the path. "Roger," said Thompson as he finished his conversation with Kevin. He turned to his remaining two men. "We still have two missing hikers," he thought to himself. "This day just keeps getting better and better." He pressed the throttle and soon caught up to Brad.

Chapter 87

Cathy awoke from her slumber. The last couple of days were a blur. She could not remember how she got to the condo. She got up and then went to the kitchen. She made a pot of coffee. As she poured herself a cup, she had a flash of Eric being tied down in a chair in her living room. She shook it off.

She walked around looking for her husband and son. Neither were to be found. Cathy opened the passage door to the garage. The bright red Honda Civic they had purchased for their son was not there. "He must be at the hospital," she said out loud. Her aspiring son was making one heck of a name for himself at Metro General. Her husband Eric must be out picking up a few things. She looked at the clock on the wall. It was 9:00am. "He is going to be so hungry when he gets back."

Cathy headed back into the kitchen. She decided to make a giant omelet for her and Eric. It would be ready when he returned from his outing. Cathy laid out two plates and cutlery then placed Eric's favorite coffee cup perfectly by his plate. She made a total of six pieces of toast, buttering each perfectly to the four corners just the way her husband liked. The omelet she made had ham and cheese with lots of mushrooms and red peppers, just the way Eric liked them.

She looked up at the clock; it was now 10:00am. Eric was not back yet. Cathy picked up the cordless phone from the counter. She called Metro General. Her son would know where his dad was.

"Hello, this is Cathy Taylor," she said to the operator that answered the hospital switchboard. "I

would like to speak to Dr. James Taylor."

There was a pause. "One moment," said the operator.

The lobby of the hospital still had investigators coming and going. The police were dealing with a missing person who had been held captive and raped. They now had what they thought to be two murders on their hands. Susan's body had just been taken to the morgue from the stairwell. Joann still lay in her hospital bed. Forensics had just finished taking all their photographs. It had been difficult to get a hold of everyone in the investigating unit. Some had gone out of town for the long weekend and were called back in.

The operator looked up as an investigator was walking by. "Sir," said the operator, "I have a woman on the line who is claiming to be Cathy Taylor."

The investigator held up his index finger to his lips. He then gathered two of his colleagues. "Put the call into that office," he said, pointing.

The operator nodded. The three detectives made their way into the small room, as the phone on the desk started to ring.

"Hello," answered the investigator as he placed the call on speaker.

"Hello, this is Cathy," Cathy Taylor said, the voice at the other end of the line. "I would like to speak to my son Dr. James Taylor."

"One moment," he said to Cathy. He placed the call on hold. "Get a shrink in here now!" he yelled. Dr. Lewis was summoned to the small office.

The investigators quickly explained who they thought they had on the phone. Dr. Lewis pressed the

hold button.

"Hello, this is Dr. Lewis," she said.

"Hello, this is Cathy Taylor. I am wanting to speak to my son, Dr. James Taylor."

"I am sorry," said Dr. Lewis, "he is currently in surgery."

"Well," said Cathy, "that's just great. I can't find my husband Eric. I made his favorite breakfast. I was hoping James knew where his father went this morning."

Dr. Lewis looked up, tears were running down her cheeks, as she looked at the three investigators. She knew full well that James and Eric were dead.

"Oh dear," said Dr. Lewis, "I am sorry, Cathy. Can I get a message to James for you? I will have him call you as soon as he is out of surgery."

"That would be wonderful," said Cathy.

"Where are you?" asked Dr. Lewis. "What number should I have him call you at?"

Cathy spoke, "At the condo. He has the number."

"That's fantastic," said Dr. Lewis. "Why don't you enjoy some of the food you made? I am sure your husband will be back shortly."

"That's a good idea," said Cathy. "I am starving. Wait till Eric gets here, making me eat all by myself. He did not even leave me a note. Thank you," said Cathy, and then the line went dead.

Dr. Lewis turned to find the investigators were already leaving the room. A trace had been placed on the call. They had an address.

Dr. Lewis ran after them, "I am going with you,"

she said.

Three police cars squealed out of Metro General's parking lot. Dr. Lewis sat in the front seat of one of the cruisers. Dispatch had sent three more patrol units to the condo. In minutes, six patrol units sat in front of Cathy and Eric's condo, the one they had purchased for their beautiful and talented son, doctor and pilot James Taylor.

Dr. Lewis stepped out of the cruiser. She was met by all the uniformed officers and investigators. She stood there in her white hospital gown. There was a quick conversation with the investigators as the ambulance pulled up on the street.

Dr. Lewis walked up the sidewalk to the front door. To her right was a beautiful porch swing. Its cushions neatly in place. The officers all had their guns drawn. Johnny Robbins was out there somewhere. They believed that he had gotten into the hospital, kidnapped Cathy, and killed Susan while making his escape.

Dr. Lewis had been given a bulletproof vest that she now wore over her hospital whites. She was nervous but had agreed to help. She did not believe that Cathy had someone with her. Dr. Lewis knew the signs of PTSD.

She reached out and rang the doorbell.

Cathy heard the bell ring. Thinking Eric had locked himself out, she jumped up from her breakfast at the kitchen table. She ran to the door and flung it open.

She was about to give Eric a piece of her mind for not leaving her a note. "Hello, are you Cathy?" said Dr. Lewis.

Cathy looked around past the doctor. She noticed all the police cars and the commotion taking place.

461

"What's going on?" asked Cathy.

"Hello, Cathy, I am Dr. Lewis from the hospital. Do you remember me? We spoke on the phone about 20 minutes ago."

"Yes," said Cathy. "Is there something wrong? Is there something wrong with my Eric, or my son?"

"Cathy, can you sit here with me on the porch swing?" Dr. Lewis pointed to the corner of the porch. The officers watched as Cathy and the doctor sat down.

"What's going on?" asked Cathy.

"We need to get you over to the hospital," said Dr. Lewis. "Your husband and son are waiting for us there." Dr. Lewis was not lying; Eric and James were in the morgue laying on slabs.

"Are they okay?" asked Cathy.

Dr. Lewis looked into Cathy's eyes. She was bound to tell her the truth but was also bound to not cause injury to her patients. The police officers had entered the house. They found some hospital clothing laying on the bedroom floor, a meal laid out in the kitchen, and nothing else. Johnny Robbins was not there.

Dr. Lewis asked for the EMTs to come up to the porch with the stretcher. Minutes later, the paramedics stood on the porch, the stretcher raised to about hip level. "Come on, Cathy, we are going to give you a ride on this nice comfortable bed."

"I don't need that," said Cathy.

"Please," said Dr. Lewis, "the sooner we get you back to Metro General, the faster you will be able to see your husband."

"Okay," said Cathy.

She got up from her position on the swing. Dr. Lewis held her hand and walked her to the gurney. "Sit here," said the EMTs. "Swing your legs up. There you go." They raised the back so Cathy was in a sitting position. One of the EMTs reached for the belts that would secure Cathy in place. He fastened the first belt around her waist. Her arms were trapped under the now tightened belt. All of a sudden, Cathy had flashbacks to being tied down in her bed at home. She saw images in her mind of strange men. Eric was tied up. She was being made to do things she never wanted to do. Cathy started screaming; she moved violently on the stretcher. She was kicking at everyone. She moved her head from side to side. Dr. Lewis called for a shot of amobarbital. The EMTs injected Cathy's arm with 10CCs of the drug.

She started to relax. "Do you bastards want to fuck me!?" she yelled. "Come on, get it over with." Her voice started to fade. She looked at Dr. Lewis. "I am God's servant," she said as her voice grew weaker. Her eyes closed, and Cathy was out. The paramedics fastened the last of the safety straps then loaded Cathy into the back of the ambulance. One EMT and Dr. Lewis stayed with Cathy in the back of the ambulance, while the other drove at a high rate of speed with lights and siren wailing. As the ambulance approached Metro General, the driver noticed the Life Flight helicopter landing on the helipad of the hospital.

Dr. Hansen and his team met their new patients, a father and son, on the first floor of the emergency room. Hillcrest had transferred the men that morning. The son, Tommy, needed plastic surgery to close wounds he had received in a bear attack. The father had been shot and sustained broken ribs, one of which had punctured his right lung. As both men were being wheeled into the operating room, Gunner was barking orders to make sure

463

they all looked after his son, Tommy, first.

"Look after my boy. He goes first," Gunner could hardly breathe, but he needed to get his message out. Dr. Hansen walked over to Gunner's side.

"It's okay," said Dr. Hansen. "We have two teams here to look after you both. Don't worry." The anesthesiologist placed a mask over Gunner's nose and mouth. "Everything is going to be just fine," said Hansen as Gunner's eyes closed.

Chapter 88

The Bell 505 lay in a crumpled heap right in the middle of the staging area for Rock Lake. Johnny Robbins had stolen a Jeep from the women and two children who were there. He left them in a pile of dust as he peeled out of the gravel parking lot. Barbara was waiting for Johnny at a little motel called the Wheel Inn. Robbins had a big smile on his face as he raced towards the motel. His plan had come together just as he expected it would. The clock in the Jeep read 10:30am. He should be at the hotel in two hours, maybe less if he could avoid the state police.

Barbara had gone to the front desk. She asked if she could look through their lost and found. She offered the manager fifty dollars for an old pair of blue jeans, a t-shirt, and a pair of runners she thought would fit her lover's feet. She went back to her room, then pulled out the ironing board. She went to work pressing Johnny's newfound duds. She laid them out on the bed. "There," she said aloud. "I hope they fit."

Barbara's cell phone rang. It was her husband. She hesitated and let it ring until the call went to her voicemail. Five minutes later, her phone rang again. Her husband was not giving up. Barbara decided to answer.

"Hello?" there was dead silence for a couple of seconds.

Then her husband started. "Where the fuck are you? The Casino has called looking for you. You were supposed to start your shift this morning at 8:00am. Where did you go last night? You fucking bitch, are you cheating on me?"

"Fuck you!" said Barbara. "Fuck you and everything you are! I hate you, I hate my fucking job, I quit! If they call back, tell them I am never coming back!"

"Fuck me!" said her husband. "I am going to find you, you fucking whore!" The line went dead.

Walter had been Barbara's husband for six tumultuous years. He had fucked around on her. As payback, she had fucked around on him. Walter came home to the trailer one night to find his neighbor's truck in the driveway. He beat the living shit out of his wife that night. He then went to the neighbor's place and waited for him to come home. Walter knifed the guy right in his own driveway. The dude survived, charges were laid. They were later dismissed when the neighbor refused to testify at the trial. The district attorney had no choice. There were no witnesses, no DNA evidence. Walter had gotten off scot-free.

He suspected his wife was still fucking around on him, but he could not prove it. Since she had taken the job at the Casino, their lovemaking had been sporadic at best. The thought of her being with another man drove him crazy. "Till death do us part." That was the commitment they made when Barbara and he took their vows. Walter had installed a tracking system on Barbara's cell. He looked at the screen on his own phone. He pressed the button to open the app on his phone. Up popped a map and a blue dot. Below it said forty minutes to Barbara's location.

"I've got you now!" he said out loud. "You bitch, just wait!" Walter got into his truck and sped out of his driveway. He was going to deal with the situation once and for all. It only took thirty-five minutes to get to the location of the flashing blue dot. Walter pulled into the

Wheel Inn parking lot.

"Fuck!" he said out loud. "The cheap whore!" He walked into the manager's office, his chest all puffed up, a package of cigarettes rolled up in the sleeve of his black t-shirt.

"Can I help you?" asked the manager.

"I am looking for a woman this tall, with Auburn hair and green eyes," Walter described his wife to a tee.

"Sorry," said the manager. "I have not seen anyone like that."

"You're a fucking liar!" screamed Walter. "I know she is here. See," he held up his phone, "I tracked her here."

"I am sorry," said the manager, "we respect our clients' privacy."

Walter turned the guest book around that sat on the counter. There was one entry that said cash. It was assigned to Room 10. Walter swung the book back around. "I got what I need," he said. Walter left the motel office.

The manager quickly picked up the phone and called room 10. "Hello?" answered Barbara.

"I think your husband might be here," said the manager. The line went dead. Barbara had no time to think; she went into the bathroom and locked the door. She opened the small window and then climbed through. She had left everything behind: her purse, her phone, Johnny's clothes. She ran as fast as she could.

Walter stood at the door of room 10. Barbara's red Mustang was parked in front. It had been behind a large four-wheel-drive truck. He never even noticed it when he pulled into the parking lot. Walter raised his

right foot and then kicked in the door. The safety chain broke free from its mounts as the door banged against the wall.

"Where are you? You cunt, you are dead!" Walter yelled. He noticed Barbara's purse on the nightstand. Her cell phone was laying on the ironing board. There were men's clothes laying out on the bed.

"You bitch!" Walter yelled. He noticed the bathroom door was closed. He tried the handle. It was locked. Walter knocked. "Come out, come out, wherever you are!" he said. There was no answer. Walter kicked in the bathroom door. Pieces of wood flew everywhere. He ran into the bathroom, pulling back the shower curtain. His wife and her lover were not there. He then noticed the open window.

"Fuck!" he said out loud. Walter went back out to the bedroom, sitting on the bed. He opened his wife's purse, dumping it on the bed. He had to look twice; there were two bundles of one hundred dollar bills staring him in the face, a box of fresh condoms, a tube of lube, and the usual shit. Each bundle of cash had a band around it that said ten thousand dollars. One of the bundles was a little loose.

"A few hundreds must have been missing," he thought. "Well, well," he said out loud, "the little whore is finally making some money."

He stuffed the two bundles into the pockets of his jeans. If the whore was going to make it, he was going to spend it. Walter grabbed her cell phone then headed towards his truck. He sat in the truck for a moment. He activated Barbara's phone. He entered her password, and the screen came alive. He scrolled through the data of the last calls. There was his call, another, and a few to Barbara's brother, all in the last two days.

Walter started his truck, highlighted the second last call, and pressed call back. Walter listened as the phone connected to the network. Donna's phone rang in the jeep. Johnny recognized the number.

"Hello, sweetie," he said. "I am about thirty minutes away."

"Who the fuck is this?" asked Walter.

"No, who the fuck is this?" was Johnny's reply.

"This is the husband of the whore you have been fucking," came Walter's reply. Johnny paused for a moment; he had been down this path before.

"Your wife fucks like a mink. She loves my cock up her ass. I hear you are an impotent little prick and can't get it up anymore."

Walter went crazy. "You fucker, I am going to kill you! Then she is next!"

In the distance, Walter could hear the sounds of sirens. The motel manager had called the state troopers. Walter threw his truck into gear, circled the hotel at high speed looking for Barbara. The dust he kicked up choked the air.

Barbara had made her way under an old beat-up motorhome that was parked at the very edge of the motel's property. She had positioned herself between the dual wheels of the back axle. She did not move. The large one-piece mud flap hanging from the rear fenders concealed her quite well. She was never going to take another beating like she had at the hands of her husband.

The sounds of the sirens grew louder. Walter slammed his fists against the steering wheel as he exited the parking lot and onto the highway. He had the number of his wife's lover. He knew she was close by.

"Their time will come," Walter said out loud.

Johnny Robbins banged his fist into the dashboard of the jeep. Barbara had been caught. He needed to get to her to get the information she had. He needed to know everything that happened at the airport. He had no choice. Johnny Robbins pressed the accelerator to the floor. The jeep was now doing eighty miles an hour. He was starting to sweat, wearing the stupid wet suit he had stolen that morning.

"Fuck!" he yelled at the top of his lungs. His plan was falling apart.

Chapter 89

Bob Gerard awoke in the Metro General Recovery room. His head hurt, but his memory was clear. A nurse walked over to the side of his bed.

"How are you feeling?" she asked.

"My head is killing me," said Gerard. "How did I get here?"

"Life Flight brought you in yesterday. They found you lying on the floor in a washroom at Rock Lake. You hit your head pretty good when you passed out."

"I did not pass out," said Robert. "I need to talk to the police. I need a phone. Can you please get me a phone?"

"You have to remain calm," said the nurse. "You had a bleed on your brain. The doctors put a shunt in your skull to relieve the pressure on your brain. You cannot get your blood pressure up. You could have a serious stroke."

"Please, I need a phone. I am a park superintendent. I need to contact my staff."

"Let me talk to the doctor," said the nurse. "I will be right back."

The nurse called Dr. Hansen and was given the go-ahead. Gerard's blood pressure would go up if he did not get the phone, so what was the difference? The first call Bob made was to the office and Betty.

"Honey, it's me," he said. "I am awake. What is going on?"

Betty started to cry. "I spent the night in the office," she said. "There is so much happening. How do you feel?" she asked.

"I will be fine," said Robert. "What's happening?"

"We lost the helicopter yesterday afternoon. It ended up in Rock Lake."

"What?" was Robert's reply. "How is Gunner?"

"He was shot," said Betty. "They airlifted him and his son to Metro General. They should be there in recovery. The son was mauled by a bear. It sounds like the bear is dead. Dan managed to get me a message. There was a jeep stolen, and there are two missing hikers. Also, I have some bad news," she said. "Gary Smith is dead. They found him on the path heading towards the cabins at Rock Lake."

Things instantly became clear to Robert. "Honey," he said, "I went to take a pee before going up with Gunner in the chopper. A guy walked in. He hit me on my neck with something. They tell me my uniform was gone. He must have taken it and then got on board the 505. That's how Gunner was shot. We need to contact the state police. The guy who killed Gary must have been the one that was hanging on the cable with the 505. Scott told you he saw a guy come in with the wreck, right?"

"Yes, that is what he told me," said Betty.

"We are dealing with above-average intelligence here for a criminal," he said.

"I have contacted the State P.D.," said Betty, "they are looking for an older jeep. The guy who took it punched a lady. He left her and two kids plus her friend at the staging area."

"God," said Robert, "I can't believe what I have missed. We need to catch this bastard."

"Honey, I love you," said Betty. "I have to go. One of the guys is on the radio."

"Love you too," said Robert. The line went dead. Robert closed his eyes. His head was throbbing.

Ten minutes later, two detectives stood beside his bed. Robert Gerard gave the men his full statement. He was then informed that they believed the perpetrator was none other than the escaped criminal Johnny Robbins. He and Matt Jones had made their escape. Jones was dead, shot in front of a burger joint in Hillcrest.

"Damn it," said Robert, "I can't stay here. There is too much to do."

"Take it easy," said the detectives.

Minutes later, Chris and Tommy were wheeled into the recovery room. Chris had a tube coming out of his chest, and Tommy was lying on his stomach with his head turned to the side. Robert recognized them immediately. Both Tommy and Chris were not awake; the effects of the anesthetic had not worn off yet. Robert would have to wait to ask his questions. He closed his eyes again and drifted off.

Back at Rock Lake, Kevin's crew was now up and about. The smell of cooking bacon filled the air. Gale was cooking up a feast as their final meal before heading out of the mountains. What a way to end a beautiful weekend. She felt bad about the crashed helicopter, but it was not her problem.

Over in RL04, David Newport and his fiancée Tammy were finishing their first cups of coffee. They had not been any help when Susan was flown out. As a matter of fact, David had been pretty ignorant. It started

when he tossed the fish away that Brad had given him by the old trapper's cabin. Maybe David was feeling guilty somewhere in the back of his mind. Maybe there was some remorse. Maybe he was actually responsible for the grizzly attack on Susan and Rachel. He shook off the doubts. Nope, no way. The girls were just too stupid to avoid the bear. He had nothing to do with it.

David walked towards the front door of RL04. He opened it, allowing the fresh mountain air to pour in. He took a deep breath. "It's a beautiful day, honey. Come have a look."

Tammy drew close, and David wrapped his arms around her. "It's beautiful but not as beautiful as you. I can't wait until we get married," he said in her ear.

Tammy gave David a long and deep kiss. "I am going to get breakfast started," she said.

"Awesome," was David's reply. "I am going to head over to the washroom." He made his way down the steps of the cabin and then walked towards the back. There was a nicely worn path that led in the direction of the outhouse. David was taking in the beauty of the morning. He could hear voices coming from the other three cabins. RL04 was the furthest cabin from the washroom, maybe a five-minute walk. But it was what he wanted. It gave him and Tammy more space and kept them away from the other hikers who had rented the three other cabins.

As David drew closer to his destination, he could smell bacon cooking. Gale had been cooking up a storm for the last half-hour. David took another breath. Not only did he have to take a shit, but he also realized how hungry he was. David heard a twig snap off to his left. Then he saw a dark brown flash.

It was the grizzly that had won its battle with the patriarch of the valley a couple of days ago, that now lay dead. Brad's knife had not let him down. The grizzly had found its next victim. These two-legged mammals were easy to catch; they had plenty of meat on them to fill its hungry belly.

David was knocked to the ground in one blow, with no time to react. He lay on his back, his fists hitting the grizzly on the head several times. David screamed at the top of his lungs. Kevin and the group heard the commotion coming from behind the cabins and ran to see what was going on. The grizzly stood over David, who now lay motionless. In David's mind, if he played dead, the big bruin would leave him alone.

The grizzly bent its head down, its claws digging deep into David's sides. In one movement, the bear put its mouth around David's neck. It clamped down, and David could feel the large white incisors puncture his throat. The grizzly's breath was rancid, and it shook David until his larynx and the skin surrounding his neck tore away. Blood squirted from David's carotid arteries. David's brain stayed active for a few more seconds. "Fuck," he thought to himself.

Kevin and his group were yelling and screaming. Kevin threw some rocks, and Jerry came running with a can of bear spray, handing it to Kevin. Kevin pulled the pin on the canister and ran towards the bear and its latest victim. The grizzly looked up, its mouth full of David's flesh. Kevin pressed the trigger on the can of spray, and a large red stream of fluid erupted from the end of the nozzle. Kevin kept his aim true, and the jet of fluid hit the bear squarely in the face. Kevin stood his ground and kept spraying. The bear inhaled as it tried to swallow its fresh kill, but it could not breathe. The fluid from the canister filled its eyes. The large grizzly let out a grunt

and then another as it ran off into the trees behind the cabins.

Kevin took three more steps towards David, and Jerry found a long pole and made his way to Kevin's side. "Stay back!" shouted Jerry to the rest of the group. The three girls from Ireland joined everyone, and Kevin knelt down beside David as blood continued to pour from the massive open wound on David's neck. David's eyes were wide open, and the ground was soaked in blood.

Tammy had come running as soon as she heard David scream, standing in shock about twenty feet away. "Do something!" she yelled. Kevin looked over at her, then back to Jerry. Kevin placed his hand over David's face and used two fingers to close David's eyes.

"I am sorry," said Kevin. "He is gone. There is nothing we can do."

Tammy screamed at the top of her lungs. The rest of the ladies in Kevin's group and the Irish girls were either crying or shaking. Jerry put his hand on Kevin's right shoulder. "That was the bravest thing I have ever seen."

Kevin looked up from his position. "If only I had been fifteen seconds faster. God damn it." Kevin stood, his knees and hands covered in blood, and walked over to Tammy, then put his arms around her. "I am so sorry," he said as he embraced her shaking torso. Tammy collapsed into Kevin's arms, throwing him off balance, but he steadied himself. "You better come with us," he said, David's blood now on Tammy's shirt.

Chapter 90

Andrew Jackson continued to speak to Norman Fisher, his lifelong friend and the owner of the old Bell 47 helicopter. Norman had worked out a pretty good gig with Andrew. The rent on the old hangar was only five hundred dollars a month. He was flying in three loads of ice from Angel Glacier every week. The Asians were paying him three thousand dollars a load. That was nine grand a week, thirty-six thousand a month. It was more money than Norm had ever had in his life, and it was all cash. Norman would land outside his hangar. Four Asian guys would meet him. They would unload the ice from the coolers on the skids of the 47. Norman never got his hands dirty. All he had to do was keep the old 47 flying.

Three times a week, the Asians would make their way to Andrew's hangar. They would leave him three aluminum insulated containers marked "Tokyo," with big bold letters marked "rush." It was Andrew's job to make sure they got on the only FedEx flight out of Hillsboro. For that, Andrew was paid one thousand dollars a week. It was easy money. Andrew never asked any questions. He did not have to. His friend told him everything.

"So what happened?" asked Norman.

"This dude had a DC-3 rented and had it all loaded with boxes of freight. The golf cart from the cafeteria somehow ran into the back of the plane, damaging the elevator and rudder."

"So?" said Norm.

"Well, I helped them unload the boxes," said Andrew. "Then the dude offered to buy my motorhome."

"What?" said Norm. "You sold the beast?"

"The guy paid me thirty grand, then told me to keep my mouth shut."

"Are you kidding? Thirty grand?" said Norman. "You only paid three grand for that piece of shit."

"I know," said Andrew. "I helped him load the boxes into the motorhome, told him a bunch of lies on how well it ran, and he drove out of here. Couldn't have taken more than half an hour."

"Interesting," said Norman. "Have you heard the news?"

"What news?" asked Andrew.

"The cops are looking for an escaped criminal. The guy's name is Johnny Robbins. I wonder if that was the guy who bought your motorhome?"

"Could be. He was in one hell of a hurry to get out of here."

"The FBI has a one hundred thousand dollar reward out for information leading to the capture of the guy."

"Really?" said Andrew. "Fuck, if I only knew that before."

"Well, he couldn't have gotten far," said Norman. "How much gas was in the motorhome?"

"Maybe a third of a tank at the most," Andrew mumbled.

"Why don't you come over to the hangar after your shift? It's getting dark. First thing in the morning, we'll fire up the 47 and see if we can find the guy. We split the reward 50/50."

Andrew and Norman spent the evening in the rented hangar, eating pizza and drinking a few beers. They were discussing how to spend the reward money. Both men eventually dozed off, sitting in their chairs. The Bell 47 sat inside the hangar doors, waiting for her next mission.

Chapter 91

Robert Gerard woke a second time in the recovery room. His head was not as foggy as it had been. He sat up and looked around the room. The open recovery area had room for about ten beds. Each could be divided with the use of curtains that moved on tracks mounted to the ceiling. In the corner, he could see Gunner. Beside him was Tommy.

"Chris? Hey, Chris, can you hear me?" shouted Robert. The nurses at the station heard the commotion coming from the recovery room.

"What's going on in here?" asked the head nurse as she stood beside Robert's bed.

"That guy over there works for me, and I need to talk to him. Can you wheel me closer to his bed?"

"He is sleeping, sir. This is the recovery room. You all need your rest."

"Please," said Robert. "Chris, can you hear me?" he shouted.

Tommy started to stir in the bed beside his father. Tommy opened his eyes and then focused on the direction from which the voice had shouted. He saw Bob and started to realize where he was. The pain in his back was killing him. An IV pole and a bag of fluid hung by Tommy's bed. The nurse left Robert's side, making her way over to Tommy.

"How are you feeling?" she asked.

"Sore," said Tommy.

"Do you know what happened?" she asked.

"Yes," said Tommy, "a bear got me. How is my friend?"

"I do not know anything about your friend," she said. "However, your father is here with you. He is going to be okay. They stitched up your back. You are going to need to see a plastic surgeon. They used over one hundred stitches to close your back."

"No wonder I am sore," said Tommy. "What happened to my dad?"

"He was shot," said the nurse. "His bulletproof vest saved his life. Just a couple of broken ribs and a punctured lung, but he is going to be okay."

Tommy moved his head so he could see Robert and then his father. "Hello, Mr. Gerard," said Tommy. "Why are you here?"

Robert's head was becoming clearer with every passing moment. "That escaped convict got me," he said. "Now I have this thing draining fluid out of my head." Robert pointed to the shunt. "Nurse, please move me closer to those two guys. I do not want to shout at them." The nurse finally complied. Robert's bed was rolled over beside Gunner's. Tommy was across the other side of the room, maybe ten feet away. "How are you feeling, kid?" asked Robert. "What happened?"

"A grizzly got me. Brad managed to put a knife in its neck. We think it was the same one that attacked those two girls." Tommy's mind was clear.

"Did they get her body?"

"No."

"I spoke to dispatch," said Robert, "there is a lot of stuff going on up at Rock Lake."

"Well, the bear is dead," said Tommy. "I

481

remember it. It was on my back. The next thing I knew, its entire weight was on me. Brad was shouting in my ear, 'Are you okay, buddy?' Dad?" Tommy shouted, "Dad, can you hear me? We are in the hospital. Dad...?" Chris started to stir. He had a tube sticking out of his chest. "Dad!" shouted Tommy again. Chris opened his eyes, then stared at the ceiling. "Dad!" shouted Tommy.

Chris turned his head, focused, and could see Tommy across the room. Gunner whispered, "Hello, Tommy." Gunner moved his head to the side and could see his superintendent. "Bob, what are you doing here?" asked Gunner.

Chris was still a little groggy from the anesthesia, but things were coming into focus. Bob spoke. "I think that convict is responsible for all of this," said Robert. "I was taking a piss, and that is the last thing I remember. Just saw a flash of light, then pain, and everything went black."

Gunner took a breath. "I thought it was you getting into the chopper. He was dressed like you, had your hat and utility belt on. He got in, pulled a gun on me. I took him up to Rock Lake at gunpoint. He pulled the trigger, I saw the flash, and the 505 went into the water. I am sorry," said Gunner. "Tommy's friend Brad managed to get me out before she went completely under."

"Don't worry," said Robert. "The helicopter was insured, so long as you're going to be okay."

Tommy pressed the button on the side of his bed. The nurse came in and stood beside his bed. "Do you have anything for the pain?" he said. "My back is pretty sore."

"Certainly," she said. "I will be right back."

Bob asked the nurse to bring him the phone again. "I will be back in a couple of minutes," she said. Robert looked at both men in the recovery room. "We are going to get the son of a bitch, if it's the last thing I do."

The nurse was back a few minutes later. She handed Robert the phone, walked over to Tommy, and placed a pill in his mouth. She took the plastic glass from his side table, then placed the edge of the straw into Tommy's tilted mouth. He drew a mouthful of water and swallowed from his face-down position. "Thank you," he said.

Robert called Betty. "Honey, it's me," said Bob. "Chris and his son are with me here in Recovery. Chris thinks that the escaped convict might have been the one to shoot him."

Betty replied, "There is an APB out for Johnny Robbins. His accomplice was killed in front of a burger joint a couple of days ago. He is on the loose. Robbins has left a trail of destruction behind him."

"It has to be him," said Robert. "What is the latest?"

"I just got a relayed message," said Betty. "There has been another attack up at Rock Lake. A hiker is dead."

"What?" said Bob. "Tommy said that the grizzly was dead."

Betty said, "This attack took place behind the cabins at Rock Lake. Also, one of the wardens had found a girl lying in the parking lot with two kids named Mark and Marcy. Her jeep had been stolen. Her girlfriend was trying to arrange transport for her to Metro General. Guess she had a nasty bump on her head. The children

were in shock after watching their Aunt get pummeled into the ground."

"What about the poachers?" said Bob. "It's Monday. They should have been before the judge this morning."

Betty said she had bad news. "Since there were no witnesses from the department at the time, the judge had them in front of his bench. He had no choice but to let them go."

"Damn," said Robert. "Well, we have their information. We have more time to pursue other charges later."

"Agreed," said Betty. "We have quite the situation on our hands."

Kevin had managed to relay a radio message through to the Ranger at Lookout Point. He, in turn, radioed Ranger Scott in the staging area for Rock Lake. Betty had received the information about the stolen jeep and the new grizzly attack. She had just arranged a flat deck trailer for the downed 505. Additional emergency transport for the woman and two children had also been arranged. Betty had contacted the sheriff's office about the stolen jeep. Betty had also notified the coroner's office about the body Tommy and Brad had reported. Now it sounded like there would be two bodies to deal with. She told Bob she loved him and would be at the hospital as soon as she could. "Love you too," said Robert. "Thanks for the update."

Chapter 92

Barbara lay under the old motorhome. The dust was starting to settle from her husband's truck speeding through the parking lot. She could hear the sound of police sirens getting closer. She was relieved that the authorities would soon be there. The gravel she was lying on was very uncomfortable. She started to move when she heard a voice. It was Jackson Hall.

"Hello, honey," he said as he paced back and forth beside the old motorhome. "How are things at the surf shop?"

Maria Hernandez replied, "We have had our best weekend ever. It's so busy. What number are you calling from?"

"I had to buy one of those disposable phones," said Jackson. "I will explain later."

"Did you get all of it?" asked Maria.

Jackson continued to pace. "Yeah," he said aloud. "The plane I rented got smashed by a fucking golf cart, can you believe it? I bought this kid's motorhome. Everything is inside, but the motorhome is not running right. I spent the night at this goddamn flea-bag hotel, The Wheel Inn. I do not know what I am going to do... Yes. All of it, I have fifty boxes total. When I get there, we can decide where we are going to go. Yes... it's a lot of cash." The sounds of the sirens were now so loud that Jackson could not hear Maria. "I have to go. I will call soon."

Three state trooper cars pulled into the parking lot of The Wheel Inn, their lights still flashing as they came to a stop in a cloud of dust. The officers stepped

out of their cruisers with their 9mm drawn. One of the police officers made his way to the motel's office. In minutes, two officers entered room number 10. One officer went out back of the motel, just in case the perpetrator made his way through a rear window.

Jackson Hall opened the driver's door of the motorhome with the old keys he had in his pocket. He released the hood latch, then made his way to the front of the motorhome. He opened the hood, propping it up with the metal rod that was neatly tucked away. Jackson took out his cell phone. He turned on the camera mode. Then he positioned the phone so he could watch the troopers without turning his head. "Brilliant," he thought to himself. Jackson pretended he knew what he was doing. He could not run away, and he was starting to sweat. There was one hundred million stored inside the motorhome. What if the cops wanted to search it? Jackson was getting a little nervous.

Barbara wiggled her way towards the passenger side of the motorhome, then crawled out from underneath it. She dusted herself off, then headed directly back behind the Motorhome. Barbara looked back, noticing a bumper sticker that said "Spending my kids' inheritance." She ensured that Jackson Hall did not see where she had come from. She made her way around the outer edge of the parking lot and then towards room 10. Tears ran down her face. "Help me," she said to the two officers.

"What happened here?" came the stern question.

"My ex must have tracked me here," said Barbara.

She saw that her purse had been overturned, and its contents were laid out on the bed. The two bundles of cash that Justin Wayne had given her the night before

were now missing. She sat on the bed, looking up at the officers. "His name is Walter," she said. "I left him a couple of days ago. He has a temper."

"Has he ever hurt you before?" asked one of the troopers.

"Yes," said Barbara, "badly. He was charged with attempted murder." Barbara never clarified that the charges were laid against Walter for trying to kill her lover at the time.

"Look at that door," said Barbara. "Who is going to pay for that? I do not have any money."

"Do you know what kind of vehicle your ex was driving?"

"I am guessing it was his truck," she said.

"That matches with what the manager told us," said a trooper. "What kind of truck is it?"

"A white Ford," she said.

"Do you know the year and license plate number?" Barbara opened a small red plastic folder that was laying on the bed. It had been in her purse. "Here," she said, "this is our old registration. My Mustang is on here as well." She fumbled to collect her belongings and organize them as she put everything back into her purse. She was embarrassed that the cops had seen the box of condoms and tube of lubricant. She gathered her car keys. Walter, in his glory of looking at all the cash, never picked them up off the bed.

"Don't worry," said one of the troopers. "We will find him."

The third trooper that had been out back now joined the two other officers in Room 10. The Trooper with the red plastic folder stepped outside. He used the

radio in his car to alert dispatch that an APB needed to be issued on a 1985 White Ford 1/2 ton, the driver Walter Kenny was wanted for domestic abuse, destruction of private property, plus uttering threats. The Trooper exited his car and then came back into the room. He handed Barbara her information. A minute later, the radios the men were wearing came to life. Dispatch had sent a message to all state troopers to be on the lookout for Walter's truck. At the end of the message, the dispatcher said, "Use caution. Suspect could be armed and dangerous."

"Do you know what direction he went?" Barbara was asked.

"Yes," she said as she pointed. "That way, down the highway."

The officers said, "South on 99?" Barbara nodded. The officers ran to their cars, hit their sirens, and spun their wheels in the gravel as they exited the parking lot of The Wheel Inn.

Jackson Hall watched as they headed south on 99. He placed his cell phone in his pocket and closed the hood on the broken-down Motorhome. "Piece of shit," he said aloud.

Norman Fisher and Andrew Jackson were up around 7:00am. They had opened the doors to the old hangar. The Bell 47 was easy to push back into the breaking sunlight.

"We better top her up," said Norman. He got on his cell phone and called the Airport mobile service. It was easier than starting the old girl up, flying over to the pumps, and then having to shut her down again. The phone rang twice.

"Fuel on wheels," was the answer. Norman had

ordered fuel many times in the past this way.

"Tim, it's Norman Fisher, I need to top up the 47."

"I can be there in five minutes," Tim said. He was accustomed to the routine, especially over the last month. Norman had been busy coming and going, almost every second day.

"See you in five minutes," said Norman. He and Andrew busied themselves with cleaning the bubble of the 47. Her plexiglass canopy had seen its share of abuse over the years. The amount of bugs and rocks that had hit or bounced off the plexiglass bubble over the years had dulled the surface. "Here," said Norman, handing Andrew a damp rag. "Wipe her down."

Andrew went back to the tail boom. He slid the covers off the aviation numbers that were assigned to the 47. He was proud of himself. The system he had developed to hide the numbers worked well.

Tim arrived within minutes, as specified. "How you boys doing this morning?" asked Tim as he grabbed his ladder. The fuel tanks for the 47 were mounted high just below the rotor. The ladder made the job much easier. "How much do you want?" asked Tim.

"Top her up," said Norman. "It's just the two of us this morning. Andrew's skinny ass should not be a problem for the old girl." Norman laughed out loud, thinking of the weight and balance of the old chopper.

Tim filled the old girl to the brim, as he was instructed. "That's $178," he said.

Norman reached into his pocket and pulled out a small bundle of hundred-dollar bills. He peeled off two. "Here you go," said Norman. "Keep the change."

Tim loved the extra cash. "Enjoy your flight," he said to the boys.

"Roger that," said Norman. In minutes, the 47 was fired up. They had been cleared to head south of the airport. Both young men wore headsets with microphones in the semi-open cockpit. Norman looked over at Andrew. "How far do you think he might have got?"

"No more than 50 miles," said Andrew.

"Then we will go 50 miles out. Highway 99 should be our best bet. If he did not find a place to get fuel, then maybe we will get lucky. Keep your eyes peeled. That hundred grand would be pretty sweet."

"You bet," said Andrew as he looked intently through the bubble of the Bell 47.

Chapter 93

Kevin walked Tammy to the front of RL03 and sat her down on the front steps. Tammy continued to bawl her eyes out. The Irish ladies and the rest of Kevin's group gathered around.

"We obviously have a serious situation on our hands," said Kevin. "Let's start packing up, ladies," he said, pointing to Aileen. "I think you should join us. We will have a look for your husbands on the way out." They nodded in agreement.

Jerry approached Kevin. "We cannot just let that guy lay there. What if that Grizzly comes back?"

"Agreed," said Kevin. "Let me see if I can get a hold of someone." Kevin pulled out his radio once more. "Guide 101 to Parks. Guide 101 to Parks, how do you read?"

Kevin's radio crackled. The voice Kevin heard was distant, and there was a lot of static. "Parks to Guide 101, Parks to Guide 101, go ahead."

Ted had received Kevin's radio message as he was getting ready to call Betty from Lookout Pass. "Guide 101, we have a serious situation here at the cabins. There has been a bear attack. We have a hiker that has been killed. Grizzly attack," said Kevin.

"Roger that," said Ted. "Understand that you have a downed hiker. Bear attack. Confirm."

"Roger," said Kevin.

"I will try to get a hold of Thompson," said Ted. "They are on their way to the Trapper's Cabin."

"Roger," said Kevin. The Trapper's Cabin was only a half mile away. Brad continued to lead Dan Thompson and the other ranger to where he and Tommy had found the body of Rachel on the trail. They pulled up on the quads in front of the dilapidated Trapper's cabin. It had been on the shores of Rock Lake for an estimated one hundred years.

Brad got off his quad. There were several items still scattered over the trail that had belonged to Rachel. "You can see the blood here," said Brad as he pointed. The bear had done a good job of ripping open Rachel's and Susan's backpacks. "There," said Brad. "That stick is where her body was."

Dan Thompson and the other rangers pulled their sidearms from the holsters on their hips. Thompson stood on the edge of the trail, looking towards the brush and side of the mountain. "I have a blood trail here," said Dan, pointing east. "It goes this way," he said. "Grab the kit," Dan said to the other ranger, "and bring the rifle." Steve had done these searches before. He grabbed the kit, a large plastic case containing a body bag, camera, flares, gloves, and surgical masks. Dan Thompson made his way along the blood trail. He looked back at Brad. "You stay here," he said.

Steve followed Dan into the bush. Within minutes, Thompson yelled back towards Brad. "We have her!" he said. Brad leaned against the quad he had been riding and bowed his head. It was the least he could do. Flies had started to accumulate on what was left of Rachel's body. She was partially covered in mud, sticks, and leaves.

Steve stood beside Dan. "Such a shame," said Steve.

"Tragedy," said Thompson. "Let's start with the

492

camera." Steve put the case down and then opened it. He handed the camera to Thompson. Dan took a series of pictures.

"Look at that wound there. Strange," said Thompson as he pointed. "They would need to corroborate their findings in a full report with the pictures."

When Dan was satisfied he had enough photographs, he and Steve put on rubber gloves and their masks. They rolled out the body bag, unzipping it in the process. The two men brushed the twigs and leaves off Rachel's body. Her clothing was shredded, and there were large chunks of flesh missing from her legs.

"What a mess," said Dan. "What end do you want?" he said to Steve.

"Legs," said Steve as Dan made his way towards Rachel's head. The men bent down to pick her up. The flies swarmed around the decaying meat that was once a human being. "On the count of three," said Steve. The men started to lift Rachel. As her body came off the ground, her bowels spilled onto the dirt.

"Christ," said Dan as Steve dropped his end. Steve removed his mask then puked into the shrubs. Flies quickly landed on the corners of Steve's mouth.

"Fuck me," he said as he pulled his mask back into place with his blood-covered gloves.

"Ready now?" said Dan. Steve nodded his head.

Both men picked up Rachel's body, placing it in the body bag from the recovery kit. Dan used a large stick to pick up the rest of her entrails and laid them in the bag with her. The men zipped up the black body bag. Dan yelled to Brad, "We could use your help here!"

Brad made his way into the brush and saw that the body bag now contained Rachel's remains. Brad was happy he did not have to contend with that part of the recovery. "Would you mind taking the case?" asked Thompson as he handed it to Brad.

Dan and Steve carried Rachel's remains ahead of Brad. The three men made their way back to the quads. The body bag was placed in the small utility trailer behind the last quad. Dan took several more pictures of the items scattered around the trail before gathering them up. Those items were placed in the trailer with the body bag. A blue tarp was then placed over the trailer and fastened into position with elastic cords.

Dan's radio crackled to life. "This is Guide 101 to Parks, Guide 101 to Parks." Dan heard Ted, the Ranger he sent to Lookout Pass. "Respond." Kevin's message was loud and clear on Dan's radio. There had been another attack.

"Guide 101, Guide 101, how do you read?"

"Loud and clear," said Kevin.

Dan spoke slowly, "Understand your situation. We are headed in your direction now. ETA about ten minutes."

"Roger," said Kevin.

The Rangers and Brad mounted the quads and drove slowly towards the cabins on Rock Lake. The body of Rachel bounced in the back of the small trailer as they made their way over rocks and potholes. Eventually, the four cabins at the north end of Rock Lake came into view.

Chapter 94

Barbara watched as the state troopers sped out of the parking lot of the Wheel Inn. The thick dust moved slowly through the air, eventually settling back onto the ground. She stood there, looking down the highway. "Justin should be here," she said to herself. She leaned against her red Mustang and started to bawl. Tears rolled down her cheeks. In a matter of two days, she had given up everything for someone she met in a hotel room. She shook uncontrollably. "Where are you!?" she screamed out loud.

In the distance, at an elevation of approximately two thousand feet, a Bell 47 was approaching in the direction of the Wheel Inn. Andrew Jackson had kept his eyes peeled for his old motorhome. "There," pointed Andrew. "There she is."

"Look at that," said Norman. "We found the old girl. Now, if we can only find that guy they are looking for, we are going to collect that big fat reward."

"Nice," said Andrew.

The Bell 47 got closer and closer. The noise from the whirling rotor cut into the air, making a whipping noise that was very distinct to the 47. Jackson Hall looked up as the chopper circled the property of the Wheel Inn. Hall ran into the motel's office. The cops had just been there. Jackson had played it pretty cool. He was now starting to feel very uneasy. "Hello," said Jackson. There was no reply.

Jackson made his way around the back of the counter. He grabbed a purple nylon vest that was hanging on the wall. The Wheel Inn logo was emblazoned across

the back. The vests were always worn by the cleaning staff. Mind you, there were only two chambermaids on the payroll these days as business had been so slow. Jackson fumbled, then dropped the vest. As it settled on the ground, he removed the other from the last hook on the wall. Jackson slipped the second vest on then bent over to pick up the first one laying on the floor.

Hall's eyes caught a glimpse of something mounted under the check-in counter. He looked closely. There, placed in two small clamps, was a fully loaded sawed-off 12-gauge shotgun. Jackson could not believe his luck. He removed the shotgun from its hiding spot. Jackson was very familiar with shotguns, even modified ones. Jackson pressed the safety release then slid the cocking mechanism back along the shortened barrel. A cartridge popped out of the chamber, landing on the floor. Jackson did that three more times. A total of four cartridges now lay on the floor at his feet. Hall bent over then loaded them back into the 12-gauge. Three into the slide, he cocked the gun again one more time. This chambered the fourth round.

The Bell 47 flew twice around the property of the Wheel Inn. There were folks standing outside of their rooms, watching as the old helicopter circled overhead. "There," said Norman, "let's set her down over there on the grass." The Bell 47 settled down gently on the only manicured portion of lawn directly in front of the motel. Norman flipped a few switches, and the 47's engine stopped producing power. Norman and Andrew waited a few moments as the large overhead rotor started to slow. Both young men removed their headsets.

With the engine now shut down, it was much easier to hear each other. "You take the office," said Norman. "I will go and check on the motorhome."

Barbara watched the two young men exit the chopper. One walked towards the motel office, the other towards the old motorhome. The motel manager had been out back in the garage that also served as his workshop. He re-entered the office through the back door of the manager's office, carrying his toolbox. It was not the first time he was going to have to repair a broken door on one of his rooms. He walked towards the counter and noticed someone was standing in the lobby wearing one of his employee's work vests.

"What's going on here?" the manager yelled. Jackson turned. "Hey, you're the guy I rented the room..." The manager did not get any more words out of his mouth as the butt of the twelve-gauge hit him square in the nose. Blood ran down the manager's face, his baseball cap went flying. Jackson hit him again. The old wooden toolbox the manager had been carrying dropped to the floor, scattering tools everywhere. The manager dropped to his knees. "You fucker," said the manager, spitting his broken teeth out. The butt of the shotgun came down on the manager's head again. This time the manager crumpled in a heap. He lay unconscious, his torso and bleeding head behind the counter, his legs sticking out into the aisle. Jackson quickly placed the manager's ball cap on his head and then dragged him the rest of the way behind the check-in counter.

Jackson crouched down, placing the shotgun behind the counter and well within reach of his right hand. Hall fumbled with the tools that were scattered on the floor, picking up a few at a time and placing them into the toolbox.

Andrew Jackson walked into the motel's office. There before him was Jackson Hall on his knees, his head down, the motel vest on, and the brim of the cap pulled forward. Andrew had no idea who he was. "Hey,"

said Andrew, as Jackson continued to pick up the tools and place them in the toolbox. "Do you know where I can find the guy that drove in in that old motorhome?"

"Why do you want to know about him?" asked Hall, doing his best to keep his voice low and his head down.

"That dude is wanted," said Andrew. "He's an escaped criminal. I sold him my motorhome yesterday. There's a one hundred thousand dollar reward for information leading to his arrest. His name is Johnny Robbins." Jackson Hall looked up from his kneeling position, and his hand reached behind the counter. "Fuck!" said Andrew. "It's you!"

Hall pulled the shotgun out from behind the counter and aimed it at Andrew Jackson's chest. Jackson Hall pulled the trigger. Andrew flew back from the point-blank blast. The hole in his chest was the size of a cantaloupe. Andrew Jackson was dead before he hit the floor. Hall stood up and walked over to the kid.

"You should have stuck to minding your own business, kid." Norman heard the commotion and the loud bang coming from the office.

He changed direction, deciding to investigate what was going on in the office instead of heading to the motorhome. Norman took two steps into the motel office. He saw his friend lying on the floor with a gaping hole in his chest. Jackson Hall stepped out from behind the open door, pointing the shotgun at Norman's head before pulling the trigger. Norman's body fell to the floor in a crumpled heap. The smell of gunpowder filled the air. Blood spurted from the arteries in Norman's neck, and there was skin, blood, and brain matter all over the walls and floor of the motel's office.

Jackson calmly closed the blinds on the window, locked the front door to the office, and then turned the open sign around to read "closed." He closed the office door as he left and calmly walked towards his motorhome. The people who had been standing outside, watching the helicopter land, had dispersed back into their rooms. Jackson's path was clear, with the shotgun tucked under his right arm, ready to use again if necessary.

Jackson fumbled with the keys until he finally got the driver's door open. He climbed in, sitting in the driver's seat, and could smell the money. Jackson took a deep breath and looked in the rear-view mirror, noticing drops of blood on his face and hands. He placed the key in the ignition, pumped the accelerator on the floor, and the engine turned over but did not fire. Jackson tried again, saying, "Come on, you bitch," as he pumped the pedal again. The engine sputtered, then came to life, with a cloud of blue smoke from the tailpipe. Jackson placed the motorhome in gear, and there was a clunk as the transmission engaged. He looked at the fuel gauge on the dashboard, which read empty. It didn't matter; Jackson Hall needed to put some distance between himself and the crime scene.

Barbara watched as the old motorhome pulled out of the parking lot. Hall pointed the motorhome south, and the sign on the highway read 'Hillcrest 60 miles'. "There is no fucking way I am ever going to make that," Hall said out loud. He continued down the highway, and the motor sputtered again. A mile ahead, Jackson could see a road crew maintaining the median leading into town. Two contracted employees sat on garden tractors, cutting the grass on the median, while their supervisor sat in a large one-ton flatbed service truck pulling a tilting trailer. Jackson pulled in front of the supervisor's

499

truck as his engine sputtered and died. The service truck had its four-way flashers on and a large electronic sign on its roof with a large orange arrow flashing to the left, indicating that drivers should move over to the far lane. Jackson walked back towards the supervisor's truck, and the supervisor gestured for him to come to the passenger side of the service vehicle. Jackson complied with the driver's motions, and the supervisor pressed the button for the electric window on the passenger side.

"What can I do for you?" asked the supervisor. Jackson looked sheepishly through the window then spoke.

"Do you have any extra gas I can buy?" he said.

"You folks in your motorhomes," said the supervisor.

Jackson explained that he had a faulty gauge and thought he had enough to make it to Hillcrest. The supervisor had been approached so many times in his ten-year career that he always carried an extra ten-gallon jug of gasoline on the back of the flat deck. The department paid for the fuel, and from time to time, he would help out a stranded motorist. For a price, of course. Depending on how much he made, the boys would go for beers after their shift. All on the department, of course. No one was any the wiser, and it cost the crew nothing to wash down the dust of the day.

"I could spare about ten gallons," said the supervisor.

"How much?" said Hall.

"Well, it looks like you're having a bad day," said the supervisor. "Where did that blood come from?"

"Oh shit," said Jackson. "Hunting. I managed to bag a deer."

"A deer?" said the supervisor. "Hunting season is not even open until the fall."

"Honestly," said Jackson. "The truth is I hit Bambi coming through the park."

"Rough start to the morning," said the supervisor.

"Rough end to a great weekend," said Jackson.

"How's a hundred bucks sound?" said the supervisor.

"Done," said Jackson.

The supervisor got out of his cab. He grabbed the red gas can from the back of the truck. Jackson and the supervisor walked back to the motorhome. They found the filler cap together. Jackson went to the cab. He removed two one-hundred-dollar bills from the box on the front seat. Jackson walked back to the supervisor. "Here's your hundred," said Hall. The supervisor set up the gas can for Jackson. He screwed the filling nozzle into place on the top of the red container.

"There you go," said the supervisor.

Jackson handed the supervisor the other hundred-dollar bill. "This is for not saying anything about the deer I hit. I don't need any stupid fines," said Hall.

"For that money, sir, I am more than happy to pour the gas for you." The supervisor wrapped the second hundred-dollar bill around the first. He placed them both in his shirt pocket. It took about five minutes; eventually, the contents of the bright red gas can were in the tank of the old motorhome. "Try it now," said the supervisor. Jackson got in and turned the key. The engine fired right up, a big cloud of blue smoke surrounded the back of the motorhome.

Jackson walked back and shook the supervisor's

501

hand. "Thank you," said Hall.

"That ought to get you into town," said the supervisor. "There's a station on your right as you're pulling into Hillcrest. It's just before Elli's Diner. If you're looking for a bite to eat, she has great home-cooked meals."

"Thanks," said Jackson. He got back into the motorhome and started down the highway again. The supervisor started walking back towards his truck, carrying the empty gas can in his left hand. He walked by his two guys on the garden tractors.

The supervisor patted his shirt pocket. Both guys on the tractors raised their thumbs in the air. They knew some cold ones were waiting after their shift.

A black jeep pulled into the parking lot of the Wheel Inn. Johnny Robbins looked around. In the corner, in front of room 10, was Barbara's red convertible Mustang. Barbara was leaning against the car. Johnny pulled up beside her. Dust swirled in the air. Over on the grass in front of the motel, the Bell 47's rotor blades bobbled in the light breeze. Johnny stepped out of the stolen jeep and into the arms of his new sweetheart.

"Justin," Barbara said, "where the hell have you been? Where did this come from?" as she pulled on his wet suit.

"It's a long story," he said. "What the fuck is going on around here?" he asked. Barbara explained what had happened with her husband, the cops asking her questions. Then she told her lover what she had heard and seen while she was lying under the motorhome.

"Which way did he go?" asked Johnny. "How long ago?"

"That way," Barbara pointed. "Twenty minutes

502

ago."

"Did you find me some clothes?" asked Johnny.

"They are on the bed, along with a ballcap and sunglasses." Barbara walked in behind Johnny Robbins. She removed her top, exposing her beautiful breasts. "Make love to me," she said. "I need to feel you inside me."

Johnny turned as he finished removing the wet suit. Barbara removed her jeans. She lay on the bed, her legs spread, and Johnny on top of her. "Oh Justin," she said. "I have missed you so much. I was so scared you would not find me." Johnny was getting hard but he did not have time to waste. He placed his hands around Barbara's neck. She closed her mouth and moaned, "Yes, yes, yes!" She wanted him so badly. He placed both of his thumbs on her Adam's apple. Barbara closed her eyes. "Yes! Fuck me, please!" Johnny looked down and smiled as he squeezed with all his might. He felt Barbara's oesophagus collapse under the pressure of his thumbs. Barbara's eyes were now wide open. The whites had become bloodshot.

When the deed was done, Johnny stood up away from Barbara's motionless body. He quickly got dressed in the clothes she had ironed for him and placed the ballcap on his head. The sunglasses were shit, but they would have to do for now. Johnny searched through Barbara's purse until he found her keys, condoms, and cigarette lighter.

"Fuck it," he said, taking the whole purse. Johnny quickly left room 10 and jumped into the Mustang, speeding it out of the parking lot. Robbins headed in the direction of the old motorhome. It was not long until he passed a sign on the road that said 'Hillcrest, 60 miles'. There was a crew out cutting the grass. Johnny took a

503

deep breath. The air smelled fresh. He smiled and pressed the acceleator closer to the floor.

Chapter 95

Clifford Jones woke to the sound of his cell phone ringing beside his bed. It had been one hell of an evening the night before. He and Billy had spent a good part of Sunday night at Metro General, only to find out that his wife, Joann, had been murdered in her hospital bed. Clifford had to fill out reports with the state police, as Joann's case was an active murder investigation. He needed to hire a lawyer. His son, Billy, had slept through most of the evening in the back seat of Clifford's car.

"Hello?" said Clifford, answering the call.

"Daddy, it is me, Donna."

"Donna, what's wrong? What's all that noise?"

"Daddy, I am in an ambulance. They are taking me and the kids to Metro General."

"What? What happened?" asked Clifford. "Where is Tommy?"

"Someone slugged me," said Donna. "They stole Tommy's Jeep. My face is so sore."

"Don't worry," said Clifford. "I will meet you at the hospital."

"Can you bring Mom?" asked Donna.

"Honey... umm, there are some things we need to talk about. I am on my way." Clifford jumped out of bed. He ran to Billy's room. "Get up, son, we have to go to the hospital again."

Billy was having none of it. There was no way he was getting up, not after spending that amount of time in the back seat of his dad's car last night.

"No, leave me alone," said Billy. Clifford did not have the energy to argue with his youngest son. Besides, he was almost old enough to be on his own.

"I will be back as soon as I can," said Clifford.

Billy pulled his blankets over his head. Clifford had a quick shower, dressed, and was out the door in ten minutes. The drive to Metro General seemed longer than normal. Thoughts of the previous evening filled Clifford's head. He pulled into the hospital's parking lot, then rushed into the emergency department.

"I am looking for Donna Jones," he said to the admitting department nurse.

"Who are you?" asked the nurse.

"I am her father."

"She is in the back. Her children are fine."

"Her children?" asked Clifford.

"Mark and Marcy."

"Oh, those kids. She is their cousin."

"Your daughter just had some X-rays. Let me take you back," said the nurse.

Clifford was escorted back to the recovery room. Mark and Marcy sat beside Donna's bed. Mark's jacket was torn, and the two children looked tired. Clifford stood beside Donna's bed. He reached for her hand. Donna opened her eyes.

"Oh, Daddy," she said.

"It's okay, honey," Clifford said, looking at his daughter's swollen face. Her left eye was completely closed, and the surrounding skin was black and blue.

"Daddy," she said, "I don't know what happened.

We were all waiting for Tommy and Brad in the parking lot at Rock Lake. A big helicopter brought in the crashed park's helicopter. They dropped it in the parking lot. A ranger walked over wearing a wet suit. That's all I remember," said Donna. "Oh, my face."

"It's okay, honey," said Clifford. "You're safe now."

Clifford walked over to the children. Marcy's feet rocked back and forth under her chair, while Mark just stared down toward the floor. Two doctors walked into Donna's room.

"Are you Donna's father?" asked one of the ER doctors.

"Yes," said Clifford.

"Your daughter is a pretty lucky girl. She has a crack around her orbital socket, but nothing is out of place. She should heal up just fine. Do you know what happened?" they asked.

"She told me about a guy in a wet suit," Clifford replied.

"When she's up to it, an officer would like to speak with her," the doctors said. "He has to fill out a report."

"Thank you," said Clifford. It was 11:30am. Clifford looked at the two kids. "Are you guys hungry?" he asked. Both nodded their heads. "Let's go to the cafeteria." Clifford reached for Donna's hand. "I am going to take the kids to get something to eat. You get some rest, honey." Donna nodded. Clifford, Mark, and Marcy made their way to the hospital cafeteria. They stood in line with several other people until it was time to order. Clifford looked down at the kids. "How about cheeseburgers?" he asked.

507

"Yes, please," both kids replied.

Clifford placed his cafeteria tray on the metal rails in front of him and held up his hand. "Three cheeseburgers and one side of fries with gravy," he said. Clifford took three medium-sized paper cups and handed one each to Mark and Marcy. The children made their way to the soda fountain dispenser. Mark chose grape soda, and Marcy filled her cup with a combination of orange and grape. Clifford filled his cup halfway with cola and quickly gulped it down. He then refilled his glass to the brim. By the time the children and he had finished at the soda dispenser, his order was sitting on the counter by the cash register.

"That will be sixteen dollars and seventy-five cents," said the cashier.

Clifford pulled his wallet from his back pocket and handed the cashier a twenty. "Keep the change," he said.

The three of them made their way into the dining room. Clifford chose a table that was next to two state troopers. The children sat down, and Marcy's legs dangled under her chair. Both kids reached for a handful of French fries; they were famished. Marcy took a gulp of her soda and looked up at her uncle Clifford.

"That man was mean," she said.

"What man?" said Clifford.

"The man that took our car."

"Tell me, honey. What happened?" asked Clifford.

"That man, he was like Superman or something. He was riding on that broken helicopter. He hit Donna and stole our car. The nice Ranger man found us."

The two troopers overheard the conversation. "Excuse us," said one of the officers. "Honey, where did the man steal your car?"

"We went camping," Marcy replied.

"Where?" asked the officer.

"Rock Lake," said Mark.

The two officers asked to speak to Clifford alone. They walked over to a corner of the dining room away from everyone else. "Sir, I don't think you are aware. However, we currently have a big investigation underway. Something the young lady said fits with some of the things we know about."

"What do you mean?" asked Clifford.

"We have an APB out for an escaped convict, a fellow named Johnny Robbins." Clifford's mind was working overtime. He started to think. Clifford had once read a letter that Joann had received from his eldest son, Matt, while in prison. It said he had met a good friend and that they were watching each other's backs. He reassured his mother that he was safe and not to worry. He ended the letter to his mother by saying he hoped to see her soon. "Johnny Robbins?" asked Clifford. "Isn't he that guy who stole a Corvette years ago?"

"One and the same," said the troopers. "He shot a helicopter pilot in the park yesterday. We just got the report. It looks like he might have escaped."

It was coming together in Clifford's mind. "My daughter is dating that pilot's son. The pilot's name is Chris. I have met him several times. He is a bit of a hero," said Clifford.

"The pilot and his son are here in the hospital," said one of the troopers. "Brought them in first thing this

509

morning."

"Tommy and his dad are here?" exclaimed Clifford. "What happened to Tommy? Did his father get hurt? I can't believe this."

"We need to speak to your daughter," said the troopers.

"Listen," said Clifford. "We just lost her mother last night. Her brother was killed the day before. He was not a good kid. He had been in trouble since he was twelve."

"Matt Jones was your son?" asked the two officers.

"Yes," said Clifford. "I don't think Donna is aware of anything. She and her friends went away for the weekend."

"We really would like to speak to your daughter," the troopers reiterated.

"She is in the Emergency room recovery area," Clifford said. "I have to look after the children."

"Let's all go and see your daughter, just in case we have a few more questions," said one of the troopers.

The children had gobbled down their lunch. Donna was now sitting in a chair in recovery when her father, Mark, Marcy, and the troopers walked in.

"Honey, these men need to speak to you for a moment," Clifford said, pointing to the officers.

"Donna, can you tell us about the man that hit you? What did he look like?"

Donna gave the deputies the best description she could. "I am sorry. That is all I remember. After he hit me, it gets a little foggy."

510

"You did well," said the deputies. One of the officers stepped outside the hospital room and keyed the microphone on his left shoulder. Quickly, the dispatch office had the officer's report, and they were 95% sure that Johnny Robbins was the culprit they were looking for. Both officers left the room Donna was in.

Clifford pulled up another chair and sat beside his daughter. He reached for her hand. Clifford's grip was firm. "Honey, I have some things to tell you."

"What?" asked Donna. She turned her head to look at her father. The bruising on Donna's face was awful, and she looked at her father through her one good eye. "Is everything okay?"

"No, honey, I'm afraid I have some very bad news. Matt escaped from the penitentiary. He was killed by the police."

"What?" asked Donna. "How?"

"There was a shootout. The cops say he had a gun." Donna started to cry. In spite of all the trauma her brother had put her through over the years, she still cared about him. Donna squeezed her father's hand.

"How is Mom taking the news?" she asked.

"Honey, that is the other thing I need to tell you. Mom is gone. We lost both of them in the last two days. Your mom took too many pills. I called the ambulance. She passed away here last night." Clifford did not want to get into the details. It was enough for the time being just to let his daughter know both her brother and mother were dead. "I am sorry, honey," said Clifford. "It has not been a good weekend. Tommy and his father are here in the hospital."

"Where?" said Donna. "I need to see them."

"Let me find out where they are, and I will see if we can go and pay them a visit." Donna was sobbing now. Her mother had made life miserable for her, which is why she moved out and found a job at the library. Donna's head tilted forward. She lifted both hands to her cheeks and wiped away the tears. Her father handed her a tissue from his pocket. "I will see if I can find out where Tommy is." Clifford made his way back to the nurse's station.

Mark and Marcy stood around Donna's chair. Both of them said, "Don't cry. We love you."

Donna looked at both children. "I love you too," she said. They all embraced in a big hug.

Clifford asked the nurse in charge about Tommy and his father. He had to explain the whole family dynamics to the lady in order to get any information. Clifford was finally informed that they had been moved to the third floor in a shared room. Clifford said, "Thank you," and turned to head back to his daughter's room. Clifford turned directly into the path of a man dressed in a black suit. "Excuse me," said Clifford.

"Mr. Jones?" asked the man. "Clifford Jones?"

"Yes," said Clifford.

"I am Agent Miller with the FBI. Can you come with me, sir?"

"What is going on?" asked Clifford.

"I would like you to come with me and identify your son and your wife. I am sorry for your loss," said Miller.

Clifford turned back to the nurse in charge. "Can you please make sure my daughter gets to see her boyfriend?" The nurse nodded her head, then picked up

her ringing phone.

Clifford and Agent Miller made their way to the hospital elevators. Miller pushed the button marked B. The doors closed, and in seconds, they reopened.

"Follow me," said Miller as they made their way down the hall to a large set of double doors. Miller hit the green button on the wall, and both doors swung open. The men moved forward. The room was brightly lit, with several desks and filing cabinets neatly placed along the walls. Above a second set of doors along the back wall was a sign that read: Office of the STATE CORONER. Agent Miller and Clifford stood for a moment or two. Eventually, the second set of doors opened, and out walked a thin young man in a white coat. He wore bright blue latex gloves, a facemask, and had a set of plastic goggles around his eyes.

"Agent Miller, I presume?" the young man said. "I am Assistant Coroner Nigel Brown."

Agent Miller reached into his breast pocket, removing his badge and identification. Miller pointed to Clifford. "This is Clifford Jones. We are here..."

"I know, I know," said Brown. He walked over to one of the filing cabinets, opened the drawer, and removed two files. He turned and then said, "Follow me."

Miller and Jones followed the young coroner through the next set of doors, entering another room. Clifford could feel the chill in the air as they entered. There were two stainless steel tables in the middle of the room, and the floor had recently been washed, making it wet. To Clifford's right was a bank of stainless steel doors, each about three feet by three feet in size, with a number and a large handle mounted to the right side.

"Let's see," said Brown. "Oh yes..." He walked over to door number 15 and pulled on the handle. The door swung open, and Brown reached inside the compartment, sliding out a long table with a body covered in a blood-stained sheet. Brown looked at the other file, then opened door 17, sliding out that table, also with a body and sheet. The sheet on this one was crisp and white. Brown looked at Clifford. "Ready?" said Brown. Clifford nodded his head.

Brown pulled the sheet back from Joann's body, almost down to her belly button. Clifford's wife lay there for all the world to see. "That is my wife, Joann," said Clifford. Her face was a light shade of blue, and her breasts were fully exposed. There were red marks around her nipples.

Brown looked at Miller. "She died from asphyxiation," said Brown. "But you two must have had some serious fun before she passed," said Brown, looking at Clifford.

"What do you mean?" asked Jones.

"Well," said Brown, "we found a large amount of semen when we did the pelvic exam."

"Oh," said Clifford as he nodded his head. Clifford had not touched Joann in years, but he was not going to let these two know that. Clifford's mind was running a mile a minute. Joann had been having an affair with someone. She must have been with the guy when he and Billy were at the car show.

"We took a sample," said Brown. "It's at the lab." Miller was making notes. Joann had been murdered in her hospital bed. Could her lover have been responsible? Miller needed to compare the DNA evidence to Clifford, just to rule out foul play.

"Cover her up, please," Clifford asked. Brown complied. He then walked over to the table in front of door 15, pulled back the sheet, and Clifford's son Matt lay before him on a cold slab of stainless steel. Several dark round holes were visible in Matt's chest, and there was a giant Y cut into his chest that had been crudely sewn together.

"Yes, that is my son," said Clifford. Brown handed a plastic envelope from the file folder to Agent Miller. It contained all the lead the coroners had removed from Matt's body. Brown next moved to a locker, opened the door, and removed a large clear plastic bag marked "evidence." He removed the blood-covered clothing, laying them out on the table. Clifford recognized the shirt and baseball cap.

Joann had kept everything for her son after he had been sent up the last time. Joann kept all that belonged to Matt in his bedroom. It was sacred ground, as far as she was concerned. No one was allowed in that room.

Clifford's mind was racing. How would Matt have gotten those clothes? Clifford was starting to piece it all together. Matt must have gone to the house, and Joann gave him his clothing. His wife not only was messing around with another guy, she helped her son with fresh clothing while he and Billy were at the car show.

Agent Miller asked if Clifford recognized the clothing. "I am not sure about the jeans," said Clifford, "but that shirt was one of Matt's favorites. Joann kept everything in his room, waiting for him to return after his sentence was over."

The three men retreated to the front office. Brown asked Clifford for a quick swab from the inside

of his mouth. Clifford complied as Brown swabbed his cheeks. Agent Miller and Clifford then left the morgue. They rode the elevator to the first floor.

"Thank you for your cooperation," said Miller as he tapped Clifford on the shoulder. "We will be in touch if we have any more questions."

Clifford made his way back to where he had left Donna and the kids. Someone else was now sitting in the chair once occupied by his daughter. Clifford went back to the nurse's station. "Do you know where my daughter is?" he asked.

"The porters just took her and the children up to the third floor."

"Thanks," said Clifford as he made his way to the elevators. Clifford's cell phone started to vibrate. He looked at the display; it was the life insurance company.

Chapter 96

Kevin's group of hikers were not really in the mood for breakfast. The Grizzly that had attacked David was gone for now. Kevin had given it a good shot of bear spray. "How long would it stay away?" he was asked by one of the hikers. That was a good question, Kevin thought to himself.

Kevin made his way to the shoreline of Rock Lake. He washed his hands that were soaked in David's blood, scooped up water, and rinsed his face and hair. His group stood in front of Tammy as she continued to cry. "Why!?" she screamed. "We were going to get married!" The ladies from Ireland were doing their best to help out. Aileen had brought Tammy a cup of coffee. Tammy gripped the mug. Steam rolled into the fresh mountain air. She just sat staring into the black liquid.

Within ten minutes, the sound of the quads could be heard off in the distance. Kevin addressed everyone. "The park's staff will be here any minute. Let's make sure we are all ready to go."

Aileen approached Kevin. "We cannot go anywhere until we find our husbands."

"Parks are going to close this entire area," said Kevin. "I have seen it before. You will not have a choice. Please," said Kevin, "gather your belongings. We will keep an eye out for your men. There are only two ways into here. We will find them," he said.

Brad continued to lead the Rangers to the cabins at the north end of Rock Lake. He was followed by Assistant Superintendent Dan Thompson, who was followed by Ranger Steve and his quad, which pulled the

517

trailer containing Rachel's body. The three men pulled into the area in front of the cabins. Brad got off his quad. He walked over to his father, Kevin. Kevin stepped forward, his hair wet and his shirt having traces of blood on it. Kevin gave his son a big hug. "Good to see you, son."

Thompson was next. Dan extended his hand to Kevin. "How are you holding up?" asked Dan.

"Okay," said Kevin. Ranger Steve dismounted his quad. He went to the back of the trailer then removed the case containing the camera. Steve then walked over to Kevin and shook his hand.

Dan Thompson turned, addressing the group of hikers that stood before him. "Ladies and gentlemen, the parks department is officially closing this area to all tourists. Please ensure you pack all your belongings. We will be clearing out in one hour." Thompson looked at Kevin. "Lead the way," he said.

Kevin walked back behind RL03. David's body lay in a pool of blood. Steve removed the camera from its case. Steve handed the camera to Dan along with a pair of gloves as the former put on a pair himself. Thompson removed the lens cap. He snapped on the gloves then started taking pictures. Kevin talked as the rangers went about their business. "Such a shame," said Thompson. "What a fucking weekend this has turned out to be. We only have the one body bag," said Thompson.

"Well," said Kevin, "I will check with his girlfriend. We can use his sleeping bag to carry him out of here."

"See what you can do," said Thompson as he continued to take more pictures.

Kevin approached Tammy. "Can we use your

fiancé's sleeping bag? We will need it to move him," Kevin said.

"Yes, of course," said Tammy, her cheeks stained from the tears she had shed.

"Brad, can you head over to RL04 and grab the sleeping bag? It's the blue one," said Tammy.

Thompson focused on the large wound on David's neck. "You see that?" he said, pointing to the right side of the gaping hole in David's neck. "There is no incisor mark on the top right side of the wound."

Steve spoke, "It's the same as the girl."

"Exactly," said Thompson. "We have a Grizzly missing a tooth. It must be an old bear or it got broken off somehow, maybe fighting."

"Maybe both," said Kevin, returning from instructing his son to get the sleeping bag from RL04. "It was a big bear, but it did not look like it was starving."

"Well," said Thompson, "it has found an easy source of food. We are going to have to put it down."

Brad returned from RL04 to the back of RL03, where his father and the two rangers were just finishing taking their photographs. "Here you go," Brad said, handing his father the sleeping bag he had just removed from the last cabin.

Kevin undid the zipper on the side of the bag. He handed it to Dan. Dan and Steve laid the bag down beside David's body. Steve took the feet, and Dan placed his gloved hands under David's shoulders then grasped his shirt. "On the count of three," said Steve. The two men lifted David's body onto the sleeping bag. They then did up the zipper.

"Is there a large plastic tie in the case?" asked

Thompson. Kevin had a look. He handed Dan the only large nylon quick tie that was available. Thompson lifted the open end of the sleeping bag as David's body slid further down inside the bag. Dan closed the open end with the quick tie. "There, that ought to do it," he said.

Steve took the camera. He placed it back into the large carrying case and fastened the clasps. Steve returned to the third quad with the trailer. He placed the case in the trailer beside Rachel's body. Steve fired up the quad and then drove to the back of RL03. Kevin, Brad, and Dan placed David's body next to Rachel's in the back of the small utility trailer. Steve pulled the quad back around to the front of RL03. Kevin's hikers were ready to go. Aileen and her three friends from Ireland were just coming down the stairs from their respective cabins.

Dan Thompson pulled Ranger Steve aside. They had a brief conversation. Steve walked over to Dan's quad then removed the Winchester 30/30 from the scabbard on the side of the superintendent's ATV. Steve returned to the back of RL03, the blood-soaked ground covered with flies. He knelt down looking at the footprints on the ground. The bear had gone due north into the trees behind the cabins. He was sure it would return from that direction.

Steve had agreed to stay behind. When the bear returned, Steve would put a round right between its eyes. Dan walked to the back of RL03 for the last time. He shook his partner's hand. "We should be back in a few hours. We will get these folks well on their way and be back for you ASAP."

"Roger that," said Steve. Brad led the way back down the trail, followed by Dan Thompson. The hikers walked with their packs in a single file directly behind

Thompson's ATV. Behind the whole group was Kevin, driving the final quad, pulling the trailer containing the bodies of Rachel and David.

Steve had climbed onto the roof of RL03. From his vantage point, he could see the hikers disappear into the distance. He cocked the lever of the 30-30 and then removed the safety. He was ready to do his duty.

Chapter 97

Jackson Hall had only ten gallons of gas left. He had at least another thirty miles to go. Hall hit the steering wheel. "Come on, baby, you gotta make it." Hall looked down at the speedometer; he kept the motorhome at fifty miles an hour. He needed to conserve as much fuel as possible.

Johnny Robbins was doing eighty miles an hour in Barbara's stolen red Mustang. Thoughts of what he was going to do to his ex-partner when he found him rushed through his head. Johnny was now 40 miles outside of Hillcrest. This was the only highway that Hall could be on.

Johnny felt something on his side. He looked down to see that blood had soaked through his shirt. He lifted it up to see that the wounds he had received in prison before his escape had torn open. Sometime over the last day with all he had been through, the work the doctors had done in the hospital eventually failed. The area around the wounds had turned bright red and was very tender. He must have torn them out when he was changing out of the wet suit. He thought for a moment about the few minutes it took to strangle Barbara. He settled his mind on the wet suit. "Fuck!" he yelled into the warm morning air. Johnny knew that Jackson was close. A reckoning was going to take place. Johnny was sure of that.

Ten miles down the road, Sheriff Gates had set up his speed trap. He parked his cruiser behind a road sign that said "Elli's Diner, Home-cooked meals 30 miles ahead." Mondays on long weekends were the best time to make some money for the county. Folks were

always in a rush to get home and prepare for work on Tuesday morning. Gates expected to write twenty tickets today.

Gates prepared his radar unit. He set the numbers at 60 MPH. The posted limit was 55. Within minutes, a red Mustang convertible blew past Gates and his cruiser. The screen on the radar unit read 87 MPH. Gates hit the switch that turned on his overhead lights, followed up with the siren. He was now in pursuit of another idiot, he thought.

Johnny looked in his rearview mirror; he saw the cop approaching at a high rate of speed. Robbins had made a mistake the last time he tried to outrun the cops. He was not going to do that again. His time in jail had etched a plan into his brain; he knew exactly what he was going to do.

Johnny raised his right hand and waved to the officer. By doing so, he was acknowledging to the officer that he saw him. Johnny had done wrong, and he was prepared to pay the price. Gates smiled as the Mustang pulled to the side of the road in front of him. Johnny came to a stop, placing the Mustang in neutral. Gates and his cruiser parked about ten feet from the back of the Mustang.

Gates pulled on the mic attached to the cruiser's two-way radio. The camera mounted above his rearview mirror had started recording as soon as the overhead lights had been activated. "Dispatch, this is car 89, do you copy?"

"Dispatch, go ahead."

Gates had already entered the license plate number of the Mustang into the cruiser's computer. Nothing came up on his screen. The troopers had been

trained to call in the plate numbers to their central dispatch as well. The system was at times slow to update. After all, everything depended on the person entering the data into the system. Gates read off the plate number, then the description of the red Mustang. He estimated the year of the vehicle and stated there was a lone male occupant. Dispatch came back a minute later. Gates's radio crackled. "No wants or warrants."

Gates grabbed his ticket book from the passenger seat. Sheriff Gates stepped out of his cruiser, placing his hat on his head. The department's instructions to their officers were to approach the perpetrator's car from the passenger side. It kept the officers out of the line of traffic coming up from behind the stopped vehicles. The officers were to walk to the back of their cars and then around to the perp's passenger side. Gates did not have time for that. He wanted to write another nineteen tickets today. Gates unsnapped the cover on his 9mm service pistol. He placed his right hand firmly on its grip. The ticket book was in his left hand. Gates ignored what he had been taught.

Johnny's hands were firmly on the steering wheel as he watched Gates in the rearview mirror. The sheriff took one step in between his cruiser and the Red Mustang. In a split second, Johnny took his right hand off the wheel, slammed the Mustang into reverse, and hit the accelerator. The Mustang lurched backward, slamming into the legs of Sheriff Gates, then pinning him against the bumper of his own cruiser.

Gates felt his legs shatter as his ticket book flew from his left hand into the traffic lane closest to the two stopped cars. Gates was in shock; he could not move. His right hand that had been firmly on his 9mm now moved freely in the air. The impact of the Mustang hitting the officer had jolted his hand and gun from its holster. The

9mm came to rest on the hood of the sheriff's cruiser directly behind him. Gates heard the pistol hit the hood, but he could not turn his body to reach for his service weapon. Gates fell forward, his torso now on the trunk of Barbara's Mustang.

Johnny opened the driver's door, then stepped out. He walked to the back of his car. Gates put both of his hands flat on the trunk. He pushed himself up. Gates was trapped, and the pain in his legs was affecting his thinking. Johnny looked at the trapped officer, then smiled. The plan he had developed in prison worked perfectly. "Oops," said Robbins, "I bet that hurts."

"You fucking son of a bitch!" yelled Gates. "You broke both my legs!"

Johnny took another step just to the left of the officer and slightly behind him. Johnny picked up the 9mm from the hood of the officer's car. Johnny then stood beside Sheriff Gates. "Were you looking for this?" asked Johnny.

Gates looked into Johnny's eyes. They were black and lifeless. Johnny moved the safety on the 9mm. He raised the barrel of the gun to the middle of Officer Gates's forehead and then pulled the trigger.

The back of Sheriff Gates' head exploded in a mess of hair, bone, and brain matter. Gates's body dropped against the trunk of Barbara's car for the final time. Johnny calmly walked to the driver's door of the cruiser. He opened the door, then slid behind the wheel and closed it. Johnny looked at the active computer screen. Barbara's plate number was highlighted. Johnny slipped the trooper's car into reverse. He backed up as Deputy Gates's body slid between the two cars, then onto the ground. When Johnny was far enough away, he slammed the sheriff's car into drive. Its overhead lights

still flashing, Johnny pressed the accelerator right to the floor. He looked at the gauges in front of him. The gas tank was full. He was soon doing 95 MPH. Johnny was pleased with himself. The stop had only taken about ten minutes. However, he still had to make up the time. The speedometer now read 100 MPH. The distance between he and Jackson was closing fast.

Jackson Hall entered the city limits of Hillcrest. He could see the sign for Mountain View Gas and Service directly ahead to his right. Hall finally started to calm down as he pulled the old motorhome up to the pumps. The station's neon sign flashed open. A young man came out from the office. "Fill 'er up?" he asked Jackson. "That would be great," Hall said to the young man. The young man placed a large block of wood under the front tire. His father had taught him to do that to stop folks from driving off without paying for their gas. It was a family-run business, and they couldn't afford to take two hundred dollar losses at the pumps.

Jackson stepped out of the cab, stretching his arms into the air. The young man asked Jackson to pop the hood so he could check the oil. Jackson complied. Jackson watched as the dial on the fuel pump passed one hundred. The kid looked up from under the hood. "She's down a quart. Do you want me to top her up?" Jackson nodded his head. By the time the pump clicked off, the dollar total read $186.93. The young man walked over to the nozzle and managed to squeeze in another three dollars worth. "That's $190.00 for the gas and $5.00 for the oil," said the kid.

Jackson handed the young man two crisp one hundred dollar bills. "Keep the change," said Hall. The young man smiled, then removed the block from in front of the tire. He walked back into the service station office.

Jackson jumped into the cab of the motorhome, turned the key, and tried to start the engine. The engine turned over but would not start. Jackson tried three more times, but the motorhome would not fire up, and now his battery was almost dead. Jackson got out of the cab and slammed the driver's door. The mirror on the door fell to the ground, shattering into a hundred little pieces. Jackson Hall made his way to the service station office. The young man who had just helped him and his father stood behind the counter. Jackson looked pissed as he said, "Do you have anyone who can take a look at the old girl? It will not start. Now my battery is almost dead."

The father spoke up. "Well, it's a holiday," said the father. "We are running short-staffed. I could probably take a look myself. We charge double time on holidays."

Jackson shrugged his shoulders. "Okay," said Hall.

Jason Booker and his family had owned Mountain View Service for the last 25 years. Jason had taken over the family business from his father. Now he was teaching his own son, Kirk, the ins and outs of making money as a full-service gas station. Jason walked out from behind the counter. He presented Jackson Hall a clipboard. Attached was a work order. In big bold letters at the top of the form, it read 'diagnostic and repairs'. In smaller print, it went on to read 'the client would be responsible for payment of all parts, labor, and costs associated with diagnosing problems related to their vehicle'. "Please sign where the X is," said Jason. Jackson took the clipboard. He signed the document, then placed it on the counter. "I will just grab the portable battery pack and meet you at the Motorhome," said Jason.

Jackson Hall walked back to the pumps. Kirk opened one of the big overhead doors of the three-bay garage so his father could roll the jumper pack out of the service bay. Two more cars pulled into the gas pumps. Kirk ran over to help the owners as his father made his way across the parking lot to the front of Jackson's dilapidated motorhome.

"Jump in and try to start her," said Jason. Jackson sat in the driver's seat, turning the key. A distinct 'click, click' was heard each time Hall twisted the ignition switch. "Pop the hood," said Jason. The hood popped into its secondary position. Jason reached under the hood, releasing the safety lever. He propped the hood up on the metal rod that the factory had installed for such occasions. Jason connected the leads from his portable battery pack. "Give her a try now."

The starter engaged with a flurry of newfound energy. The engine turned over and over; it would not start. Jason looked closely at all the wires. His son, Kirk, had done an excellent job in loosening the main distributor wire. It was just sitting in place but not pressed firmly into the distributor cap. Jason smiled. He had taught his son well. If they could get two or three more motorhomes today, the till would be overflowing with cash by the end of the day. "Try her now."

Jackson twisted the key. The engine turned over but would not fire. "I am going to have to push you over to the open bay door there," said Jason. "We will have to hook her up to the computer and see what is going on."

In minutes, Jason had fired up the old tow truck that sat on the side of the business. He pulled up behind the motorhome, placing the front bumper of his tow truck against the bumper of the motorhome. Jason got out of his tow truck and walked to Jackson's open driver's

window. "Put her in neutral," he said. "I will push you to the open bay door there," as he pointed. Jackson nodded. Jason stepped back into the tow truck, then put it in first gear.

He pushed Jackson Hall and his beat-up motorhome towards the open bay door. The gas pumps were getting busy. Kirk was running back and forth between cars. He looked over at his father as he stepped out of the tow truck. His dad gave him a wink. Kirk knew he had done well. The family was going to make some extra money today.

"Okay," said Jason to Hall, "let's get this baby hooked up and find out what is wrong. Why don't you go inside and help yourself to a fresh cup of coffee?"

Jackson agreed, and he reached over to the passenger seat. He removed the open box of cash as he stepped out. The shotgun he had stolen from the Wheel Inn, he slipped into the back between some of his precious boxes.

"How long do you think it will take?" asked Jackson.

"You never know with these things," said Jason. "Half an hour, maybe four, depending on what we find."

Jackson said, "Well, I hope it's not serious," as he made his way into the office of the service station.

Jason spent half an hour tinkering in the garage, pretending he was looking at the computer screen. All along, he knew exactly what was wrong. These folks with their big motorhomes always had extra cash, or at least a credit card. This fish was not going to get away. Thirty minutes passed, and then Jason walked into the office. Jackson had just poured his second cup of coffee.

"I have some good news and bad news," said

Jason. "It's not your timing chain. But I load-tested your battery. It is shot. You need a new one. Your spark plug wires are all cracked, and you need a new rotor for your distributor. According to the computer, that's it. The real good news is I have everything here in stock for that engine."

"How much?" said Jackson.

"With labor and the tow, excuse me," said Jason, "including the push, it will come out to..." he paused for a second as he totaled the items on the work order Jackson had signed, "seven hundred and thirty-four dollars."

Jackson looked up from his coffee. "Cash okay?" said Hall.

"Well, sir, if you're paying in cash, I can give you ten percent off. So your total is six hundred and sixty dollars and sixty cents."

Jackson nodded his head. "Let's get her done."

Jackson looked at the clock on the wall; it was coming up to 11:00am. Jackson ran the discounted numbers through his head. He always believed in signs. "666," Jackson said out loud. He knew where things were heading. Now he needed a plan.

Johnny Robbins hit the town limits of Hillcrest. He kept his eyes peeled. The motorhome that Barbara had described to him had to be close. Johnny was hot on the trail of his ex-partner. The sign for Mountain View Service and gas soon came into view. Johnny focused on the busy lot as he slowed to the posted speed limit. There to his right was an old motorhome parked in front of an open bay door. It was exactly as Barbara had described, right down to the bumper stickers and the large one-piece mud flap.

Johnny pulled into the empty lot beside the service station. He positioned the sheriff's cruiser, then turned off the overhead lights. He could now watch the movements in the station's parking lot. His planets were lining up; how lucky could one guy be? Johnny had a plan; it was now time to put it into play.

Chapter 98

Betty had been coordinating everything from her end. The parks department was stretched to the limit. Their helicopter was a pile of scrap metal laying in a crumpled heap in the Rock Lake staging area. The costs to hire the Chinook Sky Crane were going to run close to one hundred grand. The budget for the year was getting used up pretty quickly. This was the first long weekend of the year, and everything was open. It did not matter; Bob had always told Betty that human lives came first. They would deal with the cost of each situation after the fact.

Betty had called Glacier Helicopter Tours at exactly 8:00am Monday morning. She needed to get eyes into the air over Rock Lake; she needed to know what was going on. The last communication she had was when the Sky Crane crew had dropped the 505 into the parking lot. There had been a Jeep stolen there. A woman had been attacked and was down. An ambulance had been dispatched. There had been no further communication with her Ranger Scott who was on site since the ambulance had left. Betty assumed he had headed back up to Rock Lake where communications would be limited or nonexistent.

The phone rang twice. "Glacier Tours, Alice speaking, how may I help you?"

"Alice, it's Betty, we have a huge problem on our hands." There was a pause. The two ladies were very familiar with each other. "Do you have many bookings this morning?" asked Betty.

"Booked solid," said Alice.

Betty went on to describe the events of the last two days as she knew them. "I just need to have more eyes over the area."

Alice looked at her booking list. Glacier Tours ran two Bell 407s. They would carry a pilot and five tourists from the heliport in Hillsboro to Angel Glacier. Spend ten minutes allowing those that wanted, to take pictures. They then returned to the Heliport all within two hours. The company had an excellent reputation. They charged one thousand dollars a head for an experience of a lifetime. That was $5,000 per chopper times two. Four flights each per day during the busy season. The company was bringing in eighty grand a day flying lazy folks over a pile of ice. Not bad for a company that had only been in business for three years.

"How about we divert over the lake on our runs to the Glacier? If we notice anything, I will have the pilots contact me and I will call you," said Alice.

"Thank you," said Betty.

The Sheriff's department had been in touch with Betty as soon as she had reported that one of her Rangers was down. They were investigating the stolen Jeep. Now a murder had been committed and verified at Rock Lake. The Sheriff's department had dispatched their own helicopter, an EC120, to the area. With two deputy investigators on board and the pilot, they expected to be at Rock Lake within an hour. Betty received a call from the Sheriff's department stating their bird was in the air. As soon as they had more information, it would get passed on to her. The EC120 was an all-purpose helicopter equipped with everything the department would ever need. Best of all, it had a maximum ceiling height of twenty thousand feet.

The sheriff's chopper left the roof of the

533

department's office. It headed directly north to the boundaries of the park. The pilot corrected direction looking at the GPS navigation system. He flew a thousand feet above the treetops until the staging area of Rock Lake came into view. "There she is," said the pilot to his fellow members of the department. "What a mess." The twisted hulk of the 505 lay below them. The barriers to the entrance of the parking lot were in place. The only vehicles in the parking lot were park trucks. One had a large flat deck trailer attached to it. There was search and rescue half-ton letters painted on its roof and a large passenger van parked in the corner of the lot.

The EC120 gained altitude then headed directly towards Rock Lake. Within twenty minutes, the Sheriffs were flying over the calm waters of Rock Lake. The pilot flew over the camping area where Brad and Tommy had set up their tents with the girls and children on Friday. The Rangers' tents now were intermingled with Brad and Tommy's belongings. The 120 hovered above the campsite for a few moments. The carcass of the Grizzly Brad had put his knife into was clearly visible. It still laid along the edge of the trees to the west of the campsite. The pilot turned the chopper towards the north end of Rock Lake. To his right, he could see a single ranger on an ATV by the small creek feeding into the lake. There in front of his quad was a blue tarp held down with several large rocks.

The 120 proceeded slowly over the island in the middle of the lake. The sheriff sitting in the right seat pointed down towards the old trapper's cabin. "What is that?" he said. "Do you two see that?" The two bodies of Seamus and Shawn were clearly visible in the clear mountain water. Their arms seemed to move almost as though they were waving to the crew on the 120. The sheriffs could see a large group of people heading down

the path towards the south end of the lake. There were two quads, one in front and one in back with a small trailer attached. The 120 then flew over the four cabins at the north end of the lake. There was a Ranger on the roof of RL03 with a rifle, a bottle of water beside him. The 120 turned so the pilot could salute the Ranger, who in turn stood, and saluted back. Ranger Steve had only been on the rooftop for twenty minutes before the cavalry had arrived.

The 120 turned and made its way back towards the group of hikers and two rangers. It had taken a total of thirty minutes to fly over Rock Lake and assess the overall situation. The pilot dialed the radio frequency the park's department used. He pressed the button to key his mike. "This is Sheriff One, air support to Parks, how do you read? Air One to Parks, how do you read?" Dan Thompson's radio crackled.

Dan pulled his quad to a stop. "Loud and clear," responded Dan.

"Roger," said the pilot. "You have two unknowns directly ahead, 100 yards to your right, approximately twenty feet from shore. Recovery in order."

"Roger that," said Thompson. Dan knew the difference between a rescue and recovery. He had two bodies in the water ahead of him and the group of hikers. It must be the husbands of the two Irish women he had spoken to. Dan's mind was racing.

The 120 made its way back towards the campsite. They hovered one hundred feet over the tents until the downdraft from the wash of the rotors made quick work of the nylon tents, scattering them like leaves on a fall day. The Sheriff department's helicopter landed where the tents had stood just moments earlier. The pilot shut down the engine. "Let's get to work, gentlemen," he

said.

Dan Thompson led the group down the path towards his murdered coworker. He stopped his quad ten yards short of where Ranger Gary Smith lay dead. The State Troopers were now onsite. They had removed the tarp covering Smith's body. There was an extra warden's uniform laying beside Smith's body. The nametag attached to the breast pocket read 'Superintendent Gerard'. Two of the troopers held up the tarp as Kevin, his group, and the Irish ladies walked by. Everyone who was wearing a hat removed them as they walked past. The blue tarp fluttered. Each knew the gravity of the situation. Another person had lost their life this weekend; it was too much for some to handle. Emotions were running high as tears ran down several cheeks. Brad followed the group, bringing up the rear. His quad and trailer sat parked on the path, ten yards from the body of Warden Gary Smith. Brad walked by the state troopers. He joined the entire group as they made their way to where the police helicopter had landed.

The campsite Brad had shared with Tommy, Elizabeth, Donna, and the two children now looked like a warzone. The entire group stood before the helicopter. Dan Thompson pulled Kevin and Brad aside. "Follow me," said Thompson.

They walked back in the direction of the lakeshore, just far enough away from the hiking group. Dan spoke to father and son, "Kevin, I know you have a job to do. You were hired to take those folks on a journey they would not forget. I think this weekend qualifies. Gentlemen, it looks like we have two more recoveries to make. There are bodies in the water, just in front of the old trapper's cabin."

"Christ," said Brad. "It has to be the two guys

536

those Irish women have been asking about. Their husbands."

Thompson nodded and said, "Chances are it's them. Brad, can you take the quad with the trailer back to the staging area ahead of the group? Kevin, you make sure everyone gets out of here in one piece. Brad, I will need you to come back with the empty trailer. Can you handle that, son?"

"Yes," came Brad's reply.

"There is more fuel on the flat deck trailer in the parking lot." Thompson reached for his keys. He removed a small key from his ring.

"This will unlock the fuel tank," he said to Brad. "Fill the quad and get back here as quickly as possible. Good luck, Kevin, and thank you," said Thompson as he shook Kevin's and Brad's hands.

Kevin made his way back to the group of hikers. Brad, in turn, walked with Dan Thompson back to where the troopers were photographing Ranger Smith's body. Dan stopped to assist the State Troopers. Brad walked to the quad, started it up, and slowly made his way past the investigators. Brad continued until he made it to the original camp spot. He passed the helicopter and the group of hikers. The small trailer with Rachel's and David's body bounced as Brad rolled over the rocks on the path leading up to Lookout Pass.

When Brad was far enough away from the group, he sped up. There was no longer any reason to go as slowly as he had when everyone was around. The quad slowed as the engine struggled to pull the extra weight to the top of the pass. When Brad crested the hill, he stopped. He turned around and looked. He could see the old trapper's cabin. The helicopter was a small dot at the

edge of the lake. Brad continued down the path until he eventually reached the staging area for Rock Lake.

There were two additional ranger vehicles pulling into the parking lot, followed by a large black van marked with large white letters that read 'Coroner'. Brad pulled up beside the wrecked 505 that once was the pride of the park's department. Betty had done her job. Help was waiting as Brad came to a stop. The two park's trucks pulled up beside Brad. Dust filled the air as the two rangers exited their trucks. Brad quickly filled them in on what was going on. The coroner came over.

The four men walked back to the utility trailer behind Brad's quad. "These are the first two," said Brad as he pulled back the tarp covering the bodies. Blood had soaked through the sleeping bag the guys had used to hold David's body. There were several flies swarming around the trailer. "Do you have any more body bags?" asked Brad, looking at the coroner.

"I keep a half dozen on hand," he said.

"I will need three more." The coroner went back to his van and drove up behind the utility trailer. The four men loaded David's body, sleeping bag and all, into a new body bag. They then loaded both bodies into the back of the coroner's van. The coroner reached up onto a large shelf, removing three new black body bags. He then handed them to Brad. There was nothing said. Brad placed the empty bags into the back of the trailer.

Elizabeth had come running over. "Honey, stay back!" Brad shouted. "You do not need to see any of this." He covered the back of the bloody trailer with the tarp. Brad walked over to Elizabeth. "Where are Donna and the children?" he asked. Elizabeth explained what had happened. She waited for her man because she loved him. "Sweetheart, take my truck and go," said Brad. "I

538

do not know how much longer I am going to be." He kissed Elizabeth deeply. "They need me back at the lake. I love you," he said.

The two rangers and Elizabeth stood watching as Brad headed back up the trail to Rock Lake. "Tough kid," said one of them to the other. The two rangers stood guard, one at the entrance of the staging area, the other at the mouth of the path leading to Rock Lake. The coroner started the built-in generator on the side of his van. The refrigeration unit kicked in. It was going to get warm outside. The bodies needed to be kept cool to slow decomposition. It was going to be a long day.

Chapter 99

Metro General was a busy place on Monday morning. It always seemed that long weekends were the worst, especially the first warm one of the year. People cut off fingers with saws, and there were mangled feet from lawnmowers. This weekend, though, was way above the norm.

Cathy had been wheeled back into the emergency department. She was strapped down to the ambulance stretcher and was delirious. Her head was moving from side to side, and she was mumbling what sounded like, "I am God's servant." Dr. Hansen took one look at her and quickly examined Cathy for any new wounds or abrasions. There were none.

"Take her up to the psychiatric ward!" shouted Hansen. "She is in the care of Dr. Lewis now." The orderlies transferred Cathy from the ambulance stretcher to a portable bed with wheels. Cathy was headed back to a nice quiet room. "Make sure she is tied down," Hansen said. "We do not need another situation on our hands."

Two detectives followed the orderly as he pushed Cathy on the hospital gurney. The officers were there to investigate Susan and Joann's suspected murders. How could someone who had been attacked by a grizzly, then had a leg amputated, end up dead in a hospital stairwell with a broken neck? The detectives needed to question Cathy right away. Donna's mother had been admitted for an overdose. She had been doing well under Dr. Hansen's care. They needed Cathy to admit to the crime. The department needed to press murder charges. The lawyers, judge, and DA could figure out whether she was insane at the time the deeds took place. The department

just had to follow the rules if the evidence pointed to Cathy. Right now, all they had was hearsay and the testimony of Dr. Hansen.

The two officers rode in the elevator with the orderly and Cathy to the psychiatric ward. The nurses instructed the orderly to move Cathy into room 4018, almost directly across from the nurse's station. One of the detectives pulled a chair up to the outside of the door and sat down. The other detective followed the orderly and Cathy into her room. Cathy was transferred to a hospital bed, and her wrists and ankles were fastened to the frame of the bed. The detective in the room pulled a chair up beside the bed. The orderly looked over at the officer as he left the room. "Good luck," he said.

Within minutes, Dr. Lewis walked into Cathy's room. "What are you doing in here?" asked Dr. Lewis to the detective. "Get out. I will tell you when my patient is able or willing to talk to you. Don't you think she has been through enough?"

"Doctor, we need information from your patient. You do know we are investigating what we believe to be two murders here in the hospital within the last 24 hours."

"Out," said Dr. Lewis as she pointed to the door. "When my patient comes around, I will ask her if she would like to speak to you." The detective left the room and spoke briefly to his partner outside the door. Both agreed to take shifts lasting one hour. Someone had to be ready to question the suspect.

Dr. Lewis reviewed Cathy's chart for the second time in the last 24 hours. She walked to the side of Cathy's bed and placed her palm against Cathy's cheek. "You poor woman," said the doctor. "You have been through so much." She then stroked Cathy's hair. "I will

541

look after you. You're safe now." Dr. Lewis examined the restraints holding Cathy's arms and legs. The cuff on her right wrist was so tight that her hand was turning blue. Dr. Lewis adjusted the cuff, backing it off so it would not impede further blood flow. "There, that is better. I will be back to check on you soon." Dr. Lewis stopped at the nurse's station, giving the ladies instructions to have her paged as soon as Cathy started to come around. The amobarbital should be wearing off in an hour or so. Cathy had been given a strong dose when she started struggling with the ambulance attendants. "We need to treat this one extra special," said Dr. Lewis. "She is on the edge of never coming back."

The nurses assured Dr. Lewis that they would contact her immediately. Dr. Lewis left the ward, looked at her watch, and saw it was 11:30am. She headed to the elevators. Lunch would be served shortly in the cafeteria. It was time for a break. After all, how many doctors left the hospital to ride shotgun with ambulance attendants to bring a patient back? She was proud of herself. Cathy was safe and sound, exactly where she needed to be.

Donna's father, Clifford, had finished filling out his statements. The detectives were on their way to solving another crime. Joann might have had a drug problem, but she did not deserve to die at the hands of another patient in the hospital. Clifford's cellphone rang, and it was the coroner. The results were back from the DNA swabs. "Can you meet me in my office?" asked the coroner.

"As a matter of fact, I can," said Clifford. "I am here at the hospital now."

"How about in half an hour?" asked the coroner. "Will that work?"

"Yes," said Clifford. "I will meet you in half an

542

hour."

The coroner then promptly called the lead detective on Joann's case. "The DNA results are back from the lab on Joann Jones. Can we meet in half an hour in my office?" The detective responded, saying he would be there.

Clifford walked back into Donna's room and gave his daughter a kiss on the forehead. "Honey, I have a meeting downstairs. I will be back when I am finished. Mark and Marcy, you stay here with your aunt and behave." Clifford looked over at Tommy and Gunner. "Gentlemen, I will see you in an hour. Look after my girl." Clifford made his way out to the elevator. The stainless steel doors opened, and Clifford pressed the button marked B. The air in the basement seemed cooler to Clifford as he exited the elevator. He made his way down the hall to the doors marked 'Coroner'. Clifford walked in and was greeted by the detective who was working on Joann's case. Clifford spoke up, saying he had received a call stating they had the results of the DNA test.

"Yes," said the detective, "I got the same call."

Moments later, the state's coroner walked into the office, carrying a file folder. "Gentlemen, have a seat," said the coroner, pointing to the desk in the corner of the room. Two chairs were directly in front and one behind. The concrete floor behind the desk had most of its paint worn off from the constant movement of the wheels on the bottom of the coroner's chair. The three men sat down. The coroner, wearing his white lab coat, said, "We have the results of the DNA that we pulled from your wife, Joann. We have a match."

Clifford, knowing he and Joann had not been intimate for years, asked, "Was my wife raped?"

"I do not believe so," said the coroner. "There is no evidence of forced penetration. However, we were originally somewhat confused."

"Why?" asked the detective.

"Well, the DNA was a partial match to Mr. Jones."

"What do you mean?" asked Clifford.

"It was a one hundred percent match to your deceased son, Matt. We do routine swabs of a body that comes in here. We had swabbed Matt two days ago. When we ran your swab and the DNA from the sperm sample from Joann's vagina we got a one hundred percent match." The coroner repeated himself. "There is absolutely no doubt that sometime over the last two days your wife and son had intimate relations."

Clifford lost it. "What the hell are you saying!? My wife fucked my son that escaped from prison!?"

The coroner nodded his head and said, "Yes, sometime within the last two days," as he looked at the detective.

The detective asked for a duplicate copy of the report. Clifford sat in his chair with his head in his hands. "I can't believe what you are telling me."

"I am sorry," said the coroner. "The DNA does not lie."

Clifford left the office. He did not want to hear any more. He got back into the elevator, and the doors closed. Clifford punched the wall, then pushed the button for the main floor. He had suspected for years that something different was going on with his wife and eldest son.

During the few times the family would be

gathered at the kitchen table for dinners, Matt and Joann would giggle and laugh at the silliest of things. Matt always was given the opportunity for any leftovers first. Joann would say, "I have to keep my boy growing big and strong." It was around the time Matt was a junior in high school that Joann had cut her husband off from any sexual contact. It was all becoming clear. His son had been fucking his own mother for years right under his very own nose. Clifford walked out the main entrance of Metro General. He found the closest bench to sit on. Memories started to flash through his mind.

They were like snapshots in time. Clifford's cellphone rang. It was the life insurance company.

"Mr. Jones," said the voice at the other end of the line.

"Yes," said Clifford.

"We regret to inform you that the claim on your wife's life insurance policy has been denied, pending further investigation from our claims and local police departments."

"What...?" said Clifford. The line went dead. "Fucking bastards!" yelled Clifford into the air. "You fucking bastards!" Donna's father gathered his thoughts. He stood up and then started to make his way back into the hospital. As he entered the automatic doors, he was greeted by two detectives.

"Clifford Jones?" they asked.

"Yes..."

"You are under arrest for the murder of your wife, Joann Jones. Anything you say can and will be used against you in a court of law."

Clifford was forced against the wall face-first.

His hands were cuffed behind him. The state police had been informed that a claim had been filed against Joann's policy within a couple of hours of her death. They found the conduct of the claimant strange as he kept asking about when he would receive a check. They made the recording of their client available to state police. The state police were the ones that had called Clifford's cellphone moments before. Pretending they were the insurance company, they recorded the call and videotaped Clifford's response. All would be used as evidence in his murder and insurance fraud case.

Investigators believed that Clifford had found out about Joann's affair with her eldest son. That was the motive. Clifford used that opportunity to sneak into her hospital room and smothered her to death. He then slid out of her room, meeting Dr. Hansen, where Clifford played the grieving husband. It was a perfect bit of detective work, all wrapped up in a neat little package. They had the DNA evidence to prove the affair. Perfect.

Clifford was escorted from the main entrance. He was yelling that he had done nothing wrong. He did not kill his wife. He struggled with the officers then broke free of their grasp. Clifford ran down into the parking lot. He was not going to jail for something he did not do.

"Stop!" said the detectives. "Police! Stop!" Both had their 9mm Glock handguns pointing at Clifford's back. Clifford was now about thirty feet away.

"Get on your knees!" shouted one of the officers.

Clifford was having none of it. His adrenaline was flowing into his blood at top speed. Clifford spun around, yelling, "I did not do it!" as he ran towards the officers as fast as he could.

Two shots rang out. Two bullets hit Clifford in

the chest, going directly through his heart. Clifford dropped to the concrete like a leftover hotdog. Blood pooled around his body, soaking the sidewalk leading into Metro General.

The detectives looked at each other. One said, "Like father, like son." There would be no trial. There would be no further investigation. A crowd had started to gather around. Dispatch responded to the 'shots fired' call. Three more cruisers showed up. Photographs were taken of the scene. Clifford's body was taken down to the morgue. His handcuffs were removed, then cleaned and returned to the detectives. Clifford's body was placed in the refrigerated compartment directly below Joann.

"Fitting," the coroner said out loud with a smile on his face. "Mom, dad, and son all in the same place chilling out." The coroner took Clifford's file to the cabinet. It was placed in an area marked 'justifiable homicide', right in front of his son Matt's file.

Chapter 100

Johnny Robbins sat in the sheriff's cruiser, watching intently the movements around Mountain View Gas and Service. There was far too much traffic coming and going from the pumps for Johnny to confront Jackson Hall. Johnny was sure he had the right motorhome. The bumper sticker was exactly as Barbara had described. It said, 'Spending my kids' inheritance'. Johnny was like a mouse looking at a giant piece of cheese attached to one of those spring-loaded traps. He knew how good it was going to taste to get his hands on all that money. He just did not want to end up back in prison or dead. He had managed to avoid getting arrested since he and Matt escaped. There was no way he was going to blow it now.

He watched for almost an hour. Eventually, there was a cloud of blue smoke that rose from behind the old motorhome. Johnny watched as Jackson Hall came outside, walking towards the open bay door. "You motherfucker!" Johnny said aloud, recognizing his old partner. "I have you now!" Johnny started the sheriff's cruiser then headed over towards the service station. Robbins pulled in front of pump number four. Johnny pulled his baseball cap down low on his forehead. Johnny reached into the backseat. He grabbed the sheriff's jacket. Robbins then took the 9mm he had stolen from the state trooper and tucked it into the back of his pants. He pulled his shirt over the gun before he exited the trooper's car. Johnny then slipped the jacket on.

A young man came running over. "Fill her up, sheriff?" asked the attendant.

"You bet," said Johnny.

Three more cars pulled in. The kid was running around trying to make sure everyone was getting the service they needed. Johnny walked over to the gas nozzle that was on the side of the police car. He removed it as gas continued to flow. Johnny sprayed gasoline all over the exterior of the trooper's car. The young attendant saw what Johnny was doing. He came running over. Johnny turned with the nozzle still spewing gas. He directed it at the kid. "What the hell?" the kid yelled. Johnny reached into his pocket. He pulled the lighter he had taken from Barbara's purse at the motel. Johnny pressed the igniter until a flame danced on its top. The kid knew he was in trouble. The other folks getting gas saw what was happening and started to panic. They ran as fast as they could.

Johnny held the flame in front of the gas that flowed from the pump. There was a sudden rush of exploding air combined with the raw gasoline. Johnny ran back. The heat was intense. Robbins turned to see the flames engulf the cop's car and the young attendant. The kid ran around, covered in flames, screaming. It took about twenty seconds until he dropped to the ground. It was utter pandemonium around the pumps. People were screaming. Flames and smoke poured out from the burning trooper's car. The gas nozzle continued to pump fuel onto the ground under other cars. Jason Booker came running from inside the service bay as soon as he heard his son's screams.

He could not believe what he was looking at. Jackson Hall stood watching the scene unfold. Flames were now licking at the canopy over the fuel pumps. Smoke was thick. The smell of burning plastic, rubber, and flesh filled the air. Johnny Robbins walked through the cloud of smoke into the view of Jackson Hall. Johnny

reached behind his back, pulling the stolen 9mm from the back of his pants. Jackson realized just a moment too late that he was staring at Johnny. Jackson turned to run.

Johnny Robbins pulled the trigger twice. Two bullets landed in Jackson's back. Jackson was knocked to the ground on his stomach just behind the motorhome. He was still alive when Robbins walked over, using his foot to roll over his ex-partner. Jackson Hall looked up as one of the cars exploded in front of the pumps. People were on their cellphones. Johnny stood over Jackson Hall. He pointed the 9mm at Jackson's head then pulled the trigger. Jackson's skull shattered, his brains and blood flew everywhere.

Johnny ran to the driver's door of the motorhome. He jumped inside then turned the key. The engine sprang to life. Sirens could be heard in the distance. Johnny assumed the fire trucks were on the way. He backed the motorhome out of the service bay, running over the body of Jackson Hall. Jason Booker was doing his best with a portable fire extinguisher. His son's body lay in a burning heap by the pumps. The heat was so intense that the customers were now standing out on the main street.

When Robbins had backed far enough away from the open service bay, he placed the motorhome in drive. Hall's body was dragged twenty feet as Johnny made his way onto the main street of Hillcrest. As Johnny pulled away, two more explosions happened. Johnny passed three fire trucks as he headed south. He looked around. The motorhome was filled with the boxes that had been in the basement of the casino.

Johnny had made the right decision. Barbara had been right. Johnny needed to dump the motorhome. The boxes and money were another problem. Johnny knew

the cops would be looking for him and the motorhome. It would not be long until the cops were taking statements from witnesses. The clock was ticking. Johnny looked at the gas gauge. It registered full. The town of Hillcrest was hopping as tourists drove through on their way home. The main drag was clogged with traffic. Johnny needed a quick plan. To his right was a drive-in car/truck wash, one of those self-wash types: you put money into a machine then use a wand to wash your own vehicle.

Johnny pulled into the parking lot then followed the arrows to the back of the building. There was one dedicated line for trucks and motorhomes. Johnny followed the signs until he reached the large overhead door. Johnny rolled down the motorhome's window. Robbins pressed the button to open the overhead door. He pulled into the wash bay just in time to hear a helicopter off in the distance. Johnny wasted no time pressing the button on the wall to close the door he had just driven through.

He then walked to the front of the large wash bay. Johnny closed the front overhead door that led back out onto the main street. Johnny felt the back of his pants to ensure the 9mm was still within easy reach. He walked into the office of Bubbles Carwash. Standing behind the counter was a young lady wearing a light yellow tube top and a pair of cutoff shorts. Her nametag fastened over her left breast read 'Nancy'.

"Can I help you?" she asked.

"I guess I am going to need some change," said Johnny. "Can you break a hundred?"

"Umm," said Nancy, "I will have to go into the back office."

551

"Are you the only one here?" asked Johnny. "Don't you have someone to help you?"

"No, it's the long weekend," said Nancy. "I am here all by myself." She turned her back, removing a small ring of keys from the pocket in her cutoffs. She walked to the door behind her. "Is that change for one hundred?" she asked.

"Yes," said Johnny. "Can you give me four twenties and twenty tokens?"

Nancy nodded and said, "Sure."

She opened the office door, then took one step inside. Johnny Robbins sprang over the counter like a wild cougar. He was on Nancy before she knew what was going on. Johnny pushed Nancy into the office, slamming the office door behind him. Before Nancy could turn around completely, Johnny had taken the 9mm from the back of his pants. He used the butt of the gun to hit Nancy directly on the side of her head. The young lady fell to the floor, unconscious. Johnny looked around. Hanging on a hook behind the closed door was a black button-down shirt. On the left front breast pocket, it read 'Bubbles Carwash'. On the right, the name 'Dirk' was embroidered, followed by the word 'manager'. Johnny pulled the phone off the desk, ripping the wires from the wall. Johnny used the phone wire to tie Nancy's arms behind her back. A large welt was forming on the side of the girl's head. Johnny removed the shirt that Barbara had ironed for him. He slipped on the shirt he found on the back of the door. Johnny exited the office to be greeted by a customer standing on the other side of the counter.

"Can I get ten bucks worth?" asked the woman, handing Johnny a ten-dollar bill.

Johnny pressed the large button on the top of the till. The cash drawer sprang open. The tray was filled with wash tokens. Johnny took the ten-dollar bill, placed it in his pocket, and then handed the lady ten tokens.

"Thanks, Dirk," she said.

"You're welcome," said Johnny.

She left the office and Johnny sprang back into action. He rummaged through the drawers until he found some blank paper, tape, and a black felt pen. Johnny wrote 'Out of Order' on the sheet of paper. He then went outside, walking around the building to the back. He taped the sign saying 'Out of Order' to the door of the wash bay containing the old motorhome and his cash. Johnny then walked back to the office.

A police helicopter flew directly over the main street of Hillcrest. Two police cars weaved in and out of traffic with their lights and sirens on. The cops were on the hunt. So far, the prey had outsmarted them. Johnny walked back into the private office. Nancy was starting to moan. Johnny took the shirt that Barbara had found. He pulled on Nancy's hair, lifting her head. He stuffed some of the shirt into Nancy's mouth. He then took the roll of tape and wrapped it several times around her head, securing the shirt in place. There was no way for Nancy to spit it out now. Any sound she made would be muffled. Johnny was pleased with himself.

Johnny left Nancy lying on the floor. The swelling on her head had created quite an unsightly lump. Johnny left the private office, locking the door with Nancy's keys. Johnny sat behind the counter, his feet up on the desk. Two more customers walked in, looking for tokens. Johnny asked what was going on outside. One of the customers said that the cops had set up roadblocks. There had been a shooting and a major

553

fire at the Mountain View gas station.

"Oh," said Johnny. "That's what all the commotion is about." The two customers left the office after Johnny had pocketed another twenty bucks. He smiled; this was a pretty easy gig. If it were not for the hundred million he had out in the motorhome, he might think about getting a job.

Johnny heard some movement coming from the office behind him. He unlocked the door to find Nancy standing with tears running down her face. The shirt Johnny had taped into her mouth half hung down to her cleavage. Johnny walked into the office. "There, there," he said to Nancy. "I am not going to hurt you." Johnny pulled the 9mm service revolver from the back of his pants. He ran the barrel of the gun down both sides of Nancy's face. "Now you see," said Johnny, "if I wanted to kill you, I would have done that already. Do not make a sound." Johnny turned Nancy and then directed her to the chair behind the office desk. "Sit," said Johnny. Johnny sat on the corner of the desk. He noticed that Nancy was having difficulty breathing. Johnny did not care. Nancy's chest moved as she struggled to breathe through her nose. Johnny reached over with his right hand. He pulled the material of Nancy's tube top down exposing her firm and large breasts. "I would say you're a 36 double C-cup. Am I right?" asked Johnny. More tears ran down Nancy's face. Johnny ran the 9mm over her breasts. He yelled "Am I fucking right!?"

Nancy snapped out of her delirium. If she was going to survive this she needed to use her head. She nodded to the affirmative. "I thought so," said Johnny. "But really, I am an ass man. Stand up." Nancy stood, her hands firmly tied behind her back, the wire from the phone was cutting into her wrists. Johnny unfastened her cutoffs letting them drop to the ground. Johnny stood

554

behind his young captive. "Perfect," he said as he pushed Nancy down so she was bent over the desk. Her nipples rubbed against its old wooden surface. Nancy could see that at some point the desk had initials carved into its surface. Johnny kicked her legs apart and unzipped his fly. Robbins's cock sprung forth, ready for action. He laid across Nancy's back and whispered into her ear, "You are going to enjoy this." Nancy did not move. Her aunt, who raised her, said she should not ever fight back if she got herself into a bad situation. There would always be time for revenge later. Johnny grabbed a handful of her hair. He pulled Nancy's head back.

"Hello? Hello?" There was a loud voice coming from outside the office. Johnny bent back down.

"Don't you say one fucking word. No noise," he said. "If I hear anything I will take this gun and shove it up that tight pussy of yours then pull the trigger. Do you understand?" Nancy nodded her head. Johnny readjusted himself then did up the zipper on his pants. "I will be right there," Johnny yelled through the closed door. Johnny composed himself for a couple of seconds, placing the 9mm in the back of his pants. He looked back. Nancy had not moved from her position on the desk. Johnny opened the door just wide enough so he could step out behind the customer service counter. Two sheriff's deputies stood on the opposite side.

"Can I help you?" asked Johnny.

The two officers looked confused for a second, looking at the name on Johnny's shirt. "Dirk," said one of the officers. "We are looking for a guy in an old motorhome. Have you seen anyone come in here to wash a motorhome in the last hour?"

Johnny said, "No, I have not seen a motorhome for a couple of days. I assume everyone is still out

camping. We will start to get busy with camping rigs later this afternoon."

"Are you alone?" said the other officer.

"Yes," said Johnny. "You guys know what it's like on long weekends. Everyone wants them off."

The officers nodded their heads. "If you see anyone like that, call the department. We are checking all motorhomes going through town."

"Got it," said Johnny. The two deputies turned, exiting the customer service area, then headed directly towards their cruiser.

Johnny Robbins opened the office door. Nancy had not moved from her position across the desk. She turned her head so she could see her attacker. Johnny looked at her then said, "I will be back, little lady." Johnny locked the door leading out to the wash bays. He then turned the open sign on the front door to read 'closed'. Johnny fumbled with the keys he had taken from Nancy. Finding the right one, he locked the front door. Johnny walked down the sidewalk on the main street of Hillcrest. Four blocks ahead, he could see flashing red and blue lights. Traffic was at a standstill. The cops he had just spoken to were right. They were stopping every single motorhome.

Johnny eventually made his way to the parking lot of Elli's Diner. There in the lot was a large black Dodge Ram 3/4-ton truck with one of those extended cabs. Attached to the back bumper was a brand new horse trailer. The windows of the trailer were open.

Robbins peered inside; it was empty except for some hay lying on the floor. Johnny crouched low as he walked up to the driver's door. He lifted the handle. The door was locked. Johnny looked at the back window of

the fairly new vehicle. It had one of those sliding rear windows, which was partially open. Johnny rolled himself into the box of the truck. He opened the back window fully, then crawled through. Johnny pulled the 9mm from the back of his pants. He then laid down on the floor directly behind the driver's seat. Johnny covered himself with a jacket that was laying on the backseat and waited. It took about a half an hour; Johnny was getting stiff from the position he was in.

Eventually, he heard the power door locks open. Robbins heard a few voices. Johnny could see through the space between the seat and the door of the truck that the man who opened the driver's door was wearing a cowboy hat.

"Good to see you again," said the cowboy. He waved to the folks he had just finished lunch with. Johnny felt the truck move as the cowboy stepped on the running board, then slid into the driver's seat, closing the door. The cowboy sat for a moment, belched, and farted. He started the truck, then rolled down the driver's window. He fastened his seatbelt. When Johnny thought the timing was right, he placed the muzzle of the 9mm in the middle of the back of the seat. He pulled the trigger. The bullet traveled through the material of the seat. It entered the back of the driver, piercing the man's heart. Johnny's ears were ringing from the sound of the gun. The driver moaned then slumped towards the driver's door. Johnny crawled over the seats. Robbins pressed the button to unfasten the driver's seatbelt. He then reached across the cowboy and opened the driver's door. Johnny removed the man's cowboy hat, placing it on his own head, before pushing the driver out onto the pavement in the parking lot. Robbins slid into the driver's seat. He placed the truck in drive.

Johnny estimated he had been away from the

carwash for at least an hour, maybe longer. He pressed the accelerator pedal, turning to head back towards Bubbles. Johnny pulled the rig he had just stolen into the parking lot of the carwash. He pulled up to the front of the building; two of the bay doors were still open. There was no one inside. "Perfect," he thought to himself. Johnny turned off the truck. He stepped out, making his way back to the main office. Johnny reached for the door to unlock it. The door was already open. Johnny took the 9mm from his waist and went inside. The office door was open. There on the desk was the phone wire Johnny had used to tie Nancy's hands behind her back. The tape and shirt Johnny had used to keep her quiet were on the floor. Johnny ran out of the office to the wash bay that contained the old motorhome; it was still there. Johnny opened the driver's door, looking inside; everything was just as he had left it.

"Fuck!" Johnny yelled. His cash was still there, but he needed Nancy's help in moving the boxes into the horse trailer. Johnny straightened himself up. He stood with the driver's door open. Johnny heard the distinct sound of a shotgun being cocked. The shotgun Jackson Hall had stolen from the Wheel Inn was now being pointed at Johnny's head by Dirk, the carwash manager. Dirk had stopped in to check on Nancy. Nancy was Dirk's latest conquest. He had been fucking her from the first week she started at Bubbles.

Dirk was stunned to find the business sign turned to say 'closed'. When he found Nancy in his office, Dirk was pissed. Dirk had searched the carwash and found the motorhome. Dirk knew the cops were looking for a motorhome just like this one. It was all over the radio. Dirk had opened two of the boxes to see they were full of one hundred dollar bills banded in groups of ten thousand dollars. He and Nancy knew that whoever

drove the motorhome into the bay was running from the law. That person would have to come back for the cash; it was inevitable.

"Drop the gun!" Dirk yelled. Johnny held the 9mm in the air in his right hand. "Drop the fucking gun!" Dirk yelled a second time. Johnny let the gun drop to the wet concrete of the wash bay.

Nancy came out from behind one of the heavy wash curtains that separated each wash bay. The swelling on her head was turning purple. Dirk was her hero. He held the man who was going to assault her at gunpoint. Nancy had told Dirk everything. Nancy picked up the 9mm Johnny had just dropped.

Dirk pressed the shotgun harder into the back of Johnny's head. The movement tipped the cowboy hat Johnny had stolen to a strange angle. She took two steps towards Johnny Robbins. She placed the barrel of the deputy's 9mm at the base of Johnny's cock, right where it attached to his body. She pointed it down, then slightly away from herself. Dirk said nothing.

Johnny had both of his hands in the air. He looked Nancy in the eyes. "You wanted it," said Johnny. "You know you did." Nancy pulled the trigger. The 9mm fired a round, severing Johnny's cock from his body. The bullet hit one of Johnny's balls. It exploded as his sack was torn to shreds. The bullet lodged into Johnny's left leg. Blood poured from Johnny's gaping wounds, running into the grate in the middle of the floor. Johnny yelled; he was in the worst pain he had ever felt in his life. Robbins fell to his knees. Nancy stepped back.

"Are you done?" asked Dirk. Nancy nodded. She took three more steps away from Johnny. She turned in time to see Dirk pull the trigger of the shotgun. There was a loud blast. Johnny's head blew into several pieces.

His body dropped to the floor of the carwash. Blood, brains, skin, and bone were everywhere. The side of the motorhome was covered in human remains. Dirk placed the shotgun against the wall. He then lifted the grate from the middle of the floor. He rolled Johnny's body into the open drain.

He tossed the shotgun in with Johnny's body. He then replaced the grate. Dirk took two tokens from his pocket. He set the arrow on the wash box to read 'soap'. He pressed the handle on the wash wand. Within the five minutes allocated on the timer, Dirk had washed everything off the side of the motorhome, and the concrete floor was clean. Johnny's body was lying under the metal grate in the floor. Blood continued to ooze from the body, but it did not matter. Dirk and Nancy looked at each other. Nancy was shaking.

"Don't worry, sweetheart," said Dirk. "The guy was a criminal. He got what he deserved. No one is going to touch my girl like that."

Nancy walked towards Dirk. Her nipples were hard and quite visible through her damp tube top. She hugged Dirk, then kissed him. "Now what?" asked Nancy.

"The cops have already been here. They are looking for him. It won't be long until they figure out what is going on," said Dirk. "We have to do something with all that cash." Dirk and Nancy had no idea how much money they had found. Dirk had been drummed out of town once. His old man had taken away his opportunity of running the family appliance repair business. Dirk had taken the job at the carwash when he came back to town. The owners needed someone that could repair the wash equipment when it broke down. Dirk was a natural fit.

"We are rich, sweetie," said Dirk to his young conquest. "Rich beyond our wildest dreams."

Chapter 101

Brad continued down the path toward Rock Lake. Eventually, he came upon his father and his group of hikers heading toward the staging area. Brad pulled the quad and trailer as far off the path as he could, making just enough room to let everyone by. Kevin stopped as the group walked along further ahead.

"Good luck, son," he said. "Those Irish ladies have been calling out for their husbands. I'm not saying anything until all the pieces come together. If they go into shock, we might have to carry them out too."

"Thanks, Dad," said Brad. "I should be home tonight."

Brad pulled the quad back onto the trail and continued on the path until he reached Lookout Point. He paused for a moment and could see the sheriff's helicopter in what was once the space he and Tommy had set up their tents. Everything was scattered about. Brad continued down the path and the hill, eventually arriving back at the campsite. He stopped at the sheriff's helicopter.

Brad opened the pod located on the right skid and removed the box marked "two-man raft." Brad tossed the box into the back of the trailer. He then continued along the path until he reached Dan Thompson and the sheriff's deputies. They had finished taking photographs of Ranger Gary Smith's body. They now had a murder investigation on their hands. They believed the murderer, one Johnny Robbins, had flown out of the area, catching a ride when the Chinook sky crane came in to haul the crashed 505 out of the water.

Dan Thompson was beside himself. If he only knew that Gary's life was in danger. Brad stopped the quad and went back to the trailer, removing a black body bag, and then walked toward Thompson. Dan took the bag from Brad and walked over to the sheriffs. The men laid the body bag out beside Gary's corpse. They sealed Gary's body into the black bag, and placed it with the utmost respect in the back of the utility trailer.

The next step was to head up the Rock Lake trail toward the old trapper's shack. The sheriffs had seen what looked like two bodies in the water. The men mounted their respective quads. Brad led the way, moving slowly toward the old shack. When they arrived, the men dismounted their ATVs. Dan Thompson looked at the Sheriff in charge and pointed towards Rock Lake.

The tall shrubs along the pathway made it difficult to see the water. "Was it here?" asked Dan.

"Just a little past the old cabin," said the Sheriff and pilot. Dan went to the trailer carrying Ranger Smith's body. He opened the storage locker, and fumbled around until he found what he was looking for. Dan removed what looked like a three-pronged anchor that was attached to a bright orange bundle of rope. Brad and the three sheriffs followed Thompson back to the spot the pilot indicated.

"Look here," said the Sheriff, pointing towards the ground. Two sets of boot prints could be seen in the soft ground. The prints went through the shrubs to the edge of the water and then disappeared.

"Looks like they went in here," Brad spoke up. "This is the exact spot where we found that woman who had been mauled and was dead. Her and her friend were attacked by that Grizzly. Tommy's dad flew the survivor out of here. I wonder if the two men who went to help

maybe came across that Grizz."

"That is an interesting hypothesis," said the sheriff. "Maybe."

As the men stood at the edge of Rock Lake, they heard the sound of a rifle shot, then another. The air suddenly went silent.

"Sounds like Steve got him," said Thompson to Brad. They all were looking in the direction of the rifle shots.

"That is one problem other campers are no longer going to have to worry about," said the pilot. "Let's get that raft inflated."

Brad walked back to the trailer. He removed the box marked "Raft," and carried it back through the shrubs to where the other men were waiting.

"Thanks, kid, for remembering to grab this. It's going to make things a whole lot easier," said Sheriff Anderson, taking the box from Brad. He set it on the ground and opened the lid as the others watched.

Inside the box, which was about three feet long and two feet wide, was a metal canister, two collapsible paddles, and the department's latest inflatable raft. Anderson reached inside, removing all the items. He unrolled the lightweight rubber raft and screwed the metal canister to the valve on the side of the pontoon. When all was in place, Anderson opened the valve on the canister, and air rushed into the deflated raft. In a matter of one minute, what looked like a wrinkled piece of crap inflated into a usable two-man boat. Emblazoned on each pontoon was the word "Sheriff."

"That's pretty slick," said Thompson. "I am going to have to talk to my boss about getting one of these."

Anderson assembled the two paddles and instructed his two deputies to get into the raft. The two men were given the three-pronged hook and rope. Anderson pointed straight out.

"About twenty-five yards that way," Anderson said as he pointed toward the lake.

"Roger that," came the reply from both men at the exact same time. The two deputies paddled a distance of twenty-five yards from shore. Both men kept looking over the sides of the boat, looking into the clear waters of Rock Lake. It only took a few minutes until one shouted, "I see something!"

The young deputy slid the three-pronged hook into the water, moving the rope back and forth a few times until it went tight. "Got him," said the deputy to his partner. The young officer started to pull on the rope. He had pulled in about ten feet of line when the head of Seamus O'Reilly broke the surface of the water. His eyes were wide open. Staring into nothing, his head had swollen from being in the water for two days. The three-pronged hook was caught in the jacket Seamus had been wearing the evening he had gone to help.

Sheriff Anderson took his cellphone from his hip and started to record what was taking place out on the water. When the two deputies had secured the body, they paddled back to shore. Brad and the other Ranger stood knee-deep in the ice-cold water. When the boat was close enough, the two men released Seamus's body from the rope and then dragged it to shore. The two deputies paddled back to where they had recovered Seamus. Five minutes later, everyone heard, "Got the other." The body of Shawn came to the surface, with the three-pronged hook lodged under his right armpit. The sheriffs paddled back to shore, and the bodies of the two Irishmen now

lay on the shoreline of Rock Lake, face up.

"Poor bastards," said Dan Thompson. Sheriff Anderson looked closely at the swollen face of Seamus. There were three long scratches that had torn the skin down his cheek, each about three inches long. There was no blood or bruising, just white water-logged skin. Anderson snapped a picture of Seamus's cheek and then went over to Shawn's body. He lifted up Shawn's right hand, looking closely at it. He then lifted Shawn's left hand.

Sheriff Anderson removed a small plastic bag from his shirt pocket and took the duty knife he carried from his utility belt. He used it to scrape out something from under the fingernails of Shawn's hand, wrapped the plastic bag around the blade of the knife to ensure what he collected was safe and sealed. Anderson then washed the blade in the lake water, wiped it on his pants, and placed it back in his utility belt.

Anderson looked over at Dan Thompson. "They got in over their heads," said Anderson. "They were struggling to stay on the surface. This guy scratched his friend trying to survive. See the marks here?" Anderson pointed to Seamus's cheek. Dan and Brad looked closer, and they could now see what the Sheriff had noticed right away.

"The poor bastards drowned. Those boots and the clothing they were wearing were just too much. The weight, when everything got wet, took them down. They couldn't keep their heads above the water. Such a shame. Let's get these men loaded up, gentlemen. This is a closed case. We are writing these two deaths up as accidental drowning."

Chapter 102

Donna had been informed that her father had been shot and killed in front of the hospital trying to escape. The detectives had spent an hour questioning her in a back room on the main floor. She had been told that the DNA evidence had proved her mother and brother had sex within twenty-four hours of her mother's death. The cops believed that her father had discovered the truth, which prompted him while at the hospital the evening before to smother Joann while she was sleeping. It was pretty much a closed case. Donna had been given a clear plastic bag of her father's possessions. They had been on his person at the time of arrest. Donna was asked if she had any indication that something might have been going on between her mother and brother. She contemplated telling the detectives what had happened when she was younger, on the night that she used her baseball bat on her brother as he tried to molest her.

When she replied she looked directly at the cops. "Are you stupid?" she said aloud. "My brother has been in prison." She buried what she really wanted to say. She sat there, tears rolling down her cheeks. She had just lost her mother, father, and brother. All three were downstairs in the morgue. Donna grabbed the bag of belongings sitting in front of her. "I am not answering anymore of your questions," she said. "I need to go and see Tommy." Donna stormed out of the room. The detectives followed a minute later.

Dr. Hansen passed them in the hallway as he was heading off on a well-deserved break. "Poor girl," he said to the detectives. "Her mother had been doing so well. Her father was so concerned."

"Well," said one of the detectives, "he should not have killed her."

Dr. Hansen looked confused for a second. "What are you talking about? Her father had nothing to do with the mother's death. He was waiting for me in the lobby. He would not have had a clue where his wife was."

"What?" said the detectives.

"You need to question the woman upstairs, Cathy Taylor. She is being treated by Dr. Lewis," said Doctor Hansen. "I have said enough." The detectives looked at each other. They had a lead that needed to be followed up on.

Donna made her way back to Tommy's room. Matt and Marcy were still sitting in the chairs beside Tommy's bed. Donna looked at her boyfriend, more tears rolling down her face. "Sweetheart, what's wrong?" asked Tommy.

Donna climbed into Tommy's bed and spooned herself in front of him. "Hold me," she said. "Just hold me."

Marcy looked up and said, "Oh, that is so gross. You're going to get boy germs."

Donna lost it and started to cry uncontrollably. "Wait until I tell you what has happened," she said, pulling Tommy's arm tighter around herself. "You're not going to believe it."

The two detectives inquired at the front desk as to where they might find Dr. Lewis. They were told Dr. Lewis could be found in the psychiatric ward. The two men made their way to the nurse's station on the fourth floor. Sitting outside room 4018 was a familiar face from the sheriff's office.

"What are you doing here?" one detective asked.

"Waiting until we can question the woman inside."

"Her doctor would not let us question her."

"Where is her doctor now?"

The deputy looked at the two detectives. "I don't know," he said.

One of the detectives asked for Dr. Lewis at the nurse's station. After presenting his badge, he was told that Dr. Lewis would be paged. The three cops stood outside Cathy's room. Ten minutes passed, and there had been no sign of Lewis anywhere.

The two detectives entered Cathy's room. The young deputy sat in his chair. After all, the detectives were not told to leave; the two deputies were.

The two detectives approached Cathy's bedside and introduced themselves as she opened her eyes. They showed her their badges. Cathy's arms and legs were strapped to her bed. Her head had been slightly elevated. Cathy looked at both men.

"Can I help you?" she said.

"We just have a couple of questions."

"Me too," said Cathy. "Have you seen my son?"

"No, ma'am," they replied.

Cathy tried moving her arms. "What is going on here?" She looked to see that her arms and ankles were tied down.

Cathy started to struggle. "What the fuck is going on here!?" she yelled. "Are you going to fuck me too!? Come and get it, you bastards!" Cathy was now bouncing

violently on the bed.

The noise coming from Cathy's room was so loud that two nurses came running in. "Get out!" they yelled. "No one is to be in here unless Dr. Lewis is with her patient!"

"We just have..." one detective began.

Dr. Lewis walked into the room. She walked over to Cathy, putting her hand on her shoulder. "Get out!" yelled Dr. Lewis. "Can't you see that she is traumatized?"

Cathy yelled at both men again. "Come and get it, you fucking bastards!"

Dr. Lewis yelled at the two detectives. "I am calling security," she said. "You have five seconds to get out of here."

Cathy started yelling. "I am God's servant! I will kill you all!" as she fought against her restraints.

Chapter 103

Dirk and Nancy stood looking at the motorhome. "What are we going to do?" said Nancy.

"Honey, I want you to go to the office. Make up a sign that says 'closed for the holiday'."

"But--" said Nancy.

"Just do it," came Dirk's reply.

The truck and horse trailer Johnny Robbins had stolen were sitting out front of the wash bay that contained the motorhome. Dirk did some quick thinking. It had to be stolen. He was not going to touch it or get into it. Dirk made his way back to the office. Nancy was busy making her closed sign. Dirk picked up the phone, then dialed a number he knew by heart. The phone rang twice.

"Ted's towing, can I help you?"

"Ted, it's Dirk. I've got another one stuck in the Truck Bay. It's a motorhome."

"I can be there in ten minutes," said Ted.

"That would be great," said Dirk. "We have the weekend traffic coming back into town. Don't want to miss any business." Dirk hung up the phone. "Do not worry about the sign," he said to Nancy. "I want you to stay open now. Business as usual. We do not want to raise any suspicion."

"Okay," said Nancy.

Dirk went back out to the motorhome. He raised the rear overhead door. Dirk opened the side door of the motorhome. He removed a box and walked around the

571

building to his car. He opened the trunk, placing the box inside. He then used his penknife to cut the tape on the lid. Dirk opened the flaps of the box to reveal a stack of one hundred dollar bills. He then removed some cash, placing it in his pocket. Dirk heard the sound of a diesel engine pulling into the car wash lot. He looked up from behind his open trunk lid.

Ted was driving the largest tow rig he had in his fleet. Dirk closed his trunk and then waved Ted to the back of the building. Ted maneuvered the large tow truck to the open back door.

"Where is the owner and keys?" asked Ted.

"Don't know," said Dirk. "He left about an hour ago and said he was going to find someone to help. He has not come back. I am losing business."

Ted hooked his tow truck to the back of the old motorhome. He raised the back wheels just high enough so he could drive his tow truck forward, pulling the motorhome out of the bay. When the motorhome was clear of the doorway, Ted raised the back end higher. He ran a light bar to the front of the motorhome. The light bar was connected to the tow truck's tail lights, so traffic following would know if he was stopping or going left or right. Ted and Dirk spoke for a moment. Dirk then went back to the office, handing Nancy a thousand dollars from the money he removed from the box.

"I love you, sweetie," he said. "I will be back soon." Dirk got into his car, following Ted to his impound lot. Traffic on the main road through Hillcrest was backed up because of the roadblock. Ted drove through the back alleys, with Dirk following closely behind. They made their way around the roadblock, pulling into Ted's salvage yard fifteen minutes later.

Ted backed the motorhome up against the chain-link fence surrounding his yard. He lowered and then disconnected the RV from his truck. Dirk reached into his pocket. He removed two one-hundred-dollar bills and handed them to Ted. "Thanks for your help, buddy," he said.

"No worries. When the owner shows up, send him my way. When he pays the towing and storage fees, I will give you your money back."

"I know," said Dirk. "I trust you. I am heading back to Bubbles. Nancy is all alone," he said as he winked.

"Gotcha," said Ted. Ted opened the driver's side door of the motorhome. He noticed all the boxes in the back. The law would not allow him to snoop through an owner's sealed belongings. "Must be moving or something," Ted said out loud. Having a quick look inside the cab, he discovered a set of keys laying on the dirt-covered floor. He cleaned one of the old keys and then placed it in the ignition. He gave it a twist. The engine started. Ted shook his head. He had seen this before. Sometimes towing a vehicle would dislodge dirt in the fuel line. He shook his head, turned the motor off, and ensured he locked all the doors.

Ted made his way into his office, which was an old construction trailer. Lill, his office manager, stood behind the counter. Ted handed her the paperwork on the tow, along with the keys he found. Hooking fees, towing fees, and current storage charges amounted to four hundred and ninety-five dollars. Each day of storage would add another one hundred dollars to the total until the rig was picked up. If the unit was not claimed in thirty days, it would go to auction. Once a month, Ted held an auction on his property to clear vehicles that were never

picked up. The auctioneer would take ten percent off the top. Ted had done well for himself over the years, making an average of two hundred grand each year, just in these sales. It was the paperwork he hated. Lill was an expert at it. She would make sure a lien would be filed against the title. When the owner forfeited, the state would issue title to Ted's Towing so he could recoup his costs. It was a fantastic system. Lill handed him a sheet of paper. The state troopers had just called; they needed Ted to come to Bubbles Car Wash to assist in towing a truck and trailer to their forensic garage.

Ted jumped into his tow truck and made his way out of the yard. In fifteen minutes, he was back at Bubbles. Ted was met by a trooper who pointed him to the detectives standing around the black truck and horse trailer.

"We are conducting a murder investigation," said one of the detectives.

"What can I do?" asked Ted. "Do you want the entire rig in your forensic garage?"

"No," said the detective. "We have all the prints and blood we need. Take it to your storage yard."

The detective handed Ted a sheet of yellow paper from his clipboard. "You're good to go."

Ted hopped back into his tow truck and spent fifteen minutes ensuring the Big Dodge was connected to his tow truck safely.

After all, he was going to have to pull the truck and trailer in one shot. The sheriffs had left Bubbles parking lot. They were investigating a murder at Elli's Diner. They had also been informed that one of their own had been murdered on the State Freeway. A trooper's body had been found behind a Red Mustang convertible.

He had been shot, his legs crushed by the perpetrator. There was an all-out manhunt underway. The entire department was on high alert.

Ted pulled out onto the Main Road, then maneuvered his way through the back roads and alleys as he had done with the Motorhome. Twenty minutes later, Ted pulled into his storage yard. He dropped the Big Dodge and trailer in the middle of his yard. It would have been almost impossible to back up the connected units while attached to his tow truck. After disconnecting his rig, Ted made his way to his office to give Lill the paperwork.

The construction trailer was quiet when Ted walked in for the third time in two hours. He shouted Lill's name. There was no reply. Ted walked to the only closed door in the entire trailer. The sign on the door read "washroom." Ted knocked. "Lill, are you in there?" There was no reply. Ted tried again. "Lill!" he yelled. "It's Ted! Are you okay?" There was no answer. Ted put his shoulder against the door, then pushed as hard as he could. The latch gave way, allowing the door to spring open.

Lill was laying on the floor. Her jeans were around her ankles, and there was a trace of white powder under her nose. Lill's eyes were rolled back in her head. She was hardly breathing. Ted grabbed his cellphone from his hip and called 911. "Hurry," he said to the dispatch officer, "I need an ambulance sent to Ted's Towing; my assistant is hardly breathing." Ted hung up the phone and held Lill's head. Ted had no idea that Lill had a drug problem; she never exhibited any signs at all in the last ten years.

The ambulance and EMTs made their way through traffic, eventually arriving at the yard of Ted's

Towing. Ted stood on the stairs to the office trailer, frantic. He shouted at the EMTs, "Hurry, she is in here!" he said. The two EMTs ran up the stairs into the washroom.

"It looks like we have an OD. Pulse is rapid. Pupils are fixed and dilated. Does she have a drug problem?" asked one of the EMTs.

"Not that I am aware of," said Ted.

The EMTs removed Lill from the washroom, dragging her out into the open area of the office trailer. They placed a mask over her face and applied oxygen. Then, the men took the stretcher from the back of the ambulance. Lill was loaded onto the stretcher and placed into the back of the emergency vehicle. One of the EMTs sat with her in the back while the other drove. When they hit the main road, the overhead lights and siren were activated.

Ted stood on the stairs to his office trailer, shaking his head, unable to believe what had just happened. He scanned his storage yard, and to his surprise, the motorhome was gone. Ted walked to the counter and reviewed the paperwork on Lill's clipboard. Everything pertaining to the motorhome was there. Lill had stamped it "paid in full" and then wrote the word "cash" directly below the dark red ink. The only name written on the contract was Nancy. Nothing else.

Ted walked out of the trailer, locking the door behind him, and got back into his tow truck. He then drove out of his gate, stopping to lock the sliding security gate behind him. Ted made his way back to Bubbles Car Wash and walked into the office where Dirk sat behind the counter. Ted spoke first. "Did you send the owner of the motorhome to my yard?"

"No," said Dirk, "I haven't seen him. Maybe Nancy did?"

"Well, the motorhome is gone," Ted replied. Dirk was dumbfounded. Ted reached into his pocket. "Here is your two hundred bucks back. I am on my way to the hospital."

"Why?" asked Dirk.

"It looks like Lill overdosed."

"That does not make any sense," said Dirk. "She does drugs?" he asked.

"I did not think she did," said Ted.

"Damn, that's not good. I am waiting for Nancy to get back here. Is there anything I can do for you?" asked Dirk.

"Nancy?" asked Ted. "That's the name on the contract for the motorhome. Look here," he said, waving the yellow document towards Dirk. "See, she paid cash."

Dirk studied the document for a moment. When he had returned to Bubbles, his young girlfriend and coworker were missing, and the office door was locked. "Strange," said Dirk. "That's one hell of a coincidence."

"I have to go," said Ted. "I need to find out how Lill is doing."

"I understand," said Dirk. As soon as Ted had left the office, Dirk was on his cellphone. He called Nancy's number, but it automatically went to voicemail. Nancy had shut off her phone.

Dirk was angry. He had given Nancy some cash, and now she was missing, along with the old motorhome and all that money. Dirk got back into his car. It had only been an hour since he had returned to Bubbles and found

that Nancy was missing. She couldn't have gone that far.

Chapter 104

Two shots rang out from the end of Rock Lake as the wardens, sheriffs, and Brad worked to get Seamus and Shawn out of the water. The bodies of both men were now loaded into the small trailer behind Brad's quad, along with Deputy Sheriff Smith's body. The trailer was overloaded with an estimated 600 pounds of deceased human flesh, which was going to be a problem.

Dan Thompson looked at Brad. "Do you think you can make it back to the staging area?" he asked. Brad expressed his concern about the additional weight. "We need to get up to the cabins and check things out," said Thompson. "Take your time, Brad. Give these folks the respect they deserve. We need to go check on Steve."

Dan Thompson had used his two-way radio several times to try and get a hold of his Ranger. However, there had been no reply as the men were fishing the bodies out of Rock Lake. Thompson had assumed that his Ranger with the 30/30 had maintained radio silence so as not to scare off the man-eating Grizzly.

Brad mounted his quad. He needed to head down the path as well towards the cabins before he could turn around. "I will follow you," said Brad, "as soon as I can, I will turn around and head back."

"Stay at the staging area," said Thompson. "Thank you for all your help today." Brad nodded his head.

The sheriffs decided to walk back to the helicopter, leaving the inflatable boat on the shore. It was agreed that the sheriffs would fly back to the helipad in

the staging area. They would wait for Brad to arrive with the three bodies. The sheriffs would help load their coworker into the coroner's wagon.

Dan Thompson led the way towards the cabins. As soon as they made the open area in front of RL01, Brad turned around and headed back towards the campsite and the path leading to the staging area. By the time Brad had made it back to the campsite he had shared with Tommy and the girls, the Sheriff's helicopter was just lifting off. Brad looked over his shoulder as the chopper circled the lake once, then flew overhead and out of view, heading directly towards the helipad at the staging area.

Brad could only use low gear. He had the quad in four-wheel drive as he climbed out of the valley. The 500 cc engine struggled under the load. Brad was forced to stand up and lean over the handlebars of the quad to keep the front wheels from lifting off the ground. He couldn't afford to lose traction as he climbed the steep hill. The electric fan that cooled the engine turned on and did not stop. Brad was at the machine's limit. He knew that the load was over the limit of what the quad was designed to haul. He pressed on, the wheels skipping over the loose rocks on the trail. Somehow, he eventually made it to the summit that would take him down to the staging area. He looked over his shoulder and into the back of the trailer. The bodies had shifted but were still there.

He caught a glimpse of the lake, but there was no stopping to take in the view. The Sheriff's helicopter passed overhead, checking on Brad's progress. The chopper disappeared over the trees. Brad continued until he had made it to the parking lot for Rock Lake. The Sheriff's chopper was now sitting on the helipad. As Brad pulled up to the coroner's van, he was met by the department's finest. Kevin's group of hikers stood

580

quietly, watching what was happening.

Brad dismounted the quad to be met by his father. Kevin had looked into the back of the trailer. He counted three bodies. "The other two were in the lake," said Brad.

Kevin nodded his head. "I will tell the ladies that their husbands have been found."

The sheriff was right. The three bodies were removed from the utility trailer. As they were loaded into the back of the coroner's van, the people standing around removed their hats and bowed their heads. The ladies from Ireland broke down, collapsing to their knees in the parking lot. Kevin had delivered the bad news. Their husbands had set out to rescue another human being. The two heroes now lay on separate shelves in the back of the coroner's van. The van doors were closed. The noise of the generator muffled the sounds of the crying women.

Brad took in the entire scene and walked over to the sheriffs, then shook their hands. It had been a grueling weekend. What had started out as a pleasure trip with his girlfriend and best buddy had turned into a nightmare. Brad sat down on a large rock away from everyone, put his head in his hands, and started to cry. All the events of the last couple of days came flooding back.

Kevin walked over to Brad. "I am proud of you, son," he said as he put his arm around him. "You did everything you could to help these folks."

Dan Thompson parked his Quad in front of RL01 and walked over to RL03. "Steve, are you up there? Steve, it's Dan." There was no reply. The last time Dan had seen his ranger, he was climbing up onto the roof of RL03 with the 30/30. "Steve!" Dan shouted again, but there was still no reply.

Dan was met by the other rangers as soon as they had dismounted their quads. The three men walked to the back of RL03, and there, laying next to the trees, was a large female black bear. Two patches of blood ran down her fur and onto the ground. The rifle Ranger Steve had used to dispatch the large sow rested against the side of the outhouse.

Towards RL04, the men could hear some noise that sounded like a young baby crying. They moved towards the sound, and there, under the cabin, two black bear cubs were huddled away from the danger that had taken their mother's life. "What the hell," exclaimed Dan. "What are we going to do with these two orphans?" Steve had no idea the sow had two cubs before he pulled the trigger. He had watched her from the roof, thinking she was alone. The sow walked directly to the blood-soaked ground, sniffed the air, and started to lick the dirt.

Steve was positive he had his killer in his sights. Everyone had mistaken her for a Grizzly. His first shot entered her shoulder just above her heart. She spun around at the impact of the bullet hitting her. Steve fired a second round. This one pierced her heart, and she dropped like a stone. Steve watched from the rooftop as the large sow took her final breath. Steve had done his job, and the killer bear would be taken back to be autopsied.

Steve climbed down from the roof of RL03. He walked over to the large bear. He poked at it with the barrel of the 30/30. There was no movement. The bear was dead. Steve walked over to the outhouse. He had been on the roof for over three hours and needed to take a dump. He placed the 30/30 beside the outhouse door, went inside, and when he finished, he stepped back out into the fresh morning air, feeling proud that he had earned his money that day.

He stretched his arms above his head, took a deep breath, and moved his body from side to side. It took no more than a second or two when Steve suddenly realized he was laying on the ground. He tried to reach for his rifle, but the impact of the large male Grizzly knocking Steve to the ground put the 30/30 out of reach.

Steve felt the Grizzly bite into the back of his leg, and the bear tossed Steve into the air. Steve yelled in pain and attempted to reach for his can of bear spray on the side of his utility belt. The Grizzly saw the movement and bit into Steve's right shoulder beside his neck. Steve could feel the bones breaking in his shoulder. The bear's hot breath was rancid. The training the Rangers had was to roll into a ball, covering the back of their necks with interlocked fingers. Steve tried to protect himself as he had been taught, but it was too late. Steve passed out from the trauma of the attack, and everything went black.

The Grizzly pulled Steve into the trees just behind RL02, right behind a nice clump of saskatoon berry bushes. When Steve awoke, face down several minutes later, he could feel the weight of the large bear standing on his legs. The Grizzly bit into Steve's thigh, ripping a big chunk of flesh and pants from his leg. Steve felt warm blood escaping from his body, and he blacked out again.

Dan Thompson and the two other rangers shouted Steve's name again and again as they looked for him. They made their way back towards RL03 and the outhouse, shouting louder. "Steve, where the fuck are you!?" Steve thought he heard something, like he was in a trance. "Steve, can you hear us?" Steve started to stir. The pain he was in had become so intense that he did not know what was going on. His mind would not let him think clearly. "Steve! Steve! It's us."

Steve tried to say "Over here." He tried again. His mind was telling his body what to say. "Over here," he thought he said. All that came out was a gurgling sound.

It was hard for Steve to breathe. Dan Thompson stopped his men. "Did you hear that?" he asked. "Steve, it's Dan. Where are you?" Dan heard the noise again; this time, so did the other two rangers. The three men made their way towards the sound they had heard. "Steve!" There was nothing. The three men walked behind the saskatoon bushes. There on the ground was their friend and fellow Ranger. The bones on the back of his legs and thigh were clearly visible. There was a large piece of his neck torn to shreds. The three rangers pulled their service revolvers from their hips.

Dan Thompson fell to his knees beside Steve. "Steve, it's Dan. We are here, Steve. Can you hear me?" Steve tried. Dan could hear him trying to breathe. Dan rolled his coworker over. He held Steve's head in his hands. "Steve, what happened? Oh my God," said Dan. Steve opened his eyes. It took a moment for him to focus. Dan was looking directly into Steve's eyes. Dan Thompson yelled at his men to get a first aid kit. Blood was pouring from the hole in Steve's neck. Dan took his index finger. He put it directly in the hole. It slowed the bleeding just enough. Steve realized for the first time that he had been attacked. He had shot the wrong bear. The man-killer was not the sow black bear he had killed. It was a fucking man-killing grizzly.

Dan held onto Steve the best he could. His men returned with two first aid kits. They looked at Steve. There was nothing they could do. Most of his flesh and muscle had been stripped away. Bloody shreds of his park uniform lay scattered around. "Steve, can you hear me!?" Dan shouted. Steve tried to speak; he managed to

move his head ever so slightly. Dan kept his finger in the hole in the side of Steve's neck. Steve took the biggest breath he could. He was looking directly into Dan's eyes.

Steve managed to whisper, "Kill me."

Dan looked into his partner's eyes. "No, oh Steve, I can't."

Steve's body started to shake and convulse. Dan picked up his 9mm service revolver he had laid on the ground. Steve opened and closed his eyes several times. It was his way of telling Dan it was okay. Dan placed the muzzle of his service revolver under Steve's chin then pulled the trigger. The bullet entered Steve's brain, ending his life as he had asked. Dan sat sobbing next to Steve's body. The other rangers did their best to console Thompson. Thompson ordered his men to go back to RL04. The cubs needed to be dispatched. His reasoning was they had watched their mother kill and eat a human. That would be imprinted in them forever. They needed to be killed. The two rangers left Dan and Steve. None were aware a mad Grizzly was on the loose. They made their way over to RL04. The two men crouched on their knees, peering under the cabin. The two cubs were huddled together. The Rangers fired several shots from their service revolvers. When the smoke finally cleared, the two little black balls of fur lay motionless under the cabin. The same balls of fluff that Kevin's group thought were so cute. The Rangers had followed their orders. Two more potential man-eaters were no longer going to be a problem when they grew up.

Chapter 105

Nancy did not have a very good feeling in the pit of her stomach when Dirk told her to stay in the office at Bubbles. She watched as the tow truck pulling the old motorhome and her boss drove out of the parking lot. She had seen all the boxes in the motorhome. There was a lot of cash. She was not going to be left out of her cut. She had only been fucking Dirk so she could get a raise and did not have to do a lot of work around the car wash. She hated having to clean the bays and collect money from the machines. She put up with his advances until he finally had his way with her.

Nancy had been down that road a few times before. Her highschool soccer coach was the first man she had ever manipulated using sex to get what she wanted. Nancy had walked into her coach's office a few years back. He was in his mid-thirties at the time, married, with two kids. Mr. Beckman had been teaching physical education for twelve years at Hillcrest senior high since he had graduated from collage. Nancy sat down in front of Mr. Beckman that fateful day. She was wearing one of those short skirts that were popular with the girls in grade eleven. Nancy had been frustrated by what some of the other girls had been saying about her on the team. She cried and asked Mr. Beckman to talk to them. Nancy was not the type of person they said she was.

During that first office meeting Mr. Beckman got up from behind his desk. He walked over to Nancy and stood in front of her. He placed his hand on her cheek. His right thumb wiped the tears away from her left eye. Nancy stood and pressed her body into Beckman's as she

hugged him.

"Thank you," she said.

Nancy's hands slipped down his back and eventually to his crotch. She felt his member. She knew that her coach was getting excited.

Beckman stopped. He looked at Nancy. "You are so young," he said to her. "I just can't."

Nancy started to cry even harder. "Am I ugly?" she said.

"No, no," came Beckman's reply.

"I want to," said Nancy. "I have seen how you look at me."

Beckman turned. He walked over to the window of his office, closing the blind. Mr. Beckman then locked his office door. He opened his desk drawer and fumbled around under some papers. Eventually he found the small square package he was looking for. Nancy was now sitting on the corner of his desk, her purse was hung on the back of the chair she had been sitting in. The girls in school had always talked about Beckman. There had been rumors. Nancy was now alone with her coach. She had left her cellphone running in movie mode. The camera had recorded their initial conversation, its lens poked just above the zipper on top of her purse. Nancy watched as her coach removed his sweatpants. His cock was sticking straight out. He opened the package he had taken from his drawer, removing a bright blue condom. Mr. Beckman rolled it down over his erect shaft. He stood in front of Nancy.

Her seventeenth birthday was going to be in two weeks. Beckman pushed Nancy down on his desk. He lifted her skirt to find she was not wearing any panties. He placed his mouth over her moist mound. Beckman

ran his tongue over Nancy's clitoris, then back into her tight slit. He placed a finger into her vagina, making sure she was not a virgin. Nancy moaned and said, "No, please, Mr. Beckman."

Nancy's coach was whipped up. He pulled Nancy up from his desk top and kissed her deeply. Beckman spun Nancy around and lifted her right leg so her knee was on the desk. Her skirt was up around her midsection. Beckman thrust his manhood into Nancy. She moaned and said, "No, Mr. Beckman!" She said, "No, no!" as he continued to thrust into her. It did not take any longer than a couple of minutes until Beckman ejaculated into the bright blue condom.

He withdrew from Nancy's young mound. He turned her around and sat her on his desk. Beckman removed the condom from his cock. He placed the open end into Nancy's mouth. Nancy did not argue. She just sucked her coach's load from the used rubber. Beckman then kissed Nancy.

"I will talk to the girls," he said. "I sure hope you are feeling better, Nancy. I know I am." He smiled. "You are so sweet."

Nancy strightened up her skirt. She picked up her purse from the chair. She put the shoulder strap over her arm and left Coach Beckman's office. When she was far enough down the hall, she stopped and reached for her cellphone. She pressed the button to stop it from recording, then looked at her screen. The camera had recorded a twelve-minute video.

Nancy went outside. She sat on a bleacher and lit up a smoke. She hit play on the video. She watched as her soccer coach fucked her in his office. She turned up the volume. Nancy could hear herself saying "no" several times. Nancy emailed the video to herself. She

then spent a couple of hours that night on her home computer editing the video.

When she was happy with her results, she emailed a copy to "coachb@hillcresthigh.com".

The next morning, Nancy walked into Beckman's office with a smile on her face. Beckman was as white as a sheet.

"Hello, Nancy," said Beckman, in a professional tone. "Can I help you?"

Nancy lifted her skirt. She exposed herself to Beckman. "It's my turn to fuck you," she said. "I think five hundred dollars every two weeks as you get paid will keep her happy," as she pointed to her pussy. Beckman looked into Nancy's eyes.

"What is your locker number?" he asked.

"1220," Nancy responded.

"I will slide an envelope in every two weeks," said Beckman. Beckman did not want to lose his family,or his job. There was no way he was going to court or jail. He had a reputation that needed to stay intact. It was that easy. Nancy was making a grand a month and it only took three minutes of fucking to get what she wanted.

The minute Dirk had left Bubbles, Nancy got on the phone with her ex-coach. They had stayed in contact after she had graduated from highschool. Nancy had continued to turn the screws against her old coach after she left highschool. Coach Beckman continued to pay Nancy even though he thought the moment she graduated he would be off the hook. Nancy was a very conniving young lady. Her aunt had taught her how to get what she wanted at any cost. It had gotten so bad that Coach Beckman had started to sell cocaine and weed to

the the kids in school. Beckman had set up a nice little business under the roof of HillCrest High.

The grand-a-month he was still paying Nancy was now a drop in his cash bucket. Beckman had contacts. He was making more money selling the kids dope in school than he was as their coach. The only thing that bothered him was the fact that Nancy had a gun to his head. Beckman did not want to lose his wife and now three children. That video was the smoking gun that could bring his whole life crumbling down. There was no statute of limitations on the rape of a minor. If only Nancy was out of the picture things would be less stressful for the coach.

"What do you need?" Beckman said to Nancy.

"Can you pick me up from work?" she asked. "I need your help with something."

"What?" asked her old coach.

"I will tell you when you get here," said Nancy. "Yes, I am still at Bubbles Car Wash."

Beckman was at home enjoying the last day of the long weekend. "I can be there in fifteen minutes," he said. Coach Beckman kissed his wife. "One of the kids needs my help," he said. She was used to him leaving at all different hours to assist the kids in need. He was such a good husband and human being that she never questioned his integrity. She knew if one of the kids happened to be in trouble Coach Beckman would always be there.

Beckman arrived at Bubbles, and Nancy left the office. She locked the door, then jumped into Beckman's car.

"What is going on?" he asked Nancy.

"I need you to take me to Ted's Towing."

"Why?" asked her ex-coach.

"A client had left their motorhome in one of the bays. They were upset that the unit had been towed without their consent." Nancy needed to return it to Bubbles before the owner reported it stolen and called the cops. "I could get fired," she said. "I will pay you for your help."

"What?" said Beckman. "You will pay me? This must be a pretty important motorhome."

"I just have to get it," said Nancy.

Nancy and her ex-coach pulled up to the stairs of the office trailer at Ted's Towing.

"You got any blow?" she asked her coach.

"What?" asked Beckman. "Blow?"

"Don't play dumb," said Nancy. "I know what you are selling at the school."

Beckman reached into his pocket, removing a glass tube with a black plastic cap on it. Nancy took it from his hand. She got out of her ex-coach's car and climbed the wooden stairs to the door of the office trailer. Nancy walked inside.

Lill was standing behind the counter. "Hello, I am Nancy. I work over at Bubbles car wash."

Lill said, "Oh yes, dear, can I help you?"

"My boss just had a motorhome towed in. Ted was by. He helped us get it out of the car wash. The owners came back and are pissed we had it towed. I need to get it back to the car wash before they call the cops."

Lill left her coffee cup on the counter while she

went behind the wall marked "office." Lill was gone for a few moments, then returned with the documentation that Ted had left for her.

"Sign here," said Lill as she turned the clipboard toward Nancy. Nancy picked up the board and started to go through the paperwork.

"It says here that there is four hundred and ninety-five dollars owing?" Lill nodded her head and took a big gulp of her coffee. Everyone always tried to get their bill lowered, and Lill wanted to be ready.

"Where are the keys?" asked Nancy.

"In my office," said Lill. Nancy signed the paperwork and reached into her purse. Lill went into the office, removing the small bundle of dirty keys Ted had given to her. She came back to the counter with keys in her hand, but her head started spinning. All of a sudden, she was feeling dizzy, and things were out of focus.

"Oh dear," Lill said to Nancy. "I am not feeling well. Can you excuse me for a minute?" Lill made her way to the only washroom. She closed the door, then sat down on the toilet. She picked up the small plastic garbage can, placing it on her lap.

Her head was spinning. She had never felt like this in her life. There was a knock on the bathroom door.

"Hello? Hello? Are you okay?" asked Nancy. Nancy heard only mumbling. She opened the door. Lill was sitting on the toilet, her head tilted back, her eyes open. Nancy smiled. The coke she had put into Lill's coffee had kicked in.

Nancy looked around the bathroom. On the wall, she saw one of those old paper towel dispensers that give you a hard, stiff single sheet at a time. Nancy pulled a sheet and laid it out on the counter. She poured a small

amount of cocaine onto the paper, then rolled it up. She placed one end into Lill's nostril and blew on the other end. The coke went up Lill's nose, and she reacted by throwing her head back.

Nancy performed the same procedure on the other side of Lill's nose, this time using the rest of the white powder in the bottle. Nancy blew, Lill started to convulse and then fell to the floor. Nancy wiped the small glass container with the paper towel and left the vial on the counter with the black plastic lid beside it.

Nancy then flushed the toilet, throwing the single piece of paper towel into the swirling water. Nancy stepped over Lill saying, "Enjoy your trip, you old bat." She then retrieved the keys from the counter and walked outside. She waved the keys towards her old coach. Nancy walked over to the driver's door as Coach Beckman rolled down his window.

"Where's my coke?" he asked.

"Cost of doing business," came Nancy's reply. Nancy pulled down her tube top. Her breasts were now inches from Beckman's face. "There you go," she said. "You are paid in full," and laughed.

Coach Beckman rolled up his window and placed his car in drive. He made a quick U-turn in the gravel driveway and got out of there as fast as he could. For all he knew one of Nancy's friends could have been taking pictures.

Nancy casually walked over to the gates. She opened the main entrance of the storage yard, and unlocked the driver's door of the old motorhome. She slid onto the seat, and the boxes were still there. She pulled one from the back and tore open the flaps. All she could see were one hundred dollar bills, neatly bundled

together with bands that said "ten thousand dollars".

She turned in the seat and squealed. She put the key in the ignition, turning it. The engine sprang to life. Nancy took her time; she had never driven a vehicle this big, let alone a motorhome.

She drove out of the yard. Nancy glanced down at the fuel gauge, which registered full. She knew the cops were looking for this motorhome, so Nancy had to be smart. There would be no traveling on the paved roads. She had to get as far out of town as possible, and the only way to do that was on gravel service roads.

Nancy headed west, a cloud of dust thick as fog followed behind the motorhome. She rolled her window down to allow some air to circulate in the cab. She smiled and said out loud, "Screw you, Dirk. Do you think I am stupid?"

Chapter 106

Donna was in disbelief that her father had been killed in front of the hospital. The sheriffs had spent some time with her, reviewing the information they had on his case. Her entire family, with the exception of her younger brother Billy, was in the morgue. She had curled up beside Tommy in his hospital bed. Nothing made sense to her. Tommy did his best to console his crying girlfriend, while Gunner watched from across the room, trying to keep Mark and Marcy occupied. Robert Gerard was fast asleep in his bed next to Chris, with only a flimsy hospital curtain separating the two.

Two nurses came into the recovery room to check on their respective patients. Donna was asked not to lie in Tommy's bed with him because she could interfere with emergency procedures if they were necessary. The sheriffs had given Donna a plastic bag with her father's belongings, and his car keys were clearly visible. Tommy spoke, "Sweetie," he said, "why don't you take Mark and Marcy back to the house? Your aunt Mary should be returning soon."

"I do not want to leave you," she said.

"It's okay, honey. I will just lay here and get some rest. Besides, you need to check on your brother. You know what he can be like if left alone too long."

"You are right, Tommy." Donna scooped up her cousins, kissed Tommy, and then kissed Chris on the cheek goodbye. "I will call and check on you two later," she said. Donna and the two children walked out of the recovery room and made their way to the main entrance of the hospital then out to the parking lot. Several people

were outside, including staff members and the public. Donna could feel them staring at her. She felt so alone.

Donna and the kids walked through the parking lot until they found her father's car. There was a red tag stuck on the driver's window, indicating it had been searched by the state police. Donna removed the tag, as tears welled up in her eyes. Donna pressed the fob, unlocking all the doors. Mark and Marcy scrambled into the backseat, almost oblivious to what had been happening over the last day. Donna got behind the steering wheel and started the car.

"Can we go home now?" asked Mark. "I am tired."

Donna said, "Yes, we are going back to Auntie Joann's house. Your mom will be coming to pick you up soon." Donna backed out of the parking stall. The drive back to Hillcrest would take her at least forty-five minutes.

"Make sure you buckle up," she said to the children as she looked in the mirror. Donna wiped the tears rolling down her cheeks with the back of her hand. Fifty minutes later, she was pulling into Hillcrest. Firetrucks were all around the Mountain View service station, and the whole area had barricades set up around it. The local news channel was there with their van and camera. A female reporter was speaking into a microphone as Donna drove by. Traffic was moving very slowly. Donna decided to pull into one of the parking stalls in front of Hillcrest Hardware.

She turned off the engine, rolled her window down, and instructed Mark and Marcy to stay in their seats. "I won't be long," she said. Donna walked into the hardware store. Elizabeth was standing behind the service counter. She came running from behind the

counter, embracing Donna.

"How are they?" asked Liz.

Donna shook her head. "Tommy and Chris are going to be okay. It looks like Superintendent Gerrard is also going to make it." Donna broke down. "Mom and Dad are dead. So is Matt. I was interviewed by the sheriffs." Donna was shaking.

Elizabeth's father saw the commotion from his office and walked out towards the two girls. He gave Donna a hug. "Elizabeth has told me everything," he said. "Honey," he said to Elizabeth. "Why don't you go with Donna? I am sure the two of you have plenty to discuss." Donna nodded her head.

"Thank you," she said. "Why is the traffic so bad?" she asked.

"The cops are looking for a criminal in an old motorhome, some guy named Robbins. There have been three murders at the Wheel Inn. A sheriff's deputy was shot out on the interstate. It has been crazy around here. Did you see Mountain View Service?" he asked. "The bad guy set the place on fire and killed the son. It also sounds like he killed his ex-partner, ran him over. It's all over the news."

"Oh my god," said Donna. "Can anything else go wrong?"

"You girls just take your time. I am glad you are both safe," said Elizabeth's father. "Call me later, honey, and let me know if you need anything from your mother or myself."

The two young ladies left the hardware store. "Are you okay to drive?" asked Elizabeth.

Donna said, "Yes." Mark and Marcy were

excited to see Elizabeth again. Donna backed out of the parking stall and started towards her parents' home. It took almost an hour to make it through the roadblocks. The girls had never seen traffic so bad in their community.

When it was their turn to go through the roadblock, Donna had to answer more questions. She was made to get out of the car and open the trunk to her father's car. When the sheriffs were satisfied that the person they were looking for was not in Donna's car, she was waived through. Five minutes later, they pulled into the driveway of Donna's family home.

"I am hungry," said Marcy. "Let's go inside. We will make you something," said Donna. The two young ladies and children went to the side door. Donna unlocked it, and they all went inside. There on the kitchen table was an empty bowl, a box of Captain Crunch, and a banana peel. Billy sat on the living room couch, still wearing his pajamas, playing a video game.

"Where's Dad?" asked Billy. Donna thought for a quick second. "He is still at the hospital." She didn't know how she was going to tell her younger brother that their Mom and Dad were never coming home again. Mark and Marcy sat down with Billy. They watched as Billy shot at the bad guys on the screen. Donna and Elizabeth walked back into the kitchen. Donna spoke to Elizabeth about everything she knew and what the cops had said to her.

That her father had killed her mother because they had found traces of semen that came from her brother. It was all so surreal, but it made sense. Everything was wrapped up in a neat little package. Elizabeth could not believe what she was hearing. Nothing like that would ever have taken place in her

family. She looked at Donna and said, "That is so twisted."

Donna had been raised in a completely different environment. She had been pulled out of the family mess by Tommy. Her own apartment and her job had been a godsend. "I can't explain it," said Donna, yet in the back of her mind, she knew the cops were correct. She just did not want to admit it.

Chapter 107

Robert Gerard lay in his hospital bed. He was feeling much better when the duty nurse walked in, handing him the portable phone.

"Hello," said Gerard.

"Bob, it's Betty. How are you feeling?"

"Better," said Robert. "Where are things at?"

Betty brought Robert up to speed. Dan Thompson had managed to get a message out that another Ranger had been killed. This time mauled by a large sow black bear.

"Damn it," said Robert. "That is two of our men this weekend. This kind of thing never happens."

"I know," said Betty.

"What is happening with Steve's body?"

"They are bringing him out now," she said. "The coroner is waiting for the guys to get to the staging area at Rock Lake."

"What a mess," said Robert. "What about the guy that attacked me? Have they found him?"

Betty let Robert know that a huge manhunt was taking place in and around Hillcrest. "They have not got him yet," said Betty, "but they will find him."

"What about the ice poachers?" asked Robert.

"The judge had ordered them released on bail," said Betty. "We already spoke about that."

"I do not remember," said Robert. "We need to make an example out of them."

Betty said that she had arranged for field autopsies on the two bear carcasses. The Rangers were too busy with human bodies to be worried about hauling a dead bear or two out of the woods. The Grizzly that Brad had killed would be first on the list. Second would be the black bear that had taken out Ranger Steve.

"Good," said Robert, "we need to make sure we have the facts straight."

"The forensic veterinarian should be on site as we speak," said Betty. "I will call you again as soon as I hear something."

"Honey, I love you," said Gerard.

"Love you too," said Betty.

Dan Thompson and his two Rangers fashioned a rough travois. It looked similar to what the local natives had used to carry their things behind a horse. They lashed the logs to the back of Dan's quad. Steve's body was loaded onto the temporary sling. The bodies of the two dead cubs had been dragged out from under RL04, then laid beside their mother's body.

"Let's get out of here," said Thompson. "I have had enough for one weekend."

The Rangers mounted their quads. Dan took the lead. The temporary travois moved wildly up and down under the weight of Steve's body. The two poles left drag marks in the mud on the trail. In all, it held together.

The Rangers took their time, eventually making it to the staging area for Rock Lake. The men were greeted by the sheriffs, Brad, and the coroner. Steve's body was unloaded from the wooden framework and carefully laid on one of the shelves in the coroner's van. Dan Thompson appointed one of his men to stay behind and ensure that no one entered the trail that had been

closed to the public.

A three-quarter-ton truck pulled into the parking lot, pulling a trailer containing two quads with small utility trailers. On the side of the truck doors was a logo that read Hillcrest Veterinary Services. Two men got out of the truck and approached the small group of officials.

"We are here to check on your bears and make a report," said Jason Setter, the local vet. Dan Thompson drew a rough map of Rock Lake and marked two X's on the paper.

"The two carcasses are in these locations," said Dan. "We left two cubs we had to dispatch laying beside the sow." The Rangers loaded their quads onto the park's trailer as the vets unloaded theirs. "We will be returning tomorrow," said Dan, "to collect the remnants of the campsite." The two veterinarians loaded their equipment onto their respective quads and trailers. They then proceeded up the path toward Rock Lake. The coroner's wagon drove out of the staging area, followed by Dan Thompson, Brad, and two other service members. The sheriffs followed behind the park's vehicles.

The sheriff's chopper lifted off from the emergency helipad. Ranger Colby Page was left behind with a park's truck, a couple of bottles of water, and granola bars to get him through the night. Someone had to guard the trail to ensure the public did not enter the cordoned-off area. Things needed to be cleaned up before access was granted again.

Page's portable radio crackled. It was Betty contacting him from the park's office. "Base to Ranger twelve, how do you read?"

"Loud and clear," said Colby in a sleepy voice.

"How are things?" asked Betty.

"All quiet. Vets are headed toward Rock Lake as we speak. Everyone has left, including the sheriff's chopper."

"Roger that," said Betty. "Contact me as soon as you hear from the vets."

"Ten-four," was Colby's response. He went over to the park's truck, opened the door, and climbed in. Minutes later, Ranger Colby Page was fast asleep; it had been a long couple of days.

Chapter 108

Nancy continued to drive down the gravel road until she found an appropriate area to pull over. The large trees hid the old motorhome quite well from the road. A small creek flowed past the makeshift parking area. An old wooden sign nailed to one of the trees read "Parker Flats." There was an old rickety picnic table set up in the trees. Nancy shut off the engine, got out of the old camper, and took her open box of cash with her. She carried the box over to the picnic table and pulled on the flaps, peering inside and smiling. The cardboard box, clearly marked "Files," was full of one hundred dollar bills, all neatly bundled with bands that read ten thousand dollars. She threw her head back and started laughing. She still couldn't believe it. All this money meant nothing if she had no place to spend it. The whole situation was ironic, she thought.

Nancy had a big problem on her hands. She knew the authorities were looking for this motorhome and the man that was driving it. She had taken a big risk stealing it from the storage yard. She had drugged Lill so she could make her escape. The only thing that she had forgotten was the paperwork that Lill presented for her signature. She thought about going back, however, too much time had passed. She needed to get rid of the motorhome.

Nancy estimated that there had to be forty boxes, maybe more, in the back of the old RV. She sat at the picnic table, staring at the open box. Then it dawned on her. She picked up her cell phone and dialed a number she had not called in quite some time. The phone rang twice. A voice on the other end answered, "U-Haul, how

may I help you?"

"Is Bobby working today?" asked Nancy.

"He is out in the yard washing a truck. Can I leave him a message?" the voice asked.

"Please have him call Nancy. It's urgent," Nancy said. The voice said she would and then hung up the phone.

Nancy sat at the table, thinking of the events that had taken place earlier in the day. Twenty, maybe thirty minutes had gone by when her cell phone rang. Nancy looked at her call display; it was Dirk. Nancy thought for a moment before answering.

"Hello," she said, "baby, I am scared." Dirk paused before saying anything.

"Sweetie, where are you?" asked Dirk.

Nancy was sobbing. "I don't know," she said. "There is an old sign that says Parker Flats." Dirk asked if Nancy still had the motorhome; he did not ask how she was or why she was scared.

"I need you," said Nancy. "I do not know what to do."

"I am on my way," said Dirk. "Stay there. I will come as soon as I can."

A second call was coming in. "I have to go," said Nancy. She hung up. It was Bobby.

"Hello," said Nancy in a cheerful voice.

"What's up?" asked Bobby. "I have not heard from you in two years. Ever since you started working at that car wash, it's like I did not exist. Now I get a call from you, and I was told it's urgent. What the hell?"

"I am sorry," said Nancy. "I want to make it up to you."

"How?" asked Bobby.

Nancy was fiddling with the top of the open box. "How would you like to make ten grand?" she said.

"Ten grand doing what?" asked Bobby.

"I am stuck out at Parker Flats. I took a job to move some files for a guy. Several boxes," said Nancy. "The motorhome I was using has broken down. Can you come with a truck?"

"How big of a truck?" Bobby asked.

"You know one of those big ones with that extension over the cab," said Nancy.

"A twenty-footer?" asked Bobby.

"That sounds about right," said Nancy. "Then," she said, "I will pay you cash."

"Cash?" said Bobby.

"Yes," said Nancy. "Can you come right away?"

"I am leaving now," said Bobby. "It's going to take me about an hour to get there. There are several roadblocks set up in town."

"Well, I cannot go anywhere," said Nancy, "so I will wait here for you."

"I want more," said Bobby.

"More?" said Nancy. "That is everything I have. That is all the job was paying me."

"You know what I want," said Bobby.

"Fine," said Nancy, "just get here as quickly as you can."

Nancy now had two men coming to her rescue. Her boss from work that did not give a damn and her ex-high school lover that she had confided in about her coach. Bobby had always been smitten with Nancy.

Bobby went to his manager, saying he needed to take a twenty-footer to a client who was paying cash. He would ensure the company got paid five hundred dollars for the use of the truck. "I should be back in three hours," said Bobby. He then reached behind the counter, taking a set of keys for the only 20-foot truck on the lot. He then made his way out to the truck and headed directly to Parker Flats.

Dirk had to lock up the office at Bubbles before he could leave to meet Nancy. The wash bay doors were left open so the business was still making money. Dirk did not want the owners getting upset that he had shut everything down on what was to be one of the busiest days of the season. Dirk jumped in his car and headed directly to Parker Flats. The gravel road was thick with dust. He could not believe his luck. Nancy had actually answered her phone and told him where she was. There was a motorhome full of cash, and Dirk aimed to get it all. He would do whatever it took to get his hands on all that money.

Dirk eventually made it to Parker Flats. When he turned in, there was a U-Haul Truck parked beside the old motorhome. He watched as Nancy handed someone the last of the cardboard boxes from inside the old RV. Dirk pulled up beside the U-Haul. He stepped out of his car and called to Nancy. She walked out from behind the U-Haul.

"What took you so long?" she asked.

"The gravel is hard on the car, sweetie," he said. He walked towards her, extending his arms. Nancy let

607

him embrace her and allowed him to kiss her. She moaned and squirmed, turning her body 180 degrees.

Dirk followed as he clung to her. Dirk's back was now towards the rear of the U-Haul. Bobby slowly and quietly made his way up behind Dirk. There was a rustle of gravel beneath Bobby's feet as he raised the old piece of 2x4 he had taken from the back of the truck.

"What the hell," said Dirk as Nancy pushed him away. The 2x4 Bobby wielded toward Dirk's head hit with a loud thud. Dirk fell to his knees. Bobby hit his prey one more time. Dirk fell face first into the gravel. He was out cold.

"That will teach you for coming on to my girl," said Bobby. "Quick, Nancy, help me get him into the front seat of the motorhome." Nancy and Bobby struggled for several minutes until Dirk was sitting behind the steering wheel of the old RV. Bobby made sure all the windows were rolled up before he opened the valves on the three-burner stove inside the unit.

Dirk's cell phone was placed on an angle directly in front of the hole for the cigarette lighter. Bobby had crumpled up a piece of tin foil and attached it to the bottom of the phone. Bobby exited the motorhome carefully, closing the rear door behind him. He held Nancy in his arms. "I am sorry he was so abusive to you," said Bobby.

"Thank you," Nancy exclaimed with tears in her eyes. "If I did not do what he wanted, I would have lost my job."

"I understand," said Bobby. "Shall we head back?"

Nancy had just enough time to fabricate a story that Bobby would believe by the time he had pulled into

Parker Flats. Bobby bought the story, hook, line, and sinker. He and Nancy had enough time to unload the old RV and put Nancy's plan into place. Nancy had paid Bobby in cash as soon as he had showed up.

After the deed was done, Nancy loaded her box of cash into the trunk of Dirk's car. Two boxes now sat side by side. Nancy smiled as she closed the lid. There were forty-eight boxes now stacked on the floor of the U-Haul. She was on a roll. Bobby did not question her about the boxes they moved into the U-Haul, marked "files." Why would he? Nancy promised him the best fucking of his life.

Nancy got into Dirk's car; his keys were still in the ignition. "Follow me," she said as she stuck her head out the open window. Bobby followed Nancy in the U-Haul out of the parking lot and onto the gravel road heading back towards Hillcrest. As they made their way past the towing yard, Nancy noticed two police cars in the parking lot. She pulled out her cell phone and called Dirk's number.

Dirk's phone rang. It vibrated, sliding closer to the open hole of the cigarette lighter. Nancy listened to it ring two more times. The phone with tin foil attached to its base slid closer to the open hole. On the fourth ring, the tin foil sparked inside the lighter's opening. The propane that had built up inside the motorhome exploded.

The old rig blew up into a million different pieces. Dirk's body was thrown sixty feet from the blazing wreck. The motorhome the authorities were looking for no longer existed. It would look like the long-time loser Dirk had committed suicide after he had escaped, driving the only evidence that could tie the weekend events all together. At least that was Nancy's

plan.

She pulled up to the intersection that would take her back into Hillcrest if she turned left. Nancy chose to turn right. Bobby followed. Thirty miles down the road, Nancy pulled into the parking lot of the Mountain View Motel. Nancy stepped out of Dirk's car, opened the trunk, and removed a few one-hundred-dollar bills from a box. Bobby watched as she made her way into the motel's office and then came back outside with a key in her hand. Nancy dangled it, then winked so Bobby could see. She made her way to room 140 on the ground floor.

She opened the door, then looked over her shoulder. Bobby pulled the U-Haul up to the door of the room. He then followed Nancy inside.

Chapter 109

Jason Setter and Mike Stone, the two forensic veterinarians, made their way towards Rock Lake. It had been a while since Jason had been called out into the field to autopsy a wild animal. Generally, his clinic would get calls from ranchers when they found a dead cow or horse. Mike was learning the ropes from his mentor; he had just two years under his belt at the clinic. Mike never liked the idea of being in the office all the time. The forensic work always gave him a challenge. With Jason's forty-plus years in the business, Mike was soaking up as much knowledge as he could before Jason retired.

The two men carried on with their quads and equipment until they reached the summit that overlooked the valley containing Rock Lake. They paused for a moment, each taking a drink from their water bottles. Jason pulled out the rough map Dan Thompson had sketched out for him. "The first one should be on this end of the lake," he said to Mike. "Follow me."

The two men made their way down the pathway, eventually coming to flat ground. Directly ahead was the campsite that was in complete disarray. Jason turned his quad to the left, making his way past a hedge of scrub trees. The first thing the two men noticed was a backpack suspended by a rope, hanging about fifteen feet in the air. Almost directly below the hanging pack was the body of a large Grizzly.

"Look at that," said Jason. "Even with cooler temperatures up here, it's already starting to bloat." The two men gathered their kits from the back of their company quads and carried them towards the dead bear. It was important for the men to gather samples before

bacteria started to destroy evidence that the other local authorities would need. Conclusive evidence was paramount.

The men opened their kits. Each dressed in a blue paper apron that hung from their necks, latex gloves, and a plastic face shield. Mike grabbed the video camera from its case. Jason looked at him. "Ready?" he asked of his partner and student.

"Ready as I can be," said Mike.

Jason picked up his black case. It looked like a medium-sized toolbox. "Turn the camera on," he said to Mike.

The two men walked over to the carcass of the bear. It was laying partially on its side, its legs still underneath it. Blood had run down its fur and pooled on the ground. Jason looked back at the camera. The date and time were already being recorded automatically.

"We have in front of us a large Ursus Arctos Horribilis, commonly known as a Grizzly Bear. There have been several attacks this weekend here at Rock Lake, and we have been asked by the Park's service to verify that the bear responsible is the one laying before us." Jason followed the blood path up the fur to the back of the neck. He could see two vertical lines just in front of the hump on the Grizzly's shoulders. He removed two white plastic strips from a sealed bag in his case. They looked like miniature rulers, except the lines were measured in centimeters and millimeters.

It allowed for more accurate measuring. Jason scraped away the dried blood with the end of his finger. He inserted the first plastic strip into the wound closest to himself; the strip went into the beast's neck about 5 cm before it came to a stop. Jason tried again; he could

feel the strip hitting bone. He left the strip in place. Jason then concentrated on the next slit in the bear's neck. He inserted the second strip. "Are you getting this?" he asked Mike, who was standing about three feet away. Mike zoomed in with the camera lens. Jason pushed the strip into the wound; there was no resistance. The strip went into the bear's neck to its full length. Jason looked back at the camera. "Cause of death is a severed spinal cord, most likely caused by a sharp object like a hunting knife, which is consistent with reports we have."

Jason then struggled to move the large bear onto its side. He raised the left rear leg. "We have a large boar or male Grizzly," he said. Jason walked to the head and forced open the bear's mouth. "Wow, look at this," he said to Mike. "It is missing all but one of its canine teeth and several more. This boy was old." Jason composed himself. He looked back into the camera and said, "I estimate this Boar to be between twenty and twenty-two years old." He then swabbed the inside of the bear's mouth. Lab testing later would determine if any human DNA was present from around the bear's remaining teeth.

Jason then reached into his bag. He pulled out a bright stainless steel knife and removed the guard, exposing a six-inch razor-sharp blade. Jason knelt down beside the bear and carefully plunged the blade into the soft area below the bear's rib cage. He ran the blade back to just the tip of the male grizzly's testicles and placed the blood-covered blade on the body of the large bear. He reached inside with both of his gloved hands, intestines and the stomach soon fell out onto the ground. Jason looked back at Mike. "Make sure you zoom in on this." Jason took his blade and ran it along the length of the swollen stomach lining. There was a slight sound of air escaping, and then a strong smell permeated the air.

613

Jason lifted the edge of the stomach to expose a large mass of things the Grizzly had been eating. It was shaped and looked like a giant fuzzy football. Jason pulled at the mass until he had it laid out on the paper sheet he had put into place on the ground. "Interesting," said Jason as he pulled apart the contents from the bear's stomach. There were old berries, fresh grass and weeds, some tender shoots, as well as beetle larva present. There was nothing to indicate this bear had been feeding on humans. Then it happened. "Wait a minute, I have something. Focus on this," said Jason as he pulled back some more material. "It looks like a finger, yup, look here." Jason was positive he was looking at a human digit. There was man-made material also close to the area he was examining.

"What the hell?" he said. "This looks like the stuffing you would find in a winter jacket," he said. "Has to be... no, look at this," he said, holding up what looked like a finger to the camera. "It's not a finger at all. It's a goddamn sausage. You see that," he said to Mike, "you can see the casing around the meat. It's not a finger at all. This bear is not the one the guys are looking for. It may have been old, but it was not feeding on humans. We are done here," said Jason.

The two men concluded their report. They mounted their quads, then made their way towards the north end of Rock Lake. Jason and Mike pulled into the area where the cabins were located. "Should be behind cabin number three," said Jason, "according to the map." The veterinarians gathered their things, then walked behind RL03. There, laying out on the grass, was the Black Bear sow and her two cubs.

Jason, dressed in another paper apron, put his gloves on and then went to work. "Ready?" he asked Mike.

Mike held the camera up. "Ready," he said.

Jason spoke loudly and clearly. "We have here a female Ursus Americanus, commonly known as a black bear." She was lying in a pile of drying blood, and there was blood around her mouth. Jason examined the body. "We have two bullet wounds," he said. "Both could have been lethal." He looked into the eyes of the sow; they were dry and had turned hazy. "What were you doing?" asked Jason aloud. He took his large knife from the toolkit, then made the necessary cuts to extract the stomach from the body cavity.

"Zoom in here," he said to Mike. Her stomach was full of congealed blood, and there were fragments of shredded clothing and what looked like flesh, maybe muscle, in her gut. "She must have been starving," said Jason. There was no natural vegetation in her stomach. Jason followed the intestines; they were empty of any solid waste. Jason completed his report after taking more samples. "We are done here," he said to Mike. "Let's load up this Sow and her cubs."

The two men then went back to the original Grizzly. Using the winch on Mike's trailer, they loaded its carcass behind Mike's quad, placing it in their trailer. It was now 4:00pm on Monday afternoon. "Let's get going. We have to get these reports into the Sheriff's Department and Ranger Station." The two men left the cabin area on their quads. It was a beautiful afternoon.

Chapter 110

Donna and Elizabeth sat in the kitchen of Donna's parents' home, talking about everything the cops had told her. "Do you believe what they said?" asked Elizabeth.

"I don't know," said Donna. "I just don't know."

Gunner, Tommy, and Robert Gerard lay in the recovery room of Metro General. Tommy's back was really sore, and the bandages showed signs of blood and pus soaking through. Gunner's ribs were sore. As long as he did not move and only took shallow breaths, he could handle the pain. Robert was going out of his mind; he needed to get out of the hospital. There was far too much going on. He was ultimately responsible for everything that was happening within his department. He could not expect Betty to handle everything.

Robert got out of his bed, checked on Chris, then Tommy, and eventually made his way to the nurses' station. "May I borrow your phone, please?" he asked. Robert was chastised by the nurses for being out of bed. "I am checking myself out," said Robert. Robert called Betty. "Honey," he said, "I am checking myself out of here. I just can't lay on my back any longer. Yes," said Robert, "I am going to be fine. I want you to arrange for Glacier Tours to pick me up at the helipad here at Metro General. Call me back here. What's the direct number?" Robert asked the nurse in charge. Robert relayed the number to Betty. "I love you too," he said as he handed the receiver back to the nurse. "Thank you. Now, where are those discharge papers?" he asked.

"The doctor wanted you to go for an MRI. It was

scheduled for an hour from now."

"I am sorry," said Robert. "I am fine. I just do not have time for this right now. I am going to change. Please have the paperwork ready for me when I come back." Robert went back into the general recovery room. "Well, gentlemen," he said, "I am getting out of here."

Chris spoke. "What are you doing?" he asked.

"There is too much going on for me to be just laying here," said Robert. "Betty is going out of her mind. I just can't quarterback things from a bed."

"Well," said Gunner, "if you're heading out, so am I."

"No," said Robert. "You stay here. Those ribs need time."

Chris looked at Robert. "And your head does not." Gunner smiled. "I have seen guys with their legs and arms blown off. Do you honestly think a couple of broken ribs and a punctured lung are going to keep me down?"

Robert nodded his head. "I have asked Betty to arrange for Glacier Tours to pick me up here at the hospital's helipad."

"Roger that," said Chris as he started to make his way out of his bed.

Tommy heard everything. "I am going with you as well."

"Son," said Chris, "I want you to stay here. Those bandages need to be changed."

"I am going with you," said Tommy. "I need to check on Donna when we are done. Can't do that from here."

"I guess there is no point in arguing with you," said Gunner.

"Nope," said Tommy. "The apple does not fall far from the tree."

The three men dressed in the hospital track suits that had been provided. Their clothing, as bad as it was, had been sent down to the hospital laundry. The three of them looked like they had just come out of the gym. They collectively made their way back to the nurses' station. The documentation was signed by each, saying they were leaving against doctor's orders. Metro General was not liable for their well-being once they left the hospital.

The phone at the nurses' station rang. "It's for you, Mr. Gerard," the nurse handed Robert the phone.

"Thank you, honey," he said, handing the phone back to the nurse. Each one of the men was handed an envelope that contained their personal belongings. Robert opened his envelope and removed his watch. It said 3:20. "Our ride will be here in 20 minutes," he said.

The men made their way out of the hospital to the edge of the Metro General's helipad. Moments later, a helicopter emblazoned with the logos of Glacier Heli Tours landed in front of them. The three men made their way toward the helicopter with its rotating blades. Tommy and Gunner got into the back seat, and Robert into the front passenger seat. The men put on their headsets. The pilot turned to Robert. "Good to see you're up and about. Where to?" he asked.

"Back to the Ranger station. I need to look presentable," said Robert. The pilot nodded his head.

The chopper lifted off, and the pilot headed directly toward the Ranger's office. Hillsboro air traffic control granted clearance for the flight at an altitude of

two thousand feet. Thirty minutes later, they were landing on the helipad outside the Ranger station. The pilot shut down the chopper's turbine. The three men exited the helicopter while the pilot stayed in the pilot's seat, completing some paperwork.

Robert made his way to the office. He was greeted by Betty on the front steps. "Look at your head." Betty reached out and touched the shunt in Robert's skull. "I am so glad to see you," she said. Tommy and Gunner chatted for a few moments outside, then came into the office. Robert had made his way into the locker room and was changing. Gunner and Tommy soon walked in. Chris opened his locker, then removed a small shaving kit. He opened the kit, removing a set of keys. He handed them to Tommy. "Take my truck, son, go check on your girl. We will work out the details later on as to how and when you can pick me up." Tommy thanked his father, said his goodbyes to Robert and Betty, and left the building.

Tommy's back was sore, almost as though it was on fire. He stepped into his father's truck, closed the door, and started the engine. The pressure of the seat against his back made him wince. Tommy backed out of his father's parking stall and headed towards Donna's parents' house. The events of the weekend filled Tommy's head as he drove. If it were not for Brad, he would not be alive.

Gunner and Bob quickly got out of the hospital track suits and dressed in their respective spare uniforms.

There was always a spare change of clothes handy; it was part of the department's mandate that Bob had implemented years earlier. The two men exited the locker room. Robert asked Betty if there had been any more updates.

"We have heard back from Ranger 12 and the Forensic Veterinarians. They have examined the two bears up at Rock Lake. They say it looks like the Sow Black Bear was the one responsible. There was blood and shredded clothing found in her stomach. The DNA would prove conclusively that she had been responsible for the deaths of Rachel and the mauling of Susan. Obviously, there was conclusive evidence that the female Black Bear had been responsible for consuming some of Warden Steve. The shredded clothing in her stomach turned out to be portions of a park's uniform."

They had their man-killer. That was what had been radioed in to Betty. Robert nodded his head. "Good," he said.

Chapter 111

Dan Thompson pulled up in front of Brad's house. He extended his hand towards the young man who had been so instrumental in helping over the last two days. "Could not have done everything we did without your help," he said to Brad. "I think it's time for you to decide whether or not you want to come to work for the service."

"I have a pretty good job at the Mill," said Brad.

"That's not something a young guy like you should be doing as a career," said Thompson. "I am talking a full-time job with the department, benefits, and you will always get to work in the outdoors. Think about it." Brad nodded his head. He stepped out of the park's truck and made his way up the steps of his father's home. Kevin opened the door to greet his son. Brad stepped into his father's arms, and they embraced each other.

"Are you okay?" asked Kevin.

"I am going to be fine," said Brad. "I have to check on Tommy and Elizabeth."

Brad made his way to the kitchen, picked up the phone, and called Metro General Hospital. He asked about Tommy and was told that he had checked himself out a few hours earlier. Brad called Elizabeth's cellphone next. She answered. "We are here," she said. "We are all here at Donna's mother's house. There is so much to tell you."

"Me too," said Brad. "I am going to take a shower, then I will be right over. I love you."

"I love you too," she replied. Elizabeth ended the

call.

"Brad is home. He is going to have a shower, then he is coming over," Elizabeth said.

Tommy nodded. Everyone he cared about was safe. Mark and Marcy sat in the living room watching TV with Billy. It was like they were completely oblivious to what had taken place over the weekend.

Tommy asked Donna for the remote control that worked the small TV in the kitchen. He adjusted the channel to the news. "This is Christie Mathews live in front of Mountain View Service Station. Behind me, you can see the authorities mopping up the scene of a major fire. We have reports of gunshots in the area." The camera panned to two yellow sheets on the ground. "One by the burned-out pumps and another about thirty feet from the open bay door of the garage. There are two bodies we can see, maybe more inside. This is Christie Mathews reporting live." The screen then flashed back to the newsroom. The two reporters sat side by side. It was unusual to see two reporters behind the desk in the newsroom.

Tommy turned up the volume. There was footage taken from a helicopter of a red Mustang on the freeway. Its trunk and rear bumper were dented. Behind the car was another tarp covering the body of a sheriff's deputy. The headline read "Officer killed in the line of duty. Patrol car missing. Massive search underway in the communities of Hillsboro, Hillcrest, and Crestview." The screen then flashed a picture of Johnny Robbins. "Escaped Convict on the loose. Wanted for questioning in the deaths of a Park Ranger and Sheriff's deputy. If you see this man, do not approach. He is considered armed and dangerous. Call 911 immediately."

The anchor then flashed to a reporter outside the

Wheel Inn. Several police cars were in the parking lot. The reporter was interviewing some people who had been staying at the motel. "We went in to pay our bill. That's when I saw the bodies," said the man with the microphone pointed at him. "The noise from the helicopter woke up my wife and me." The camera panned to the old chopper in the field across from the motel. "It's just a mess," said the man.

The reporter managed to get the attention of one of the officers. "Can you explain what happened here?" asked the reporter.

"All I can tell you is that we have four bodies. One is a woman in a lower room, three in the office. We are trying to piece it all together."

The reporter turned to the camera. "There you have it, ladies and gentlemen. This is Brent Hunter live at the Wheel Inn. Back to you in the station."

The screen flipped back to the reporters. "Investigators continue to investigate a small plane crash that happened a few days ago. In other news, the Park's service has reported that the area around Rock Lake has been closed due to bear activity."

Tommy looked at Donna and Elizabeth. "Holy shit," he said. "This whole weekend has been one clusterfuck after the other." Tommy apologized to the girls. "I am sorry about my language. I just can't believe what has happened over the few days we were out of town." The doorbell rang at Donna's parents' home. "I will get it," said Tommy as he stood up slowly. He made his way to the front door. Brad stood in front of him on the porch of Donna's parents' home. Tommy broke down. "Buddy," he said, "you saved my life." The two young men embraced carefully. "The back is pretty tender," Tommy said.

"Ah hell," said Brad, "you would have done the same thing for me. I am sure it is sore."

Brad walked into the house. He said hello to the children. By the time he had taken three steps inside, Elizabeth was on him like flies on a fresh pile of bear shit. She jumped into his arms, and Brad held her tight. A few moments passed, and then Donna got a big hug from Brad. "We are all safe and sound," said Brad. "Where are your folks?" he asked Donna.

"Sit down," said Donna, "we have more to tell you."

Chapter 112

Cathy woke up in the psychiatric ward. She was groggy from the medication in her system. The nurses were alerted to her room by the sound of the restraints moving on the rails of her hospital bed. Dr. Lewis was on the ward and summoned to Cathy's room.

"Hello, Cathy. Do you remember me? I am Dr. Lewis," she said.

Cathy looked at her. "No, I am sorry," said Cathy. "What am I doing here? Why am I in restraints?"

"Do you remember anything that has happened in the last couple of days?"

Cathy shook her head. "I am sorry," said Cathy. "I assume I am in the hospital, Metro General?"

"Yes," said Dr. Lewis.

"Have you seen my son?" asked Cathy. "He is a doctor here. His name is James."

"No, I am sorry," said Dr. Lewis, "I have not. How do you feel, Cathy?"

"Sore," came the reply. "This bed is very uncomfortable, and I have to go to the bathroom."

"How about I release these," said Dr. Lewis as she reached for the restraints on Cathy's wrists. "We wanted to make sure you did not roll out of bed."

"Funny," said Cathy.

"Let me help you," said Dr. Lewis as she placed her hand under Cathy's arm. Cathy steadied herself.

"I am fine," she said to Dr. Lewis.

Cathy made her way across the room towards the open washroom door. She walked in, then sat down on the cool white plastic seat of the toilet. She adjusted her hospital gown. Cathy's ear was sore. After she had finished, she rolled up some bathroom tissue and proceeded to wipe herself. She was sore down there and did not know why. Cathy flushed the toilet and then made her way back into her hospital room.

"Everything okay?" asked Dr. Lewis.

"I am just a little sore," said Cathy. "It's nothing. I am sure I will be fine."

"Okay," said Dr. Lewis, "why don't you have a seat here in the chair, and I am going to order something for you to eat. You must be starving."

"I am," said Cathy. "I would kill for a nice chicken dinner."

Dr. Lewis handed Cathy the remote control for the TV that hung from the ceiling. She gave the nurses instructions to call down to the hospital kitchen. "Make sure she gets a nice pureed chicken breast, along with whatever else they send up." Dr. Lewis was following Dr. Hansen's orders to make sure nothing rough passed through Cathy's system. "Keep her door locked but allow her some freedom," she instructed the nurses. Dr. Lewis was then paged to the emergency department downstairs.

The ward was quiet, and thirty minutes later, one of the hospital's catering staff showed up with a tray. Cathy sat in the chair staring at her TV. She heard keys in the lock on her door. The staff member walked in with a tray of food. Cathy noticed there was a blue plastic dome covering the main plate. The tray was placed on a small table beside her chair.

"There you go," said the staff member, as she lifted the cover. "There is some nice mashed chicken breast under here."

"Thank you," said Cathy. "That looks horrible but it smells good."

"Enjoy," said the dietitian as she left Cathy's room. The food was nothing to look at, but Cathy's appetite had returned. She moved the tray over onto her lap and started eating. She devoured her dinner in minutes.

Dr. Lewis walked back into Cathy's room a half hour later. "How are you feeling?" asked Dr. Lewis.

"Good," said Cathy. "I am full. For mashed hospital food, that was not bad. Have you heard from my son James?"

"No, Cathy, I am sorry I have not," said Dr. Lewis. "Cathy, there are a couple of gentlemen out in the hall that would like to talk to you if you're up for it. What do you think?"

"Sure," said Cathy. "Who are they?" she asked.

Dr. Lewis opened the door and said, "Gentlemen, she would like to speak to you." Two men entered Cathy's room.

"Hello, Cathy. I am Detective Miller, and this is my partner, Detective Anderson. We are with the FBI." The two men presented their badges for Cathy to look at. Dr. Lewis watched Cathy's reactions very closely as the detectives started to ask their questions.

"Cathy, do you know this man?" asked Anderson, flashing a picture at Cathy.

"Of course, I do," said Cathy. "That is my son James. He is a doctor, you know. He works at Metro

627

General."

"Do you know where he is?" they asked.

"I know he went out of town on a conference. He is a pilot too, you know. We bought him a plane years ago after he got his license. He is such a bright boy. What day is it?" asked Cathy.

"Monday, May 23rd," said Agent Miller.

"My boy will be at work in the emergency department. I remember him telling me that he had to be back home to work on the long weekend."

"Okay," said Agent Miller, holding up a picture of Susan. "How about this lady, do you know her?"

"She looks familiar," said Cathy. "Oh, yes! She helped me! I remember now! I had a heavy amount of weight on me, and I could not move. She came over to my bed... oh yes... It was like magic. She did something, and it was like a ton of weight had been lifted off of me. We left our room together. She was very nice. Missing a leg, the poor girl."

"How about this lady?" asked Anderson. He showed Cathy a picture of Joann.

"I remember her very well," said Cathy. "She is the woman that... oh my God!" Cathy started to cry. "She is the mother of a man... oh no..." Some of her memories came flooding back. "That bitch's son and his partner held my husband and me as hostages! Oh my God! I remember now! I saw her somewhere... I am not sure where, but I know I could not stand looking at her. I covered her face. God told me what to do."

"Thank you," the detectives said. "I think we are done here for now," said Miller. "Do you mind if we come back and speak with you later if we have more

questions?"

"That would be fine," said Cathy. Agents Miller and Anderson left Cathy's room with Dr. Lewis.

The agents made a call to the local Sheriff's department. Sheriff Paul Ryder was informed that the FBI had a partial confession on the murders at Metro General. "We believe that your officers may have shot an innocent man in front of the hospital. We are continuing to investigate."

Ryder was under the impression that his men had performed admirably in their line of duty. He had his hands full investigating the murder of a trooper on the interstate. The weekend had been tough. The department was running with a full staff. There had been a big fire at Mountain View Service Station with bodies. They were still looking for an escaped convict. Sheriff Ryder hung up the phone. That call was going to create a ton of paperwork.

The phone in Donna's parents' home rang. She walked over to the wall and picked up the receiver. "This is Agent Miller with the FBI," said the voice. "May I speak with Donna?"

"This is Donna," she said.

"We have reason to believe that your mother may have been killed by someone other than your father. Our investigation is open, and we are following up. I will call you as we learn more."

Donna hung up the phone, then sank to the floor. Tommy went to her side. "Who was that?" he asked.

"The FBI," said Donna. "They think someone else might have killed mom."

"What...? Holy fuck," said Tommy. "You mean

your dad could be innocent? But the cops shot him!"

Donna was sobbing. Elizabeth and Brad did their best to help console her. "Oh my God," said Donna. "I can't believe what I am hearing."

Chapter 113

Nancy and Bobby finished their sexual encounter. Nancy had fulfilled her end of the bargain. It had only taken Bobby two minutes of thrusting as Nancy was on her knees to satisfy himself.

"That was awesome," said Bobby.

"Great," said Nancy.

"We will have to get together again."

She rolled her eyes. "Why don't you relax?" said Nancy. "I am going to go and find us something to eat."

Nancy grabbed the keys to both Dirk's car and the U-Haul. Bobby had started to drift off. He never noticed what Nancy was doing as she removed his wallet from the back pocket of his jeans. She tossed it back onto the floor. Nancy walked out of the room, closing the door behind her. She opened the trunk to Dirk's car, removing both boxes. She placed them in the front cab of the U-Haul. Nancy then placed Dirk's keys in the ignition of his vehicle.

Nancy got behind the wheel of the U-Haul. She started the truck then drove out of the parking lot.

"911, what is your emergency?" came the answer as Nancy held her cellphone close to her ear.

"I think the man you are looking for is at the Mountain View Motel in room number 140, that escaped criminal." Nancy hung up. She then tossed her cellphone out the window as she pulled onto the interstate. There was no way the authorities were going to track her; she had seen way too many movies.

Nancy drove back towards Hillcrest. Within twenty minutes of her being on the road, at least ten state trooper cars with their lights flashing passed her heading in the direction of Mountain View Motel. Nancy smiled and thought to herself as the day's events filled her mind. She opened the flap of the box on the seat beside her. She pulled a bundle of one hundred dollar bills from inside the box then held it to her lips and kissed it. She had outsmarted a criminal, her boss, her ex-teacher, and now Bobby. Nothing was going to stop Nancy now.

State troopers pulled into the gravel parking lot of the Mountain View Motel. Dust filled the air as officers hid behind the doors of their cruisers. Room 140 was surrounded. Whoever was inside was not getting away. A trooper picked up the mic for his car's public address system.

"This is the state police! We have you surrounded! Come out with your hands above your head! This is the state police! You have five minutes to comply!"

Bobby woke from his slumber. He heard the announcement a second time. Bobby slipped his pants on. His head was still groggy from his short nap. He pulled the corner of the curtains back so he could see outside. There were police everywhere. The U-Haul was missing. Then it hit him. Nancy had set him up.

"That fucking bitch!" he said out loud. The cops were after him for helping Nancy deal with her boss. The dude got everything he deserved.

"Come out with your hands above your head! Johnny Robbins, this is your last warning!"

"Who the fuck is Johnny Robbins!?" Bobby said out loud. He pulled the curtain back again. Bobby

opened the door to Room 140 just a crack.

He then shouted out loud, "Who the fuck is Johnny Robbins?" The troopers were on edge, their fingers rested on the triggers of their department-issued weapons. They knew, or thought they knew, that Robbins was responsible for the death of one of their brothers.

Bobby opened the door with his foot. Bobby raised his hands over his head. "I am coming out!" he said. Bobby took one step out into the daylight. His eyes squinted, then started to water. Bobby reached into his back pocket to grab the black rag he used while working. He pulled it from his pocket to wipe his cheek.

Someone yelled, "Gun!" All hell broke loose. Each member fired on Bobby as he stood in the doorway. Blood and parts of his flesh splattered all over the wall and the door behind him. Bobby dropped face-first onto the concrete sidewalk of the Mountain View Motel. "Hold your fire!" came the order.

The sheriffs walked over to Bobby. One of the officers rolled him over with his boot. Bobby's eyes were open, and he was lying in a pile of blood. Bobby was trying to speak. Blood was coming from his mouth; he coughed, and blood splattered onto his face. Bobby took his last breath. The officers present radioed into Dispatch. "Suspect down. Shots fired."

The deputies looked around for the reported gun. Nothing was found except for the rag in Bobby's hand. Bobby lay motionless, his body riddled with bullets from the deputies' guns. One of the officers grabbed a copy of the all-points bulletin. The department had issued it in the morning. Attached was a photograph of Johnny Robbins, the escaped criminal. The officers stood looking at the body. Bobby's face was a mess because of

the way he fell. When he spat up the blood, it made matters worse. The officers could not tell if it was Robbins or not.

"Grab a kit," said Deputy Harris. One of the officers produced a black plastic case. Harris opened it. He removed an ink pad from the case. Harris lifted Bobby's right hand, placing his index finger on the black pad. Harris rolled Bobby's finger against the soft sponge-like material. He had one of his deputies hold a clipboard with a blank sheet of paper next to Bobby's hand. Harris rolled Bobby's finger across the paper, leaving his print behind. Harris then took the clipboard and placed it on the hood of his cruiser. He then took his department-issued phone out of his pocket and snapped a picture. He sent the photo to the state forensic lab. He stated, "Suspect Johnny Robbins, right index finger."

It was not long after that when an ambulance showed up on the scene, followed by the FBI. "Has anyone touched this body?" asked Agent Anderson.

"Of course," said Harris, "I printed his right index."

At that moment, Sheriff Harris heard his phone ping. Harris looked at the screen. All it said was, "Print is not a match." Forensics had compared Johnny's prints from his prison records to what had been sent in thirty minutes earlier. Harris showed his phone to Agent Anderson. Room 140 was searched for ID. The office records showed a Jane Smith paid for the room in cash.

Anderson looked at Harris and said, "Well, good luck." He continued, "You're going to need it," as he walked back to his car. The sheriffs had shot someone, but they still did not know who. Dirk's car was now being searched, and the identification team was on site, taking prints from Room 140 and Dirk's car.

Nancy was still smiling as she drew closer to Hillcrest. She had the air conditioning going full blast in the cab of the U-Haul. As she got to the edge of town, she noticed police cars pointing in each direction. Traffic was slow, but the officers seemed to be waving everyone through. Nancy rolled her window down as she approached the trooper standing beside his cruiser. "Are you alone?" asked the trooper.

"Yes, just me and my stuff," said Nancy. "I have been moving this weekend." The trooper nodded his head and waved Nancy along. The sheriffs' radios had been active. Robbins had been taken down at the Mountain View Motel, and they were just waiting for the word to shut down the roadblocks. There was no point in delaying the public any further.

Nancy rolled up her window and proceeded into Hillcrest. She pulled into the parking lot of Elli's Diner. Nancy walked in and then walked directly back into the kitchen, where she found her Aunt Elli. The two embraced for a moment. "Aunty, I think we are going to be okay."

"What do you mean?" asked Elli.

"Come outside with me," said Nancy.

"We are really busy, honey," said Elli. Nancy insisted, and Elli walked to the passenger door of the U-Haul with her niece. Nancy opened the door and showed her aunt what was in one of the boxes on the passenger seat. Elli gasped. They then walked behind the truck. Nancy opened the overhead door, and the back of the truck was full of boxes, all the same.

"Where did you... are they all...?" Elli stopped herself. "It's a miracle!" said Elli. She gave Nancy a big hug and a kiss on the lips. "Let's take the two open boxes

inside. We'll put them in the cooler. Then I want you to go over to the house and wait for me. We will unload everything when I get home into the garage."

Elli was beside herself. She lasted two more hours at the diner. Elli gathered the two boxes she and Nancy had placed in her cooler and carried them out the back entrance. Elli's old derelict car, which had not run in years, sat in the back corner of the parking lot. Elli fumbled with her bundle of keys until she found the one that fit the trunk's lock for the old car. Elli placed both boxes in the trunk and closed the lid. Then, she got into her five-year-old Ford Taurus and headed home.

Nancy had backed the U-Haul into her aunt's driveway. In the two hours she had been alone, Nancy had managed to unload all the boxes into the garage of her aunt's home. Elli had raised Nancy from the time she was eight years old. Nancy's mother had been arrested for trafficking narcotics and child endangerment, resulting in a twenty-year sentence. Someone had to step in and look after Nancy.

Elli had treated Nancy well and taught her how to survive on very little. After all, it was not easy running your own business, no matter how popular it looked to outsiders.

"Oh, honey, it looks like you've worked up a bit of a sweat," Nancy wiped her brow, and her tube top was stained with perspiration.

"I have," she said to her aunt.

"Where did this U-Haul come from?" asked Elli.

Nancy lied to her aunt, "Someone left it in the parking lot at Bubbles. It was in the way, so I had a look inside. The keys were in it. I opened one of the boxes. Then I went back into the office. I was going to call the

cops when I heard on the radio that there was an escaped convict they were looking for." Nancy did not tell her aunt any of the actual facts.

"Oh my God!" said Elli. "This must be drug money. There is going to be someone looking for all of this. There must be millions of dollars here!"

Nancy shrugged her shoulders. "There is quite a bit," she said.

"How many boxes?" asked Elli.

"I counted forty-eight," came Nancy's reply.

"Well, let's lock up. We need to drop off the truck to its rightful owner," said Elli. "Follow me, honey. There is a depot just around the block across the road from the Mountain View service station." Nancy followed her aunt as she was instructed. They pulled into a gravel lot across the road from the burned-out service station. The fire department and cops were still on the scene. The news crew van was still there filming the chaos. Elli pulled in behind the U-Haul in her Taurus. Nancy stepped out of the cab of the U-Haul and locked the door. She walked over to the small office on the lot. There was a sign on the door that said, "Drop keys here." Nancy placed the keys in the slot and then made her way towards Elli's waiting car.

The two women stopped at the diner to check on the daily activity. When Elli was satisfied that all was running smoothly, Nancy and her aunt left. The women then drove straight to Elli's home. They pulled into the driveway and walked into the garage through its side door. Nancy pulled a box down from the pile, she opened it. Elli and Nancy stood looking at bundles of one-hundred-dollar bills. Elli put her arm around her niece's shoulder. "Wow," she said, "does anyone else know

about this?" Elli asked her niece.

"No," said Nancy, looking directly into her aunt's eyes.

"How could someone just leave this behind?" Elli asked.

"Maybe something happened to them," was Nancy's reply.

"We need to think about this," said Elli. "Maybe there is a reward." The two women left the garage, making their way into the home they had shared for twelve years. Elli turned on her coffee maker, and she sat down at the kitchen table. Nancy had excused herself to have a shower and change. Ten minutes later, Nancy slipped quietly into the kitchen. Her aunt had a fresh cup of coffee in front of her, and fresh cookies were laid out on a plate.

Nancy stood behind her Aunt as she watched Elli take a bite from one of her world-famous chocolate chip cookies. Nancy took the plastic bag she had removed from the garbage can in the bathroom and slipped it over her Aunt's head as quickly as she could. Nancy held the bag over her Aunt's nose and mouth. Elli struggled, and within a minute, her Aunt had passed out. Nancy held the bag in place for another minute, just for good measure. She then slipped the bag off her Aunt's head, and Elli fell forward, her face hitting the kitchen table.

Nancy returned the bag to the bathroom can, then replaced the garbage she had removed moments before. Nancy made her way back to the kitchen and screamed at the top of her lungs. She picked up the phone, calling 911, sobbing. "I don't know what happened," Nancy said. "I was in the shower. No, she's not moving."

"Do not hang up," said the operator. "I am

sending you an ambulance."

Nancy stood looking at her Aunt's lifeless body. "Hurry," she said to the operator, "she is all I have." Moments felt like hours, and eventually, Nancy heard the sounds of the siren. She ran to the front door. "Hurry," she said, "my Aunt is in here."

The two EMTs followed Nancy into the kitchen, removed Elli from the chair, and laid her body on the kitchen floor. The two men checked Elli's mouth, which was full of pieces of cookie. They commenced CPR, injected Elli's heart with a shot of adrenaline, and then shocked Elli's chest. "I have a pulse," said one of the EMTs. Elli's chest started to rise as she began breathing. The EMTs placed an oxygen mask over Elli's mouth and nose. Nancy was asked to give one of the attendants a hand bringing in the stretcher. Nancy obliged, as she wanted it to appear that she really cared. Elli was loaded onto the stretcher, and the ambulance took off with lights and siren activated. They were destined for Hillcrest General Hospital, and Elli needed to be stabilized before she could be sent to Metro General.

Nancy took her Aunt's purse off the hook on the front door and found her Aunt's car keys inside a zippered pocket. She got into her Aunt's car and made her way to the local hospital. Nancy found her way to the emergency department and was escorted to a waiting area outside an emergency room. "Stay here," said the nurse. "When the doctor knows something, he will come and talk to you."

Two hours later, Dr. Leonard Steel met with Nancy in the waiting room. "I have some good news and bad news," said Dr. Steel. "Your Aunt is still alive. However, she is not showing any signs of brain activity. Her pupils are fixed and dilated, and they are not

responding to light. The EEG shows no activity in her brain. To be sure, we need to do an MRI to see how much damage there is. Does your Aunt have insurance?" asked Dr. Steel.

"I don't know," said Nancy. "She owns Elli's Diner."

"We need you to fill out some paperwork," said Dr. Steel. "Are you her guardian?"

"No, she raised me," said Nancy. "My mom went to jail when I was young. I have lived with my Auntie for twelve years." Nancy completed the paperwork the best she could. She checked the box that said "self-employed" and then wrote the name of Elli's Diner as her Aunt's business. The paperwork was forwarded to admitting. Someone in the accounting office glanced at the documents. With a stroke of a pen, Elli was sent for her MRI. In fine print on the contract, it read, "Hillcrest General reserves the right to sue or obtain any assets and estates legally. The named patient declared herein is obligated to pay any balance owed. Hillcrest General does not assume any financial liability for the patients it treats." Nancy had signed this admission form on behalf of her incapacitated Aunt. After all, she had to keep up appearances.

Nancy sat in the waiting room looking for Dr. Steel to come out and give her an update on Elli. Three hours later, Dr. Steel approached Nancy. "I am sorry," he said. "The MRI shows that there are portions of her brain that have ceased functioning. This is caused when the brain is starved of oxygen for too long. Based on the EMTs' report, it looks like your aunt choked on her cookie. It's too bad you were not there to help her."

"I was in the shower," said Nancy. "She was just laying face down on the kitchen table when I went back

640

into the kitchen."

"You need to decide what you want us to do," said Dr. Steel.

"What do you mean?" asked Nancy.

"Your Aunt is brain-dead, and there is no hope that she will ever come back to us. Did she leave any instructions about donating her organs?"

"This is too much," said Nancy as she ran to the end of the room and fell to her knees, sobbing.

Dr. Steel came over, placing a hand on her shoulder. "I will come back in half an hour," he said. "You can let me know what you would like to do then."

Chapter 114

Robert Gerard had been briefed on all the information Betty had. He asked her to schedule all the Rangers to report for duty here on Tuesday. There was one hell of a mess up at Rock Lake and Angel Glacier. The ice poachers had been released, and that pissed off Robert. However, the perpetrators' information had been recorded by the department, courts, and local authorities. Robert would press new charges again later after he knew how much the cleanup costs would be. Rock Lake was another matter. The bear carcasses had been hauled out by the forensic veterinarians. There was still the matter of the cabins being cleaned up and the campground where Brad, Tommy, their girlfriends, and local sheriffs had stayed.

"I want Dan Thompson back up at the lake," he said to Betty. "He knows how to coordinate and handle things."

"I will make sure of that," said Betty. "What about the funerals?"

"Make sure we send flowers to Gary's wife."

"Christ," said Dan, "they had only been married for two years. Call her, please, Betty, and let her know the department will be looking after all the expenses for the funeral." Betty nodded to confirm that she would look after things.

Gunner came out of the locker room. "How are your ribs?" Robert asked his pilot.

"Sore," was Gunner's reply, "but I have had worse. How about that thing in your head?"

Robert touched the shunt, and droplets of fluid wet his fingertips. "I am fine," said Bob. "Do you feel like going for a flight back into the park?"

Gunner knew there was unfinished business his boss needed to wrap up, and he wanted to keep an eye on his friend. "Let's go," said Gunner.

Robert Gerard walked behind the counter then removed a digital camera with a telephoto lens from a box by Betty's desk. "I am ready," Bob said to his pilot and friend. The two men, now dressed in their park uniforms, made their way out to the Glacier Tours helicopter. Robert had ordered his ground personnel to top up the bird while Gunner and he had gone into the office to change.

"Where to?" asked the tour pilot, Darcy Brown.

"First stop is Rock Lake," said Robert. "I want to get some overhead pictures of the area."

"Roger that," said Brown. Gunner took the front passenger seat, and Robert sat in the back directly behind the pilot. In moments, the chopper was warmed up and flying. Brown had entered the coordinates of the lake, and air traffic control had given him a new squawk code for the helicopter's transponder, allowing them to be tracked on radar. They were cleared to an altitude of 5,000ft on a path directly towards Rock Lake.

Once inside the restricted airspace of the park, the helicopter was again free to move about as the pilot saw fit. The airspace over the park was only accessible to the park's chopper and those with specialty permits, ensuring no conflict with other aircraft in the area. Glacier Tours was the only outfit granted permission to fly in the restricted space, which is why they went above and beyond to help when the park needed assistance.

They did not want to jeopardize their yearly permit. Without it Glacier Tours' business would collapse.

The helicopter entered the park's airspace thirty-five minutes later. The men flew directly over the staging area and parking lot for Rock Lake. Ranger Colby Page, now awake, was sitting in his park truck, making sure that the public got turned away from the area. The helicopter proceeded over the mountain until it dropped into the valley. Rock Lake lay directly ahead. Robert Gerard asked Darcy to hover over the campsite while he took photographs.

"Keep her at about 1,000 feet above everything," he said. "I don't want to be blowing stuff into the lake." Robert took a series of photos, and they then maneuvered over the inflated emergency raft, capturing several more shots. "Now the cabins," he said to Brown.

"Roger that."

Gunner sat in the passenger seat, thinking, "This is great." It was the first time he had ever been in the area and not been in control of the park's helicopter. The chopper made its way over the cabins, with things looking in order for the most part, except for the dark red stain behind RL03.

Robert snapped several more pictures. "Okay," he said to Brown, "let's get over to Angel Glacier."

Darcy Brown turned the helicopter around, applied power, and started his climb out of the valley, ascending to 10,000 feet to clear the ridge directly ahead. He applied more power, but suddenly, there was a loud bang, and the helicopter started to spin wildly. "We have lost the tail rotor!" yelled Brown into his microphone. Gunner was on the controls right away, but there was absolutely no response to the pressure he applied with

his pedals on the floor. "I have got it!" said Brown, looking over at Gunner. "Fuck, fuck!" he said. "I cannot control her! We are going in!"

Gunner pressed the red button on the control yoke in front of him. "Mayday, mayday!" he shouted. "This is Glacier Tours! We have lost our tail rotor! Mayday, mayday!"

Robert Gerard was holding onto the handrail above the door. Everything was happening quickly, and he could hear Gunner in his headphones yelling "mayday, mayday." Darcy Brown did everything he could, but the helicopter hit the side of the mountain approximately 1,500 feet below the tree line. The helicopter's main rotor caught on some spruce trees as it went in. The crash was violent. Branches came through the front windshield. The helicopter ripped apart as it hit the ground. Gunner had managed to maintain his composure.

The chopper ended up partly on its left side, with the engine still running, drawing in pieces of spruce bows. Gunner reached over, flipping the switches to turn the damn thing off. Chris could harldy breathe. The seatbelt and shoulder harness had caused additional damage to his previous injuries. He looked over at Brown. There was a branch that had come through the front window and pierced the pilot's neck. Brown was motionless. Gunner removed his headset. "Bob! Bob!" he shouted. "Can you hear me? We have to get out of here!" The smell of jet fuel filled Gunner's nostrils as the fuel tank had obviously ruptured. "Bob, we have to get out of here!" said Gunner, managing to unfasten the seatbelt that held him in place. Chris did his best to reach Robert. "Bob, wake up!" he shouted.

Smoke was pouring in from the engine area.

Suddenly, there was an instant rush of heat, and the air filled with smoke. Flames were coming into the cabin from all around. There was only one thing for Gunner to do. He crawled through the smashed windshield and away from the wreck as best he could. When he felt he was far enough away, Gunner turned and rested against a large rock. He looked back as the entire helicopter became engulfed in flames, staring in disbelief. Just five minutes before, they had been sitting in the comfort of a helicopter. Now, Chris was alone, having trouble breathing. It was all too much for his body to handle. Gunner passed out. His head slumped forward, blood draining from the side of his mouth.

Several hours passed before Gunner was awoken by the sound of a helicopter overhead. The Emergency Location Transponder (ELT), as it was known to the public, had done its job. The force of the impact had set it off. The signal was sent to a satellite, which was then downloaded and sent to the Sheriff's department. Gunner awoke to see the sheriff's bird hovering over him. The terrain was too steep with too many trees around to allow them to land. Gunner raised his right hand to shield his eyes.

"We have a survivor," said the spotter hanging out the side door. "He's alive! We have to set down!"

"Negative," said the pilot. "Mark the coordinates."

"Drop a survival pack," said the co-pilot. "Make sure you include a note that we will be back."

"Roger," said the spotter. The pack was dropped, landing about twenty yards from Chris, among some of the shattered trees. Wisps of black smoke still emanated from the downed helicopter, and the burned bodies of his boss, Robert Gerard, and Darcy Brown, could be seen.

646

Gunner had seen worse during the war. Summoning all the strength he had left, he looked down at his legs. His right foot was facing completely backward, and the pain was now starting to register.

"That's not good," he said aloud. Chris crawled his way over to the bright orange emergency pack, then opened it. The first thing he found was two bottles of water. He opened one and drank the whole thing. Chris started to choke. When he coughed, he spat out a large volume of blood. His chest was killing him, the pain was worse than his broken foot. Gunner removed the blanket from the bag. He found a utility knife, matches, and several granola bars neatly bundled together. He also found the note the flight medic had written for him: "The ground rescue team would get there as soon as they could".

Chris wrapped the blanket around himself as he was getting cold. The hulk of a helicopter that once carried tourists around the park lay in a burned-out heap, with its main rotor sheared off in several places. What was left bobbed up and down in the fresh mountain air. Chris dozed off, knowing the rescue team would soon be there to retrieve him from the mountain. He had been through a bunch of shit over the last few days, and it was all finally catching up to him.

Chapter 115

Nancy sat in the waiting room, pondering her next move. Thirty-five minutes had passed since she last spoke to Dr. Steel. She watched as there was a bunch of commotion around the entrance to the room where Elli was being treated. Several minutes later, Dr. Steel came out, his head bowed. He stood in front of Nancy.

"I am sorry," he said. "Your Aunt passed five minutes ago. There was nothing we could do."

Nancy started to sob. She needed it to appear that she really was upset.

"I am sorry," said Dr. Steel. "Someone from the administration department will come and speak to you. We have a family counseling office here as well," said Steel. "Would you like to speak to someone?"

"No," said Nancy, "I just can't believe that she is gone. She was my role model."

Dr. Steel apologized a second time and then left Nancy sitting in the waiting room. Soon, someone from admitting came and spoke to Nancy.

"Your Aunt's body will be transferred to the morgue. We will hold her body for up to 48 hours. That should give you enough time to make the necessary arrangements."

Nancy nodded her head, then wiped her eyes and blew her nose. "Thank you," she said. Nancy then signed a document that Dr. Steel had signed twenty minutes earlier. Nancy had officially acknowledged that her Aunt was deceased.

Nancy left the hospital and drove directly to the

house she had shared with her Aunt. Nancy parked in the driveway directly in front of the garage door. She got out of her car and went into the house through the back entrance. Nancy stood in the kitchen, smiled, and started a little dance. She twirled around once and then sat in the chair where she had killed her Aunt.

Nancy reached for one of the cookies her Aunt had placed on the plate. She took a bite and looked up at the ceiling. "I am sure going to miss your cooking." She smiled again and then laughed. Nancy had a garage full of cash, millions of dollars, she thought. She was thinking of ways to spend it.

Nancy had not been sitting at the kitchen table for more than fifteen minutes when the doorbell rang. She got up and went to the front door. Nancy opened the door to be greeted by two detectives from the FBI.

"Are you Nancy May?" asked one of the men.

"Yes," she replied.

"Do you mind if we come in?"

"Why?" asked Nancy. "My Auntie just passed away a few hours ago. I am very sad."

"This will only take a few minutes." The men entered her Aunt's home. They were breaking a ton of rules, but Nancy had not said no. The three of them made their way into the living room. Nancy was asked if she knew a gentleman named Dirk.

"Of course," she said. "He is my boss at work."

"How about a young man named Bobby?"

"Yes," she said, "he was an old boyfriend from high school."

"Nancy, we believe you might have been

involved in the murder of Dirk Benning."

"What?" she said. "What do you mean Dirk is dead?"

"Don't play dumb, Nancy, we have you on video."

"What do you mean?" she said.

"You and your Aunt dropped off a U-Haul truck several hours ago. Do you remember that?"

Nancy was feeling the pressure. "No," said Nancy. "I do not."

"Well," said the oldest agent. "When you and your Aunt dropped off the truck, the news cameras were rolling across the road at Mountain View service. When your Aunt turned her car around, the camera captured her license plate number. Bobby had been killed. His fingerprints pointed us to the U-Haul franchise. You see, Nancy, we have a body and a burned-out motorhome. We believe that to be Dirk Benning. His car magically was found at the same motel Bobby was shot at. When we spoke to Bobby's boss at the rental company, she said he left in a truck to meet a female client. How did you get the truck, Nancy?"

Nancy looked at the detectives. "Fuck you! I am not saying another word. I want a lawyer."

"Fuck us!?" said one of the detectives. "No, fuck you, missy! Stand up! You are under arrest for the murder of Dirk Benning." Nancy stood and turned around as handcuffs were placed on her wrists. She was placed in the back of the detectives' car. They had called into the office requesting a search warrant for Elli's home. A half-hour later, two more cars showed up, each carrying a lone detective. One of the detectives had the warrant in hand. It was shown to Nancy.

The four agents began searching Elli's property, eventually making it out to the garage. They opened the overhead door. Sitting in front of them were forty-eight cardboard boxes. The agents opened a box and peered inside.

"Holy fuck," they said. "Look at this. There has to be a couple of million in here." They opened a second box, and it was full of bundled one-hundred-dollar bills as well. "Scratch that. There has to be one hundred million in total here. Where the fuck would all this have come from?"

Nancy sat in the back of the agents' car. She started banging her head against the window until it shattered. Blood ran down her forehead. Nancy was hauled out of the car. Her feet were bound as she lay on the grass in front of Elli's house. Her hands and feet were then tied together, and Nancy was tossed back into the agents' car face down on the back seat. The FBI agents stood around talking for a few moments. Nancy was escorted to the local office for her interrogation. She waited, her hands bound in handcuffs. The interrogation room was small. There was a small metal table, the chair she sat in, and one more. The wall she faced had a window; she couldn't see through it, but she had watched enough cop shows to know it was one-way glass. The door opened, and in walked Agent Douglas McCarthy.

"Hello, Nancy, do you remember me? We met at your front door a few hours ago." Nancy nodded her head. "Nancy," he said, "everything you say to me is being video recorded. You see that camera up there in the corner?" Nancy looked up, seeing a small black lens directed right at the table she was sitting at. "I am sorry for the loss of your Aunt," said Agent McCarthy. "How did she die?" he asked.

Nancy fidgeted in her seat. "Where is my lawyer?" she asked.

"On his way," said McCarthy. "Long weekend and all, the public defender's office is running late. Answer my question!" snapped The Agent, slapping his hand on the table.

Nancy jumped; his action scared her. "My Aunt was eating a cookie. I found her like that after I got out of the shower."

"Did you now?" said McCarthy. "I don't think so. We have evidence that suggests otherwise."

"What do you mean?" said Nancy.

"I know the truth," said McCarthy. "I know you did it. How do you know she was eating a cookie if you were in the shower?"

"There were cookies on the plate. The ambulance guys said she choked on a cookie. I saw them take stuff out of her mouth."

"What about Dirk Benning?" asked McCarthy. "We found what was left of his body in a burned-out motorhome. Blown to bits. How did his car get to the Mountain View Motel?"

"How do I know?" said Nancy.

"We have video of you paying cash for a room from the front desk. There is also video of you getting out of Mr. Benning's car in the parking lot moments before we have your prints."

"All right, all right," said Nancy. "I borrowed my boss's car to meet Bobby. He called me. We met at the motel. We fucked, and I left."

"That makes no sense," said McCarthy. There

was a knock at the door. In walked Todd Sterling, the public defender.

"Nancy, I am your lawyer, Todd Sterling." The lawyer bent down and whispered into Nancy's ear. Nancy then whispered into his. Sterling presented a single sheet of paper to his client. Nancy immediately signed the document with Todd's gold pen. "Now," said Sterling, looking at Agent McCarthy. "Have you been questioning my client without me being present?"

"We were chatting," said McCarthy.

Nancy started to cry. She pointed to the FBI agent. "He accused me of killing my auntie. I am so upset. He was asking me about my boss, Mr. Benning."

"That's okay, Nancy. I hope you did not say anything. I have had a chance to review your search warrant. It is not valid," said the lawyer. "The warrant was issued to search Elli May's property. She was already deceased. Technically, the property belonged to Nancy May the moment her aunt died. Your department has made a grievous error. My client will be suing." McCarthy sat back in his chair. "Do you have anything to hold my client on other than your damn speculation?" asked Sterling.

McCarthy excused himself from the room. He walked next door. Two of the other agents that had helped search Elli's home had been watching through the one-way glass. "You know what to do," said McCarthy.

The two men nodded their heads. FBI Agent McCarthy walked back into the interview room. "You are free to go, Nancy."

Sterling had given Nancy one of his business cards. He placed a hand on her shoulder and then said, "We will discuss the lawsuit later. Call me tomorrow."

Nancy nodded her head and wiped the tears from her eyes. She held out her hands so McCarthy could remove the handcuffs. Nancy was then escorted out of the building. She walked to the corner of the street, where she managed to wave down a cab. Fifteen minutes later, Nancy was back in front of her aunt's home. "Wait here for a moment," she said to the driver. "I will get you your money."

Nancy went to the front door of the house. It was closed and locked. Nancy moved the flower pot on the front step, which revealed a hidden key. She opened the door and walked into her bedroom. Her purse and its contents were turned upside down on her bed. She removed a twenty from her wallet, then went back outside to pay the driver. Nancy waved as the cab backed out of her driveway. She walked back to the garage. The side door had been damaged; it was broken around the lock, wood splinters were everywhere. Nancy opened the door, then turned on the light. She stared into the garage. The bare concrete floor was all that she could see. Every single box that had been there hours before had disappeared.

Nancy yelled at the top of her lungs. "You motherfuckers! Fucking cops!" she said aloud. Nancy turned to leave the garage. Standing in her way was a large man wearing a black ski mask. There were two small muffled thuds. Nancy felt something hit her in the chest. She dropped to her knees. The perpetrator placed the silencer of his gun against Nancy's forehead, then pulled the trigger. Nancy fell face-first onto the concrete floor. Blood poured from her wounds. A bundle of one hundred dollar bills was scattered around her body. The man in the ski mask took his time. He hid the gun and silencer under his jacket. The mask he placed in his pocket. The man walked toward a black sedan that had

654

government plates on it. He opened the passenger door and got in. The two men drove away from Elli's home. Several blocks later, they were crossing the bridge that Brad had always watched, the one with the gauge that indicated the height of the water in the river. The passenger rolled down his window. The gun and silencer used to murder Nancy were thrown from the moving car. They landed in the cold rushing water.

"Did you see that gauge?" said the passenger. "Water is up to the eighteen-foot mark." The two men bumped their fists together. "No one is ever going to find that piece."

"Perfect," said the driver. "Everything is wrapped up in a nice neat little package."

Chapter 116

Gunner was sound asleep, his back against the large rock. The blanket was doing its job, keeping him warm. The bag that had been dropped by the sheriff's chopper sat beside him. His mind drifted as he slept. One moment he was back in the war, the next he was chasing down bad guys in the new 505. His hands twitched as he dreamed of working the controls of whatever helicopter his brain told him he was flying. His mind paused for a moment; his dream was not making sense. There was a smell that he detected, nothing like he had experienced before.

"What is that?" he thought. His dream was now a fleeting thought. Chris was coming back to reality. He started to move; the pain in his chest and leg turned on all his senses. His eyes were still closed when he heard heavy breathing beside him. There was a deep rumbling sound, almost like a growling dog but ten times lower than that.

Gunner heard the emergency bag being dragged away from beside him. Chris opened his right eye. Laying five feet beside him, its snout inside the bright red emergency bag, was the largest grizzly Chris had ever seen. It had deep scars on its side. The old boar, the new patriarch of Rock Lake Valley, was there. It was the one that had attacked Susan and Rachel. Gunshots it had heard in the valley forced it up the mountains. It was now a few feet from Chris.

The smell of rotten flesh, blood, shit, and urine permeated the air. Its front feet held the bag down as the bear moved its head back and forth. Gunner watched as it pulled out the bundle of granola bars. It was just laying

there. It would use its front teeth to tear at the packages. When it realized that was too much work, the grizzly just started to devour everything, wrappers and all.

Gunner did not move. He knew if the grizzly's attention was diverted, things could get a lot worse. Its tongue flicked back and forth until it spit out the white tape that had kept some of the bars bundled together. The grizzly looked up. Its wet snout flickered as it smelled the fresh mountain air. It kept moving its head back and forth; one second it smelled jet fuel, the next burned grass, the next burned flesh.

The old boar was intrigued. It stood up. It used its right front paw to dig into the ground. Chris watched as it covered the emergency bag in dirt and twigs. The grizzly turned; its rump now faced Gunner. There was shit all down the back of its legs and ass.

The smell was too much for Chris to take. He started to choke and then coughed. The grizzly spun around, looking for what made the noise. The big boar stood in front of Gunner. Chris watched as the bear sniffed the air. The pain in Gunner's chest got the best of him. He tried to hold his breath, but it was impossible. The big grizzly was on Gunner in a split second. The bear bit down on Gunner's leg, then started to shake its head wildly from side to side. Chris could not stay silent any longer. He screamed. The grizzly paused for a moment, then went back to work. The bear bit through the blanket. It was now biting into Gunner's mid-section. Chris could feel his skin being torn from his stomach. It was too much. Chris passed out.

The bear rolled Chris over with its left front paw. Its six-inch nails tore into Gunner's ribs. The bear bit down on the back of Gunner's neck. The boar straightened its stance, dragging Chris away from the

large rock. The bear dragged Chris between its front and back legs. As the bear walked further ahead, the blanket covering Gunner got caught on a branch. Gunner's intestines were spilling from the large gaping wound on his stomach. As the bear moved forward, it looked like sausages were being pulled along behind Gunner's feet.

The grizzly stopped, content with the location it had found. It stood over Chris, biting into his left leg. It had learned after attacking Rachel and Susan that there was good and easy meat to be had in this very spot. The boar bit down hard through Gunner's pant leg. It shook its head twice. Gunner's calf muscle ripped from the bone as his pants were shredded. The grizzly chewed a few times, then swallowed. It then did the same on the right leg. Both of Gunner's tibias were exposed, and blood poured from the wounds.

Gunner woke for a moment. He moved his right arm and then remembered the grizzly. He was no longer in any pain. "Was it over?" he thought. The old boar saw the movement in Gunner's arm. The grizzly moved to Gunner's head and bit down. It shook Chris violently. The boar stood over its prey. It had enough food for several days. The old bear walked back twenty feet or so. It then laid down beside the big rock Chris had been using. The sun felt good. Its belly was full, and there were no other rivals around to challenge for territory, food, or breeding rights. The grizzly dozed off, a few flies settled on its snout and around its rump. Nature had a way of ensuring everything had something to eat.

Chapter 117

Donna sat on the floor of her parents' home, crying her eyes out.

"Sweetie, let me help you up," said Tommy. He bent over to extend his hand and arm to Donna. He could feel the sutures pulling on the skin of his back as he helped Donna off the floor. Tommy pulled a kitchen chair out from the table. "Sit here," he said. He handed Donna a couple of tissues from the box on the counter.

"What a frickin' weekend," said Brad.

Elizabeth ran the water in the sink until it was nice and cold. She filled a clean glass, handing it to Donna.

"Thank you," said Donna. "You all have been so kind."

The young adults spoke about the weekend events.

"It's hard to believe," said Brad. "Tommy's father is out there right now, with Superintendent Gerard. They will find the guy that shot Chris and killed Gary Smith. The law will bring him to justice."

"What about Dad and Mom?" said Donna. "It is crazy what happened to them."

Moments later, Donna's father's cellphone rang. Donna looked at the call display. The screen displayed State Farm and a number. "Hello?" said Donna.

"Hello," said the agent. "May I please speak to Clifford Jones?"

"I am sorry," said Donna. "He passed away

yesterday afternoon."

There was silence for a moment.

"Who am I speaking with?" asked the agent.

"I am Donna, Clifford's daughter."

"I am calling about your mother's life insurance policy," said the agent.

"What policy?" asked Donna.

"Your mother had a life insurance policy. There was a question as to the legitimacy of the claim your father had made a couple of days ago. We have completed our investigation. Based on the information we have from investigators from the state and federal departments, it has been concluded that your mother's life was taken from her."

"What do you mean?" said Donna.

"The report we received from the FBI shows they have a confession from a patient in the psychiatric ward of the hospital."

"But," said Donna, "the Sheriffs called me and told me something different."

The agent spent another twenty minutes explaining things to Donna. "You should be getting a call from the local police department soon. I want you to know the folks here at State Farm are very sorry for your loss. I mean the loss of your mom and dad. We will be proceeding with the claim your father started. It will be necessary for you to submit a copy of your mom's death certificate."

"Yes," said Donna. "May I ask how much my mom was insured for?"

"The policy was for two hundred and fifty

thousand. However, there was a clause that if your mom died accidentally, the policy paid double. In this case, the policy will pay five hundred thousand."

Tommy watched as Donna listened intently.

"Thank you," said Donna. She ended the call. Donna looked at Tommy. "Mom had life insurance. That was the insurance company. They are going to pay five hundred thousand."

Brad and Elizabeth looked at each other. Tommy was rubbing Donna's back. The doorbell rang. Donna's Aunt Mary stood at the front door. Brad took it upon himself to answer. Mary stood there with a big smile on her face. The trip to Vegas with her new boyfriend had been awesome.

"Hello, Mary," said Brad. "I have not seen you for a while."

Mary stepped inside her sister's home. Her children sat on the couch, watching Billy play his video game. "Look at you two," said Mary. "You are both my beautiful babies. I love you so much." She went over and kissed Mark and Marcy.

"That's gross," said Mark.

Donna heard her Aunt at the door. She left the kitchen to greet her Aunt. "Hello, Aunt Mary," said Donna.

"How did things go?" asked Mary.

Donna stared blankly at her Aunt. Tommy was now by her side. Tommy was about to say something when Donna put her arm around him. She put some pressure on her fingers, pressing them into Tommy's ribs. Tommy said nothing. Donna said, "Things went great. We did a little camping together."

"Where are your mom and dad?" asked Mary.

Mark spoke up, "They are at the hospital."

"The hospital again," said Mary.

Donna nodded her head. "Yes," she said. Brad and Elizabeth stood listening to Donna's conversation with her Aunt.

"Someday your mother is going to kill herself with all those stupid pills she takes. I don't know how your poor father puts up with it. Have him call me later." Donna nodded her head. "Come on, Mark and Marcy, it is time to go."

"Oh, Mom, we're tired."

"Now!" said Mary. "Get your stuff. Greg is waiting in the car."

The kids gathered their things. Donna bent down and gave both a hug goodbye. She whispered into each of their ears. "Remember," she said, "Santa is watching. We have to keep our secret."

Both kids nodded their heads. Mary opened the front door. "Let's go, you two little rascals." Mark and Marcy bounded towards Greg's car. He stepped out, then opened the trunk. He placed the kids' belongings alongside Mary's suitcase. Donna stood in the open entrance of her parents' home. She waved goodbye as Greg pulled away. Donna closed the front door. She turned towards her friends. "Thank you," she said. "Thank you for not saying anything about the current situation. I just did not have the energy to explain everything to my Aunt."

The four young adults walked back into the kitchen. Billy continued to play his video game. The house was far more quiet now that Mark and Marcy were

not there. Donna felt a sense of relief knowing she no longer had to care for her cousins.

"I am going to stay here tonight," Donna said to Tommy. "Someone has to look after Billy. All his things are here. There is no point in moving some of his stuff over to my apartment. He needs to be in his own bed."

"Agreed," said Tommy. "I will keep you company. Besides, I think you might need to change the dressing on my back."

"Oh, Tommy, you are so good to me," said Donna.

"I would do anything for you."

Mark and Marcy sat in the back of Greg's car. Mary turned slightly towards her children. "Did you have fun with your Aunt Donna this weekend?" she asked.

Mark spoke up right away. "You should have seen the bear," he said. "Its breath was real bad. It ripped my jacket, see," said Mark, holding open its shredded side.

"Don't be silly," said Mary. "Bears don't do that. Stop making up stories. Marcy, did you have fun?"

"It was okay, Mom, but I am tired. I just want to go home. We walked a lot."

"Good," said Mary. "The exercise is great for the two of you. Maybe your Auntie Donna should look after you every weekend."

Both kids shouted, "nooooo," at the same time. Mary and Greg laughed as they headed out of Hillcrest.

Chapter 118

The crash scene of the Glacier Tours helicopter had been locked into the GPS of the search and rescue helicopter, as provided by the sheriff's office. The chopper flew back to the Rock Lake staging area. Betty had been contacted by the Glacier Tours office. They had received a message from the sheriff's office that had responded to a transponder signal inside the park. They had observed the Tour Helicopter on the side of the mountain. One person was confirmed alive; there was no one else visible. Betty was beside herself with grief. "It had to be Bob," Betty thought to herself. "The poor man had been through so much the last few days."

Betty called Hillsboro Airport Search and Rescue. The rescue chopper had landed on the emergency pad for the staging area at Rock Lake. A plan had been formulated. They would fly back up to the crash site as soon as they were able to refuel. They needed to make the necessary modifications to the winch cable. There was only one hundred and fifty feet of line on the main reel. With the slope of the ground at the crash site and continuous updrafts, another one hundred feet of line needed to be attached to the existing cable. The pilot had made the right call to make sure they too did not end up on the side of the mountain.

It took two hours for the fuel truck to arrive at the staging area. The men were anxious to get back to the scene. After all, a human life was at stake. The rescue crew laid out the steel stretcher that was carried under the belly of the helicopter. A webbed four-point harness was attached to each corner. The additional cable would be clipped into the ring on the top of the harness. Then,

the other end of the extra cable would attach to the hook on the one hundred and fifty-foot line already on the rescue chopper. The problem was that the reel on the helicopter's winch could only handle the regulation one hundred and fifty feet of line. Someone was going to have to ride in the stretcher, dangling one hundred feet below the helicopter, back up to the crash scene. They would then have an extra one hundred and fifty feet of line they could raise and lower to the survivor. It was risky but was the safest thing to do so a rescue could be implemented.

The chopper was refueled. The additional cable had been attached to the existing line. Out of the three Search and Rescue members, Braden McFadden volunteered to ride in the basket. The co-pilot would work the winch cable from the open side door while the pilot kept the helicopter under control. Braden climbed into the stretcher with his rescue duffle bag. Three belts lay in the open. They looked like seatbelts from an old car. Braden fastened a belt around his hips. The whine of the helicopter's engine soon muffled everything in the area. The co-pilot stood in the open door, and the chopper lifted off. The slack in the new hundred feet of line was soon taken up by the rising helo. The co-pilot kept in constant communication through his headset to the pilot.

The stretcher soon dangled below the crew's bird. The helicopter rose to a height of five hundred feet above the trees, still giving them four hundred feet between the treetops and the stretcher. As the rescue bird moved forward, the stretcher started to turn. Braden laid down and closed his eyes. He hated those rides on the county fairs that spun you around until you got sick. This had the same effect.

The chopper took twenty minutes to fly back to

the coordinates of the crash site. When Braden sensed the helicopter was no longer moving forward, he sat up in the basket and leaned over the side. He vomited his lunch into the air. The downdraft from the rotating blades one hundred feet above dispersed his vomit into a fine mist with chunks. The co-pilot was hanging out of the window. Braden looked up. The co-pilot gave Braden the thumbs up, and he replied with his own thumb in the air. Braden looked down. The wreck of the Glacier Tours helicopter was about four hundred feet below him.

The pilot reduced power to the engine, and the rescue bird started to descend. "More... more," said the co-pilot into his mic as he watched Braden get closer to the treetops. "There, that ought to do it. Hold her steady here." The pilot concentrated on his altimeter and position to the mountain directly in front of him. The co-pilot pressed the button to lower the stretcher. "Seventy-five feet," said the co-pilot. "Fifty feet, twenty feet. Basket on the ground."

Braden unfastened his safety belt and climbed out of the basket, grabbing his duffle bag. He ran toward the burned-out helicopter and looked inside. Braden could see the burned remains of two people. The body in the pilot's seat had a burned tree branch that stuck through its chest. The smell of burnt flesh filled the air. Braden knew there was nothing he could do for these two.

"Hello? Hello?" he shouted over the noise of the helicopter two hundred feet overhead. Braden walked toward the large rock Gunner had used to rest against. The emergency bag he had tossed out several hours earlier lay fifty feet in front of him. The blanket that was in the bright red bag was lying ten feet away, now covered in blood. One end was caught in a broken tree branch. There were wrappers from the granola bars lying

about, plus a half-full bottle of water sitting on a rock. "Hello? Hello?" Braden shouted at the top of his lungs. He then realized what he was looking at and froze. Gunner's body lay about twelve feet from the blanket. A trail of blood and intestines lay behind his feet.

"Oh no!" he shouted. Braden walked toward Gunner's body, then knelt beside him. Chris was laying face down in the dirt. Braden was shaking as he turned Gunner over. He recognized the mangled face he was looking at. Braden had been inspired to join the Search and Rescue department after he had read the story of the Hero Pilot. That magazine article had changed Braden's life as a teen. He pressed his fingers to the side of Gunner's carotid artery in his neck just to be sure. There was no detectable pulse to be felt.

Gunner felt some pressure on the side of his neck. He couldn't be sure if it was the grizzly back for another round. Braden radioed to the helicopter overhead. "Our survivor did not make it," he said.

"Roger," said the pilot.

Braden looked back down at Gunner's face. Chris opened both of his eyes and stared directly into Braden's. Gunner managed to utter the words, "Help me."

Braden quickly radioed the crew overhead. "He is still alive! My God, he is alive! I can't believe it!"

There was still no detectable pulse. "Ten-four," came the reply from above.

Braden quickly assessed Gunner's injuries. The muscles on the back of his legs were missing, and blood had congealed around the gaping wounds. Braden reached for two straps he had in the rescue bag and used them as tourniquets on both legs. He found the one bag

of saline IV fluid he carried but had to find a vein to insert the needle from the IV line. It was impossible. All of Gunner's veins had collapsed from the lack of blood. Braden didn't have a choice. He inserted the needle directly into Gunner's carotid artery. If Chris was going to have any kind of chance for survival, his heart needed more fluid to pump. It was a huge risk. Braden placed the IV bag on a small rock beside Gunner, about two feet higher than the level of his head. The fluid started to run into Chris's neck.

Next, he had to collect Gunner's intestines in a plastic bag so more wouldn't spill from the open wound in Gunner's stomach. Braden did his best to pack the wound with the little gauze he had on hand. Braden radioed to the crew above that he was ready. The helicopter and basket were maneuvered directly overhead. Braden lifted Gunner and the bag with his intestines into the basket, then secured his patient in place. Braden put his feet on either side of the basket and clipped his harness to the swivel attached to the cable. He radioed that he was ready.

Power was applied to the engine, and the helicopter climbed, then turned to head back towards the emergency pad at the staging area. The Search and Rescue helicopter made its way back to the parking lot and staging area. Braden, Gunner, and the basket were lowered into the parking lot. The extra length of cable was unfastened by the co-pilot.

Ranger Colby Page came running over to offer his assistance. "My God," he said to Braden, "that is Gunner. What happened?"

"Looks like a bear," said Braden. "A fucking big bear based on his wounds. We need to get him loaded and to the hospital right away."

668

Chris opened his eyes and felt the two men carrying the stretcher to the waiting rescue helicopter. Gunner was loaded, and Colby held Gunner's hand for a split second. Braden then slid the door closed as the Search and Rescue helicopter left the ground. He hung the almost empty bag of IV fluid from the hook in the helicopter.

Braden was looking for a fresh bag of fluid when he noticed Gunner had opened his eyes. Chris could feel the surge of the helicopter as it lifted from the pad and started to bank. Braden wore a headset, communicating with the pilot. "We are forty minutes from Metro General. They are aware we are coming in hot." Braden put his hand on Gunner's shoulder. "We will be there in forty minutes," he said.

Gunner felt a sense of peace come over him. It was unlike anything he had ever experienced in his life. He was exactly where he wanted to be, in a beautiful bird flying as fast as it would go. Chris looked into Braden's eyes. Gunner took as deep a breath as he could. Then, he closed his eyes for the last time. The hero pilot was gone, and his soul was finally at peace.

Chapter 119

Todd Sterling had been informed by the state police that the neighbors had found Nancy's body in her aunt's garage late on Monday night.

Sterling had been doing some legal work for his client over and above his public defender duties. With Nancy's mother in prison and being estranged from the family, Sterling was filing paperwork to ensure that the title to Elli's home was registered in Nancy's name. He needed to ensure the documents were filed with the state's title office immediately after her aunt's death. If the state accepted his filing, then the search warrant was void, as Sterling had stated in the interview room.

Now, with Nancy's death, Sterling had his hands full. Todd opened the file containing the contract Nancy had signed when he first met her. Paragraph four clearly stated, "Any remuneration and fees not covered by the state and charged herewith by your public defender, Todd Sterling, may be collected using chattels and/or property described herein." Elli's Diner was clearly written into the blank space, along with Elli's home address, right there on page two.

Sterling had to draft up documentation he could submit to the judge first thing on Tuesday morning. It was a bitch being a public defender. He looked at his watch when he had finished preparing the necessary documents. It was 11:00pm on Monday night. Sterling needed to get to bed, so he was fresh and at the courthouse by 9am sharp. He wanted to be ready and presentable so the judge would see things his way.

Chapter 120

A large black van pulled into the vacant parking lot across the street from Hillcrest Saw and Lumber. The smell of freshly cut timber filled the air. The driver inhaled deeply as he stepped out of the vehicle. Shortly, three unmarked black Ford Police Interceptors pulled into the parking lot beside the van.

The rear doors of the van were opened, and each driver took one cardboard box, then walked it back to the trunk of their own car. The driver of the van closed the rear doors. The cars started to drive out of the lot, followed by the van. The four vehicles looked like they were in some kind of parade.

As they drove down the main street of Hillcrest, traffic in front of them had come to a standstill. The roadblock set up to look for the fugitive, Johnny Robbins, was still in operation. The black Interceptor in the lead activated its flashing red and blue lights. The hidden strobes in the grill and rear window became evident to anyone paying attention. The four government vehicles maneuvered around the blockade of cars ahead, driving up on the curb and part of the sidewalk, heading through town.

Once at the front of the line of cars, the lead Interceptor drove off the curb ahead of the waiting cars to go through the roadblock. The sheriffs waved all four black vehicles through the blockade without asking questions. The Interceptors and van quickly accelerated, putting as much distance between themselves and the town of Hillcrest as they could.

Two hours later, the four vehicles arrived at the

city of Metro. Fifteen minutes later, they pulled into the secured parking lot of the local FBI headquarters. Each man parked his government-issued ride in the appropriate assigned parking stall. The man who was driving the van opened the rear doors. There was one cardboard box left for him in the rear.

The four men each carried their own box to the staff parking area. Their individual boxes were loaded into the trunks of their personal cars. The men then walked over to the booth where agents signed out cars at the start of their shifts. The old man working behind the window passed a clipboard through the slot. The four vehicles that had just returned had been signed out on a single sheet of paper. All four agents needed to sign them back in.

The sheet of paper showing the vehicles had been taken from the lot for official duty was then removed from the clipboard. Each of the four men clipped a one-hundred-dollar bill under the clasp of the board, which was then passed back to the man behind the window. There were no words spoken. It was common practice for agents to use government vehicles on their own time. The old man behind the glass couldn't care less who was driving what, so long as everything was accounted for. Everything was back where it belonged. He nodded his head.

The four agents turned and walked towards their personal cars. They all drove out of the secure employee parking area in a single file at the same time, each heading to their own home. It had been a long day.

Chapter 121

Tuesday morning arrived quickly. Todd Sterling had arrived at the courthouse in Hillcrest at 8:30am. He filed his documents with the court clerk immediately and was given a time of 9:30 to be in the courtroom in front of Judge Harry White. White was known among local lawyers to be fair but harsh, disliking attorneys trying to take advantage of the system. Sterling sat in the courtroom while Judge White reviewed the documents he had prepared.

"How am I to grant your request?" said White to Sterling. "There are no death certificates attached to the paperwork here."

"I am aware of that," said Sterling. "The long weekend has created quite a backlog. I should be able to present the necessary documents later this afternoon."

Judge White spoke, "I will then reserve my judgment at 3:30pm. This application will be held over until that time." Sterling thanked the Judge and left the courthouse. He had a lot of running around to do to meet the Judge's 3:30 deadline.

Tommy and Donna woke up Tuesday morning. They had slept in her parents' bed. "I have to get to work," said Tommy. "Old Pete will have a fit if I don't show up for my shift."

"What about your back?" Donna asked.

"I'll deal with it. Everything should be fine. Brad can do the lifting today." Tommy quickly had a shower. Donna replaced the gauze on her boyfriend's back. "I'll come back here when I'm finished with work."

"Okay," said Donna. Billy's bedroom door was still closed as Tommy walked down the hallway. "Take Dad's car. The keys are in the bowl at the front door."

"Thank you, sweetie. I'm going to have to call my insurance company and get the claim going on the Jeep. Do you have a copy of the paperwork the cops gave you with your statement?"

"In my purse," said Donna as she came down the hall in her mother's bathrobe.

"Got it," said Tommy. "I love you. See you around six tonight."

Donna ran to the door. She kissed Tommy deeply. "I love you too. Have a good day."

Tommy drove to the mill, parking in the employee lot. He noticed a state trooper's car parked close to the main office. Brad's truck was in its usual spot in the lot. Tommy made his way into the employee staff room. He grabbed his employee time card to punch in. The time on the clock of the machine read 7:52am. Tommy shook his head. After everything he had been through on the weekend, he had managed to make it to work on time.

Brad walked into the staff room. "How did you sleep?" he asked.

"Okay," said Tommy. "Donna is really worried about things and was up several times."

"Old Pete wants to talk to us," said Brad. "He is waiting in his office."

"Okay," said Tommy. "Is something wrong?"

Tommy followed his childhood friend into Pete's office. Tommy entered first, followed by Brad, who closed the door behind him. Two state troopers stood

beside Pete's desk while Pete sat in his worn-out leather chair. "These men have some things to tell you," said Old Pete.

Tommy stood looking at everyone. He looked at Brad. "What is going on?" he asked, puzzled.

One of the troopers spoke up. "We have found your Jeep," said one of the troopers. "It was found outside a room at the Wheel Inn Motel."

"I know where that is," said Tommy.

The trooper continued, "Do you have any idea how it got there?"

Tommy shrugged his shoulders. "All I can tell you is that someone slugged my girlfriend up at the staging area for Rock Lake. He stole the keys then took off in my car."

"Yes," said the other trooper, "we have a report from your girlfriend. According to your friend here, you were attacked by a bear and were flown to the hospital with your father."

"That is correct," said Tommy. "What is going on here?"

"Son, your jeep was found in the parking lot outside a room where a woman was murdered. Do you know anyone named Barbara?" asked the trooper.

"Sorry," said Tommy, "no, I do not." Both troopers nodded their heads.

"We have something else," said the larger of the two officers.

"What?" said Tommy. "What the hell is going on here?"

"Tell him," said Old Pete. "You have asked your

questions, now tell him what you are here for."

Tommy looked at Old Pete. "Son," said one of the troopers, "the helicopter your father was flying in yesterday crashed. Search and rescue reported there were no survivors. We have no further details at this time. We tried to contact you last night, but there was no one at your address."

"No," said Tommy, "I was at my girlfriend's. My dad, he said my dad is dead?"

"There were no survivors," said the trooper. "We still do not know the full details."

Tommy's knees felt weak. He looked at Brad, "Did you know?" he asked.

"I just found out when I got to work," said Brad. "I told these guys you were at Donna's last night, and you would be in this morning."

Tommy looked at everyone in the room, tears started to well up in his eyes. "Forensics is going through your jeep," said one of the troopers. "We will let you know when we have completed our investigation so you can pick it up."

"Thank you," said Tommy.

The troopers left Pete's office. Brad put his arm around his buddy's shoulder. "I am sorry," he said. "Your father was one hell of a man." Tears ran down Tommy's cheeks.

"Take some time off," said Pete. "Come back in a week. Your job will still be here."

"No," said Tommy, "I need to work to keep my mind off of things."

"Are you sure?" asked Pete. Tommy nodded his

head.

Brad and Tommy walked out of Pete's office. "I am so sorry to hear about your father," said Brad. "They told me not to say anything, just bring you into Pete's office."

Tommy looked at Brad. "I understand, but I would not have said a word if you told me."

"I know," said Brad. "Let's have a coffee in the staff room before we head outside." Tommy nodded his head; he was still processing everything he had been told.

"I can't do it," said Tommy. "I just cannot stay here. I need to go see Donna and tell her in person what has happened to Dad." Tommy left the table then walked back to Old Pete's office. "I have to go," said Tommy.

Pete nodded his head. "Okay, son," he said. "Don't worry about this place." Tommy headed out to the employee parking lot. He jumped into Donna's father's car. Tears welled up in his eyes. He finally lost it and began sobbing like a baby. Tommy's mother and father were dead. He felt alone and empty.

Chapter 122

Todd Sterling made it back to the courthouse at 2:45pm with barely enough time to compose himself before presenting his new documents to Judge White. The judge had had a long day and was in no mood for misfiled paperwork by a sloppy attorney. Sterling's case was recalled at exactly 3:01pm.

Judge White spoke first. "We are here to determine if Attorney Todd Sterling has a claim against... a deceased individual's property, a Mrs. Elli May." Todd Sterling asked if he could approach the bench as he waved copies of official death certificates in his right hand.

White spoke in a firm voice. "If you have more documents for the court to review, you may hand them to the clerk." Judge White motioned with his right hand. Sterling stepped forward, the clerk snapped the documents from Sterling's hand, then walked calmly towards the judge. The judge reached over his bench as the clerk placed the paperwork in his right hand. Judge White adjusted his reading glasses on his nose. He reviewed the documents then cleared his throat.

"I now have everything I need to render my decision," said White. "Son," he said to Sterling. "I worked in the public defender's department for five years before starting my own practice. Sometimes things just work out the way they do. You may feel like you are entitled to extra money. However, I find that the amount of time you spent assisting Elli May's niece," he fumbled through the documents, "a Miss Nancy May does not give you a claim to the entire estate. There is a sister involved here, incarcerated or not."

Sterling's stomach sank. The judge was going to rule against his claim. "However," said Judge White. "I am very familiar with Elli's Diner. I have eaten there many times. We do not want that landmark shut down. Therefore, I appoint you as custodian of Elli's Diner and residence until such time that the sister who is incarcerated is released or you find a buyer for the business and personal property. If you want to earn more money than you are entitled to as a public defender, you are going to have to work for it. You are now in charge of making sure that business stays running, and the residence is maintained. You may submit a billing to the court every thirty days for your time looking after things. Upon review of the monthly financials for the diner, the court will determine if your billing statements can be paid. Congratulations, and good luck. You may pick up a copy of my decision from the clerk's office at 3:30pm." White hit his gavel on the wooden block sitting beside the blotter on his desk. "Court is adjourned for the day."

Sterling looked stunned. The last thing he wanted was to be responsible for running a business. He thought everything was going to be cut and dry. After all, he had his client fill out the paperwork the public defender's office used all the time. Sterling made his way to the clerk's office. He requested a copy of the judge's decision. Sterling placed the documents into his briefcase. He walked out to his car, then got inside. He rolled down his window, and his cellphone rang. The office was calling. Some guy was in jail; his wife had been murdered in a cheap motel room, and he needed a lawyer.

Chapter 123

Maria Hernandez had not heard from her lover in two days. She was getting worried that something had happened to Jackson Hall. She opened the Locate A Phone app on her cell. Jackson's phone did not appear to be on or working. There was no indication of his location, and it was not sending a signal. She then remembered the GPS tracking tag Jackson had placed in one of the boxes stored in the basement of the casino. Wherever the money was, Jackson had to be with it. The tracking device was one of those units people used to track down their parents who had dementia and got lost. So long as the tag was in a cellphone service area, the signal could be pinpointed.

Maria switched over to the Find Me Safely app that Jackson had loaded on her phone. The app zeroed in on the town of Hillcrest. Maria expanded the screen with her fingers. The flashing red dot was stationary. Now Maria knew something was seriously wrong. Jackson said he was heading home two days ago. She hated the thought of him getting into trouble again. Maria had a good thing going with the surf shop and looking after the books for the Blades. She also loved Jackson.

Maria knew why Jackson had gone to Hillcrest. He had unfinished business with his old partner, and he needed to get to Robbins so Jackson could access his key to gain entry to the vault at the casino. There was one hundred million waiting. Jackson and Maria had a beautiful spot picked out in Mexico where no one would ever bother them again. Maria was aware of everything.

Maria called her younger brother, Carlos. "I am worried about Jackson."

"Why?" asked Carlos.

"He should have been home yesterday," she said.

"Where is he?" Carlos asked. Maria said that he had gone to meet an ex-business partner. Carlos listened as his sister gave him the basics. She did not want to tell him too much, as Carlos could make things difficult for Maria and Jackson if he ever found out about the one hundred million.

"Where are you?" asked Carlos.

"At the surf shop," was Maria's reply.

Carlos agreed to meet Maria within the hour so they could discuss things further. Maria called Calmer Air in Modesto. She needed to charter a plane into Hillsboro. Maria spoke directly to Arthur Anderson. "Can you get me to Hillsboro?" asked Maria.

"How soon do you want to leave?" asked Anderson.

"As soon as I get to the airport."

"The company's Lear 45 Jet was just back from a client's trip to Mexico. It will be fueled and ready to go as soon as you get here."

"How much will that cost?" asked Maria.

"We will discuss that later," said Arthur. "You make sure you take care of your business, then we will worry about my compensation later."

Maria convinced her brother to fly with her to Hillsboro. They would then rent a car upon their arrival and drive to Jackson's location. Maria turned the sign around on the door to the surf shop to read 'closed', then locked the front door. It took her and Carlos one hour and twenty minutes to make it to Calmer Air's hangar in

Modesto. Maria and Carlos walked into the office of Calmer Air. They were greeted by two pilots.

"Hello," said Maria. The pilots asked if she was the friend of Arthur. Once formalities were out of the way, Maria and Carlos were escorted out the back of the building to the waiting Lear.

Carlos smiled and spoke to his sister as they boarded. "I feel like a millionaire," he said.

Maria sat directly across from her brother. "You never know," she said, "maybe someday you will be one."

The door was closed on the jet. The pilot had informed Maria the flight time into Hillsboro would be one hour and twenty-five minutes once they left the ground. The pilots had filed a flight plan at an altitude of 47,000 feet, well above all regular commercial traffic. They pulled out onto the runway, hit the throttles, and were off.

"This is air traffic control, have a great flight, Calmer Air."

Chapter 124

Todd Sterling had his marching orders. The judge had ensured that Elli May's estate was going to be looked after until things could get sorted out. Sterling sat in his car, reviewing Judge White's orders. The sister that was in prison was now the rightful heir. She would not even be aware of the events surrounding Elli's death. It would be up to Sterling to bring her up to speed.

Todd had just finished handling his latest public defender case. Some local named Walter Wood had been charged with the murder of his wife, Barbara Wood. Her body had been found at the Wheel Inn. The cops knew her husband had been there earlier in the day. They had Barbara's own testimony. Walter had been in trouble with the law before. He had been arrested later in the day at a local watering hole. His truck was sitting right out in the middle of the parking lot for all the world to see.

Sterling had argued before the judge that if his client had actually killed his wife, would he not be in hiding? He would not have left his truck out where the cops and everyone could see it. Judge Parks set bail at one hundred and fifty thousand dollars. Ten percent had to be paid upfront. Walter smiled. He had the cash he had taken from Barbara's purse in the hotel room less what he had spent on his beer and wings. That would still leave him a few bucks when his bail was posted. Sterling had Walter sign off on some paperwork so he could access his personal belongings that were on Walter's person when he was arrested. Sterling took fifteen thousand out of the brown envelope marked "Wood, Prisoner 6943." Sterling posted the bail, allowing his client the freedom he required to prove his innocence.

Sterling finished reviewing Judge White's order. It was clear that Todd Sterling was running things for Elli's estate. He decided it was best to head over to Elli's Diner and introduce himself to the management and staff. Sterling pulled into the parking lot of the diner. He walked through the main entrance. Behind the front counter stood a young lady.

"Table for one?" she asked. The dining room was full.

"No," said Sterling. "Can I speak to the manager who is on?"

"Well, the manager, owner, is Elli, but she has not been in for the last two days. However, Enrique, our main cook, is in the back. He looks after things when Elli is not feeling well."

"May I speak to Enrique?" Sterling said, handing the young lady his business card.

"One moment," she said, and disappeared into the kitchen. She came back out one minute later.

"He is too busy," she said. "If you want to talk to him, he said you can go into the kitchen. He has a lot of meals to get out to the dining room."

"Lead the way," said Todd. The girl escorted Sterling through the kitchen door. There were two cooks busy preparing meals for the customers out in the dining room. A large wheel with written orders sat above the opening in the wall. Plates were put up on the shelf. The cook would ring a bell, placing the written order under the plate. The system had worked flawlessly for over forty years.

Sterling walked over to the older of the two cooks. "Enrique?" asked Sterling.

The older cook looked up. "What can I do for you?" asked Enrique.

"My name is Todd Sterling. I am a public defender for the state. I have some terrible news for you and the staff here."

"What is wrong?" asked Enrique.

"It's about Elli," he said. "She passed away. Choked on a chocolate chip cookie."

"What?" asked Enrique.

"She passed away."

"Oh my God," said Enrique, in a thick Mexican accent. "What about Nancy? How is Nancy doing? She is like her Aunt's own child."

"I am sorry," said Sterling. "Nancy May is also deceased. She was found in her garage at home." Sterling did not go into the details. "Judge White has issued some paperwork. It will allow us to keep running Elli's Diner until we can get everything straightened out."

Sterling fumbled for the paperwork he was carrying. "I can't believe what you say to me," Enrique said, his eyes starting to well up with tears. "Nancy was just here on Sunday. She and her Aunt carried some boxes outside to the old car. They were so close. When Elli left on Sunday, she was so happy. What are we going to do? Who will make sure we get paid?"

"That is my job," said Sterling. "Is there a photocopier here?"

"Si," said Enrique. "In the office. Do you want to tell the staff, or should I?"

"I will tell everyone," said Enrique, "after they finish their shifts."

"That is a good idea," said Sterling. "You will make sure the diner stays open, run things as usual."

"Si, si, no problem," said Enrique, as he wiped the tears from his cheeks, flipping the burgers in front of him. "Si... business as usual."

Sterling found his way to the back office. It was a mess. There was paperwork everywhere. He photocopied the judge's order, granting him custodianship of Elli's business and personal home. He then posted everything on the back of the office door. Todd sat in Elli's chair behind her desk. He started to fumble through some of the invoices on her desk. Most were past due. Sterling sat back in the chair. He opened the top drawer of the desk. Pens, paper, blank name tags, and a bundle of keys slid around as the drawer stuck slightly while it was opened. Todd grabbed the bundle of keys. He assumed they were Elli's.

Todd walked back into the kitchen. "Enrique, I have left the paperwork for you on the back of the office door. These keys, are they for the restaurant?"

"Si, si," said Enrique, "they are Miss Elli's."

Sterling placed the keys in his suit pocket. "What happens with the deposits at the end of the day?"

"I show you," said Enrique. He stepped away from the grill momentarily. He opened the freezer door. He stepped inside, then picked up a wooden box from the floor. He lifted the lid. The day's receipts from Sunday, plus a bag of cash, half-filled the box. "This is all of Sunday," said Enrique. He handed the box to Todd.

"You just leave everything here?" said Sterling.

"Si," said Enrique. "We lock all the doors and go home. Miss Elli looks after the rest."

Todd placed the box back on the floor from where Enrique had removed it. "Business as usual," said Sterling. "I will let you get back to work." Todd took the bundle of keys from his pocket. He fumbled around until he found the key for the freezer door. "Anyone else have a key for this door?"

"Just me, Señor Sterling, just me."

"Very well," said Todd. Sterling made his way out of the kitchen. He walked around, trying different keys in different locks. He was getting a handle on his surroundings. Todd walked to the back of the diner. Tucked in the corner of the rear parking lot was an old, beat-up Camaro. The old expired license plates read "Elli 1." Sterling estimated it to be from the mid-seventies. Its paint was blistered, it was rusted, and the four tires were flat. The car was an eyesore. "More shit I have to deal with."

Todd walked over to the car. He tried the door handles. The doors were locked. Todd rubbed the dirt off the driver's window. He peered inside. He was looking at old boxes marked with the word "receipts" and "year." Todd fumbled through the bundle of keys. He looked and then saw two that had "GM" stamped into them. Todd was familiar with this type of key. His father had owned a Camaro similar when he was just a boy. One key had a square end, and one had a rounded end. Todd chose the rounded end. He placed the serrated end of the key into the door lock and turned it. Todd pulled up on the door handle. The driver's door opened. The smell of mice, urine, and shit permeated his nostrils. "Damn it." He was looking at boxes that were marked twenty years ago and had long since been forgotten. Sterling shook his head. He locked the door, then closed it, walking away from the car. "Fuck," he said to himself out loud. He turned, then walked back to the trunk of the car. Fighting low-

hanging tree branches, Todd inserted the same round key into the lock of the trunk. It snapped open. Todd lifted the lid. What looked like two brand new boxes lay in the trunk. The tape on the upper flaps had been cut open. Sterling lifted one flap and looked into the box. All he could see were one hundred dollar bills. All were bundled together with paper bands that said "ten thousand dollars." Todd looked into the second box. It was exactly the same. Both were full of cash. Sterling quickly closed the trunk. He smiled. The old lady that owned the place had been using the trunk of this car as her personal bank. Forty-some years of business had created quite a little nest egg.

Sterling walked around the front of the diner. He got into his car and drove to the back parking lot. Sterling pulled in beside the old Camaro. Todd opened his trunk. He then opened the Camaro's. Sterling looked around and when he felt no one was watching, he transferred the two boxes of cash into his car. He closed both trunks. Todd Sterling climbed into his car, driving out of Elli's parking lot. He drove out of town past the taped-off Mountain View service station. The smell of the burned-out business washed through the air vents in his car. "Jesus," he said aloud. "The garbage stinks here in town."

Chapter 125

The manhunt in Hillcrest for Johnny Robbins had been shut down. The Sheriff's department still had an APB out. The FBI had put Robbins on their most wanted list. The dragnet that had been thrown around Hillcrest had failed to turn up the criminal. The Deputy's car that had been stolen and burned had been examined for any evidence that might have escaped the fire. Robbins' prints were all over the interior of the Mustang on the Interstate. Johnny was wanted for murder in the first degree. There was also the matter of the Trooper's sidearm. It was missing. The authorities assumed Robbins had it. So the APB said "considered armed and dangerous."

Robbins had slipped through the roadblocks somehow. His picture was all over the news. "If you see this man, do not approach. Call 911 immediately," said the reporters. It did not matter which station you turned to; Johnny was in the news.

Donna had just made breakfast for Billy. She flipped through the local stations. Hillcrest and what happened on the weekend was the lead story. She started to cry; everything was just starting to sink in. Donna had called into the Library. She explained what had happened to her boss and said she would need a couple of days before returning to work. The best thing about living in a small town was that information traveled fast. Her boss was aware of the news regarding Donna's family. "Take as much time as you need, sweetheart. We have things covered here." Donna felt better after she ended the call.

Donna heard her father's car pull into the

driveway. She looked out the window to see Tommy heading towards the side door. Donna walked through the kitchen. She opened the door to meet Tommy. One look at his face, and she knew something was terribly wrong. Tommy looked Donna in the eyes. He started to sob. "My father is dead."

"What?" said Donna. "How is that possible?"

"The Sheriffs were waiting at work to tell me. The helicopter they were in yesterday afternoon went down."

"How the hell is that possible?" asked Donna.

"I don't know," said Tommy. "All I know is Search and Rescue had reported that there were no survivors. That is all I know."

"We have to call someone," said Donna. "There is just so much that does not make any sense. So many things that happened this weekend. It just seems to be all tied together somehow. The news, I have been watching the news. It is on every channel. My brother escaped from prison with this guy they are looking for, this Johnny Robbins guy." Donna used the remote until his picture flashed on the screen. "See! There is a woman in the hospital. She claims that Robbins and my brother attacked her and her husband. Her son's plane crashed, and he was killed, his body burned in the wreckage."

Tommy's mind cleared for several moments. "That face is the guy they are looking for?" Tommy asked. "Just before dad's helicopter crashed, I am sure I saw that face through the window of the helicopter."

"He is the guy who hit me in the parking lot," said Donna. "We need to tell someone."

Donna picked up the phone. She called the local number for the FBI. She asked for Agent Miller. There

was a pause on the line as her call was forwarded to Miller's cellphone. It automatically went to voicemail. "This is Miller, leave a message." Donna left her message, saying that she and Tommy might have some important information regarding their investigation.

Tommy and Donna waited an hour. They consoled each other. Donna was getting tired of waiting. She called the FBI office again. "I have very important information," she said to the operator.

"We have had a very busy weekend," said the operator. "Agent Miller will return your call as soon as he can."

Donna was fed up. "We have something to say that someone needs to know." She called Hillcrest News and asked to speak to her cousin, Christie Mathews. Within an hour, Christie sat in the living room of Donna's parents' home. The interview took about two hours. "Thank you, cousin," said Donna. "Both Tommy and I think the story needs to be told."

"Watch the news at 6:00," said Christie. She hugged Donna, then exited the house with her cameraman.

Chapter 126

Maria Hernandez and her brother arrived at Hillsboro Airport. The Learjet touched down almost exactly as scheduled. Maria had tried calling her father, Jesus, but there had been no answer. Maria and Carlos stepped off the plane. As they walked towards the chain-link fence close to the airport's small restaurant, Maria noticed a damaged golf cart up against the fence. Two men of Spanish descent stood on the other side of the gate, tattoos covered their arms and necks. Both wore blue denim shirts with the sleeves cut off. One of the men waved to Maria. She waved back and said to Carlos, "That is our ride."

The two men were lifelong members of the Blades. They had been retired out to Hillsboro along with Maria's father, Jesus. The Blades always looked after their members. That is what made the gang so strong in the first place. As members got older, they were shipped off to communities where they did not have to worry about who was looking for them around the next corner. As the gang and membership got larger, more and more money flowed into the accounts Maria managed. Her father had made sure his men were always going to be well-cared for. They received an allowance every month, courtesy of all the criminal activity the younger members brought in. Everything was funneled through Maria. The surf shop had worked out to be the best cover. Hardly any of their daily clients used credit cards. The business was mostly cash. When blended with the daily take from stolen property, drug, and gun sales, Maria had managed to make things look legit over the years. Any of the Blades retired and receiving their allowance always had loyalty to the Blades. It did not matter how old they were.

If a call came in, they were to assist, no matter what. It was part of the code. Maria's father had implemented the plan when he was running things. It was perfect. It kept everyone loyal to the gang; no one wanted to lose their monthly allowance. In all the years, there had never been a rat. No one ever turned in another member. Maria had made sure she stuck to the original pledge her father had promised all the original members.

Bruno and Daniel had been lifelong members from the time they were twelve years old and jumped in by Maria's father. They were both now in their late sixties. The four adults climbed into the white van Daniel had borrowed for this occasion. "Good to see you, Maria," said Bruno. "You must be Carlos. I am Bruno, and this is Daniel. Where to?"

Maria handed Daniel her cellphone. The app that showed Jackson Hall's location flashed on the screen. "There," said Maria. The signal indicated a location between Hillsboro and Hillcrest. It was a storage facility.

"I know the place," said Daniel. "It's one of those storage places, the ones with the roll-up doors. Someone put it up a few years ago. It's a big place, surrounded by a chain-link fence."

"Good," said Maria. "I have not been able to reach my father. How is he doing?"

"I saw him on Wednesday last week. We talked about the old days, had a beer and some wings while we watched some playoff hockey."

Maria nodded her head. "Have you been receiving your money okay?" she asked both men.

"Every month like clockwork, thank you," said Daniel.

The white van pulled out of the parking lot at the

airport. "It will take about a half-hour to get there," said Bruno. Maria tipped her head back, then closed her eyes. The day's events were starting to catch up with her.

Chapter 127

Donald, the owner of Glacier Tours, circled over his downed helicopter. He watched as the search and rescue chopper left the area with Chris and Braden suspended below its belly. Three men started to scramble up the hill, then over a small ridge that hid the crash site of the downed tour helicopter. The three search and rescue members walked towards the burned-out Glacier One helicopter. The smell of burned plastic and burned flesh permeated the air as they got closer.

The three men walked around to the front of the burned-out wreck. The two bodies still in their seats were unrecognizable. Their lips had burned away, exposing the whites of their teeth. Their burnt clothing, what was left of it, clung to blackened skin. Sections of their skin had split open, exposing raw flesh underneath. The fire had been intense, burning out quickly as its supply of fuel dissipated.

Charles, the lead rescue member, noticed what was left of a camera beside the body in the back seat. The body in the pilot's seat had what was left of a large tree branch piercing its torso. "Fuck, what a mess," said Charles. He needed to confirm for his own curiosity who it was in the back seat. He had a good idea but needed to know for sure.

Charles reached into his emergency pack and removed two blue latex gloves. Placing them on his hands, Charles stood outside the wreck beside the body in the back seat. He used a broken tree branch to push the body onto its side. The process of moving it ruptured the burnt skin around the stomach area. Internal organs and fluid spilled forth like a raw poached egg. The two other

search members turned away, then proceeded to vomit. The bottom of the pants that clung to the body were scorched but still recognizable.

Charles reached into the left rear pocket and removed a leather billfold. Chuck stood away from the helicopter and opened the leather folder. Recessed in the right side of the wallet was a silver badge that read "Parks" and the name "Superintendent." On the left side were the singed remains of the official certificate issued by the Government parks branch that said "Robert Gerrard."

Charles turned to his men. "It's Superintendent Gerrard," he said. "Betty is going to go out of her mind. We need to make arrangements to get these two out of here."

Chapter 128

Todd Sterling's head was spinning as he left Hillcrest. He had never seen that amount of cash, not even when he had to represent some of the local drug dealers in town. The amount of cash they were busted with did not compare to what was in Todd's trunk. Sterling got onto the interstate, heading north. He needed to figure out what he was going to do with all those one hundred dollar bills. How many did he have? His mind was racing.

Maria Hernandez, her brother Carlos, and the two retired Blades made their way towards the storage facility. "There it is," said Daniel. "See, I told you it was in the middle of nowhere." The van pulled into the parking lot of Ponderosa Storage. The entire yard was surrounded by a chain-link fence. There was one of those large electronic gates that rolled back and forth, allowing clients to access their units. There was a pin pad to the left of the entrance. To the right, a small blue building stood, its white door gleaming in the sunlight. Above the door, an official-looking sign read, "Office. Manager on duty 24/7." Attached to the sliding gate were two signs that read, "BEWARE GUARD DOGS ON DUTY."

The van came to a stop in front of the office door. Maria looked at her phone with the location app open, showing they were one hundred yards from Jackson's location. "He is here," she said aloud. "Look, we are so close." She held her phone up in front of Carlos. "How are we going to get in there?"

"Don't worry," said Daniel. "I have an idea." He stepped out of the van and made his way into the office. Daniel walked up to the front counter. The smell of

cooking bacon permeated the air. A small silver bell sat on the counter, and a sign beside it said, "Ring bell for service." Daniel proceeded to tap the bell.

A moment later, the manager, Ernie Wilson, appeared from the back room. "Can I help you?" he asked.

Daniel spoke, "I would like to rent a unit," he said, fumbling with a brochure he had taken from the display.

"What size are you looking for?" asked Ernie.

"Ten by twenty," said Daniel.

Ernie looked at all the tattoos on Daniel's arms and neck. He had sized up many individuals since he and his wife opened the storage facility. Ernie knew when and how to ask the right questions. "That's one of our most popular sizes," said Ernie. "Seems a lot of folks own too much stuff these days and have no place to keep it." Daniel smiled while he looked at six color TV monitors that pointed down each aisle of the outdoor facility. In the upper corner of the office, a camera recorded people coming and going from the office.

Ernie had to be in his mid-sixties or so. He fumbled around on the computer for a minute. "Can you excuse me," he said, "just for a second? I left my bacon on the stove. My wife left ten minutes ago, headed into town, so I am fending for myself."

"Sure," said Daniel.

Ernie walked through the doorway that led to the married couple's private residence.

"I will be right back." Ernie walked to the stove. He removed the frying pan from the glowing element. He was looking forward to a nice meal of his maple

bacon and eggs. His wife, Valerie, always nagged him about how much he would eat. Today he was not going to have to listen to any of that. It was going to be a peaceful lunch. Ernie turned to head back to the business counter so he could look after his new client. In front of him stood Daniel. "What the hell?" said Ernie, pushing Daniel away from him.

"I wish you had not done that," said Daniel.

"What are you doing back here?" yelled Ernie. "This area is private."

"No one touches me," said the former Blade. Daniel pulled out one of those retractable razor knives from his back pocket. He moved his thumb along the black slide, exposing the blade to its full length. Ernie reached for the frying pan; its hot grease and bacon slid around as Ernie threw the contents towards Daniel's face. Daniel yelled as the hot grease burned his eyes, his exposed skin blistered. The partially cooked bacon hit the floor. Daniel lunged towards Ernie. The bacon and grease now on the floor caused Daniel to slip and crash to the ground.

Ernie moved quickly to the utility drawer beside the stove. He opened it with the speed of an attacking rattlesnake. His thirty years of service with the SEALS had taught him a thing or two. Before Daniel could get off the floor, Ernie was pointing his old 9mm directly at Daniel's chest. "My eyes!" screamed Daniel, his skin was now heavily blistered.

"Don't move a muscle!" said Ernie, as he kicked the razor knife across the kitchen floor. "Don't you fucking move!" Ernie reached for the portable phone on the wall, then dialed 911. "I need the cops!" Ernie shouted to the operator. "Someone just tried to kill me. Yes, that is correct, Ponderosa Storage. I have my gun

on him right now."

"The sheriffs should be there in minutes," said the operator. "Do not hang up."

Daniel heard the conversation with the operator. With his past and what had just taken place, he could not be there when the cops showed up. Daniel started to get up. "Don't move!" shouted Ernie, the phone in his left hand. "Don't move! I will shoot!" said Ernie. Daniel shouted more profanities at Ernie. His shirt was covered in grease. "I said do not move!" yelled Ernie. "I will shoot you!" The recording equipment in the 911 office was capturing every word. Daniel lunged in the direction of the voice in front of him. Two shots rang out. Ernie watched as Daniel's body and the spent shell casings fell to the floor. The two rounds had hit just to the left of the center mass just as Ernie had been trained. The bullets ripped through Daniel's heart. He was dead before he hit the floor.

"What the hell was that!?" yelled Maria.

"We got trouble!" shouted Bruno, as he reached for the glove box. By the time he had his gun in his hand, Ernie stood in the entrance of the office, his nine-millimeter pointed at the driver through the van's windshield.

Ernie could see the driver had a gun in his hand. He fired twice more. The bullets pierced the windshield and entered Bruno's chest. The deflection off the glass had changed their trajectory just slightly. Bruno took three or four more breaths before the gun he held dropped to the floor of the van. Broken glass and blood were everywhere as Carlos scrambled for the gun.

Ernie ran to the side of the van and watched through the side window as Carlos sat upright with the

black 9 mm in his hand. Two more shots rang out. Both hit Carlos; one of the rounds went through his body and entered Maria's chest, puncturing her right lung. Ernie slid open the side door of the van as broken glass fell everywhere. He realized then he still held the cordless house phone in his left hand.

Ernie looked at the carnage in the van. Carlos was slumped forward against the back of the passenger seat. He watched as Maria struggled to catch her breath. Blood covered her blouse. Maria lifted her right hand, and Ernie saw something black. It glistened as she moved. Ernie fired one more shot, believing Maria was raising a gun. The bullet hit Maria center mass. Her body jerked once then lay still. Ernie watched as Maria's cellphone dropped onto the seat beside her. The operator was yelling into the phone, "Sir? Sir! Are you okay?"

Ernie held the phone up to his ear. "Hello," he said.

The operator asked, "Sir, are you okay?"

"Fucking punks," said Ernie. "These fucking punks." Ernie could hear the sounds of the sheriff's cars' sirens in the distance.

"They are almost there," said the operator.

"I can hear them," said Ernie. Ernie reached into the van. He removed Maria's cellphone. When he turned it over and looked at the screen, a blue dot flashed: "300 feet to your destination." Ernie slid the cellphone into his back pocket. "They are here," said Ernie, as two sheriff's cars screeched to a stop in front of his office.

"Drop your gun!" yelled one of the sheriffs as he hid behind his door. "Drop it!"

Ernie placed his gun on the roof of the van. He shouted back at the cops. "They are all dead!"

701

"Put the phone down, sir!" the cops shouted.

"I am going to hang up now!" Ernie said to the operator.

"Go ahead," she said. "We have recorded everything, sir. The sheriffs will look after you."

Ernie hung up and put the phone next to the gun on the roof of the van. "Sir, put your hands on your head, turn around, and walk backward towards my voice!" shouted one of the sheriffs.

Ernie complied with the instructions. His mind was starting to clear, and the adrenaline was leaving his system. "I am Ernie Wilson!" he shouted to the cops. "My wife and I own this place."

"Get on your knees!" shouted one of the sheriffs. Ernie dropped to his knees. "Hands behind your back, sir!" Ernie placed his hands behind him. One of the sheriffs walked towards Ernie with his gun pointed directly at Ernie's skull.

"You got him?" shouted the one sheriff to the other.

"Got him!" The second sheriff had stepped out from behind his door. His gun now pointed at Ernie's head to protect his partner as the second sheriff placed handcuffs on Ernie's wrists. "Stand up," said the sheriff. Ernie complied as the sheriff helped him to his feet. "Sir," said the sheriff, "the cuffs are only temporary. My partner and I need to figure out what is going on here. You understand it's for our safety."

"Yes," said Ernie.

"Thank you for complying," said the sheriff. "Do you have any ID, sir?"

"Not on me. It's on my nightstand in the

bedroom."

One of the sheriffs entered the business and then the private residence. He found Ernie's wallet just where he said it would be. The officer opened the wallet. The driver's license verified Ernie's claim as to who he was. The officer stepped out of the front door of the business and walked over to Ernie, then released him from the handcuffs. The officer handed Ernie his wallet.

"What the hell happened?" asked both sheriffs.

Ernie rubbed both his wrists. "Fucking punks," he said. "I have seen this type before. One of them was going to kill me in my kitchen. Then the other three were going to shoot me."

The officers looked at the carnage in the van. One of the sheriffs radioed into dispatch. "Code 10-40, send investigators and a coroner. 10-4," said the sheriff's operator. "Have a seat, Mr. Wilson. This might take a while to straighten out."

Ernie walked over to the bench by the front door of his business. The flowers his wife, Valerie, had planted in the pots on either side were in full bloom. Ernie took a deep breath and then sat. Ernie looked around. Without knowing it, he had just dispatched four notorious members of the Blades gang, past and present. He took another deep breath and shook his head. He removed Maria's cellphone from his back pocket. It now said, "280 feet to your destination."

Chapter 129

Cathy woke up in her hospital bed on Tuesday morning. The sun was shining brightly through the window in her room. She stretched her arms out as far as they would go, then swung her legs over the side of the bed. She remembered that she was in the hospital but couldn't remember why. She felt fantastic. Her ear was a little sore, but other than that, she was in great spirits.

Cathy walked over to her washroom, lifted her hospital gown, and did her business. She was in the mood for a shower, so she turned the faucet on. She moved her hand under the stream of water that flowed from the showerhead above. When it was just the right temperature, Cathy let her gown drop to the floor and stepped into the enclosure. The water ran off her as it beaded up, and it felt wonderful. Cathy turned her back to the water, tilted her head back, and closed her eyes. Her hair hung down the back of her neck, clinging to her skin. Her nipples grew hard as the water and air combined to stimulate the flow of blood to specific parts of her body.

In the corner of the shower stall was a built-in dispenser with two buttons she could push. One was marked "Shampoo," and the other was marked "Body Wash." Cathy placed one hand under the dispenser and pushed the "Shampoo" button. A small circle of product dropped into her palm. "That's not enough," she said aloud. She pushed the button again, making sure there was enough shampoo in her palm. Cathy went to work lathering up her hair. When she was done, she tilted her head back, allowing the water to rinse the soapy water down her back. Cathy then reached for the body wash,

running her soap-covered hands over her body, between her legs, and her bottom. She kept her eyes closed, enjoying the sensation.

As she began to play with herself, her mind wandered, and flashes of Eric's face filled her thoughts. She was reaching a point where she was going to climax when other images started to flash in her mind. She could see Matt and Johnny's faces intertwined with flashes of Eric's as her fingers worked their magic. Cathy stopped, fell to the floor of the shower, and began sobbing. The water continued to run over her body.

A nurse unlocked Cathy's door. She entered with a food tray for breakfast and placed it on the portable table beside Cathy's bed. She could hear the water running behind the closed bathroom door. "Breakfast is ready!" the nurse shouted as she knocked on the door, but there was no answer. The nurse raised her voice and knocked harder. "Cathy, your breakfast is here!" Still, there was no response. The nurse tried the handle on the door and opened it ajar. The bathroom was full of nice warm steam, with moisture running down the mirror above the small white sink. "Cathy, your breakfast is ready," the nurse said, but there was still silence. The nurse entered the bathroom and pulled back the shower curtain. Cathy was curled up in a ball on the shower floor, rocking on her side, sobbing out loud. "Cathy!" the nurse said as she turned off the water. "Cathy, are you okay?" The nurse crouched down beside her patient. Cathy turned her head, her eyes looking hollow.

"I remember," said Cathy. "I remember everything. I was raped in my own home!"

The nurse helped Cathy to her feet and wrapped a towel around Cathy's torso.

"Here is one for your hair," said the nurse.

"I was raped!" said Cathy.

"I know, sweetheart," said the nurse. "I am so sorry."

Donna and Tommy were discussing the events of the weekend. The interview with Christie Mathews had gone well. There was a short three-minute segment on the six o'clock news about what the young adults had been through on the weekend. The focus of the story had been edited to highlight a Grizzly bear attacking Donna's boyfriend, Tommy. The camera focused as Tommy lifted the back of his shirt to show the blood-stained bandages on his back. There was no mention of Johnny Robbins or Donna being hit in the parking lot; all of that had been edited out of the story. The news director had decided they had enough from the authorities on the escaped convict, the death of a sheriff, and the burned-out Mountain View service station. They needed another story, so it became "Parks Department hunting a Large Grizzly in the Rock Lake area. Hikers are warned that all trails in the area are closed until further notice."

Donna was disappointed in how their story had been presented. The doorbell rang, and Donna stood up from the couch. She opened the front entrance, where a young man in his mid-thirties stood in the doorway.

"Donna Jones?" he asked.

"Yes," said Donna.

"I am Jack McLean with State Farm. I have some documents for you to sign."

"Please come in," said Donna. "Tommy, this is Jack McLean from the insurance company."

"Yes," said Tommy. "I heard. Please have a seat."

Chapter 130

The Chinook Sky Crane returned two hours later. The three search and rescue members had managed to remove the two bodies from the wreck, placing them in their respective black body bags. It was a horrendous job, as the bodies were being moved, the charred and burnt skin would pull away or crack. It was one of the worst scenes the three men had ever had to clean up. If the bodies had been left for another day, wildlife could have made quick work of the corpses.

The Sky Crane hovered overhead, and its rescue basket was lowered to the three men below. Both bodies were loaded and stacked together for the first lift. The basket was removed when the bodies were in the helicopter. The extra-long winch cable was lowered down. Both of the younger search and rescue members stepped into their safety harnesses, fastening the large rings of their harnesses to the winch hook. They were then raised to the hovering helicopter.

The cable was lowered a third time, with an empty harness attached. Charles Bailey unhooked the harness and stepped into it. He then fastened and adjusted the clips and hooked the large ring onto the winch cable. He took one last look at the crash site and lifted his right hand into the air, rotating it in a circle. The winch operator pressed the green button on the wall, and Bailey was pulled up and into the open sliding door of the helicopter. The rescue members had done their jobs, as gruesome as it was.

The pilot gained altitude and pointed the big helicopter towards Hillsboro. It would take them an hour, maybe a little more, to get back to the airport. Hillsboro

Traffic Control vectored the large helicopter to the search and rescue pad that was used strictly for emergencies. Waiting on the tarmac were two local ambulances.

As the helicopter touched down, the group of men noticed a familiar face sitting in the front seat of the first ambulance. Betty had been waiting for more news from the crew. It had been impossible for them to communicate with her while in the back of the Sky Crane or on the mountain. The big bird settled on the ground, and power to the rotors had been backed down to idle. The three search and rescue members helped the winch operator unload the two black body bags. The engines were then shut down completely on the Sky Crane.

Betty, sensing it was safe to get out of the ambulance, opened the passenger door. She ran over to the four men. "Where is he?" asked Betty. "Where is Robert?" The three search and rescue members cast their eyes toward the black body bags, then back at Betty. "No!" she yelled. "I need to see him." Betty collapsed to her knees, shouting Robert's name over and over as she reached for the zipper on the closest bag to her.

Charles Bailey reached for Betty's arm, moving it away. "No!" said Charles. "You do not want to open that!"

"But," said Betty, "I need--"

"No!" said Charles. "I am sorry, Betty, but Robert would want me to protect you, and that is what I am going to do!" Charles helped Betty to her feet, and she collapsed into his arms.

The ambulance attendants had removed their gurneys from the backs of their units. The two younger search and rescue members assisted in lifting the body

bags onto the waiting gurneys.

"Come on, Betty," said Charles, "I will drive you back to the station."

The ambulances left the tarmac with only lights flashing. It was a matter of respect, but there was no urgency in getting these two to the morgue.

Ernie Wilson had been dealing with the authorities for about three hours on his own when his wife, Valerie, pulled back into the parking lot of the storage facility. She was stopped halfway down the driveway by a sheriff's car blocking her way. Valerie stepped out of her car. "What is going on here?" she said. "That is my husband over there."

"Ma'am, we have a crime scene here. You cannot go any further."

"What do you mean, a crime scene?" she shouted. "Ernie!" Valerie shouted at the top of her lungs. Her husband got up from the bench he had been sitting on. Ernie walked towards his wife. "I am going to see my husband," she said, running past the deputy. The two met and embraced about seventy-five feet from the trooper's car. "What happened, honey?"

Punks," said Ernie. "These punks showed up. One of them got into the house. He was going to stab me."

"How many?" said Valerie.

"Four," said Ernie. "They are all dead."

"That's all," said Valerie, "just four? That's pretty light work for my SEAL." Ernie looked into his wife's eyes. She knew what he had been through while in the service. That is why their marriage had lasted forty-three years.

The coroner's wagon that had been up at Rock Lake the day before now sat in front of the business entrance of Ponderosa Storage. Pictures had been taken of the scene inside and outside the house. The van with the three bodies had been photographed. Each body had been fingerprinted on-site. The knife had been bagged from the kitchen floor, and the gun from the van was tagged, unloaded, and bagged for evidence.

When the four bodies were loaded into the coroner's van, the lead investigator approached Ernie. "We are pretty much finished here," said the investigator. "We have all the evidence we need. There will be no charges, Mr. Wilson. You had every right to defend yourself. We have two confirmed matches on some of our fingerprints. These were pretty badass dudes. Here is a card of someone you can call if things are bothering you."

Ernie shook the investigator's hand. "Thank you," said Ernie, looking at his watch. Four hours had gone by very quickly.

"There is still a bit of a mess in your kitchen. We have the HAZMAT crew coming to see you. They have been busy with the cleanup at Mountain View Service Station."

"I understand," said Ernie. "I heard it was quite a mess."

"A real mess," said the investigator. "Call us if you need anything."

"Again, thank you," said Ernie, as he took Valerie's hand and walked back towards their business. Valerie and Ernie stood at the office entrance as the authorities drove out of the parking lot. Ernie's gun had been taken for evidence, but he carried the portable

phone with him. "I am sorry, honey," he said. "It's a bit of a mess in the kitchen."

The two walked back into their private residence. Ernie hung the phone back into its cradle. Blood had pooled on the floor. It was thick and had dried along the edges, gelling in the middle. Ernie remembered the cellphone in his back pocket. He had taken it from Maria's hand. Ernie wanted to make sure the cops did not have any doubts when looking at the scene. By removing the cellphone, there was no mistaking what Ernie had told them. They all took turns reaching for the gun in the van. After all, the whole event had even been recorded by 911.

"What is that?" asked Valerie.

"One of the punks had it," said Ernie. As Ernie was about to show Valerie, the phone screen flashed, saying "low battery." Then the app re-opened. The blue dot flashed. It now said, "You are one hundred and sixty feet from your destination."

"What is this?" asked Valerie.

"It looks like some kind of tracking system," said Ernie. The two of them walked out the back door and into the storage yard. Ernie walked in the direction of the arrow on the screen, with Valerie following behind her husband. When they arrived in front of locker 225, the screen changed. It said, "You have arrived at your destination."

"We need to check to see who owns this locker," said Ernie. "Obviously, the punks were interested in what is inside."

Valerie went back into the office with her husband. She got onto the computer, logged in, and called up Locker 225. "Look here," she said. "That

locker was rented yesterday. I remember the two guys. They came in here around 3:00, paid cash for six months. Clean-cut fellows, driving a very large black van."

"What is the name and phone number?" asked Ernie.

"Jason Davis," said Valerie. Ernie dialed the phone number that Valerie gave him. The phone rang once, and an automated message came on, saying, "The number was no longer in service."

"Interesting," said Ernie. "Do you smell smoke?" He winked at Valerie.

"Yes, I do," she said. Ernie was now holding his cordless angle grinder in his right hand. The contracts that everyone signed when they leased space from Ponderosa Storage stipulated that the owners had the right to enter any rented locker or space in the event of a potential or ongoing emergency. Fire was on the top of the list, even though it might be an imaginary one. Ernie and Valerie made their way back to locker 225. Ernie went to work on the lock with his grinder. Sparks flew in different directions until the shackle finally gave way. The lock dropped to the ground, and Ernie slid the locking mechanism to the left. He then lifted the door, exposing the contents of locker 225.

The storage unit was filled with forty cardboard boxes, all exactly the same. It was an unusual sight. Normally, the boxes would be of all random sizes. Ernie had never seen anyone move or be in the process of moving and use all identical boxes. Ernie took the closest box to him off the top of the pile, slid his fingernail along the clear tape on the top of the box, and then ripped open the flaps. Both he and Valerie peered inside, finding neat bundles of one hundred dollar bills stacked inside the box.

"Look at that," said Ernie. "No wonder they wanted to get in here."

"You don't think that they are all like that?" said Valerie.

Ernie took another box down and opened it, finding it stacked exactly the same as the first. "Holy shit," said Valerie.

"It has to be drug money," said Ernie.

"What are we going to do?" asked Valerie.

"I know exactly what we are not going to do," said Ernie. He handed a box to Valerie and picked up the second box. He rolled the door closed, and the two of them walked back into their private residence. They made their way back into the office. Valerie emptied the contents of her box on the office desk and started to count the bundles of one hundred dollar bills. She counted two hundred bundles.

"There is two million dollars here," she said. "Do you think this is real? With that box, that is four million in cash."

Ernie smiled. "Do you remember that drug guy Escobar? He had so much cash he did not know what to do with it. Yes, honey, I believe it's all real."

"What are we going to do?" asked Valerie.

"I have a plan," said Ernie. "Take this money and put it in our company safe. I have work to do. Make sure you put the empty boxes in the burn barrel out back. Get rid of them."

Ernie walked past the blood-stained kitchen floor, shaking his head. "Fucking punks!" he shouted. Ernie walked outside into the sunlight, jumped into his old CASE backhoe, looked up to the sky, smiled, and

said out loud, "God bless you all!"

Chapter 131

Cathy had gotten dressed and finished her breakfast when the FBI entered her room. Two agents stood before her with Dr. Lewis off to their right.

"Cathy Taylor," said the closest agent to her, "I am charging you with the murders of Joann Jones and Susan Higgins."

"What are you talking about?" said Cathy. "Murder? Who are those people?"

"We have been instructed to advise you that you will remain here under the care of Dr. Lewis until such a time that you can be released into our custody to face criminal charges."

"What in the hell are you talking about?" Cathy yelled. "I want to speak to my husband. Where is Eric?" Cathy shouted to Dr. Lewis.

"Do you understand the charges as I have explained them?" asked the agent.

"No!" said Cathy. "I don't know what you are talking about."

"That is enough, gentlemen," said Dr. Lewis. "Please step out into the hallway. I will be with you in a moment."

Cathy sat down in her chair, breaking down sobbing. Dr. Lewis placed a hand on Cathy's shoulder. "It's okay, dear. We have a lot of work to do. Do not worry."

"I just do not understand," exclaimed Cathy. "Is someone going to tell me what is going on here?"

"We will get to that," said Dr. Lewis. "When it's the right time. Can you please excuse me for a few minutes? I have to speak to those gentlemen in the hallway." Dr. Lewis left Cathy's room so she could address the agents who were waiting for her.

"I told you gentlemen that she would not understand what you were saying. My patient has Traumatic Amnesia. She does not have a clue what you are trying to do. Her brain has blocked out all the events of the last four horrendous days. No one should have to deal with what she has been through."

Both agents nodded. It was a matter of formality that they explained to Cathy she was being charged. The law required that the attending physician be present so they could act as a witness. "Please sign here," said the FBI agent, handing Dr. Lewis his clipboard. As soon as Dr. Lewis signed off, the agents could move on to their next pressing case. Cathy would remain in the custody of Metro General and Dr. Lewis until such a time she was deemed fit to understand the charges she faced. Dr. Lewis handed the clipboard back to the agent after signing. She had been down this road before.

"Have a good day, gentlemen," she said as she turned her back and walked back into Cathy's room. Cathy sat in her chair, her mind continuing to search for something, but she would have a moment, and then there was nothing.

Betty was beside herself. Charles had kept her from seeing the man she had worked with and grown to love. Robert Gerrard now lay in the county morgue, along with two other Rangers. It had been a busy weekend for the two coroners on duty. Betty now had to arrange three funerals that the department would be responsible for. She also had a job to do, ensuring the

717

crash sites were cleaned up.

The area at Rock Lake needed to be opened up again as soon as possible for the general public. Betty had placed a call to Dan Thompson, asking him to meet her in the office first thing in the morning.

Dan arrived bright and early. He was actually there before Betty. He climbed the stairs to the office door, then used his key to enter the warden's headquarters. Papers were scattered on Betty's desk, and he walked over to the coffee maker, proceeding to make a full pot. Betty had spent the night in the Superintendent's Warden Quarters, alone. She lay in the bed she had shared with Robert and kept smelling his pillow until she could no longer stay awake. She managed to get an hour or two of sleep. When she walked through the front door of the office, she had dark circles under her eyes.

Dan walked over to Betty and gave her a large hug. Betty started to cry. "I am sorry," said Dan. "I know this is hard on you. Robert always kept things on a professional level, but I know he loved you."

Betty looked up into Thompson's eyes. "Thank you," she said. "We tried to keep our relationship quiet."

"Robert left something for you," said Betty. She walked over to her desk, opened her top drawer, and removed an envelope. Written on the front, in blue ballpoint pen, were the words: For Dan Thompson in the event of my death. "He wanted you to have this. Robert said it might help if something happened."

Dan could not contain himself any longer. Tears formed in his eyes and ran down his cheeks. Dan opened the envelope, and the letter read as follows:

"Dear Dan, if you are reading this, then I have

met my demise. I am giving this letter to Betty the day after you were promoted to Assistant Superintendent. I want you to know how proud I am of you. If anyone can make sure things continue to run the way we want them to, you can. After all, everything I know, I have shared with you, inside and outside of the job. Look after our park, do what you need to do to protect it. Keep it in your heart. She is now yours to run as you see fit. I have one final request. I know there have been rumors about Betty and me. Betty has been a very important assistant to me and also a close friend. That friendship blossomed into a romantic relationship, as you know. She is as close to me as a woman could be. I love her as much as being out in the wilderness with the smell of the damp pines filling my lungs. Please make sure you watch out for her. She will be going through a pretty rough patch. You are now the Superintendent. Good luck and all the best. Your friend, Robert Gerrard."

Dan Thompson held the letter in his hand. There would be formalities later with the State, but the succession plan had been laid out the day he had been promoted.

"Thank you, Betty," said Dan.

"What did the letter say?" she asked.

"That we have a lot of work to do," said Dan. "Are you feeling up to it?"

Betty nodded her head. "Call the men," said Dan. "I want you to arrange a meeting for noon. Then we have to get that damn helicopter off the mountain. We have things to clean up at Rock Lake and Angel Glacier. We need to prepare for the funerals. We have a park to run."

Donna and Tommy had finished with the insurance representative. He had handed Donna a slip of

paper that said the insurance company would pay $500,000 upon receipt of her mother's death certificate. Donna and Tommy sat looking at the numbers. Donna had never seen that amount of money in her life. All the problems she had encountered with her mother Joann over the years now amounted to dollars and cents.

"What are you going to do with all that?" asked Tommy.

"I don't know," said Donna. "I have to talk to the bank. I have to arrange to get the paperwork. Then there are the funerals, for Mom, Dad, and Matt. My head is just spinning."

Tommy had spoken to Betty about his father. She had confirmed that there had been a report that Gunner had not made it. Tommy was told the department would make arrangements for him to view his father's body. He also did not have to worry about paying for his funeral service. There would be a service for all four Rangers that lost their lives on the weekend. It would be a large affair. Never in the history of the parks service had four members died all within a day or two. It had been a totally unbelievable weekend. Betty had reassured Tommy she would keep him up to date as she got more information.

"What are you going to do?" asked Donna as she held Tommy's hand.

"I guess I will have to take it one day at a time. So long as I have you," said Tommy, "then I think I will be okay."

"Me too," said Donna.

Things had gotten quiet up at Rock Lake. The Grizzly responsible for the attacks on Susan, Rachel, David, Ranger Steve, and Chris had been scared off the

mountain by the large helicopter that had hovered over the Glacial tour crash site. It ambled down the Glacier Creek trail leading back to Rock Lake. The old bore sniffed the air as it made its way uninhibited by any human intervention toward the clear waters of the lake. The Grizzly walked along the pathway until finally reaching the old Trapper's cabin. Its nose told it that there was a kill close by. It walked by the side of the cabin, clawing at the leaves and sticks that once covered Rachel's body. It licked at the ground. Its food source was gone. There was a smell of human presence lingering on the foliage. The Grizzly huffed and stood on its hind legs. It looked over the area, making sure it had not missed anything. The Grizzly dropped down to all fours then made its way a little further along the pathway. The scent of humans was everywhere. But there was also something else. The Grizzly made its way to the water's edge, right to the very place that the sheriff's department had dragged Seamus and Shawn's bodies from the water.

The inflatable raft was pulled up on shore and had not moved from where it had been left. The bear sniffed around the rubber raft, with its front feet in the water. In the bottom of the raft were two partially eaten granola bars. The two young sheriffs who had fished Seamus and Shawn's bodies out of the lake could not finish their snacks once they saw the bodies of the two men.

The large boar clambered into the raft. Its claws made quick work of the inflated chamber on the left side of the boat, and air hissed from the punctures. The grizzly spun around to see where the noise was coming from and bit down into the now deflated side. The grizzly shook its head until it managed to tear a large hole through the nylon and rubber. Satisfied that it had

721

eliminated the threat against it, the grizzly devoured the remains of the bars, wrappers and all.

The old boar ambled slowly out of the half-deflated raft and into the clear water of Rock Lake. The grizzly swam until it reached the small island in the middle of the lake. It climbed out of the water and stood on the edge of the rocky shore, shaking the water from its fur. The old bear and new patriarch made its way up the rocky incline until it stood in front of the entrance to its den. It sniffed around the rocks, with the scent of humans lingering in the air.

The grizzly climbed to the highest point just above its den, sat down, and looked across the lake towards the cabins. It then turned, facing the mangled tents at the south end of Rock Lake. The old male lay down. The sun was now heading towards the western ridge of the valley, and the warmth it provided felt good. The light glistened off his fur, and flies started to swarm around the grizzly's rear as it closed its eyes, its belly full. Rock Lake was quiet. The old male felt safe from any threats. The new Patriarch of the Valley was where he belonged.

Manufactured by Amazon.ca
Acheson, AB

13441768R00404